Zero Hour

For my loving wife, Courtney.

Without you none of this
would be possible.

I love you!

The soldier above all others prays for peace,
for it is the soldier who must suffer
and bear the deepest wounds
and scars of war.

~Gen. Douglas MacArthur

<u>Part 1</u>

Prologue

Wakeup Call

Sept. 29th 0430 MST

Navy Lieutenant Commander Marcus Attledge dug his thumbs into the corners of his eyes and rubbed hard. He was tired, and it was becoming more difficult to hide it. As the forward reconnaissance teams and intelligence operatives were sent out, the staff at the facility had been steadily drawn down. They were on a true skeleton crew now with less than two hundred people total, and half of those were special operations retirees that Price had called back into service.

Between the two shifts of facility technicians, they had enough people to keep the automated drive systems up and running and address problems as they occurred, as long as they didn't get too complex. For anything major, they would need to bring both shifts online at once and could only operate that way for a limited time. The whole thing made Attledge feel exposed in a way that was unsettling, given how far they were from anyone who had clearance to even know the facility existed.

The Signal Control and Acquisition Room was called the "SCAR" by the staff, who had a seemingly pathological need to assign acronyms to everything. This room had received active satellite feeds for days when the data transfer had been initiated just prior to the Blackout. However, since the Russian attack on the secure

Sat-Net systems, the room had been maintained but not actively used. Too many earthly concerns needed attention for the staff to devote time and resources to satellite signals that may or may not be there and may or may not have helpful information.

Attledge was in the last stages of powering up the signal acquisition system, but it was slow going. As the various systems came online, status reports began showing up on the terminals. All nine antennae were reporting back in good working order because their shielded housing and hardened circuits had protected them as designed. With the faraday cage enclosures open, the receivers would be vulnerable, but it would take an amazing coincidence of timing for an enemy to choose this very instant to detonate another EMP device over an already devastated continent.

He knew the odds, such as they were, rested in their favor.

Finally, the acquisition system came to life and showed a status report on the screen. No active scans or searches were running so there were no results to report. A screen full of blank readouts and zero values was not the most promising way to start this operation.

At nearly the same instant the acquisition system came online, the door to the SCAR opened and Commander Terry Price, United States Navy, stepped inside. The chief stayed in the hall, watching for threats as always. Price's face was grim and shadowed, his cheekbones more prominent than Attledge remembered, and his eyes were set deeper in his face. He looked tired, exhausted even, but determined.

"What's the status, Commander?" Price asked.

"All of the systems are up and ready for input," Attledge answered, stifling a yawn. "There are no active signals in reception, of course, but the lines are open and ready."

After checking three of the monitors himself, Price dropped heavily into one of the chairs and fixed Attledge with an indiscernible expression before asking, "How many of the old Nav-Sat network birds have we been able to activate?"

"Seven are up and running, and another three have begun sending telemetry back. We're working on getting the other systems online. That will make ten total."

Price shrugged his shoulders slightly. "That will have to be enough."

"Commander, if you don't mind my asking," Attledge began, stifling another yawn behind his fist, "why was I dragged out of bed at 0300 to come down to a shuttered signal acquisition room to tell you there were no signals to acquire?"

Price leaned back in the chair and closed his eyes for a moment. Attledge waited, but when he didn't respond, or move, he wondered if the man had fallen asleep. Finally, Price sat up and shook his head roughly.

"There is a secondary network of satellites that we are going to start bringing online tonight. The first one is a true dark bird, and it's never been brought fully online. Between the two of us, we're going to wake that bird up before sunrise."

"How many satellites are in the network?" Attledge asked, not looking forward to the added workload of finding and activating them. It was a slow and tedious process—one he didn't relish the thought of growing longer.

"I'm not sure," Price admitted with a short chuckle. "We won't have to worry about that, though, and your team won't have to worry about tracking them down and reactivating them either. This is a newer generation of satellite and operating system than the one

4

you're working with. This one parent will send signals out to other active satellites it can see in the area. If those have the proper software installed, the signal will activate their program and initiate a takeover of the parent system. Return signals will be sent once that process is complete, making those new nodes in the network."

"What if no return signals are sent? If those satellites have no mal-ware installed, then the signal won't have an effect."

Price kept an eye on the monitors. "The targets that fail to send confirmation are registered, and then any signals coming from their coordinates are automatically isolated and filtered."

"The exposure . . ." Attledge began, but Price cut him off.

"Is minimal and necessary. Don't mistake this for a request. Now, we've got a lot of work to get done and a rapidly closing window of opportunity, so let's make the most of it."

Price began laying out plans and instructions for how various pieces would come together, with order, timing, and precision of the utmost importance. When he was done, they both began working on separate tasks. Attledge focused on moving the signal receivers into position to follow and track a certain point in the sky. Nothing registered on any of the radar frequencies other than a dim echo on the infrared spectrum that could have been a reflection or an atmospheric lensing effect.

That done, Attledge turned to the signal transmission systems to set the parameters that Price had specified. Power settings and signal bandwidth were critical. He also set up an auto loop resending program that resent the original full signal on a very specific rate of repetition.

Meanwhile, Price set up the encryption and decryption protocol as well as the signal authentication and reciprocation protocols. There were apparently some things that he still was not comfortable sharing because when Attledge finished his tasks and asked if he could assist, Price shook his head.

Attledge pressed the issue, and, finally, Price growled, "I'm the only one with the encryption and decryption protocol, and it stays that way. If for some reason something happens to me, there are precautions in place to make sure that you have access to certain critical information, Lieutenant Commander. Until then, you will be content to operate with what I give you. Is that clear?"

Attledge didn't answer but instead sat back in silence and watched as Price finished his work. It bothered him how much Price still kept secret, but it was at least partly his own fault. Attledge's own reaction to some of the things he'd been asked—no, ordered—to do thus far had caused the distance between himself and the commander. He recognized that, but he didn't know how to fix it, or even if it *could* be fixed.

After a few moments, Price breathed a heavy sigh and pushed back from the keyboard. "The transmission file is done. I'm going to send it to the input port on the transmission terminal. Bring the packet in and auto-run it through the transmission program, and it should take over and begin the message cycle."

Attledge began keying in the necessary commands. "How long will it take to get a response?"

"Depends on whether the satellite we're sending it to is still operational. If it's in good working order, we could get an initial response in minutes. If it's not, we might not ever get anything."

"What are the contingencies?" Attledge asked.

Price snorted a short laugh. "This is *the* contingency. If this doesn't work, there isn't anything else."

Silence fell between the two men as the transmission terminal indicated the cycle was transmitting. A small status bar in the top right corner showed only two percent of the cycle completed. The percentage points clicked by slowly, but eventually the full cycle completed and the status bar began blinking one hundred percent. At that point, all they could do was watch and wait for a return signal.

After a few moments of intense anticipation, the receiver systems whirred to life, and a green dot began blinking on the incoming transmission display. The actual content of the message was not displayed and wouldn't have been even had it not been heavily encrypted. The standard practice was to store all incoming transmissions in a buffer system to be examined before being brought fully into the integrated systems.

Several layers of authentication and reactivation remained ahead, but the first major hurdle had been successfully crossed. Attledge felt and saw an unmentioned tension drain from Price's body language and demeanor.

"Good work, Commander. Go back to your quarters and get some rest. I can monitor things from here for the duration."

Attledge hesitated, but it had been a clear dismissal. He knew if he tried to linger or offer help, he'd be turned down with increasing firmness. He stood and made his way to the door where he hesitated again. The commander was still holding back; he knew it. But he also knew that for the moment, there was nothing he could do about it.

Attledge stepped out into the hallway and let the door close behind him, leaving the commander and his secrets on the other side.

*

Price watched Attledge leave and then counted to fifty. He went to the door, pressed his ear against the wood, and listened. There were no muffled sounds from the other side, so he turned the handle and eased the door open slightly.

The hallway was empty.

Price returned to the signal terminal. He called up the encryption and transmission protocol that Marcus had so carefully tuned, and he made sure to double save the settings in two separate configuration files so they could easily return to them later. As soon as that was done, he erased the input details and began working on a new set of protocols.

Price worked from memory, his fingers flying over the keyboard. Even as a young boy his memory had impressed his parents and teachers, though his peers had found it odd and used it as a pressure point to ruthlessly taunt and torment him throughout grade school. But as he had grown older, that steel-trap memory had served him well.

It took only a few moments to encode the transmission settings and to encrypt the message. But Price's finger hesitated over the upload command. Once he pressed that button and sent his message up to the master satellite hub, there would be no way to cancel it. A fail-safe that he had insisted be written into this system was the fact that no message histories could be erased once they were created and no messages deleted or canceled once they were sent.

He'd spent years laying the careful groundwork for this very moment, thinking the entire time that he'd never actually have to use it—hoping that he'd never be sitting exactly where he found himself. The commander wondered briefly if he would have accepted the position decades before if he'd known where this path would lead.

Drawing a deep breath to steady himself, Price pressed the final command. The message was sent. A progress bar appeared on the transmission screen and rapidly filled as the encryption headed upstream along the connection. From the central hub, the message would be disseminated throughout the network of communication satellites as they came online. Those satellites would then send the message both to active receivers already on the network and to new nodes as they came online.

Price had no way of knowing whether his message would be received or not, but he'd done what he could. A sudden wave of exhaustion rolled over him, and he leaned back in the programmer's chair, kicked his feet up onto the desk of the neighboring cubicle, and closed his eyes. He was asleep in a matter of moments.

Chapter 1

Non-negotiable

Oct. 2nd 0715 EST

The Lowe's in Bennett was one of the biggest stores in the area, and it sat by itself in what had been the beginnings of a strip mall that never really took off. Joe and Eric split up, taking positions on opposite sides of the large bay door at the front loading entrance. For the past two mornings, just at sunrise, that door had opened and two guards stepped out to do a patrol around the building. They walked in opposite directions and met at the front entrance a while later.

The eastern sky was barely showing a pearly pink tint when Joe took cover behind one of the trash cans. It wasn't much, but it would hide the bulk of his form enough to allow him the element of surprise. Eric crouched between two model sheds and gave a thumbs up sign to Joe before disappearing completely.

It had begun to grow light, and when the sun had just barely crested the horizon, Joe heard the metal door roll up and slam into place. He checked his watch and counted ten seconds before he stood and locked his weapon on a kid that wasn't a day over twenty.

"Hands!" Joe barked, stepping around from behind the trashcan and placing the young man's back squarely facing Eric as he

10

stepped out and took aim on the second kid. "Show me your hands!"

The young man held his hands out, carefully. Joe saw a shingle hammer tucked into one side of his belt and nodded toward the hammer. "Take it out with your left hand, slowly, and toss it over by the wall. You can pick it up later if all of this goes to plan."

The young man followed Joe's orders and tossed it well out of reach.

Joe pointed to where Eric had the other guard kneeling in the street. "Okay, turn around and walk back to your buddy." The young man started to say something, but he thought better of it and turned around. His shoulders slumped as he realized that he was thoroughly caught. Joe made him kneel next to his friend and zip-tied their hands.

Joe stepped to one side so that he could face Eric and the door, then raised his pistol to fire into the air. A voice from the other side of the glass doors stopped him, though.

"You don't have to shoot that," a woman called. "If you'd meant to kill the guards you'd have done it already, and there's no need to let me know you're here. Obviously."

Joe lowered his gun but held his ready. "We have your attention," he said easily. "Good. There are a few things we need from inside, and we are willing to pay for them. But we have to do a job first. Once we're done with this job, we'll need more stuff. I'll leave a list of what we're taking and what we'll need. When we come back through, we can talk it out and come to some kind of agreement on a price that we're both happy with. And then I'll double it. Sound good?"

"Look, put down your guns and you can come in and talk," the woman called from inside the store. Her words sounded far more rational than her voice. She was terrified. "There's no need for us to negotiate through a wall."

Joe shook his head. "You don't understand, Miss. This ain't a negotiation. You take my deal or I shoot your guards and leave. Then we'll come back with more people, and we'll take what we need and everything else with it. I don't want it to go that way, but it will if it has to. I gave my word to do a job, and I need some of the tools you have in that store to get it done. Once I give my word, Miss, I see it through. My name is Captain Joe Tillman, and you can ask around."

Joe stepped up and put his face against the glass door, and he could just barely make out the shadowy silhouette of a woman standing in the entrance a few feet back.

"But you don't get to negotiate. You get to choose which way it's gonna be. If I were you, I'd take the way that gets a lot less people dead at the end of it."

He stepped back from the door and waited.

A long two or three minutes passed before the inner doors slid open and a woman that looked as if she might be in her early forties stepped out into the foyer. She unlocked the outer doors with three different deadbolt locks and opened the door.

"My name is Marsha. I'm the manager of this store, and these two work for me. Please, don't hurt them."

Joe holstered his pistol. "I take it we have a deal, then?" When he extended his right hand, Marsha shook it and nodded with a bit more enthusiasm than was strictly necessary.

Joe turned to Eric. "Keep your eyes open, son, and keep your gun on them. If I don't step out of this store first, you know what to do."

Eric nodded but didn't speak. He positioned himself so he could watch the door and the two captives at the same time. When he was satisfied, he nodded to Joe.

When Joe stepped inside, Marsha stepped in front of him. "I'm going to need your sidearm. We don't let strangers go armed in here."

Joe shook his head. "Not part of the deal, Marsha. My gun stays with me, period. Now, here's the list of supplies I told you about. I'll get what we need now and we'll be out of your way."

Marsha looked down the list, and her eyes grew wide. It was extensive and would have been expensive, even before the Blackout. Her eyes narrowed, and she hesitated. "How do I have any guarantee that you'll come back?"

Joe met her gaze and calmly smiled. "Because I gave you my word."

Marsha stepped out of his way. "Go ahead, but be quick," she said. "The fewer people that know you're here, the better."

Joe took a cart and his own copy of the list and went around the store collecting items one by one. He grabbed a few heavy engineer's hammers, some ball pings of various sizes, and two camp axes. He added a large pair of linesman's pliers and some vice grips, wrenches and sockets of every size. Finally, he picked up several pairs of elbow-length rubber chemical gloves and a pair of heavy welding gloves.

When he was done, Joe took the cart back to the front of the store and let Marsha check off the items one by one to make sure the list matched the goods he'd taken. When she was satisfied, they both initialed the two copies.

As Joe headed to the door with his loaded cart, Marsha shook her head and gave him a sidelong look. "I hope I didn't make a mistake here."

For a moment Joe met her gaze, then turned and pointed to the two guards Eric still had at gunpoint. "You're smart to do patrols, but get them off the ground and up on top of the building. Tell them to keep low, and use the building's shape to help hide them. They'll be able to see ten times farther from the roof than they can down here. Maybe give you enough time to make a difference if they're serious about their watch and don't get spotted."

Marsha's eyes narrowed again. "You make me nervous, Captain Tillman," she said honestly.

"I hear that a lot, ma'am," he chuckled. "But I'm not all that bad, really."

Joe nodded to Eric, who let the guards up and motioned for them to walk toward the door. As the hostages passed Joe, their faces were masks of anger mixed with fear. There had been no way around humiliating them, and that was unfortunate. But Joe and Eric had needed the leverage, whatever the cost. Once Joe was back with Eric and the two sentries were back with Marsha, Joe turned back to her. Eric raised his gun, dropped the magazine and tossed it to Marsha. She caught it instinctively and then realized what she was seeing.

She whipped her arm back as if to throw the magazine at Eric, her face twisted in an angry snarl. "Empty?" she screamed. "You had an empty gun this whole time? Do you think this is some kind of joke?"

Eric didn't say anything but bore the full force of her outrage. "I was nervous," he said when Marsha had run out of breath for a moment. "I didn't want to pull the trigger on accident. It's one thing if someone's coming at me, but not this. I told him I'd do it only if my gun was empty."

"Why even pull this charade if the threat wasn't real?" Marsha growled in return.

Joe stepped between Eric and Marsha and shook his head. "The threat was real. I told you that if you refused *I* would shoot your guards, and I meant exactly what I said. His gun wasn't loaded. Mine is."

The rage drained from Marsha's face, and she suddenly looked very tired. Joe stepped forward a few steps and held out his hand. She handed the magazine over to him and, with a heavy sigh, lifted her eyes once. If she had anything to say, she kept it to herself as she turned and ushered the two sentries back inside the store.

Before closing the outer doors, Marsha looked back over her shoulder. "I'll have a price ready when you come back. No need for the guns next time, just knock."

Joe opened his mouth to reply, but the metal door was already rolling down from the ceiling, so he turned and pushed the cart over to Eric, and the two started across the parking lot. In the quiet morning air, the cart clanged and jerked across the rough asphalt loud enough to be heard from miles away. But for the moment, Joe wasn't concerned about keeping out of sight.

They had an appointment to keep.

Chapter 2

Outside the Wire

Lieutenant Commander Attledge stood next to a cluster of six solar panels mounted to a fixed steel bracket. The bracket was welded onto the end of a solid steel pole nearly as thick as Attledge, and that pole was set in a fifteen-foot-deep bed of concrete. The winds in the Henry Mountains could get strong in the stormy winter and early spring months, and the solar panels that powered much of the living and working area of the facility had been built to ride out those storms.

Still, the mounts needed to be checked from time to time, and that gave him the perfect excuse to be out in the pre-dawn darkness with Commander Price and a security detail of eight men who had set up a tight perimeter around each panel installation they checked. A cluster of panels had been set in similar fashion closer to the helipad and the main entrance into the facility, but there were three times as many like this one in hidden alcove installations on the surrounding hills. They were intended to be difficult to see and target from the air or the ground and still be useful to collect power and transmit it to the facility.

Price looked out over the mountains. "You feel confident we've rooted out the last infiltrator?"

Attledge thought about it for a moment and nodded. "I'm as sure as I can be. We've had no action since the execution. That was weeks ago."

Unsure of how to go on, Attledge hesitated, and Price stopped in his tracks. "There's something you're not telling me, Marcus. Let's hear it."

"Sir, even assuming we have gotten rid of the last traitor in our midst, they're still going to look for your daughter. And if they find her, they'll hurt her to get to you. Shouldn't we be trying to find her first?"

Price shook his head slowly. "If I tried to find her now, I wouldn't even know where to start. Besides, all that can do is end up getting her hurt one way or another, assuming she's still alive. The whole reason I gave her up for adoption in the first place was because I saw a day like this coming, and I wanted to make it as difficult as possible to find her when it did."

"And if they do find her?" Marcus asked.

"Is this really what you brought me out here in the freezing cold dark to talk about?" Price shot back. "These people have killed millions, Marcus. Do you really think I'd hand the keys to the kingdom over to animals that could do that? Do you really think I'd hand the go codes for the nukes over to those monsters?"

Attledge met the Price's tirade without flinching. "You've ordered me to do some horrible things, Commander. Things I never would have done if you hadn't forced it. I need to know that you're committed to seeing this through, no matter what. I've followed every one of your orders, so you owe me at least this much."

"Fine," Price grated through clenched teeth, "I've answered your questions. Now you'll answer mine. Why am I out here?"

Attledge handed over a sheet with coordinates and times marked on a map. "I've been monitoring the Nav-Sat channels as ordered. He's on the move. They were on the southwest corner of town for two days. Then they went basically due west and stopped. Now, they're moving north and angling back to the east slowly."

Price took a deep, slow breath. His eyes were down, and a deep frown creased his face. He rubbed his left ring finger absently, his fingers tracing the pale circle where his class ring had been.

After a long moment, he gave a rough shrug and straightened. "Whatever Captain Tillman is involved in, he's on his own for the time being. We have to get ready for the first strike, and that's going to take all of our resources. The communications network we activated a few nights ago is growing. Nine nodes are confirmed active already."

"What do you mean *active*?" Attledge asked.

"When we got enough coverage, I sent a message out on a secure channel," Price answered. "Over the last ten years or so I've distributed secured sat-phones to some of the more trustworthy commanders and officers I've met. It seemed prudent, given the facility I was put in command of, to take steps to create my own network of support should communications with the command structure break down."

Attledge was having trouble believing what he had just heard. "You sent an active signal over satellite? Are you insane? Anyone monitoring for strong comm signals from orbit would be able to pick that up and possibly triangulate back on us."

Price shook his head. "Not likely. It was a one-time burst transmission, not a repeating or sustained signal. All it did was send a coded message on a secure, encrypted channel potentially to eleven secured sat-phones." Price put a reassuring hand on

Attledge's shoulder. "Besides, Marcus, the people we are fighting already know exactly where we are, so there's no real sense in hiding our location."

"What was the message?" Attledge asked, still not sure what to expect.

"I'm activating them as assets. If any of them get the message, they are instructed to report here for debriefing and new orders."

Attledge frowned at the potentially low number of respondents. "Do you really think any of them will come?"

"The message was sent out with an official presidential seal and operation code. If they still consider themselves part of the service and bound by their oaths, then that should be enough to convince them. Several Presidential Directive Authorities were granted to my office similar to the one that allowed me to immediately draft the staff of this facility. There is another that allows for the activation of assets from among existing military and other governmental agencies for immediate deployment in defense of the nation. They may not like the idea, but they won't be able to ignore it."

Marcus turned and looked out at the eastern horizon. He noticed how the land fell quickly away from the Henry Mountains and the desert plain stretched out, empty and stark as far as he could see. The grass on the slope was covered with a thin layer of frost that sparkled in the dim light of the coming sunrise, and its tingling smell floated on the breeze. The smell of frost is akin to that of snow but lighter and more transient. It's sharp and dry but doesn't linger like the more permanent smell of snow.

Marcus leveled his attention back on the prospect of retaliation that he fully expected would come in one form or another. "Will they hit us so soon, do you think? You took out one of their over-confident upper management, locked out the databases, hardened this facility, and cleared out all of their operatives here. Maybe they'll regroup before striking out across the country to come after us."

Price snorted as he stepped up next to Attledge and gazed out at the brightening sky. "You misunderstand me, Commander. This man who calls himself president has overthrown the government, betrayed the Constitution, and seized the country for himself. And he meant to do worse than that. He meant to sell us over to Russia."

Price paused, his jaw clenched in an effort to forestall his rising anger, and just then, the sun rose over the mountain. The hillside was strewn with millions of tiny jewels as the frost caught the first rays of the light and scattered them in tiny shards of rainbow colors. Almost instantly, though, the heat of the sun began melting the frost, and the dew started to evaporate in the cold, dry wind.

Price turned to Attledge, his face a stony mask. "We're not preparing to get hit," he said through clenched teeth. "We're going to hit them first, we're going to hit them hard, and we're going to hit them where they least expect it."

Chapter 3

Morning Coffee

Oct. 4 th 0705 EST

Beth opened her eyes and stared at the dark ceiling. It was still early enough for only a little gray light to filter in through the two windows in the bedroom, and it was cold. She reached her hand out, knowing that she would find an empty pillow next to her. Even after all the years, she still wasn't used waking up alone in her bed.

She frowned and sat up; she also wasn't used to waking up this early for no reason. She strained her ears, but the only sound she could hear was the steady breathing from all of the sleeping bodies inside the farmhouse and the faint rumblings of snoring from the assortment of tents that were still set up in the front yard. It seemed Bill and Gilbert had a competition going for who could be the loudest the longest, and how either of their wives got any sleep at all was still beyond her understanding.

Satisfied that nothing was out of the ordinary, she stretched out to try and get a few more minutes of rest before sunrise. She was just starting to feel the heaviness of sleep settle over her when a new noise caught her ear and triggered her mothering instinct. Someone was retching and sick outside. Beth was up and out of the bed by the time her brain had consciously recognized the sound for what it was. This was the noise that had roused her from her sleep, as it had years before when Eric was a child.

Grabbing her heavy housecoat, Beth slipped into a pair of fleece-lined slippers and moved quietly through the living room. She eased open the wooden interior door and the metal storm door and stepped out onto the front porch. There was a light breeze blowing down from the north, and her breath fogged in front of her face. It was early in the fall for it to be this cold, and that wasn't a good sign for the coming winter.

Beth listened and after a moment heard the faint sound of someone dry heave to the left, where the yard met the edge of the old scrub brush and young timber. She stood still and listened as whoever it was coughed softly a few times. Then she heard the sound of delicate footsteps in the dry leaves. Whoever had just gotten sick was coming toward her and was trying to be secretive about it. Beth sat down on the top step and waited.

In a few moments, Christina came around the front corner of the house wrapped in a quilt and wearing a pair of Eric's boots. She was so focused on carefully putting one foot down after another that she didn't notice Beth until her foot was on the bottom step. When she looked up, she jumped, her eyes wide with surprise.

"Oh!" she exclaimed softly. "I didn't wake you up, did I? My stomach wasn't feeling well . . . "

Beth stood and helped her up the steps. "It wasn't something you ate, was it?" she asked, draping one arm around Christina's shoulders and pulling her over to sit on the wooden bench. "I hope no one else is feeling ill."

Christina leaned against Beth's shoulder, her fingers picking absently at the old patchwork quilt as the sky lightened with the coming sunrise. "I don't think anyone else is going to be sick," she said softly.

Beth frowned for a moment, unsure how Christina could be so sure. If something she'd cooked had turned sour or had somehow made Christina sick, then it only stood to reason that someone else could also be affected, unless it wasn't Beth's cooking that had made Christina ill in the first place. If it wasn't the cooking, that really left only one explanation.

Beth's eyes went wide, and she took in a sharp breath. "You aren't . . ." she stopped, unable to finish the question.

But she didn't need to finish for Christina to know what she was being asked. She nodded her head, a tear dropping from the tip of her nose as she looked at her fingers. "We didn't mean for it to happen like this. We wanted to wait, but everything fell apart after the Blackout. We were on the run and then we ended up here. We were both so scared and it just happened a few nights after the Blackout. Once we figured out I was pregnant, we wanted to have the wedding first and then make the announcement. You're not angry, are you?"

Beth wrapped her arms around Christina and pulled her closer. "Angry? Why on earth would I be angry? I'm going to be a grandmother! I'm thrilled, darlin!" Beth wiped a tear and kissed the top of Christina's head.

"But what are we going to do?" Christina asked, trying to pull away. "There aren't any working hospitals, or OBGYNs, or anything. What are we going to do when it's time for the baby to come? What if something goes wrong?"

Beth pulled Christina's head back against her shoulder. "Shhh. We'll have plenty of time to worry about all of that when the time comes. We've got months to answer those questions and no need to work ourselves up over them this early. Right now, let's just focus on being happy that you're pregnant and a new addition to this crazy family is on the way! And you can stop trying to hide your morning sickness from everyone."

Christina gave a firm shake of her head. "Not until Eric's home and we can tell everyone together."

"Okay," Beth said, patting Christina's shoulder reassuringly, "we'll wait until Eric and Joe get back. How long has it been?"

Christina shrugged her shoulders slightly. "A few weeks now. It's not every day, but when it hits it can be pretty bad. This morning was a rough one."

Beth nodded. "When I was pregnant with Eric, I couldn't stand the smell of coffee. Some women go green at the smell of meat cooking, but for me, it was the smell of freshly brewed coffee that just twisted me up in knots. Joe, God bless him, can't start his day until he's had at least two cups of strong black coffee. He's been that way since the Academy."

Christina stifled a yawn with the back of her hand. "Oh no. What did the two of you do?"

Beth pulled part of Christina's quilt over her own shoulder and snuggled a little closer on the bench. "Well, the first time it happened, we didn't know what it was. I used to love coffee myself, but not as much as Joe. He would wake up, brew a pot, and have his first cup before I got out of bed. That first morning, I smelled the coffee start brewing, it was like someone stuck a blender in my tummy. I jumped out of bed, ran down the hall to the only bathroom in our tiny place and proceeded to make some of the nastiest noises a human can make."

"By the time it was over, I didn't want anything but to brush my teeth, rinse my mouth out, and go to bed," Beth chuckled. "It wasn't until the same thing happened the next day as soon as the coffee started brewing that we put two and two together. After that, Joe got up at four in the morning and drove his motorcycle down to the donut shop on the corner. He would be there when the store opened, get two cups of coffee, and be back home again before I was even awake. The morning sickness would still hit sometimes, but nowhere near as bad. Joe did that every day for nine months, and on Sundays he'd bring home a dozen donuts for breakfast."

Christina mumbled something against Beth's shoulder, but judging from her breathing, the young woman was already deep in sleep. Beth shifted her weight a little to get more comfortable and enjoyed the warmth and comfort of another person to hold onto as the sun rose. Joe and Eric had been gone for two full days now, and Beth was beginning to get worried.

"Whatever happens," Beth whispered softly, "we always seem to find a way to get through it and come out the other side. But Lord, I pray for this child and the world that its coming into."

Her only answer was the cold breeze drying her few tears and the warm sunlight shining on her face.

Chapter 4

On the Road Again

Oct. 4 th 0745 EST

The sun was up, but it was still cool enough for Mike to see his breath fog in front of his nose and mouth every time he exhaled. He was crouched between two large tractor trailers in the shipping and receiving yard of a huge warehouse complex. The building across from him was dark and quiet, but that didn't settle Mike's nerves.

The doors were all shut tight and none of the windows had been broken out. From the outside, the warehouse looked intact, and that made Mike nervous as well. If people were holed up inside, they might have made it difficult for the curious to get out once they got in. With no open windows or access points, that could pose a serious problem.

Then again, the entire building could be intact because no one had thought to check it for anything valuable. There were no signs on the trucks or the exterior of the building itself. Across a small industrial drive was an obvious FedEx shipping hub with their logo painted across transfer trucks and vans, but this warehouse was much more inconspicuous.

Whether the warehouse was occupied or not, Mike knew he had to check, and that meant going inside for a look around.

Satisfied that they weren't going to learn anything else from the outside, Mike turned and tapped Arthur on the shoulder, and the older man nodded. They made their way as quickly as they could across the concrete parking lot and up one of the ramps to a closed metal garage door.

The rolling doors along the row of loading bays were solid, and they made a tight seal with the side of the building. Neither Mike nor Arthur could get the edge of their crowbars in the gap between metal and concrete to try and pry the doors open. After a few unsuccessful attempts, Mike shook his head and pointed to the front office. If they couldn't get in through the metal bay doors, then perhaps there was a chance with the glass-fronted office.

Mike stuck his crowbar back into the almost empty pack on his back and pulled out a rock hammer. The tool had a stout chisel on one side and a sharp pick of hardened steel on the other. Arthur followed him back down the ramp and around to the double glass front doors. Mike cupped his hands around his eyes and peered inside as best he could in the gathering light. Arthur watched his back while Mike searched the dark interior for signs of movement and found none.

When he was satisfied the place was empty, he tapped Arthur on the shoulder. "I'm going to break the glass with the rock hammer. It might shatter out of the frame, and it might not, but it'll definitely break. Step back and watch your eyes."

Arthur nodded, took three big steps back and covered his eyes with his forearm. Mike stood with his back to the glass door, just to the side of the door frame. He raised his rock hammer high over his head and brought it down hard, striking the center of the glass. There was a muffled *thwack*! and the glass shattered into a spider web of fine cracks.

Mike cursed softly under his breath.

The door was safety glass, and the central film held it firmly in the frame in spite of being shattered into thousands of tiny shards.

Mike pointed to a thick, black rubber seal that closed the edges of the glass and held it in the metal frame. "I'm going to have to try and rip the seal out. If I can get enough of it out, then maybe we can kick that sheet in. It's a heck of a lot heavier than it looks, so once it starts falling, get out of the way. There's no way to do this quietly, so keep an eye out for anyone who notices the noise. Are you sure this is going to be worth it?"

Arthur smiled and shook his head. "No, I'm honestly not. I have no idea what is or isn't inside that building. All I can tell you from my past experience working in places like this, there's got to be at least a snack machine and a first aid kit. If no one else has thought to look inside, maybe that stuff is still there. And at this point, anything we can get would be a big help."

Mike couldn't really argue with him there. They had been searching buildings and houses in an increasingly large radius around the White Water Center, looking for anything salvageable among the deserted neighborhoods and industrial parks. For the most part, they found that others had beat them to it. A few homes had medicines that Arthur recognized as valuable in the long run because without high technology, producing them would be difficult in the future. Pantries and cupboards had been stripped bare, as had just about everything else. After coming back with sparse supplies at best, and often empty-handed, they had agreed that less obvious sources would have to be found if they were going to scavenge enough supplies to last them on the road to Bennett. And the longer it took to gather the supplies, the more likely the weather was to break cold on them before they made it.

Mike knew from his park ranger training that cold made travel through the brush difficult at best. He had done simulated rescues in cold and icing conditions three different times and used different terrain each time. One thing had been the same, though, the way the cold leeched the strength and stamina out of the body. It worked from the outside in, numbing as it went, and could creep up on even an experienced outdoorsman.

If the group didn't soon begin their trip toward Bennett, they would have to spend the winter holed up in the outskirts of the city with already dwindling supplies. Mike wanted to avoid that at all costs.

These thoughts raced and tumbled through Mike's mind as he hung the rock hammer from a loop on his belt and pulled a long-shafted flat screwdriver from his pack. He jammed the flat point into the crevices between the door face and metal frame. He had to work the point behind and then under that rubber gasket, but eventually, he had pried up enough to get his knife blade in a position to move.

The screwdriver scraped with high pitched squeals as Mike worked it down the frame, scraping the rubber seal off as he went. With his other hand, Mike pulled the gasket out a few inches at the time. He worked slowly, deliberately, and efficiently. Still, it was far from easy work, and despite the cool morning breeze, Mike was sweating by the time he had the top edge and the left side of the gasket removed. He started pulling from the right corner, and when he'd taken down about a foot of that side of the gasket, the glass began to sag.

Mike let go of the gasket and stepped back. "Okay, we count to three and then kick hard in the center. "One--Two--Three!"

Both men leaned back and put their full weight behind their kicks. The glass sheet sagged in as the rest of the gasket tore away, but it caught on the long handle on the other side. As the force rebounded, the sheet of shattered safety glass began to sag outward, and Arthur stumbled. Mike bent and jerked the older man out from under the glass as it fell, barely getting him clear before the two-hundred-pound sheet hit the ground.

Mike helped Arthur up and the two stood back to back, listening. Mike watched the inside of the warehouse, now exposed through the gaping doorway, and Arthur watched everything else. Nothing moved for a few moments, so Mike stepped inside, careful to avoid brushing the edges of the door frame in case splinters of glass were still attached. Arthur followed him in, and the two men waited in the entryway for their eyes to adjust to the dim light.

Both checked their holstered side arms to make sure they were clear. Two hallways faced them, one to the right and one to the left. The bulk of the warehouse was to the right, so Mike turned to the left. If there was a break room with vending machines, it would be on the climate-controlled side of the building, not the open warehouse side.

Mike took out one of a handful of green chem lights he'd taken from the White Water Center gift shop. He snapped it and dropped it just inside the hallway, lifting some of the darkness. As they came to each office door, they cleared the room and closed the door. The first two had been open, but now they faced their first closed door and hesitated.

Mike drew his Beretta and nodded. Arthur tried the door handle and it turned. He pushed the door open, and Mike stepped forward. He had his pistol in his right hand resting on his left wrist. In his left hand, he gripped a small Streamlight flashlight and clicked it on.

The bright white light from the high-intensity LED flooded the dark, empty room. Mike scanned twice from side to side, making sure he covered every inch of what looked like a reservation booking center. There were three desks, each with a computer, a phone, and a fax machine on top of them. Three large filing cabinets stood along the back wall, but there was no other furniture in the room. The row of windows that cut across the back wall above the filing cabinets looked out on the two tractor-trailers that Mike and Arthur had crouched between earlier.

The room was empty, so Mike lowered his pistol and engaged the thumb safety before holstering it. He closed the door as they left the room, snapped and dropped another chem light, and moved to the next door down the hallway. This was the first door on the right side of the hallway, and it stood open. When Mike turned on his tiny flashlight again, he saw the room was at least twice as large as the offices they'd passed, and he could make out the shapes of what looked like a refrigerator, at least two vending machines, and a row of cabinets both above and below a metal kitchen sink.

Mike pointed to the two vending machines. "Looks like you were right about the snack." Arthur started to step toward the machines, but Mike shook his head and stopped the older man with a hand on his arm. "We need to clear the rest of the building first. Never know when someone might be hiding behind a corner or on the other side of a closed closet door."

Arthur frowned, a question behind his eyes, but he nodded, and they stepped back out into the hallway. They cleared the rest of the offices on the hall, two bathrooms, and two storage closets. Mike dropped two more chem lights, and even that dim light stood out to their eyes.

The two then stepped out into the warehouse and listened, shining their flashlights down rows and rows of huge wooden

31

crates stacked like building blocks on top of each other and on a giant metal shelving system. Mike wondered what was in the crates, but they didn't have time to check anything at the moment. They made sure the warehouse was empty and then made their way back inside to the break room.

Mike used his rock hammer to smash the glass front of the snack machine, which was much easier to break than the door had been. He and Arthur split the load of toaster pastries, potato chips, pork rinds, honey buns, white cheddar popcorn, corn chips, and candy between their two bags. They took everything, even the chocolate bars because when starvation threatened, calories were calories.

They tried to break into the drink machine, but the metal frame and solid lock proved too strong. Mike even hit the hinges several times with a sledge hammer retrieved from the warehouse, but the door didn't budge. Reluctantly, he gave up on the drink machine that Arthur had already abandoned in favor of the cabinets. Arthur showed off four cans of soup and a small first aid kit. He also pulled down two full salt shakers, a pepper shaker, and three full canisters of Folger's ground coffee.

Mike opened the refrigerator, and immediately the smell of soured food filled the break room. He found four bottles of warm soda in the back as well as six unopened bottles of filtered water. The rest of the contents were unfit to eat, and the putrid smell made the breakroom unfit for people, so they left and checked each of the offices more thoroughly.

They collected another first aid kit, two pocket knives, and two small flashlights. On an impulse, Mike grabbed a long spool of dark green para-cord they found in one of the closets. The spool was heavy, but the rope was thin and strong.

Satisfied that they had everything they could carry, Mike led the way back to the shattered front door. As he stepped into the entrance, a sound to his left made him turn his head just in time to see a large man swing a stout length of wooden dowel a little thinner than his wrist. The wood connected with the bridge of Mike's nose, and there was a loud crack. His eyes watered immediately, and he tasted blood in the back of his mouth.

Mike fell to his knees with a muffled groan, and on his way down, he saw a man with a long-bladed knife step over him toward Arthur. The man above Mike raised his wooden cudgel, and Mike knew the blow that was about to connect with his head would be enough to kill him, but he couldn't get his arms to respond fast enough to stop it. The first strike had stunned him, and all he could do was watch as the killing blow was about to fall.

Suddenly, two loud cracks came from behind Mike, and he rolled his head enough to see smoke curling from the barrel of Arthur's snub-nosed revolver. The man in front of him had dropped his knife and was holding his side with one hand and pulling at his pants pocket with the other, no doubt reaching for a gun.

The man standing over Mike dropped his wooden club, and it clattered to the tiled floor in front of Mike's nose. His assailant lifted his shirt, and Mike saw the wooden handle of a pistol tucked behind the man's waistband.

Somehow, Mike was moving. He grabbed the wooden dowel in front of him and brought it up end first into the man's groin. He heard a loud wretch as the man doubled over. Mike stood and brought the wood up hard again, connecting with the man's gaping mouth. He spit a few teeth on the floor and collapsed to his knees. Mike brought the wooden club down one last time, striking him just above and in front of his right ear.

The man twitched once and fell to the side, blood trickling from his ear and from his nose. Mike turned toward Arthur, finally, drawing his Beretta as he did, but there was no need. Arthur stood over the man with his own revolver in one hand and the attacker's small semi-automatic in the other. Arthur's face was ashen and he seemed unsteady on his feet.

The assailant sat hunched over his wound, looking much worse. The man's lips writhed as if he was speaking, but no sound came out. A trickle of blood ran down the side of his mouth and neck, and the dark pool of it beneath him was growing. Whatever Arthur had hit, it had been important.

Mike pulled at the older man's sleeve as he pulled off his T-shirt and wiped the blood from his broken nose. Arthur shook himself, turned, and stumbled out of the broken door. Mike could hear him heaving in the bushes just outside.

Reaching down, Mike pulled the gun from his attacker's waistband. He took the two spare magazines from the man's back pocket, as well as his long-bladed belt knife. The other knife he left where it lay. If Arthur didn't want to claim it, Mike certainly wasn't going to. He took one last look at the dead and the dying men, each in turn, and felt a disturbingly cold detachment as he turned his back on them and stepped out into the fresh autumn air.

"Come on, Arthur. We've got more than two miles to make it back to the White Water Center, and we'd better get a move on. The last thing we want to do is wait around for anyone who might have heard what just happened."

Arthur wiped his mouth and nodded, some of his color restored. The two men put the warehouse behind them as they turned back down Performance Road and began the long hike back to their base camp. Neither of them looked back a single time.

Chapter 5

Helping Hand

Oct. 4th 0900 EST

Eric climbed carefully, making sure to keep three points of contact with the pole. Every two or three footholds he would unclip the safety line and move it up level with his eyes. The strap wrapped around the pole and clipped with a solid carabiner. If he were to slip, the rope would pull itself tight as he fell, and the handholds would keep it from sliding down with him. It was a simple, but apparently effective, safety mechanism, but Eric hoped he wouldn't have to put it to the test.

It was a warm day but not hot. Still, sweat stung Eric's eyes and soaked his shirt by the time he reached the top of the pole. He pulled up a sealed bag of tools that hung from a rope knotted on his belt. A rough diagram was scrawled on a piece of cardboard in black permanent marker. Eric took out a long, heavy screwdriver and then tied the tool bag around the steel arm that supported the street light so he wouldn't have to hold its weight.

Above him, a broad, flat bracket held three solar panels in a row. The panels were connected with a short cable to the control circuitry that was housed in the large metal cabinet Eric currently faced. He unscrewed the heavy bolts that locked the access door and placed the bolts, nuts, and washers carefully into his tool bag.

The bolts and washers fit perfectly into the small zippered pouch in the side.

He checked the diagram one more time and then carefully secured it in the bottom of the tool bag. He pulled on two layers of thick rubber chemical gloves, flexed his fingers as best he could and got to work. He knew the solar panels had been covered by blankets. He'd held the ropes while his father and Danny tied them on the previous morning. The street light had spent all of its light already and had drained the circuits, but for that brief moment when Eric, forty feet in the air, reached in with a metal tool, his pulse raced. Until the screwdriver actually touched the first cable connection, he wasn't really certain whether all of the juice was out of the circuit or not.

When Eric grabbed the power cable and began unscrewing it from the modulator, nothing sparked and nothing jolted him, and he let out a breath he hadn't realized he'd been holding. Once that tense moment was over, the process was relatively straightforward. He unscrewed a few cables, took off mounting brackets, and stored the components and cables in the tool bag. He collected all of the hardware that he hadn't dropped and then came down as carefully as he'd climbed.

By the time Eric reached the ground, his arms and legs were shaking and cramping. He climbed out of the safety harness and handed it off to his waiting father. Eric stumbled over to the shade of the tall pines lining the highway. He found a few bottles of Gatorade there and opened one. It was warm, but Eric didn't care as he drained half the bottle before screwing the cap back in place.

When he turned back to look at the light pole, Joe was already at the top, and Eric could only shake his head. Sometimes he forgot how strong his father was, and it was good to be reminded of it. Joe looped a rope over the arm supporting the street light and then tied it off to the cross arm of the bracket holding the solar panels. He carefully unbolted the entire bracket assembly and lowered it onto the support of the rope he'd tied.

Danny stood on the ground with the rope looped around the light pole and a fire hydrant, slowly letting the load down hand over hand. As the panel got lower, Eric walked back out onto the roadbed. He stood under the bracket and caught the weight as it came down so the panels wouldn't be damaged. They lowered the contraption the last few feet until it settled on the grassy bank of the road.

Joe climbed down slower than he had climbed up, and his face was red and sweaty by the time he got to the bottom of the light pole. "I think this will be the last one," he said and wiped his forehead. "You'll have twelve panels total, Danny, and if even half of them and half of the components work, you'll be able to power freezers, well pumps, and filters. Maybe even have climate control in the house on good days—ventilation, if nothing else. You can come back and get some of the lights if you figure out a way to take them down whole. They'll hook right up to the power boxes and they're durable."

Danny stood for a long moment, mopping sweat from his brow with one hand and fanning himself with a broad, sweat-stained straw hat in the other. The frown on his face looked like someone had just told him his dog was dying. The silence stretched until he shook his head and straightened.

"I still can't guarantee anything. I told you that from the beginning. But when you said you had a down payment to make in good faith, I had no idea. Captain Tillman, these have got to be worth a fortune now. Are you sure? What if the rest of them still say no? What if no one will fight?"

Joe smiled and gave a half shrug. "Whatever they say, we need to help each other these days. These panels and the power systems could help you preserve enough food to get you through the worst of the winter, if you're careful and if you're lucky."

Danny shook his head again and fixed Joe with a long, quiet stare. "I'll see you back at the normal meeting place next week, and I'll have their answer, okay?"

Joe stuck out his right hand to Danny, who took it immediately. "One more thing, though," Joe said quietly, and Danny tensed. "Nothing big, I promise. I just need you to stop by a hardware store with me to show a woman I can pay her what I promise to pay her."

"That really creates more questions than it answers, Captain," Danny said, his frown deepening.

"We didn't have the tools we needed to get these things apart," Joe admitted, "but I had to promise you something big to get you to listen. So, I convinced a lady at a hardware store to sell us the tools on credit. Now I need to show her that if I promise things like solar panels, I can actually deliver them."

Danny nodded toward the array of solar panels. "Speaking of delivering, how are we going to get those back? They're heavy and I can't put more than one on the shopping cart without it tipping over. It's tough to control even with one."

Joe patted Danny on the shoulder. "Well, Danny, I'm not sure. We'll tie the one array on the shopping cart and help you hide the rest. You can bring your horse and cart out later at night to collect everything and take it back in one trip, if you're serious about it and bring help."

Danny turned and faced Joe one more time and offered his hand. "Captain Tillman, you're a good man, and I thank you for everything you've done for me. Whatever my uncle and the rest of them say, I'll go with you when the time comes."

Joe took Danny's hand and shook it firmly. "I appreciate that, Danny. We're going to need all the help we can get. After seeing what those bastards did at Forest Hills, I don't think this is going to be any kind of an easy fight. But it's one that we're gonna have, whether we like it or not. Might as well be on our terms rather than theirs."

There wasn't much to say after that, so they got busy securing the shopping cart. Two bags of components and two tool bags went into the bottom, along with a few thick branches from a deadfall pine to balance the weight. They lashed the array of solar panels across the top. Once they were finished, it was heavy and awkward, but it would roll and turn without tipping over if Danny would be careful.

When they were done and had walked the small area to make sure no tools or scraps were left behind to indicate they'd been there, Danny turned a questioning eye to Joe. "Are we making camp for the night here?"

Joe considered it for a moment but shook his head. "If it's all the same to you, I'd like to get a little distance behind us tonight. I've been away from my wife for too long, and I'd like to see her by tomorrow evening if possible."

Danny nodded once and pulled the straps on his backpack tighter. "Sounds good to me."

"Good," Eric said with an exaggerated sigh of relief, "the quicker we get back home, the quicker I can get some of Nanny's hot biscuits."

"What, do you mean lukewarm water and hard granola are getting old?" Joe asked with a short chuckle. "Is everything about food for you, son?"

"When you're talking about hot biscuits, something battered and fried in the middle, and a side of mashed potatoes and gravy, then yes," Eric replied with a grin as they walked down the edge of the highway.

It had taken them a while to lash down the solar panels and collect the tools, and before long the sun was low enough to be hidden by the pines on the left, their long, dark shadows stretching across all four lanes of empty blacktop. Joe walked in front, keeping a close eye on the road ahead of them and stopping every now and then to check around a curve or peer through his scope to make sure the way was clear. Danny walked in the middle with the cart and supplies, and Eric took up the rear.

Every fifty yards or so, Eric turned around and walked backward for a few paces, checking their back trail for followers. Once, while he was looking back, Eric caught a glimmer of swift movement on the shoulder of the road and he froze. He whistled softly and motioned for the other two to take a knee. Eric put the scope on his AR-15 to his eye and adjusted the magnifier until he could make out the area of the road where he'd seen the movement. He scanned from side to side but could see nothing in the gloomy half-light and shadows.

Another flicker of movement alerted Eric. The clip holding his rifle on his shoulder sling clinked against the side of the receiver with a clear metallic ring, and Eric saw it again. A bobcat the size of a large dog slowly turned its face to stare directly at Eric. Its green eyes shown in the gathering darkness, collecting the dim light and throwing it back at him. The eerie sight sent shivers down his spine and goosebumps racing along his arms.

The bobcat was there only for a brief moment, and then with a dim impression of swift, fluid motion, it was gone. Eric stood and let out a breath he hadn't been aware he was holding. "It was just a bobcat," he said to the others' questioning looks. "Not a big bobcat, but a bobcat. And I think he didn't like sharing the road, so he ran back into the woods."

"Well, keep your eyes peeled," Danny said with a shudder. "Them things are mean if they get backed up in a corner, or if they think you're after their den. Might not look big and scary, but they can do a lot of damage to a person if they take a notion."

Eric nodded, and they moved on again, none of them in a big hurry to set up the evening camp in a bobcat's backyard.

Chapter 6

Over Breakfast

President Hall spread thick, yellow butter over one piece of dark, steaming rye toast and then laid three thick strips of crispy bacon over the other piece. He spread it liberally with orange marmalade and made a kind of bacon sandwich. Senator MacArthur sat on the other side of the table, his face a pale, gaunt mask of grim determination and silence.

He refused even so much as a glance at the food.

The president took a large bite of his sandwich. "What's it been, Senator? Fifteen days? No, seventeen, if memory serves. You've lasted far longer than any of the guards guessed in their wagers, and from what I understand, they've started taking bets again on how long before you either eat or die." He finished chewing his bite and swallowed before arching an eye brow and asking, "Would you like to know what the pot is up to now?"

MacArthur didn't flinch. He simply stared back with implacable patience and resolve. It was infuriating. Hall had tried everything he could think of, short of direct physical torture, to break the man, and nothing had so much as dented him. This personal hunger strike of his was becoming more than tiresome—it was dangerous. If he persisted, the man might actually kill himself. He was that stubborn.

If that were to happen, it could absolutely destroy the president's standing with the rest of the Senate. And while he had set things in motion in such a way that he could carry the rest of it out single-handedly if necessary, having the Senate share some of the administrative burden and lend at least the appearance of legitimacy to his actions was helpful. But they were only helpful so long as they remained obedient and satisfied. If this rogue MacArthur were to convince them that they could stand against him, then it could all end in disaster.

The man had to be brought around to reason somehow, and that was why Hall had him here for this conversation over breakfast. Even now, he remained absolutely unreasonable in his determination.

"Senator, there has to be some common ground we can find," President Hall said for the tenth time. "I will not require you to change your vote on the floor. I will simply require you to take the new oath of compliance and that will be the end of it. Once you've signed your verification of the oath, you will be allowed to take your rightful place in the Senate, and you will be allowed to vote your conscience. On some matters, of course, unanimity will be necessary, but we will inform you of those matters ahead of time. In every other instance, you will be the leader, *the* voice of opposition in the government. What do you say?"

McArthur didn't move a muscle. He glared back at the president from his stony mask of hunger and deprivation with that overwhelming sense of resolve.

"Senator, if we're to have a dialogue, then at some point you will have to answer me," Hall said.

McArthur's face twisted into a snarl of disgust. "Dialogue?" He turned his head to the side to spit. "Is that what you call this? You dictate to me the terms under which I will be *allowed* to live, and you call that a dialogue? You don't understand, Mr. Hall. The worst you can do is kill me, and I've already accepted the fact that I may end up killing myself with the course I've chosen. I've already given my life to this, and that means there's nothing left that you can take."

Hall's jaws clenched so tight that he was worried he might shatter a tooth. He was seething with rage as he looked across the table at MacArthur, and only the greatest exercise of personal restraint in his life kept him from lunging across the table and ripping the man's throat out with his fork.

After a long moment of silence, President Hall chuckled a laugh that was anything but humorous and made his brutal intentions unmistakably clear to the senator. "You think not? I'll strap you to a hospital bed and put it in the middle of the Senate floor. I'll have my doctors shove a feeding tube through your nose and down your throat to fill your belly with just enough to keep you alive, to keep you breathing without withering away. I'll let you die, eventually, but I'll drag your demise out day by day so that by the end, your fellow senators will be scrambling over each other to kill you themselves, just so they won't have to endure the spectacle of your suffering any longer."

McArthur flashed a deep grin. "Do it." He leaned forward, his eyes so intense they seemed to shine. "Do it, you bastard. The others might be able to ignore my quiet withering if it's by my own hand. They'll admire my conviction for a while and then laugh it off at dinner parties as the fool-hearty display of a backward and ignorant cretin who simply failed to grasp the realities of the situation. They'll explain *me* away if I do this to myself. But if *you* do it, they won't be able to ignore it. They won't be able to explain it away. They'll *have* to see you for what you really are, then."

"And what will you accomplish with your defiance?" President Hall spat back. "You will be dead and I will still be in power. I will still be standing while you rot in an unmarked, unremembered grave and your fellow senators laugh at each other's jokes."

Senator MacArthur stood slowly, wincing with the pain of the effort. His bones and his joints stood out far more than they should have, and a thick blue vein at the side of his temple throbbed once he was on his feet.

"I'd rather be remembered as the only patriot martyr who died standing against you, Mr. Hall, than be remembered with the traitors lapping at your feet."

Without another word, the senator turned and stumbled for the door. Before he reached it, Hall nodded for the two security guards to let him return to his room. When McArthur and the guards were gone and the room was once again empty, he sat for a long time and stared at the cold breakfast on his plate. He considered hurtling the plate against the wall but quickly dismissed the thought.

Such a childish display would accomplish nothing and would serve only to alert the staff to his anger and frustration. Instead, he began eating mechanically, barely pausing to notice some of the more succulent flavors. He had work to do, and his body needed the fuel to accomplish it. Try as he might, though, he could not get Senator MacArthur out of his head.

Finally, President Hall pushed the plate away, his food half-eaten. It troubled him that while he was well fed and rested, his starving enemy was somehow stronger and more resolved. As he sat, he saw the beginnings of a plan to take the sting out of the McArthur's death. If the senator was willing to give his life for his beliefs, then it was up to President Hall to make sure that death served his own purposes rather than the senator's defiance. The only way to do that was to take the matter out of his hands. He'd hoped for it not to come to that, but the man left him no choice.

Like the senator, President Hall was willing to go as far as necessary.

Chapter 7

War Council

Commander Price stood in the briefing auditorium, the wall of screens behind him displaying an expanded satellite view of the Midwestern United States. A tangle of interlacing lines shown in red represented major railroad lines, and a similar network of blue lines represented major highways. Often the thicker and more traveled highways paralleled some of the largest and most heavily used railroad shipping lanes.

Sometimes those thick red railroad lines bent far away from the major cities and highways, striking their way across the open prairie states. Those railroad lines provided the nation, and a good portion of the world, with grain and other food staples. Price tried not to think about the fact that those rail lines were empty this fall and what that would mean for the millions who depended on the food they provided. Instead, he focused on the tangled masses where those various lines re-converged.

Those twisted knots of red and blue were the shipping and freight hubs, the beating heart of the Republic. The ability to easily move people and goods from A to B was one of those small things that had made a huge impact in the history of America. That entire system was, at best, horribly crippled. If there was to be a restoration it would be measured in decades; Price knew that.

47

The image was at his back, but he could feel the weight of it sitting squarely on his shoulders, pressing at him, pushing him down. It was more than a man could bear—this weight of responsibility. He couldn't bring himself to turn and look at the map, not yet, not with an audience. It overpowered him to see the names of so many towns and wonder if anyone was still alive.

A knock at the door interrupted Price's private thoughts, and he took a moment to compose himself before responding. "Come in."

Lieutenant Commander Attledge marched into the room, while his bodyguard remained in the hallway. He wore his service dress khaki uniform, pressed and polished despite the fact that it was 0400 and still hours before dawn. He strode to the middle of the room, executed a flawless right turn and marched to a distance of three paces and presented at attention, but he didn't salute.

"Lieutenant Commander Marcus Attledge reporting as ordered, sir."

"At ease, Commander," Price said, and Attledge relaxed a hair as his eyes wandered to the map of the Midwest. "I ordered you here this morning so you could be a part of a very special meeting. The signal I sent out a few days ago was pinged back to the satellite by three of the encrypted phones I distributed. That means those three phones were active and received the signal. I have no idea about the others, but those three at least got it."

Price gestured to a stand in the third row that held a forty-two inch LED television and a small webcam attached to a laptop. The screen displayed a video chat window that was currently blank and waiting an input signal. "One of the phones was in the hands of the captain of the USS George Washington. He dialed in our frequency using his own shipboard secured transmitter and gave us a return call. He'll be joining us for the briefing via satellite transmission. The second phone was with a commander training special operations forces in the Idaho mountains. He arrived at the base with a small detachment of his troops just a few hours ago and should be here shortly."

"Wait, you said three phones pinged you back," Attledge interjected. "What about the third phone? Who has that one?"

"I gave it to the man who is now in charge of the Arizona Air National Guard. There hasn't been any response from that phone, so I have no idea if the man is even alive or if he keeps the phone around anymore. The two we have are all we have to work with for now."

Attledge started to ask another question, but Price held up his hand. "Marcus, I know you have questions, and I swear to you I will answer every question you have, but we don't have time right now. What I need from you is to be another set of eyes and ears for me. Look for the things I don't see and listen for what I don't hear."

Attledge's voice dropped to a whisper. "Do you think one of them could be a traitor?"

Price's face was grim. "Anyone can be a traitor, Marcus, even these men. But we need them and the people under their command. If we're going to make a fight of this, we need men, we need officers to train them, and we need air power. It's going to take more than a few hundred of us huddled under a mountain in Utah and a few hundred more sent off on probable suicide missions of recon and recruitment. But as much as we need them, I can't afford to trust them—not yet. So that's where you come in. If you're asked a direct question, give a direct and brief answer, but otherwise just be here and keep your head on a swivel."

Attledge nodded and kept his other questions to himself. The far-left seat on the front row of the auditorium had a bottle of water, a notepad, and a pen waiting for him. Price told him to take general notes and appear to be occupied but to stay focused for any signs of treachery or deceit from the two others attending the meeting.

After a few moments, there was another knock at the door. Price took a deep breath and let it out slowly. With a firm, loud voice he called, "Come."

The door opened, and a tall, broad-shouldered man dressed in forest green camo marched formally into the room and stood at attention. His right hand twitched as if it wanted to salute.

"Lieutenant Colonel Charles Darius reporting as ordered, Commander."

"Thank you for coming, Colonel. I will set up the video link with the captain now. Give me a moment."

Darius' jaw tightened slightly, but he held attention and waited. So far, he was willing to at least give the show of deference to the orders Price had cited, and that was promising. Price's fingers raced over the wireless keyboard as he keyed the signaling commands into the telecasting platform. In a few moments, a video window was up and running with a feed from the captain's Carrier Ready Room. A small cut out image in the upper left corner of the screen showed the auditorium broadcast to the ship.

The captain was waiting at the head of a short, empty conference table.

"Thank you for coming, Captain," Price said. "This is Lieutenant Colonel Darius of the Army Special Forces. Lieutenant Colonel, this is Captain Willard Haley, commanding officer of the USS George Washington."

Darius gave the camera a nod, and Haley did the same on his end.

"Who is that on the end?" Haley asked.

"That is my second-in-command," Price answered, "Lieutenant Commander Marcus Attledge. I have him here to take notes and minutes, which will be sealed to the room unless we vote otherwise."

Darius started to ask another question, but Price had had enough. "Gentlemen, I'm sure you have questions, and I would love to answer them," he said, firmly steamrolling over the colonel before he could get a word out. "Right now, though, we have limited time to discuss what we need to do. Captain, I need you to write down these numbers: 38° 36'29.8"N 131° 05'50.4"W."

Price repeated the numbers twice as he handed the colonel a folded piece of paper. When Haley nodded that he had them down, Price clicked a button on the remote. "I just handed Lieutenant Colonel Darius a similar string of numbers. Those are GPS coordinates for where the two of you were when you powered on your satellite phone and received my message. You can cross check the times and positions down to the second, if you like, and I'm sure your own memory or records will confirm."

Price gestured to the screen behind him that now showed a series of green dots alongside the red and blue lines. "The point of this little demonstration is to prove my ability to pinpoint the location of assets in the field. That kind of overview of the theater will be invaluable. The indicators you see now are advanced reconnaissance and intelligence forces I have already deployed.

Reports from some of the teams should begin filtering back to us within a matter of days, but we can lay the groundwork now."

"I'm sorry, Commander, but I think you've lost me," Haley said from the screen. "You're throwing around words like theater and recon like we're in a combat zone or something. Just who are you fighting, Commander Price? You're in Utah, if I'm not mistaken."

Price didn't miss a beat. "We're fighting the people who did this to us. The man who has claimed the presidency is a traitor, a mass murderer, and a terrorist. From what I've been able to piece together, this was a plot that had been more than four years in the making and involved at least heavy support from the Russians as well as a group of knowledgeable, ambitious, and well-connected collaborators here at home. This man who calls himself President Hall was the leader of that group. That's who we're fighting, Captain."

There was a moment of tense silence in the room, and finally Haley broke it. "I assume you have proof for these charges, Commander? Or evidence, at least?"

"I do, and you're welcome to come here and examine it yourself. The Lieutenant Colonel has already been provided with copies of everything we have gathered, though I doubt he's had time to do more than skim the high points. But, one thing I must stand firm on—I will not, under any circumstance, transmit my evidence until the traitor Hall has been either captured or killed. Until then, I will safeguard the evidence by controlling it."

The captain took a minute to consider his options. "We've picked up radio transmissions on official emergency broadcasts from the mainland, just at the edge of our reception, even on the long-range radio. The messages are ordering all Navy vessels to report to San Diego for re-tasking according to the orders of 'acting

President Hall and the Federal Senate,' whoever in the blue hell that is. Something has had my hackles up since I heard the repeating automated messages the first time. My old sailor's gut telling me things, I guess. I'd still like to see what you have, Commander, but I'll take what you've said at face value."

Price relaxed visibly and used the laser pointer to highlight a particularly dense junction of red and blue lines on the map. "The first thing we need to do is make sure we can move men and material across the country. This is Kansas City Missouri, one of the largest railroad and highway hubs in the nation. If we can control those junctions, we control access roads and railways that touch every corner of the lower forty-eight states."

"You're talking about taking a city. An operation like that takes men, equipment, supplies. We'll need a way to move all of this stuff," Darius said, his deep voice quiet and thoughtful.

"Strategic Command kept a fleet of hardened diesel train engines for emergency transport," Price answered. "There were two hundred kept on constant alert and readiness standby. There are a few scattered across the central US, but most have been housed in the more populated coastal states. I know for a fact that two of those engines are stored in a secure facility in the Colorado mountains. We can use those two to help stage supplies and move men, if we can gain access to them fast enough. Otherwise, we'll just have to improvise."

Price clicked another button on his remote before Darius could ask another question. The view of the map changed, focusing in on an expanded aerial shot of the entire metropolitan area of Kansas City.

"This is our target. Between the railroads, the highways, and the rivers, there are no cities more strategic this side of the

Mississippi River. Much of the nation's food has always come through this city in one form or another. Metric tons of beef, chicken, pork, grains, potatoes, and vegetables move on barges and railcars—non-stop—throughout the year. We're going to need that kind of leverage."

Haley leaned forward. "What do you have in mind, Commander?"

Price clicked, and the next screen showed an image of an F/A-18 Super Hornet fighter. "How many of these do you have on board, Captain, and are they loaded?"

Haley smiled. "How many do you need, Commander?"

Price thought about it a moment. "Four at the least, with a good mix of air to ground and air to air hardware. I think I will have some A-10s for you to rendezvous with, but I can't be sure yet. I will let you know when I find out, but if I don't yours might be enough."

"Their targets?" Haley asked.

"Any assets the enemy has that are worth it. I don't know what they have, but I know they're there. Satellite images I gleaned from other people's orbiting hardware show right now that they have moved in personnel carriers at the very least. The resolution is crap, so I can't be sure, but there are definitely some large vehicle formations on the north end of town. It can't be coincidence that the main rail and freight yards are also there."

"If you don't have the resolution to tell what the vehicles are," Darius began, a thoughtful frown on his weathered face, "how can you tell it's the Federal Security Service? From what I understand, those guys are pretty discrete about their tags and logos."

Price relocated the pointer onto the map. "That is why three of the teams I sent out are headed for that part of town. They should get there in a matter of days and begin reporting back. That's where you and your men come into play, Colonel. How many trainees do you have with you this run?"

"Thirty-eight total with me, including outriders. I've got another two hundred or so back at the Wilderness Combat Survival, Evasion, Resistance, Escape School. Some are military or former military, some are civilians, some instructors. I guess everybody's a soldier now, though."

Price clicked the next image that showed a digital layout of the northern section of Kansas City and a series of tiny images, icons, and lines. "Colonel Darius, your men are going to have a lot of ground to cover in a relatively short time. How are their legs?"

Darius smiled. "You just point us in a direction and watch us go, sir."

Price nodded and began detailing the diagram on the screen behind him. The officers asked questions here and there, but for the most part they took Price's presentation as straight forward. When Price finished, a long and somewhat uncomfortable pause settled among the men.

Haley cleared his throat and broke the silence. "You realize all of this could be for nothing, right? Those vehicles could be friendly forces and all of this might just be an overblown knee jerk reaction."

"You're right," Price admitted. "It could be. But I'd rather over-react and be ready if something goes south than assume things are going to go smoothly until thcy don't."

Chapter 8

Unnecessary Violence

Oct. 8 th 1325 EST

Tom drove the post hole diggers into the dirt again, yanked the handles apart to catch a scoop full of dirt, and pulled them out of the hole. He dropped the plug of dark soil to the side with the rest of the pile. They had no quick mix concrete around, so Tom slid the fence post that he'd cut from a cedar sapling into the hole. Brant and Steven packed sand and small gravel around the base of the post and then filled in the rest of the hole with the dirt Tom had removed earlier. When they finished, the post stood with three feet of length buried tightly in the ground and another four feet or so exposed.

Grabbing the top of the fence post, Tom pushed and pulled on it to test its stability, and, to his relief, it held fast. Satisfied, he nodded and leaned the post hole diggers against one of the small pine trees that dotted the edge of the pastures on both sides of the highway. He sat in the shade of the pine and took a sip from the plastic canteen that sat next to the lunch basket his wife and two sons had brought earlier. The food was long gone, as was to be expected with a teenager and an early-twenties college student around, but the water was refreshing even if it was warm.

Tom handed the canteen over to Brant. "You boys drink up. It's not hot out today, but we're sweating a lot. With the breeze drying you off, you can get dehydrated without realizing it. So, what's the next step, Brant? This is your rodeo. I'm just along for the ride."

Brant swallowed one last gulp of water and passed the canteen on to Steven Gandry. "Well, when we've done this in the past, it was always a temporary thing to move the cows from one side of the road to the other. I guess we can go ahead and cut the fence where we measured yesterday. We'll take each strand and fold it out toward the road. If we measured right, we'll have more than enough to cross the road and tie it off so the fence is whole again. We'll put loops in one side of the wire and attach the spring hooks on the other. When you pull the barbed wire tight, the spring hook goes in the loop and closes it. To the cows, it looks like just another piece of fence."

Tom nodded and thought for a few moments. "How much excess do you think we'll have?"

Brant shrugged. "Tough to say exactly, but at least a few dozen feet on each strand."

Tom rubbed the thick stubble on his chin as he thought. "What if we cut some thick timbers and lashed them together in groups of three or four to make a shape kind of like the barricades the Germans set up on the beaches of Normandy back in the forties? We could wrap them with the extra barbed wire and make it tough to get a good grip on them to move them around."

Brant handed the canteen back to Tom. "If you think we can do it, I don't see why not. What would that do, though?"

"Well, it would slow down anyone trying to steam roll their way through here, for one thing, and maybe just the appearance of the obstacles would be enough to make people think twice about trying to screw with us."

Brant liked the idea, but they both agreed the fence was the top priority. Before Joe and Eric had left on their scavenging trip with Danny, they'd all agreed that cutting off the road was a major priority to slow down the advancement of the violent group in Bennett. Until that threat was addressed, they had to do everything they could to protect themselves, and making travel more difficult was just one way to do so. Joe had left it up to Tom to figure out, but using the pasture fencing had been Brant's idea.

The young man had proven resourceful in finding the parts they needed, including several of the hook-and-loop gate kits. After a brief rest, Brant grabbed the wire snips first and volunteered to do the cutting. He had Tom stand on his right and Steven on his left to pull the barbed wire toward each other near the middle of the road that bordered the upper pasture.

With the fence now slack, Brant easily snipped the wire, and then Tom and Steven carefully released the tension they were holding. If Brant had simply cut the wire, it would have snapped wildly from the tension of being strung tightly. Barbed wire was always dangerous and someone could end up with stitches, a blind eye, or even missing fingers with that kind of mishap.

The three men repeated the process for each of the four runs of wire. They unhooked the runs from three posts in each direction from the cut. When they had cut the runs on the other side of the road the same way, they started hanging the wire on the posts, pulling each run as tight as possible as they went. Brant would need to find a wire stretcher to stretch the fence tight, but for now hand-drawn would have to do.

They worked on the side of the fence that faced town first and had finished three of the four runs by the time the sun was halfway to the horizon. All three men were hot and exhausted, but they'd made the decision to finish this part of the fence before they took another break, and they were committed to seeing that small goal accomplished.

Steven was busy threading the barbed wire through the closed end of the gate kit handles and twisting it into a tight knot with a pair of vice-grip pliers. It was an easy but tedious task that the teenager had tackled with gusto. Meanwhile, Tom pulled the barbed wire tight between the fence posts they had planted earlier, and Brant hammered u-shaped clamps into the fresh wood. He used three per post for each run of fence.

Brant hammered the last clamp into the first of the posts on the fourth run of fence. "I used to work like this with my dad. I hated it at the time. We'd work for hours, and I wouldn't say a word just to spite him. I wanted to be in the woods hunting, or out with friends—anything but stretching some damned wire fence."

He nailed the next three clamps in silence and after a long moment said, "I'd give anything to have it back, though. One more boring, grumpy Saturday stuck running fence with him."

Tom wasn't sure what to say to that, so he reached down and gave the young man's shoulder a comforting squeeze. Brant was so large, and with his now full-grown and quite bushy beard, it was easy to forget how young he really was at twenty-six. Tom got the impression that Brant had matured a great deal the last few months, though he had little on which to base his hunch. Often, he seemed withdrawn and somber, but out here in the open air and sunshine that undeniable sense of youthful innocence returned.

They began stretching the fence from the other side, working their way back to the middle of the road. Tom and Brant were both on the town side of the fence hard at work, their backs facing down the road. They never saw the men until Steven looked up and whispered, "Someone's coming. *Strangers.*"

Tom caught Brant's eye and gave a very small shake of his head. He stood and acted like he was stretching his back from pulling the fence. As he did so, he managed to glance over his shoulder and see three men coming at them. Tom motioned with his hand for Brant to stand as he turned to face the strangers.

Now that he was facing them, Tom took in the details, cataloging them as his eyes flicked back and forth among them. All three were armed with side-arms, but none had a rifle or shotgun. They all had knives on their belts and probably more hidden. Along with the holsters on their hips, Tom saw at least one ankle rig bulging inside the too-tight camo pants of the man on the right.

The center man was walking a little forward of the others, and he had on dark sunglasses, but no hat. The other two wore ball caps and sunglasses. Though the man in the center was the most forward of the three, and he walked with a purpose, Tom's eyes were drawn to the man on the left. Something about the way he moved, the way he held his head and his hands, the slope of his shoulders as he walked, or some other indiscernible quality screamed to Tom's instincts that this man was dangerous, and no matter how it seemed, he was the man in charge.

The three strangers, their faces streaked with dust, soot, and sweat, stopped, at most, ten feet from Tom. The man in the center was close enough for Tom to smell his sour sweat when the breeze shifted. The man on the left kept walking until he had placed himself directly between Tom and the pine tree where his M-4 carbine and Brant's 12 gauge pump shotgun were leaning.

The hairs on the back of Tom's neck stood on end as he felt the tension instantly go up a notch. The guy on the right kept checking the woods and back along the road as if he expected an ambush at any moment. Nothing about the situation smelled right to Tom. These three were trying to look the part of hicks with their faded blue jeans, hand-me-down camo fatigues, and cheap Ray-Ban knockoffs. But underneath the thin coating of miscreant, they moved like operators.

Trying to sound somewhat congenial, the man in the center spoke without preamble. "What are you fellas out here doing this afternoon? You can't block a public right of way, y'all. There are all kinds of reasons it's against the law, but the bottom line is you can't do it."

Tom held his right hand out. "I'm Tom." The man looked at it but didn't make a move to take it, so Tom let his hand drop. "There aren't any emergency services to get blocked. That's all over a long time ago, so there's no harm in it. Where you guys headed? Maybe I can tell you a detour to take."

Tom could hear the edge as the man's tone grew more serious. "Won't be any detour, mister. I told you that you can't block a public right of way, and I mean that. Either you and your boys are gonna take down this barricade, or me and my boys are gonna take it down for you. What's on the other side of your fence, anyway, old man?"

Tom frowned. He was in his fifties, though barely. And his father had lived to be ninety-eight, so he felt far from old. With an effort, he kept his voice calm. "Look, we already told you that we're not going to take the fence down, and there's no need for you to know what's on the other side of the fence. So, I can help you find a detour that will be short and direct, or you can find one yourself. Either way, you're not getting through here."

At that moment—the worst possible moment—one of the cows in the upper pasture mooed so loud it echoed from three directions. Tom saw the light of recognition in the men's eyes as they understood what they had stumbled across.

61

"So, you're the ones we've heard the rumors about," the man in the center said, a slow grin spreading across his face. "Y'all are the ones with the guns, the cows, the salt, the medicine, and near everything else you can think of. I was starting to think y'all were a myth."

Tom's pulse was pounding. "Look, I don't know what you've heard. All we're doing is trying to keep our families, and a lot of other families, alive out here. Yeah, we help people whenever we can, but sometimes we just can't help. And we can't help you men."

The man in the center spat at Tom's boots, his face growing red with impatient rage. "You're hoarders. You're hoarding vital supplies while others starve. You are in violation of the First Emergency Order of the new mayor of Bennett. We are the mayor's collection officers, and we are here to collect what you owe to the community."

"This isn't part of the city," Tom said, his pulse suddenly smooth, and even. He saw what was coming, and he knew there was no way of stopping it. Options rolled through his mind a thousand a second, racing for alternatives for how to handle the coming gun fight. These men were going to try and take the cows—they all knew it. It was just a matter of working up to it. The man in the center, his face an even darker shade of red, was still going on about equitable allocation of food, or something.

The man on Tom's left had been steadily closing the distance between himself and Tom since the trio had stopped. Tom had purposefully ignored the motion, though he'd swept the man with his eyes several times. Now, the man was just a few strides away. If he waited any longer, it would be too late.

Tom abruptly turned and started toward the man on his left. The man in the center was so startled he cut off in midsentence, and into the sudden silence, Tom yelled, "Steven, RUN!"

The man on the left hadn't expected Tom to charge him, so he hesitated, but that was all Tom needed to close the gap. By the time the man's right hand was on his gun, Tom's left hand was too, holding it in the holster. With his right hand, Tom drove his fist hard into the man's chest, dead center, below the midline where his heart would sit, and snapped the man's solar plexus.

The man's air went out in a ragged retch and he doubled over. Tom grabbed his head with both hands and drove it down as his knee came up and connected with his temple. There was a crunch from the man's neck and he crumpled to the ground.

Everything happened so quickly that it was over before either of the man's companions could reach for their weapons. Tom drew his own Beretta from a holster on his right hip as he turned toward the other two strangers. The man on the right was bringing his gun up, so Tom focused on him.

Tom pulled his trigger three times in rapid succession, striking the man twice in the chest. As Tom turned toward the man in the center, he noticed out of the corner of his eye that Steven was gone and Brant was on the way to the pine tree to get a weapon.

He also realized that Brant would be far too late.

Tom watched as the man in the center aimed and squeezed the trigger on his .45 caliber 1911. There was a flash from the muzzle and an explosion of white hot pain in his lower right chest as the bullet tore into him. Tom sagged a bit on his feet but managed not to fall. He raised his own pistol and squeezed off four rounds that struck the man in the center of his torso. As he fell, the man had the strength to pull the trigger one more time, and Tom felt the bullet shatter his left knee.

Suddenly, Tom was falling forward, a loud ring piercing his ears. Everything faded to black before he hit the ground.

Chapter 9

Paid On Delivery

Joe held up his right hand in a closed fist, and Eric stopped. It was early afternoon, and the sun was warm enough to be nearly hot. They were at the edge of the hardware store parking lot and completely alone as far as Joe could tell. A familiar sensation was itching its way up his spine from between his shoulder blades, though, and that meant they were being watched. After decades down range, Joe had learned to trust his instincts at such moments. He rarely knew what had alerted him, but once his hackles were up, those hunches usually proved right.

Eric was confused by their unexpected stop. "Aren't we going to keep going?"

Joe shook his head slightly and whispered over his right shoulder. "Something doesn't feel right. If this lady followed my advice, they should already know we're here. They can come out and meet us, or we can go home. It's her call."

"How long do we wait?" Eric asked, but his question was answered before Joe could speak.

The large, rolling door that covered the bay clattered up, and Marsha, the store manager, stepped out into plain view. She waved to Joe and Eric, then put her fingers to her lips and whistled a shrill signal.

Joe nodded to Eric, and they started walking. Joe kept his hands on his M-4, and Eric's was placed in the cart so that he could pull it in a flash. They both had their side-arms in case things went completely sideways. Joe had hoped that when they were called inside, the feeling of hidden eyes would dissipate, but it hadn't. If anything, it had grown more acute and more uncomfortable.

Joe stayed two paces behind and two to the right of Eric, and he constantly checked their flanks and their back trail. As they got closer, he could see Marsha's smile.

"I honestly didn't think you'd be back," she said. "When you left I..."

Joe cut her off in midsentence. "Ma'am, we'd better finish this inside." She started to say something else, but Joe shook his head and let Eric push the cart inside.

Marsha could tell he was serious but she still didn't like getting bossed in her own store. "Sure. It will be good to get into the shade for a bit," she said somewhat bitingly.

Joe ignored her snarky comment and nodded for her and Eric to lead the way. Only when they were all inside the store with the door rolled down was Joe able to relax and somewhat shake that feeling of being watched. He hated feelings like that, but he knew better than to simply brush them aside just because they were unpleasant. Until he could understand what was going on outside, Joe was more than willing to tolerate the stifling heat in the store.

"Marsha, have you seen any strangers around the store?" Joe asked without preamble. "Have you noticed trash cans in the shopping center turned over, ransacked, anything like that?"

Marsha shook her head.

"What about droppings? People, not animal."

"Droppings?" Marsha asked, her face twisted into a grimace. "You mean like crap? No, the patrols haven't seen evidence of anyone taking a dump around the store. Why are you asking? Did you?"

Joe chuckled at her blunt inquiry. "No, I didn't see anything, and I certainly didn't do the deed myself and leave it lying around for someone to find. But I got the feeling that we were being watched out there, and closely. Did you have any security out in the bushes at the edge of the parking lot? Any scouts doing wide perimeter rounds?"

Marsha shook her head again. "I had four look outs up on the roof and four walking and looking close to the store, but nothing farther out than fifty yards at any time. If you didn't see anything either, maybe you're just being paranoid. It could be nothing."

Joe frowned but didn't say anything. He was used to figuring things out and was unsettled by his reaction to what had, so far, been nothing more than a gut feeling. He turned to Wanda and gestured to the cart. "We have the components and the panels we promised. The panels won't power the store or anything, but they'll be enough to charge the batteries for the lights and give you some visibility around the perimeter at night. I can get more for you later, after we negotiate a new deal. But this balances us out, right?"

"Not so fast," Marsha said. "Not much good to me if I don't know how to hook it up."

Joe smiled. He reached into a zippered pocket of his vest and pulled out a pocket-sized memo book. He held it up for Marsha to see. "These are diagrams and instructions for how to hook up the panels and the components—how to set them up to charge, set them up to run, set them up to test. Everything you need to know. Principles, anyway, I guess you could say. Some trial and error will be needed to fine tune things, but this will get you on paper, as they say."

Marsha's smile returned, and she reached for the notebook, but Joe pulled it back. "Not so fast. When we negotiated this deal, we agreed you would trade the tools for the components, the light, and the panels. Nothing was mentioned about setting it up or instructions. This little notebook isn't part of the original deal. It's part of a new deal."

Marsha's eyes narrowed and her lips stretched into a thin, angry line. "That's low, and you know it," she practically hissed.

"What I know is that this notebook is now very valuable, agreed?" Joe asked, his voice calm and even. Marsha didn't speak; she simply glared at him. "Good. We agree on that. I want you to know that *I* know exactly what I'm doing here. I know *exactly* what I'm handing over to you, free and clear."

Joe held the notebook out, and Marsha hesitated, but she accepted it. "That's leverage, and I don't operate that way," he said. "I don't apply pressure or exert influence on friends and people who deal squarely with me and mine. Now, people who cross me— that's a different story. We understand each other?"

Marsha nodded as she tucked the notebook into her pocket. "Perfectly. Is there anything else you all need while you're here?"

"Interesting that you should ask," Joe said. "We could use a couple of axes and hatchets, a splitting wedge, and a couple of hand saws if you have them. We can talk about trade . . ."

A shrill whistle echoed from the back of the store and Marsha held up a hand, silencing Joe, much to his surprise. A young woman, breathless and sweaty, came running up. Marsha bent, and the young woman whispered to her and then ran toward the back of the store. Marsha turned back to Joe and Eric. "The lookouts on the roof have spotted someone riding a bicycle from the direction you both came. Is it someone you know?"

Joe shrugged. "I have no idea standing in here, but I'm certainly not expecting anyone. If it is someone I know, I'll be as shocked as you are. It's just one person?" When Marsha nodded, Joe checked the safety on his M-4 and then pointed toward the door. "I've been feeling edgy all morning, to tell you the truth. Let's see who this is together, and one way or another we'll handle it."

Without waiting for a response, Joe turned and nodded to a young man standing next to the bay door, and he began slowly cranking it up. Joe dropped to one knee so he could peer out as soon as the door was open a few feet. Eric stood behind him, his rifle already in his hands.

When the door was high enough, Joe stepped out and moved to their left, and Eric rolled to the right. They spread out until both could see the man on the bicycle. It was Cage, peddling as hard as he could.

Immediately, both Eric and Joe dropped their muzzles and let the slings catch their weight. Joe reached Cage first and held the bike while the hulking man climbed off the seat. Cage was drenched in sweat, so Joe handed him his half-full canteen, and Cage drank it all in three massive gulps.

As soon as Cage could get words past his ragged breathing, he said, "Mister Tillman, you got to come quick. Mr. Tom got shot and he's bad off. They were all talking late last night about who to send when the sun come up, and couldn't none of them decide on who should go and who should stay, or why. So, I wrote them all a note and left once they was all in bed. The boy Steven, he let me out the gate and said he wouldn't tell anyone until they started looking this morning. I took a bike cause I can't walk too fast these days. I guess I can't ride too fast either. He fell into a fit of hard coughing and had to catch his breath.

Joe let the bike fall over. "Slow down, Cage. Tell me what happened, or what you know, but tell me quickly."

Cage nodded and filled Joe in on what Brant and Steven had told the others of the attack. Joe listened and the itch between his shoulder blades grew stronger with each word, but he barely felt it, now. A new, more troubling feeling was growing in the pit of his stomach. As Cage described the attack and where Tom had been hit, a cold knot of dread and fear began to twist deep in his gut.

When Cage finally slowed down, he picked up the bike and pushed it at Joe. "You should hop on here and ride back, Mr. Tillman. They need you back there. I'll get your boy home."

Joe looked at the bike for a moment but finally shook his head. "We're going back together. That means you're going to need the bike to keep up, Cage. No one gets left behind today."

<u>Chapter 10</u>

Last Leg

Only one in five of the overhead light panels was lit in the Capitol building at this time in the afternoon, and windows let in most of the light in the hallways. The massive banks of solar panels arrayed on the National Mall supplied an impressive amount of power to the compound when the sun was up, but the majority of it was stored in massive battery systems for the night time darkness. With the perimeter lights eating up a lot of the available kilowatt hours at night and in the day, the interior of the Capitol was left in gloom.

The dim light fit President Phillip Hall's mood as he strode through the halls, his six-man security team forming a diamond shape around him as he moved. Even here, in the dead of the night, the president had to maintain his vigilance. He knew that if he faltered now, or if he fell victim to the plots and schemes of ambitious or fearful men, then everything he had carefully built would fall apart.

He had already been betrayed by the Russians; that much was clear now. They had never even intended to help him seize power, not really. They just dangled the carrot a little too close— intentionally, of course. The final straw was sitting face to face with the first deputy premier and being handed a written guarantee of forces with the signature of the Russian president himself.

Hall still had that letter in a maple writing case that once sat on George Washington's writing desk, one he'd had relocated from the Smithsonian. One day he would show it to the Russian president and remind him that they could have been allies. That would be after he had taken everything from the man and reduced his life to ashes for his betrayal.

But those thoughts of revenge were of no use to him at this time, so he ruthlessly strangled that train of thought and refused to allow his attention to return to it. He had to focus on the present first, solidify his position and his control, and then rebuild what he could with what he had.

If he couldn't manage that, there wouldn't even *be* a later to exact his vengeance.

In the here and now there was trouble enough to deal with. The Senator who was initially an annoyance had become a real threat to Hall's already tenuous grasp on the Senate. With his every ragged and defiant breath, Senator MacArthur refused to bow to his will, and the rest of the Senate saw it.

Hall had, of course, fabricated a charge of treason and conspiracy to besmirch Senator Timothy McArthur and to justify clapping him in irons in the middle of the Senate Chamber. After his audacious speech in the first assembly, it wasn't difficult to get the rest of the opportunistic politicians to turn on him. Whether they really believed the charges to be true or had simply justified them to their own consciences, their conviction of the senator could be expedient. They were enthusiastic about the hearing, and some even pushed openly for conviction and exile. Before the senators worked themselves into a lynch mob, Hall had been forced to call for a recess so that he could consider the matter in private.

Throughout the entire ordeal, Senator MacArthur hadn't said a word.

Hall ground his teeth as he remembered feeling uncomfortable under the McArthur's unwavering glare. The man had shown such contempt in his expression that it practically rolled off him in shimmering waves like heat over a road in the summer.

As Hall rounded a corner and found himself in front of the Senate Chamber doors, he paused for a moment, his breath coming in deep, heavy pants. His adrenaline was up, and he needed to bring it into control. In order for his plan to have any hope of success, he had to have at least the appearance of calm authority.

When he was ready, Hall gave a single nod, and the man at the forward point of the security formation opened the doors. As he did so, he stepped aside, and his detail poured through. Three men fanned out and swept the corners as they went. The four regular security guards stood frozen in place as they were patted down and disarmed.

A few days before in an unfortunate misunderstanding, a young security guard had been shot just as Hall stepped into the Senate Chamber. The young man had very bad timing, and when he reached for the flashlight that was clipped to the same side of his belt as his pistol, one of the Special Security Police had seen the movement and assumed a threat. He'd responded accordingly by shooting the security guard three times in the chest.

The Special Security officer was given a bonus and a promotion.

Now, to avoid those kinds of mistakes, the guards inside any room the president entered were immediately disarmed. Once the guards were secured, they stood at attention and waited as the rest of the detail set up an interior perimeter. They were all in place before the president had taken three steps into the room. Senator MacArthur sat as upright in his seat as he could, but the chain holding him to the table was short and gave him very little slack to maneuver. His shoulders were hunched forward slightly, but he had enough room to bend his neck and look someone in the eye.

The senator looked strong, considering it had been more than two weeks since his last real meal. He'd eaten little bits and pieces of food that he'd acquired on his own through stashing and trading, not to mention the refreshments he kept on hand in his own congressional offices. Those supplies had remained his when he first agreed to serve in the Senate.

But a snack could stave off starvation, at best, for a short length of time. It certainly wasn't enough to satisfy that gnawing, burning sensation of hunger. And now, chained to this table for several days, he'd been deprived even of that small amount of sustenance. The senator's eyes were a little more deeply set, and his cheek bones seemed more prominent beneath the stubble on his hollow cheeks. He was hungry and in pain, that much was clear in his eyes, but he refused to allow it to show anywhere else.

President Hall felt a grudging admiration for the man and his steadfast determination, which didn't help his mood at all. He stood silently over the senator for a long moment, forcing the captive man to crane his neck to look up at him. The president dragged a chair over and sat opposite of MacArthur, putting them roughly on eye level, or what would have been eye level had the Senator been unrestrained.

Hall turned to the lead security officer. "The regular guards may be dismissed." One by one the disarmed guards filed out of the chamber without a word or a moment's hesitation. When the last one was gone, the head of his security detail stepped back inside and gave Hall a salute. He would remain in the hall with the regular guards in case anyone tried to force their way into the chamber.

"If any word of what is said here is uttered outside of these walls," Hall said calmly, his eyes never leaving the senator's, "I will personally kill every single man in this room. Is that understood?"

As one, the Special Security Police saluted, right arms across their chests at a right angle, right hands over their hearts in a fist. "Yes, sir!" they sounded off in unison.

MacArthur still didn't flinch, and he didn't say a word. The implacability of a man committed to dying was a powerful thing to behold, and an impossible one to withstand. Eventually, the president dropped his eyes to the senator's hands and his thin, bruised wrists.

"I understand you didn't even fight when they bound you in these chains," Hall spat, the vehemence in his own voice startling. "How pathetic. Such a brave man, unwilling even to defend himself."

McArthur sneered in contempt. "What good would it do to try and harm the men carrying out your orders? I can't harm you, not from my current position. All I can do is refuse to be compromised. I can refuse to bow to your will. I can remain free."

Hall leaned down into McArthur's personal space, mere inches in front of his face. "Yet, here you are, bound hand and foot in chains. How free do you feel, *Senator?*" the president hissed.

Hall could see it. Hidden there behind the hatred and the resolve in the senator's eyes was a deep, dark pit of cold fear. He was a man just like any other, and he didn't really want to die; he just didn't see a way out of it—not yet, anyway.

Hall leaned back and straightened his suit. "I told you once before that I would chain you to a hospital bed and force feed you to keep you breathing. I have reconsidered that particular decision. Instead, I think I would like to see you waste away and die rasping and begging either for food or a bullet. Sure, there will be some who see it as a moral victory for you, but you'll still be dead, and they'll still be too terrified to even think about opposing me. You want the principled, moral victory? Fine, it's yours."

Hall paused to let his words sink in. His lips curled in vile contempt, and he sat back in his seat. "On the other hand, if you were to confess to having succumbed to a momentary lapse in judgment, combined with an intense desire to protect the already crippled nation and a misplaced suspicion against me, then perhaps some accommodations might be made. If you then agreed to a period of probationary custody, dependent, of course, on continued good behavior and loyalty, companied with an unconditional and public oath reaffirming your allegiance to your office, and to mine, then you might be able to forego execution by starvation."

For the briefest of moments, MacArthur's eyes lifted with the unexpected prospect of hope, and he instantly hated himself for it. Still, the promise was too tempting, too good to pass up. Even if he didn't believe a word of Hall's promise, it was an opportunity to delay death and possibly work out an escape and a resistance. If he did buy into the offer, it would give him a way to move back into the fold. Either way, he couldn't just walk away from a deal like this without considering it.

The senator's eyes narrowed as he considered his options. "On one condition. I get to pick who takes my oath, and I get the chance to practice with him beforehand. I want it to be someone I trust, and I don't want to look the fool doing it."

President Hall was a little startled that McArthur had agreed so quickly and asked for so little, but rather than look a gift horse in the mouth, he simply nodded. Agreed. Tell me who you prefer, and I'll have him brought to you. I'll give the two of you until sunrise the day after tomorrow, and no later."

"The Senator from Kentucky, Mr. President," MacArthur said without even a moment's hesitation. "I've known him for several years, and I trust him more than any of my other colleagues."

Hall furrowed his brow as if considering McArthur's request. "I will have him brought here immediately. I will leave a guard, of course, but he will be out of earshot while you practice the message of confession and oath of loyalty."

The president offered his hand to seal the deal, but MacArthur looked at it as he might a dead fish that had been too long in the hot August sun. Hall couldn't really blame him. Had their positions been reversed, as impossible as that was to conceive, he would have done the same. He would have refused to bend right until the end.

But he would not have broken. Not like the senator had. Not that quickly.

"I must say, Senator, I'm surprised you sacrificed your principles so quickly."

"You said it yourself, Mr. President. I don't want to die. Not like this, not chained to a table. And you wouldn't either."

The simple, naked honesty of the reply caught Hall by surprise. He stood, and without another word, left McArthur to the torture of the demons he'd seen behind the man's desperate eyes.

Outside, he pulled aside one of the Special Security Police. "You are to get the senator from Kentucky and bring him here

77

immediately. Neither of you are to speak to anyone else beyond what is necessary to carry out my orders, understood?"

"Yes, Mr. President," the man said, saluting across his chest.

Hall stood for several moments after the regular security guards had their weapons returned and were ordered to their posts to wait for relief. He couldn't shake the feeling that he'd missed something important and missed it so thoroughly that he had no idea what it was or what it could mean. It was a feeling he was unaccustomed to, and it gnawed at him.

With a conscious effort, Hall pushed away his nagging concerns about the senator. Regardless of what the man planned and schemed, he was still the one chained to a table, and he was still the one who was living not only on borrowed, but on mortgaged time. If he proved more troublesome than useful, then Hall would simply finish what he'd already started. He would crush the man.

Chapter 11

Deadline

Mike was awake as the sky outside became gray. He stood and carefully disentangled himself from Alyssa so he didn't wake her. He couldn't quite remember when she had first come and laid her head on his shoulder while he slept. They woke that way one morning, and neither said a word about it for the entire day. That next night, Mike was asleep when he felt a nudge and was startled awake to find Alyssa sleeping soundly, her head resting on his shoulder. Every night since had been the same.

Arthur had taken the last watch of the night and was still awake, sitting just outside the door to the administration building. He had a steaming cup of instant coffee in one hand, his other resting on the 12 gauge shotgun in his lap. As Mike walked down the hallway, Arthur turned back and nodded to him.

"There's more coffee in the pot back inside. If you drink it when it's still too hot to taste, you can almost believe it's the real thing."

Mike didn't get a cup but rather sat next to the older man and watched as the coming sunrise softened the shadows and spread a bluish gray twilight across the scene in front of them. "Did you see anyone last night?"

Arthur shook his head. "Nothing, thank God. First quiet night we've had in over a week."

"We need to talk about that," Mike said. "You and I keep going farther and farther out on scavenging runs, and we keep coming back with less and less. And then there's the business from a few days ago. Other people are pushing out further and further too, and that means we're going to keep running into some. Eventually, one of them will be tougher than we are. It almost happened the other day."

For a moment, Arthur looked like he might try and argue, but he shook his head and remained silent. After waiting a moment to be sure, Mike continued.

"I'm stronger now. You can't deny that more often than not I'm the one with the heavier pack at the end of the day. Besides, we've already got more stock than we can carry on the road. We're limited in what we can take with us, and as a result we have always known that there will come a point out there where we run out of supplies. There's just no way to avoid it unless we find a car or something, and I'm not gonna count on that slim hope. At some point, we will have to restock en route, and that's always been a part of the reality. That means we need to get going *now* when there might still be some stuff out there to restock with."

Arthur breathed a heavy sigh but still didn't say anything. This wasn't the first time Mike had brought the subject up, but this time he didn't plan to let it drop. As Mike had grown stronger, the older man had seemed increasingly reluctant to leave. Even by the best estimates, Mike was a good two weeks ahead of schedule on his recovery, and he'd been ready to leave for days. Arthur, on the other hand, had dug in his heels.

"I know you're worried about being on the road, Arthur," Mike began, but the older man cut him off with a whispered curse as he stood up from the steps and walked down onto the sidewalk.

"Look, it's not that I'm scared or worried, or whatever. You haven't been out there since before the camp. Not really, not in any clear, conscious way and not for any time. You don't know what it's like."

Arthur paused and turned away for a moment, his shoulders hunched. When he finally turned back, his eyes were grim. "You think you'll see less of what we had to do a few days ago out there on the road? There will be more of it. A lot more of it. It seeps into you after a while and gets into your bones. It's like a sour taste you can't get clean of, and then after a while, you don't want to. That kind of thing changes a man after a time, and it isn't something I'm in any rush to wade back into."

Mike was silent as he considered the other man's words. He rubbed the scar along his forearm. It still burned if he worked his hands or arms too long, and it would ache when the chilled morning air hit it. That scar served as a constant reminder of how quickly a simple injury can go from inconvenient to life-threatening when basic first aid supplies are rare luxuries. The infection that had taken hold of him had entered rapidly, struck his bloodstream, and spread throughout his body like an invading army crashing through enemy gates. The fight that resulted nearly killed him, but he was past that now.

He couldn't afford to look back and lament what he hadn't been able to fix or prevent at the time. All he could do was look ahead, and what he saw was a rapidly closing window of opportunity. If they waited much longer under the guise of gathering more supplies that they couldn't possibly carry, the weather would turn on them and they would be stuck waiting out the winter with whatever they could find. If something worse didn't happen first.

"Arthur, I am leaving in two days," Mike said with quiet finality. "Alyssa and her sister will be coming with me, and we are taking all of the supplies we can carry. We're going to rest and feast for those two days and get ready. And then we're hitting the road. You and your wife are welcome to come with us if you want."

Mike stood and fixed Arthur with a hard gaze. "I appreciate everything you've done for me, Arthur. You saved my arm and the use of it, and I can't even begin to think about how to repay that. But if you dig in on this, I will leave you and your wife here."

Arthur shook his head and started to speak, but Mike rolled right over him. "If we stay here, eventually someone bigger, tougher, and meaner than we are is going to find us. They're going to want everything we have, and we're not going to be willing to give it to them. They'll kill us and take it all anyway. You and I both know as bad as things are, it's only a matter of time in a place this densely populated."

Mike leaned forward, his eyes intent. "I'm not going to let that happen. We're leaving. I encourage you to come with us, but if you choose not to, then you can consider the White Water Center and whatever supplies we can't carry as a gift. If we have to, Arthur, we *will* leave you."

With that, Mike turned on his heel and walked back inside the administration building. By the time he made it back to where the women were sleeping, the sun was half-way up and bright sunlight streamed through the windows. Alyssa and Maria were both already up and about. Arthur's wife Cheryl was nowhere to be seen, which meant she was probably down in the bathrooms getting herself ready for the day.

The toilets and other plumbing had stopped working the night of the Blackout, when the municipal water pumps had been knocked out along with everything else. Still, there were mirrors and a drain in the tile floor. With the help of some carefully collected and boiled rain water, a pan bath was possible though it was a poor substitute for a hot morning shower. Cheryl always liked to be last to use the facilities, making sure everyone else had enough water first.

Alyssa was heating water on the small gas camp stove. A sealed plastic pouch next to her held several pieces of salt-cured pork shoulder that could be kept for months without refrigeration. As the water began to boil, she dropped the pieces of meat into the water to soften them. She would use the water to cook an oatmeal porridge that was hearty rather than tasty. Maria rolled their sleeping bags, tying them carefully. When not in use the thermal sleeping bags stayed tied onto their hiking packs just in case they needed to move quickly. Mike had encouraged them to start that practice more than a week before, and it had proven useful to teach the rest of the group about the right knots to tie and how to secure their packs. With his experience in the coast guard and as a park ranger, those kinds of skills were second nature to Mike, and he often incorrectly assumed they would be for others as well.

Still, with a little practice, Maria and Alyssa were both showing real promise. Maria was already comfortable enough with her knots not to ask Mike to check them and, more importantly, good enough at them not to need him to. Alyssa had become a skilled cook, which was one of the most important elements on a long trek. A bad cook would make people not want to eat, and that could be fatal on a long-distance hike. They were going to need every single calorie they could get, and a decent cook went a long way toward making sure people stayed nourished.

Arthur and his wife both had experience hiking and camping outdoors and had gotten more experience on the road since the Blackout. Mike wasn't worried about making sure they could handle the trip, but he was worried about convincing them it was time to leave. Cheryl, surprisingly enough, seemed far more willing to travel than Arthur, and Mike had hoped to get the chance to talk to her about convincing Arthur to relent. If Cheryl could help sway her husband, then Mike wasn't above using that to his advantage. If it came time to go, Mike was prepared to leave them to their own defenses, but he would rather avoid that if possible.

"How are you feeling?" Alyssa asked, nudging his shoulder with her elbow as he sat next to the stove and her.

"Good," Mike answered with a smile. "Stronger than I have in weeks. What about you?"

Alyssa shrugged, a strand of her hair falling down across her face. "Restless. I want to be moving again. This place was nice at first, but it doesn't feel right anymore."

Mike couldn't help but nod in agreement. They were all starting to feel the same indescribable, yet inescapable, pressure to move— except for Arthur. Every day the feeling of urgency grew stronger, and every day Arthur pushed harder against it. Mike was rolling the issue around in his mind, trying to find some new angle to come at the problem when Arthur and Cheryl stepped into the room together. Mike immediately noticed a difference in Arthur's face.

"We talked it over," Arthur began without preamble, "and we're going to come with you. In two days, we all leave together."

Mike closed his eyes as he felt the terrible weight of having to leave without them suddenly lift. He said a silent prayer of thanks for an unexpected resolution that spared him from having to make the choice to abandon people who had grown close to him. Mike stood and stepped over to shake Arthur's hand.

"Well," Arthur said with a thin smile, "the good news is we get to have a party now."

Mike couldn't help but laugh as he slapped Arthur on the back and ushered him over to sit by the camp stove. They had a lot of things to discuss and plans to make as far as provisions and routes. But for now, it was good simply to enjoy a moment of peace and friendship in the last bit of comfort they were likely to know for some time.

Chapter 12

Sunsets and Starlight

Oct. 10 th 1230 EST

Chris moved as quietly as he could and avoided the places he knew the plank subflooring would creak beneath his feet. He wasn't sure if Tom was really asleep or just out of focus from the pain and fever. Either way, Chris was doing his best not to disturb his patient, but he had to check the wound and the dressing on Tom's chest. When he reached the bed, he knelt and pulled out a small, high-intensity pen light to help him see.

Chris lifted the outer layers of the dressing carefully, but it didn't take long to see blood staining both sides of the binding. This was the fourth time he'd packed pressure bandages around the wound and wrapped it, and the bleeding still hadn't stopped. As gently as possible, Chris lowered the bandages and stood. He turned to leave, but Tom's hand shot out and caught his wrist with an iron grip. Chris turned and was surprised to see Tom's eyes open and staring at the ceiling. His skin was pale and slick with sweat, and the part of his eyes that was normally white had already taken on a slight yellow tinge from the damage to his liver. Toxins were building up in his bloodstream, and that was a bad sign.

"Steven? Brant?" Tom managed to whisper in a soft, strained voice.

"They're safe," Chris answered. "You took out the threat and kept them safe, Tom. You did well."

Tom took a deep breath, and a spasm of painful coughing shook him from head to foot. When he quieted, he opened his eyes again, but they seemed clouded and less focused. "How bad?" Tom managed to ask after a moment.

"Bad," Chris answered, putting his hand over Tom's. He could feel the intense heat radiating from Tom's skin. "The round that hit your chest ripped through more than half your liver and shattered two ribs. It missed your spine, but that's the only blessing, if you can call it that. The one that hit your leg wasn't as bad, but it destroyed your knee and several major blood vessels."

Chris paused and swallowed hard, trying to find a way to say what he had to say next, but Tom beat him to it. "How long?"

Chris had to fight past the lump in his throat to answer. "It's tough to say, Tom. Infection has already set in, and the living part of your liver is being overwhelmed. I'd say you have twelve hours at least, but it's tough to tell. It could take days. To be honest, more than once over the past thirty-six hours I thought you were done already. It's just a matter of time now." Page 68 you say Chris tries to forget the bloody events of the past 24 hours.   Reconcile the hours.

Tom shook his head slightly, and tears fell from the corners of his eyes. His face twisted into a tortured mask as he fought for the strength to speak. "I can't—" he whispered hoarsely. "The pain—I can't take it. Can you help?"

Chris shook his head slowly. "There's nothing I can do, Tom. If I had a full surgical ward, a transplant liver, and unlimited 0-neg for transfusions, maybe I could, but even then, it'd be a long shot. I don't have any of that. There's just nothing I can do."

Tom shook his head again. "I don't mean fix," he whispered, "I mean help."

Chris was silent for a long time. Finally, he squeezed Tom's shoulder with his other hand. "Yeah, Tom," he said softly, "I can help. Jen is outside with the kids. Should I send them in?"

Tom barely shook his head. "Not yet. Not ready. Does she know?" When Chris nodded, Tom squeezed his eyes shut again, and more tears flowed silently down his cheeks.

Chris wanted to look away; he wanted to tear his wrist from Tom's grip and run from the room. But this was his friend, a man he'd grown closer to over the past few weeks than he'd been to anyone since he left active duty. Seeing him in this much pain, knowing the end was coming for him was almost more than he could take. He'd left this world of maimed and dying bodies behind years ago, and for good reason, and now he was back in the middle of it, with the stench of blood and death thick in the air around him. Chris felt his stomach turn. He hated seeing people in pain, knowing that there was nothing he could do to cure them.

"The captain," Tom whispered raggedly. "I need to see Captain Tillman."

Chris squeezed Tom's shoulder again, "Tom, your wife—" he began, but Tom shook his head and cut him off.

"I told you, not yet. Bring me Captain Tillman first. Then I'll see my family."

Chris nodded and patted Tom's shoulder. "Okay, Tom. I'll go get Joe. You've got to let go of my arm, though."

Tom let Chris's arm go. His eyes closed, but he didn't fall back asleep as far as Chris could tell. Chris eased himself out of the front bedroom and made his way through the house to the large living room where Captain Tillman was waiting with Jen and Tom's two oldest sons. The other two children were outside playing under the watchful eye of Beth, Beth-Anne, and some of the others.

"Can I go in to see him?" Jen asked, fresh tears staining her cheeks.

Chris shook his head. "He's awake, but he was adamant about seeing the captain first."

Tillman put his hand on Jen's shoulder and squeezed. "I'll talk to him, Jen. He'll want to see you when we're done."

Jen nodded and pulled the two of her children in the room to her. They were the two boys, the oldest of Jen and Tom's four kids. As Tillman went to speak with Tom, Chris motioned for Jen to take a seat in one of the arm chairs as he pulled a foot stool over in front of her.

Chris chose his words carefully. "Jen, I've done everything I can, but Tom isn't going to get better from this. It's a matter of time now, and there's nothing I can do about it." Jen nodded but didn't speak. She couldn't even bring herself to look Chris in the eyes, and instead focused on her two children as he spoke. "At this point the only thing left is to make sure Tom is in as little pain as possible. There are things I can do to make the end easier for him so he doesn't suffer."

Jen shook her head. "It wasn't supposed to be like this. He quit the teams and came home. He wasn't supposed to get shot. We were going to see Europe one day."

Chris wasn't sure what to say to that, but thankfully Tillman came back in the room and saved him from finding a response. Without a word, Tillman pulled Jen into a fatherly hug and held her

89

as her shoulders shook with sobs. When Jen had finally cried herself out, the captain took a step back and gripped both of her shoulders. He looked into her eyes as she dried them.

"Jen, you and your children are family. I want you to know that no matter what, your home is here. Be strong. Tom needs that. He's ready to see you, but he asked that you leave the kids out here with me. He's in bad shape, and he doesn't want them to remember him like this."

The oldest of the children, an eleven year old boy, stood his ground and shook his head, clinging to Jen like a drowning man holding onto a life line. "I want to see daddy!"

"Daddy's hurt, Trey, and he's tired," Jen said, trying to sooth the boy. "I'm just going in to tell him goodnight."

"You're lying!" the youngest son, Matthew yelled, his face red and stained with tears. "I know you're lying! Daddy's not getting better. I heard Mr. Chris say so!"

Jen pulled the eight year old boy to her and hugged him tight as he sobbed. "You're right, Matthew. Daddy's not getting better. But I need you to be strong for me right now and take care of your brother and sisters. I need you to be strong so I can help Daddy be strong, okay?"

Finally, Matthew nodded and followed his older brother and Captain Tillman through the house toward the back yard. Jen took a moment to collect herself and dry her eyes. When she stood, Chris stood also and walked with her to the door of the front bedroom. Before Jen could open the door, though, Chris put his hand on the knob and held it shut. He reached into one pocket and pulled out two capped syringes. He handed Jen the one that was about a third of the way full.

"This is morphine. It will take away the pain." Then Chris held up the larger, full syringe. "When he's ready, let me know and I will administer this. It will be like he's falling asleep—no pain, no suffering."

Jen took the smaller syringe and stepped into the room, closing the door behind her.

Chris crossed to the opposite side of the middle bedroom and sat heavily on the floor. He was exhausted. He leaned his head back against the wall and closed his eyes, trying to forget the hectic, bloody events of the past day and a half. Within moments, though, sleep overtook him and he dreamed troubled dreams.

*

Jen leaned her back against the door as it closed. She stood for a moment, looking down at her husband's pale, sweat-soaked face. The faint coppery smell of blood tingled the back of her nose and turned her stomach. Thick bandages wrapped around Tom's waist and leg, and both showed fresh stains where blood had soaked through. His eyes were closed, but his breathing was far too shallow and too rapid for him to be asleep. Looking down at him, Jen felt a knot of pain, fear, and uncertainty begin to roll and twist deep in her guts. She did her best to ignore it, but she couldn't.

When Tom had quit the teams, she'd been thrilled. Finally, after more than a decade of marriage, she was going to have her husband to herself. Then he got the job at the Joint Special Operations Command, and things had been stable and good for a while. The pay was awesome, the job fit right in Tom's wheelhouse, and he had more time at home than he'd enjoyed in years. When the Blackout happened, and Tom told her they had to run, she'd taken it in stride. With Tom by her side, Jen had been able to face the uncertainty of the road, the fear and the unknown, even taking their children from their home to a place they'd never been to live with strangers in some weird compound of last resort.

In spite of herself, Jen couldn't stop thinking that none of this was supposed to happen. Tom had quit the teams to be safe, so he could be there for their children as they grew up and so he could be there for *her* as they grew old together. That was how it all was supposed to end—with the two of them in their old age, happy and surrounded by family. Not with Tom bleeding into his bandages while she watched helplessly.

Jen swallowed the taste of bile in the back of her throat and dried her eyes, steeling herself for what lay ahead. She'd known since the day she met Tom while he was still in the Academy that this kind of end was possible. She'd always thought that if it came to this, he'd be lying alone on some foreign battlefield calling her name. That thought had kept her up nights while he'd been deployed with the SEAL teams, but she'd let go of it since. And now she found herself face to face with it. But that was what she'd vowed when they'd married twenty years ago—that no matter what, for better or worse, she would be by his side. And she meant to fulfill that vow, whatever the cost. Jen took a step away from the door, and the floor creaked. Tom's eyes shot open and he turned toward her. As soon as his eyes fell on her, he smiled in spite of his obvious pain. It was almost enough to break Jen's heart and her resolve all at once.

"Hey, baby. You look like you've seen a ghost," he said as he barked a short laugh. Again, his body erupted into a painful cough that left him gasping for air.

Before he stopped coughing, Jen was by his side. She eased herself onto the edge of the bed and stroked his hair away from his forehead, comforting him with her touch. "You shouldn't joke like that, Tom," Jen scolded him. "You need to save your strength."

Tom managed a weak smile. "Save it for what, babe? There's not much left for me to save now."

Jen swallowed back tears and held up the small syringe that Chris had given her. "Chris said this will take the pain away." She pointed to the IV still in the back of Tom's left hand. "It will make things more bearable."

Tom shook his head. "No, babe," he whispered, "I don't want my head foggy and clouded with that stuff. Not right now. I want to see you and touch you, and I want it to be real."

Tom took Jen's hand in his, and she felt the intense heat of his fever. Tears blurred her eyes for a moment, but he reached up and wiped them away for her. His smile never wavered. "Do you remember the first day of our honeymoon?"

Jen laughed in spite of herself and nodded. "I thought that taxi ride from the airport to the ferry on St. Thomas was going to be the end of our married life. That guy was crazy."

Tom chuckled, and this time he didn't cough. "Yeah, that was intense. But I was talking about later. After the drama with the taxi, the car rental place forgetting our reservation, the cabin rental office losing the keys to our cabin, and everything else. At the end of that long, hard day, when we were sitting on the balcony of our cabin looking out over Coral Bay, and you looked so beautiful and so peaceful. I'd never seen you look that happy before, and I remember thinking how much I love you."

Jen smiled and shook her head. "I remember the balcony, but I don't remember looking beautiful. I was tired, sweaty, and grumpy from the plane ride and all the drama we had to fight our way through. What I remember most is the last night. We sat on the beach at East End Bay with the stars and the moon overhead, and we talked all night. That's where we made the plans for our life—your career with the SEALs , the number of kids we'd have, all of it. Then the sun rose over the ocean that morning while we watched. You said, 'The road goes on forever from here, babe. As long as we're on it together, there's nowhere we can't go.'"

Tom reached up and touched her cheek again with his fingertips as a single tear ran from the corner of his yellow-stained eyes. "I'll still be with you, babe," he whispered, "every step of the way."

Unable to hold back her grief, Jen began to sob. Tom pulled her close, and they held each other.

*

Chris woke with a start, his right hand going for a gun that wasn't on his hip, his left hand groping in front of him for the threat. Instead, he found himself holding onto Jen's shirt. Jen gently gripped his hand and forced Chris to look into her eyes and focus. He blinked a few times and tried to clear his head. Sunlight slanted through the windows on the wall of the bedroom facing west, and he was stiff from having been hunched over asleep for a few hours. Jen's face was streaked and her eyes red and swollen from crying.

"Is he . . ." Chris started to ask, but Jen shook her head and cut him off.

"Not yet, but the pain is getting worse," she said, her voice strangely calm. "I gave him the syringe, but he made me wait until the pain was so intense he couldn't take it anymore. He's ready for you now."

Chris nodded and stood. He stretched his muscles as best he could and followed Jen into the bedroom. As he opened the door, Chris could smell the beginnings of gangrene from Tom's wounds. His patient's face had lost more color, and his breathing was ragged and gurgling now. Jen stood with her back against the wall next to the door as Chris checked Tom's vitals out of professional habit. The entire time, Tom never stirred a muscle. It was the first time Chris had been in the room without waking him, and it was a sign that things were taking a bad turn.

"Do you want me to try and wake him?" Chris asked.

Jen shook her head. "We've said everything we need to. The last thing we did was say a prayer, and he fell asleep. He's ready to go."

Chris turned back to his patient, took the large syringe from his pocket, and injected it into the main line he'd started on Tom's hand.

"Will it take long?" Jen asked, her voice barely loud enough to be heard.

Chris shook his head. "A few minutes at most," he answered.

Tom's breathing began to slow. The space between the rattling, gurgling gasps became longer until, finally, they stopped. Jen sank to her knees by Tom. Chris eased himself out of the room and closed the door.

A pain like Jen's was too deep to be shared.

Chapter 13

Complications

Joe was standing under the massive oak tree in the back yard watching the children play when Chris stepped out the back door. One look at his face and Joe knew that Tom was gone. Joe closed his eyes and said a quick prayer that his brother-in-arms' soul would find peace and rest, and he prayed for peace and comfort for Tom's wife and children. They would have a difficult few weeks ahead.

As he watched those children run and play, Joe couldn't help but feel a pang of guilt. He'd promised Tom and Chris both that he'd keep them and their families safe, that he'd watch over them. They had trusted him and taken him at his word, and now Tom was dead, his wife widowed, and their four children left without a father. Unlikely as it was that Joe could have done a single thing to stop or avoid the tragic confrontation at the pastures, he couldn't shake the deep feeling of guilt and responsibility.

Chris came and stood next to Joe, but for a long moment neither of them spoke. Joe put his hand on the younger man's shoulder reassuringly. "I know you did everything you could, Chris."

"Listen, Captain, there's something else you need to know," Chris said finally, reaching into the pocket of his jeans. "Before Tom got shot he sent Steven running. Brant tried to get to his gun, but he wasn't quick enough. Steven made it here, screaming at the top of

96

his lungs for help. I grabbed Gilbert, Levy, Steven, Beth, and Beth-Anne and we took off for the pastures with as many guns as we could carry. Everything was done by the time we got there, though."

Joe patted Chris's shoulder and turned back to watch the children. "Even if you'd been there, you might not have been able to stop it," Joe said. "Those men were intent on taking what was ours, and we were intent on stopping them. That kind of thing can really only end one way."

Chris shook his head. "That's not why I'm telling you this. We got Tom back here, and I left Steven and Brant and his two friends to finish closing up the cow pastures and securing the fences. When they were done, I told them to drag the three bodies into the edge of the woods on our side of the pasture and make sure they weren't visible. They collected the weapons and ammo and checked their pockets before hiding the bodies."

Chris pulled two plastic cards from his pocket and handed them to Joe. "Two of the men had those in their pockets."

The cards were the size of a credit card, though a bit flimsier. On one side were a magnetic strip and a digitized code scanner panel. The other side had a picture, presumably of the card's bearer, and underneath were the bold black letters **FSS** and the seal of the Department of Homeland Security. No names or ranks were indicated on the cards.

Joe stuck the cards in his pocket before anyone else could see them. "Did they have anything else? Badges, anything?"

Chris shook his head. "Two of them had packs, but they just had a few extra magazines, some water, and about three days of rations each. One of them had a local road map marked up with lines, circles, and X's."

"These guys weren't geared up to travel far," Joe said as he ran a hand through his growing beard, "and that means they've got friends somewhere within a day's walk. When they don't come back, someone is going to start looking for them."

"What are we going to do, Captain?" Chris asked.

Joe's face was grim as he turned and looked out at the fields and woods around the farm. "First, we're going to bury Tom," he said, "and then we're going to find the others out there before they find us. And we're going to kill 'em all."

Chapter 14

Dress Rehearsal

Oct. 11th 0100 EST

Senator MacArthur felt dizzy and weak under the Senate Chamber lights. He could feel his strength fading with every passing hour. The bone-deep pain of hunger that had gnawed at him for weeks was suddenly gone, and that was more troubling than the pain had been. His eyes were blurry and tired, and he had read the oath so many times that he'd had it fully memorized for hours. Still, he needed to create some space between him and the guards or he would never be able to broach the subject of resistance that had led him to ask for this particular practice partner.

The junior senator from Kentucky Shawn Coleman was the only surviving member of the Kentucky delegation to Congress from either the House or the Senate. He was young for a senator and had skipped the early stages of a political career that most of his colleagues had suffered through, Senator MacArthur included. Instead, the Kentucky native had attended West Point straight out of high school and then Army Ranger School. He had served one deployment in Afghanistan and two in Iraq, leading his men through some of the worst fighting of the war in Anwar Province and Fallujah. Coleman had a reputation as a dogged fighter and ferocious patriot, which was why Senator MacArthur had chosen him as the man to deliver the oath to.

"I promise," Senator MacArthur began, reading the pledge aloud for what felt like the ten thousandth time, "to uphold and obey..."

Coleman cut him off with a frustrated sigh and a shake of his head. "We've been over this, Senator. The opening line reads, 'I solemnly swear to uphold and honor all orders of the President of the . . .' If you don't get the beginning correct, the rest of it won't matter."

"I'm sorry," Senator MacArthur answered, exaggerating his exhaustion. "I just can't think with these guards hovering right over top of us, staring down at us." Senator MacArthur looked around and purposefully shuddered. "I need some space to think."

Coleman looked at the closest of the guards and raised an eyebrow. "What do you say, Captain?" he asked, flashing a classic politician's grin. "Can you and your men back off a bit and give us some space to practice?"

The man shook his head. "I'm not a captain," he answered, "and our orders were to stay close."

Coleman put on an apologetic look and heaved a heavy sigh. "That's unfortunate, I suppose," the younger man said with a small shrug. "I'll leave it up to you to explain to President Hall why we're not prepared to deliver the oath tomorrow morning as expected. I'm sure he won't be happy about it, but at least it will be you and not me that has to face him. I just need your name and ID number so I can pass it along when the president wants to know why we failed to meet his deadline."

The guard's face paled, and he looked far less sure of himself.

"No?" Senator Coleman asked, sarcasm dripping from his voice as he stood and turned to face the guard. "You mean you don't want that responsibility? Well, then I suppose it's still my job to see that this prisoner is ready tomorrow, and it's my job to explain why if he isn't. So, if you're not going to stand up and say it was *your* fault when the president starts asking questions, then you're not going to stand in my way right now and force me to do it for you. Now back up and give us our space."

The guard hesitated for just another second, then dropped his eyes and backed away, motioning for the other guards to do the same. When they were safely out of earshot, Coleman slid the copy of the oath of allegiance back across the table to Senator MacArthur. "Now, let's try this again, from the top."

Senator MacArthur picked up the copy of the oath and held it in trembling fingers. He set it back on the table without reading a word. "Listen, I don't know how long we have," he whispered, his voice barely loud enough to be heard, "but I need to say some things and I didn't know who else to say them to. I didn't randomly ask for you to be a part of this. I know your resume. You're a patriot and a warrior. If there's anyone here that can land a blow against the enemy, it's going to be you. If someone like you starts a resistance movement, I know others trapped here will join in and work with you."

Coleman looked at the senator for a moment, his face unreadable. Then he pointed to a section of the oath and leaned forward, his voice low. "You mean like they joined you and helped you? Keep focusing on this oath like we're talking about it or the guards are going to come and see what we're really saying. I don't think either one of us wants that."

MacArthur nodded and leaned in, his eyes on the piece of paper. Coleman pointed to another section, but cut his eyes at the senator. "Now, let's get one thing straight old man," he whispered. "Just because you read some *USA Today* article about my time in the service or some crap typed up by a staffer doesn't mean you know one thing about who I am. Right now, I'm a survivor and that's all that matters. You think I want to end up chained to a table with the rest of the Senate watching me starve to death one long day at the time?"

"Do you really think I *want* to be here?" MacArthur asked, his voice rising dangerously. With obvious effort, he controlled his tone. "Son, I took an oath to uphold and defend the Constitution, same as you. *I* took that oath seriously. *I* don't make it a habit to give my solemn vow to something and then tuck tail and hide at the first sign of danger."

"Are you calling me a coward?" Coleman asked, his eyes narrowing. "You're not the only one that can read a resume old man. When I got into Congress I read up on every single member, just in case I had to work with someone on legislation. I checked your service file too, and the closest you ever got to action was filing paperwork in Fort Benning, Georgia, while Grenada was going on thousands of miles away. I've been in the shit, old man. When I was in Fallujah there were bullets snapping over my head while I carried a guy out of the line of fire. He died a few minutes later, but I was already back out there pulling another guy who'd been hit out of the middle of a street. So, don't talk to me about getting in the fight, sticking my neck out, or God and country and all of that. I've been there and done it. If I need a report filed about it, I'll let you know. Now, I was told to have you practice this oath so you can deliver it tomorrow, and that's what I'm going to do."

"Look at me, son," Senator MacArthur said, lifting the chains that held his hands bound to the table. "Look what they're willing to do. Yes, I started this as a hunger strike to make a point to the rest of you that we were violating every oath we'd ever taken. And look at what that monster Hall was willing to do to prove that *he* is the only one who decides who lives and who dies. Can you really serve that kind of man with a clear conscience? If you can, then I've made a pretty big error in judgment, and I'm not typically known for those kinds of errors."

Coleman was quiet for a moment before giving his head a small shake. He pointed back at the sheet as if pointing out a mistake the senator had made in his recitation. "It's wrong. I know it is. This guy, the situation, the attack—all of it is nine different shades of wrong. But I can't change it and I can't stop it. I can either do what I need to in order to survive, or I can stand up and take a round to the face, like you're doing."

Coleman leaned in, his eyes narrow and his voice intense. "Now here's the thing, old man. You're going to die with those chains around your wrists, or you're going to die some other way when you break this idiotic oath in six days or six weeks. Either way, you're going to eventually wind up on the wrong side of this monster, and he's going to kill you and probably take his time doing it. And when he's done, this tyrant that has claimed the nation for his own will keep right on going as if nothing happened. If you want to throw away your life like that, it's your business, but if I'm going to go down swinging I want at least to know that I'm taking the other guy down too."

Senator MacArthur was silent for a long time as he pretended to study the oath before him. Finally, he raised his eyes, his face suddenly unreadable. "I have a cousin in Tennessee in the National Guard. He's part of an elite mountain search and rescue helicopter team. His name is James Withers. If you ever change your mind and decide you want to live up to the oath you've taken and defend the Constitution, then you find James. I guarantee if there's a fight, he'll be in the absolute middle of it."

Coleman didn't know what response he'd expected, but this wasn't it. The starving Senator had gone from passionate and committed to completely withdrawn in the space of a heartbeat. Senator MacArthur sat back in the moment of silence that fell between them and shoved the typed copy of the oath across the small table. "Thank you for your help, Senator," MacArthur said in a voice loud enough that he clearly meant the guards to hear. "I think we have practiced this as much as we can for now, and we both need some rest so that we are at our best for the presentation tomorrow."

Coleman studied the senator's thin, haggard face. He leaned over, slid the paper back across to Senator MacArthur, and growled a reply in a rough whisper. "You'd better not screw me tomorrow, old man. I don't know what angle you're working, but I mean to make it out of this alive. Got it?"

Senator MacArthur actually managed to smile. "Don't worry, son," he responded, "whatever happens tomorrow, your reputation with the man calling himself president will be secure. That much I can guarantee you."

Coleman hesitated as if he wanted to say more, but the guards were back within earshot by that point, so he held his tongue. Instead, he fixed MacArthur with a hard glare before turning on his heel and striding out of the Senate Chamber. The guards went back to their posts watching the entrances to the Chamber while at the same time steadfastly refusing to acknowledge Senator MacArthur's presence.

Exhausted, the senator put his head in his hands and began to pray.

Chapter 15

First Look

Oct. 11th 0500 MST

Commander Price stood in the operations center, his eyes glued to the massive LED screen that occupied the front wall. The video playing on the screen was grainy, and it froze repeatedly, but there was enough clarity and detail to get the job done. It helped that the operator on the other end of the open phone line was narrating as the video transmitted. They didn't have enough bandwidth available to transmit live video yet, so it had to be compressed and played back in sync with the narrator to make any sense out of the images. Colonel Darius, the only other man in the room, had his eyes glued to the screen as well.

"Four guards posted at each entrance to the stitching yard," the former Army master sergeant reported over the phone. "No guards visible at the perimeter fences, though, and no towers. It looks like they have a camp set up right inside the shipping yard. Difficult to tell exactly how many, but based on the movement we observed over the course of an hour, I'd have to say somewhere between seventy-five and a hundred and fifty."

Commander Price looked over at Darius. "Will your men be able to handle that many?"

The colonel snorted, his face twisted into what Commander Price had come to recognize as his thoughtful grimace. "Shouldn't be a problem. We couldn't take them head on, but we'll nibble at the edges a bit and soften the target. As long as we can get some air power to handle the reinforcement and resupply problem, and maybe take out a hardened target or two, it shouldn't be a problem. Any word on that?"

Price shook his head. "Still no contact from my guy in Arizona, and that's starting to worry me."

The image on the screen had shifted, and the camera was filming through an opening in a chain link fence. "There seems to be at least one team of mechanics or engineers," the sergeant said. "I couldn't get close enough to get a clear view, but it looks like they're working on two or three of the engines, trying to get them up and running. When they're working, there are several groups of armed guards that keep watch. I didn't want to linger too long and attract attention, so I kept the filming short here."

As if on cue, the video image shifted again. This time the view was looking at the entrance to the shipping yard from a few hundred yards down the street. A wooden barricade wrapped with barbed wire spanned the entrance, and several well-positioned cars with their tires missing littered the street for fifty yards or so. The cars made a decent road block that would stop everything but a heavy assault vehicle like an Abrams tank or a Bradley fighting vehicle.

"This is the main entrance," the sergeant relayed. "I was filming around daybreak and caught something interesting. There were teams of three leaving the compound and a couple of teams that seemed to be returning. As the teams passed through the gates, a single agent checked their IDs with some kind of pen reader and a tablet. You'll see a shot of it here in a minute. The ones coming back in were carrying supplies with them and were likely foraging parties."

Price watched as two teams of three men left the compound. As they passed the gatehouse, a guard stepped out with what looked like a small tablet. He scanned each man's ID card with a small pen-style scanner as they handed it to him. The guard also reached up to tap the side of his glasses when he looked each man in the face, likely taking a snapshot with a pair of smart glasses. As the two teams split, each taking a different side street, another team entered the compound. Two of the three men in the returning team carried bulging packs, and the third had a bundle that was covered in blankets and tied with rope. The guard scanned their IDs and snapped their photos as well.

The video transmission ended, and the sergeant logged off the secure data transfer network. The signals for the data and the voice transmissions used the same satellite network but operated at slightly different frequencies, allowing the recon teams to relay video and still images while reporting by sat phone. The only drawback was that the video and images couldn't be uploaded in real time.

"That's the end of this report," the sergeant said. "What are our orders moving forward?"

Commander Price unmuted the speaker phone sitting on the console next to him before answering. "Keep an eye on the rail yard, Sergeant, and stay out of sight. Do not engage the enemy unless you are fired on first. I'll be in contact sometime over the next twelve hours with more orders, but for now just find a place to hole up."

"Roger that, sir. Farstrider 117 signing out." There was a click and the line went silent.

Price and Darius walked over to the smart table that sat on the right side of the operations center. Price entered a few commands to unlock the system and then called up a satellite view of the

Kansas City, Missouri. He keyed in a few more commands, and the view zoomed in to show a detailed overhead shot of the area around the shipping and rail yard. A series of red dots zigzagging around the southern perimeter of the rail yard marked the path the sergeant had taken.

"How many troops do you think you'll need to overcome the FSS presence?" Price asked, looking at the layout of the rail yard. "Assume the worst, that there's a hundred and fifty enemy there at the very least."

Darius thought about it for a few moments before answering. "Well, it depends on how quickly you want it to happen. If I had two thousand troops and a few pieces of heavy artillery, I could take the whole city inside a day and have it secured within a week. Bare minimum? Sixty of my men plus whatever recon troops you have already on site. We'd hit them on their foraging parties for a few days and draw their numbers down. Plant IEDs to take out the patrols they'll eventually have to send out to look for the foraging parties. Asymmetrical warfare at its finest."

"How long will it take to crack them?" Price asked.

"Tough to say," Darius said truthfully, "but if we can keep them from getting resupply and reinforcement, a week or two at the most. They won't be able to last long without their foraging parties bringing in fresh supplies. Eventually, they'll have to come out, and that's when we'll hit them hard."

"Keep the engineers and mechanics alive if you can," Price said. "We may need them to get the trains running again."

Darius nodded. "One problem, though, Commander. How are we going to get there? I've got only a handful of Strykers back at the training facility, and we can't get two of them running. Even packed

108

to the gills, that means we're more than thirty men shy of our target."

"I can get you the vehicles you need, Colonel," Price said evenly. "Just let me know how many, and I'll have them for you, ready to leave tomorrow morning."

"You just happen to have some extra armored personnel carriers laying around unused?" Darius asked, the sarcasm heavy in his tone.

Price gave a small shrug. "As a matter of fact, I do, in a manner of speaking. The Department of Defense has had a standing protocol for decades now called the Strategic Contingency Stockpile Initiative, or SCSI for short. It's part of a system of black budget projects put into place during the Cold War that were quietly, yet monumentally, expanded in the years following the collapse of the Soviet Union. Under the original charter, the program was designed to store for long periods of time critical food and medical supplies that could be distributed rapidly to the public. As it expanded, though, the list of items eligible for stockpiling by the government grew to include weapons, heavy machinery, money, fuel, and just about anything else we wanted. "

"That's all fascinating," Darius said, "but how does it help us?"

"I have the coordinates of all of the secure stockpiles located throughout the nation," Price replied. "There are over two hundred separate facilities, an average of four per state, housing everything from food rations to tanks and armored personnel carriers. The inventory was updated and expanded following 9/11 to include state of the art electronic surveillance technology as well as enough small arms, ammunition and equipment to outfit the armed services and the National Guard three times over. The idea was to have a sufficient stockpile to arm the people if the worst ever happened and a terrorist insurgency gained a foothold on the mainland. It was considered an absolute worst-case contingency, planned for but never actually needed."

Price keyed a few commands into his console and brought up an inventory search database. He typed in a search for Stryker vehicles within a one-hundred-and-fifty-mile radius of the base and got a hit on a hardened facility fewer than twenty miles away. The refurbished mineral mine housed construction equipment, armored personnel carriers, and a small fleet of Bradley Fighting Vehicles. The inventory listed fifteen Stryker vehicles along with several crates of maintenance supplies and spare parts.

"I have four working Strykers for you and whatever spare parts you need to repair the two that aren't working," Price said. "The facility has everything we need. What's your prep time for this mission?"

Darius carefully considered his answer. "Give me a day to get back to my men, two to travel and go over the details of the op— three to be safe. We can be rolling on this inside four days."

"Can you do it without air support, if need be?" Price asked.

The Colonel made a sour face, like he wanted to turn and spit. "Can I?" he repeated. "Yeah, I *can*. But there will be a lot of casualties. We'll take it and we'll hold it, but it'll cost us. Even a little air support, like a couple of A-10s to lay down some cannon fire, would do a lot."

"I'll do what I can, Colonel," Price said, his voice and his eyes grim. "You have my word on that. But I can't guarantee anything. One way or another, though, in four days we're going to take Kansas City."

"And once we have the transportation lines, we can push east and attack?" Colonel Darius asked.

Commander Price hesitated, uncertain how much he could reveal to the colonel, even now. After a moment, though, he gave a slight shrug. "Not east, not yet, at least," he replied, somewhat cryptically. "First, we're going to need to raise an army, and that means food. A lot of people out there are hungry and desperate. They need help, and we're going to take it to them."

"And in return for a full belly, you think they'll fight for you?" Darius asked.

Price shook his head. "Not in return for," he replied, "in exchange for. If they'll fight, we'll feed them."

The words hung in the air for a moment, and an uneasy silence fell between the two men. Darius started to speak again, but Price cut him off. "Four days, Colonel," the commander said. "By then we'll have enough satellites online to carry the video feed and voice on the same signal, so we should have live footage. I will have my men load three Humvees with the transmission gear and whatever supplies you need. You and your men can get on the road at daybreak. By then I will have maps and instructions for accessing the stockpile. The system operates on an emergency generator system once main power is lost, and it is designed to operate for a year or more at minimal consumption levels. If you run into any problems, you know how to contact us here."

"I'll check in at least every twelve hours with a sit rep," Darius said. "Once we're within fifty miles of the city, though, I won't contact you again until we launch the operation. I don't want to risk some random signal getting picked up on their equipment."

Price nodded and felt his pulse begin to hammer in his temples. He walked around the table and stopped, standing face to face with the colonel. As he looked him eye-to-eye, Price found himself envying the old soldier. He was actually going to engage the enemy and take the fight to them. Price had gotten a taste of that in these very halls, and he found that combat agreed with him. It was a personal realization that was both surprising and troubling.

Commander Price extended his hand to the colonel. "God's speed, Colonel Darius, and happy hunting. Give 'em hell."

Darius took the Commander's hand and shook it firmly. "With pleasure, sir."

With that, the colonel turned on his heel and strode out of the operations center.

Chapter 16

The First Oath

Senator Coleman stood at the center of the room, waiting. He could feel the sweat rolling down the back of his neck and on past his shoulder blades. He had dressed in the best three-piece suit he had left in his office, a tailored dark grey Italian silk-wool blend, with navy blue pin stripes. He'd spent the last hour before the call to convene shining his simple black oxfords to a mirror polish.

Even with the fine layer of dust and grime on the suit, Coleman cut quite the dashing, albeit sweaty, figure. His face was a calm, stony mask, but behind it his mind was running a mile a minute trying to find his safest course of action in the face of any surprise that could come his way. The old man had been desperate the night before, and desperation, Coleman knew all too well, could make people do some very rash and unpredictable things.

The Senate Chamber was crowded and unbelievably hot with the full Federal Senate, a contingent of more than fifty FSS agents, and the president's own Honor Guard and Secret Service, all crowded into the cavernous room. President Hall stood alone on the central dais where the vice president would have stood when the Senate was in session before the takeover. His personal guards formed a double ring around the front of the dais and faced the Senate. In fact, all of the guards inside the Chamber, including the

FSS agents, faced the Senators. The threat was clear, and it was palpable. Coleman was fairly certain that even had it been the dead of winter with no heat, something he'd actually experienced in this very room once before, he would have been sweating more than shivering.

Although they tried to hide it, one by one the senators eventually glanced at the table that still sat in the center of the Chamber. The shackles that had been attached to Senator MacArthur's wrists and ankles were on the table, empty and open. A handful of senators glared at the iron restraints, and a handful leered at them almost lustfully, but most glanced at them only once and turned away.

He was watching the seconds tick by on what had once been his grandfather's watch, so Coleman knew that the ornate and precision-tuned grandfather clock that had been pulled out of storage was about to chime. Still, when the gongs began to sound, echoing through the perfectly silent Chamber, Coleman jumped in spite of himself. That clock had been used to keep the official time of the Senate for more than a century. For decades, though, it had been rotting in some cellar as the official time ticked by on a red monochrome digital display above the vice president's head. Now that display was dark, and the old clock chimed again.

Coleman took a deep breath to steady himself and let it out slowly as he looked up at the faces before him. "Attention Federal Senate," he called, "you have been convened by order of the acting President of the United States Phillip Hall. I now call you to order. We are here to bear witness to the Oath of Allegiance of Senator Thomas MacArthur of Tennessee. Per the request of the attainted, I will be administering the Oath of Allegiance. I call Senator MacArthur forward by order of the president."

Everyone in the chamber held their breaths, waiting for a response to the call. Into the silence, the massive double doors at the back of the Chamber swung open, and the emaciated Senator McArthur strode wearily, yet purposefully, to the center of the room. His head was high and his eyes were clear and confident. Of all things, he looked well rested, and that irritated Coleman to no end. Thanks to the good senator, they both had been up, nearly sleepless, the night before, and now he actually had the gall to look rested.

A group of six Secret Service agents flanked the man—two in front, one on either side, and two behind him. The senator marched forward, seeming not to notice anyone else in the room, and the Secret Service agents, for their part, pretended not to be aware of the man walking at the center of their formation. Their eyes were on the crowd, constantly scanning for weapons and threats to the president. The man in their midst was the absolute least of their worries.

When MacArthur reached the table, he looked down at the manacles and shackles, crossed his arms and rubbed his wrists with opposite hands. A shudder rippled through his wasted body as the past and future converged upon the present. The light from the banks of suspended LED panels cast deep shadows across his face, and for a moment he resembled a tired skeleton looking longingly at his grave. Then he tore his eyes away from what had been his bindings and looked out across the sea of faces staring at him.

He never glanced at the chains again.

Senator Coleman turned to face the senator. "Senator MacArthur, you know the charges that have been leveled before you." He had to rush to get the words out ahead of the rising taste of bile in the back of his throat. "The charges have been read to the

Senate and entered into the public record. Do you wish to hear the charges again?"

McArthur sneered, first at Coleman and then at the president. "Charges?" he spat. "This man dares to bring charges? He took power when he saw an opportunity, declared the Congress dissolved and anointed the Federal Senate with the legislative authority. Your first act is to ratify a so-called amendment to the Constitution in the name of the fifty states without their knowledge or consent."

The Senator turned to regard the rest of his colleagues, his eyes burning with righteous fury. "And the rest of you? You belly lickers. *You* went along with it. All I did was say I disagree, and look at where I am."

"Senator," Coleman growled, cutting the older man off mid diatribe. "Do you waive the reading of the charges or not?"

"You can save your charges," McArthur replied. "It's not like they matter anyway. The charge was never the issue and neither was the verdict. Those were both determined before either was announced. Let's just get on with it. Do what you came here to do."

"Then will you swear the Oath of Allegiance to the new Federated States and to President James Hall of your own free will as an admission of guilt and a supplication for clemency?"

"I'll do no such thing," MacArthur snapped without hesitation. "The only oath you'll get out of me is the one I swore the day I enlisted in the Marine Corps."

"I don't understand." Coleman replied, genuinely confused. "You're here to give the oath of Allegiance, not join the Marine Corps. Besides, I've read all about your military service, Senator.

116

You were an officer in the United States Army, not an enlisted Marine."

"Son, I could fill a book with what you don't know." MacArthur said as he raised his right hand, his eyes never leaving Coleman's. "I, Thomas Andrew MacArthur, do solemnly swear that I will support and defend the Constitution of the United States against all enemies, foreign and domestic; that I will bear true faith and allegiance to the same; and that I will obey the orders of the President of the United States and the orders of the officers appointed over me, according to regulations and the Uniform Code of Military Justice. So help me God."

The senator's eyes bore into Coleman's, and then he turned to face the Chamber. "Our first duty is to the Constitution because *that* is what safeguards this nation and her people. Not a man in a suit spouting lies. He's the *enemy,* and if you don't realize that, so are you. That man . . ."

Without warning, Coleman's eardrums nearly ruptured from the deafening blast of a handgun at close range, and he felt a hot rush of wind fly past his head. He was deaf from the ringing of a thousand cathedral bells deep in his head, and his eyes stung from the acrid scent of spent gun powder. Senator MacArthur turned slowly back to face him, his eyes wide and his face pale. Both of the Senator's hands clutched at his chest and blood flowed in thick scarlet ribbons between his fingers.

MacArthur took one unsteady step toward Coleman, his lips moving as if he were trying to speak. When he tried to take his next step, he stumbled, fell to his knees, and slumped slowly over to the side. A stunned silence settled over the Chamber as Coleman turned to face President Hall who stood on the dais with a mirror polished 1911 style .45 caliber semi-automatic pistol still in his hand.

A woman screamed behind him, but her shriek barely cut through the ringing in Coleman's ears, and then all hell broke loose.

Guards began rushing everywhere, herding the Senators out of the Chamber. Coleman was seized from behind and felt the cold barrel of a pistol pressed briefly on the back of his neck. The pressure eased immediately, and he was shoved forward and almost tripped over MacArthur's body. Coleman didn't risk a glance back toward the president until he was being prodded through the double doors at the back of the Chamber.

Hall remained on the dais, the pistol still in his hand. He leaned on the podium and glared down at Senator MacArthur's corpse, the contempt for the patriot at his feet obvious. Then Coleman was out in the hallway, and the doors slammed shut in his face.

Chapter 17

Laid to Rest

Joe was a captain again in his dress white uniform. He had expected it to be tight as he buttoned down the front of the jacket. It had been years since he'd had it out of the vacuum-sealed garment bag that he'd placed it in the day he retired from active duty. The stress of the past few months had taken a toll on him, though, and he had shed a good thirty pounds. He lifted his custom-forged captain's sword from the black stand in the corner of his closet and hung it from the left side of his belt.

The standard issue officer's sword was a sword in name only and would be worse than useless on the battlefield. It was designed to catch the eye—nothing more—with the blade made of cheap steel that wasn't sharpened to a cutting edge. Joe had always thought if a man was going to wear a sword, it should be one that he could bet his life on if need be. After his commission as an officer, he went to great lengths to find a renowned master blade smith and paid an exorbitant amount for a sword made to be used in battle, not parades. It had the same look as the standard officer's sword, but the steel was much better, folded and forged by hand, and sharpened into a razor's deadly edge. The clay-tempered blade was hard, resilient, and durable enough to be used in combat for years before it needed to be sharpened again.

119

The sword was heavy, and Joe felt the weight of it today more than he would have otherwise. When he had been in the Teams, he had spent decades leading men into some of the worst combat zones on the planet. In the process, he'd lost more than one man under his command and had been called upon to perform the funeral rites for several of his fellow SEALs. It was a process he was sadly very familiar with, but today felt different somehow. Joe reached onto the top shelf of the closet and pulled down a folded American flag.

With his hat tucked under his arm, he looked himself over in the mirror one more time. The uniform was old but still crisp and bright white. He took a deep breath and let it out slowly, preparing himself for what he would do for Tom and Tom's family in the next couple of hours.

Joe stepped out the back door of the farmhouse and walked down the steps. Bill, Eric, and Steven were standing guard at the pasture, but the small tribe of friends stood in the shade of the towering oak. Beth and Meg were doing their best to comfort Jen. Chris was already out at the grave site and Christina were watching over the kids with Beth Anne and Maimey. Levy, Blanche, and the rest stood in a loose circle, talking in hushed tones that all fell silent when Joe reached the bottom of the steps.

The sun was already low in the western sky, and long shadows crept across the small cluster of solar panels at the edge of the field as Joe led the funeral procession around the perimeter of the field to the old cemetery. Not even Levy knew when the first grave had been laid in the small burial plot hidden in the edge of the trees, but the oldest legible grave marker was from 1763. With dates stretching that far back, there were fewer than three dozen individual graves that were clearly marked.

With limited hand tools, the men had been able to dig only four feet down for Tom's grave. The bottom and sides were lined with smooth stones carried in buckets up the quarter mile from the river bottom. Everyone had helped carry the stones that morning with Blanche and Maimey leading them in old hymns like "Amazing Grace" and "Old Rugged Cross" while they worked. The grave was just inside the woods at the very outside edge of the old graveyard, and more stones were piled next to it.

Tom's body, wrapped carefully in several old bed sheets, lay in the bottom of the grave. Jen knelt briefly by the grave and whispered a goodbye while the rest of the group stood back, allowing her space and as much privacy as possible. When she finally stood, Beth and Meg went to her immediately and helped steady her. Jen's lips were tight and her face pale, but she had dried her tears, and her face was a mask of rock-solid resolve.

She met Joe's eyes and nodded that she was ready.

Still holding the flag in his hands, Joe stepped to the head of the grave and spoke. "I've known Tom for a long time. He joined our team at Joint Forces Command Center more than ten years ago. The first day I met him was like meeting an old friend, and standing the watch together over the years gave us a chance to become close— really close. Tom saw me working on Sunday school lessons and studying my Bible, which led to many discussions about faith and God. One night, after 9/11, Tom shared all of Psalm 139 from memory. He said it was his favorite part of the Bible and the one part he always turned to when he needed strength."

Joe reached into his back pocket and pulled out a small leather-bound copy of the New Testament that had been his pew Bible at the Naval Academy. "From the 139th Psalm, verses seven through eighteen: 'Where can I go from your Spirit? Where can I flee from your presence? If I go up to the heavens, you are there; if I make my bed in the depths, you are there. If I rise on the wings of the dawn, if I settle on the far side of the sea, even there your hand will guide me, your right hand will hold me fast.

'If I say, "Surely the darkness will hide me and the light become night around me," even the darkness will not be dark to you; the night will shine like the day, for darkness is as light to you. For you created my inmost being; you knit me together in my mother's womb. I praise you because I am fearfully and wonderfully made; your works are wonderful, I know that full well.

'My frame was not hidden from you when I was made in the secret place. When I was woven together in the depths of the earth, your eyes saw my unformed body. All the days ordained for me were written in your book before one of them came to be. How precious to me are your thoughts, O God! How vast is the sum of them!

'Were I to count them, they would outnumber the grains of sand. When I awake, I am still with you.'"

Joe closed his Bible and looked up at his family and friends. "That was Tom's philosophy of life in a nutshell. God knows what is happening, and He is in control. Everything else is just the details. God was in control two days ago, and Tom trusted that control. Tom was the voice of calm that more than once backed me down a precipice or smoothed out a disagreement among the brass. In the months after the Blackout, Tom became more than a close and trusted friend. He was someone we could all depend on to get the job done, whatever that meant. That kind of selfless determination to see the mission accomplished is a rare thing."

Joe cleared his throat as he looked down at the flag in his hands. "Tom was a man of deep honor and lived every day of his life with his oath of service foremost in his mind and in his heart. But his love of country was a pale thing compared to his love for his family. Tom was a devoted father and husband and talked about Jen and the kids every day at the office. But his sense of family went far beyond his own wife and children. He saw each and every one of you here as his family. In the end, it was his love of this family that put Tom between Brant and his friends and three strangers bent on doing them and all of us harm. He stopped the threat even though it meant sacrificing himself. I can't think of a better testament to the man Tom was than that. The Bible says, 'Greater love hath no man than this, that a man lay down his life for his friends.' Rest in peace, brother. "

Joe turned and marched over to Jen. He held the flag out to her but didn't release it when she put her hands on either side of his. "Jen, on behalf of a grateful nation and a grateful family, I present this flag to you in honor of Tom's life, his service, and his sacrifice. This flag was presented to me when my father was buried, and I hope one day to explain to your children how their father earned it."

Jen nodded, her eyes filled with unshed tears. Joe came to full attention and raised a slow salute, his left hand on the hilt of his sword. He held the salute for a long count of three seconds and then dropped it. He marched to the foot of the grave and stood at attention. The group walked by the grave and paid their last respects to their friend. Some knelt to whisper a few words, some said a prayer. Gilbert knelt and dropped a handful of dirt into the grave and closed his eyes. When he finally struggled to his feet, Joe saw the old farmer pull a red paisley handkerchief from his back pocket and dab at his eyes.

Jen was the last to stop at the graveside, the flag still clutched tightly in her hands. She knelt on both knees and sobbed softly as she fought to breathe. Her tears spent for the moment, Meg stood, and Amy and Beth walked with her back to the house. The children followed along, though her eleven-year-old son Trey, the oldest of the four, looked back often at his father's grave.

Brant, Oscar, and Oscar's brother were standing off to the side, still in their work clothes. The three young men had been with Tom when they were ambushed, and in spite of reassurances to the contrary, they all felt responsible for Tom's death. Brant, though, carried the weight more than the rest. Once the rest of the group moved on back to the farm house, Brant and his two friends stepped forward.

They had asked to dig the grave and to fill it in once the service was done. It was a grim task, and they saw it as part of their penance for not doing something foolish or heroic in Tom's place. They had survived, but Tom was gone. Nothing could change that. Joe had seen that kind of guilt eat away at men until it destroyed them, and he meant to address their guilt now to make sure that didn't happen to Brant and his friends. Not only did they not deserve the guilt, the group couldn't afford to lose them. The clan needed every pair of fighting hands they had.

The young men shoveled a layer of earth over Tom's body, being as careful as they could. Once the layer was about a foot deep they set their shovels aside and began stacking the large river stones into the cairn. The stones would make certain that scavengers like foxes, wild dogs, and raccoons could not reach the body without enormous effort. The process was slow and meticulous, but the three young men worked steadily in spite of being clearly exhausted by their work earlier in the day.

An hour and a half after the young men had begun their work, Brant laid the next-to-last stone on the cairn and stepped back. All three young men were winded and sweating, but they had done a good job in a short time. Joe walked over and picked up the last stone. He placed it on the very top of the cairn and bowed his head.

When he straightened, he turned and regarded the young men. "You three blame yourselves for Tom's death," Joe said without preamble. "You think if you'd only acted, drawn your gun and fired first, put yourself between him and the attackers, or some other fool business, Tom would still be alive and breathing."

"Sir, I . . ." Brant started to say, but Joe cut him off.

"I'm not done, son," Joe snapped. "And that wasn't a question. It was a statement. I see it every time I look in your faces—the way you hold your shoulders, and in the way you drop your eyes whenever anyone looks your direction. I've seen soldiers, sailors, marines, and SEALs go through this before, and I can tell you if you don't find a way to face it and overcome it, this guilt will eat you alive. And that ain't gonna happen on my watch. Got it?"

Joe fixed each one of the young men with a hard stare before continuing. "Now the truth is Tom was a former special operations operator with decades of the absolute best cutting-edge training and front-line military experience the world has to offer. He saw a threat, he responded the way his training, his instincts, and his experience had taught him, and he neutralized the threat. If any one of you had even had the time to react—which you probably didn't—you would have none of the advantages Tom had, and you see how it worked out for him."

An uncomfortable silence settled among them, as each young man shifted his weight from foot to foot and confronted the uncomfortable truth that his guilt was uncalled for. Regardless of what any of them had done, someone was going to die in that gun fight. If either of them had been able to react in the split second it took Tom to spring into action, all they could have possibly done was get in the way and cause more casualties. It wasn't an easy thing to hear or to accept, but Joe was telling them the truth.

"Now, I get that you're angry," Joe continued. "I get that you're pissed off at the world and at the assholes who did this, and so am I. But there isn't any blame or guilt for you three to carry. Not one ounce of it. You need to direct that anger the same way Tom did—toward the people that deserve it."

Joe stepped forward a few paces, cutting the distance between him and the three young men in half. He locked eyes with each of them in turn, his face serious. "I thought we could stay here, on the farm, and miss everything else that was coming. I should have known better when those first strangers clipped our fence. I was wrong. War is coming, whether we want it or not, and it's time for you men to start training for it."

Chapter 18

The First Step

Mike closed the doors of the admin building and wrapped the handles tightly with a bicycle chain. He closed the padlock and tested the doors, putting his weight against the chain and pulling as hard as he could. The doors opened slightly, but the chain didn't slip and the padlock held. Satisfied, Mike turned and helped Alyssa finish tightening the shoulder and waist straps on her pack so the weight would be distributed more to her shoulders and hips than riding only on her back.

Maria, Arthur, and Cheryl were all waiting for them at the end of the concrete walkway that led from the front doors down to the main parking lot. The sun was gone and a high layer of thin gray clouds rolled in with the twilight. By the time the almost full moon had risen, the clouds were thick enough to dim it to a small spot in the sky. Some light filtered through and settled a muted purple glow over the landscape so that the soft shadows made seeing anything more than about ten yards away impossible.

At the end of the walkway, Mike dropped his pack and pulled out a folded Rand McNally road atlas and a flashlight. He and Arthur had spent the past two nights planning their route and had agreed that until they got well out of the city, their number one priority was avoiding other people. That meant staying off the roads as much as possible.

"All right," Mike said, pointing to the highlighted line on the map, "this is the power line cut through that Alyssa and I used to get back to Maria's place. We'll follow that up past the Latta Plantation, all the way around the north side of town. That will keep us off the main roads until we get to the northeast corner of the city. From there we'll hit Highway 49 and take it out of town. It's rough terrain, so keep your eyes on your feet. We should be able to make it at least to the other side of Latta Plantation before the sun comes up and we break for rest."

"What if we see someone?" Maria asked, checking the shadows around them as if she expected someone to be lurking behind them already.

"Hopefully, we won't," Mike reassured her, "but if we do, just keep your head down and keep walking unless you hear me or Arthur tell everyone to stop. I'm hoping a group this size, moving at night, and obviously armed will be enough to convince anyone who might see us to give us a wide berth."

"And if it's not?" Alyssa asked, a hard edge to her voice.

"We'll cross that bridge when we get to it," Mike answered. "No sense making problems for ourselves by imagining what might happen down the road. Right now, we need to focus on getting our feet moving and putting some distance behind us."

Mike made good on his word by closing the atlas and returning it to his pack. He left the small LED flashlight hanging from the elastic lanyard around his wrist, but he clicked off the power. With the dim moonlight filtering through the clouds, he could see well enough without it, and they were keeping a low profile. A human eye can see a single candle burning at nearly ten miles under ideal conditions, so even in thick brush a trail light with a thousand lumens of brightness would be like a beacon.

Mike had walked this section of the power line cut through twice before in the dark, and he was becoming rather familiar with it. Leading their short column, he stayed a good twenty yards ahead of the group and kept his eyes peeled for any motion in the open path ahead of them and the woods to either side. Overhead, the clouds shifted on the winds and cast a moving blanket of mottled dimness and darkness in alternating ratios. Every time a shadow passed in front of the ghostly image of the moon, Mike's paranoia ratcheted up another notch.

After a mile or so, Mike's eyes were more accustomed to the darkness, and he wasn't as distracted by the shifting moonlight. The breeze coming down from the northwest was cool enough to feel cold against his forehead, but sweat still beaded there and rolled down the side of his face and neck. Walking with a sixty-pound pack loaded down with supplies and sleeping bags was difficult, even on relatively even terrain. The ground under the power lines alternated between smooth, almost pastoral grass and rough, unbroken scrub brush making it at times easy going and at times a real chore to get from one step to the next.

By the time they reached the point where they would leave the main line, they'd covered almost five miles. Based on how high the moon had risen, Mike guessed they'd been walking around two hours or so, which meant they were on a decent pace for their first night. Mike and Arthur had planned to cover fifteen miles before they made camp to wait out the dawn, but Mike was also concerned about pushing the group too fast too early and having someone get injured. If they made that mistake, it could add days or weeks to their travel, and that they couldn't afford. Better to start off slowly and build their pace than to sprint and burn out in the first couple of nights.

Mike turned the corner and walked another hundred yards or so down the smaller side branch. The new line would lead down to another offshoot that would take them across Mountain Island Lake and into the Latta Plantation nature preserve. He reached the top of a small hill and set his pack down next to the tree line. Alyssa and Maria were next to reach the top of the rise. Then came Cheryl and Arthur. They all sat down and breathed a few deep, refreshing breaths before trying to talk.

Mike was the first to speak. "We just hit right at five miles. I want to get twice that much distance behind us tonight. It will get tougher as the night goes on, so we need to rest now and pace ourselves until dawn."

Arthur unzipped the small front pouch of his backpack. "I have granola bars for everyone. They've got a good amount of carbs and some protein, so they should keep us going for a while."

Arthur gave Mike his first and then distributed them to the rest of the group. The snack bars were made of rough cut oats mixed with crushed nuts and granola, all held together by honey. Mike tried to chew as quietly as possible, but it seemed as if the crunching echoed off the trees on the other side of the power line cut. He knew that was only his over-active imagination being fed a healthy dose of paranoia, but it still made him nervous.

As Mike was chewing on his granola bar and on his worries about the loud chewing, a new sound began to intrude on his awareness. At first, it was a low-pitched rumble that was so far down the frequency scale it was as if he felt it more than he heard it. As he strained his ears, though, Mike saw some of the group looking around with puzzled expressions that mirrored his own. They were hearing it and feeling it too.

Then the pitch changed and began to rise. Arthur stood, facing southeast toward the Charlotte Douglas airport, his eyes wide with recognition. "I know that sound," he said softly, his voice barely more than a whisper. "That's the sound of an A-10 throttling up for a high-G takeoff."

As Arthur finished speaking, the sound rose suddenly and sharply in pitch and volume. The rumble was more of a roar at this point, and despite the few miles between them and the airport it was still impressively loud. The roar faded and was gone just as suddenly as it began, though the dull rumble of the jets lingered.

"Arthur, how do you know what an A-10 sounds like on the runway?" Mike asked.

"When Cheryl and I first got married we didn't live in Charlotte. In fact, for more than twenty years, we lived near Fort Bragg and Pope Air Force Base a few hours northeast of here. All through the 80s and into the early 90s we heard A-10s, C-130s, and all kinds of other aircraft taking off and landing. Before the first Gulf War in the early 90s, they used to run training missions at night with the A-10s making high-G takeoffs on full throttle. It was loud enough to rattle the plates in the cabinets sometimes."

Mike scratched the thick stubble that covered his face as he thought. "It's the dead of night, though. Why would they be launching jets in the dead of night?"

"The only reason I can think of is to carry out a strike," Arthur replied. "They sure aren't going to waste fuel on a training mission—not now, anyway."

As Arthur spoke, another sound far to the south caught their attention. At first, the distant rumbles sounded almost like thunder, but there was something off about them. Mike couldn't put his finger on it, but something just didn't sound natural. The sound lasted a bit too long to be thunder, and it reminded him more of the sound an old burlap sack would make if it were slowly being ripped open. Whatever the sound was, he didn't like it.

Just then, four jets screamed overhead, moving so fast they were almost past the stunned group before the sound of their engines reached them. The aircraft were low enough that Mike could just make out their dim shapes in the soft moonlight. Once past the group, the jets kicked on their afterburners and lit the night with four plumes of flame as their engines roared even louder. Mike tracked the tiny bright points of light as long as he could, but he lost sight of them after only a few seconds. The rumble of their engines lingered, though, and they could hear the jets maneuvering in the sky overhead.

A series of reddish orange flashes lit up the horizon to the north and east of the group, each followed by a hollow sounding thump almost like thunder. The flashes came in groups of two and moved steadily south. The first two were so far north they could barely hear the booms that accompanied them. The next were closer, and the set that followed immediately afterwards was closer still. They saw a few flashes to the south, and the rumble of the jets faded, but just as silence settled over them again, a series of rapid flashes lit up the sky to the southeast, and from the direction of the sounds they were right over the airport.

"Is that thunder?" Maria asked in a soft whisper. "That doesn't sound like any thunder I've ever heard."

Mike and Arthur shook their heads at the same time, but it was Mike who answered first. "That's not thunder. It's an air strike. One hit right next to our camp that first night and blew up the bridge over Lake Wylie. I don't know who those jets belong to or what they were hitting, but they hit it hard."

"If that was the airport, they could have been cratering the runways," Arthur said. "In every war since World War Two, one of the first things an invading force does is destroy the enemy's

132

runways to prevent their use of air power. We did it both times we went into Iraq."

"Yeah, but just because they're going after the FSS doesn't mean they're on our side," Mike said as he stood and dusted off his pants. "One thing it does mean is that this area is a lot less safe than we thought it was, and that's saying something. We need to get moving."

Mike shouldered his pack as the others stood and did the same. As they started walking again, Mike couldn't help but think of Robert Frost and the first poem he'd ever read—and the only one that had stuck in his memory. Tonight, like the man in Frost's poem, Mike found himself with miles to go before he slept.

Chapter 19

The Unknown Unknown

Oct. 12th 0330 MST

Commander Price sat at the long conference table in the Operations and Command Center, which the handful of remaining personnel had taken to calling the OCC. It was late enough that most people would call this time of day early morning, but to Price, who hadn't been to sleep in more than twenty-four hours, this was simply the closing act in a very long play. He rubbed his eyes with the heels of his hands and tried to clear his mind, but to no avail. He had never been the best at compartmentalization, even back when he was on the Teams and going downrange on missions into hostile territory.

An untouched glass with three fingers of eighteen-year-old Macallan single malt Scotch sat on the table in front of him. He spun the glass idly on its coaster but didn't take a sip. He knew that what they were about to do was necessary, and he knew deep down that it was the right thing to do. Yet the idea that he was about to lead an attack against what was now the official and declared, albeit wildly unconstitutional, government of the United States of America was enough to threaten his sanity. His entire adult life had been built around an oath to protect and defend the nation and the Constitution, and now, in order to fulfill that oath, he would have to attack the very nation he'd sworn to defend.

Price was exhausted, both physically and mentally, and it was beginning to wear on him. He rested his head on his right hand, his elbow propped on the table. For a moment, he closed his eyes. Over the past few hours a dull, but persistent ache had developed deep behind both of his eyeballs. His eyelids were so dry it felt like they'd been coated with fine-grit sand. At some point, he must have dozed off because when he felt someone's hand gently grip his shoulder he jumped so hard he nearly fell out of his chair.

"I'm sorry to wake you, Commander," Lieutenant Commander Attledge said, "but I thought you'd want to see this right away."

Attledge dropped a file folder on the table and walked around to sit across from Price, who couldn't help but chuckle at the stamps across the top of the folder marking its contents as compartmentalized intel, unreachable even by those with top secret clearance. Anyone who worked at this facility had already been cleared up to top secret, and all of those involved with the actual operations of the facility held write-in clearances among the most expansive ever delivered. They needed these clearances since this facility handled some of the most sensitive and important intelligence the nation possessed. For weeks now, with the skeleton crew running the day to day operations, they'd been able to narrow that field even further. The idea that anyone who lacked the proper clearances would ever find this place and risk seeing what they shouldn't was hopelessly optimistic.

Inside the folder were printouts of some high-resolution images taken by a weather satellite they had commandeered and incorporated into their growing Sat-Net. The time stamp showed that the images were only a half hour old and had been taken on the East Coast. The time difference meant it was considerably lighter in the photos than in Utah at the moment. Price could clearly see the residential neighborhoods and commercial districts that bordered each other, but he didn't recognize the city.

135

"It's zero-three-thirty, and I'm so tired I can't see straight. What am I looking at, Commander?"

Marcus pointed to specific points on the printout. "These are images of Charlotte, North Carolina. One of the east coast NOAA weather satellites we have re-tasked picked up some odd infrared signatures a few hours ago, so we set it to record video of the area. The last few are enlarged to show the detail of the highlighted boxes."

Price flipped to the last few images in the stack and whistled softly. The images showed what appeared to be the aftermath of an airstrike. There were several precision hits on mobile surface-to-air missile sites, one destroyed radar tower at a small regional airport, and some impressive destruction on the main runways at the Charlotte-Douglass International airport. The last images showed rows of buildings leveled and still smoldering, cratered runways, and a completely destroyed radar tower at the main airport. Whoever hit the place had hit it hard.

"Do we know who launched the attack?" Price asked, uncertain he wanted to hear the answer.

Attledge shook his head. "Our best guess is that it was an element of the South Carolina Air National Guard. Probably the 157th Fighter Wing. They have F-16s with the capability to carry out a precision strike like this in the dark."

"This is the part that eats at me," Price said as he dropped the photographs back onto the table. "I tried to plan for everything, anticipate every unforeseen contingency. But there's still the unknown unknowns that I just can't see. The things I don't even know to look for, the things that can come out of nowhere and just blindside everything."

Attledge frowned. "I don't understand, Commander. If it was the South Carolina Air National Guard, that's a good thing, right? More people like you standing up to the FSS and trying to put a stop to it."

"Maybe, but I don't know. I don't know anything about their commander. I don't know anything about their people or their mission. I don't know if this is a patriot trying to put the country back together of if it is some nut job crazier than this man who calls himself president trying to make a play for themselves. We don't even know if this was the SC ANG or if it was something else. There's just too much that we don't know, too much that we *can't* know."

Attledge still had a frown on his face. As Price talked, he poured another glass of the scotch and slid it over to him. Price took a sip of his own before continuing.

"When you're planning any military operation, you have to consider what you know, the known. Then you have to try to account for the things you don't know, the known unknowns. These are always gaps in your intel, questions you can have answered and questions you can't. But you also have to at least plan for the things you don't know that you don't know, the unknown unknowns. The problem is, there is an infinite number of those things, and you can never anticipate or plan for all of them. So, at some point, you just have to accept that you've planned and plotted as much as possible, and you pull the trigger. You act."

Price drained his scotch in one large gulp and slid the photos across the table to Attledge. "And then something like this happens and throws all of those nice neat plans right up into the ceiling fan along with the proverbial crap. If whoever launched that attack ends up a bad guy in this whole thing, it could completely unravel all of the plans I've tried to put into place. On the other hand, if they're on our side, it could be the final straw that breaks the camel's back and makes this a war rather than a valiant but pointless effort." Price pointed to the photos. "The problem is, I just don't know."

"We could try sending redirect commands to the satellite that took the photos of Charlotte," Attledge said. "That's the closest bird we have in the area and it's worth a shot. We'll have to try moving some of those satellites around eventually, and we might as well start with this one."

Price nodded. "Get the signal group to work on it. I want those instructions mapped out, planned out, coded and debugged ASAP. Whatever side these folks are on, that airport just became a player in this whole thing, and that means we need to get to know them."

Attledge drained his glass and had to cover his mouth with the back of his hand as he coughed hard. "I'll get them to work on it right away, sir."

Price shook his head and stood. "Not tonight, Marcus. Tomorrow. It's late and you need to get some rest."

"Yes, sir." Attledge set his glass down and fixed the commander with a serious frown. "And if you don't mind my saying, so do you."

Price nodded, but didn't answer. When Attledge had gone, he poured himself another glass of scotch and set it on the table. He stared into the amber liquor, his mind running at full speed. He had been operating as if he were the only officer left who was working on a way to stop the FSS and Hall, but the incident in Charlotte had him doubting those assumptions. If there were other forces and other units around the country who saw this attempted coup for what it was, then there was hope. As long as there were people willing to take a stand and fight against the FSS, he knew what he had to do. He just had to find a way to get it done.

The problem he'd been wrestling with was the fact that the FSS was already united, coordinated, and on the offensive. They had the initiative, and they had the momentum on their side. He'd been playing defense ever since the order was given to begin the data dump into the secure backup system. From those first moments, he'd been trying to figure out what was happening and who was behind it. All the while the other side was busy executing their plans and achieving their objectives one by one. He had to find a way to shift that momentum and seize the initiative from the enemy, but that was like finding a way to catch an avalanche and redirect it after it has started.

Price studied the map he had projected on one wall of the OCC that showed the approach to Kansas City. A line of red dots had been moving steadily closer and closer to the cluster of tangled highways and rail lines that was Kansas City. If they kept their pace, the convoy would reach the outskirts of the city in less than a day. In two, they'd be in place and ready to launch their first offensive with a real objective. Everything depended on Colonel Darius and his ground forces being able to overcome the entrenched FSS forces already in control of the rail yards. If they could take the city, they would open the door to the East Coast and the FSS headquarters in Washington, D.C. If they failed, it could mean the end of their short-lived rebellion before it even got started.

Having air superiority would go a long way to deciding that issue, but Price still had not heard from the man he had in place in the Arizona Air National Guard. At this point he had to assume that either the officer in command had been killed during the initial chaos after the attack or he had decided not to join Price's resistance. In any case, that was help he could no longer count on but help he desperately needed.

He downed the glass of scotch in one gulp and put the stopper back in the bottle. He had two cases of the liquor in storage, but there was no guarantee when they'd be able to get more, so he wanted to make it last as long as possible. He stood and made his way to his quarters. He had to get some rest.

As he lay in bed, his mind still racing through plans and contingencies, the commander's last thought before he faded to sleep was that at the very least he was moving, and a moving target was always tougher to hit.

Chapter 20

Under the Fence

Oct. 12th 1100 EST

Eric stood just inside the edge of the woods with Brant next to him. Bill and Oscar were keeping guard on the lower pasture, but they were across the road and well out of sight. The sun was up, but it was still early enough that the trees cast long shadows over more than half of the pasture. The sliver of sun lay along the far edge of the pasture on the side closest to town. Steam rose from the grass as the sun slowly warmed the air and evaporated the heavy dew that had fallen.

Brant pointed to a spot near the far corner of the fence. "I saw him when I was on patrol on the other side of the pasture," he said. "I've never seen him before, but he doesn't look dangerous. He's dirty, got some dried blood on the left side of his face, but he doesn't have any weapons I could see or bags of any kinds. He didn't even have a fire, just a ragged old sleeping bag he was huddled under. If I hadn't been keeping a hard eye out, I might have tripped over him."

The small pair of field glasses Brant carried with him had come in handy in their search for the stranger. Eric handed them back to Brant. "When he woke up, which way did he start moving?"

Whoever the man was, he was still deep enough in the woods that Eric couldn't see him, even with the help of the binoculars.

"He didn't really start in any direction," Brant answered. "Just started looking around under logs and rocks like he was looking for bugs and worms to eat. Made my stomach turn."

Through the years, Joe had shared some of his own survival stories and had pointed out numerous simple but effective strategies to Eric. As unsavory as the traveler's breakfast might have seemed to Brant, Eric understood its implication. "That's smart, and it shows he's a survivor. More people in the world eat bugs as a stable form of protein than eat cows. And that was before the Blackout. Do you know if he'd seen the pasture yet?"

"I couldn't tell. He didn't start moving this direction, but I could hear some of the cows from where I was hidden. If I could hear them, so could he."

Eric ran through several possible outcomes if he let the stranger go and didn't like any of them. Better to be safe than sorry and have to explain his decision to his dad. He thought for another moment and shrugged. "Dad said he didn't want anyone left out here roaming around. We've got to get him and bring him in, even if it's just to let him go a few miles on the other side of the river."

"Your call, Eric," Brant said, while he checked the chamber on his lever action Henry Big Boy .357 magnum rifle. He carried a Ruger Vaquero pistol chambered in the same caliber, and Eric knew he was dead-eye accurate out to nearly a hundred yards with both.

"Brant, we want to bring him in alive," Eric reminded his friend. "And you said you didn't see any weapons anywhere around this guy."

"That's right," Brant said as he put his arm through the shoulder strap on his rifle, "but you never know what someone's going to try and pull."

Eric let Brant take the lead. They stayed in the woods rather than cut across the open pasture. Brant wove his way among the tree trunks along a semi-cleared trail. They had intentionally left the trail rough to keep it somewhat concealed, but if a person knew what they were doing, it could be traversed at a steady, quick jog. Brant set a tough, but sustainable pace, and Eric followed, scanning the woods for any unseen threats.

After a solid ten minutes of jogging, they rounded the last corner of the pasture and headed into the woods. Brant slowed and began to pick his way from tree to tree, keeping a generally westward heading. After a while, he stopped and motioned for Eric to crawl up to him. Eric crept as quietly as he could and stopped at Brant's right shoulder, both of them concealed by a large windfall from one of the big storms back in early September.

"Last time I saw him," Brant whispered, "he had eaten a few worms and crickets. After that he went and laid down and was sleeping twenty yards up the hill. There's a cedar leaning against a split oak. He was huddled up under the branches. No fire, just him and the sleeping bag."

"I'll go around to the right and flank him," Eric said. "You come at him straight on from here. I'll whistle like a bobwhite when I'm in place, you whistle back when you're getting ready to move. I'll advance in from my side. If he tries anything, we'll have him in a cross fire."

Brant nodded, and Eric moved twenty yards to the right and then advanced twenty yards and stopped. He checked the chamber on his M-4 carbine and clicked the safety to the fire position. The plan was to take the stranger alive, but his father had always said that plans were made to deviate from later. He checked the 9mm he had in his Alien Gear holster as well, and then he whistled the call of a bobwhite quail. A few seconds later, he heard Brant answer him with the same call.

Eric stood and started moving. He saw the leaning cedar as he moved up through the pines. Brant was coming in from his left, already yelling for the man to stop moving and keep his hands still as he crawled out from under the branches. The man started to turn to his left, but saw Eric and his eyes went wide. He froze, kneeling with one hand on the ground, one in the air, and his back half still hidden by the cedar branches that were brushing the ground.

Eric trained his rifle on the man's chest. "We don't want to hurt you, but if you don't do exactly as you're told, or if we think for one second that you are going to be a threat to us in any way, we will not hesitate. You understand? Nod, don't speak."

The man nodded but didn't move other than that. It was a good start.

"Okay," Eric continued, "for starters, keep both hands where we can see them. You reach for something, you get shot. We won't wait to see what it is." When the man nodded again, Eric continued. "Now crawl very slowly the rest of the way out from under the tree. Move over to my partner on your hands and knees, then lay down with your ankles crossed and your arms stretched out, palms up. Stay that way until I tell you otherwise."

The man crawled over to Brant. Once he was within a few paces, he lay face down on the ground as instructed. Eric caught Brant's attention, pointed at his eyes and then at the man lying on the ground. Brant nodded that he understood and trained his Henry on the prone man. Eric ducked under the branches of the cedar tree and pulled out the man's rolled sleeping bag. Eric could feel shapes and bulges wrapped in the bag, but he didn't open it to see what was inside.

Eric showed the bag to the man and then tucked it under his arm. "I'm going to keep this. I won't take anything out of it, and when you meet my dad he'll look through it with you watching. We're not thieves."

The man tried to nod, but the movement was awkward while lying prone in the dirt. His thick plastic-framed glasses wiggled off his face in the attempt, and he squinted up at Eric. "Who's your dad?"

Eric hesitated a moment, but there was something vaguely familiar about the man. He felt as if he should recognize that face, but he couldn't quite place from where. "I'm Eric Tillman. My dad is Joe Tillman."

The man began to laugh. At first it was a sound so soft and low in his throat that Eric thought he was imagining it. But it grew from there, and soon he was laughing so hard that he could barely breathe. Tears streamed down the sides of his face, cutting clean tracks through layers of soot, dirt, and grime. After a time, he regained some composure and lay panting in the dirt, tears still trickling from the corners of his eyes.

"Captain Joe Tillman," the man panted, "he was there. He was there the day it all started, the day it all fell apart. He came to my store and robbed me—saved my life, probably, but robbed me all the same. They burned it then. Burned it and whatever they couldn't carry, they burned with it. I watched from the hill west of town as the smoke rose. I knew it."

Eric looked at Brant and saw his own confusion mirrored in his friend's face. The man was babbling now, repeating something about the smoke and his store. Then, Eric's memory clicked, and he remembered kneeling with Chris and watching his father make his way around to the back of the pharmacist shop on the edge of town. He remembered the angry mob gathered in front of the store and the way his father had bluffed his way in the front and out the back with most of the stock and the pharmacist. He'd been in that store dozens of times as a child when he'd gotten sick with strep throat two and sometimes three times a year.

Now he looked down at the small, haggard man lying in the dirt, and he remembered the face he'd seen on the other side of the counter for so many years. "Mr. Benny?" Eric asked as he slowly lowered his rifle. "Mr. Benny MacPhail, the pharmacist?"

The man made another sound in his throat, but this time it wasn't laughter. "I was—but that was before. Before the Blackout. Before your father and the mob. Before the others came. Before it all."

The man suddenly lurched into a kneeling position, and Brant raised his rifle and took aim. Eric caught his eye, though, and shook his head.

"Can't be a pharmacist without a pharmacy," the man said with a weak smile. "Take me to your father, Eric. I know your family and have for a long time. And there are some things he needs to hear."

"Mr. Benny, I have to pat you down," Eric said cautiously. "I remember who you were, but things are different now. I have to, you understand?"

Benny nodded and held his arms out. Eric stepped forward and lightly ran his hands along each arm and down each side of the older man's torso. He felt Mr. Benny's ribs and shoulder blades more strongly than he should have. He had lost a lot of weight and barely looked like the cheerful, smiling man from Eric's childhood.

146

Eric patted the outside and inside of each leg but found no weapons of any kind, not even a pocket knife.

Of course, there was still the rolled up sleeping bag and whatever it held.

"Okay, Mr. Benny," Eric said when he was done, "we're going to take a walk now. What I said before still holds. If we think you're a threat or think you're going to try anything to put our group in danger, we won't hesitate to put you down, understand?"

"I understand," Benny said, climbing slowly to his feet. "Things are different now."

Chapter 21

Breaking Camp

Oct. 12 th 1400 EST

Mike sat with his back against a large pine tree. The Latta Plantation Nature Preserve was one of the most densely wooded areas around Charlotte, and the trees here were large and old. The towering pines shaded out a good amount of the undergrowth, and the small scrub hardwoods that did manage to find enough patches of sunlight to take root were few and far between. He had a decent line of sight for the entire thirty yards of sloping hillside that led down to the power-line cut.

They had gone around the slim finger of Mountain Island Lake rather than swimming across the way he and Alyssa had done the last time. The detour had added a few hours to their walk, but it kept all of their supplies dry, and that was well worth it to Mike. He was sitting the last watch while the rest of the group rested and caught what sleep they could beneath a makeshift tent made from stringing a rope between two trees and draping a blue and silver tarp over it. The corners of the tarp were staked to the ground to form a crude triangle.

Once the tarp was tied down, Arthur had offered to sit watch while they slept. Mike said yes only because he was too exhausted to argue. The hike the night before had taken more out of him than he'd expected. Arthur had agreed to wake him at noon, though, and he'd been true to his word. Now Mike was waiting for the sun to get a little lower in the sky before they began walking again.

The woods were quiet except for the birds tweeting and squirrels chattering to each other. The breeze was cool in the shade, but thankfully it lacked the acrid, stinging smell of smoke that had become so prevalent the night before. Shortly after the airstrikes hit, the breeze had changed and brought with it waves of thick, choking gray smoke. It wasn't the sweet, pleasant smell of wood smoke that rises from country homes in the cold fall weather. This smoke had stunk of burning rubber and plastic, melted vinyl siding, and diesel fumes. With every breath it left a thick, oily after taste on the tongue and in the back of the throat.

Whatever the air strikes hit had sparked off secondary fires that had blazed for hours at several points on the horizon, flickering and sending up their own columns of thick, black smoke. Thankfully, shortly before dawn, the wind had shifted from a wandering breeze that could come from any direction in a moment's notice to a steady, strong wind out of the northwest. It was cold and carried the dry smell of an early-season freeze, but it had cleared out both the clouds high overhead and the heavy smoke lingering over the terrain.

Tonight, would be colder still, but with the filling moon it would at least be easier to see. That would hopefully make for a quicker pace and greater distance. Mike couldn't shake the feeling that things were about to become much less safe in and around Charlotte, and the air strikes had only deepened his apprehension.

A twig snapped in the silence behind him and Mike rolled to his right, bringing his M4 up to his shoulder as he rolled. He came to a stop resting against the side of the next tree and scanned the slope behind him. The camp they'd made was on the opposite slope of a low ridge that fell on one side down to a creek and on the other sloped down to the power line cut through and Mountain Island Lake beyond. They'd used fallen limbs, leaves, and saplings to conceal the rough camp from anyone who might have approached from the creek side, so it was possible someone had walked right past the camp and stumbled on Mike.

Mike caught a hint of motion out of the corner of his eye and turned just in time to see a large doe flick her white tail in the air and go bounding back across the ridge to the creek. Mike took a deep breath and let it out slowly as he relaxed and took his finger off the trigger. When he turned back toward the downward slope, though, he froze. Two men were squatting just a few yards from him, both with pistols in their hands. The man on the left had a long, fresh scar down the left side of his face that barely missed his right eye.

The man on the right smiled, but it was a cold and calculating greeting. "You a little jumpy there, son," he said with a heavy southern drawl. "If a deer got you spooked, I'd hate to see what you been through to get here. Now, you do yourself and me a favor and set that purdy rifle over to the side nice and slow. Wouldn't want anyone gettin spooked and accidentally shooting a toe off or somethin."

"You gonna set your pistols down?" Mike asked.

The man on the left raised his and pointed the barrel at Mike's forehead. "What do you think, asshole? Now do what he said before we decide it's less trouble to shoot you and just take it."

The man on the right placed his hand lightly on the other stranger's wrist. "Come on, Trigger, we don't want to give him the wrong impression." Trigger lowered his pistol and the other man continued. "Look, I don't know what you've been through the past couple of months. To be frank, I just don't give a little rat's furry turd, either. Truth is, you got a good rifle and, I'm guessing, some ammo. Hell, you probably got a camp somewhere around here with some clean water and food in it. That's all we want, really. Just your stuff, that's all. We don't *want* to shed any blood over this. You get my meaning?"

Mike felt his pulse begin to race and his hands started to shake. A sudden sheen of sweat erupted from his forehead despite the cool breeze and the shade. He swallowed and took a deep breath to steady himself. If he could just keep these men talking, maybe he could work something out to his advantage. Mike lowered his rifle to his lap, careful to keep the muzzle pointed well away from both men and to keep his finger far from the trigger.

"I think so," Mike said, watching the stranger's face carefully. "You mean you're not looking to hurt anyone, but you won't hesitate to if it comes to that. Is that basically it?"

The stranger turned to Trigger and slapped him on the shoulder as his cold smile broadened into a chilling grin. He gestured at Mike with his pistol. "See, Trigger, I told you he'd see through to common sense. Now, as soon as he lays that rifle aside and tells us where his camp is, he can be on his way, right?"

Trigger didn't answer and he didn't twitch a muscle. His gun was half lowered, but that only meant that it was now pointed at Mike's gut rather than his face. Still, it was enough to let him breathe easier.

"There's a problem, though," Mike said as he deliberately set the rifle to his side. He was careful to keep one hand on the sling and he casually rested his right hand on his upper thigh, right next to his holstered Beretta. "I'm not from around here, and I'm just passing through. I don't have a camp to take you back to, mister."

The man smiled his cold smile again, his teeth bared like fangs. "I'm sorry, I forgot to introduce myself. I'm Steag Jenson. People know me around these parts and they know I mean business. Now, you say you got no camp, but I don't see a single scrap of food. I don't see any bedroll or sleeping bag, and you got not one drop of water anywhere in sight. And that don't add up son."

Steag gestured to the hills around him. "You see, there ain't but so much game in the woods here, and I ain't heard any shots in these parts for a long time. So, you ain't hunting to eat, but you damn sure are well-fed. And you ain't tryin to claw my throat out to get a drink, which means you got plenty of water, too. And not one drop of it in the lakes or streams around here is fit to drink."

"Now, what do you think that all adds up to?" Steag scratched his chin as he pretended to ponder the question. "If you ask me, it adds up to you tryin to feed ol' Steag a load a bull. I know you got some place, someplace with a bottle of water and maybe a can of Beenie Weenies if nothing else. So why don't you cut the crap and tell me where your camp is. If you tell me, you can go. If you make us work it out of you, then you stay."

Steag pointed his pistol at the dirt in front of Mike. "And son, trust me. You don't want to stay."

Trigger made a sound in his throat that may have been a chuckle, but sounded more like a growl to Mike. He wet his lips with his tongue and wished he'd been smart enough to bring at least one water bottle or canteen with him. He was suddenly terribly thirsty.

"I'm sorry, but it's like I told you," Mike said as he tried to keep a steady voice. "I'm just passing through. I don't have any place like what you're talking about. I just don't. I'm on the move going somewhere. I don't even know where yet, just moving."

Steag shrugged. "Have it your way, son." He turned to Trigger and pointed back at Mike with his pistol. "Keep your eye and your gun on him. If he moves for that rifle, you tap 'im. Got it?"

When Trigger nodded, Steag turned back to Mike and holstered his pistol. As he closed the distance, he pulled a long, slightly curved hunting knife from a sheathe on the right side of his belt. Steag knelt and pointed the razor-sharp blade at Mike's nose, holding the razor sharp tip only inches from his face.

"This is going to hurt, so you go ahead and be loud," Steag said. "I doubt anyone's close enough to hear you anyway."

"Wait!" Mike shouted and Steag froze, a true smile suddenly splitting his clean-shaven face.

"The knife gets 'em every time, Trigger." Steag said with a chuckle.

"I wasn't talking to you," Mike said softly.

Steag stopped laughing and his mouth closed so hard his teeth clicked. His eyes narrowed just a tad, and he started to turn and drop his hand to his holstered pistol. Just then, Arthur racked the slide on his twelve-gauge shotgun, and Steag and Trigger both turned to find themselves face to face with Arthur and Alyssa. Cheryl and Maria whistled from the top of the ridge behind Mike, who was now smiling.

"See I was telling my friends to wait," Mike continued, his voice suddenly steady and calm. "I didn't want them to kill you. Not yet. You haven't actually harmed me, just threatened me. A lot. But I don't think that should get you killed, even now, with things the way they are."

Trigger and Steag turned back to Mike.

"Trigger, why don't you set that pistol down and move over next to Steag. Both of you, take off your clothes. All of them. Slowly. If we even think you're going for a weapon, I will kill you myself."

Mike picked up his rifle and stepped over to get Trigger's pistol and tuck it into the waist band of his pants. He took two steps back from the men and held his rifle at a low ready. Arthur and Alyssa moved to stand on either side of the men so they were out of Mike's line of fire.

Steag turned his head and spat to the side in disgust, but he stood and began to unbutton his sweat-stained plaid button down. Trigger pulled a grimy undershirt that was more brown and yellow than white over his head and dropped his ragged blue jeans with a glower. Steag also stood in his boxers and socks, both men refusing to look at each other. Steag had a faded swastika tattooed over his left breast and lightning bolts on one arm. Aside from the scar on his face, there were two more on his right ribs, and three on his left. Trigger had scars that looked like cigar burns across his chest, shoulders, and back. He also had what looked like two old stab wounds and a healed gunshot to one shoulder.

Either before the Blackout, or since, these men had led hard lives.

Mike motioned for the men to take a couple of steps back, and they complied. He then piled their clothes to one side. "Now, walk over to that great big pine tree over there. Steag, you stand on one side, Trigger you on the other. Face each other, and hug the tree. I want you each to hold the other's wrists. Not hands, wrists. Got it?"

The men nodded, their faces burning with indignation and rage. They did as they were instructed and reached around the four-foot diameter trunk of an old loblolly pine. The pine bark was rough and more than a little uncomfortable, as were the large black wood ants that made nests in the pines from time to time.

Mike turned to Arthur and Alyssa. "You two stand behind me at all times and watch these two. If either of them lets go of the other, even for a second, you shoot. Got it?" Arthur and Alyssa both nodded. "Arthur, do you have the zip ties and rope?"

Arthur nodded and pulled a bundle of zip ties from the back right of his belt and caught a coil of rope tossed down from the ridge above. He handed both over to Mike and then took position next to Alyssa. He hung the shotgun from his shoulder sling and drew his revolver.

Mike stepped up to the two men. "You see, we aren't going to kill you, although we'd probably be doing this world a favor. We're just going to take your guns and your blades. That way you won't be able to use them to rob or hurt anyone else. I think that's fair."

Mike waited.

"What about us?" Steag asked finally, his face twisted in grimace.

Mike smiled. "I'm going to tie you together and leave you here hugging this tree. Eventually, you'll be able to work yourselves free—maybe. That is, as long as you don't die of thirst first. Or as long as someone else comes along and finds you."

Mike stepped up to the tree while both men stared at him with wide eyes that clearly showed their fear of what lay ahead. He slipped two zip ties around their touching wrists and zipped them down as tight as he could. Steag started to move, but Arthur cocked his revolver and he stopped. Alyssa and Arthur moved with him as Mike stepped around to the other side of the tree and secured the men's hands on that side.

Once that was done he caught a deep breath and relaxed a bit. The men were secure, and he could tie their wrists together with rope. He hated to use both, but he wasn't sure that the zip ties alone would hold them long enough for the group to get a good lead. If the two broke out of their bonds too quickly, they might catch up and still do harm. He wrapped the rough hemp rope around the wrists of the two would-be robbers and tied several knots. Mike pulled at the rope every way he could, but the knots didn't loosen.

"You can't do this," Steag said, his voice suddenly thin and reedy. "You can't leave us tied up like this. Someone will find us and kill us."

Mike shook his head and started tying their other two wrists together.

"What about our clothes, man?" Steag asked. "What about them? If we get out, we're gonna need our clothes.

Mike looked Steag in the eye for a long time, hoping the man could feel his hatred. "Listen. I'm not your son. Got it? As far as your clothes, we should burn them, judging by the smell. But, as long as you don't mind going swimming, I'm sure you'll get most of them back. The boots, belts, guns, and knives we're taking with us, of course."

Steag's face turned from red to almost purple as he struggled against the zip ties and ropes. "You can't do this man!! You can't do this!!"

"This is gonna hurt," Mike said, a twisting feeling in his stomach, "So go ahead and be loud."

He turned his back on the two men and started sifting through their belongings. Mike pulled their belts and holsters off first, along with three knives each. The boots and knives he gave to Arthur. He handed the belts, holsters, and pistols over to Alyssa, and she started up the hill with them, her face pale. Mike sifted through the men's pockets and found sixteen silver coins, four gold ones, another two pocket knives, two packs of matches, a Zippo lighter, and a pack of Camels that was half hand-rolled joints.

Mike started to toss the cigarettes to the side, but Arthur caught his arm and shook his head. "We might need those to trade at some point. Never know when something like that might . . . come in handy."

Mike shrugged and handed the pack over to him.

Careful not to touch either the underwear or socks directly, Mike gathered the rest of the clothes and walked down to the shore of the lake. He tossed them as far out into the water as he could.

When he reached the tree with Steag and Trigger attached to it, Arthur was there and waiting with the rest of the group. He was holding Mike's pack. "When you didn't come back to wake me up at the right time, we broke camp like we discussed. We wanted to be ready to move in case something really bad had happened. Looks like it's a good thing we did."

Arthur handed Mike his pack and he settled it in place.

"You're really going to walk away and just leave us to die?" Steag asked. "Man, you people are messed up. If you're gonna kill someone, just put a bullet in their head."

Arthur whirled on Steag and leveled his rifle. "If it were my call right now, asshole, that's exactly what I would do"

Without another word, Arthur turned and started down the hill toward the power line cut. Mike and the rest of the group had no choice but to follow.

Chapter 22

Uninvited

Joe sat at the dining room table, a glass of cold sweet tea in front of him. A dark ring of condensation had soaked into the table cloth at the base. Across the table from Joe, Benny MacPhail sat devouring a tuna salad sandwich with such enthusiasm that he worried for the man's fingers. After a few minutes, the sandwich was gone and Benny pressed his fingers onto a few crumbs left on the plate, licked them off, and then sat back with a smile.

"I used to hate tuna when I was a kid," he said after a moment. "I've always liked fish, just never could get on board with fish from a can. But that was just about the best sandwich I think I ever tasted. Thank you."

Joe smiled and took a sip of his tea. "Benny, what happened to you? The last time I saw you, you were at least healthy. How did things go so badly for you?"

Benny snorted, his eyes suddenly darting around the room wildly. "The last time you saw me. Yes, I remember *that* day very well, *Mister* Tillman. You robbed me."

"I also saved your life," Joe said without hesitation. "Yeah, I took some stuff. Stuff you weren't going to be able to hold onto anyway. And I got you out of there before that crowd could roast you alive in your store when you didn't have enough to go around. So, do you really want to bring up who owes who for what?"

Joe waited for Benny's reply. "You saved my life, all right, Captain Tillman, but I'm not sure if that means I owe you or you owe me. Anyway, that was the start of it. The start of things turning ugly. That night four guys showed up in a pickup truck. They were from out of town, but they had supplies and some of them were hard to come by—stuff like insulin and blood pressure regulators, beta blockers, things like that. There was food, too. They had the military meal things. I forget what the guys called them, but there were cases of them."

"MRE's," Joe offered and Benny looked up from the table cloth, a frown on his face. "The meals, they're called Meals Ready to Eat, or MRE's for short. Not important."

"That's how it was in the beginning," Benny continued. "Those guys had stuff, and they started just handing it out to the people in town who needed it. They worked in teams and got volunteers from the crowds to keep an eye on things and keep things orderly. People just kind of got used to taking instructions from them. And then the first theft happened."

Benny paused for a moment, and his eyes grew blank. It looked as if he were focused on things that weren't in front of him now, things that were in the past. The color drained from his face.

"A man broke into the storage shed these guys had their MRE's in and took two boxes. He had a wife and two kids, plus two older family members looking to him to provide. He got scared and he got desperate, and then he did something stupid. He turned himself in two days later with only one of the meals gone. That evening at sundown the head guy—Masterson was his name—he had a big meeting with everyone who could come in town and showed off a

159

new truckload of supplies—cases of meals and water and some clothes, even. He never did say where they were getting their stuff, just implied that they had a stockpile and they were willing to share it for the good of the community."

Benny's hands shook as he took a sip of his tea, but his voice stayed eerily calm and steady. "Then they brought out the man who had stolen the meals from the storage unit. Masterson walks up calm and cool as a cucumber and shoots the guy in the head. Just like that. Then he looked at the rest of us and said that the things they have are limited and they can't have anyone that tries to horde for themselves at the expense of the community, especially if they're willing to steal to do it."

Joe leaned forward on his elbows. "Wait, he shot the man in front of the whole town? No trial, no charges, just shot the man?"

"Everyone was so shocked we didn't know what to do. Before anyone could think, Masterson was back in his truck, driving off to the supply shelter. Three more people showed up the next morning. They had a smaller pickup, but they also had guns and ammunition. Masterson knew them and made them in charge of groups going around and gathering supplies. Anyone not on one of those supply teams caught 'looting' was dealt with immediately, just like the first man. It only took three more executions for people to get the message."

The room fell silent and Joe could hear the clock above the mantle tick away the seconds. He waited for Benny to gather his thoughts. "Those guys, they took over. More kept showing up, and Masterson kept putting them in charge of something. After the scavenging teams used up all of the stores, they started going into the neighborhoods and taking stuff out of the empty houses. They cleaned out what little hadn't already been taken pretty quick. Once they had all of that together, they started going house to house and collecting everything people had. At first some people objected, a few even fought back. But they were treated the same way that first guy was. Shot, in front of everyone, and then their stuff was loaded up and taken anyway. You see that enough times, you get the message and you stop fighting."

Benny took another sip of his tea and his voice grew quiet, not much more than a whisper. "When they came for me, I didn't fight. I gave them everything I had. I cried. I begged for my life—for my wife's life. They took everything we had, every scrap of food in the house, all of our medicine. They even took the three rifles and the one shotgun I inherited from my dad. I never even shot any of those guns, wouldn't know how to. They just remind me of him. And now they're gone. I saw one of the thugs from town that joined their group carrying it when he went out on a supply run with them. I wonder if he's shot anyone with that gun."

"Why didn't the people in town get together? Make a stand against them?" Joe asked. "If you had moved together, you all could have stopped them!"

"You don't understand," Benny said as he shook his head. "They had food. They had water. It had already been eleven days when they showed up and just started handing out stuff. People were starting to run out. Some had died. They were getting desperate. We didn't want to fight. We just wanted to live."

"What happened, Benny?" Joe asked again. "You get kicked out? You run? It matters which one it was. If you ran, they'll be looking for you, which means they'll probably be tracking you. I can understand this Masterson keeping you alive, knowing you're a pharmacist with at least some knowledge of drugs, medicine, and treatments for certain conditions. You'd be helpful to recommend an antibiotic for an infected cut versus an ear infection, for instance. That's the kind of information that could mean the difference between someone living and someone dying. I can't imagine there are many people in town that would have that kind of knowledge."

Benny shook his head. "Probably not. There was a CVS up on the north side of town, but that pharmacist lived in the Bennett Woods golf community. I'm not even sure if he made it through the first few days, and then the fire that went through there."

Joe and Eric shared a look and Joe shuddered. The things they'd seen at the gate to that community had prompted him to find a way to eliminate the group that was responsible. They were brutal and showed absolutely no regard for human life. For decades, Joe had seen those same kinds of people at work in some of the worst places in the world. He knew just how deep that kind of depravity could run once its roots took hold.

People always justified it by claiming they were doing what was necessary, what was best, what would keep them alive. That was a convenient defense in that it removed all possibility of argument, disagreement and doubt. In the end what did it matter? If the alternative was death, then what measure wasn't worth the cost? Nobody wants to die. It was a self-justifying defense and the preferred excuse of tyrants and monsters alike throughout human history.

Plato said it best, "Only the dead have seen the end of war."

"Benny, did you run or were you kicked out?" Joe repeated. Startled, the former pharmacist jumped.

"I ran," he said, his voice shaky. "They had my wife. Said they would do things to her. That's why I went with them in the first place, to keep her safe. Masterson swore he'd have her protected and see that she had enough supplies, enough of everything, to make it. He told me she would be safe, so I went and I helped him. When his men would get hurt, or sick, I would help them figure out what meds to take. I treated them with first aid. I helped them. I knew what they had done, and I helped them."

Benny put his face in his hands and tears dripped off his chin. "Then I ran into my neighbor. He was working for the men but not like the others. He didn't go on runs or anything. He just carried stuff for the men. He loaded trucks, carried water buckets, even carried latrine buckets and dug the burn pits when they were full. Anyway, he said he was outside two days after I left and my wife, Donna, she ran out of the house screaming. She was half-naked and her face all bruised up. A guy followed her out into the yard and stabbed her in the throat."

Benny's hands clenched into fists and he banged them down on the table hard. "We all knew the man who did it. He was a local drunk and troublemaker. He'd start bar fights, and people thought he'd done a few break-ins in the area, but no one could ever prove it. He was just an all-around bad guy. It was him. He even admitted to it. But he was on Masterson's crew, so he got a pass. Nothing happened. Nothing."

Benny looked up at Joe and shook his head slowly. "I had no reason to stay there after that," he said. "I figure if they catch me they'll probably kill me. But that's okay too. I'd rather die free and on my feet than go back to that knowing what Masterson and his men did. Knowing what I'd helped them do. I'd rather be dead than go back to that. I never even thought about them tracking me because I didn't really care if they caught me."

"But what if they catch you here, with us? What then?" Joe asked. "These people don't sound like the kind that would let you go just because you took shelter with some family."

"Just let me go," Benny pleaded. "I'll keep running. You can take me back to the cow pasture, and I'll go a different way. They'll never know I was even here and you and your family will be safe."

Joe shook his head. "I couldn't do that even if I wanted to, Benny," he said sadly. "Truth is, I can't let you go now. For one thing if these people are trying to track you down, we don't know how far behind you they are. Could be you got a few hours head start, could be they left right after you did and they'll be here any moment. We just don't know, so we can't risk taking you back out into the open like that. If we get caught with you, there's no explaining that away. As long as the people trying to get to you don't know that we have you, there's a chance we can throw them off if we needed to."

"But I . . ." Benny began, but Joe held up a hand.

"No, Benny, I mean it. We can't let you go now, even if we knew for a fact that no one was after you. You see we're not planning on just sitting here waiting for those maniacs to make it out this far and start taking our stuff and harassing or killing our people. We're going to hit them first, and we're going to hit them hard. You've seen this Masterson and you've been inside his headquarters. You know the layout, where people stay, where they keep their supplies, the whole nine yards and then some."

Joe leaned forward on the table, his eyes intent. "You've got information I can use, Benny. Information I need. And you're going to give me every bit of it."

"What are you going to do once I give you what you need?" Joe leaned back and drained the last of his iced tea before answering calmly. "I'm going to track them down and kill them. All of them."

Chapter 23

Hindsight

Mike crouched next to the highway, his rifle held ready. Across four lanes of black top and a grassy median was a cluster of parking lots. Two gas stations, a CVS pharmacy, a Subway, and a Papa John's formed a small block where two large subdivisions branched off the main highway. It was after sunset and the sky was beginning to fade from a pearly purple-gray to a velvety, inky black. Already a few stars and planets were shining bright along the eastern and western horizons.

The light was fading fast, and it would be night soon. The moon was three, maybe four days from being full, yet it gave off a good amount of light. Mike could make out the empty parking lot and the black windows of the pharmacy, and nothing was moving that he could see. Two large neighborhoods were nearby, and he could see the roofs outlined against the fading light still hugging the darkening sky. They had passed the other neighborhood to the north east on their way to the stores.

If people were inside the pharmacy, now would be the best time for them to come or go without being seen. Mike strained his eyes as hard as he could, but there wasn't even the flicker of a stray cat crossing the street or the parking lot beyond. All of the stores were empty and silent. The whole thing seemed a tad too quiet and

165

it made the small hairs on the back of Mike's neck stand on end, but there was nothing he could do about that now. They were here, and before they moved on down the trail, they needed to see if there was anything they could use in any of these stores. The longer they could live off the land now, the longer they'd be able to live off their packs later.

Mike turned and motioned for the rest of the group to join him. Cheryl, Alyssa, and Maria came first at a low trot. Once all three made it to Mike and dropped to the ground on his right, Arthur came across and dropped next to his left side.

"You sure we need to do this, Mike?" Arthur asked for the tenth time.

Mike's patience was wearing thin. "Arthur, we've been over it. If we can find supplies in here, we can use them now and make what we have stretch longer on the road. We might even find stuff we need, especially if the pharmacy hasn't been looted yet."

"Look around, Mike," Arthur whispered. "There are houses all over the place. You really think someone hasn't been through here yet?"

Mike shrugged. "These are the suburbs, Arthur. How many of these people do you really think would consider kicking down the doors to a drug store? And how many of those would actually do it? I can see glass in the windows of the pharmacy from here, the moonlight is reflecting off it. If they didn't break the windows out, there's a good chance that the place was never even hit. Only one way to tell, though, and if I'm right the payout could be huge. If I'm wrong, we wasted an hour and a half. So what?"

Arthur wasn't finished. "What if you're right, the place hasn't been looted but you're wrong about it being empty. What then?"

"We'll cross that highly unlikely bridge when we get to it," Mike said, purposefully avoiding answering the question. "If we get to it. And I highly doubt we will."

"How can you be sure, though?" Arthur asked.

Mike drew an impatient breath through his nose. "You smell anything, Arthur?"

Arthur frowned, but took a deep breath and shook his head. "Nothing out of the ordinary. Just wet ground, grass, and pine trees."

Mike nodded. "Exactly. We're down-wind from this place and neither of us smells a latrine, trash, anything. There's not one single smell to tell you anyone is anywhere nearby, not even old ashes from a cooking fire. If someone were here, living in this place for the past two months, you'd be able to smell it by now."

"Oh," Arthur said, blinking, "I hadn't thought of that. You're right. I don't smell anything at all, not even a hint."

"As long as we keep our heads, we should be able to clear these buildings," Mike said gesturing at the pharmacy and other stores. "And there's bound to be some stuff left in there that we can use. We're pretty far out and I don't see any damage from looters here."

Arthur held up a hand. "Okay, I give. It's a good idea. We'll see what we can use and maybe get some food out of it."

Mike nodded and breathed a sigh of relief. He pointed to the grassy ditch on the other side of the road. "The bottom of that ditch is a good eight feet down from the parking lot level. Maria, Alyssa, Cheryl, I want ya'll to get on the other bank of the ditch, use the shrubs for cover, and keep an eye on the front door to the pharmacy. Arthur and I are going to go in. When we clear the entry,

I'll flash my light at you twice. You come up and station yourselves inside the doorway with your backs against the wall. Anyone tries to follow us in the store and pen us in, you shoot them in the back as they pass. Don't give them time to get weapons on you. Just point, aim, and squeeze the trigger."

Mike turned to Arthur. "You have your revolver?" Arthur nodded and took out a small penlight as well. "Good. When we go in, you stick to the right wall. I'll stick to the left. We'll meet in the back in the middle. Clear down each aisle as you pass it. If you see anyone, keep your pistol on them 'till I get there. If you see a body, check it good. We don't want anyone to be able to sneak up behind us as we go. When we get to the back of the store we'll clear the closets, bathrooms, and pharmacy stock together. We've got to do this right. We didn't the last time I did one of these and one of our people got shot, almost got killed. To tell you the truth, wouldn't surprise me any if he died afterwards, given the wound he took."

Mike fixed Arthur with a hard glare. "I don't want that on my conscience again, understand? Let's do this right the first time."

Mike drew his Beretta and handed his rifle to Alyssa. "You got pretty good with this thing at the White Water Center. You were consistently hitting empty soup cans at fifty yards. Take your time, control your breathing, and make your shots count. You've got this."

Alyssa nodded and checked the chamber and safety of the rifle as she took it. Mike smiled and was genuinely impressed with how far she'd progressed. She'd asked him to train her as he recuperated from his injuries, and he'd been happy to oblige. For Alyssa's part, she'd soaked up every instruction like a sponge. She was such a fast learner that in very short order she no longer needed any instruction, simply practice.

Those skills had paid off and now Mike was more than comfortable placing his life directly in her hands. Mike dropped his pack and Arthur did the same. If they needed to move fast, they couldn't have the extra weight. The two men climbed up the last few feet of grassy embankment to the level of the paved parking lot. They paused just on the edge of the pavement and listened to the wind rustle in the dry leaves of the small Bradford pear trees planted in what had been neatly manicured beds of shrubs and flowers.

Mike nodded and pointed toward the door of the pharmacy. He and Arthur ran at a low crouch and stopped on either side. The glass was intact and the door seemed solid enough. In fact, it was so unexpected to see the glass in one piece that Mike half-way expected it to slide open as he stepped in front of it. But instead, he found himself staring at his own reflection. The steel security doors were rolled up, and Mike wasn't quite sure what to make of that. He reached out and pushed tentatively on them, but they were locked.

Mike waived at Arthur to get his attention. When the older man looked his way, Mike pointed to his eyes and then pointed out to the parking lot. Arthur stepped over and scanned the dark parking lot as Mike bent and rummaged through his camel pack backpack. He pulled out a mason's hammer and a bath towel. Mike folded the towel and placed it against the store window. He held the towel in place with one hand, and with the other reared back with the Mason's hammer, ready to strike the towel with the pointed chisel end.

"Stop!" a man inside yelled just before Mike's hammer fell. "This place is occupied! You've got to get your own!"

Mike looked up and found himself staring at a man with a sweaty soot-stained face, wide eyes, and a very large handgun pointed right at his face. Mike let the towel and the hammer drop to the sidewalk and stood slowly, keeping his hands away from his body.

"Look, man, just put the gun down, okay? No one wants to get hurt here, and no one wants any trouble, okay?"

The other man took one look at Arthur and Mike and shook his head. "You two have guns, both of you, and you're about to break my door down. And you say you don't want trouble?"

"Arthur, lower your revolver," Mike said over his shoulder. "Listen, this place looked deserted," he continued to the man on the other side of the door. "We didn't think anyone was here and needed to check for supplies. We're on the road and will be for a long time. There may be some stuff in there we'll need down the line. Maybe some stuff you could spare?"

The man hesitated for a moment. "How do I know you won't just cut my throat and take what you need once you get inside?"

"You're just going to have to trust us," Mike said. "I mean my friend here could have shot you as soon as you stepped to the door, but he didn't and he hasn't shot you yet. Heck, you probably could have taken us both out before we knew what hit us, but you didn't. I don't think anyone here wants to shoot anyone, okay? We've all seen enough death the past two months to last the rest of our lives. Let's not make any more tonight."

The man still seemed unsure, but at least he lowered his pistol. "You willing to leave your guns outside and come in to look around?"

Mike shook his head. "We'll keep them holstered, but we're not going in there unarmed. It's just not going to happen. You've got your gun, we've got ours, but as long as no one draws them, we shouldn't have a problem." Mike returned his Beretta to its holster and motioned for Arthur to do the same with his revolver.

The man holstered his pistol and reached up to unlock the sliding doors. He pushed the doors open just wide enough for Mike and Arthur to get through, then stepped a few paces back and waited.

Arthur hesitated and leaned over to Mike while keeping his eyes on the stranger just inside the doorway. "Are you sure about this, Mike? He could have a dozen people in there waiting for us."

Mike paused long enough to shake his head and flash his flashlight to the women waiting back at the edge of the parking lot. "Am I sure about this? No, but we don't really have any choice. We're not going to just shoot this guy, but we need to get more supplies while we can, especially medical stuff. And if he had a dozen people in here, I doubt he'd be letting us in at all. If he wanted to kill us and take our belongings, he wouldn't bother getting his floors messy to do it."

Arthur didn't seem quite convinced, but he nodded anyway. "Okay, let's go," he said, "before I change my mind."

Mike stepped inside, keeping his hands away from his waist. Arthur followed behind him, and when they were both inside, the man stepped up and closed and locked the door again. "Who were you signaling with that flashlight?" he asked Mike.

Mike pointed to the back edge of the parking lot. "I told you we have other people with us. There are three women who were watching our backs with rifles. I was signaling to them that we're okay and not to start shooting. You're welcome."

The man relaxed a little and clicked on a small LED flashlight. "Okay, what were you looking for as far as supplies?"

Mike stuck out his right hand. "I'm Mike. This is Arthur. You are?"

The man blinked for a moment. "Oh, jeez, I'm sorry. It's been a while since I came across someone who didn't know me. My name's Carlton Marshall Davis, but everyone calls me Chip."

"Chip it is, then," Mike said with a smile. "Thanks for letting us in. We don't need much, just looking for some medical supplies mainly, and maybe enough food for a meal. We've got rations for the road, but as long as we're this close to town, I didn't see any need to dip into them."

Chip shrugged. "Well, the medical and first aid stuff we have plenty of. We've got food too, but not a ton of it. We might be able to spare a little, but not much."

"What about the gas stations and restaurants here?" Arthur asked. "Have you checked those places for more supplies?"

Chip smiled. "Yeah, we cleaned them out right after we got here. Moved everything into the pharmacy. I work here, or I guess worked would be the right word. Not like I'm punching a time clock these days. When everything went down, my neighborhood got rough really quick. My roommates wanted to stay, but I just didn't feel safe. When we started hearing gun shots every few hours the fifth night after the Blackout, I hit the road. I didn't really know where else to go, so I came here. Jess, one of the girls that worked at the BP, she was here too and we've been together ever since. We kept waiting for someone to come—police, fire and rescue—someone."

"What about the neighborhoods? Did anyone from any of the houses around here come by to get supplies?" Mike asked.

"Nope," Chip answered, "we haven't seen anyone. I thought that was kind odd, so about a week and a half ago I went into the neighborhood across the street. First house I came to had some weird graffiti on the front door. A huge X and some numbers that didn't make sense. I knocked a few times on the front door, but didn't get an answer. The back door was unlocked, though, so I went in and that's when I smelled them. There were four people dead inside. Looked like two parents and two kids, the oldest one was probably ten or so, but it was hard to tell they'd been dead so long."

"Probably died of thirst," Arthur said.

Chip shook his head slowly. "Not these people. Their hands and feet were tied, and they'd all been shot twice in the head."

Chapter 24

Unpaid Debt

Levy, his morning glass of sweet tea in his hand, stepped out onto the front porch, and froze. Cage stood against the iron railing watching the sunrise, his broad back to the door. Levy turned and started to go back inside, but the screen door creaked loudly as he opened it, and he heard Cage turn around.

"Good morning, Mr. Levy," Cage said, a broad smile splitting his face. "No coffee? I brewed a fresh pot, and I know it ain't gone yet."

Levy shook his head and let the screen door close. He walked over to join Cage and watch the sun rise over the trees along the eastern edge of the field. The morning was cool, but the sky was clear and it was still early enough to get warm later in the day. A thin layer of fog hugged the ground and rose slowly as the sunlight hit and warmed the ground.

"I don't drink coffee anymore," Levy said after taking a sip of his sweet tea. "I used to start every morning with the Bennett Daily Gazette, two Camels, and two cups of black coffee. Twenty-five years ago, I was holding Eric in my lap and coughing hard enough to make me see spots. He was only a year old at the time and it scared him so he started crying. Blossom, that's my wife's nickname, she told Eric not to worry, I wouldn't live to see him grow up 'cause of my smoking."

Levy chuckled and shook his head. "Well, I put the cigarette I was smoking out, and I never lit another one. That was also the last day I drank coffee. Even to this day just the smell of a fresh cup is enough to make my fingers itch."

Cage looked down at the steaming cup of coffee in his hands and slid a little further down the rail away from Levy. Levy chuckled a bit at that. "Don't worry, Cage, it's been a long time since I had a craving for a smoke that was anywhere near strong enough to make me fall off the wagon. You're fine."

Levy took another sip of tea, and a somewhat uncomfortable silence settled between the two of them. He didn't know what to say anymore, but he could feel that something needed to be said. Levy's hands began to twitch slightly and he had an irresistible itch between his shoulder blades. He had suffered from that same nervous itch as a child, and it developed whenever he was confronted with a socially awkward situation or when he was embarrassed or feeling guilty. But it had been a long time, longer than he could remember, since he'd felt it.

Levy's hands twitched again and Cage looked down at them. "You okay, Mr. Levy?"

Levy shook his head and looked down into his glass, avoiding Cage's eyes. "To tell you the truth, no. Not really."

Cage dropped his eyes to the coffee cup in his large hands. "It's okay, Mr. Levy. Most folks I talk to, soon as I tell them where I come from and what it is I done . . . well, they don't usually want to be round me much after that. I understand. It's okay."

Levy turned to face Cage and waited until the other man turned to face him. "It ain't that, Cage. Hell, I done things in my life that I wouldn't want my daughter to know. Things I never told to anyone who weren't in the war. Dark things . . . bad things. I'm the last

175

person to make a judgment about someone cause of what they done."

Cage frowned. "Then what is it, Mr. Levy. What's wrong? I know you don't like me much. I see you tense up whenever I come around, and I guess that's why I been walkin more and more these days. I thought it was cause you didn't like thinking about the things I done and the fact I used to be in prison. If that ain't it, then what is it?"

Levy took a deep breath and turned to stare out at the field and the rising sun. "I'm an old man," he said, finally. "And I guess as I've gotten older, I find myself thinking more and more about some of the stuff I done when I was a younger man. There were times in the past that I did things and said things to colored—no, that ain't right—to African Americans. Things no good Christian man ought to do or say. I never thought twice about it cause that's just how things were then."

Levy grew quiet and stared down at his hands for a long time. "And then here you are, in the middle of everything breaking down and falling apart all around us, and you come walking through the world pretty, well, untouched by it all. The Father, He reached down and plucked you right out of that jail cell and set your feet on a path that led you to this door. To my door. Like He's reminding me I got debt that ain't been paid."

Levy chuckled softly. "And what's more, you're a good man. I can see that. I ain't blind. You might have done something bad way back when, but you ain't a bad person cause you made one mistake. Was a time I wouldn't been able to see that. I woulda been blind to who you are cause of what you are. I spent a lot of my life looking at a man's color first and his character second, and it took me too damned long to realize it."

Cage drained the last of his cool coffee in one large gulp and set the cup and saucer down on the brick and concrete floor of the porch next to the black iron railing. He reached over and put one large, warm hand on Levy's shoulder and gave it a squeeze.

"Mr. Levy your family took me in when I had nowhere to go. You gave me food and water. You gave me shelter and safety in a time where there's little of any to go around. Never asked nothing back in return, just handed it over to me like I was one of your own and brought me into the fold. I don't know who you were back then, what kind of man you were. But I see who you are now—the man you are today. And I can tell you, Mr. Levy, you ain't owe me a thing. If anything, it's me that owes you."

Levy smiled. "Forgive us our debts, as we forgive our debtors, right? I guess that takes on a whole new meaning these days don't it Cage?"

"Boy ain't that the truth," Cage replied. "Look, Mr. Levy, I'll tell you something a preacher told me thirty some years ago in the pen. He was preaching to a big group of us one Sunday morning, but 'bout half of them in the pews was sleeping and most of the other half was only there to check it off on their list for the parole boards. Me, I was in there cause Momma always said it was what you did on Sunday mornings that counted. Well, this preacher man was talking and he tells this group of murderers, thieves, rapists, and whatever else, 'Never let the man you were destroy the man you are or kill the man you could be.'"

Cage leaned his bulk against the iron railing and it creaked dangerously, so he stood up again. "I didn't understand what that preacher was trying to tell us at the time, but that stuck with me. I thought about it a lot over the weeks and months and years. And I think I got it figured out now. What he was trying to tell us was that we all, every single person out here walking and breathing, got something in our past we wish wasn't there. Most everyone's probably got way more than one something, to tell the truth. But when you get right down to it, the Father, the Son, and the Holy Ghost all three of 'em are more interested in what comes next than they are in what we done been through. It ain't the past that tells you who you are. It's what you do now and what you do tomorrow and every day after that. That's how people know what kind of man you are. That's how they know who you are, Mr. Levy."

Again, the porch fell silent for a moment, but this time it wasn't uncomfortable. There wasn't a heaviness between them, and Levy's shoulder blades had stopped itching. He breathed easier and enjoyed the quiet this time, and it felt good to stand on the porch with Cage.

"I guess it's hard to let go of a guilt you've carried for so long," Levy said after a while. "You just get so used to carrying it that you don't feel quite whole without it. Not at first, anyway. And that makes it both heavier to carry and harder to lay down."

"Brother, don't it?" Cage said.

They enjoyed the rest of the morning in silence. Levy sipped his sweet tea and pointed out a line of six deer as they walked along the back edge of the long field of old, dry soybeans. Cage cupped a hand to shade his eyes from the rising sun and then nodded. The two men watched the deer as they ran and played. Behind them, the house was waking up.

Chapter 25

Ready, Set . . .

Oct. 13 th 0930 MST

Commander Price woke with a start, his hand darting for the pistol beneath his pillow. He stopped when he saw Lieutenant Commander Attledge's face in the dim lamplight, but he kept the pistol in his hand. With the back of his left hand, he rubbed his eyes and glanced at the clock on his nightstand.

"Commander, you wanted me to wake you when we had something," Attledge said. "The signal team got the re-tasking program finished and uploaded to the satellite. It's in place and transmitting now, sir." Attledge straightened and stepped back from the bed.

"Well, what did you see, Commander?"

"You're going to want to see this for yourself, sir."

Price nodded and waved toward the door. "Give me five minutes to get dressed and wake up. I'll meet you in the hallway."

Attledge closed the door behind him as he stepped out into the hall. Price sat up and stretched as best he could. He'd gotten some sleep, though nowhere near enough. Still, he felt better than he had in days. He wanted to enjoy this brief moment before facing whatever waited him in the Operations and Command Center.

He dressed quickly in his khaki uniform and made sure the nickel-plated Colt .45 pistol was secure in a leather holster low on the outside of his right thigh. It was a rig he had designed himself while in the Teams and one that had served him well for years. It had been a long time since he'd worn it every day, but it still fit like a glove and he was used to the extra weight and bulk. Now he didn't feel dressed without the comfort of the sidearm in its holster.

Price stopped and checked himself in the mirror that hung on the back of his door. His uniform was pressed and in order. The laundry service ran like clockwork and was a much sought-after position now. The work could make the time go by quickly, which made the down-time more enjoyable. Plus, because it was laundry, the stakes were very low and it allowed people to decompress every now and then. The result was a constantly rotating staff thankful to have the break, and that made for lots of very clean laundry.

He noticed a fine gray stubble on his cheeks and neck, more than he had let grow in a decade. He needed a shave, bad, and at least another five hours of sleep to feel truly rested. But he was presentable, and that would have to be enough for the moment.

Price stepped out into the hall and joined Attledge and the master chief who was also his personal body guard. As they walked down the hall toward the OCC, Attledge filled him in on the broad strokes of what had happened since he'd retired to his quarters for the night.

"The weather satellite took photos as it was re-tasked, and those images have been processed. We've got some good images of the Charlotte area and down into South Carolina. We now have a live video feed up from that same satellite. It's on a bit of a delay, but it's at least something. The satellite is holding station with a dim view of the state line and a direct view of the SCANG base. I think you'll be interested to see what it shows."

Price rounded the last turn, and an officer waiting by the door to the OCC snapped to attention and opened the door. As he stepped into the room someone in the back corner called out, "Officer on deck, room attention!" And everyone in the OCC snapped to attention.

Price responded, "As you were," and continued to the display monitors mounted along one wall. Three screens on the far right-hand side showed still images from the Satellite's re-tasking, but the rest were full of video showing the airstrip in South Carolina. As Price watched, two fighter jets took off and veered north toward the Charlotte area.

"This is live video?"

"Like I said, there's a few minute's delay between what happens and when we see it on the screens," Attledge answered, "but it's as close to real-time as we can get right now. In some of the images on the right, when you zoom in on them, you can see where other airstrikes have happened recently. And it looks like there was some kind of battle around this airfield in the not-too-distant past."

Price nodded, a mixed sense of relief and uncertainty eating at his thoughts. "So, this is who hit the FSS, then?"

"Everything we've seen so far would seem to indicate it is, sir," Attledge replied.

"We need to find out everything we can about the commander of this fighter group," Price said. "I want to know what kind of person he or she is, inside and out. What are their values, what are their objectives, and who are they working for? This is what we took for granted, Commander. What we had come to expect—the easy, immediate access to information. It was so easy to forget that for most of human history just getting knowledge and information from one place to another was often more than just a hassle. It was at times down right impossible."

"The fog of war," Attledge said.

Price blinked in surprise. "That's right! I see you're familiar?"

"Only in general," Attledge admitted. "I read about the principle and how it was applied to the actions and command structures in both World Wars. I'm a history nerd of the worst kind and I've read books and books about the wars. Military history has always been a fascination of mine, and I guess that's why I was drawn to this assignment. I'm better with data and computers and that kind of stuff than with people anyway. Throw the DoD in the mix, and it was an easy choice for me."

Price pointed to the screen and the video of fuel trucks moving about the tarmac. "The principle was first put into words in the West by von Clausewitz, a Prussian general and military theorist. Basically, it means that in war, the key decisions often turn on details that are shrouded in at least some level of uncertainty and ignorance. The key to becoming a successful general or tactician revolves around clearing as much of that fog as possible. Gather intel, information, whatever you can. And then act based on what you know and try to plan for what you don't. Sun Tzu wrote about it in different terms. It's a principle common to war and one every great general throughout history has had to deal with."

Price shook his head. "When things were—well, before the Blackout, that is—we had nearly destroyed the fog of war. Surveillance was approaching a point where it would have been impossible to do or say or even *think* anything that was truly private. Once we reached that point, there would be no more fog.

Not in any meaningful sense, anyway. Now, though, there's just so much we don't know. So much we don't understand."

"The way I understand it, sir," Attledge said, "one of the reasons the Allies won in World War II was that they gave the battlefield commanders tactical and operational override authority. They were the ones on the ground, dealing with the problems directly, so they were the most likely to know and recognize how to respond to them. It created the shortest possible line between information acquisition and command decision."

"That helps some," Price admitted, "and it certainly gives the battlefield commanders more flexibility to respond to the unknown. However, the only real way to combat the fog of war is to gather information. Without that, you're still operating at least somewhat blindly, and that is dangerous. We took for granted the satellite over-watch, instant communications, and live video feeds that had become such a backbone of US military operations. Now, without all of that technology, we're going to have to re-learn the basics of fighting a land war with time delay in information processing that is on the order of days rather than minutes. There were whole classes at the Academy that focused on these issues, and while I took several, I really wish I'd paid closer attention in them."

Attledge started to respond, but just then the screen flickered and brought up a message of an incoming video transmission on the secure and encrypted satellite frequencies. Price and Attledge both froze for a brief moment, staring at the blinking message waiting to download. Only one person had been given the access codes required to transmit video over the satellite feed, and that was Colonel Darius. And he was under strict instructions not to break radio silence until his teams were in place, which shouldn't be for another ten hours at least.

Price keyed in the commands to authenticate the encryption package and accept the transmission. The screen flickered again and a blurry, digitized image began to form. The image slowly resolved into the broad, grinning face of Colonel Darius, a fat cigar clenched in his teeth.

"Commander Price, Lieutenant Commander Attledge," the colonel said, his grin growing wider. "We made better time than we had planned and our men are in position early. I've got sharp shooters on the roofs of four of the tallest buildings facing the railway stitching yards. There are assault teams and ambush teams standing by. No contact with the enemy reported as yet. It looks like we slipped in the back door without waking up the parents."

"That's good to hear, Colonel," Price said, and he relaxed a bit. "How are the men?"

"I pushed them hard to get here," Darius admitted, "but they're tough and they're ready. I've got them chowing up right now and hydrating. Nothing worse than getting caught in the middle of a fire fight and having an empty stomach. They'll be rested and ready when the sun sets this evening, don't you worry. We're gonna hit these sum-bitches with everything we got."

Price shook his head and pounded his right fist into his left hand, obviously encouraged by the colonel's report. "Good to hear, Colonel. I wish I had air support to offer, but the Arizona ANG is a no show on this one."

"No worries, Commander," Darius answered with a laugh. "The Army was winning wars a long time before we had birds in the air. We're just getting back to our roots is all. I'm hopping off here unless you got any new orders or intel. I'll fire it back up when the action starts, give you a bird's eye view of the whole thing. I already got a nice spot picked out on a tall building that sits at the northwest corner of the rail yards. It's the tallest in the area and should give me a clear line of sight to most of our boys on the ground."

"Until then, Colonel," Price said, raising his coffee mug, "good hunting and God's speed."

The colonel smiled. "We'll give 'em hell, sir." And with that, the picture on the screen froze and then went black.

Price checked his watch and did some quick math in his head. Two and a half hours to noon and another six to sunset, maybe a bit more. That meant in less than nine hours the battle would be officially joined, and with any luck in ten hours the rail yards in Kansas City would be theirs.

In ten hours, they'd know if this was going to be a war or a lost cause.

Chapter 26

Shake On It

Joe and Eric walked point as they made their way to make another trade with Danny. With any luck, he would have his uncle's decision about whether the rest of his group would join the fight. Eric was also excited about this meeting because it would give him a chance to bring up the wedding and hopefully nudge his father into making a deal that would seal the date. As of yet, they had talked only in oblique terms about the wedding happening "soon" or "before the winter."

Now it was time to pin down a day.

Behind them Brant and Bill guarded the cart and lead the horse to make sure he didn't spook. Pounds of frozen beef had been carefully wrapped and packed into six large coolers. Along with the frozen beef, Joe had included a bundle of spiced beef jerky sealed in plastic bags. Eric's granddaddy Levy had come up with the recipe and hadn't shared much of it yet. Whatever he did gave the meat a sweet and spicy flavor with strong smoky overtones. It was tough, but delicious. The other group hadn't asked for jerky, but Eric was hoping they'd want to buy some or possibly trade for some hardware and other things the farm needed. If nothing else, it could serve as a nice snack on the way back home.

Eric and his father were far enough ahead of the cart to be out of earshot when Eric broke the silence between them. "Christina and I have been talking, and we are thinking that Thanksgiving would be a good time to have the wedding. It's about a month away, so it gives mom a chance to go a little crazy with the plans. But it still gets done before winter sets in because who knows what will happen by then, right? What do you think?"

Joe was silent for a time before answering. "I think it sounds good, son. That will give the people something to look forward to that's positive for a change. I think we could use that after everything that happened with Tom. How is Christina doing?"

"The morning sickness is rough on her," Eric admitted. "It's not that it's hurting her really, it's just uncomfortable as crap. She's tougher than she looks, though, and she's not losing any weight or anything. So that's good." Eric paused, lost in his own thoughts for a moment before continuing. "To be honest, Dad, she's scared. We both are. We didn't mean for this to happen, it just did. She's scared."

"Maybe you should think about sticking closer to home for a while," Joe suggested. "You're about to get married, Christina's pregnant. You've got a lot on your plate, and a lot riding on your shoulders, son. Maybe you need to take a step back and play it safe for a little bit until things settle down."

Eric was already shaking his head before his father quit speaking. "That's just it, Dad. I have to be out here now more than ever. I have to make sure it's safe for Christina and the baby. I mean, for the rest of them too, but especially for her and the baby. I couldn't stay behind. It would drive me insane."

Joe stopped and put a hand on Eric's shoulder, turning him around so they were face to face. "Son, you have to understand something. There isn't anywhere that's safe. We're less than twenty miles from the home you practically grew up in, and we're having to go armed four deep just to feel like we have a shot at making it down the road and back. Like I said, nowhere is safe anymore."

"You're wrong," Eric replied. "The farm is safe. The pasture is safe. If the town isn't safe, we can make it safe. We have to, that's why we're out here. It's something we have to do because no one else is going to do it. That's why we're fighting that war you were talking about at Tom's funeral, right? To make it safe again? Otherwise, what's the point?"

His father was silent for a long moment, his face unreadable. "Right now, we're out here to get some pork, salt, and sugar, and maybe trade for some hardware or something. We'll worry about the rest of it when the time comes."

Eric nodded and they started walking again. He watched the right side of the road while his father scanned the left. These roads were lightly traveled even before the Blackout took everything down. They'd made nearly a dozen runs like this and hadn't seen any unexpected travelers. Because of what happened in the pasture, they kept their eyes peeled more than ever.

Joe and Eric reached the crossroads first. The intersection wasn't really an intersection but an area where three roads came together in an off-set y-shape. The area had been a swap meet of sorts, and a few stalls had been built like a flea market, but when the tobacco markets west of Bennett closed down, these roads all but closed with them. It had been years since the traffic made it worth trying to sell anything here, so the stalls were all faded and falling in on themselves.

The few houses that had been occupied around the cross roads stood with their dark, windows facing the road. Joe and some of the men had cleared the homes before the first meeting and they'd all been empty. It looked as if the people had gathered only what they could carry and nothing more.

Bill and Brant caught up to Joe and Eric and pulled the cart around so the horse was facing back down the road. If an unexpected threat happened, Joe had instructed Brant to jump in the cart and drive the horse as hard as he could back home. Hopefully the attackers would focus on the cart and give the group time to take them out.

Thankfully, all of their transactions had gone smoothly, so they'd not had to use any of the contingency plans Joe had in place. Still, with the group from town pushing farther out into the country, they couldn't afford to let their guard down for even a second. The last thing they needed was a foraging party stumbling up on their trade with Danny. That could do more than cost them a few dozen pounds of beef, pork, and dry goods. An attack could create suspicion and sour the whole trade relationship between the two groups. Joe couldn't afford to lose a reliable source of something as valuable as salt and sugar.

The group waited for a little more than a half hour before Danny arrived with his crew of three men. They had a horse-drawn cart as well, but their cargo was different this time. The cart held a bundle as usual, but tied to back of it was a pair of pigs that looked nearly full grown. They were snorting and digging at the grass and weeds along the side of the highway, which likely accounted for the late arrival. Danny also had his usual two-man guard detail, but there was also a fourth man with the group this time—a stranger that neither Joe nor Eric had met before.

The new man was older and walked with a sense of purpose and determination. His thick gray hair was pulled back in a ponytail and his equally white beard fanned out across most of his chest. He wore Carhartt khaki work coveralls and a pair of stout work boots. As this unfamiliar man strode up to Joe and Eric, he looked them over from head to toe, cataloging every detail. Joe, equally observant, took immediate notice of the lever action rifle he carried and the revolver holstered on his right hip that was balanced by the long-bladed bowie knife on his left.

The stranger extended his right hand to Joe. "You must be Captain Tillman. I'm Danny's uncle, Jerry D. Williams. It's a pleasure to finally meet you, son. I heard a lot about you and your group."

Joe took Jerry's hand and shook it. "I hope everything you heard was good," he said with a smile.

Jerry clapped a large hand on Joe's shoulder. "Considering your first introduction to my hard-headed nephew was him poaching one of your cattle and all he lost was a pair of horses, I'd say that set the tone pretty well. We miss the horses from time to time but sure am glad you let Danny come back to us in one piece."

"Just a misunderstanding that worked out best for everyone in the end," Joe said.

"I see you two met," Danny said as he walked up and shook Joe's hand. "Good to see you again, Captain Tillman. I brought everything that you asked for last time like we agreed."

"I wanted to thank you, too," Jerry interjected, "for helping Danny get those solar panels. We were able to hook a couple of them up and we've got working freezers again for the first time since the lights went out. They ain't producing much power, but it's enough to keep food from going sour on us, and that's a lot these days. Between that and giving us some lights on the outside of the shop at night, things have gotten a lot more comfortable around home thanks to you boys and your hard work."

"Glad you could get some use out of them," Joe said, casting a sidelong glance at the older man. "Did Danny also mention why I sent those panels to you all practically free of charge?" Joe asked after a moment.

Jerry nodded slowly. "He did, as a matter of fact. Way I understand it you want to go off all John Wayne on that group causing a ruckus and a trouble up on the north side of town. That about right?"

"Those people are dangerous," Joe said. "They're killing people and sucking up all the supplies and resources for miles around and then killing anyone who disagrees with them or objects to being robbed and extorted. If we don't do something now, we'll find ourselves bending knee to them soon enough."

"Danny said he's seen them doing some pretty nasty stuff," Jerry admitted, "but we haven't had any trouble with them where we are. How about you?"

Joe nodded. "A group came through our area a few days ago. They tried to confiscate our pasture and our cows. Said something about 'hoarding' being against the law now."

Jerry whistled through his teeth. "Were they serious about it?"

"Serious enough to draw on one of my men," Joe said. "He shot all three of them, but took a bullet to the liver and one to his left leg. He ended up with a blood infection and died."

Jerry shook his head, a deep frown creasing his forehead. "That's some serious business, Captain Tillman, serious business all the way around. You catch any blowback from it?"

"Not yet," Joe admitted, "but I imagine we will. It's only a matter of time until they notice those men missing and send someone to

191

find out what happened to them. So, one way or another, we got trouble coming. If you want to keep this trade relationship working, then that means you got trouble coming too."

Jerry tugged on his beard, thinking about Joe's words. "I guess you're right. If they're branching out from town and looking to take what people have, then eventually we're going to rub up against them the wrong way just like y'all folks did. Cause they ain't gonna get what we got. And that's just that." Jerry paused for a moment and heaved a heavy sigh. "Truth be told, I ain't got that much in the way of help to offer. I got maybe a half a dozen men like Danny who might be useful in a fight, but most of the people up my way are older. They got health problems and a lot of 'em got spine problems too."

"Spine problems?" Joe asked, confused about the difference between that and a regular medical problem.

"Yeah," Jerry said with a grin, "I'm sure you know the type. They talk tough, but when the shit hits the fan, they suddenly develop the problem of not having a spine to keep their asses from hittin the dirt."

Joe chuckled a bit at the joke. "Anything you can spare will help a lot. It's not about the numbers, not yet anyway. What we need is people willing to step up and take action. People willing to fire the first shots and let the rest of the community know they aren't alone. Let people know that others out there are willing to stand up to these monsters and stop them. Once people see that, I hope they start standing up on their own to help us take out the trash."

"If people don't stand up, though, do you think you can see this thing all the way through with just the people you got and the handful I can lend?"

Joe didn't hesitate. "Absolutely. We'll lose some people, without a doubt. We'll lose more if the people still living in the area don't stand up and fight, but we'll lose people either way. But we'll take so many of them with us that they won't have any choice but to tuck tail and run."

"Okay," Jerry said, sticking his hand out again, "You say you can do it, and I believe you Captain Tillman. We'll work with you and do whatever we can to help. What do you need from us?"

Joe accepted Jerry's handshake. "We'll need the men, first off. As soon as you can send them to our place, get them on the road. Have them bring clothes, tents, any guns and ammo that you can spare while still keeping enough to defend your place and your property. And if any of them knows how to use a bow, that would help."

Jerry frowned. "A bow? Like a bow and arrow?"

Joe nodded. "A lot of deer hunters around here have very nice compound bows. We're going to make good use of them. They're a lot quieter than a rifle and will do just as much damage in the right hands. Even more. There's a psychological aspect to finding a fellow sentry with a few arrows sticking out of him that's hard to ignore."

Jerry's face went a little pale. "Boy, Danny won't kidding. You are one ruthless SOB when you have to be, ain't ya? Well, when we get back I'll talk to the fellas. We'll get them on the road back out to you first thing in the morning. Any idea how long they'll be gone? Some of the men I have in mind have families and they won't take too well to their men folk being gone too long with the holidays coming up."

"Hopefully no more than a few weeks," Joe said. "I want them to get basic training in movements and signaling, assault and retreat tactics, that kind of thing. We'll run a few missions together. Then I plan on turning them loose to harass the group on the northern edge of the town while we hit them hard on the southeastern edge. If we can get them to spread their defenses, it will be a lot easier to hit them and hurt them."

Jerry jerked his head back toward the carts where Brant was helping Danny's two men transfer the goods one to the other. "Let's go see if there's any work left to do now that we've done the talking."

Jerry led the way as Danny hung back a bit to speak with Joe and Eric. "Uncle Jerry insisted on coming out to meet you in person this time. After the solar panels worked and we were able to get electricity back to a few things that are still functional, he was really impressed. I think that went a long way to him agreeing to help y'all out."

"Is that why you brought us two pigs?" Eric asked, pointing at the two hogs chewing on the grass by the edge of the road.

Danny shared a look with Joe and then shook his head. "That's something else. Something your father and I worked out, so you'll have to ask him."

Eric looked at his father and Joe smiled a broad smile. "I knew you were going to pick a date for the wedding that was before winter, and I figured we'd want to have a big party for it. Well, right now a barbecue is about the only big party we can really throw with what we have available, so that's what it's got to be. One of those hogs is for your wedding celebration and the other is to have sausage, salted shoulder, and other pork for next year."

Eric was speechless. For a moment, all he could do was stand and stare at his father. He didn't even want to think what had been promised for two live, almost full-grown hogs. They would have been more expensive than anything the group had traded for, and one was solely for his wedding reception. Eric found himself blinking back tears and threw his arms around his father in a hug that Joe returned just as tightly.

"I love you, son," Joe whispered to Eric. "Everything is going to work out all right in the end. You'll see."

Eric pulled back after a moment and dried his eyes. Danny had already walked over to the carts to give them some privacy, so Joe and Eric followed. By the time they got to the carts, all of the goods had been transferred and the men were chewing on some of the beef jerky Eric had brought.

"This stuff is good," one of the men said, biting off another chunk.

"First piece is free, but the rest will cost you," Eric told him, and the man grinned.

"Your buddy here already told us. If you can bring more of this next time, we'll have screws, nails, bolts, nuts, and everything else you could possibly want. We'll work something out, don't worry."

Eric nodded. "Sounds good."

"That reminds me," Jerry said, "we need to talk about the trade situation here. Now that we've got cold storage up and running we can stockpile a little more fresh meat, and we won't have to keep swapping salt and sugar for beef. I think you're probably stocked up on dry stuff too for a little while, am I right?" When Joe nodded, Jerry continued. "Well, I think we can still meet here once every other week or more if we need to, but we'll just be trading different things. Like the beef jerky your boy brought and hardware, things like that. What do you say?"

"I'll talk it over with my people," Joe said, "but I don't see it as being a problem. We've got a good stock pile of salt and sugar built up and we won't need that much more until we start canning again next season. Do you have anything in particular you need that we can maybe help you with?"

Jerry thought for a minute before giving a small shrug. "To tell you the truth, I'm not really sure. We'll put our heads together back home and come up with a list for next meeting."

Joe nodded. "We'll do the same, then, and I want to thank you for sending your men to us. I want you to let all of your people know that if anyone wants to come, we're having my son's wedding on Thanksgiving Day. You're all welcome to come and eat and celebrate with us if you want."

Jerry smiled and stuck out his hand again. "Well, Captain, I'm glad I finally got to meet you. We could stand here chewin the fat all night, but we've got a long way back and you do too, so we'd better get moving."

Jerry turned to Eric. "And for you, Eric, congratulations on getting married. I know Danny will be there when you have the cookout and there will probably be some others who want to come too. Thank you for opening up your home and welcoming us in. We sure appreciate it. We can use all the friends we can find these days."

Eric shook Jerry's hand with a firm grip. "Thank you, sir. We look forward to seeing you at the wedding."

Eric stood with his father and watched Danny and the others make their way back west. They disappeared around a curve just as the sun touched the horizon. He felt like something big had happened and he didn't quite have the details yet. Something about the way that Danny's uncle had looked at his father said that this was the beginning of something that would change their lives.

"Son, I'm proud of you," Joe said after a moment, and it caught Eric off guard. When he didn't say anything, his father continued. "You've taken on a lot the past month, and the family depends on you just as much as we depend on anyone else. You're going to have a big part to play in what's coming. I want you to know I have faith in you. I've seen a lot of men at the point you are now, and they weren't ready for lay ahead. You're ready."

Eric tried to speak but found his throat was tight, and he couldn't quite get words to form, so he nodded instead and pretended to wipe the dust away from his eyes.

Joe turned and stepped out onto the road that led them home. "When we get back to the house, you need to get your bow. Tonight, we're going hunting."

Chapter 27

The View

Oct. 13 th 1805 EST

President Hall sat on the open balcony outside his suite and watched the sunset over the National Mall. The angry red ball was nearly gone now; just a sliver of it peaked over the horizon as he sipped a good bourbon and enjoyed the cool breeze. The afternoon had been warm, but the breeze had shifted as the sun set, and thin, wispy clouds had begun to move in from the north and west. As the sun set, those clouds first glowed a bright gold and then turned a deep orange that bled into a rich scarlet. Now, Hall watched them shift to a soft, dark violet against the fading sky.

Daniel was waiting for him inside, but the president was in no hurry to listen to another status report about falling morale and uncertainty in the Senate. He'd thought the dead Senator MacArthur would have served as a lesson, and to some he had. But to others, the effect was the opposite of what he'd hoped. They'd gone from quiet uncertainty and being noncommittal to near open dissent. That, thankfully, was a line no one had crossed yet, but if he allowed attitudes to go unchecked, it was only a matter of time.

President Hall did not want to have to shoot anyone else on the Senate floor. Once was a statement, more than once became a pattern. And that was too easy to portray as inhumane and cruel. The president knew he had to handle things delicately, and that was why he hadn't made any more moves. He was waiting to see how the dust had begun to settle and where it hadn't.

He stared at the satellite phone on the table next to him. It hadn't rung in more than a month. His last conversation had been a call that he'd made, and the one before that as well. And even that last conversation had been preemptively cut short while he was on hold for some minor delegate of the Russian entourage. Suddenly, the line had clicked and gone dead. He'd tried to redial the number more than once, but he received only busy signals.

The phone might as well be a paper weight.

He knew the problem. He'd rushed with the Senator when he should have taken his time. He was too eager to move, too eager to pounce. That had always been a failing of his, and it was one that was difficult to resist at times. But Hall knew deep down that the years of planning and scheming for this moment were done. Now he simply had to let the action unfold. But that meant exercising patience.

He grabbed his bulb-shaped glass of bourbon and stood. He walked to the western railing of the balcony and looked out over the Mall as the darkness deepened. Banks of LED flood lights were just coming on as they drew their power from the solar-charged batteries on each pole.

White tents lined the entire Mall in rows so tightly ordered, hardly any grass showed between them. Each tent held four people and each day more people from DC and surrounding cities showed up to join the new Federal States Army, the FSA. The ranks were swelling, and already groups were being tasked with missions outside the city limits.

Hall looked down on the FSA, the army . . . *his* army . . . and smiled.

This was the moment he had been born for—the reason he existed. For a thousand years, his name would be etched into human history as the man who conquered America. The Federal Senate was a temporary nuisance for him and a popular nostalgic relic of days gone by for the masses, but it would never again wield any real power.

The power was his, and everyone who had stood in that chamber and witnessed the execution of the traitor MacArthur knew it.

There was a cough behind him, and Hall spun to see who had so rudely interrupted his reverie. "Daniel, I thought I told you to wait for me inside. Was I not clear enough?"

Daniel nodded. "Yes, Mr. President, you were clear enough. But you need to hear this. There is news from Charlotte, sir, and it isn't good."

"Someone really hit us, then?" President Hall asked, half in denial. "Someone domestic?"

Daniel nodded. "Looks like it was South Carolina Air National Guard, Mr. President. They hit our aircraft and supply depots hard at the airport. They also totally destroyed eight road-mobile surface-to-air missile launch systems at six different sites, and they dropped two radar towers, one at a regional airport and one at Charlotte Douglas. The damage was extensive, sir."

Hall's face went from an impatient red to white with rage, and his hand trembled. "I want you to find out where the attack came from, exactly where. And I want to hit them with everything we have. Obliterate them. Do you understand?"

Daniel hesitated to push the issue, but Hall had to understand the facts. "Mr. President, I'm not sure you understand the impact here. I have seen pictures from one of our satellites, sir. The damage is, as I said, extensive. We may not have enough to hit them, and even if we do, it's unlikely the planes would be able to land back at the airport, which means it will be a one-way trip for whoever goes."

"Just what exactly are you trying to tell me, Daniel," Hall asked, his voice suddenly very calm and cool. "Because it sure didn't sound like, 'Yes sir, Mr. President. Right away Mr. President.'"

Daniel's face flushed. "I'm trying to say, Mr. President, that if we launch this attack it may fail."

Hall stepped up face to face with Daniel and fixed him with a dangerous glare. "Don't fail. You've got a lot riding on the success of my order. You, personally. If you fail to bring these traitors to justice, I will kill you. Failure is not an option."

The president turned his back on Daniel and stepped back toward the rail. "Now go, and come back when you can tell me how hard we hit these mutinous bastards. Is that understood, Daniel? Don't make me come find you so I can ask."

Daniel relented. "This is not the kind of thing I'm comfortable handling, but if you insist, sir, of course I will agree. Is there anything else I can get for you, sir?"

Hall smiled over his shoulder and took another sip of his bourbon. "No, Daniel. I'm just enjoying the view."

On the Mall below cooking fires were being lit at pre-determined points along the grid and the smell of burning wood drifted up on the breeze.

Chapter 28

Tango Down

Oct. 13th 1930 MST

Commander Terry Price stood at the front of the Operations Command Center with the long bank of high-definition monitors at his back. The remaining staff was gathered in front of him and filled the auditorium-style seating with another twenty or so people along the back and sides of the room. This was the first time he'd seen the skeleton crew of ninety assembled in one place. They all looked tired and a bit worn but still determined to get the job before them done.

"We are all that remains here at the facility," Price began, "but we are not alone. Recon teams have been sent to several cities, and crews are tapping into some of the strategic surplus depots nearby to gather more equipment and supplies for the coming war. We are all doing our part to push that larger objective further toward the goal line, and tonight is a big moment in that drive."

A restless stir went through the audience as some involved in isolated parts of this operation from the beginning had their suspicions confirmed. In an operation this size, even with a small staff that compartmentalized information and tasks as much as possible, it was inevitable that a few would realize that something big was in the works. But, to their credit, whatever their suspicions had been, the staff had enough professional integrity to keep their suspicions to themselves. Nothing had leaked at any point in the operation.

"Some of you have seen bits and pieces of this building," Price continued, "and I appreciate your discretion in keeping theories and speculations to yourselves. Now I can tell you, we are about to hit the enemy and hit them hard. The target is Kansas City, Missouri. Specifically, we'll engage an enemy outpost at the rail yards in this city. Our objective is to secure the city and use it to serve as a supply depot and transportation hub. With the rivers, roads, and rail lines radiating out from that city we can move men and material all over the country."

Price nodded to Lieutenant Commander Attledge, and he powered up the displays behind Price. Two of the screens showed satellite images of the rail yards with near real-time video feed. Four of the monitors, reserved for live streaming video feed from the battlefield, currently displayed static as the transmission channels weren't yet active.

"Colonel Darius will be commanding the ground forces in the attack," Price said. "He will make contact shortly via satellite phone and we'll establish a video uplink. Once that's done, we'll serve as the Colonel's eyes and ears—clear the fog and give him what he needs to make decisions about how to advance the assault. This is a big moment, and there's a lot riding on what we do over the next few hours. I can't think of a better team to have behind me than you folks. If anyone can get this job done and get it done right, we can. And, gentlemen, we are the ones who have to do it."

Price paused and fixed each member of the audience with a firm stare. "Our grandchildren will read about these days and the things that are happening around us, and they will be proud to know that we were here at the beginning. Now, you all know the jobs you have to do, so go do them. Department heads, if you run into trouble, don't hesitate to bring it up. I want to know the solution before it becomes a problem. Dismissed."

Price stepped away from the front of the room as the team dispersed to their various departments. Their primary charge was routing the signals coming in from various sources and patching them through the OCC communications network. Attledge was already waiting at the smart table that served as the command interface terminal. From that station, Price could access the direct communications to any of the platoon commanders or to Colonel Darius himself. He also had access to each of the satellite feeds and could isolate videos to create still images and manipulate them while bringing up the 2-way video chat with each department head.

Attledge was looking over the topological map of the city blocks surrounding the rail yards. The elevation contours around the buildings marked out the ridges and valleys of the Kansas City skyline. They had highlighted the troop placements Colonel Darius had reported earlier so they would know where the friendly troops were stationed and where they would make contact with enemy forces.

"You can analyze it to death," Price said, "but all you'll do is give yourself heartburn. This is what we have and what we know at this point and there's nothing we can do to change that. We're just going to have to play it out and see where the chips fall."

Attledge started to reply, but the signal group buzzed in on one of the smaller communication terminals, and a young technician's face appeared on the screen. "Colonel Darius is patching through on the main channel, Commander. The channel is secure."

The tech disconnected the transmission, and the central screen powered on at the same time. At first the large screen showed only static, but after a moment it flickered to an image of Colonel Darius, his face illuminated by the eerie green light of a night vision optic.

"Commander Price, it's good to see you," Darius said in a whisper. "I'm on a small point of land on the edge of a residential neighborhood across the Missouri from the FSS installment. We're a little exposed but more than a mile away and in the dark. Plus, from here I have a clear line of sight to one of the checkpoints, and we can control the Nightingale from here. I'll have a good view down to the rail yards and the surrounding battlefield. I've got four platoon commanders wired up and their connections should be activating soon."

"Thank you, Colonel," Price replied. "God's speed tonight, Colonel, and happy hunting. How has the drone performed?"

"We've used it a few times scouting ahead of the convoy on the way here. It also came in handy setting up Third and Fourth Platoons' positions. The pilot has gotten pretty handy with it, and that's become my primary means of directing engagements whenever possible. That feed should come up with the platoon commanders in a few moments. Now, if you need me, you'll probably have to scream my name to cut through the chatter. I'll have all four platoon commanders and the over watch coming in over the comms, so I'm going to be a bit distracted."

"Understood," Price said. "I'll leave you to your work."

Price muted the input channel for the Colonel's feed at the same time the four platoon commanders signed onto the satellite feed one by one. The connections were somewhat intermittent and prone to freezing every few seconds if the soldier moved too fast. It wasn't perfect, but it was the best the systems and signal engineers had come up with considering they had only a few dozen satellites answering commands at this point.

Once the four platoon feeds normalized, a fifth input was directed to one of the desktop monitors facing them. The image was of the rail yards from fifteen-hundred feet altitude. The view was magnified several times, and the camera also transmitted the telemetry for the small backpack drone that was operating it. The controller would be on the rooftop with the colonel, who could see the images in real time and plan his battle accordingly.

From the colonel's video and photographic recon, they knew there were two main gates leading into the stitching yard. Both had been manned by DHS agents but were now home to Federal Security Service guards. Manually operated cross bars blocked the entrance, and leading up to both guard shacks, rows of sandbag and concrete obstacles were staggered to make the approach a series of tight, slow switchbacks. Banks of halogen construction lights drew power from towable DOT solar generators and cast bright pools on the gate itself as well as the approach. From the drone's altitude, however, all that was clearly visible were the pools of light and the guard shacks. A few vague figures moved around the streets, but they were indistinct when the image zoomed out and less than clear when it was more focused.

In the pictures, four armed guards stood at each gate, and though they never split into four separate directions, they made an obvious effort not to stay grouped in one place for long. At least one guard was always posted inside the shed where additional weapons and supplies were likely stored close to hand. They were professionals and it showed.

Beyond the gate, people congregated around the rows of tents and cook fires or in front of one of the maintenance buildings where it appeared engines and cars were being repaired. No guards were stationed within the perimeter of the FSS camp, and only two more guard towers covered the rear of the camp and the two main roads into the back of the property. The silent drone circled several times and zoomed in on various zones in its field of view. The images reflected in real time what the colonel had captured with his camera at ground level.

Darius clicked on his communications link. "Okay, First Platoon, you're a go. Hit them now and hit them hard, then pull back to the alleyways. Get cover and keep firing and giving ground. Make sure they follow you in. That's when you're up, Second Platoon. Third and Fourth, you hold until I give the order. Let's get it done, gentlemen."

The four platoon commanders gave their response in unison. "Yes, sir."

First Platoon's commander gave his orders, and two three-man teams took off at a trot up the narrow alley. Two of the men on each team carried regular M-4 rifles with scopes and night-vision optics. The third man carried two side-arms and a short-barreled pump-action shotgun, and strapped to his back was the large tube of a Javelin AGM-148 missile.

The view from the drone switched to a passive infrared image where hotter objects showed up as lighter colors of gray and white. The six men were clearly visible against the black landscape as they moved north on Hwy 269 to the point where the road ran into the trees that lined the bank of the Missouri river. Each team had a clear view down one leg of a triangle with Front Street as the base and both guard check points approximately 1.3 kilometers away.

The two fire teams deployed slightly offset from each other, one facing the east checkpoint, one facing the west. A white flash signaled that both teams had fired their Javelins in unison. A small charge had sent them airborne, and then the main rocket engine took over the flight and trajectory of the projectile. The missiles flew to a height of one hundred and fifty feet before angling down and targeting the roof of each guard shack.

The drone panned out to a wide angle and captured the two bright flashes that ignited at nearly the same instant. When the surge of heat and light cleared, the two guard shacks were gone. An instant later the resounding detonations could be heard on all four platoon commanders' satellite uplinks.

"That's our cue, boys," Second Platoon's commander said. "Hit them with everything you have. Make your shots count, keep them engaged, and keep your feet moving!"

The drone feed recorded a moment of stunned silence from the stitching yards as the impact of those two explosions rippled through the FSS encampment. Then the small dots that were people all began moving at once. The FSS members closest to the gates ran toward the wreckage and were immediately cut down by Second Platoon's sharp shooters. The FSS forces quickly recovered, though, and began making their way to the wreckage at the front gates much more carefully, keeping themselves low and using transfer trailers and broken-down rail cars as cover.

Price watched with a strange mixture of fascination and horror as the real-time firefight unfolded before him. First and Second Platoons were fully engaged with the FSS forces that were trying to mount an effective counter-assault. If they had pushed right then, the two platoons could have made their way into the fenced-in compound of the stitching yards, but that was what the FSS anticipated. Price knew the two machine gun installations inside the compound would shred his forces if they rushed into the gap in the FSS defenses that had been created by taking out the checkpoints.

The FSS forces finally gave up waiting for the attackers to push into the camp and broke through the outer perimeter in a sudden rush of men and rifles. White flashes in the green-tinted image broadcast by both platoon commanders indicated the FSS forces were returning fire and gaining ground. A few of the FSS shots found their mark and Price heard cries of pain or muffled groans as members of Darius' assault force fell.

"First fire team, pull back!" Second platoon's commander called out above the noise.

The four-man team at the front of the column Second Platoon had formed along Front Street wheeled and sprinted to the back of the formation. Once they had taken position along the left and right shoulders of the street, they began firing again. After a few moments, the platoon commander repeated the order and the second fire team peeled off and sprinted to the back of the formation. As they moved, the FSS troops saw them retreating and began advancing in their own staggered formation.

Price cursed. He'd hoped the FSS troops would be so eager for action that they would charge the assault teams and make it easier to draw them in. This kind of slow advance could put a serious kink in their plans. The assault teams had a limited amount of ammunition, and with Third and Fourth Platoons waiting on the signal to advance from the back side of the compound, there was no hope of relief or resupply. If they ran out of ammo, they'd be cut down.

"Sir, First Platoon's assault team is taking heavy casualties," Attledge said, pointing to the screen on the smart table. Four red dots clustered at the beginning of First Platoon's assault area meant there were four men killed in action.

"There's nothing we can do about it from here.," Price growled. "I'm sure Darius is aware."

At that moment, Darius shouted over his broadcast feed. "First Platoon, break contact and head for rally point alpha-one-three! Set up interlocking fields of fire and try not to take any more casualties. Second might need you as reserves if they can't get these guys moving. Second, what the fuck is the hold up? Get those assholes moving towards you or this whole thing's gonna come unglued!"

"I'm a bit busy, sir!" Second Platoon's commander screamed back over his own video feed. "I'll get to you in a minute! Third fire team, switch to side arms. Let's make them think we're low on rifle ammo."

The men in the fire team switched from rifles to Berettas one by one. When the FSS soldiers saw the switch, they took the bait and assumed the men were running low on rifle ammo. The FSS ranks surged forward and broke formation, hungry for the kill.

"Second Platoon, fall back before we're overrun!" the platoon commander called.

Together the men rose and began running back down Front Street to an old freight track that ran between two rows of warehouses to the left. The platoon took the rail track while four men dropped to their knees to provide cover at the corner of the ware houses. The FSS troops advanced quickly and were closing the gap. Chunks of brick and mortar began flying off the walls of the warehouses as the FSS soldiers returned fire. When the last of the platoon had cleared the edge of the building, the covering fire team peeled off contact and followed on their heels.

Protected by the buildings, Second Platoon sprinted down the track as fast as they could. They had lost three men already and two more had shoulder wounds, but they still moved quickly. The men were about two thirds of the way down the track when the FSS soldiers came around the corner and started after them. A few were shooting, but most were running, trying to close the distance.

Then Second Platoon stopped, spun, and dropped to their bellies except for the platoon commander. He stood tall, raised a flare gun, and fired a single flare into the air. As he fired, three bullets tore into him; one cut through his left arm just above the elbow, one took him in the right leg just below the knee, and one impacted his chest hard enough to knock the wind out of him and drop him to his knees. To his credit, the platoon commander didn't fall or collapse completely. Instead, he drew a ragged breath and screamed at the top of his lungs, "Fire from above!"

The other half of second platoon that had been hiding along the rooftops of the warehouses sprang into action. They rose as one mass on both sides of the narrow ravine created by the backs of the warehouses and opened fire on the FSS troops below. With an elevated position and the benefit of the flare, the massacre was over quickly, and the few FSS troops that made it out of the narrow track were downed by First Platoon as they advanced to reinforce Second.

As soon as the flare hit the air, Third and Fourth Platoons sprang into action. They were waiting in their armored Strykers at the back side of the compound. When Second Platoon launched their flare, both Third and Fourth Platoons fired up their Strykers and gunned the throttle. Each platoon had three vehicles for their leg of the assault, and they were loaded with the remaining infantry and special ops soldiers. Two main roads led into the fenced off stitching yard from the back end, and both had simple checkpoints to maintain security. In spite of the fighting and explosions on the other side of the compound, the FSS personnel manning these stations had stayed at their posts.

When the Strykers hit, the FSS guards were totally unprepared. Most of the FSS soldiers had their backs to the assault team and were watching the smoke rise from across the rail yards. They never saw the vehicles coming. Massive belt-fed .50caliber machine guns on each of the Strykers opened up and cut down the half dozen FSS security personnel without slowing down and then tore through the chain link fence like it wasn't even there.

The Strykers converged on the maintenance building that served as a command post and cut down any FSS personnel they saw running through the stitching yard or attempting to return fire. Groups of FSS troops were laying down their rifles and dropping to their knees in surrender. As soon as the Strykers formed a semicircle in front of the maintenance building, the back doors dropped down and troops offloaded and secured the surrendered prisoners.

None of the attack force made a move to enter the building and no one else came out as the drone circled overhead. For a few tense moments, the scene was at a standstill, until the front door of the building opened and a man holding a rifle high over his head stepped outside. The drone zoomed in and Price watched as one by one a line of men in tactical clothes came out and set various rifles and pistols off to the side. They were taken into custody and led to the attack vehicles.

Third Platoon's commander oversaw taking the prisoners into custody while Fourth Platoon's commander secured the command-level prisoners. Price muted their channels and spoke to Darius directly.

"Congratulations, Colonel," Price said. "It seems you have taken the objective with a solid victory."

"There are a few active combatants still out there," Darius replied. "A small group by the western checkpoint is offering resistance to First Platoon, but they'll be either killed or captured in the next few minutes. First Platoon is moving into position on their flanks, and they're about to have that group in a hell of a cross-fire. But other than that, yes sir we have taken the objective."

"What's the toll?" Price asked quietly.

"I'll let you know in the morning," Darius answered. "A few of the injured may make it, and a few probably won't. Some are already gone. When I know, I'll let you know. But I can tell you this, we lost a lot fewer than they did."

"I hope that's enough," Price said to himself. "Colonel you and your men did well. Secure the rail yard and celebrate. You've earned it."

Before Darius could respond, Price turned and walked out of the Operations and Command Center.

Chapter 29

Hunter's Moon

Oct. 14th 0130 EST

Joe was running point for the small column jogging down state highway 902, known to the locals as Jerry Frye Rd. Behind him Eric, Brant, Henderson, and Chris formed the rest of their assault force. Joe would have liked to have had three or four more people, but they needed guards back at the pasture and at the end of Cutler's Run to keep an eye on things. He was also nervous that FSS search parties might be out and about by now, and he didn't want them to stumble on the cow pasture or the Run without someone there to defend the farm.

Overhead the sky was clear, and the full moon was bright enough to read a newspaper. The abundance of light was a double-edged sword, though, in that it made navigating the roads easy, but it also made them easily visible to anyone keeping a tight watch on an encampment. The men were dressed in hunting camouflage with tree patterns to mimic underbrush and bare trees or in military grade digitized camo fatigues. Either way, they would be difficult to see as long as they made good use of the stark and clearly defined shadows cast by the moonlight.

As they approached the intersection of Highway 902 and Highway 42, Joe slowed his advance. The road had cut through heavy trees on both sides, but it opened up as it neared the intersection. Without speaking, he turned to the men behind him and with a series of hand signals split the column into two groups, and one group moved to each side of the road. They advanced slowly, looking for any signs of activity or surveillance. Once Joe was convinced the intersection was clear, he walked out and stood in the crossroads.

The road they had traveled continued for about another two thousand feet and then crossed Bernard Purvis Road—the road Benny had identified as the FSS checkpoint for their regular "foraging parties," as he called them. Joe dropped to one knee and pulled out a satellite map he had printed of the area years before when Eric began hunting. He'd wanted Eric to know the area around their home and the town in case he ever got lost and needed to find his way to a highway or back to the farm.

Joe clicked on his red LED flashlight and pointed to the small point where two thin ribbons of gray crossed on the map as the rest of the group gathered around him and took a knee. "Okay, this is where we are. About two thousand feet to the west this road goes through another intersection. That's where Benny said the FSS has one of their main checkpoints set up, and that's what we're going to hit tonight." Joe pointed west as he spoke. "You can just see the glow from their fires if you look hard enough low on the horizon, so we know they're still manning that post. There's a big field to the left up here where the road starts around a short bend. When we get there, we're going to break off the road and cut across the field. I want to come at them from the south so if we don't manage to get the whole crew and they start pursuit, that's the direction they'll head."

The rest of the men nodded and Joe continued. "Eric, you and Brant creep up this line of trees until you're just about at the intersection. Stay back in the shadows so you can't be seen, but get your bows ready. Benny said they have four sentries in two pairs that walk a circuit around the camp. One pair goes clockwise and the other goes counter clockwise. Those are going to be your targets. Once the pair circling counter-clockwise passes you, you'll have a clear shot at their backs with your bows. Take them down. Aim for the point where the shoulders and the neck come together, and they'll drop. Once they're down, I'll hit the two coming at me with my suppressed Beretta. That should clear the perimeter."

Joe turned to Chris and Henderson next. "I want you two to circle around to the west from the row of trees here and get about a hundred to a hundred and fifty yards down 902 from the checkpoint. Once the sentries are down we'll signal by radio. Eric, you and Brant will head south until you have good cover in the trees. Then take a few shots with your rifles and hit what you can. Once they turn to face you, Chris and Henderson will open up from the west and I'll open up from the northeast flank. That cross fire should be more than they can handle. They won't have anywhere to run."

"Chris, you and Henderson are our backup. If things go sideways and you hear me call 'Broken Arrow' over the radio, fall back about two thousand yards to this store. That will be our rally point. If everything just goes to shit, head there and we'll regroup. Any questions?"

Everyone understood their assignments. "Okay," Joe said as he reached into a pouch on his camel pack and pulled out a small two-way radio, "Eric and Brant have one walkie with them, Chris and

Henderson have another, and I've got a third. Everyone keep their radios on channel 3. Eric, when you and Brant are in position click the broadcast button once. Chris, you and Henderson click it twice when you're ready. I'll click three times when I have a clear shot from the trees to the northeast. When you get a clear shot at the sentries' backs, you take it, son. Once the pieces start falling into place it will happen quickly, so stay on your toes, and stay moving. If you get rooted, you get routed. With any luck they won't get off more than a handful of shots before the whole thing's done."

"What if they try to break and run?" Chris asked.

Joe shook his head. "No prisoners, and no one gets out. We can't afford to have them report back what happened, and we don't have the resources to take care of prisoners. That's how it's got to be."

"Understood," Chris said grimly.

Joe fixed each of the men facing him with a serious look. "This is going to be tough. We're going to hit these guys while they're looking the other way. It's messy, it's dirty, but it gets the job done. And that's what we're here to do. Get the job done. Once it looks like we've taken all of them out, I'll go in first and clear the camp. Once it's cleared I'll signal with three bursts of three. Let's get to it."

Joe folded the map and clicked off his pen light. The moon overhead was bright, and they were going to need their night eyes on the trail ahead.

Chapter 30

In The Pale Moonlight

Oct. 14 th 0210 EST

|*Click.*

Click.

Click.

Eric heard the three slow, deliberate clicks over the broadcast channel on his radio. He glanced at Brant five yards behind him and gave a thumbs up, which was returned. The next time the pair of sentries going counter clockwise passed them, they would strike. Eric tried to swallow, but his mouth felt suddenly dry and his palms slick with sweat.

He had acted in self-defense before, but that was different. It had always been in the heat of the moment with a direct threat in his face. No time to think about it, plan it, or dread it. The thing just happened, and then it was over. He was alive and the other guy wasn't. That was all that mattered in that moment, and after.

But this was different. He had time to think about this, to think about what it would mean. He had time to think about the cold hard reality of cutting someone down from behind. It was cold, it was inhuman, but it was necessary. He saw that and understood it; he just didn't like it.

Eric watched Brant, and Brant was watching for the two sentries. Shortly, Brant held up two fingers on his right hand to indicate that he had made visual contact with them and slowly eased back behind the tree he was using as cover. Eric took a deep breath and attached the trigger release to the bow string on his Rage compound bow. An arrow with a four-bladed razor-sharp steel broad head tip was nocked and ready to fire.

When Eric saw the two sentries walk by him, he turned and nodded once to Brant. They stepped out of the trees at the same instant. Eric drew his bow with three fingers on the string and heard Brant do the same behind him. He was pulling seventy pounds, but the cams kicked in and reduced the pull by seventy percent once he got the string all the way back. That meant once the bow was pulled, he was holding only twenty-one pounds. The reduced hold weight made it easier to steady the bow and aim through the peep-sight.

The sentries were still headed away from Eric and Brant and hadn't heard anything to alert them. Eric slowly relaxed his fingers and let the trigger release strapped to his wrist take the weight of the tension on the string. He aimed and put the neon point of the pin between the shoulder blades and neck of the sentry on the right. He took a slow breath and let half of it out as he allowed himself to take note of and feel his heartbeat. It was faster than usual, but that was to be expected. Eric's hands stopped trembling and the pin steadied.

Eric pressed the release and just a fraction of a heartbeat later heard Brant do the same. There was a whisk of air to Eric's left and a flash of pale white as the fletching of the arrow sped by. The arrows both found their targets with barely offset thwacks. The two sentries were an eerie mirror of each other as they dropped their rifles and raised their hands to their throats. They sank to their knees, made some muffled gurgling sounds and fell forward. They kicked at the dirt for a long moment before finally lying still.

Eric stood rooted to the ground, stunned by what he'd done. He knew he was exposed, knew he was supposed to grab cover as soon as the arrow was loosed. But he couldn't move. His eyes wouldn't leave the tiny neon orange dot of the arrow nock. That one had been his and he couldn't look away. In his mind, he kept hearing his father's voice on his thirteenth birthday saying, "Once you let that arrow fly you own everything it hits. Whatever that is, whatever it maims, injures, or kills, that's on you. So, make damn sure you know what you're shooting at."

There were hands that seemed to come out of nowhere. They grabbed Eric's collar and his right sleeve and pulled hard. That was the wrong way, though. That was away from the other FSS soldiers and the fires. He looked over and saw Brant, his face pale and his eyes wide, pulling Eric towards the dark shadows and the safety of the trees. He shoved Eric to the ground behind a large pine and dropped to his belly, inching around to look back to where the bodies were lying in the dirt.

"Eric, signal your dad," Brant whispered. "He's got to get those other two before they see those bodies."

Eric suddenly snapped back to the present. He blinked and nodded. His fingers shook badly, but he managed to click the broadcast button once to signal his father that their part was done. There was a long stretch of silence and Eric shook as if he were freezing. Finally, the silence was broken with three long clicks over the broadcast channel.

Eric and Brant exchanged an uncomfortable glance, hung their bows from makeshift shoulder straps, and drew their handguns. They took aim at the small cluster of fire barrels and men in the middle of the intersection. Eric held up fingers on his left hand and counted down from three.

Both fired five or six rounds into the camp and heard several groans and shouts as men either hit the ground or scattered. As soon as the last shot rang out, Eric and Brant ran at a low crouch back through the trees. The shouts behind them changed from alarm to anger, and in a few seconds, the first shots rang out in return fire. When they heard the snap of that first bullet fly past them, they both hit the ground and began crawling. At that same time they heard gunfire start from the other side of the camp as the rest of their party engaged the enemy.

They moved as quickly as they could at a crawl, keeping the tree trunks between them and the intersection. When they'd gone far enough, they each took cover behind a large oak tree. Overhead, bullets still tore through the tree limbs, far off their target, but in enough volume to be troubling. With that much lead coming down range at them there was always the chance that blind luck would find its mark in a meaningful hit.

The bullets stopped coming at Brant and Eric, but they could still hear gunfire. This was a different gunfire, though, coming from a good distance to the west where Chris and Henderson were and from the northeast where Joe had taken a sniper position covering the only avenue of retreat left to the FSS. The next couple of minutes seemed like a century, but they waited behind the oaks until the gunfire from the west slowed and stopped. There were three more isolated shots from the northeast, and then silence.

click-click-click

click-click-click

click-click-click

Eric looked at Brant as he stood. "Look, I don't know what happened. I took the shot and something just snapped. For what it's worth, I'm sorry, and thank you for saving my life."

"You almost got us both killed, Eric," Brant hissed. "Yeah, you made the shot. That wasn't the end of the plan, though."

Eric couldn't think of anything to say in response, so he turned and started walking toward the encampment. As he approached the intersection, he headed for the two sentries they'd hit with their bows. Barely swallowing back bile as it rose in his throat, Eric retrieved the two arrows. He placed his back in the quiver that was attached to the right side of the bow.

Eric turned and held Brant's arrow out to him, but Brant could only look at it.

"Exactly," Eric said. "This is different from anything else we've done, and you recognize that too. That's why you don't really want to take your arrow. It's not damaged and it's too valuable to leave behind. You have to take it. It's yours."

Brant met Eric's gaze for a moment longer and swallowed hard, but he took the arrow. His disgust was obvious as he rammed it back in his own quiver. The two friends didn't say a word on their way to the intersection.

The FSS had four flat-bed trucks, one blocking each leg of the four-way intersection. In the center of the intersection three oil drums had been converted into fire pits, and over to the side, a spit stood over a small cook fire that had been fueled with coals from the barrels. Some kind of meat—probably deer—was roasting on the spit and the smell made Eric's stomach growl.

As the men surveyed the camp and took inventory of all the FSS had at their disposal, the wind shifted and Eric caught the thick coppery smell of blood and his stomach turned.

"Fourteen people," Joe said as the rest of the group gathered around the fire barrels. The dead lay all around them. "Four of them had regular FSS identification cards and seemed to be the leaders. The other ten had a card similar to a driver's license that had 'local asset' printed in large red letters on both sides."

"Local asset," Brant said. "I don't understand. What does that mean?"

"They're people who joined after the Blackout," Joe answered. "Some of them are actual locals and their addresses are from around here. Some of them were picked up by this FSS unit along the way here. A couple were from Tennessee and one from Arkansas. Two from Georgia and five from here. Then the four actual FSS officers who were in charge."

Joe pointed around the encampment, his grim face a reflection of the danger these dead men represented. "Look around you, all of you. This is what we are getting ourselves into. It's going to be bloody and in your face, and it is going to be people that look just like me and you that we're fighting against. It isn't going to be easy, but this is what has to be done."

Joe pointed to Eric and Brant. "Check all of their packs for food, weapons, ammo, paperwork, anything we can use. Make sure you don't take a transmitter or anything the FSS can trace." He turned to Chris and Henderson and motioned toward the bodies. "You two check the bodies and see if there's any intel. Collect weapons and ammo, any valuables, including jewelry and wedding bands. Use their shirts to cover their faces."

No one said anything. They all went about their macabre tasks in grim silence. They'd won, but it wasn't the kind of victory they could cheer about. Eric walked over to a stack of backpacks waiting by the handful of tents set up in the grassy medians of the intersection. He opened one and began carefully sifting through the contents.

It felt wrong on many levels to invade someone's personal property, knowing they were lying dead somewhere within fifty yards. Eric opened a small notebook just long enough to realize it was a personal journal and set it aside. There were a few inventory lists and some sort of check-out stubs for the weapons the dead man had carried. A few zip-lock bags held various toiletries and basic first aid supplies. A side pocket held a water-proof canister full of matches and some cotton wadding for kindling, a six-inch hunting knife, a compass, and a signal mirror. The other side pocket had been modified into a magazine pouch that held four magazines for the AR-15 he'd signed out and two for an FNX-9mm signed out on the other ticket.

The front pouch held a small Bible and a picture of a pretty young woman and little twin girls. Eric stopped and stared at that picture for a long time, forcing himself not to think of his own child yet to be born. Finally, he put the picture in the Bible and closed the front pouch. As carefully as he could, Eric re-packed the bag and stood.

"I can't do this—not right now. Maybe if we take the packs back to the house and look then, but not right now."

"Suck it up," Joe replied. "No way we can take those packs back and risk bringing a transmitter with us. You've got to check them, at least for that possibility. I know it sucks, but it's gotta be done. That's how it is."

Eric nodded and pulled the next pack out of the pile and started sorting through it. Brant had a pack in front of him and was doing the same. He looked up once and smiled weakly at Eric, but his face was just as pale and slick with sweat as Eric's. They worked their way through the packs but didn't find anything that looked like a radio or a transmitter. Around the same time Eric and Brant finished with the packs, the other three men finished checking the bodies.

Eric and Brant began loading the packs onto one of the flatbed trucks along with the weapons, ammo, and valuables collected from the bodies. They transferred the supplies that were loaded on the other three trucks down to one. When they finished, they had two empty flatbeds and two full ones.

"Eric, you and Brant take one of the cans of diesel and go douse those tents," Joe said. "When the can's empty, just toss it inside one of them. Then get a tree branch or something and light it on fire."

Eric and Brant set the tents ablaze as they'd been instructed. By the time the flames and thick black smoke were rising from the pile of melted nylon and canvas, Joe had the two full trucks pulled onto the road and pointed toward home. The two empty trucks were parked next to the burning barrels. The fuel tanks on both trucks had been punctured with screw drivers, and Chris had poured a generous amount of diesel around them, splashing fuel inside the cabs and all over the hoods and beds.

Chris drove the lead truck, and Henderson rode in the back with the supplies while Brant rode shotgun in the cab. Joe drove the rear truck with Eric in the bed. As he slowly pulled away from the intersection, Joe handed a road flare to Eric through the window on the back wall of the truck's cab.

"Light it," Joe yelled back to Eric, "then toss it back into the intersection."

Eric pulled the cap of the road flare off and struck the end of the flare. An incandescent jet of red flame burst out of the end, and Eric threw it overhand back toward the intersection. It bounced off the roof of the right truck and fell to the ground. As soon as the flare hit the dry, fuel-soaked grass in the median, it burst into flames. The fire quickly engulfed the trucks and the tents.

Joe sped up as he pulled away, and after a while he reached up and slid the back glass closed, leaving Eric alone with his thoughts and the wind as they headed east and back home. The flames must have spread quickly because as they topped a hill a few miles from the intersection, a dark stain of smoke rose against the gray pre-dawn sky. With the fuel that Joe and the others had spread and the spare wood the FSS had stacked to feed the barrel fires, the bonfire and makeshift funeral pyre they'd built would burn for hours.

The bodies had been left where they had fallen, and now that Eric watched the smoke rise above the tree tops he wondered how much of that smoke was made of the men they'd killed. He shivered in the wind as the diesel flatbed bounced down the rough blacktop. The back of the truck had an open frame of wood slats that made three-foot walls on either side, but they offered no protection from the wind. He pulled his coat tighter around his chest, but he couldn't get warm.

Behind him the sun rose and cast its first deep ruby-red light across the trees. In the distance, a church bell began to toll.

Chapter 31

Sunrise Service

Levy stood just outside the doors of the Rocky Creek Presbyterian Church, waiting. The sky had finally cleared, and the morning was cool but not cold. Though, in truth, the older he got he found it more difficult to tell the difference between the two. The east, a bright glow of orange and red, hinted of sunrise. Crows chattered across the trees, and to the south a flock of blackbirds took flight and faded from a dense, dark cloud to a dim splotch on the horizon as they continued their long journey south. Everything was still, quiet, and peaceful, but Levy didn't notice any of that. His eyes were locked on a column of thick black smoke rising into the sky a few miles to the northwest. He knew what that smoke meant and what had caused it. That was why he was here.

Just then, the sun crested the horizon and red morning light flooded the landscape. "Okay, Cage, you can start," Levy said.

Cage nodded and reached over to grab the long, braided rope that hung from the ceiling of the church vestibule. He pulled the rope with his strong, massive arms and high overhead the church bell, cast in 1815 to commemorate the end of the War of 1812, rang out from the steeple. The deep gongs reverberated throughout the building and spread out into the cool morning silence. The church sat atop a small plateau that farmers had cleared generations ago, affording it some of the best views in this part of the county. That clear line of site for miles and miles meant the tolling of the bell would be heard far and wide.

"How long do you want me to ring it?" Cage called over the echoing peals.

"Until they start coming to see what the fuss is all about," Levy replied.

Cage nodded and kept ringing the bell as the sun rose a little higher.

Levy breathed in the fresh morning air as memories of times and people gone by washed over him. That church bell had been rung more than few times in his life, but it had been decades since it rang this loud and this long. As a child, he'd heard it ringing every Veteran's Day in remembrance of those lost in the Great War that was meant to end all wars. Then, as a young man, the bell had rung to announce the attack on Pearl Harbor and America's entrance into World War II. He was told it rang along with every other bell in the state to celebrate the end of that war, but he hadn't heard that one because the war was over, and he was on his way home from Europe.

He remembered the bell ringing when one family or another had a death or a fire or other need that called for helping hands. It called the community together to rebuild and heal and share whatever burden needed sharing. They'd rung the bell to mourn President Kennedy and then six years later to celebrate landing on the moon. They'd rung the bell for Beth's wedding in '79 and for his fiftieth wedding anniversary in '04, though those were more personal than noteworthy occasions. The last time it had drawn the community together was on November 9, 1989, the day the Berlin Wall fell. Levy had pulled the rope himself that day, his eyes wet with tears. All of those moments and more rolled through his mind in a jumble as he listened to the steady tolling of the bell and the dim echoes of its sound bouncing off the distant trees.

It didn't take long for the people to come. At first, just a few folks within walking distance showed up, but then groups of two or three from farms farther out rode up on horseback. The people kept a wary distance from each other and from Levy at first, but their curiosity overtook them, and they began asking questions about why they were there, why the bell was ringing, and was there news from the government.

Finally, when the crowd was about forty people, Levy stopped Cage from ringing the bell. He stood on the top step to address the people. "Y'all are wondering why we're here and why we're ringing the church bell. That'll be answered in a little bit. But I want y'all to know I'm not with the government or anything of that sort. Some of you know me, but there's a lot of faces here I don't know, so I'll introduce myself. I'm Levy Withers, and I grew up around here. Lived here my whole life except when I went to fight the Germans. We started ringing this bell 'cause there's something y'all need to hear, and the man that's gonna say it is pulling up now."

Levy pointed over to the driveway of the church where Joe had just pulled a flatbed truck into the parking lot, followed by Chris driving the other truck. Joe got out of the cab and climbed onto the roof of the truck and faced the crowd. He waited while Eric, Brant, Henderson, and Chris formed a semi-circle in front of the truck, their rifles in hand. The crowd turned to face the truck but kept their distance, forming a loose ring about ten feet in front of Eric and the other men.

"I'm Joe Tillman. I used to be a captain in the Navy SEALs, and Levy is my father-in-law. I don't know what you've had to do to survive since the Blackout, but if you're like us, it's been tough. And

I hate to tell you, but it's about to get a lot tougher. There's a group in Bennett right now trying to put down roots so they can take over, and they mean to take every single thing we have. They call themselves the Federal Security Services, and I'm sure some of you have heard of them."

Several people in the crowd murmured to each other, and one man shouted, "They took my family's water and food, the neighbor's too. Shot their boy when he tried to stop them!"

More people began to shout, but Joe held one hand up and stomped hard on the roof of the truck to get their attention again. "I've seen their handiwork first hand in Norfolk, Virginia, and here. They're evil, they're ruthless, and they are hell bent on being *the* authority when this is all over. Well, I'm here to tell you that my family and I are not going to let that happen." Joe pointed back over his shoulder at the column of black smoke on the horizon. "We hit the FSS last night, and we hit them hard. We took out close to fifteen of their members, gathered some intel, torched two of their trucks, and got two flat-beds loaded with supplies. These guys are not invincible. Hell, they're not even that good, if last night was any indication. They're counting on people being too scared, too hungry, or too weak to fight back."

"We're not soldiers," someone in the crowd yelled. Another voice shouted, "We're not SEALs!" And another called out, "They've got more guns!"

"No, you're not soldiers," Joe admitted. "But you don't have to be. I've spent years in some of the most violent places on the planet and I can tell you there's more to fear from a man protecting his home and his family than from even the meanest, most well-trained, paid soldiers in the world. And that's who we are, people fighting to protect our homes and our families. We all had to fight to get where we are in life, and since the Blackout happened, we've all

230

had to fight a lot harder just to survive. We've been doing it on our own, keeping our own families afloat day by day. But that's not enough anymore."

"You're talking about starting a war!" a man yelled and several others joined him.

"No!" Joe yelled back. "They started this war. I don't know if they started the Blackout, but I think it was probably them. I do know they've killed civilians, including women and children. I've seen it with my own eyes. I've watched them shoot women who were tied hand and foot, watched them dump bodies on railroad tracks and neighborhood streets to spark terror, and I've watched them sort through a neighborhood and execute whole families based on orders written out on a clipboard. They've already got control of most of the town, and now they're pushing out into the country, gobbling up every resource they can find. They found our pastures a few days ago and demanded we hand over everything we had. When we refused, they tried to kill three young men and a good friend and long-time colleague of mine named Tom. Tom was quick enough to save the three young men's lives but paid with his own in the process of killing the three FSS soldiers."

Joe climbed down from the roof of the truck and faced the crowd eye-to-eye, fixing each of them with a cold, hard stare. "I know you're scared. I'm scared. We all are, and that's okay. But it's time to set that fear aside and do something. If we don't stand now and stop these bastards, they'll chip away at this community, at this country, a piece at the time until they've broken it. I've spent my whole life fighting, spilling blood on foreign soil to keep this country and the people I love safe and secure. I'll be damned if I'm going to stand by now and watch while a force just as dark and evil as any I've ever seen rips it apart and devours it from the inside."

Joe stepped forward, and the crowd parted in front of him. Eric and the rest of their group followed close behind him as Joe walked across the churchyard and up the front steps to stand next to Levy and Cage.

"Independence, freedom, liberty. These things are not genetic. We don't pass them down to our kids like our hair color or our dimples. They have to be bought and paid for in sacrifice, hard work, diligence, and, at times, in blood. I know what I'm asking isn't easy. I won't pretend that it is, but it's necessary. If we don't stand together then we'll either die together or we'll spend the rest of our lives living under the boot of the FSS. I don't know about you, but my family has made our decision. We'd rather die fighting to be free than live the rest of our lives a slave to some false government, depending on them for everything—food, water, clothes, and shelter. This country was begun because a group of farmers, tradesmen, and trappers decided they were tired of living like slaves to give their lords a better life. They stood up and demanded their freedom, fought for it, and won it. Now, it's our turn."

Joe looked at the faces before him, taking time to commit each one to memory. "Today is Wednesday. Go home and talk this out with your families and with your neighbors. Tell them what I've told you. And anyone who wants to join this fight should be here at the church in three days."

"What happens in three days?" a man at the back of the crowd asked.

"We're going to start building an army."

Chapter 32

Tagged and Bagged

Oct. 14th 0900 EST

Mike stood at the entrance to the neighborhood, his finger on the trigger of his M-4 carbine. On the sign for the neighborhood, a large circle had been spray painted. It was divided into quadrants by an X painted in its center, and markings had been painted in each quadrant. Mike had already seen that pattern on several doors, but this was the first time he had gotten a look at the key. Inside the top quadrant was a large R, the left side was marked AoA, the right DoD, and the bottom UA.

Alyssa stood next to Mike looking at the strange markings. "What do you think it means?"

"I'm not sure, but it's similar to the coding we used in search and rescue. When we were doing house by house searches after Hurricane Katrina, we'd put the unit we were in and the date we inspected the house in the top quadrant and any threats like biohazards in the bottom. The left and right quadrants were for alive and dead. If I had to guess, I'd say this was something similar, but I don't recognize the codes."

"I don't like this place," Alyssa whispered. "It feels like we're being watched or something—like there are ants crawling all over my skin. Are you sure we have to go in there?"

Mike nodded. "Chip said he looked into only a couple of houses at the entrance to the neighborhood and they were all the same. The people inside were dead, apparently executed, and the doors marked like this. We have to check because we might find supplies we could use. Besides, I need to see what it's like for myself." Mike turned and gave Alyssa an unreadable look. "You don't have to come with me. I can manage on my own, and you're not going to want to see what's in these houses."

"You think I can't handle it?" Alyssa demanded. "I'm tougher than you think I am, Mike."

"I don't doubt how tough you are, Alyssa. It's just . . ." he shook his head and gave a small shrug. "Look, I was just trying to look out for you. But if you want to come, I'm not going to stop you."

"Like you could stop me if you wanted to," Alyssa said with a toss of her head. "Let's go, Mike. We're burning daylight."

Alyssa turned and headed into the neighborhood, her back stiff and her head high. She refused to glance back at Mike and he refused to speed up his pace to catch her. Alyssa was carrying a twenty-gauge pump-action shotgun that Mike and Arthur had found during one of their scavenging runs while they were still at the White Water Center. It was a little smaller than a twelve gauge but still packed enough punch with 00 buckshot to put down even a large attacker. Despite her tough talk, she kept the shotgun at a low ready with her finger never far from the trigger, just in case.

At the first house, Alyssa stopped in the front yard and stared at the bright orange paint on the door. That was the house Chip had described finding the dead children inside, and she hesitated. "I'll stay out here and watch your back while you're inside. I'd hate for someone to sneak up on you."

Mike climbed the steps and paused at the front door. The top, left, and right sections of the circle had the number four painted in them and the bottom had a zero. The front door was slightly ajar from when Chip had run out of the house after he'd seen the bodies. Mike reached out with his right foot and pushed the door fully open and waited, his rifle ready in case anyone or anything moved inside. He stepped over the threshold and waited for his eyes to adjust to the dimness.

The floor plan for the house was open, allowing Mike to see well into the rooms. The front door led into a wide foyer with an office to the left and a sitting room to the right. Pictures of a happy young family hung along the walls, but Mike tried his best not to see them. The air smelled of old rot, but it was less overpowering than he'd thought it would be. Ahead of him in the large family room area, four bodies were lined up on the floor. The carpet beneath them was stained a dirty brownish green, and ragged pieces of blackened flesh and dry skin still clung to the bones in places.

Mike swallowed hard and focused on breathing through his mouth as he climbed the stairs to the second floor. The smell of old death was less pronounced in the upstairs rooms, and Mike breathed a little easier. He passed by the two kids' rooms without looking too closely. The master bedroom at the end of the hallway had a gun safe but it was standing open and empty. There were two nice leather coats in the closet, one sized for a man and the other for a petite woman. They would come in handy if the weather turned cold or if they got caught in the rain.

Mike took the coats, a couple of knitted wool sweaters, and a bottle of prescription cough medicine with hydrocodone. Satisfied that he had checked the upstairs, Mike made his way back down to the first floor. He avoided the bodies in the family room and made a quick check of the kitchen and pantry but found no food or bottled water.

On his way out Mike took a quilted throw from the back of the couch and gently laid it over the remains of the family. It wasn't much, but it didn't seem right to leave the bodies exposed like that. As he stepped back out into the sunshine and fresh air, Mike's hands were shaking.

"What did you find?" Alyssa asked.

"A couple of leather coats and some cough syrup. The rest was just like Chip said."

Alyssa nodded but didn't say anything. The two moved down the street and checked the next few houses. As they moved from door to door Mike began to understand the code. At the fourth house, the door was marked with a five on top, a four on the left and right, and a one at the bottom. Inside, he found four bodies in the same state as all the rest. They were lined up in the main room on the first floor, hands and feet bound by zip-ties, bullet wounds to the back of the head.

In this house, though, the pictures showed five members of the family. The mother and father were a little older, and they had two daughters that looked to be about the same age and a son that was quite a bit older than the girls. Upstairs, the son's room was decorated with high school athletic photos and one wall was dedicated to Appalachian State University. On the desk was a photo of the son and a young woman at their high school graduation, both wearing their cap and gown.

Suddenly, the code clicked and Mike understood what the numbers meant. That realization sent a cold chill through his blood. He gave the rest of the house a quick run through, but he didn't find anything useful. Once back in the front yard, Mike walked over to Alyssa and looked over what they'd found so far. They had two leather jackets, two hiking jackets from the North Face company, a pair of telescoping fishing poles, and a small tackle box with hooks, weights, a few lures, and several spools of fishing line. The medicine cabinets in most of the houses had been emptied, but Mike had managed to find the cough syrup from the first house and a few bottles with amoxicillin and Cipro, both useful antibiotics to fight off bacterial infections.

"Look, I think we have enough," Mike said when they'd inventoried their take. "I think I've figured out their code, and if I'm right it means we need to get the heck out of here. Now."

"What is it?" Alyssa asked.

"I think this was a kill squad. When you look at the code spray painted on the door, the number at the top is the number of residents on some kind of record at that address. The number on the left is the number of people they found alive on arrival, or AoA. The number on the right is the number they left dead on departure, or DoD. And the number at the bottom is the number of people unaccounted for."

"Why?" Alyssa asked. "Why would they go through and just kill everyone like that?"

Mike shook his head as he started walking back toward the entrance to the neighborhood. "I don't know. Maybe they're trying to thin the population because resources are so scarce. Maybe they're trying to keep the people from fighting back by using terror and murder to subdue the population. But they didn't kill everyone."

"How can you tell?" Alyssa asked.

Mike pointed to the third house he'd checked. "That door has a four painted on the top, four on the left, two on the right, and zero at the bottom, and there were only two bodies inside that I could find. That means there were four registered occupants, four found alive, two left dead, and zero unaccounted for, if I'm reading their code correctly."

"What happened to the other two?" Alyssa asked.

Mike was quiet for a long moment before answering. "I think they were taken."

"Taken? Taken for what?"

"Labor, probably, or to serve as conscripted soldiers. The FSS has got to be losing people and they need replacements. The two taken out of that house were probably teenage boys they can indoctrinate and turn into cannon fodder."

Alyssa covered her mouth with one hand. "That's horrible! That's like turning them into slaves!"

Mike nodded. "That's exactly what it is. And if that FSS unit comes back through here to conduct a more thorough sweep of the area while Chip and his girlfriend are hiding out here, they'll either be taken or executed like everyone else."

"Then we can't leave them here. It's not safe for them by themselves. One way or another, they've got to come with us."

Mike nodded but didn't say anything. They made their way back to the pharmacy in silence. Once inside, Alyssa laid out everything they'd found in the houses as Mike explained what he'd seen and what he thought the code painted on the doors meant. When he was finished a stunned silence fell across the room.

"You mean they went through and killed or captured every person in that neighborhood?" Arthur asked, finally breaking the silence.

"That's what it looks like. There certainly wasn't anyone left alive when they got done. Some people might have made it out before their houses got searched—I don't know. But everyone they found inside was either executed or taken." Mike turned to Chip. "Did you see any trucks or buses coming out of there when the FSS was doing their raid?"

Chip shook his head. "We stayed back away from the windows as much as possible those first few days after we got the supplies moved in. I never saw the group that went through there, but I didn't get here until a few days after the Blackout happened. Jess might have seen something, though."

Mike turned to Jess, a young woman with hair so blonde it looked almost white, except for one stripe of hot pink that hung down by her right eye. She had a nose ring and the edges of a tattoo that showed at the bottom of her short-sleeved shirt. "Did you see anything, Jess?"

Jess nodded, and her eyes looked faraway as she spoke, her voice barely more than a whisper. "There were three things that looked kind of like tanks, but with wheels. They rolled in first. I could hear the screams . . . and the gunshots . . . it went on for hours and hours. Then came the buses. They looked like old school buses, but instead of windows they had metal grates over the window openings." Jess trailed off as tears began to roll down her cheeks. "When one was going by the gas station, I hid in some of the bushes. I could see little fingers sticking out through the holes in the grates . . . I'm sorry, I can't . . . I didn't know. I couldn't do anything to stop them."

Jess broke down in sobs, and Chip put his arm around her shoulders and pulled her close. The heavy silence was broken only by the sounds of her crying softly into his shoulder.

"You can't stay here," Mike said, finally. "If they come back, they'll be looking for supplies this time instead of people, and that means this pharmacy will be one of their first stops. If they find you two here, they'll kill you."

"We could hide from them," Chip said, but Mike was already shaking his head.

"No, you can't. Once they see evidence that someone has been here they won't stop looking until they find you. And you know how that will end. One day you're going to run out of canned soup, potato chips, and beef jerky, so you'll have to leave eventually. You might as well leave now, with us."

"Where are you guys going?" Jess asked softly as she dried her eyes.

"We're going to a small town called Bennett," Mike answered.

"I've never heard of it," Chip said. "Why should we leave our shelter and supplies to go out on the road with you to a place we've never heard of?"

"We have friends there," Mike answered. "And it's a small town, out of the way. The longer you stay near a big city, the more likely you're going to run into trouble. At least out in the country, it'll be safer."

Chip looked at Jess and she gave a small shrug. "I think he's right. We can't stay here forever, and we're better off with more people. Strength in numbers, right?"

"All right," Chip said. "I guess we're going with you guys, then."

Mike nodded and stood. "Chip, let's you and I go through some of the houses in that neighborhood this afternoon. We should be able to find some clothes and packs for you and Jess. We probably won't find any food, but you've got plenty here for the trip."

"What if we don't find your friends?" Chip asked.

"We'll find them," Mike said as he pulled Chip up to his feet. "We have to."

"Then what?" Chip asked.

Mike fixed Chip with a grim look. "Then we survive, and we find a way to fight back."

Pt. 2

Chapter 33

Foothold

Commander Price watched the satellite uplink from the over-watch drone on the main screen in the command center. The image was of the base in Kansas City, and it showed a man with two road flares signaling the engineers of two diesel train engines as they pulled slowly into the center of the stitching yard. Each train was more than a half mile long and carried troop reinforcements and resupply provisions for the force holding Kansas City.

Once the trains stopped, the drone footage panned out and showed men already unloading crates from the flatbed cars and from three passenger cars. They were volunteers and draftees that had joined as the trains made their way from Utah to Missouri. They were men that Commander Price had never met, and he was going to order them into battle to shed blood and possibly die.

He felt ill.

When Price turned his back on the screen, he found his second-in-command waiting patiently behind him, a satellite phone in his hand. "Commander, you have a call from Colonel Darius."

Price took the phone and turned back to the screen. "Good morning, Colonel Darius, what do you have to report?" the commander asked without preamble.

"Commander Price, we have two hundred and thirty-seven new recruits on this train. That's more than twice what the last train pulled in, and the supplies are as recorded in the logs, sir. Is there anything else?"

"No, Colonel," Price said. "I'll report back when I have new orders for you. Freedom One out."

Price turned and motioned to the communications station, and the line was disconnected. The image on the main screen switched to static and the phone line went dead at the same instant. He put his hands on the table in front of him and leaned forward, his eyes closed. There was a sore stiff knot growing between his shoulder blades, and it seemed to get tighter and bigger and heavier every day.

"Commander, we have nearly a thousand troops waiting in Kansas City now," Attledge said.

Price raised his head, his face drawn and haggard. "I know how many men are there, Commander. I wrote the conscription orders that forced most of them into service. I ripped men and boys away from their families and forced them there at the barrel of a gun— the ones that tried to fight it anyway. I did it because we're going to need them soon. We're going to need them to kill, and some we're going to need to die."

The commander's eyes fell to the table again. "Trust me, I know exactly how many men we have waiting in Kansas City," he said softly. "And that's why we can't rush this. We have to give the scouts time to report back. If we run blindly into a city the size of St. Louis, we run the risk of running into a larger, more well-equipped force. We just can't take that chance."

"And if we stay put too long," Marcus shot back, "our men become a very tempting target to either the FSS or some power-hungry war-lord. We're already getting probing attacks at some of our outposts and supply depots. It's only a matter of time before one of the larger gangs decides to hit us full force. And that could be bad. Even if they don't get through, they could weaken a garrison to the point that a subsequent attack would wipe them out."

"We can't move without intel, Commander," Price said.

"Maybe not toward St. Louis, sir, but we could send a small force south in two or three Strykers to map out an alternate route in case St. Louis is impassable. At least that way we would know how to get some of our men and supplies out of there."

"You want to divide our forces?" Price asked, shaking his head. "We can't do that, not now."

Attledge pulled up an image of the stitching yards and surrounding areas. Five camps were marked, and each camp held approximately four-hundred men. "Sir, our forces are already divided. At least this way we have some men doing something productive. You're the one that had me read all of those strategy manuals and handbooks about tactics and operations, right? Well, all of them said know your contingencies."

Confident that Price needed to listen to him, Attledge pointed to the map and a rail line that ran to the southeast. "That rail line is still in use as a freight line, Commander. I checked the database and confirmed that it's an open line last night. Why wouldn't we want to make sure it is passable, just in case we need it?"

Price looked up at the map for a long moment, his brain moving more slowly than it should have. After a while he began to put the pieces together and as he did a cold wave of shock rolled over him. Attledge was right. He had *bccn* right the entire time, and Price should have seen it.

"You're right, Commander. That's a sound tactical move and I should have seen it a long time ago. I don't know why I didn't."

"When was the last time you got some sleep, Commander? And I mean real, deep sleep, not a five or ten-minute nap at your desk."

Price thought about the question and realized he didn't know the answer. It had been so long since he'd actually lain in his bed asleep that he couldn't remember the last time. Sleep deprivation was a hazard of command—one he'd felt before—but it was also dangerous. If he allowed it to go on, he would miss things, had already *begun* to miss things. And that kind of negligence could get men killed.

Price turned his back on the screens. "Commander Attledge, I am temporarily placing you in command. I've allowed my judgment to become compromised and I can't allow that to compromise the mission."

"Wait, I'm not ready for command. There's got to be someone with more experience. Chief, maybe, he's got decades of military experience."

"As a non-com," Chief said from the side of the room. "I'm no officer, sir, with all due respect. I can advise, but that's it."

"Commander Attledge, you saw the obvious tactical necessity and I didn't," Price said. "Right now, I can't afford not to put this on your shoulders, whether you feel like you can handle it or not."

"Colonel Darius will be calling for an update in four hours." Attledge said. "What do I tell him?"

Price was already headed for the door to the command center. "Tell him what you just told me. And then give him his orders and tell him I will be back in command as soon as I can be. Until then, he's to follow your orders and directives."

"But the Colonel, he already . . ." Attledge tried to find a tactful way to say what he was trying to say.

"The man already wants to cut my throat the next time he sees me," Price said with a wave of his hand. "At this point how much worse can I really make it? I don't care if he wants to kill me. All I care about is that he follows orders and wins the battles we need him to win. I'll worry about the rest of it later, when I have the luxury."

Price stopped in the doorway long enough to turn back to Attledge. "I have full faith in you, Commander. You may not think you're ready for the burden of command, but I know differently. I've seen enough young officers at this point in their careers to recognize leadership when I see it. You're ready and you'll do fine."

Before Attledge could think of a reply, Price stepped out into the hall and closed the door behind him. The corridors were empty at the moment, so he made his way back to his quarters in silence. His two-man personal detail stayed a good fifteen feet back, closing that gap only when they rounded corners so they could keep him in sight at all times.

When Price reached his quarters, he waited as one of the security detail opened the door, stepped inside with his weapon at the ready, and cleared the room before allowing the commander to enter. The two men took station on either side of the door as Price closed it and pulled his uniform off one piece at the time. He was exhausted, and now that he was an arm's reach from his bed, he suddenly felt that exhaustion washing over him like a tidal wave. His fingers trembled slightly as he unbuttoned his shirt and untied his shoes.

The commander was asleep almost before his head touched the pillow. And thankfully, he was too tired to dream.

Chapter 34

Strength In Numbers

Oct. 22nd 2200 EST

Mike watched as Arthur and Alyssa crept closer to the intersection. They were well past the tree line now and in the exposed triangle that formed as Highway 49 and Highway 8 neared the vertex of the y-intersection ahead. From the safety of the shadows beneath the trees, Mike could see their dim silhouettes moving as darker shadows against the already gloomy night.

At the point where the two roads met, two men rose from the shadows and confronted Arthur and Alyssa. The two strangers flashed bright lights in their faces and aggressively patted them down for weapons. One of the men began asking questions, his tone rough and demanding, but Mike didn't listen to or care what his words were; his eyes were trained on the shadows standing in the small pool of light.

Mike had anticipated guards at least this far out and had planned for them. As the men patted down Arthur and Alyssa to confirm they had no weapons and were not a threat, four people came out of the trees at a rush. Before either guard could react, they each had two handguns in their face. They were frisked twice, disarmed, and forced to kneel under the light of their own flashlights.

249

At that point Mike stepped out of the bushes and approached the guards, his M-4 carbine at the low ready and a wool hunting scarf covering the bottom half of his face. He pulled the scarf down and looked at the two men, carefully weighing their reactions. "If you listen and do what you're told, I won't hurt you," Mike said. "If I think you're about to do something stupid or threaten my family in any way, I will kill you. Understand?"

The two men didn't speak, and neither made a move to nod their heads.

"I don't want to hurt anyone," Mike continued as if they had agreed. "But I will if I am backed into a corner. If you're serious about getting out of this alive, you'll help me convince who I need to convince to let me and my people get across the bridge you're holding up ahead. You understand me?"

"I don't know about any bridge," one of the men said.

The other was shaking and looked as if he was going to be sick.

Mike leaned down in front of the shaking man's face and spoke in barely a whisper. "I think that other guy might have made up his mind already. How about you?"

"I'll help you," the man stammered, tears running down the side of his cheeks. "My uncle is one of the men on the bridge. His name is Silas. He'll let you through. You won't have to hurt anyone."

Mike turned to the first guy. "Is what he saying true? Cause if it's not, I'm not gonna start with him. I'm gonna start with you. He scares easier."

The tough guy swallowed hard and suddenly didn't look so tough. After a long moment of silence, he nodded. "Silas isn't in charge, but a lot of the local guys look up to him."

"What about the guys that aren't local?" Arthur asked, breaking his silence for the first time.

The tough guy turned his head to spit. "Those guys are messed up. They're hard as nails and twice as bitter. They'll chew you up and spit you out if you let them get their hooks in you."

Mike pointed the muzzle of his M-4 at the obstinate man, "I'm going to tape your mouth closed. If you're not quiet when we do this, I'll probably put a bullet in you just to prove a point. I won't kill you unless you make me, but if you push me I'll damn sure shoot you. Now shut your mouth and keep it shut, got it?"

The man's eyes widened slightly and he nodded once.

"You, tell me how many people you have between here and the bridge," Mike said as he turned back to Silas' nephew. "And be quick before they realize something didn't go as planned and come looking to find out what."

"There's two more in a power line cut through on the left side of the road just before you get to the bridge," the man said. "They got shotguns and rifles, and so do the men out on the bridge. There's more than one group out there, and they switch up how many goes at one time. I can't tell you how many is on the bridge right now, mister. Can we go now?"

"Jesus, Calver, you can't tell people stuff like that or you're gonna get somebody killed," the tough-guy growled.

Mike had had enough. He pulled a roll of thick, black duct tape and a gauze pad from his pack. He stepped in front of the man and dropped to one knee to put them on the same eye level. He fixed the man with an even stare and considered him for a moment. He didn't look like the type that had real violence in him, just frightened bravado, but it was difficult to tell. Mike had people, a lot of people, depending on him. He couldn't afford to take chances—not now.

"Listen to me carefully," Mike said. "You have survived this long by doing whatever you had to do. I know what that's like, and I know how heavy it gets. But you made it. And I don't think you have survived this long to get it all cut short here, now, over a bridge."

Mike was quiet for a moment, then tapped the pistol at his side. "Don't prove me wrong. Please. I don't want to have to carry that too."

Mike leaned forward with the duct tape and the prisoner recoiled. Mike paused and took a deep breath. "If you resist, it's going to get worse. And if it gets too bad, one of the people standing around us will put a bullet in your head, so please calm down. This is for your protection as much as mine. Now this is happening, one way or another. You got it?"

The man's breathing was coming in quick, ragged gasps now and his eyes were wide, but he nodded. The bravado gone, all he had left was the scared. Mike saw it, knew what it was like to feel it, and he felt his stomach twist. He was doing what he had to do to get the group across the river. That was all that mattered at this point.

They had traveled more than forty miles since picking up their first new people, Chip and Jess. Their group had grown from five, to seven, to more than thirty. They moved in a tight group and kept a steady pace that wasn't fast but allowed them to cover ground at a predictable rate. With a group their size, food and clean water was always a struggle; however, the safety that such a large number of people provided was well worth the added effort of scavenging, bartering, and foraging for supplies on the road.

On two occasions, their sheer size had persuaded hostile groups not to harass them. And once, when their size hadn't been enough deterrent, their numbers had made the fight a foregone conclusion. Most of their party had some kind of weapon and knew how to use it, and the marksmanship of the handful of proficient hunters had come in handy in more ways than one. Mike focused on those memories as he carefully placed the gauze over the man's mouth and wrapped duct tape around his head to gag him. He used zip ties to secure the man's wrists but left his ankles free so he could walk. Mike then did the same to Silas' nephew who didn't resist at all, which was almost worse. When he was done, Mike felt drained.

He took no time to focus on that, though. He climbed to his feet and told the rest of the people around him his plan. "Okay, there are two more people between us and the bridge. Arthur, you and Alyssa go get the others and bring them up to here. I'll take the prisoners and the rest of you, and we'll go secure the other two watchers. I'll take the prisoners into the woods and work around behind them and come in loud enough to be heard. They'll turn to see what's up, and I'll start negotiating. Then you four come in from behind them just like you did here."

Mike took one of the flashlights. "I'll use this to show them that these two haven't been hurt. That should buy me at least a little good will and enough time to distract them so you guys can get in place and come in. Remember, once you go, you can't hesitate. If you do, you lose that element of surprise."

As she turned to go with Arthur, Alyssa gave Mike a look that was somewhere between disgust and pity. She couldn't bring herself to look at the men still bound and gagged at his feet. Mike closed his eyes for a moment, and his jaw clenched as he ground his teeth. When he opened his eyes again, thankfully, Alyssa and Arthur were out of sight. He took another deep breath to steady himself, then nodded to the four young men around him.

They all had been practicing together in the afternoons and evenings, doing simple group drills so they could coordinate better, and so far, their time and effort were paying off in a big way. Two of the young men took the prisoners, and Mike took point as they moved northeast along the highway. They slowed when they came to another small intersection where a two-lane country road came in from the left. Mike pulled out his map and checked.

The map showed the power line cut through as it dropped south across the highway about two thousand feet ahead. Mike led the group into the forest to the left of the road, and they pushed their way through the hardwoods and evergreens for a while. The underbrush was thin and brittle in the cool late fall air, which made it easy to move, but twigs snapped and leaves rustled with every step.

Mike was ready to tell the rest of the group to bear to the right when they broke through the woods onto a narrow gravel road. The transition from dense woods to open road was so quick and complete that Mike actually stumbled a bit. He looked both directions and instinctively dropped to one knee to make himself a smaller target. He was pleased to see all four of the young men with him do the same while the two prisoners stood still, not sure what to do. There were no shouts and no shots to indicate they had been spotted, so just as quickly as they'd dropped to the deck, they were up and moving again. Mike headed to the right, and the young men formed up around him with the prisoners. Mike stopped when he saw the power line opening through the bare tree trunks ahead. He pointed to the two prisoners and to the ground. If they were on their knees, they would be less likely to run. He turned back to the four young men with him.

"All right, two of you go across as quick as you can and work your way down through the trees. The other two stay on this side and work your way down. Go slow and stay quiet. I'm going to walk straight up the cut through until they hear me and stop me. If I see them first, I'll cut on the flashlight to signal them. Hopefully they're not the shoot first and ask questions later type."

Only one of the young men forced a chuckle. They were on edge, and Mike could understand why. They'd all been in fights where the adrenaline surged and the nerves got frayed, but the hurting and killing weren't getting any easier. These young men were handling the stress for the moment, and that was all he could really ask of them.

Mike waited until he couldn't hear the young men moving through the woods and then pulled the two prisoners to their feet. He looked them both square in the eye before speaking. "I may not want to kill anyone tonight. but if things even smell like they're going sideways out there, I'll use you both as human shields and kill your friends. I'm not going to let anything put my family in danger. Got it?"

The two men nodded, and Mike pushed them both lightly with the muzzle of his M-4. They started walking down the gravel road toward the power line cut through. Within a few moments they were standing under the open sky and the thin power lines. Mike turned the men to their right, angling back to the highway and the waiting assailants.

He was about five hundred yards back from the highway when the two men he expected finally stepped out of the woods ahead of him. One of them shined a flashlight in Mike's direction, so he stopped. He kept both hands visible, with one arm around the tough guy's neck and the other pointing his flashlight at the still shaking prisoner.

"I've got two of your men," Mike said in a clear voice. The two men, twenty yards from him, would have been able to hear him with no difficulty, but his voice wouldn't carry far beyond that. "All I want is to go over the bridge with my family. If you let me do that, you can all live."

The two men facing him snorted, and the one with the flashlight spoke. "Well, if you pay the toll, you can go across no problem. Although we might have to have a talk about your manners, treating our friends the way you have."

"They're still breathing," Mike said, "and that's after they assaulted two of my friends at an intersection a ways back. Besides, you seem to think this is some kind of negotiation. It isn't. I'm telling you how it is. You either let me and my family go across, or you try and stop us. There's no third option."

"There's always another option," the man with the flashlight countered smoothly. "You just have to be willing to take it."

Just then a soft click caught his attention and the man with the flashlight looked behind him, right into the barrel of a sawed-off shotgun. The other man had two revolvers in his face when he broke eye contact with Mike and turned to help his compatriot. The four young men had moved at the same instant, and before either of the two hostiles could respond, they were outnumbered and outflanked.

Reluctantly, both men handed over their handguns, heads hanging low as Mike walked up to them. "I meant what I said. I don't want to hurt anyone, and if they let me through at the bridge, I'll let you all go at the end of this. But I'm not paying you any toll for a bridge that you didn't build. And I've got enough people with me that I don't have to. It's as simple as that."

Mike had the two men patted down and their hands zip-tied behind them. "I trust I don't have to gag either of you the way I had to gag these two. Both men shook their heads in the affirmative.

"Good. I'm glad we understand each other. Now, how many people are on the bridge tonight?"

"Six," the man who'd had the flashlight said at the same time that the other man said "Four."

Mike stared at them for a moment. "Well, you can't both be telling the truth, but you could both be lying, I suppose. Either way, it doesn't matter."

"You think you're tough because you can sneak up on someone?" the man who had been holding the flashlight asked. "It's a different thing to actually pull the trigger."

"Ain't it, though," Mike said as he led them toward the road. He stepped out into the middle of the black top and turned his back to the bridge, a smile on his face. "Let me introduce you to my family," he said with a sweep of his arm.

The four prisoners reached the road just as the group of more than thirty armed people came into view. Arthur, Cheryl, and Alyssa led the column, and they each had long guns of some sort in their hands and at least one handgun on their belts.

"Like I told you," Mike said as he turned back to his temporary hostages, "we're getting across that bridge tonight, one way or the other."

Chapter 35

Price of Admission

Oct. 22nd 2330 EST

Mike pushed Silas' nephew lightly in the back to get him moving. The man wasn't trembling anymore, but he stumbled as if he were dazed. Exhaustion was beginning to take its toll, and he wasn't holding up well. Mike needed him moving for just a little bit longer, though, and then, hopefully, the whole ordeal would be over.

The bridge was actually two bridges, each with two lanes. One had been blocked off with burned out cars and concrete construction barriers and was mostly impassable. The other had a few concrete barriers and a few burned out cars, but they were staggered to create a series of switchbacks. Mike followed close behind Silas' nephew, partly to make sure the man kept putting one foot in front of another and partly to use the large farmer as cover.

They were nearly a third of the way across the northern-most span when four banks of construction lights clicked on and suddenly blinded them.

"Stop right where you are," a voice called from behind the lights. "You've got rifles on you, and if you try anything we'll shoot."

Mike stopped and held his hands out wide from his body, careful to keep them in plain view. "Okay, I've stopped," he called. "I

258

just came to talk. I don't have any guns or knives on me, and I brought Silas' nephew unharmed. Is Silas here? I was told Silas would be willing to talk."

"All right, come forward," the same voice answered. "Keep your hands where we can see them and move slow."

Mike nodded and he and Silas' nephew began moving across the bridge. When they were about ten feet from the construction lights, three men came out to face them. The man in the middle was one of the largest men Mike had ever seen. He stood at least six and a half feet tall and had to weigh more than four hundred pounds. He wore a brown field jacket over dark blue work coveralls and carried a double barrel shotgun in his hands and a pair of forty-five caliber pistols on his belt.

"I'm Silas, and that's Calver, my nephew. If he's been hurt, things ain't gonna go well for you, son. But I'll listen to what you got to say, either way."

Two of the men stepped forward and gave Mike a pat down, but neither made any move to bind his hands or feet. After they were satisfied that he didn't have any weapons or hidden surprises, they cut the zip ties on Calver's hands and took the gag off his face. Calver blinked and answered questions, but it was clear he was still in shock and needed some rest. One of the men put a firm hand on Mike's shoulder and forced him to kneel.

"What do you have to say?" Silas said as he patted Calver on the back and sent him behind the lights.

"My family and I are going to cross your bridge tonight," Mike said calmly. "How we do it is up to you. I have three other men waiting with my family that I'm sure you know as well. Men who probably have families that would like to see them again. If you let us cross your bridge, we will release them on the other side as we leave. We're just passing through and don't want anything from you, just to be on our way."

"Okay, and what if I told you that we don't let people cross unless they can pay the toll?" Silas asked. "That's something the two towns agreed on in the treaty. We need that income to buy things. It's that simple."

"We are paying a toll," Mike insisted. "But our toll is in lives. We have three of yours that you know with absolute certainty will die if you force our hand. We'll kill them first and then the rest of you. We'll lose people, but I have over thirty and you have at most six from what I've seen and heard. We have you at a five to one disadvantage. You can't hold out, so you'll be overrun."

"Yeah, but you'll die too," Silas said, "which means it's not a great deal for you either."

"Oh, I agree," Mike said, and he slowly stood, keeping his hands well clear of his body. Even on his feet he wasn't nearly on eye level with Silas. "If things go sideways I'll be dead, and so will you. I have some people in my family that are dead-on accurate with their deer rifles."

Mike pointed to one of the blazing halogen lights on the twelve-foot stands. The cluster of lights was connected to a solar generator with DOT spray painted along one side. The lights were intense and designed to be rugged. But as Mike pointed to the top right bulb in the stand in front of him and just behind Silas, it exploded in a shower of sparks and glass shards. A few moments later the report of a high-powered rifle reached them and echoed off the trees.

"How many of those bulbs can one of those lose before it shorts out the system?" Mike asked. "My guess would be not many, not like that. Now, are you going to let us through or are we going to have a pointless and bloody fight first?"

Silas turned and huddled with the other two men. Mike could hear their whispers and see the other three members of their party as dim shadows just on the other side of the construction lights. No doubt they were nervous, and with good reason. Finally, Silas turned back to Mike, his frown reflecting the seriousness of Mike's intent. "And we have your word that once you all are on the other side of the river that you'll keep going?"

Mike nodded. "We're just passing through on our way somewhere else."

"Mind if I ask where?" Silas said carefully.

Mike smiled. "You can ask all day. But I can give you my word we're not sticking around. We're just passing through."

"Why are you out on the road? Isn't it dangerous everywhere you go."

"It's better than where we were," Mike said softly. "We came from Charlotte, and things are getting bad there. People are desperate. And then there's the FSS."

Immediately, Silas' eyes narrowed and he leaned forward. "The FSS? What about them?"

Mike's teeth clicked as he closed his mouth and shook his head. "No," he said. "Nothing else until I have your assurance that we can pass—all of us. Once we're on the other side, we'll release your people back to you. Don't try to follow us, don't try to find us. We go our separate ways. Agreed?"

Silas nodded with an impatient wave of his hand. "Yes, fine." One of the other men started to protest, but Silas silenced him with look. "You're giving us three hostages and information that could be more valuable than anything else we could ask for, so we'll call that your toll. And if someone back in town has a problem with it, they can come find me. I'm hard to miss."

Silas turned back to Mike. "You were saying, young man?"

"Look, I've seen the FSS do some terrible things, and I've seen what they've left behind. They shot someone I was close to right in front of me after swearing for her safety. I don't know what their agenda is, but they're ruthless. If you find anyone with an FSS badge, you put them down, period."

Mike turned and gave a series of shrill whistles. The column of thirty-four people trotted up from the foot of the bridge. Under close guard, the three hostages led the group between the two banks of construction lights. Silas and his men gave way, and Mike's group crossed in silence. As the last few people passed by, Mike fixed Silas with one long stare. "I'm serious about the FSS. If they're already in your town, you've got to get them out. Now. If they get a foothold, you'll never get rid of them."

"These people aren't all your family, are they?" Silas asked. "They can't be. There's too many of them."

"They're the only family I have left. We're all that's left for each other."

Mike turned and started walking away. "We'll send your people back across the bridge when we're gone," he called over his shoulder. "Remember, don't try to follow us."

Before Silas could respond, Mike had disappeared into the shadows beyond the light cast by the construction lights.

Chapter 36

Restless

Eric sat up in the bed, sweat soaking his hair and his pillow despite the chilly air. The sound of snoring from rooms on both sides of their small bedroom was clear, even through closed doors. But that wasn't what had awakened him. In fact, without the soft rumblings, Eric doubted he'd be able to fall asleep now. The different tones and rhythms had become a baritone white-noise machine that lulled him to sleep many nights.

Eric shivered without the warm covers around him. He swung his feet around and stood beside the bed. He couldn't remember the dream that woke him up, and he was glad for it. All he had was the feeling the dream had left him with—a throat closing kind of panic that was difficult to shake. He moved as carefully as he could, and Christina shifted in her sleep but didn't wake.

Just enough light filtered in through the windows for Eric to pull on a shirt and some socks. He grabbed a thick wool sweater from the closet and picked up his M-4 by the door. He slipped his head and shoulders through the strap and stuck his FNX 9mm pistol in its holster on his belt. Two thick bladed tactical knives were in secure sheaths at the small of his back.

No one went anywhere unarmed. The risk was too great—too real after the pasture. Eric picked his way through the living room and out the front door. He was careful to be quiet as he left the front porch and crossed the yard between two tents. As he approached the gate, Steven Jacobs came out to meet him. The young man had grown a lot in the last month, and he was much more serious, predictable, and reliable now.

"Mr. Eric, do you want me to open the gate for you?" Steven asked.

"Sure, Steven, and close it behind me. I'm feeling restless and think I'll take a lap around the fence to check for weak spots."

Steven nodded. "Well, as long as you're back before sunup, I'll be here to let you back in. After that it's next shift, and I think that's Bill."

Eric stepped through the gate and waved to Steven as he moved off into the woods. He followed the barbed wire fence around in a wide curve that encircled the farmhouse compound. He knew that the fence didn't really need checking. Teams checked the perimeter three times a day every day, a lesson they had learned from the first breach that had nearly cost several people their lives. Checking the fence was a convenient excuse to get some time outside, especially at night.

Whenever Eric spent too long at the farm, he grew restless, restive even. He would pace at night, get mild flare ups of claustrophobia at random times, lose his temper more quickly than usual. The nightmares didn't help and often drove him out of bed, as they had this night. As he moved silently through the trees, he thought about how long it had been since he'd gotten a full night's sleep.

When he was around the halfway point, Eric slowed his pace and eventually stopped next to a large oak tree that stood on the edge of the valley between the plateau that was their farm and the next one over. At the bottom of the narrow valley, a creek eventually fed into the river that ran along the back side of the property. This creek wasn't as big as Culver's Run that had given the road its name, but it was still a decent size.

Eric could barely hear the water as it tumbled over a few small boulders below. He put his back against the trunk of the broad oak and slid down until he was sitting on one of the massive roots that jutted up through the soil and the old leaf litter. The root was covered by a soft coating of moss so it made a decent seat.

He leaned his head back and looked up at the stars and the thin sliver of moon. The hunter's moon was long since gone, and the next time it was this bright would be around the time of his wedding. It felt odd to think of things in those terms. He had known he would get married one day—had even begun laying the plans—but to have it so close was a shock.

The friend of a friend was a few years older than the rest of their group, and he was the first one to tie the knot. They made a huge deal out of the bachelor's party, and a big group flew out to Las Vegas for a four-day weekend. Eric hadn't been able to make the trip, but he'd helped plan the local party, and that had been its own kind of spectacle. The last one of Eric's friends to get married before the Blackout was barely twenty-one.

Now, he was the oldest guy in his circle of friends, and not many of them were even engaged yet. He'd been looking forward to his own party and celebration, but now things were different. He was different. He felt it, and he didn't know how to reconcile that feeling with who he had been. When things started going bad here at the farm, Eric had been forced to do things to keep himself and the rest of the group safe. They were terrible things, but he knew why he had done them. His back had been against the wall.

When he thought about Christina and their child she was carrying, he tried to think of even one thing so terrible that he wouldn't do it to keep them safe. But there wasn't a single thing, no matter how shocking or how evil, that he wouldn't do to protect them.

And that frightened him.

As he thought about these things, Eric's hand went to his neck where his fingers found a leather cord strung with a row of bottle caps. The newest was only a couple of weeks old, so the points and edges were still sharp enough to be uncomfortable. Some, though, were already worn and smooth.

As Eric sat, lost in his thoughts, the eastern sky slowly shifted from the velvety purple of night to the pinkish-gray of the coming dawn.

Chapter 37

No Words

President Phillip Hall sat on his balcony overlooking the National Mall. The entire lawn below him, except for a parade ground set aside for practicing formation marching, was covered with neat rows of tents. The ability to coordinate movement over distance played a huge role in modern warfare and, for the unseasoned soldier, required copious practice. One of his favorite pastimes was watching his recruits drill for hours. It soothed him to watch such order imposed on the chaos of the time.

As Hall watched, two squads of special operations candidates practiced hand-to-hand combat techniques on one side of the parade ground while two more squads practiced transitioning different positions for firing a weapon in urban terrain. As they walked around the formations, the instructors used a series of coded whistle blasts to transition the fire teams from one position to the next. Even though there was no sequence to the positions, cadets were expected to make the transitions flawlessly. Any mistakes were called out and ruthlessly punished.

Successes were ignored.

Behind him, Hall heard someone clear his throat but didn't have to turn his head to know that Daniel was behind him. He was

267

the only person in the world that the security services would let through unannounced.

"What do the reports say, Daniel?"

"Charlotte has been attacked twice more. No word on casualties or lasting effects. The FSS team that was en route to Fort Bragg is now on its way to Charlotte to check the status of our forces there. The column is divided into four main units traveling separate routes, with a fifth expeditionary unit, the Tennessee Mountain Tactical Team, mapping and securing an ex-filtration route for post mission operations."

"I want those unit commanders checking in every twelve hours on the dot," Hall said, and Daniel made a note in his hardened tablet.

"We have not heard anything out of Kansas City, Missouri, in more than two weeks," Daniel continued. "We sent a dozen scouts from St. Louis, but none have reported back as yet. Satellite over flights show a new occupying force and evidence of recent mass graves."

"How many men?" Hall asked.

"Two hundred and thirty-seven. We aren't sure if they all were contained within the main camp at the time of the attack, but as I said, we have had no reports of survivors. If not for the satellite over watch, we wouldn't know they have been hit."

"Send word to our forces in St. Louis. They are to tighten their control and increase their hostile activities. I want that area boiling in blood and chaos by the end of next week. All restraints are off and all leashes cut. And when the local citizens are in a frenzy, find a way to lay it at the feet of the soldiers in Kansas City. That should convince them to get a war party together go after those Kansas City rebels."

Daniel made more notes on his tablet. "Is there anything else, Mr. President?"

Hall turned and regarded his vice president carefully. One of the reasons he had hired the man as a nondescript staffer years before had been his shocking lack of ambition. He had struck the president as the only applicant who wasn't secretly trying to push a private agenda or pad his own resume. Now, though, seeing how Daniel had risen through the ranks to his second-in-command, Hall wondered if that initial assessment had been mistaken.

Had Daniel desired such a powerful position or was he merely the beneficiary of benign chance? Perhaps the office of the vice president had given him too much power—power that could make Daniel a threat to Hall's power and, ultimately, a threat to his carefully crafted plan.

A small part of the president's mind screamed that he was being unreasonable, but that small voice was drowned out by screams that said Daniel was about to betray him and had to be stopped.

"Daniel, call a full session of the Senate. I want to see them all at dawn tomorrow morning. I will make several announcements, and they all are to be in attendance, and they all are to be attentive. I want you there as well."

Daniel blinked in surprise and started to ask a question, but Hall raised his hand sharply. "I will not answer your questions about this. You are to carry out my orders. Is that understood?"

There was the briefest of hesitations before Daniel regained his composure. "Of course, Mr. President. It will be as you ordered,"

Daniel said as he put his right fist over his heart. "I am simply surprised at the suddenness of this call. The Senate is usually given at least two days' warning. The senators will not be happy with having been rushed."

"That is neither your concern nor mine. I don't need them to be happy. I need them to be there, and I need them to be compliant."

Daniel nodded and added another note to his growing list. "Is there anything else, Mr. President?"

"Am I boring you, Daniel?" Hall asked, his voice barely more than a whisper.

"Of course not, sir," Daniel stammered. He not only was surprised by Hall's question, he was frightened by the unmistakably vicious tone beneath the whisper.

"There's something on your mind, then?" the president asked, though in truth it wasn't a question. He'd known Daniel long enough to recognize when the man was chewing on an unasked question or trying to conceal an intractable problem for his own sake. The man was a competent assistant and had no discernible intent to eliminate his superiors in order to achieve his own advancement, but he was ruthlessly protective of the president. And, at times, that kind of smothering could get tiresome.

Daniel, still unsure of Hall's current demeanor, hesitated but continued. "Sir . . . ah . . ., the team you diverted to Charlotte, they were . . . ah . . . originally tasked with establishing your foothold in Fort Bragg, sir. Not to be blunt, but we need that military base or we risk losing the entire East Coast, including DC"

President Hall allowed a smile, just at the corners of his mouth, though it was more of a sneer. "I know that, Daniel. If you recall, I'm the one who told you that very fact standing over a map more than two years ago. But you're absolutely right. We *must* take Fort Bragg or the entire war is lost before it begins."

"What will we do?" Daniel asked with a little hesitation before the 'we.'

Hall turned and waved his hand to the training men below. "We're going to build this army into a giant fighting machine, and then we're going south. We're going to take Virginia and the Carolinas. This nation's government might have been built around the lecture tables in a Pennsylvania State House, but it was won on the battlefield by soldiers and generals."

When Hall turned back, a feverish light blazed in his eyes. "We're going to war, Daniel," he whispered.

Chapter. 38

A Good Supper

Eric watched as the two young men performed the same move over and over again. First, one of them would come in low and fast at the other and thrust up with the point of a butter knife aimed at his target's heart. At the same time, the other young man stepped smoothly to his left and grabbed the aggressor's wrist with both hands. The would-be victim turned his hips sharply and used the attacker's own momentum to spin him up into the air and down onto the grassy ground with a controlled thud. He then twisted the attacker's wrists and disarmed the knife while pretending to drop a knee onto his temple.

The two stood again and reversed roles, carrying out the same choreographed moves in slow, controlled steps. Eric nodded approvingly. He had spent years sparring with his father, learning the same moves in same fashion.

"Good job," Eric told the two young men, patting each of them on the shoulder. "The key to these skills is to learn them slowly at first and then practice them over and over. You may never be attacked with a knife like this. But there could be that one time you're out on an ambush mission or on a snatch and run, and it happens. This maneuver could save your life. Also, remember that in the field you're going to either drop a knee on the guy or boot stomp his head. It's brutal, but you need to visualize doing that and harden yourself to it."

Eric looked at each of the half dozen or so young men facing him and the two in front of him. "Because out there, when it's just you and the other guy, one of you is not walking away. Don't let that man be you. We need every single man we have. Got it?"

"Yes, sir!" the young men said in unison.

Eric cringed inwardly but kept his doubt off his face. These young trainees from the surrounding farms had taken to calling all of the men and women either sir or ma'am, with only a few exceptions. Eric's father was now known as Captain Till, his moniker for years while on the Teams. And though Eric's granddaddy wasn't called by rank, somehow most of them managed to make Mr. Withers sound even more revered than Captain Till. It also helped that Mr. Withers was a legend for his campfire stories about World War II.

Eric was uncomfortable with the respect he received and felt he hadn't earned it. Most of the people who gathered at the church were either five years younger or twenty years older, and they all called him "sir" every time he turned around. They didn't know who he really was or any of the things he'd done.

And he didn't want them to.

As the handful of young men walked away, Brant came up. "This is strange," he said, and Eric nodded, but didn't respond. "How did your group do?"

Eric gave a small shrug. "Once they got the forms down, it was just a matter of repetition. They're not smooth yet, but they are functional. There's a couple of them that show promise and will probably be good at the gritty part of what goes down."

Brant nodded. "Same here. I had three that looked like they could get it, but the rest are iffy at best."

Eric made no move to respond. After a while, Brant shifted his weight to his other foot and grunted. He was trying to find something to say. Eric knew it, but he wasn't in any mood to attempt conversation. He'd respond if he had to so as to avoid being rude, but that's all.

"Look, about what happened back at the crossroads . . .," Brant began, but stopped as Eric turned to walk away.

The crossroads was the one thing he couldn't stand to BS his way around. It was too much, too real, and too fresh in his mind to try and rationalize it or explain it away. He had frozen, and in the process, had nearly gotten both of them killed. If it hadn't been for Brant's quick thinking, Eric would have been standing there dumbfounded when the other two sentries came around the curve, and that would have been it. The alarm would have gone up, and at the very least Brant and Eric would have been cut down where they stood.

The others would have at least had a chance, but they likely would have died too. Instead of running for cover, his only real option for survival, Brant had pulled Eric to safety first. Eric remembered freezing, staring down at the body of the man he'd just shot with his bow, and he remembered thinking how this was going to be the last moment in his life. He was going to leave the world staring at a man he'd just shot in the back.

He'd felt cold and numb, as if he were watching the scene from outside his body, totally removed from his actions. From behind and above his own right shoulder, he had watched the empty caricature of himself stand there and stare at a dead man with an arrow sticking out of his back.

Eric shook his head, and with no small effort dispelled that image to keep from getting sucked into the miasma of paranoia, introspection, and guilt that threatened to take hold of him. He just wasn't ready to deal with the crossroads, yet. He wasn't ready to cope with what he had done and how he had reacted. The experience had shaken him far more than he was willing to admit to anyone, especially himself.

He certainly wasn't ready to talk to Brant about it.

Lost in his thoughts, Eric hadn't taken more than three steps when he almost ran into his father. Joe gestured for Brant to join them. "You men make sure your groups get a good meal tonight. The cooks have been working overtime on two big pots of venison stew. Everyone gets their fill, understood?"

Both Eric and Brant nodded, so Joe continued. "After you all eat I want you to pick your three best guys. Gear up and meet over by the flag pole by 2100. We've got a recon op to get to and need an escort for the long walk in and out of the area. If everything goes according to plan, the backup team won't run into anything and they'll stay backup. But they have to be ready if we call on them for help."

"They're still very new," Eric said. "This makes me nervous."

Joe smiled. "Don't worry. I'm going to put Chris in command of the backup unit and leave Henderson in charge of the training group. The trainees will be ticked they're not going, but they need the extra training to get whipped into shape."

"Are you expecting there to be trouble, Captain Till?" Brant asked.

Joe shook his head. "I'm not expecting it, exactly, but it's a distinct possibility. We're going farther than we usually go on foot,

275

and we're headed to what we think will be a secret meeting between the FSS garrison in town and their supply and command chain. It's a rare opportunity and worth a little risk. That's why we're leaving the greenhorns a couple of miles out from the actual meeting point and we three will go in on our own."

Joe started to walk away and called over his shoulder, "Bring extra mags." And then he was out of earshot, leaving Brant and Eric in the lengthening shadows as the sun dimmed on the horizon.

Chapter 39

Last Light

Oct. 23rd 1638 MST

Commander Price stood among the solar panels that helped power the facility nearly a quarter of a mile back down the ridge. He liked this vantage point because he could see both the eastern and western horizons, depending on the direction he faced. He often came here to watch the sunrise and then would return to see it set on the same day. Since the Blackout, Price had needed the sunrises and sunsets to hang on to the natural rhythm of living.

By being there each day, he could live the lives of the millions who would never see another dawn or dusk. He kept telling himself that it was millions, though deep down he knew the number had surpassed the one billion mark long ago. America had been the world's breadbasket, and global starvation would have pushed the casualties to near sixty percent by this point, which meant more than four billion people were dead or dying.

Recoiling like a spider from a sudden light, Price's mind shied away from that number. It seared its way across his mind, but he wouldn't allow it to sink into his consciousness. If he ever stopped to fully accept the magnitude of what he had witnessed and its consequences, it would overwhelm him. He knew that, and he fought daily against it. These brief moments of solitude helped him regroup and prioritize his thoughts.

Price faced west at the moment, watching the sun sink beneath a blanket of low steel-gray clouds that looked and smelled like an early snow storm brewing. The air had gone from pleasantly warm a few days before to uncomfortably cold, and even without the fat Dominican cigar in his left hand, his breath would have fogged the air.

The commander took a long, slow drag on his cigar and held the smoke. He let the flavors soak in slowly until his tongue and cheeks tingled with absorbed nicotine. As he exhaled, he tried to blow a smoke ring but failed. The breeze was too strong and too steady to allow them to form, so the smoke whipped away from his mouth.

He heard a cough behind him and the commander smiled. "Decide to take me up on the offer of a smoke, Marcus?"

"Yes, sir," Commander Attledge said, his breath fogging the air as he climbed the narrow path to the top of the ridge. "How are the panels doing?"

Price passed a cigar and a butane torch lighter to Attledge. "They're holding for now. There are maybe three more that will have thermal failures sooner than they should, but the rest don't show any damage from the pulses. I think with the possible exception of those three, we're going to be good."

Attledge took the cigar and busied himself lighting it, so Price continued. "How did Colonel Darius take my temporary absence?"

"He wasn't happy," Attledge admitted, "but he took it in stride. He's setting up security check points and recruiting stations around the city in an effort to win over the local population, which seems to have splintered. Some have sided with the more unsavory elements in town. He's trying to fight that tendency by bringing a larger order to the area, but Kansas City is a big place. He still doesn't have enough support to reach the outer edges and into the suburbs. He expressed concern about being overrun should the civilian population realize how tentative their hold is."

"Yes, he's said as much to me on more than one occasion. He seems to forget the heavy weapons, armored troop carriers, and artillery that we have moved into the stitching yard. No local gang is going to try their hand against that, at least not for a long time, and by then, we'll have even more reinforcements in place."

They smoked in silence as the sun sank lower over the far ridges, more than half of it now below the horizon. The clouds that had been a sullen gray were beginning to reflect shades of pink and orange, and Attledge felt as though he could see the sun inching closer to dusk. At last, his perception grew into an undeniable reality, and the last slim sliver of red disappeared.

"The colonel is going to want an answer tonight. Do you have orders for him that you would like me to relay, sir?"

Price shook his head. "No, Marcus, I will be speaking with Colonel Darius myself later this evening. Whatever I have to say to him, and him to me, we can get it out of the way then. For now, I would like simply to spend some time in peace. One question before you go, did Colonel Darius send a contingent south to look for an alternate open rail line to either Georgia or Tennessee?"

Attledge nodded. "Yes, sir. Two Strykers with four men each left this morning. Each group was sent down different legs of the freight rails that head generally south by southeast. If either of them is open all the way, then we'll have our alternate path. If, by some stroke of luck both lines are open, then we will have two roads where we're headed. That could give us a strategic advantage."

Price smiled. "You've been reading the World War II books I gave you, haven't you?" he asked, and Marcus nodded. "The tactics our troops learned fighting their way through Europe are still used today. You're learning to see those tactical principles in what we're actually doing, which is a good sign. So, what do we do if we have a best-case scenario and find two paths open into the deep south? Which one do we use?"

Attledge thought about it a moment before answering. "If it were my decision, I would send a train loaded with men, supplies, and equipment down both tracks. That way you're increasing the odds that at least one of the trains will make it to the target destination."

"You could do that, but that would mean dividing the troops and weakening your force. You would be more vulnerable with longer and more complicated supply lines. And, in the end, it would use more time to reach the objective because one of the paths your forces take is necessarily going to be longer than the other."

Price took a pull on his cigar and let the smoke out slowly. Light was fading from the clouds and darkness was coming on fast with the low blanket of clouds blocking any hint of stars and moon alike. The air smelled sharp and cold with a dry, tingling taste. It smelled of snow.

"In that case," Price continued, "you're giving up security for a minor increase in odds. You'd do better to determine a path of least resistance, or shortest travel time, or whatever other variable you decide is important enough to determine your choice, and you throw everything you have at that one option. You make a call and you gamble on it."

Price stared out at the landscape of hills and mountain ridges. The tree line was low here and the tops of the ridges mostly bald.

They made the perfect place to plant solar panels, and several hills in the area had similar arrays that transmitted power back to the main facility. This one was closest to the facility's access point and, therefore, the one he was most familiar with.

"We'll give St. Louis two more days at the most. If we don't hear back from at least one of our scouts by then, we'll have to make a move south. Are the two advanced teams equipped with satellite phones?"

"Yes, sir," Attledge said. "They should be checking in tomorrow at sunrise to report what they've found so far on their respective routes."

Price took another puff on his cigar but didn't hold the smoke this time. The cigar was growing shorter and the smoke hotter and harsher. His cheeks and lips were already tingling with the absorbed nicotine and his fingers were beginning to shake; although, to be fair, that could have been the cold.

"I'll be honest with you, Marcus," Price said as he looked down at the nub of his cigar, "the fact that it's been this long with no word from any of the people we sent to scout St. Louis can't be good. Whatever we hear back from there, *if* we hear back from there, won't be good either. I think we'll end up going south on one of those two paths the men are scouting now."

Price took one last long pull on the cigar and held the thick, acrid smoke as long as he could. That last bit of smoke from a cigar was always the most potent. When he finally blew the smoke from his mouth, his eyes and nose were stinging.

"And Commander Attledge, when we do, you'll be going south with them." Price dropped the nub of cigar and ground it into the dirt with the heel of his boot. In the dim light, he saw that Attledge's eyes were wide with shock and his cigar hung forgotten from his right hand, ashes still glowing hot. "Careful," he said as he walked past. "If you drop it lit like that you could send this whole ridge up in smoke and half the mountains and hills around us with it. It's cold, but it's been dry lately, and I'd hate to survive the end of the world only to die in a wildfire started by one of my own cigars."

Before Attledge could think of a reply, Price was headed back down the ridge to the facility. He was left to finish his cigar, alone with his thoughts and the lengthening shadows around him.

Chapter 40

Lay of the Land

Oct. 24 th 0130 EST

Joe stopped beneath a large oak tree and checked his hand-held GPS. The thing was more than ten years obsolete, but the satellites that ran its operational network were solar powered and stationary. These units were so old that not many people still used the system, but it worked, and the signal strength had been better than most of the more modern systems before the Blackout. It was accurate down to about twenty yards, where as a newer one was accurate to two or three feet, but he didn't need that level of precision for what he was doing.

This was the waypoint he'd set two days earlier after hiking this path with Chris and Henderson. That first trip had been to get the lay of the land and make notes in his GPS about landmarks they could use to navigate. Even though he had the GPS as a back-up, Joe still preferred to rely on low-tech solutions in the field when possible. That instinct had served him well on the teams, and it certainly served him well now that the only solutions were low-tech solutions.

Joe turned to the six men that Eric and Brant had selected for this mission. "You men stay here and stay out of sight. Take up watch positions covering all approaches in a loose ring around this tree. Stay out of sight unless you absolutely have to engage, but you do not lose this ground. Got it?"

The men all nodded and said, "Yes, sir!" in unison.

"Good. This is our fallback position, and we need to know that you're going to be here if we come running. We are going ahead to scout out a place for a potential ambush. The area is under heavy enemy surveillance, and we might be coming back with trackers or hostiles hot on our heels. If we do, you men will provide us the covering fire we need to get here and then escape. This is important, men. Our lives may depend on you."

The young men looked nervous as they glanced at each other. More than one seemed about to say something but thought better of it. Joe let the moment of doubt stretch just a tad longer, then gave a hand signal. "Of course, I am going to leave you some support so you won't be alone."

At that instant, Chris stood up in the midst of them, rising from the ground in a ghillie suit with bits of twigs, leaves, and branches tied to it. His appearance was so sudden that a couple of the young men actually stumbled backwards, but none raised their weapons. Joe had warned Eric and Brant, so both of them just stood back and watched with smiles on their faces.

"Easy, men, there's no threat here. This is a lesson in concealment," Joe said to the young men once they'd settled down again. "Chris here is a master at disguise and camouflage. Just goes to show, you never really know what's around you, so you'd better act like you're always in someone's crosshairs. Chris brought along a few rough suits for you gentlemen to customize with local plant matter. He'll teach you to blend in with the ground and the shadows around you."

Joe looked deep into the eyes of each of the six men. "You were picked because you show promise. If you prove yourselves in this exercise, we may train you as snipers and recon specialists. If nothing else, these suits will make you tougher to spot if an enemy patrol should come through here before we get back. Make no mistake, gentlemen, we are now in hostile territory."

Joe turned to Chris. "You got this?"

Chris nodded once. "Yeah, Captain Till, I've got this. We're good. Keep your head down, eyes sharp."

Joe nodded and turned to Eric and Brant. "I'm going to set a hard pace. We've got a long way to go and not a lot of time between now and sunrise. We need to be in position before it gets even a little bit light. You two ready?"

Eric and Brant nodded, and Joe smiled. "Well, what are we waiting for, then?" He turned and trotted off into the deep shadows of the forest around them.

Joe could hear Eric and Brant behind him as they followed his trail. They weren't loud, just careless. Here and there a twig snapped in just the wrong way or a pile of leaves rustled just a little too loudly. If he slowed, he knew they could move much more quietly, but they had to make up some time. Just a few days ago, Benny, the former pharmacist, had given him the schedule for this meeting, and Joe had already scouted the location twice but had seen no enemy activity.

He knew that from the point they left the other men with Chris, they could afford to make a little noise for the next five miles, but for the last two miles, they would have to move quietly. If they could cover those first five miles in an hour and a half or less, they would have plenty of time to move slower and more carefully on the last two miles into the target area. Stealth would definitely

285

decrease their risk of being exposed once dawn broke. If they took longer than an hour and a half, that cushion of extra time evaporated. And the last thing Joe wanted was to be moving with it light enough to see. That would put their entire objective, not to mention their lives, at risk.

After a while, Joe detoured from his path and headed for a small clearing he'd marked as a landmark the day before. When he broke through the trees and out into the opening, he scanned the sky and found a few familiar constellations. Eric and Brant came out of the trees behind him just as Joe was aligning his position and getting his bearings. He knew he could use the GPS, but he didn't want to risk turning on an active signal in what could be a monitored air space.

"Listen, both of you," Joe said softly. "We're about a mile and a half deeper into enemy territory than either of you have been, and we've got a lot more to go. This area could be under digital surveillance and signal monitoring, so no radio comms whatsoever until I tell you otherwise. Don't even turn them on, and same thing goes for flashlights. Keep all noise to a minimum, including chatter. I may have to use the GPS, but for the most part I want to keep that off as well. That means navigating by the stars. We need to move fast so the stars I'm using don't set on us."

Eric and Brant caught their breaths and took a few small sips of water. Joe noted that they didn't guzzle the water but sipped a little at the time to avoid getting cramps. He took a few sips from his camel pack, then stood and motioned for the other two to follow him. With his rifle on a sling across his back, Joe slipped noiselessly back into the shadows among the trees.

They followed what looked like an old logging road that long ago had been cut through the woods. It was wide, flat, and devoid of most trees and large shrubs and reminded Joe of a section of a colonial-era road that had been preserved at the King's Mountain National Park. He'd taken Eric there the summer before his thirteenth birthday, and they had walked the two-hundred-yard section of the old road that was little more than a slightly open path between two rows of trees.

After reading the historical marker, Joe couldn't help but see that road for what it was. It was just a bit too straight, too flat, too precise to have been the work of nature. It had the stamp of man's planning and attention to detail written in its course. Once he'd seen that, the road had leapt out at him, and this path had done the same on his first trip through these woods. And now he was taking full advantage of the straight and open path, whatever its origin.

He ran until his legs ached and his lungs burned with every breath. He was pushing hard, probably even harder than he really had to, but he didn't know what lay ahead of them—what kind of delays could slow them down. Joe couldn't afford to feel his age at the moment, so he pushed through the pain and kept his pace.

After another half mile or so, spots started to creep into the edges of Joe's vision and he felt his lips and face going numb. He slowed to a jog and sucked air in through his nose and blew it out through his mouth quietly, but forcefully. His vision cleared, but he was still more than a little light headed.

Eric and Brant caught up to him, and they all three slowed to a fast walk. Joe sipped water through his camel pack, and Eric and Brant both took small sips from their water bottles. They had been pushing hard, and Joe needed to get his bearings again. After a few minutes of walking to cool down his legs and lungs, he paused in the shadow of a towering pine tree.

Joe dropped to one knee and pulled his outer jacket over his head. He saw Brant's and Eric's boots from under the edge of his coat as they took up positions guarding him, and he heard the unmistakable metallic clicks as the two young men switched their rifles from safe to fire. He clicked on a small flashlight with a red LED and looked a printed satellite image of the area. There were several waypoints marked with coordinates, and Joe clicked on his GPS.

It took the unit a moment to power up, but when the screen finally cleared, Joe read the coordinates and quickly copied them onto the notepad he kept in his pocket. He looked at the plotted line on the image compared to their actual position and realized they had veered right and would have to backtrack to the south in order to get back to their intended path. Still, it had been only forty-five minutes since they had started running and already they'd covered just over three miles.

That meant they had a little less than two miles to go and another forty-five minutes to get it covered. If they could keep their original pace, they would have more than enough time to get to the meeting place and get in a well-concealed position. Eric and Brant were less winded than Joe, but he was the only one who knew where they were headed, so it was up to him to set both the pace and the direction. He had to keep pushing.

Joe stood, took a quick reading of the landmarks around him and picked a line through the trees that would take them back to their original path. They had stayed on the old road too long and now had to make up some time and distance. He clicked the power button on the GPS, popped off the back, and removed the battery. One of the reasons he liked these old models was the battery was easily removed, which killed the high-powered transmitter and receiver that made up the guts of the unit.

Newer models with integrated batteries could never be powered down completely by the user because the battery constantly supplied power, allowing the system to be activated if the right codes were intercepted. That meant circuits independent of the user's power controls were set to activate when those codes were received. Such hidden codes and traps could easily turn a navigation tool into a tracker at the flip of a switch.

Joe felt a lot more comfortable with the GPS in one pocket and the battery wrapped in a balloon in the other pocket. He took one last sip out of his camel pack and, pointing off through the trees, nodded to Eric and Brant. They ran for a while, dodging the tree trunks and deadfalls as they went. Joe kept a close eye on his watch, and when they'd been running for a little more than five minutes, he checked the GPS again.

This time their dot was right on the intended path, and they were a mile and a half away from the next waypoint. As they grew closer, Joe would have to check the navigator more frequently to make sure they could find their target, but for now, a general bearing was good enough to cover some distance. Joe sped up as he removed the battery from the GPS again. When he set the pace this time, it was more manageable and steady enough to maintain.

Even with a slower pace, the last mile and a half seemed to go the quickest, and before long Joe had the GPS out again, working his way toward the next to the last waypoint. As he got closer, he shut the GPS down and looked for landmarks. He recognized a white quartz boulder the size of a recliner jutting out from the side of the ridge they were following. He walked over to it, put his back against it, and walked straight ahead.

After about ten paces, Joe came to a hollow left by the remnants of a giant wind-fall oak. The root ball of the old hardwood had been enormous and had gouged a deep and wide bowl in the forest floor when it fell. Tucked back against the lower lip of the hole was a bundle covered with leaves. Joe pulled it out, untied it, and handed

Eric and Brant their own ghillie suits. Joe had used his suit to wrap the bundle and secure it, so all three had their own camouflage.

Joe had taught both young men how to tie the two parts of the suit together to make a bundle that could be slung over the shoulder when not being worn. It wasn't exactly comfortable, but it was better than trying to move long distances over uneven terrain while wearing the things. Even in cool weather, that was an exhausting and sweaty endeavor. With night-time temperatures still in the high fifties , and the heavy packs they were carrying, Joe didn't want to risk any of them dealing with heat exhaustion. They would carry the suits a while, and when they reached the target area, they would mold them into an extension of the surroundings by attaching local plant matter that would conceal them.

"We're two miles out now," Joe said as he finished tying off the arms and legs of his suit. He slung the bundle over his head and one shoulder, shifting it so the bulk was riding on his back between his shoulder blades. "From this point on, we've got to move slower and be a lot more careful about our noise level. There could be patrols this far out, though I doubt it. If there are, I want to hear them coming before they hear us. And remember, we are on a recon mission, so no firing weapons until you're fired upon. Got it?"

Eric and Brant both nodded, so Joe continued. "If you have to take someone down, do it quietly—knife or garrote if possible. We want to draw as little attention to ourselves as possible, and dead bodies draw a lot of attention. We're going to scout a location for a possible ambush on a resupply route. The town group uses this road to meet their handlers, so we'll have a chance to hit both of them at once. To do that, we need the information we're about to gather. Keep your heads down, your eyes open, and follow my lead."

Eric and Brant pulled their ghillies over their heads, and when the three were ready, Joe checked his GPS one more time. Once he got his bearings and picked his heading, he disconnected the battery and stuck it and the GPS unit in his camel pack. He led the way into the shadows among the trees, and Brant and Eric followed behind him, both quiet as a mouse as they moved through the darkness.

Joe glanced at his watch and noted that they had a good two hours before light would begin to creep onto the forest floor. In that two hours, they had to cover just under two miles and take a position overlooking what Benny MacPhail swore was the overpass the FSS used as a meeting point. Barring the unexpected, they should have plenty of time to be in place, but Joe was still anxious.

He had scouted this route twice with Chris, and they hadn't seen any sign of patrols or scouts, but Joe still couldn't shake the feeling he was being watched. It was like an itch deep in his back between the shoulder blades. Whenever he was down range and felt that itch, it meant trouble ahead.

Chapter 41

The Road Less Traveled

President Hall sat in his office in the Capitol, a map of the southeastern US displayed on a monitor mounted behind him. The still image, taken the day before, showed all of the major cities, roads, highways, and intersections, along with county and state lines. Light blue lines depicted rivers and small red lines showed railroad tracks.

Two paths were highlighted and President Hall stared at them both. On the right was the path the Senate had debated, deliberated on, and eventually approved. It ran along Interstate 95 south from Washington, DC, to Fort Bragg. Hall had mapped out the second path that followed highway 29 south, a smaller road that was much less direct but offered the benefit of avoiding several major cities. The more circuitous path would also allow his army to approach Fort Bragg from the northwest without passing through the entire city of Fayetteville first.

Daniel stepped into the office and closed the door quietly behind him. "The Senate is assembled and ready for you, Mr. President." He glanced over at the map and his lips tightened. "Are you still planning to use the alternate route?"

"It was never an 'alternate' route, Daniel. I never intended to use the I-95 path the Senate outlined. It's too obvious and too

292

heavily traveled. I had them map that route so that if the information is leaked, our enemies would have false information in hand. They can't betray the route the FSS will take south if they don't know it, after all."

"Sir, they will not be happy at having been kept in the dark. They spent days working out the details and planning the supply routes and camps for the FSS to use."

"Yes, well, that will give them something to focus on for a bit, then," Hall said with a smile. "As long as I can direct their collective angst where I want it, I control it, and, therefore, it's not a threat to me. If they ever start planning and plotting over grievances that are not of my choosing, then I will have a problem. For now, though, I'm not worried."

"It seems like grabbing a tiger by the ears," Daniel said with a shake of his head.

"It is, but sometimes that's the only way to keep from getting your throat ripped out by the tiger. One of the problems with that, however, is I can't trust this Senate enough to leave them here alone so I can take direct command of the FSS army we're sending south, as much as I wish I could. And that brings us to you, Daniel."

"To me? Oh No! Mr. President, I assure you I am the worse person for that kind of job. I have no military experience, I have no command authority, I am not a person that soldiers would even take seriously on the battle field, sir, much less as the literal head of an army. I ..."

Daniel's voice failed him as his throat suddenly went dry. President Hall, on the other hand, was actually smiling, trying to suppress a laugh.

"Of course, you won't be in command of the FSS, Daniel. You will be my personal attaché and liaison officer to the Commander-in-Chief. I will sign orders granting you executive-level authority commiserate with a three-star general. You will exercise my directives and my directives only. I will make it clear to the commanding officer that you do not fall under his chain of command, but alongside it. And, in certain matters, your authority will outweigh his own."

Genuinely concerned at the thought of being sent into battle, Daniel appealed again to the president's better judgment. "But if you send me south with the army, who will serve in my place here? Who do you trust enough to stand beside you and guard your back?"

President Hall smiled again. "There are some things you do not need to know, Daniel. Suffice it to say that I will find a way to manage in your absence, though it will be difficult, I'm sure. Since I can't accompany the FSS forces myself, I need someone I trust completely to go along with them, and there is no one I trust more than you. You will be responsible for delivering my orders and making sure they are carried out by the FSS command structure. I want you to watch for any signs of betrayal, treason, or insubordination. I know this isn't your area of expertise, but there really isn't anyone else I can trust."

Daniel searched for some other objection, anything that might relieve him of this task. Finally, though, his shoulders slumped slightly and he let out a defeated sigh. "I guess this is one of those things I don't really have much choice about, isn't it, sir?"

Hall walked around from behind his desk. "I'm glad we understand each other, Daniel. Look at it this way, at least you'll get out of the city for a while and travel. Aside from the time on the road, though, I doubt you'll see any excitement. Even if we're met with resistance at Fort Bragg and it turns into a siege, you'll be far enough removed from the fighting not to be in any real danger. And then, once we've taken the military base, you'll be back here in the Capitol with me before you know it."

Daniel looked far less certain, but he straightened his back and nodded. "I serve at your pleasure, Mr. President. You know that. If you need me to march with the FSS when it moves south, then that's where I'll be."

Hall turned back to the screen and pointed to the alternate route. "I knew I could count on you, Daniel. The route you'll be traveling is just under four hundred miles long. Six months ago, you could have made that trip by car in less than nine hours, depending on traffic. Now it'll take you the better part of a month, and that's if we push the soldiers to the brink of exhaustion and there are no delays or detours on the way. This is why we need to take Fort Bragg, Daniel. With the hardware that's on that base, we can mobilize our entire force in hours rather than weeks."

"Sir, when do we leave?"

"Eager to get on the road already?" President Hall joked.

Daniel's tone was much more serious. "Eager to return home, sir. The sooner we leave, the sooner we can accomplish our objective and I can return here, where I belong."

"You'll leave at first light tomorrow. Orders were given day before yesterday and the commanders of the two brigades we have stationed across the Potomac have spent these two days readying their men and supplies for the move. With the men we have here in the city and the ones we have stationed on the south bank, you'll have nearly ten thousand soldiers with you when you march. Not all of those will survive the trip south, but the commanders have been ordered to fill the ranks with volunteers and conscripts as they march. My goal is to arrive at Fort Bragg by the end of November with no less than thirty thousand men ready for a siege if need be."

President Hall reached into one of his desk drawers and pulled out a thick manila envelope. "Inside you'll find your orders and your commission as the senior executive vice president of the FSS, a rank that puts you on par with the top-ranking battlefield commander, though your authority will be limited to areas I designate. Included is a key to the storage locker I had delivered to your quarters a few hours ago. There you'll find your new uniforms, a sidearm, and a satellite phone with a solar charging pack. You'll ride in one of the two dozen armored personnel carriers with the commanders, so don't worry about finding a pack or good walking boots. Other than that, everything you need will be provided for you on the march."

Daniel looked at the packet for a moment before reluctantly taking it. "What should I do if any of the commanders *do* show signs of treason or betrayal, sir?"

"That's why you're getting a side arm." Hall placed a hand reassuringly on Daniel's shoulder. "I know you're anxious, and you should be. This is a big responsibility to have thrust on you, but it's one I have absolute confidence you can carry. You're helping us take the first real step toward establishing firm control over the entire country. Once we take Fort Bragg, the Southeast will be open to us. And once we have that opening, we'll take the rest of the country. When our grandchildren read about this time in their history books, your name will be right alongside mine, like George Washington and Nathanael Greene. Together, we'll forge a new nation out of the ashes of the old, and this is where it begins."

Daniel still looked more than a little nervous as Hall ushered him out of the room. It was time for him to prepare his address to the Senate, and when he glanced back at the screen, he couldn't help but smile with satisfaction. He had always been more a man of action than a man of strategy, and now after so much planning and waiting and deliberating, it felt good to put things in motion again. If things went according to his vision, the entire country would be firmly within his control by spring. Then he would have the time to deal with those who had resisted him and betrayed him, and he would make them suffer.

Hall clicked a button on his wireless mouse, and the screen changed to a satellite image of Moscow. He felt his pulse begin to pound as the adrenaline of rage flooded his veins. His entire body trembled with barely contained fury as he stared at the image of the Russian capital.

Yes, he thought to himself, he would make them *all* pay.

Chapter 42

Intersection

Oct. 24 th 0652 EST

It was still half an hour before sunrise according to the old *Planters Almanac,* but it was getting light enough to see short distances. Overhead, a blanket of high, thin clouds had moved in and glowed a faint pink, as the sky bloomed low on the horizon. Joe, Eric, and Brant were in place high on the northeast bank of a four-lane highway as it approached an intersection. Joe knew these roads well, and he knew the overpass ahead was called Spies Road, a fitting name given the circumstances.

Joe was on point with Brant and Eric flanking him deeper in the shadows of the trees. Joe was confident in their abilities, but he didn't know if snipers had slipped in place or not. And, when in doubt, he liked to play it safe. That meant keeping his son alive, regardless of how hard he might protest the protection.

They had been in place over an hour and a half, watching and waiting as the shadows around them paled in the early dawn. Now they could see the overpass and the deep shadows beneath, but still, nothing moved. Joe was tense, and he could sense the tension in the two younger men as well. They were all on edge and had been all night as they crept through the darkness.

Above the early-morning sounds, Joe became aware of the faint hum of engines moving in his direction. This was the reason they had come—the moment they had to witness.

The sound of a diesel engines grew louder from behind Joe's right shoulder, and shortly, a line of pickup trucks, some with dual rear axles, passed on the other side of the road, their headlights off. The trucks pulled up to the overpass and turned in a wide U-turn to face the way they had come. Five trucks in all—four of them lined up behind the lead vehicle.

The doors opened, and two or three men stepped out of each vehicle. Joe noted that two men sat in the bed of the lead vehicle. Through the infrared spotter's scope, he could see that all of the men carried long guns. At this distance and in such poor light, he couldn't tell what they were, but it hardly mattered. He imagined they would be similar to the mix they'd collected at the church, with possibly a skew toward higher-end equipment since there were government sponsored.

The two men who had stepped out of the lead truck stayed back from the group that milled around under the overpass. It was almost light enough to switch off the infrared filter on the scope, but Joe could still see tiny flashes when they lit cigarettes and the brief spikes of flame sparkled across the image, so he left it on. He wished for the thousandth time that he had a parabolic microphone in his field kit and made a mental note to work on plans for how to construct one out of scavenged material.

If he'd had a microphone, even a small one with the correctly shaped parabolic focus, he could have heard at least some of what the two men closest to him were saying. With only his ears, he heard murmurs and mumbles but nothing more concrete. It was frustrating, so he focused on the men themselves rather than their conversations.

He made mental notes of their height and build, their clothes, and how they stood. Some of them shifted weight constantly; others preferred to half-lean with their weight all on one side or the other. A handful stood with their knees slightly bent, weight balanced on the balls of their feet, ready to move in an instant. Their heads moved the most as they checked their flanks and looked at their back trail. Most of them put their backs against a truck or one of the concrete supports so no one and nothing could get behind them.

Those were the most dangerous ones. Some men would crumble under fire. But there were those dangerous few who looked for others like themselves. They would be the most trouble in a fight.

A new set of headlights drew Joe out of his thoughts. A line of vehicles approached from south, and the group under the overpass parted as it grew near. The two men in the lead truck walked to the overpass and stood shoulder to shoulder. The sky was brighter, and Joe could see a pattern in the blue flannel shirts the men wore. Coupled with identical khaki pants, they were definitely part of a civilian group, but what group, Joe wondered.

The approaching vehicles resolved into a delta formation of Humvees that had massive brush guards over the front end and high-intensity trail lights on a roll bar that extended across the roof. Two of the vehicles had fifty caliber machine guns mounted on the roof, but they were unmanned. They slowed and parked a few dozen feet in front of the two men.

Joe reached up with his right hand and adjusted the focus on his scope. When the view stabilized again, the front passenger door of the lead Humvee was standing open, and a man in black and gray tactical gear shook hands with one from the lead pickup and slapped the other on the back as if they were old friends. Joe saw both men stiffen and knew immediately that they were not friends with the man or comfortable with the situation.

The man in tactical gear waved to the civilians by the pickups, and to Joe's surprise, they began walking forward. At the same time, more than a dozen men wearing tactical gear got out of the Humvees and began unloading supplies. They took packages, boxes, and crates off the vehicles and scanned their barcodes as they handed them off to the men in flannel shirts. Joe noticed that a few of the civilians shook hands with the tactical leader, while others looked past him as if he wasn't there. Could that mean a rift in the ranks he wondered? Some weak links in a breakable chain?

Joe also kept a close eye on the two civilian leaders. They did their jobs well, making sure the supplies kept moving and were organized in the pickups. He couldn't help but notice, though, that after their initial greetings, both men maintained more than a little distance from the tactical leader. Were they afraid of the man? Had Joe seen a glance of contempt cast in the leader's direction? Even from a distance he could sense that they wanted nothing to do with the man. They were there out of obligation or fear but definitely not because of any freely-given allegiance. Joe committed to memory as much detail about the men—civilian and military—as he could. He would likely see at least some of them again.

When the last of the supplies were loaded, the men in uniform got back in their Humvees, and the men in civilian clothes climbed back into their trucks, except for the two leaders. They stood together for a moment, their heads together in obvious discussion, and then walked over to the tactical leader. A few words were exchanged, and the tactical leader turned and walked back to his waiting convoy.

Once the leader was inside, the Humvees pulled a series of tight turns, and in a matter of seconds all of them were headed back south down Highway 74. Two men popped into view in the gun turrets and raised the .50-caliber belt-fed machine guns to face the men in the pickups. For a heartbeat, Joe's breath caught in his throat as he half expected to hear the guns tear into the civilians, but nothing happened, and the whir of the engines was soon lost to the distance between them.

The two civilian leaders, still rooted to the asphalt, exchanged a look that was both horrified and relieved and walked back to their truck without a word. Their doors slammed shut, and the convoy started moving. Joe sat motionless as the headlights swept over him. He was thankful they were in the opposite lanes, but he doubted they'd have seen him either way.

Still, Joe remained motionless long after the sound of the engines had faded to nothing behind him. Brant and Eric were both under strict instructions not to move a muscle until he did, and Joe hoped they listened. One of the most effective counter surveillance and counter recon measures was to deploy your own surveillance and reconnaissance team to watch the objective while concealed. This was a long-distance game of chicken with an opponent who may or not even be there.

Time dragged by, though, and after an hour sitting motionless, Joe was beginning to think it could be safe to move before sunset. It was around then that he began to hear the unmistakable hum of engines again. As he watched the intersection, two of the Humvees returned, one with the mounted weapon and one without. As the vehicles pulled up on the side of the road just on the other side of the overpass, Joe watched as two shapes that looked far too large to be men walked down the angled embankment of the highway onramp.

They were snipers in ghillie suits, and one climbed into the back of each of the waiting vehicles. The two Humvees pulled tight

U-turns and sped away into the distance. Joe waited until the sun was high overhead and hot enough to make him sweat in his stifling camouflage despite the cool breeze before he risked standing. He moved slowly at first, partly from being stiff and partly from a fear that there might still be a hidden pair of eyes in the distance. If that were the case, he wanted to expose the smallest areas possible first, so he raised his hands and feet, stretched his arms and elbows, then his knees. He finally worked into a squatting position before fully standing and signaling for Eric and Brant to join him.

"Who were those men?" Eric asked as he wiped sweat from his forehead.

"That was the enemy. This is one of their meeting points for resupply. Benny was brought here a couple of times to inspect medical shipments and catalogue the contents, so he remembered the area."

Brant fidgeted from one foot to the other, visibly frustrated that they had come and would leave empty handed. He hated the FSS for what they'd done to Tom, and he had turned that hatred into anger and aggression. "Why did we come all the way out here just to watch them get more stuff that we don't have?"

"Don't worry, Brant," Joe reassured him, "the next time we come out here it won't be to watch."

Chapter 43

War!

President Hall stood silent before the assembled Senate. The senators had been gathered for hours, waiting, before he had finally arrived to give his address, and now he stood silent for another fifteen minutes. A few had started whispering to each other in hushed tones, careful to become silent and avoid his harsh gaze when it passed their way.

Finally, the clock on the wall chimed ten o'clock, and as if at that signal, the president gripped the podium before him and began speaking. "For fifteen minutes I've stood before you," he said suddenly into the silence. "Now, imagine that ten million people were dying each minute for those fifteen minutes. That would be a hundred and fifty million people dead. Picture now, if you will, that these one hundred and fifty million people were all Americans. And not soldiers, mind you, though that would be bad enough. No, these are women and children, the elderly and the ill, the people who need our help and our protection the most. And we let them down, We let them die."

Hall paused here, looking at each senator in turn. "Well, it's the truth. They *are* dead, though it didn't happen in the span of fifteen minutes. It's been more than two months since the Blackout, and the death toll here in the US has probably reached a hundred and fifty million. If it hasn't yet, it will before long. Starvation, thirst, dysentery, violence raging in cities and suburbs alike. People are dying out there right now, slow and painful deaths, isolated and alone.

"Sitting here in our comfortable halls and plush apartments with full bellies and clean water brought to us at our leisure, it's easy not to think about such things. But it's our job to think about them. We are the leaders of this country now, and our fellow citizens will be looking to us for shelter, for sustenance, and for protection.

"I know it's probably the last thing any of us wanted to be faced with in our tenure, but there is a war raging right now, right outside these walls," Hall said, sweeping his arms around him. "The city itself is relatively safe, but how far does one have to go into the countryside on either side of the Potomac to run into bands of thieves and worse? Desperate people do desperate and terrible things just to survive. That's what our countrymen are facing out there every single minute of every single day."

Hall paused, his breath heaving in and out as passion and adrenaline took over. "And in the middle of all of that, we now face yet another threat. The small contingent we sent south to help restore order to Charlotte, North Carolina, has come under heavy attack. Another group in the Midwest, working to reactivate the railway lines that have pumped with our nation's lifeblood for more than a century, has also gone silent. These brave men and women serving with the Federal Security Services in Charlotte represent our front lines, and they are under assault."

What had been whispers moments before had turned to murmurs of uncertainty and a few hints at anger. The president saw his opening and he pounced. "But we are not going to let them suffer this assault alone. We are going to respond. At my direction, some of you have been involved in drawing up marching plans for our forces to head south. This has become far more common knowledge than I had intended, but at this point that doesn't matter anymore. There it is. We are marching south, ladies and gentlemen of the Senate. We are marching to war!"

There was a brief pause as Hall's last word echoed in the silent chamber. And then, from somewhere in the back of the assembled Senate, one man started to cheer. The Chamber followed suit and erupted in a cacophony of sound as the senators and the security service personnel alike roared and cheered at the tops of their lungs.

The reaction startled President Hall a bit, and he blinked as the waves of approval rolled over him like waves thundering against the shore. As he looked out at the Senate, one man caught his eye. He was standing and clapping like the rest, but his face was unreadable, emotionless. He never cheered, only clapped and moved lifelessly with the crowd.

It was Senator Coleman, the young man from Kentucky who had been scheduled to administer the oath of allegiance and obedience to the late Senator MacArthur. Even as he thought the name, the president had to fight the urge to look down at the dark stain where the senator had fallen.

He often thought about that moment when he first realized that he was going to kill the man, and he wondered what might have happened if he had decided differently. There were nights he would wake up in a cold sweat, gripping the sheets with clenched fists. He could never remember the dream that had jolted him awake, only the name whispering in his head for the rest of the night.

Hall thought it ridiculous that the man responsible for the millions of deaths he'd just described could be haunted so deeply and so darkly by the ghost of one old and largely forgotten senator who had decided to buck the system at the wrong moment in his career. He just could not understand how that was possible. But there it was.

As Hall's eyes met the eyes of the Kentucky senator, all of those thoughts flashed through his mind in an instant. His mood shifted, and he slammed his fist down on top of the podium hard enough to make the microphone ring in the speakers. The sharp, high-pitched feedback cut through the cheers and echoed off the walls for a moment before fading.

In the silence that fell, President Hall cleared his throat before speaking. "This is not a time for celebration," he said somberly. "There will be Americans put in harm's way. This is a time for reflection and a time for commitment. And that is why my Vice President Daniel Arnold will help lead the charge south. He will accompany the column as they make their way to Fort Bragg, and from there on to Charlotte, and then into South Carolina. Vice President Arnold will be my eyes and ears on the ground with our forces, and he'll be in direct contact with me via satellite communications. Based on his advice, the field commander's advice, and my own tactical directive, we will track down and destroy whoever is attacking our security forces and putting the safety and security of this nation at risk."

Before cheers could erupt again, Hall held up a hand and said, "Senator Coleman, you will report to my office later. My officers will show you the way."

"Thank you, Mr. President," Senator Coleman answered without hesitation, "but I know the way to your office."

Hall smiled. "I'm sure you do, Senator," he replied. "The officers will be along just the same."

The Senator nodded, but he suddenly looked as if he didn't feel well. President Hall smiled in spite of himself before turning back to the body as a whole. "The rest of you are to begin finding ways to fund the food and medical supplies this force is going to need. We have access to a limited number of supply caches this side of the Mississippi at the moment, and that limitation has our hands tied. We need food, ammo, and medical supplies, and it's your job to find them so our soldiers have what they need to get the job done."

The Senate responded in unison with a resounding, "Yes, sir!"

Hall gave a jerk of his head toward the doors of the Chamber. "The Senate is dismissed," he said.

The Senators stood and filed out of the Chamber in orderly rows, each waiting their turn. Whatever might have happened differently if he'd chosen another path, it was clear to President Hall that executing the senator had cowed the Senate. But he feared it had also planted some deep-seated seeds of hatred and malice against himself in some of their minds and hearts.

Those were the kinds of seeds that could take years to sprout but could bear some terrible fruit. That much the president knew for certain for he had experienced the fruit of those seeds himself. And that fruit of long-harbored vengeance often tastes the most bitter to the one who first cultivated it. Even if that were the case, there was little he could do about it now except remain vigilant.

Once the senators were gone, Hall turned to Vice President Arnold and smiled as he shook his hand. "You are doing your nation a great service, Daniel. Your name will be written in the history books alongside names like Sherman, Grant, and Washington."

"Yes, but those men all knew what they were doing," Arnold mumbled. "I'm a complete novice at war."

Hall smiled a cold, calculating smile that never quite reached his eyes. "Well, there's only one way to solve that particular problem, isn't there? Good thing you're going off to help lead a war. And good thing you'll have me on the other end of a sat-phone telling you what moves to make and when. Don't worry so much, Daniel. It's going to be fine."

Daniel didn't say anything else, but he looked far from convinced. Still, the President had other things that needed his attention. "Good luck, Daniel, and God's speed. I'll be in touch."

Before Arnold could respond, Hall turned and headed for the hallway beyond the Senate Chamber as two men in uniform opened the doors. His security detail enveloped him as he stepped into the less-secure area, cutting off his view back inside even before the doors swung closed. Aside from his security detail of more than a dozen men, the president was alone in the hall. For a brief moment, despite the marble floors and ceiling and despite the blast-resistant windows, he felt exposed.

Hall adjusted his belt, and as he did so he checked his pistol to make sure it was clear and ready to draw. He had two spare magazines in a shoulder rig on his left side and the forty-five caliber Colt on his right. He still felt alone and exposed, but at least he felt less vulnerable.

He walked into his office, poured himself a bourbon from the glass decanter on a side table, and sat behind the massive oak desk that had spent years in the Oval Office. The Resolute Desk, it had been named, and for good reason. Behind it, many of the decisions that had shaped the world for the last half century had been made and delivered. Hall planned to carry that small bit of history from the old country over to the new, but his nostalgia for the old Republic ended at fine furniture, good liquor, and the weapons of war. That was why he had moved the seat of power from the White House to his new Presidential Palace.

He took a sip of the bourbon and then tapped a small wooden gavel on the side of the desktop. A security service agent opened the door and stuck his head inside. "Send for Senator Coleman. Have the guards arrive with him in exactly twenty minutes."

The agent nodded. "Yes, Mr. President," he said as he pulled his head back and closed the door.

Hall sat back in his overstuffed leather executive chair and collected his thoughts. He held the glass of bourbon in his hand but didn't take another drink. He enjoyed the taste, and the bourbon he'd poured was a long-time favorite of his from a small distillery deep in the hills of Kentucky. At least, that was what the bottle said, and he'd never had any desire to destroy that particular illusion, if that's what it was.

As much as the President wanted to finish the glass, he couldn't afford even the smallest impairment right now. Still, he wanted the smell of it on his breath and he wanted the Senator from Kentucky to see that he recognized fine American liquor. Those subtle, unspoken connections would begin to form, and if he played his cards right, he might get the man off balance. That was his only shot at finding out what really happened on the night he'd spent preparing Senator MacArthur to take his oath.

He'd read the transcripts that Senator Coleman provided, but now he wanted to hear it from the man himself. Hall wanted to read Coleman's face as he answered questions without a chance to prepare his response. He wanted to see how deep this story went because he had a strong suspicion that there was a great bit of detail that the Senator had either conveniently forgotten or deliberately omitted, and he meant to find out every single thing that was said between the two men.

A firm knock at the door was followed a few moments later by another. President Hall took a deep breath and let it out slowly. "Come in," he called. As the door opened, he stood and leaned slowly forward, timing his movements so that he was just setting down his whiskey glass on a cork coaster as Senator Coleman stepped into view. "Thank you for escorting the Senator," Hall said to the guards. "You can wait in the hall."

The leader of the security detail nodded and motioned to the rest of his men. They filed out of the office tactically, the first three men out taking watch stations so the other two senior members could step out into the hallway with protection.

Hall let the door shut without acknowledging the senator, and he continued to stand in silence for the next two or three minutes. The senator stood with his back rigid and his jaw clenched but refused to even turn his head the few inches it would have taken to look in the president's direction. Hall had set the tone by speaking politely to the guards and dismissing them first, and Coleman was determined to remain just as aloof.

Finally, Hall gave the senator the slightest smile that wasn't really a smile. "Thank you for coming, Senator. Please, take a seat."

Coleman sat stiffly in one of the two armless chairs that faced the massive Resolute Desk. Hall took off his coat and hung it from a spare hanger he kept on the wall behind the desk. When he turned back to face the senator, Hall noticed the other man's eyes go immediately to his nickel-plated pistol. His face paled slightly and he swallowed loudly in spite of himself.

"Yes, it's unfortunate what happened with Senator MacArthur," Hall said, breaking the silence so abruptly that Senator Coleman

311

actually jumped in his seat. "Sorry to startle you there, Senator Coleman, would you like a glass of bourbon?" Hall raised his own glass and nodded. "It's a fine small-batch distillery that tends to operate somewhat off the books. They benefit from the fact that many of their best clients are also very powerful men. I knew several senators before this all happened who were on a permanent guest list of the distillery's owners. Very good stuff."

Senator Coleman glanced at the bourbon, and his face somehow paled more as he shook his head. The sight of the pistol had unnerved the man more than Hall would have thought.

Hall leaned back comfortably and looked directly into Coleman's eyes. "Senator Coleman, let's discuss what you and the late Senator MacArthur talked about on his last night on this earth."

Coleman shifted slightly in his seat and Hall smiled. He didn't want to admit it, but he actually liked interrogations. It wasn't the opportunity to inflict physical pain that excited him so much as the chance to wring every inch of information—every secret—from the one who fought with every fiber of being to stop him. It was the ultimate test of wills and wits, and he relished in it.

He knew he would get the answers and the secrets he sought. He always did, in the end. The only question was how long and how difficult the fight would prove.

Chapter 44

Sticks and Stones

"What's your name again?" the young man asked.

"I'm Hunter Tyson, but everyone calls me Sticks," Sticks answered. It was the fourth time the young man had asked, and Sticks was getting a little tired of answering the question.

"Oh, okay," the young man said. "I'm Tippy. I can remember faces real well, but it takes me a while to catch on with names."

"So I've gathered," Sticks said in return.

"Why do people call you Sticks?" Tippy asked.

Sticks chose to take that as a good sign. It was the first question he'd asked that the answer wasn't someone's name. The rest of their eight-man team was already ignoring Tippy, and Sticks feared if Tippy continued his chatter, the others might turn violent.

Sticks pulled Tippy over to the side. "Look, they call me Sticks because I've had the best batting average on every baseball team I've been on since I was seven years old. Not too many homeruns, but I had a decent number of RBIs and a ton of base hits. The name started in little league and it just stuck, I guess. I thought it would wear off when I quit playin ball, but it didn't."

313

"Hey, where are we going?" Tippy asked, suddenly concerned that they were starting to lose sight of the others.

"I'm pulling you over here into the bushes. You're loud, and if you draw a scout or a sniper to you, I don't want them coming down on the rest of us and taking us out too."

"Are you going to leave me here?" Tippy asked.

Sticks shook his head. "No, Tippy, I'm not going to leave you. But you need to be quiet, okay? There are people trying to find us and we don't want them to. So, we have to be quiet."

Tippy nodded. "I can understand that. It's like a game I used to play, but more serious. Dad tells me that sometimes. And then I have to be really still and quiet. Who are the men he's talking to?"

"They're my boss," Sticks answered. The kid was observant and smart; he just had an awkward way of asking questions. "Your dad had some information my bosses needed and he was nice enough to bring it to them."

"What was the information?" Tippy asked, looking down at his shoes.

"I don't know," Sticks admitted. "I'm not important enough to know, I guess, in the grand scheme of things."

Tippy smiled. "There are things Dad doesn't tell me, too. But I find them out anyway. Sometimes he whispers in his sleep."

Sticks couldn't help but chuckle at that. He turned in a slow circle, keeping watch all around them. "Seriously, though, Tippy," he said again in a whisper, "you need to keep it down. We have to go back with the others, but to do that you need to be quiet, okay? No more questions."

"One more, then, before we go," Tippy continued without waiting, "Are your bosses going to send us back home?"

Sticks had to pause for a moment as he suddenly felt overwhelmed with empathy for the young man. He was scared, isolated in strange place, and it seemed all he really wanted was to be home. A feeling Sticks could well identify with.

"I wish I had more answers for you, Tippy," Sticks said. "But I just don't know."

Tippy was quiet and very still for a while and continued to stare at his feet, but his face had a blank look like his focus was entirely somewhere else. "I don't want to go home," he said. "Home scares me."

Sticks didn't know what to say to that, so he didn't say anything. He just pointed off through the woods and held a finger to his lips. Tippy nodded and they walked in silence back to the forward outpost. This was the outer-most perimeter for the Kansas City Brigade, as they had taken to calling themselves. They were fifteen miles outside the city at a crossroads on some back-country highways. This was not a likely place to get to by accident, and that's why it had been chosen as the rendezvous point for the scouts sent into St. Louis.

Tippy and his father strolling into camp with white flags raised was quite unexpected. The father immediately claimed he'd been sent by one of the allied scouts and then shared a code-word that the commanders had taken without hesitation. Sticks had watched the whole thing happen while he was standing watch at one of the outposts.

At first, he had counted himself lucky to be privy to such intel, but then he was put on protection detail and told to watch out for the kid while the father met with the higher ups. He had trained for a lot of things in the military and then while in the National Guard, but he had never trained for this. He felt like he was making a complete blunder with all of his efforts, but the kid was still tagging along with him, and when Sticks joined the rest of the advance recon team manning the outpost, Tippy stayed within a few steps of him with his back turned to the others. He clearly didn't trust the rest of them.

"I don't think the other men like me," Tippy said after a few moments. He was staring at his shoes again. "I can tell by how they look at me and whisper. Kids at my school used to do the same thing when they didn't like me. They thought I didn't notice, but I did."

"Do you like school?" Sticks asked, trying to change the subject.

Tippy snorted. "I hate it," he growled. "I already know most of what the teachers are trying to teach and the other kids don't like me." Tippy kicked at a few pieces of dirt by his right toe and didn't say anything for a minute. "I'm different, and they pick on me and make fun. Mom used to say it doesn't matter cause they're all stupid heads, but it matters to me."

"I'm sorry, Tippy. Kids can be really mean sometimes."

This new topic wasn't making Sticks feel any more comfortable. When he'd been in school, more often than not, he was one of the kids doing the picking, not the one being picked on, so he knew the kinds of kids Tippy was talking about. He wanted to tell the young man that the kids picking on him didn't mean to hurt him and that they were really just joking around, but he remembered his own time in middle and high school too well to lie to the kid. Instead, he tried to shift the topic of conversation and his own guilt.

"Why did you and your dad come out here Tippy? Did something go wrong at home?"

316

Tippy's head snapped up and his eyes suddenly narrowed. "Dad said I'm not supposed to talk about that to strangers. He said it might be dangerous."

"Do I seem dangerous to you, Tippy?" Sticks asked, and Tippy's eyes dropped to the M-4 carbine in Sticks' hands. "Besides, I'm not a stranger anymore, not really. We know each other's names and you've been talking to me for nearly two hours now. We're friends, right?"

Tippy nodded hesitantly. "I think so. You haven't picked on me or been mean to me, and that's part of being a friend, right?"

Sticks nodded. "Exactly. So, why are you and your dad here? Are you running from something?"

Tippy shook his head. "A man came to our house," the young man said hesitantly. "He was hurt bad and bleeding, and he was really scared. Dad tried to help him, but the man got sick. It was the same kind of sick Mom got when she cut her leg after the lights went out, so we knew what was going to happen. The man got worse and worse, and he was in a lot of pain."

Tippy pushed at a half-buried rock with his foot, but the rock didn't budge. "The man started talking about Kansas City and how important it was for him to get word back. I don't know what he meant cause dad told me to go into the other room and put my fuzzy ears on. That's what he calls my ear muffs. I used to call them that, but then I grew up. My fuzzy ears make loud noises not as scary, and they make it so I can't hear stuff my dad don't want me to hear."

"What about the man?" Sticks asked. "What did he say? What happened to him?"

Tippy gave a small shrug. "Dad never told me what he said. He just told me we had to take a trip. The other man died like Mom did. He went to sleep that night and he just didn't wake up the next morning. I was glad too, cause that means he's not hurting anymore. He was really hurting bad."

"How did you know where to come to find us?" Sticks asked.

"The man told my dad," Tippy answered with a smile. "He pointed it out on a roadmap and everything. Dad said it was important for us to come here to tell you what the man said and to show you what he gave us."

"What did he give you?" Sticks asked.

Tippy shrugged again. "I'm not sure what it is, really. Dad thought it was pretty important, though. It looks like a credit card, but a lot thicker. On the front were some numbers like on a clock, but they didn't tell the right time. And on both sides was a big yellow circle with red triangles inside."

As Tippy described the object, Sticks felt a cold knot of fear growing in the pit of his stomach. Sticks had an uncle who had been in the navy and had worked on the reactors in nuclear submarines for more than twenty years. Above his uncle's fireplace, sitting on the mantle in a frame, was a small badge just like the one Tippy had described. It was an early warning badge designed to show when the person wearing it had been exposed to radiation. The only people Sticks had ever heard of who were given those badges were the people who worked on nuclear reactors and the ones who handled nuclear weapons.

Sticks started to ask Tippy another question, but the two were interrupted. The post commander had come back with Tippy's father, and the boy ran straight to the older man. Sticks looked at

318

the father again but with a different perspective on who he might be. This time he saw things he had missed before.

This man was no stranger to violence, for one thing. He had scars across his face and forearms that were fresh and bright, but there were older scars there too, some deep. And the way he carried himself said that he knew how to move when he needed to and could dish violence out at least as well as he could take it— probably better, given the fact that he was standing here now. He had a small skinning knife at his left side, a longer, thicker knife on his right hip, and another in his right boot. There might have been more hidden that Sticks couldn't see, but those were enough.

Tippy's father put his left arm around the boy's shoulders and pulled him close, his right hand staying close to the handle of the knife on that side of his belt. It was a practiced move and one that he was comfortable making. If the situation were to go badly, they'd have a difficult time keeping the father restrained in close quarters like this. Things could get very messy very quickly.

The outpost commander was a former army lieutenant, but he seemed to know his stuff. He was a little older than the typical lieutenants, but he was still in impeccable condition. Sticks had heard that LT, as he preferred to be called, was a former enlisted who was commissioned shortly after the Blackout, but he didn't know for sure if that was true. What he did know was the man was intimidating. He stood five feet, ten inches and was built like a UFC fighter. He was one of the best in the brigade at recon and advanced operations and had been put in command of the best recon platoon in the brigade.

As the commander approached, one of the men called out "Officer on deck!" and the men all snapped to attention.

Sticks wasn't sure who had called it out, but it might have been one of the former SEALs with their group. These were the best of the best of every branch of the armed forces cobbled into one group and they were trained to be on the absolute front lines of the war. They were also meticulous when it came to following military protocol and showing respect due the officers leading them.

That's why Sticks was here. He always had a knack for excelling at whatever he put his mind to, and the military had proven no different. His short career in the army had been one of intense action overseas, and he'd been decorated more than once for his dedication to duty and his bravery. Now he'd earned a spot on Romeo Recon Platoon, and that had landed him at this outpost at this moment, where he had landed babysitting duty.

The commander took one look at Sticks and froze. "Jesus H," he started, shaking his head. "You spoke to the boy, didn't you, Sticks? Damnit, Specialist, I have told you a thousand times, if I don't tell you to say it, keep your lips pressed firmly together and breathe through your nose!"

"Sir, you told me to keep an eye on him," Sticks said.

"I know what I told you, Sticks. I'm not a moron," LT snapped back. "Did I tell you to have a friggin heart to heart with the boy?"

"Sir, I had to talk to him to get him to trust me. And I had to get him to trust me so I could get him away from the other guys. He was already talking a mile a minute, and they were about to lose it. Some of those guys have a pretty short fuse and I didn't want one of them to snap at him."

"Well aren't you just as sweet as a buttercup angel?" LT asked sarcastically. "Now back to my original question, what did the boy say to you?"

"Sir, he described something to me," Sticks said hesitantly. He was starting to wonder if he'd blown the whole thing out of proportion. He hadn't actually seen a radiation badge, and the boy could have been mistaken or dreaming the whole thing up.

"Well, Specialist, what was it?" LT asked again. This time there was a sharpness in his voice that sounded more like worry.

"He said it was something that looked like a credit card but thicker and with digital numbers on top. And he said it had a very specific symbol on the front and back, a yellow circle with red triangles."

"Something a lot like this, then?" LT asked as he stuck a hand into one of his shirt pockets and pulled out a small zip lock bag and tossed it to Sticks.

Sticks caught the bag and found himself holding a small gray rectangular badge. On the front was a digital display with some numbers, and on the background of the front and back was the unmistakable radiation symbol. And when Sticks flipped it back over, he looked at the numbers and felt the small hairs on the back of his neck stand on end.

"Sir, have you looked at the numbers?" Sticks asked.

"Obviously I have looked at them, but I don't know what they mean," LT answered. "Do you have any ideas?"

"I had a cousin in the navy who worked on the reactor for a sub," Sticks answered. "He was retired, but he kept his radiation badge in a frame on his mantle. I asked him one time what the numbers meant. He said if they were all zeroes then the badge had never been exposed to radiation, and if there was a reading on it, then it had been. The higher the numbers and the more of them that showed, the worse the radiation dose. These numbers mean whoever was wearing this badge, they were exposed to radiation, and a good amount of it too. My uncle worked for twenty years around reactors and his number was barely half that."

"How do you remember so much about this?" LT asked. "Weren't you in the army? Last I checked, not much nuclear submarine talk in the army, Sticks."

Sticks smiled. "I would listen to my uncle's stories when I was a kid. That's why I ended up joining the military when college didn't work out the way I thought it would. I started out talking to the navy recruiters cause I wanted to work on a sub like my uncle did. Then I got to tour a sub, and those things are tiny. I don't do good in small spaces like submarines, dorm rooms, that kind of thing. So, I thought to myself, who's outside a lot? The army's outside a lot."

LT smiled and shook his head. "A genuine American hero, ladies and gentlemen."

Sticks shrugged. "Look, if I would have known we'd all end up outside marching around playing soldier anyway I would have gone and been a lifeguard at the beach somewhere. Hindsight and all that, I guess."

"Shut up, Sticks," LT said. "I've got to think something like this is important enough the commanders need to hear about it from the horse's mouth, so to speak. Sticks, you are going with me and these two back to the city. The rest of the outpost will carry on and keep a watch for any returning recon scouts. I want you at my tent and ready to move in ten minutes flat. You got it?"

"Yes sir," Sticks said and turned to go and gather his gear from the tent he shared with two other men.

"And Sticks," LT called over his shoulder as he led Tippy and his father to the edge of camp, "bring everything! I'm not sure where we're headed after this."

Chapter 45

Who We Are

Mike sat in a clearing next to a small pond, his back to the water. The group had pushed hard for two days, working their way steadily deeper into the Uwharrie National Forest, but they had gone less than twenty miles. The terrain was rough and full of hills and valleys that had to be navigated carefully. Thanks to a satellite trail map printed by the Fish and Wildlife Department, Mike had been able to keep the group off the main roads and out of sight, for the most part. But now they were running low on food and water, and people were starting to get nervous.

For a few days, the group had been scraping by on food and water they scavenged from gas stations, business parks, and abandoned homes along the way. This deep in the Uwharrie, though, there were far fewer targets of opportunity. Without food and water, the group had been slowed to a crawl, so Mike decided to set up camp for a couple of days next to the small pond. He'd caught a few fish, as had some of the others, but not enough to make a full camp-wide meal. And while the fish seemed clean enough, they questioned whether or not the water was safe, so the group had decided not to drink any of it. The last thing they needed was half the camp coming down with giardia or some other water-borne illness.

The two scouts Mike had sent out the night before to look for food and water had come back far sooner than he'd expected. Both men now sat across from him on the other side of the small campfire he'd built. "So, what did you find?" Mike asked.

"There's a group not far from here," Carter, the man on the right, said. "They're set up at a church a couple of miles east of here on that main road to the south."

Mike dug around in his pack and pulled out the trail map. He spread it on the dirt off to the side and dropped a rock on each corner to hold it down. "Okay, if we're here," he said, pointing to a clearing off of Horseshoe Bend Road, "where is the church?"

Carter traced the line of Flint Hill Road and stopped at a sharp bend to the right. "It's in this bend right here. It's a small white church right along the road. Thing is, they've got enough supplies to last a group our size two weeks, but there's only ten of them at the church. And only two of those look like they're on watch or even armed."

"Did you see anyone else come to the church while you were watching?" Mike asked. "It could be a trading post or a supply depot for a larger group. That would take fewer guards because you've got less to guard against if you assume the entire surrounding area is in friendly hands. And if that's the case, then we may have stumbled into the middle of something larger than we realize."

Carter shook his head. "I don't think so, Mike. We haven't seen signs of anyone else in this area for two days. They're all back on the other side of that bridge in one of those two towns we dodged. That means this side of the lake is pretty much fair game, unless I'm mistaken."

"What do you mean 'fair game?'" Mike asked. "You said yourself they have ten people down there. Even if that's their entire group, what right does that give us to go take what we want?"

"Not what we want," Carter snapped, "what we need. Don't you get it? We have hungry and thirsty people up here and we don't have enough clean water and good food to go around. And that's gonna get worse, not better, the longer we sit here. Those people have what we need to get on our feet again. Right now, it's survival of the strongest, and there's strength in numbers. You said that yourself when you convinced me to come with you. Now it's time to press that advantage, man."

"And what if those people don't want to give up what they have?" Mike asked. "You said you saw at least two of them with guns. What if there are more you didn't see? Or what if those two don't roll over the way you're assuming they will?"

"Like I said, we outnumber them at least three to one even if every single one of them has arms," Carter shot back. "And if it's just the two and they're stupid enough to really try and stop us, then their blood won't be on our hands."

Mike was stunned into a shocked silence. He couldn't believe what he was hearing. Carter, the man who had refused to eat so another couple's kids could have food just a week before was now ready to go down and murder people in cold blood and take what they had.

"This isn't us," Mike said softly. "This isn't who we are. This isn't who we are going to become. It can't be. We didn't survive everything we have survived this far to start just ripping each other's throats out for some food and water. We're not those people. That's why we're here."

Carter tried to look away, but Mike grabbed his collar and turned him back around. "That's why *you're* here," Mike growled. "If we were that kind of group we'd have gutted you and taken your kids and your supplies when we found you. Did we?"

Carter sat silent, and his scout partner Lewis looked like he wished he could magically disappear. He was stoically looking off to the left, refusing to acknowledge either of the men enough to even be dismissed.

Mike shook his head. "You don't get off that easy. Not after suggesting something like that. Did we gut you and your family, Carter? I want an answer."

Carter shook his head. "No."

"No," Mike agreed, releasing the man's collar. "We didn't gut you and rob you. We took you in and helped you. We protected you, and in time you helped protect us. And now you come to me with this?"

"We're desperate, Mike," Carter pleaded. "I don't know what else to do."

"Anything but that," Mike answered, holding the other man's gaze for a moment longer. Then he looked at Lewis and the rest of the small crowd that had gathered at their raised voices. "And let me be clear, in front of witnesses. Anyone caught trying to assault this group, or any other group we run across, without first being attacked will be dealt with swiftly and permanently. That kind of action will not be tolerated, and things being what they are, there's only one punishment for murder."

Mike looked around at the faces staring back at him, some of them disappointed. "If you're found guilty, I'll pull the trigger

327

myself." He paused to make sure he'd made his point. "Okay, now that that's settled, you all know your jobs. Get to them."

Mike turned back to the two scouts. "Lewis, you stay where you are and wait for Arthur to come and get you. You're going to guide the first contact group. Arthur will have the rest of the details. Carter, you're coming with me."

Mike stood and walked over to the main group of tents and ground tarps that made up the bulk of their campsite. He found Arthur already awake and sitting by a cold fire pit, a blanket wrapped around his shoulders. There had been a heavy dew the night before and everything was soaking up the moisture, which made the little bit of chill on the pre-dawn air feel ten times as cold as it really was.

"Arthur, I need you for a special project," Mike said, somewhat cryptically.

Arthur frowned. "Okay, Mike," he said hesitantly. "You know I'm right here when you need me."

"Thanks," Mike said, patting the older man on the shoulder. "Let's take a walk and I'll explain our situation."

Arthur stood and stretched a bit before following Mike down the path toward the small pond and Mike's own tent. As they walked, Mike outlined the basics of what he knew so far about the church and a possibly well-supplied group there.

By the time Mike had filled Arthur in they were back at his campfire. He stopped in front of Carter and fixed him with a withering look. "Carter here suggested that we simply raid the group at the church and take what they have because we need it. Which I, of course, rejected out of hand." Mike turned back to Arthur. "There isn't anyone else I could trust to be level-headed enough to handle this without stomping on some toes and creating an incident where one doesn't need to be."

"Handle what?" Arthur asked. "What incident? What are you talking about?"

"Arthur, I need you to go to this church and meet these people," Mike said in a rush. He held up a hand as Arthur started to protest. "You'll have three people of your choice watching your back as you talk to whomever will talk to you. From a distance, too, please. Don't get right up next to any of them—not until we know more about them."

"What do you want me to say to them?" Arthur asked. "I've got to say, Mike, we've gone out of our way not to come into contact with people as much as possible. So far that's been a pretty good way of moving and operating. Why change that?"

Mike nodded his head toward Carter. "Because of people who possibly agree with Carter here that we should just go in guns hot. Eventually, enough people will side with him, and they'll go in shooting everything that moves first and asking very few questions after. And once that starts, that mentality becomes the new normal. How do you think some of the violent groups we've seen got that way? It didn't happen overnight, I can guarantee you that. It was a slow slide from who they were to who they became."

Mike paused and fixed Carter with a look that should have bored holes straight through him. "We aren't going to start that slide. I've already made it clear to the group, and now I'm making it abundantly clear to you personally, Carter. If you try anything at all or encourage others to try something like what you suggested at first—just going in and taking what we need from the strangers— I'll shoot you myself. That's not who we are."

Carter swallowed, his face pale yet tinged with the rouge of humiliation, but he managed to nod his head. Mike turned to Lewis and officially introduced Arthur, though he was sure Lewis had at least heard who the resident medic was and would recognize Arthur's name. Carter sat on the sideline as instructed and didn't say a word.

"Arthur, Lewis is going to guide you and two support-team members to the church," Mike said. "I want Lewis to stay behind on a peak that's across the creek from the church. It's an elevated position so he should be able to keep a good over watch on your progress. The other two will shadow you down to the edge of the road, and they'll watch your back as you go in to make contact."

"I'm guessing no gun for me when I go to talk?" Arthur asked.

Mike nodded. "We need them to trust you and to at least open the door. Only way to get them to do that is if you go in alone and unarmed. They won't see the pair of rifles watching your six, though, and that's your advantage. Stay within line of sight of the spot you come out of the trees and you should be good. We've got some dead-on shots with us, so pick your team with that in mind."

"You're not coming?" Arthur asked. "I figured you'd want to be at least within earshot."

Mike shook his head. "I can't afford to leave Carter here alone with the rest of the group. He might get it in his head that he could do better convincing the others than he did me. And I don't want to take that chance."

"Jesus, man, I said I had dropped it," Carter growled. "What's it gonna take?"

Mike shook his head. "I don't know, Carter. You hurt a lot of trust with this. I don't know what it's going to take to build that back. Until you do, I'm going to keep a close watch on you. And that's just how it's going to be."

Mike turned back to Arthur. "I'll get everyone ready to move, and I'll take a group down where this road intersects Flint Mill Road. We'll wait for you there, just in case you need some help getting out." Mike stepped over to his tent and rummaged through his pack. When he came back he handed Lewis an orange pistol. "This is an emergency flare gun. It's only got one shot, and it's simple to use. Cock the hammer back, point it up, and then drop your aim about ten degrees from vertical. Pull the trigger."

Mike caught Lewis's eye as the man took the flare gun. "I've got two extra flares for this and no more, so use it only if the shit really hits the fan. Got it? I mean there better be bullets flying. Otherwise save the flare."

"I understand," Lewis said. He stood and followed Arthur back to the main camp so Arthur could pick the other two members of his team and they could be on their way.

From the other side of the fire, Carter stretched his legs and looked up at Mike. "So, can I go back to my tent or am I still grounded?"

"I don't care what you do, Carter," Mike replied, "so long as you stay in camp. Until this whole thing is resolved with the people at that church, one way or another, I want you in camp."

"You know this isn't some military unit, right?" Carter asked, his temper flaring. "And you're not some general with stars on your shoulders. We're just people, and you're just some guy that people listen to. That's it. You can't force me to do anything and you sure can't force me to stay here or anywhere else."

Mike's eyes narrowed and he leaned forward, one hand resting casually on the handle of his Beretta. "You're right. This isn't the army or the military, and I can't force anyone to stay. In fact, if you really want to leave and go your own way, that's your call. But you should understand one thing. If you going your own way means you attack this church or the people camped there, then you'll find me standing between you and them."

Mike leaned back and shook his head. "That's the part you don't get. I brought you people here. Me. No one else did that. I did. So, I am responsible for everything that you all do and everything that happens as a result of you being here. And I'm not going to be responsible for some massacre."

"I know you think you were protecting the group and providing for us," Mike said after a moment. "But you have to realize that if we give up who we are in order to survive, then survival isn't worth it anymore. There are plenty of people out there willing to do whatever it takes just to keep breathing another day. But if we're going to have any hope of rebuilding after this, we have to be some of the people who don't lose the part of themselves that's civil, that's restrained. There may not be any law out here, but there's still right and wrong. If you can recover that belief and that principle, then you can find a place here with us."

Mike paused for a long moment to let his words sink in before continuing. "But if you can't get back to that place, if you can't wrap your head around the two fundamental concepts of love thy neighbor *and* defend you and yours to the absolute end, then you won't have a place with us—you can't have a place with us. And it's best you figure that out now, before we go any further."

"What, are you exiling me?"

Mike shook his head. "No, not yet, anyway. I just want to be honest on where we stand. And you've got to know that's a possibility. I hope it's one that stays just a possibility, but that's more up to you than anyone else."

"What if others want to go with me?"

"I'm not going to stand in anyone's way," Mike answered. "I've made it clear from the beginning that I have a destination in mind, and anyone who wants to come with me is welcome to tag along. I'm not forcing anyone to take one step they don't want to take, but if you're going to follow me, then you follow my lead. Period. That's not negotiable, Carter. You've got to understand that."

Carter stood up and faced Mike head on. "If I had it to do over again, I'd just get me some people together and do it," he said. "We could have had this done by now and no one else the wiser. Three to one advantage and we could take the high ground on both sides. It wouldn't have been a real fight. And you know it. What happens when the day comes that a group says no? Will you be able to do what it takes to make sure our people survive? Cause on that day, surviving *will* be enough."

"I'll cross that bridge when and if I come to it," Mike answered. "For now, you're here, and that means you're going to follow my lead. Get the rest of the camp on their feet at sunrise. Cold meals only for breakfast, so jerky and meal bars. That kind of thing. No fires. And I want all six three-man forage teams to report to my tent as soon as they're done eating and gearing up."

Mike pointed to the full expanse of the camp around them. "The rest of the group needs to start breaking camp as soon as possible. It's your job to make sure everyone here is ready to move as quickly as possible. If they're not ready and the word comes to move, I'm coming after you personally to find out why. Now, you've got a lot to do and only about an hour and a half to get it all set up, so you'd better get moving."

Carter turned to go, but Mike caught his arm and held it. "I'm putting a lot of trust in you to handle getting the camp ready to move, but I want you to know that it's not blind trust. There will be people—not just me—keeping an eye on you."

Mike held Carter's stare and then let go of his arm. As he watched him walk away, headed for the main body of the camp, the sun broke over the edge of the horizon and bathed the tops of the low mountains around them with a deep, ruby red light. Mike tried to push thoughts about Carter and what he'd tried to get the group to do out of his mind as he ducked into his tent and began gathering his rifle, extra magazines, and a few bottles of water. The rest of his meager belongings went into a pack. He rolled up the tarp he'd been using as a makeshift tent along with the sleeping bag and foam pad he slept on. He tied the bundle to the bottom of the pack and set the bundle by his campfire.

Already, the foraging teams were beginning to show up with their weapons, ammo, and field packs. When they were all assembled, Mike pulled the three youngest aside. All three boys were under the age of sixteen but had proven themselves skilled at hunting, fishing, and shooting. Mike motioned for them to take a knee.

"Okay, I have a special task for you three. I want you to go back to your families and get out of your field gear. Help around the camp as much as you can, but keep Mr. Carter in your sight at all times. Don't be too obvious about it, but make sure there's at least one, preferably two of you who can put eyes on him at any given moment. If he starts meeting with people individually, one right after the other, or if he has a group meeting and he seems like he doesn't want anyone else to see it, one of you come and find me. I'll be at the end of the road with the rest of the men. Do you understand?"

The three young men nodded. They might not understand why they were being told to watch Carter, but he knew they would do it. And for now, that was enough. Mike stood and turned back to the rest of the team members who watched the youngsters go. That was their unspoken signal that whatever they were about to do was going to get serious.

"All right, I'll keep this short and sweet," Mike began. He laid out the situation as quickly as he could. "If things go badly at the church, or if they have more people than we think they do, then it could get really nasty out there. If there's anyone who wants to opt out, I won't hold it against you. You can go with the others and maybe help flank the church from the hill on the other side of the road."

He waited, but no one moved. "All right, then. I guess that means we're all in. Arthur should be heading to the church to test the waters. That means we need to get in place, so let's hit the road."

Mike led the group as they jogged down Horseshoe Bend Road toward Flint Mill Road. Around them, the sunlight had already made its way down the edges of the hills and low mountains. It would be a while before the valley bottom was in sunlight, but morning was well on its way. As he ran, Mike kept glancing to his left, to the east, looking for the flare that he hoped he wouldn't see.

Chapter 46

The Messenger

Commander Price clicked on the monitor, a warm cup of coffee in his hand. The screen flickered a moment as the video feed went through the verification and decryption protocols and then flashed to life. The image on the screen was the headquarters that Colonel Darius had established in a fortified warehouse that also served as a temporary garrison for incoming recruits and soldiers.

At one glance, Price knew that the colonel was not happy. "All right, Colonel, out with it. You didn't get me out of bed this early for nothing, so what's going on?"

"Sir, there's something you need to see.

He held a small rectangular badge up to the video camera on his end of the feed. The image was clear and unmistakably showed a commonly used radiation detection badge. Price felt his hair stand on end. The numbers were not zeroed out. In fact, they were quite high if the badge had been worn by a single individual per the design.

"Where did you find this, Colonel?"

"Actually, I didn't find it," Darius replied as he dropped the badge onto the desk next to him. He sat on the desk and absently wiped his fingers off on his pants. "The badge came to me. A man and his son showed up at an outpost that was supposed to be top secret, need to know. He knew exactly where to find us and just walked into camp without anyone seeing him first. The scouts were all freaked out, and some of them were more than a little pissed that he was able to bypass the security measures that way."

"Colonel, the badge?" Commander Price prodded. Darius was brilliant tactically, but he rambled constantly.

"Yes, the man said he found one of our scouts on the outskirts of St. Louis," Colonel Darius replied. "The scout was badly injured and near death, but the man brought him into his home and tried to treat his wounds. The scout stabilized for a time, but infection set in, and he faded pretty quickly. Near the end, he gave the badge to the man and told him it had to come back here so we could figure out what to do about it. He told the man how to find us and told the man's son the GPS coordinates. The kid is a savant or something, but he remembered the coordinates and was able to plot a course for the dad on a road atlas. They stayed off the highways and made it right to our doorstep without coming across anyone else the entire time."

Price tried to process this information dump a piece at the time. He was looking for any gaps in the story, anything that didn't make sense. He was suspicious of such a perfect lead falling into their lap like this, especially after so long without any word from any of the scouts they had sent to St. Louis. It seemed like bait to him.

"Did the scout tell the man he'd seen a bomb or missile?" Price asked after a moment.

Darius shook his head. "Nothing like that. He said the scout never told him where or how he came to have the badge, just that he had taken it from an enemy soldier. Apparently, the scout held on until the very last few moments of his life, trying to relay the information, and he was having trouble getting it out clearly. He was barely able to repeat the GPS coordinates twice before he died, from what the man and his son both said."

"Colonel Darius, this could be a serious threat or it could be an elaborate hoax," Price said. "Either way, I don't see how we can allow it to affect our original plans."

"Sir, I'm not sure I follow. If this badge really came from an FSS officer in St. Louis, then they could have a nuke there. How can that not affect our plans?"

"Colonel, this man and his son made it to you undetected," Price began, "and that's after taking care of our injured scout. Whatever the FSS has or had in St. Louis, if they wanted it in Kansas City it would be there by now. I'm not convinced that's their target, but if it is they've had ample time to get there, and if a man and his son can make it here without running into any problems, you can bet the FSS can, too."

"Do you have any Geiger counters in your supply dumps?" Darius asked, and Price nodded. "Send as many as you can spare in the next shipment to KC. We'll deploy them as fast as possible and begin sweeping the area around our key installations. With any luck, nothing will be detonated between now and then."

"It's unlikely that the FSS would have been able to gain access to the codes to arm a nuclear weapon," Price said. "I designed the protocol that resets those codes in the event of a cyber-attack or a power interruption, and I know how fast they work. The codes would have been reset on the computers on site once the power was disrupted. Enough power would be left in capacitors and slow-bleed diodes that the software would have no problem running simple algorithmic calculations and keying the access code answers to the predetermined code set for an Omega level event, the worst possible scenario. The only facility that has access to those Omega level preset codes is this one, and I can assure you that we have *not* been compromised."

"Maybe," Darius conceded, but he didn't sound reassured, "but what about the possibility of a dirty bomb. That's not a far step below a full-fledged hot detonation. The affected area may be smaller, but within that area the casualties can approach a hundred percent from radiation poisoning. And even if the enemy didn't gain access to the codes to arm a nuke, they could have gutted one and made a hell of a dirty bomb or maybe a couple dozen smaller charges with some of the ordinance I've seen deployed so far. Either way, it would be enough to rain hell down on our extended ass supply lines."

"You make a good point," Price admitted, "but we cannot lose sight of our objective. The FSS forces in and around DC have begun to move south. We have to find a way to get our forces south ahead of them so that we can stop them. If the FSS secures the entire eastern seaboard, we won't be able to dislodge them. We simply won't have the numbers. We've got to keep them isolated or the entire thing falls apart."

"So, if Kansas City has to burn, that's though shit," Darius grated, "but the cause must march on. Is that it? How do you suggest I tell my men that, or this man and his son?"

"You think they don't already know, Colonel?" Price asked. "Look around you. If it's not perfectly clear to them by now that this is an all-in game, then it never will be. And yes, if Kansas City must burn so that this cause has a chance to win, then so be it. If this facility I'm standing in has to go up in smoke with me standing in the middle of it, then so be it. The price cannot be too high if it purchases victory for America, Colonel. You should remember that."

"Do you really think we're going to rebuild the Unite States, Commander?" Darius asked in disbelief boarding on contempt.

Price snorted and shook his head. "No, Colonel," he said softly, "we're not going to rebuild anything. At best before we're all killed, we'll be able to kill enough of the FSS that they can't rebuild anything either, and the people who are still alive will have a chance to do it. That's at best. But I have no illusions about our chances of survival or the chances of us being able to rebuild anything of what we've lost. My only hope is that enough good people out there will still be alive that they can do it when we're gone."

Price leaned forward. "And if that means that we have to sacrifice Kansas City and every other city from there to D.C. to get the job done, then that's what we do. But we get the job done, understood?"

Darius nodded. "Yes, sir. What should I do about the man and his son?"

"They can stay with you or they can come here, but they can't go back to St. Louis and they can't go anywhere else. We don't know enough about them to trust them, and they know too much about us to let what they know out into the world. Our best defense right now is that no one sees us coming; otherwise, they'd have started hitting us already. We have to keep it that way as long as possible."

"Understood, sir," Darius said. "You should know that the men and I, we're ready to do what's needed. I just have to look out for them as long as I can as much as I can. You understand."

Price nodded. "Lieutenant Commander Marcus Attledge will be coming out with the next convoy. They will be loading the train in the morning, and he should be there in a day or two. He is on a special mission and under my direct command on certain issues. That means there are going to be parts of his mission that you aren't informed about and parts that you will have to step back from and let him assume operational and tactical command. Can you handle that?"

"Whatever you need to get the job done, sir," Darius said without hesitation. "And as far as the father and son, I'll ask the father what he wants to do. On our next communication, I'll let you know his answer."

"How secure is this information, Colonel?" Price asked after a moment.

"Well, the regulars that are involved will keep their mouths shut, of course. The others? It's anybody's guess, really. Some of them seem to have their heads on straight, while others seem to be looking for a way to inflict violence on people and get a meal for their trouble. And with a base this size, once a few people outside the chain know, everyone will."

Price gave a small shrug. "I suppose there's nothing to be done about that. Attledge and the convoy will leave once we've tracked down the Geiger counters for you. Until then, stay as safe as you can."

"We'll do all we can while we can," Darius said with a nod.

The Colonel reached up and the feed went dead as Price took the first sip of his cup of cold coffee.

Chapter 47

First Impressions

Arthur crept forward, keeping his body as low as possible as he moved toward the edge of the trees that lined both sides of the old logging road. Ahead of him was a screen of small scrub oaks and other sapling hardwoods, their branches cloaked in full fall colors ranging from bright yellows all the way to deep burgundy, depending on the species. Through the trees Arthur could see across the small two-lane road to the white-washed wood church. As he watched, Arthur counted a dozen different people, though it was difficult to keep an accurate count as the people moved around too much to follow them all at the same time.

To the right, up the gentle slope from the church, was a small graveyard with simple stone markers shining in the early morning sun. At the far-right edge of the cemetery a cluster of tents huddled among a stand of towering old pine trees. A few people were milling around in the camp, but Arthur couldn't make them out clearly or tell how many were there. The left side of the church was a small gravel parking lot that had been transformed into a makeshift open-air market. Stalls built of spare lumber and rough-cut trees lined the sides of the parking lot with people selling firewood, canned goods, quilts and other clothing items, and more.

As Arthur watched, an old and rusted Chevy pickup pulled up to the side of the road in front of the church and four people climbed out, two from the bed and two from the cab. They waved to an elderly woman sitting in a rocking chair on the front porch of the church, and she looked up from her quilting square just long enough to wave back as they passed her. As the new comers came up to the first stall, a man that Arthur hadn't noticed in the edge of the trees on that side of the road came out to meet them. They talked for a moment and then all four people from the truck stood with their arms out to their sides, feet spread a little more than shoulder width apart. The man that Arthur had missed patted down each of them in turn, checking for any hidden weapons.

When he was satisfied that none of them had weapons, the security officer motioned them to go ahead as he walked back to the edge of the trees and settled in to watch the road. Even knowing the man was there, Arthur had a very difficult time picking him out of the trees as he was wearing hunting clothes with a woods pattern that blended in nearly perfectly with his surroundings. Arthur was uneasy. He'd counted three people in the church yard who were obviously carrying some kind of long-gun and he'd assumed they were the only ones armed in the area. Now that he had seen the camouflaged sentry, he was uncertain and wondered how many other pairs of eyes might be hidden in the woods around him.

The only comfort Arthur had was knowing that the other members of his team were somewhere off to his left and right flanks covering him. He had chosen the three men carefully, two former police officers and an avid hunter. All three could shoot and all three had demonstrated uncommon coolness under pressure and even under fire. Plus, Lewis was on the hill a few hundred yards behind them, waiting to call in reinforcements if needed. Finally, unable to justify procrastinating any longer, Arthur stood and dusted off the leaves and twigs clinging to him as he made his way back to the logging road and started toward the church.

The old logging road intersected the newer paved Flint Mill Road directly across from the small church. The trees around the intersection were thinner than the rest of the woods, almost as if it were once a clearing that had slowly been overgrown through the years. As soon as Arthur left the dense undergrowth, the woman on the porch set her quilting in her lap and her eyes locked on his as he approached. She sat, tapping her foot lightly, waiting for him to cross the road.

As soon as Arthur's feet touched the grass on the church side of the road, the elderly woman stood and held up her hand. "That's far enough for now, stranger. We don't mind visitors, but we got a few questions for you first."

Arthur nodded. "Whatever you need, ma'am," he said, trying to sound reassuring.

"Where are you coming from and where are you headed?"

"I'm coming from Charlotte," Arthur replied, "and headed to Bennett, North Carolina."

"Are you armed?"

"Not at the moment," Arthur answered truthfully.

"We'll still have to pat you down. Only way to be sure. Can't be too careful with strangers these days, you understand."

Arthur nodded but didn't respond. He was careful to keep his hands well clear of his body, though.

"And last question," the elderly woman said as she pointed to the woods across the road, "are your friends out there in the woods something we should be worried about?"

Arthur shook his head, his mind racing. "They're just keeping an eye on me, making sure nothing bad happens. Like you said, can't be too careful these days."

"Come on over, then, and we'll show you around," she said as she set her quilting square on her rocking chair.

Arthur did as he was instructed and stepped off the shoulder of the road and onto the gravel driveway of the church. The camouflaged sentry came over to pat him down and Arthur could see a hunting rifle propped against one of the trees a few feet inside the edge of the woods. As Arthur was getting patted down, the woman climbed down the steps and retrieved an old, gnarled walking stick propped against the side of the church. She leaned on the stick as she walked, but not heavily, and Arthur wondered briefly if the stick was really necessary for her to walk or if it was her way of having a nice, solid cudgel in her hands if something went sideways.

When the sentry was done, he turned and nodded once to the woman and then returned to his post. Arthur got his first clear view of her as she stepped in front of him and gave him an appraising look. Her face was lined with age and with the effects of a life spent outside, and faded white scars crisscrossed the backs of her hands. Her hair was stark white shot through with bands of sparkling silver, and although she was definitely old, her eyes were bright and sharp behind her clear acrylic-framed glasses as she inspected him.

"Well, what's your name, stranger?"

Arthur tried to relax as he extended his hand. "I'm Arthur. It's nice to meet you . . ." Arthur waited as the older woman just looked at his hand without saying anything. Having weighed her options, she gave a small shrug and shook his hand with a surprisingly firm grip.

"I'm Sue Ellen Prichard, the head of the Women's Circle here at the church and the official welcoming party for all strangers, drifters, and passers through. Which I guess hits you on pretty much all three, don't it?"

Arthur chuckled and nodded. "Yes, ma'am, I suppose it does."

"I guess I might as well show you around a bit." Sue Ellen turned and started walking toward the shop stalls without so much as glancing back to make sure Arthur was following. This woman was used to being obeyed. "There ain't much to see, really," Sue Ellen said over her shoulder. "We got a few people out here selling and trading what they can, but there ain't all that much to go around these days."

Sue Ellen stopped at the first stall where stacks of firewood and bundles of kindling stood in neat rows. "Angus sells firewood, obviously, and he can sharpen any axe, hatchet, or saw you've got. He does work on knives too, but not as much." Sue Ellen moved down to the next stall and smiled at the woman in the back. "This is Margaret and she has some of the best canned vegetables and fruit in three counties."

Arthur tried to keep track of the names as Sue Ellen went through them, but his memory wasn't as good as it had been when he was younger. Sue Ellen led him around each stall and pointed out the goods that the proprietors were selling. One had leather belts, straps, and holsters that were all hand-stitched and hand-tooled. Another had hardware and tools that looked like they had come out of a local hardware store a half a century ago, but nothing was broken to the point it wouldn't function. Another had jars of honey and bundles of various dried herbs. The last stall had quilts and clothes, all home-made from spare fabric or from home-spun cotton and wool. Sue Ellen had a few pieces for sale or trade in this stall and took the time to point them out to Arthur.

At the end of the brief tour, they found themselves back at the front of the church. Sue Ellen climbed the steps and set her walking stick against the wall next to her rocking chair. She lowered herself into her chair and picked up her quilting square and went back to work stitching scraps of cloth together in a complex pattern of triangles, squares, and diamonds. Her fingers moved with confidence and speed that came from decades of practice and experience.

"So why are you here, Arthur?"

"I told you, ma'am, I'm passing through on the way to Bennett."

Sue Ellen shook her head. "That's why you and your group are in the Uwharrie," she said, "but that's not why you're here, in front of this church, talking to me. So, I'll ask you again, why are you here?"

"Group?" Arthur asked, trying to sound surprised. "What group? It's just me and the two people in the woods that came here with me. We don't have a group."

Sue Ellen put her quilting square in her lap. The brightness was gone from her eyes, and she fixed Arthur with a glare that bore right through him. "You mean to tell me you're not part of the big group that's camped off of Horseshoe Bend Road? Our lookouts have been following that group for two days, just about since they crossed the bridge. You want to try your answer again, Arthur?"

347

Arthur was quiet for a moment, his thoughts racing. "Okay, I'm sorry I lied to you. I'm with the big group, just as you said, but we weren't sure what kind of people you are, so I came to check you out. Like you said, can't be too careful with strangers these days."

"There's one thing I can't abide, Arthur," Sue Ellen said, her voice still sharp and her eyes narrow, "and that is someone telling me a lie. Don't do it again." When Arthur nodded, she continued. "What is your group planning to do to us?"

Arthur was quiet as he tried to think of the best way to answer the question. After considering it from every angle, and with the camouflaged sentry in mind, Arthur decided that the truth was the best option available. "We're not sure," he admitted. "There are people in our group, at least a couple, who wanted to come down here and massacre all of you and take what you have for ourselves. We're low on food, low on water, and some of the people are getting desperate. Those people have been put in their place, though, and we won't let that happen. They decided to send me here to talk to you and see if we could work out some kind of trade deal."

"And what if we said we didn't have enough to spare?" Sue Ellen asked. "What if we told you we couldn't do any trades and you'd have to find your supplies somewhere else? What then?"

"Some of our people wouldn't be happy about it," Arthur admitted, "but we could handle them. We'd just have to move on quicker than we had planned."

"You know there's some groups with numbers like yours who would try to get us to lower our guard first. They might think we're easy pickings so they'd send in someone to talk to us and make us feel safe, and then they would attack us anyway. How can we trust that you won't do something like that?"

348

Arthur gave a small shrug of his shoulders. "Well, Sue Ellen, you can't be sure of it. Bottom line, there's no guarantee that we won't attack you beyond my word. But, then again, there's no guarantee that you don't have a hundred armed men hidden in the woods waiting to attack us, now is there? I guess that means either we take a chance and trust each other, or we don't and we go our separate ways. But no matter what happens, as long as you all don't start shooting first, I can promise you that you have nothing to fear from me or my group."

Sue Ellen picked up her quilting square and began stitching again. "What did you do before the lights went out, Arthur?" "I was a veterinarian for more than thirty years," he answered. "I had my own practice and loved every minute of it, right up to the moment I sold the shop and retired four years ago."

Sue Ellen nodded as she stitched. "I was a school teacher. I taught just about every grade there is this side of college, but I spent most of my career teaching high school English grammar, composition, and rhetoric to kids who thought they already knew everything the world had to offer. I think when a person does a thing for as long as I taught school and for as long as you worked with sick animals, it changes who they are. Like it or not, what you do becomes a part of you. Teaching taught me a lot about myself and about people. One thing I learned in the classroom was how to tell when someone is either lying or holding something back. I spent nearly five decades in front of a bunch of young'uns and alongside a bunch of adults, and in that time, I got real good at telling when people were lying to me."

Sue Ellen paused and looked up at Arthur. "You're not lying to me, Arthur, but I don't think you're being entirely honest with me, either. And that worries me."

Arthur opened his mouth to respond, but Sue Ellen shot out of her rocking chair so quickly that it almost toppled over backwards. She pointed over Arthur's head toward the sky, her eyes going wide. "What is that?" she asked in a whisper.

Arthur turned and saw the bright red ember of an emergency flare drifting slowly down from the pinnacle of its arc, and it suddenly felt like his stomach had fallen through his shoes. He whispered, "Oh shit."

Chapter 48

Mixed Signals

"What is that, Arthur?" Sue Ellen repeated, worry creeping into her voice.

"It's a signal. I don't have time to explain it right now, but I need to go and meet my people. If they saw that flare, and I have to think they did, then they are already on the way. If I don't get to them, they're probably going to shoot first and ask questions later."

Sue Ellen shook her head. "I don't understand. Why would they come here looking for a fight?"

"Look, I know you don't trust me," Arthur said, already backing away from the church, "but you're going to have to put that aside for the moment. You said you can tell when someone is lying to you? Well I don't want anyone, your people or mine, to get hurt over a mixed signal. Am I lying about that?"

Sue Ellen's eyes narrowed, but she shook her head. "No, you're not lying. Go ahead and go, but if you want any hope of doing business with us, you'll come back by yourself and empty handed, just like you are now. We ain't done yet, Arthur."

Arthur was running before Sue Ellen finished talking. He sprinted up Flint Mill road as fast as he could, adrenaline already

351

pumping through his veins. He had gone less than a half mile when he rounded a bend and almost ran into Mike at the head of the column from the camp.

"Whoa!" Mike yelled, catching Arthur before they collided. "We saw the flare and thought the worst. What's going on?"

Arthur shook his head as he gasped for breath. "I don't know," he said finally. "There were no problems at all at the church. I was talking to one of the leaders of their group, an elderly woman named Sue Ellen, and all of a sudden, the flare went off. No shots were fired, nothing threatening at all that I can tell. I don't know what's going on."

"Well, let's go find out," Mike said and he started to push past Arthur, but Arthur moved to block his way.

"Not so fast, Mike," he said. "Listen, these people at the church weren't threatening, but they weren't exactly friendly either. And I get the feeling that there's a lot more going on here than it appears. They knew about the people I had with me in the woods, and they already knew about our camp too. I've been trying to feel them out and see how much more they know, but Sue Ellen is very guarded. If you show up with ten armed men, it's not going to go over well, I can tell you that. And who knows what will happen with the rest of the group back at the camp. They might be under guard already, we don't know."

"We can't just leave Lewis out there on his own," Mike insisted. "He might be in trouble."

"The old woman already sent people to check," Arthur replied. "Whatever is happening, we won't be able to get to him before they do. And I don't think Lewis is in any kind of trouble since they didn't seem to be aware that he is out there. I know it's difficult, but the smart move right now is for you to go back to camp and keep an eye on things there."

Mike clenched his jaw for a moment but finally nodded. "You're right, but I don't like it. Here, take this."

Mike tried to give Arthur a snub-nose revolver, but Arthur shook his head and took a step back. "They've got sentries, and they pat down everyone who comes to the church, even people they know. If I show up with that we won't have any chance of dealing with them. I guarantee it. It's not easy, but we're going to have to trust them."

Mike still hesitated but finally relaxed and put the snub-nosed .38 special back in his ankle holster. "If you say so, Arthur. I don't trust them. I trust you. Find out what happened to Lewis, please, and don't keep us waiting too long. I might have to come looking for you, and that could get tense."

Arthur nodded and then extended his hand to Mike. When Mike took his hand and shook it, Arthur pulled him close. "Be careful what you say and how loud you say it," he whispered. "I'm pretty sure our group is being watched."

Mike kept a smile on his face as he leaned back, but there was a tightness around his eyes that said he'd gotten the message. With nothing more to say, Arthur turned his back on Mike and the rest of the group and started jogging back down the road toward the church. He was still winded, and the jog back was downhill, which would help him recover before he reached Sue Ellen. Still, his legs and back were aching by the time he reached the gravel parking lot.

"Looks like you saved the day, Arthur." Sue Ellen said without looking up from her quilting.

"What happened on the hill?" Arthur asked. "I told you I had a man up there, and he had only one of those flares. He was told not to use it except in a last chance scenario, so what happened?"

Sue Ellen shrugged. "I don't know yet," she admitted. "I have two men out looking, and I assume your two are probably looking as well?"

Arthur shook his head. "They were told to keep their eye on you, and they wouldn't have abandoned an order like that. My guess is they're still out there."

"Why don't you tell them to come on over?" Sue Ellen asked.

"Because I think you might have a problem with some of the tools they're carrying," Arthur replied, being very careful with his wording.

"What kind of tools?" Sue Ellen asked, suddenly interested. "Screw drivers? Hammers? Saws?"

Arthur smiled, though he was still a little out of breath. As he stepped off the shoulder of the road, the sentry came out of the woods to frisk him again. The man had a face sleeve that hid the lower part of his face up to his eyes. His wide-brimmed hunting hat hid the rest, and a pair of dark sunglasses covered his eyes. It was unnerving to have a featureless man that looked like a moving part of the woods walk up and pat him down. Arthur couldn't help but admire the disorienting effect. Whether it was intentional or not, it was definitely effective.

Satisfied, the man nodded to Sue Ellen and returned to his post.

Arthur turned and regarded the elderly woman with a thoughtful look. "Let's talk about the idea of trading some things, Sue Ellen. Are we talking about a wish-list here, ma'am? Are there things you people need that you'd be willing to trade for? Or are we still getting to know each other?"

Sue Ellen smiled. "You are direct, aren't you, Arthur? What's your last name, again?"

Arthur smiled back. "Arthur will suffice."

Before Sue Ellen could respond, Arthur heard footsteps behind him and turned. Coming down the road was a group of people so jumbled it took Arthur a moment to make sense of it. Lewis, one of the men Mike had sent with him, was helping a tall, broad-shouldered stranger carry a young man whose left leg was bandaged. Another young man followed them with a slightly smaller, much older stranger, and the last two members of Arthur's team brought up the rear carrying the packs and weapons of the others, as well as their own.

Arthur watched as the group approached, but Sue Ellen was already up and down the stairs before they had crossed the blacktop. Her gnarled walking stick stood against the wall behind her rocking chair, and Arthur almost grabbed it for her but thought better of it. Instead, he followed her over to the young man that Lewis and the stranger were carefully setting on the ground. Lewis cradled the young man's head and chest, keeping them elevated above his leg.

The boy was unconscious and pale, a slick sheen of sweat over his forehead.

"That's Micah Pagliio," Sue Ellen said as she knelt next to the young man. "What happened?" she asked, shooting the other young man a sharp look.

"We . . . we . . . went out looking . . . for . . . some squirrels," the young man stammered. "Thought it might be a good day to . . . get . .

. to get 'em coming out of their nests early. I got four and Micah got two, but . . ."

"I don't care about squirrels, boy," Sue Ellen snapped. "What happened to his foot?"

"Well, we was on the way back to camp, and Micah stepped over an old windfall pine without checking first," the young man said in a rush. "He yelled and fell over on his side holding his foot. I saw a big timber rattler's tale going back up under the old tree trunk, so I drug him back away from it. I tried to help him walk, but he wasn't moving too well. I started screaming, and this stranger showed up." The young man pointed at Lewis. "He took one look at Micah and me, and he threw Micah over his shoulder and started running."

"When I got back to the clearing at the top of the hill, I fired my flare," Lewis said. "One of ours and two of yours came to check it out and we all started this way. Can you help him, Doc?"

"Doc?" Sue Ellen asked, her head snapping around to Arthur.

"I told you I was a veterinarian, remember?" Arthur said absentmindedly. His attention was focused on the boy's foot, which was already swollen and discolored. The hiking shoe Micah was wearing had cut off much of the circulation as a result of the swelling and had served as a natural tourniquet. The snake had spun when Micah stepped on it, and it sank its fangs into the top of his foot through the nylon webbing of the tongue of his shoe, leaving two deep puncture wounds. Venom from the bite was starting to seep out of the young man's foot, though, and angry red lines were already tracing their way up his slightly swollen ankle.

"The boy's going to lose the foot," Arthur said in clinical tone. "If we move fast, I might be able to save the leg, or most of it. But the foot's gone. If we don't do anything, the venom will probably kill him."

"There's a hospital in Troy," Sue Ellen said. "It's about eleven miles from here. You think they could help?"

"Even if that hospital was fully staffed, they wouldn't be able to help," Arthur said. "The antivenin serum has to be kept in cold storage or it breaks down and is useless. And there's no guarantee that a hospital that size would have any on hand to begin with. I'm sorry, but this is the best I can do. Do you have a doctor of your own?"

Sue Ellen shook her head. "We did, but the fool man up and had a heart attack six weeks before the Blackout."

"Where are the boy's parents?" Arthur asked.

Sue Ellen gave a small shrug. "His daddy had a pacemaker and it went out the same time the lights did. His momma and him live on the other side of Ophir, but he stays around the church for the most part. It'd take us a half hour to track her down and get her here."

Arthur shook his head. "That's too long. If we wait that long the venom could spread to his heart by then. Once it gets far past the knee, I won't be able to do anything. It'll be in his major arteries, and I won't be able to amputate without him bleeding out or going into shock. The decision has to be made now."

"Can't you just tie off his leg and wait?" Sue Ellen asked.

Arthur pointed to Micah's foot. "If I tie a tourniquet around his leg and they decide not to amputate, it'll be a death sentence. The venom is bad enough, but as it kills tissue and cells, chemicals are released that kill other cells and other tissues. The effect spreads and it's cumulative. Meaning after a certain point, there won't be anything anyone will be able to do. So, it's either I cut the shoe off his foot and let the venom run its course, or I amputate and try to save his life. If I amputate now, he's got a fifty-fifty shot, and those odds will only get worse as time goes by. If I don't amputate, I'd give it seventy-thirty odds that he doesn't make it."

"You can't expect me to decide if this boy keeps his foot or not," Sue Ellen protested.

"Well someone has to," Arthur shot back, "and you seem to know him best. So yeah, it's gotta be you making the call. And I need an answer, now!"

Sue Ellen patted the young boy's hand, but he was either unconscious or so overwhelmed by the pain that he couldn't respond. After a long, agonizing moment, she finally looked up at Arthur and nodded. "Do what you have to in order to save this boy's life."

Arthur stood and pointed to one of the men on his team. "You run back to the group and get Mike. Tell him to bring his medical kit and as many bandages as he can round up on short notice." He turned to the stranger who had not helped carry Micah down the mountain. "You, I need boiling water. Start enough pots to add up to about ten or fifteen gallons if you can. Drop a little salt in the water if you have it and that will help sterilize it."

Arthur put a hand on Sue Ellen's shoulder. "We're going to do everything we can for him, but right now I need you to step back."

"You're going to operate here?" Sue Ellen asked, shocked.

"Unless you have a clean, sterile room stashed around the church that you left off the tour," Arthur replied as he wrapped the young man's belt around his leg a few inches above the red lines on his ankle, "then I guess it isn't going to make much difference. The lighting is good, so yeah, we're doing it right here. I need some space to work. If you can find me a few large sewing needles and some good, strong fishing line, I'm going to need it to stitch things up when I'm done."

As people started moving, carrying out Arthur's orders, Lewis looked up and raised one eyebrow. "You really think you can pull something like this off, Doc? I mean, if you end up killing this kid . . ."

Arthur knew what he was trying to say. "I don't know," he admitted, "but I do know that if I do nothing, the boy's going to die. And I just can't sit here and let that happen. If there's a chance, even a small chance, that I can save his life, then I've got to take it, right?"

Lewis gave a small shrug. "Whatever you say, Doc. Just make sure those rifles aren't too far out of reach in case things go downhill."

Arthur didn't want to say it, but he had a sinking suspicion there was more to this group than met the eye, and even if the rifles were in their hands they wouldn't have much of a chance if the right person gave the right order. Right now, he was focused more on keeping peace than having the means to fight within arms' reach.

Arthur glanced up at the small brass cross that hung over the double oak doors of the church and said a quick prayer. "Lord, if you're up there, this boy sure could use a hand right now . . . and so could I."

Chapter 49

Double Bit

By the time Mike came jogging up with his med kit and a full pack of supplies, the young man's foot was turning purple and green. The tourniquet around his ankle held, and the poison was no longer spreading up his leg. Arthur gave Mike a brief rundown of what had happened and what he was planning.

Mike opened the pack and started laying out the supplies Arthur had asked for on a clean sheet that had shown up, probably from one of the stalls. "What are you going to use to cut the leg?" he asked as he worked.

Arthur gave a small shake of his head. "I'm not sure. There's not a bone saw in the pack, and the only other saws they have are those." He gave a jerk of his head to a display of assorted hacksaws and crosscut saws, all with blades in various stages of wear and tear. "If I try to use one of those, it will shred his leg and probably get the thing infected."

Mike nodded. "I don't know that we have any other choice, though."

Arthur looked up at the first stall across the churchyard from them. "That may not be true, but I don't think the people here are going to like it much."

Mike followed Arthur's eyes and then looked back to the older man. "Are you sure that's your only option?"

Arthur nodded. "We need something sharp and clean, something that can take it in one blow and leave a somewhat clean edge so I can stitch the arteries and veins. I'll have to cauterize parts of it, most likely, but that can't be helped. At least with an axe, he'll have a shot."

"What can I do to help?" Mike asked, his face a little pale.

Arthur used his finger to trace a line around Micah's shin a few inches above the tourniquet. The young man groaned and shifted but didn't waken. The pain and probably the fear had made him pass out before they'd made it to the churchyard, and the fact he hadn't woken up yet was a blessing. "That's where we'll cut. I need you to clean his leg with iodine and alcohol. It won't do any good to get rid of the venom in his foot if we let an infection set in and kill him. I'll go talk to the wood cutter and see what he has that we might be able to use."

Arthur stood as Mike wiped the young man's leg with a wet-wipe from his pack. The iodine stained Micah's skin yellow when Mike poured it over his leg and cleaned the area with a gauze pad. With a deep breath, Arthur turned his back on his patient and walked across the churchyard to the woodcutter's stall where a group of people had gathered to watch, Sue Ellen among them.

"Why is it taking so long, Arthur?" Sue Ellen asked. "Didn't you say time was of the essence in this?"

"If I rush through this, it will kill him just as surely as the snake bite would. I am doing what I can for him, but I need patience. And a favor."

Sue Ellen frowned. "What kind of favor?"

"I need you to convince the wood cutter to let me use one of his axes. The saws I've seen are either too rusted or too dull to do the job. With an axe, he'll have a clean wound."

Sue Ellen looked momentarily horrified, but she nodded her head. "He won't like it. Angus is rather particular about his axes."

Sue Ellen parted the crowd with an imperious wave of her hand and led Arthur into the wood cutter's stall. Angus, was a tall, broad-shouldered, barrel-chested man with a shiny bald head. A fringe of red hair streaked with gray that matched his beard hung down to his shoulders. They found him sitting on a stump at the back of the stall, a file in his hand and an axe across his legs. He looked up when the two stepped into the rough wooden structure, his darkly tanned face set in a deep scowl.

"Miss Sue, I don't know what you're after, but . . . "Angus began.

"You're right, Angus T. Shaw, you don't know what I'm after," Sue Ellen said, planting her fists on her hips, "so why don't you shut your fool mouth and listen. Maybe I'll tell you what I'm after once your jaws ain't flappin."

Angus kept a steady rhythm with the file until the older woman was done. Then he looked up at her. "Yes, ma'am?"

Sue Ellen nodded and gave a short snort. "That's better. I need your best axe."

Angus gestured beyond the stall to a pile of wood. "If you need firewood, Miss Sue, I have plenty already cut."

"You heard what happened to Micah?"

Angus nodded. "A cryin shame for that boy. I saw a grown man bit by a big rattler when I was a kid. He was dead within a day and a half. It's a bad way to go. But I don't see what that has to do with my axe."

Sue Ellen pointed over her shoulder at Arthur. "This man is a veterinarian, and he thinks he might be able to save Micah. But we need your axe to do it."

Angus was quiet for a long moment before shaking his head slightly. "You'll end up mutilating the boy before his death, maybe even hastening it. Better to let things play out the way they were meant to, rough as that is. Sometimes that's what it takes."

Sue Ellen started to say something else, but Arthur place a hand on her shoulder. She whirled, ready to snap, but something in Arthur's face stopped her.

"You don't know me, Mr. Shaw," Arthur said, "so I understand that it's difficult to put much faith in me. Believe me, I get it. But I was a good vet, and I did hundreds of complex surgeries over the years. I think I can do this, but I will be successful only if I have the right tools. Even then, to be honest, it's not a great chance that he'll survive. But it's a hell of a lot better than he'll have if we just stand here talking about it."

Angus's brow furrowed but he still offered no axe.

"Look, I'm not trying to step on your toes, Mr. Shaw," Arthur said. "But I know that Micah will die if I do nothing. A sharp, relatively clean axe will go a long way toward giving Micah a chance to come out of this alive. But either way, with your axe or without it, I'm going to try."

Arthur leaned forward, his voice dropping. "Do you really want me to saw that boy's foot off with a rusted hacksaw? Then you can sit around for the next few days and listen to him as gangrene sets in and slowly eats him alive, knowing the whole time that if we'd used your axe, he might have lived. Now, what's it going to be?"

Arthur held Angus's glare and straightened, but he didn't step back. His face was red and his breaths were heavy with indecision, but his eyes never left Arthur's. After what seemed like a century, he stood slowly and pulled an axe from the rough-hewn log wall behind him. The axe head was covered with a double-bit leather sheath and the handle was marbled hickory that was sanded and polished into a deep, velvety sheen.

"This is a Helko Hinterland axe," Angus said, his voice a deep guttural growl. "It's a fine, hand-crafted felling and splitting axe."

Angus extended the handle to Arthur, and when he let go of the steel axe head, Arthur was surprised at its weight. It was well balanced, despite the heaviness, and the wood felt good in his hands. Still, this was a tool that was totally unfamiliar to Arthur.

Angus looked him over once and fixed him with a critical eye. "Have you ever felled a tree or split a cord of wood?" he asked suspiciously, and Arthur didn't answer. The wood cutter's eyes narrowed further. "Have you ever even swung a proper axe?"

When Arthur still didn't answer, Angus reached over and took the axe back with his right hand and rested the sheathed axe-head comfortably on his right shoulder. "That's what I thought," he growled. "I wasn't just agreeing to you borrowing my axe, I was agreeing to be the one who swings it."

Arthur opened his mouth to reply but didn't get the chance.

Angus shifted his gaze from Arthur to Sue Ellen. "I don't want to hear it. I'll do it. Now get out of my stall. When you need me, come back and get me. Until then, both of you get out."

Neither Arthur nor Sue Ellen could find anything to say to that, so they turned and left.

Arthur raced ahead of the stooped and slow Sue Ellen. He nodded to Mike as he passed and ran on to the cook fire where water was boiling in four large pots set on a grate over a bed of hot coals.

"Good," he said, a little out of breath. "Drop all of the metal implements from the medical bag into one pot and take it off the fire. Once the water stops bubbling count to two hundred, then drain the water. Dump the utensils into the next pot of boiling water."

Arthur pointed to a pot with a black enamel finish flecked through with white. "Make that the last pot you dump them in. Leave it on the fire until I ask for it, okay? When I call for it, dump the water and leave the implements in the pot. They should be sterilized at that point, but pour some of that pure grain alcohol they're selling in the fourth stall over them anyway, just to be safe. Just don't do that next to the fire."

When the four people watching the pots nodded, Arthur returned to Mike. The supplies they had were laid out on the sheet in the order Arthur imagined he'd need them. He would use the black magic marker he'd asked for to draw the cut line for Angus. Long tweezers called a hemostat would clamp off the major vessels, arteries and veins that would be severed. He would tie them off with the strong monofilament line. A large-bladed butcher's knife was waiting next to a small fire he'd had Mike build. He would heat the blade to cauterize the areas he couldn't tie. Next to the knife was a pile of gauze padding and rolled gauze bandages and five tubes of antibacterial ointment that would be used to bandage the stump once he was sure the major bleeding had been staunched.

The one item on the sheet that held Arthur's attention, though, was the tourniquet he would use to tie off the boy's leg above the cut. Once he tightened that thin strip of tightly braded high-quality nylon fabric, they were on the clock.

"Once I tie his leg off, Mike," Arthur said, getting the other man's attention, "we'll have ninety minutes. That's ninety minutes, start to finish, or we run the risk of causing tissue damage due to lack of oxygen. If that happens, his leg will start to die and gangrene will set in. Let's go over this one last time, okay?"

Mike nodded, so Arthur continued. "I tie off the tourniquet. Mr. Shaw makes the cut when I give him the signal. Once the cut is made, you apply pressure while I start the first tie-off. I tie-off the major bleeders as I find them, largest first and so-on. Then we use the hot butcher's knife to cauterize the rest. Once I think I've closed every bleeder, we loosen the tourniquet real slow. I'll work on any areas that start to bleed, and then we'll repeat the process."

Mike's face was pale, but he nodded that he was following.

"Once that's done, the hard part is over. Then we coat the whole face of the wound with antibacterial ointment, pack it with sterile gauze as tightly as we can, and then wrap it so the dressing doesn't come off. If we've done our job right, when we loosen the tourniquet there will be no bleed through. Any sign of blood is a bad sign that we've missed something. Any questions, Mike?"

"What am I going to do while you're tying all of this stuff off and everything else?" Mike asked, his voice a bit unsteady.

"Whatever I ask you to," Arthur replied. "I want you to stay focused on me, not the wound. I'm going to need you handing me things and doing small things for me while I focus on the wound."

Mike nodded.

Arthur swallowed hard. "Well, I guess that's it, then." He stood and waved to Sue Ellen, who nodded and stepped into the wood cutter's stall to get Angus.

Arthur drew a line around Micah's leg and slipped the field tourniquet over his foot and up three inches beyond the line. He tightened the straps on the tourniquet first, making it snug against Micah's leg. Then he twisted the handle on top of the band, cinching it down until it was clear the circulation had been stopped. Arthur slipped the handle into a Velcro band that held it tight and kept it from unwinding.

Angus strode up with the axe resting on his right shoulder, a two-foot thick section of round, flat tree trunk under his left. He set the chopping block down and pointed to it with his left hand. "Put the boy's leg on there. It'll make it less likely to roll. You're gonna want to hold him."

Mike carefully lifted Micah's leg onto the stump and then moved up to the young man's shoulders. Lewis came to help hold him down, and Arthur took Micah's distended and discolored foot. Micah groaned and winced as Arthur gripped his ankle firmly.

Arthur looked up at Angus and nodded once.

Angus took a deep breath and raised the axe high over his head. He paused there for just a moment, holding the axe nearly vertical, his wide eyes locked on the black line around Micah's shin. For a heartbeat, Arthur thought Angus had changed his mind.

And then the broad-shouldered wood cutter brought the axe down in one swift, solid motion.

THUNK!

Micah's entire body arched backwards in a sudden convulsion so violent that it knocked both Mike and Lewis off their balance. Then Micah spasmed the other way and sat bolt upright, his eyes bulging, a scream unlike anything Arthur had ever heard rising from deep within him. His hands clutched his leg just above the tourniquet, and he stared at the bloody stump. He screamed until all of the air was gone from his lungs and continued trying to scream afterwards, his open mouth gaping silently.

Micah's eyes rolled back in his head, and he fell limply back into Mike's and Lewis's arms as they struggled to regain their balance. The pain had overwhelmed the young man again, and he was thankfully unconscious.

Arthur turned to the side and laid the young man's leg on a folded towel. He donned a pair of blue nitrile exam gloves from the medical pack. Arthur took a deep breath, grabbed a four-inch length of pre-cut fishing line and a pair of hemostats.

"Mike," Arthur said, but Mike didn't respond. Arthur leaned over and nudged Mike's right arm. "Mike," he repeated, and this time the other man turned to look at him. "I need you to put on a pair of gloves and take that pad of folded gauze over there and sponge away some of the blood so I can see."

Mike nodded and did as he was instructed, moving to position himself at Arthur's right elbow so he could reach Micah's leg without blocking Arthur's view. Mike dabbed the wound and exposed the blood vessels and the cleanly sheered bone. Arthur swallowed once and wished he had a bottle of water close by to sip, and then he got to work. First, he found the largest vessels and tied them off with two separate strands of fishing line placed close enough to touch each other.

With the major vessels tied, Arthur began tying off the smaller vessels, working as fast as he could, despite his shaking fingers. He lost track of time as he worked, his mind allowing only thoughts of the task immediately before him. He focused on carefully looping the fishing line over the tiny tubes of the vessel walls, tying the knots carefully and then cinching them closed and tying them off. His fingers were guided more by muscle memory than by his conscious direction.

Now came the hardest part. Arthur took the broad-bladed butcher's knife that had been heating in the fire and cauterized the parts of the stump that were still oozing blood. The blade was hot but not quite to the point of glowing, and it sizzled as he pressed it against the wound. Each time he closed off a new part of the wound, Micah would groan and twitch, and it turned Arthur's stomach to think that even with everything else the boy had been through, he was still feeling the burn from the hot blade. Arthur moved quickly and when he was done, he handed the knife to someone he didn't recognize and told them to put it back in the fire in case they needed it again.

Arthur dabbed the wound clean again and looked for any places he'd missed, but he didn't see any. "Okay," he said to Mike, his voice hoarse and rough. "I think we're ready to loosen the tourniquet. I'll slowly let the tension off. You look for anyplace that starts bleeding, and if you see something let me know so I can tighten back down."

Mike nodded, though his face was pale, and he looked like he would rather be anywhere else but there with Micah. Arthur began loosening the tourniquet, unwinding the handle a quarter of a turn at the time. Arthur watched, but Mike never gave him any signal to stop, so he kept loosening the tourniquet. After a few turns, the band was loose enough to pull off, and Arthur removed it. He checked the end of the stump again, but it wasn't bleeding anywhere that he could see, at least not more than a few minor drips here and there—not enough to stitch closed or try and cauterize.

"Okay, we need to get it dressed," Arthur said.

Mike began opening tubes of antibacterial ointment and handing them to Arthur, who emptied three tubes directly onto the bloody end of the stump. He then took sterile non-stick gauze pads and pressed them firmly into the gelatinous mass of ointment. He added more pads of plain gauze over the non-stick pads and then wrapped the stump with rolls of gauze. The bandages were thick and almost twice as big around as Micah's shin when Arthur finished, but they were tight and held firmly when he tugged on them.

Mike looked across Micah's leg to Arthur. "Do you still need my help? Are you good?"

Arthur shook his head. "No, Mike, I don't need your help. But I couldn't have done this without you."

Mike didn't seem to be listening, though. He stood and turned, his hands trembling and his face pale. He made it a half-dozen steps across the church yard before dropping to his knees and emptying his stomach.

Sue Ellen stepped up next to Arthur and kneeled to place a hand lightly on Micah's shoulder. "Will he live, do you think?"

Arthur gave a small shrug. "His breathing is steady and the stump isn't bleeding. But it's too early to tell.

Sue Ellen gave Micah's shoulder another pat and then squeezed Arthur's shoulder as well. "Whatever you and your people need that we can spare is yours. God knows you've earned it."

Chapter 50

Along the Road

Oct. 25 th 1445 EST

Joe pointed to a small country road that was traced in red felt-tipped pen. "This is the road the convoy uses to get back to Bennett," he said to the others gathered around the table with him. "Benny said they used to drive different ways to get to the rendezvous site, but they always used the same set of back roads to get back to Bennett. We'll hit them here."

Chuck, the head of one of the larger families that had come to the church to join Joe's army, shook his head. "Why don't we hit them at the meeting point and get two birds with one stone?"

"The others have too much heavy weaponry," Joe replied. "Two up-armored hummers with belt-fed .50 caliber machine guns mounted to the roof. Even one would be difficult to overcome. Two working together would shred any kind of serious threat we could put together. I've seen those weapons at work, and we wouldn't stand a chance. Besides, we've got to hit the group from town once they're far enough away from the rendezvous so that help from their suppliers isn't an option."

Chuck frowned but finally nodded. Joe looked at each of the other eight men standing around the table and they all nodded in turn.

371

"We can put a few people up in tree stands along the road," Joe continued. "They'll have an elevated view of the ambush and can provide sniper support. If we do it right, we can have four snipers, one on each corner of a kill box. Then a team on each side of the road that will approach from the north with interlocking fields of fire. We create a kill box that is covered from every angle possible. As long as we can stop the convoy and force them into a fire fight, we should be able to pull it off."

"How do you plan on stopping them?" Chris asked. "It's got to be something big if it's going to stop the whole convoy in its tracks."

"I've got a few ideas, but nothing definite," Joe replied. "We can work on the details as we put this thing together. What do you all think?"

"It's a good area for an attack," Chris said. "The road's narrow and there aren't any turn-offs for them to use to escape. But that also means we'll have a hard time getting the supplies away from there unless we take their pickup trucks."

Joe was already shaking his head. "I don't want to risk bringing a tracking device home with a truck," he said. "We'll have to come up with another idea."

Chuck cleared his throat. "I know that road pretty well. If we move the ambush point to here, another three quarters of a mile down the road, there's a power line cut through that runs north and east. We can use some ATVs on that cut through to carry most of the stuff we take. The rest of the assault force can split up on foot and use different routes to leave the area. That'll confuse anyone who tries to come and track us too."

"Do we have enough ATVs that we can count on?" asked Marshall, another patriarch who had brought several men with him to train and fight.

Chuck shrugged. "I know of a half-dozen families that had them. If we ask around I'm sure we'll find enough to make it work."

"This is going to be the biggest hit we've pulled off yet," Joe said. "There's a good chance that we'll end up losing people, but we could also do some serious damage to the enemy. These guys rely one hundred percent on resupply from the outside. If we can disrupt that supply chain enough, we could force them into a situation where they have no choice but to surrender or starve."

"You know they'll try to hit back," Chris said. "Up until now our group has been the only ones doing any of the heavy lifting, and we've hit them only a handful of times—small raids here and there outside of that first big statement. If we take things to that level again they're going to come after us."

Joe looked around at each of the men at the table with him. These men represented the leadership in their small guerilla force. They were family men, not military men. Most had been farmers or factory workers before the Blackout. But now they were more. They were survivors.

"We won't let them," Joe said, his voice grim. "We are going to spend the next few weeks training for this. We're going to get it absolutely right, and then we're going to hit them. And once we hit them out here, we're not going to stop. Any time they send anyone out of town, they'll get hit. We're going to start doing raids in town too. That's the only way this works. Because if we don't do that, then Chris is right. They'll get reinforcements and they'll come at us with everything they've got."

Joe watched as the full weight of what he'd just said sank in on each face.

"You're talking about all-out war," Chuck said after a moment.

Joe nodded. "That's what it's going to take. That's the only way we can make sure our families are safe. We have to eliminate the threat, no matter what."

"Do you really think we can?" Chuck asked.

Joe turned and grabbed his rifle from where it leaned against the low wall that separated the pulpit from the choir loft.

"We don't have a choice," he said as he turned and walked out the double doors and into the late October sunshine.

Chapter 51

Under Orders

Oct. 25 th 1950 CST

The train lurched slightly as the brakes were applied, and a faint high-pitch squeal cut through the sound-proofing on the passenger car. Lieutenant Commander Attledge looked out his window and saw the stitching yard lit with dozens of clusters of high-intensity halogen lights, each with its own small solar generator attached. Men in digitized camouflage filled the gravel lot as they moved among the train cars on one of the other tracks. They were either loading or offloading supplies; he couldn't tell at this distance. More men marched in formation over to the side as a drill instructor called orders to them. Marcus crossed to the other side of the car and looked out the windows there to see men in the distance practicing with pistols aimed at cardboard silhouettes. Another group went through hand to hand combat drills in pairs.

A tall flagpole had been raised in the center of the stitching yard, but with the sun already set, it was empty.

Attledge felt another small shift in inertia as the train finally slowed to a complete stop. Outside his window the air brakes hissed as they released the excess pressure in the lines. As soon as the train stopped, men waiting by the tracks opened the doors on the cargo carriers and began offloading the supplies.

Attledge stepped into one of the washrooms on his car and checked his uniform in the mirror. He straightened the green and brown digitized camo outer blouse and tucked his undershirt back into his pants. He wanted to make a good impression on the colonel, and that meant he had to at least look the part of a naval officer despite the fact he still felt completely out of place in a uniform. As he looked in the mirror, Attledge drew the Beretta holstered on his right hip and took aim at his reflection. One of the last places he would have expected to need a sidearm was this makeshift military base in the heart of the American Midwest, but if he needed it, he wanted to know he could get to it in a hurry.

Satisfied that he could draw if necessary and that his uniform looked as good as it was likely to look, Attledge grabbed his duffle bag and headed for the door. As he stepped outside onto the gravel of the stitching yard, he was greeted by an older man in a uniform similar to his but without a name tape and with no marks of rank or insignia. The man had silver hair, a face lined and weathered by years of working outdoors, and a warm smile. There was a faded tattoo of an anchor and globe on the backs of both of his hands as he held the door open for Attledge with one and took the duffle bag with the other.

"Good evening, sir," the man said with a nod. "You'll forgive me if I don't salute. There have been snipers taking shots at what they think are officers from time to time, and we'd rather not tempt them. Not a huge threat given how dark it is, but with all of the lights around you never know. Colonel Darius sent me to meet you and bring you back to his command operations center. If you'll follow me, please."

The man turned and started walking without waiting for an answer, leaving Attledge little choice but to follow him or be left standing there with no idea where to go. He followed the man's back across the broad gravel yard as the last echoes of the recruits' target practice faded and in a few steps caught up with him. Attledge looked back at the train as they left it behind and saw the group of sniper trainees gathering their brass shell casings under the watchful eye of an instructor.

"What do you do with the brass?" Attledge asked.

"We have several reloading stations in one of the supply depots," the man said over his shoulder. "We save all we can and reload them. A few will be cracked or bent beyond repair, but we try to recycle the ones that aren't."

Attledge thought about all of the thousands of rounds he'd shot in his lifetime and how much brass he could have accumulated if he'd saved it. He had been an avid target shooter and hunter and had put tens of thousands of rounds down range over the years. He'd never had a reloading press, though, so all of that spent brass had wound up in trash cans and range buckets. He wished he had it all back again so he could contribute to the cause. Ammunition was one thing they simply could not have too much of at the moment.

Though he appeared at least twenty years older than Attledge, his guide had a quick and strong stride. It was difficult for him to keep pace without jogging. The older man walked with the duffle bag in his left hand, and every now and then his right hand would twitch when they passed another officer.

"Were you in the military before?" Attledge asked.

"Yes sir, Commander. I enlisted in the Marine Corps in 1962, when I turned eighteen. Three years later we entered the Vietnam war, and I found myself overseas. I served nine combat tours from '65 through '71. More than once I skipped a rotation home or spent just a few weeks before jumping back in. I never felt at home when I was home, not after that first week in combat."

The older man snorted hard and shook his head. "Six years when everyone I knew was doing anything they had to so they could stay out of that hell-hole, and all I could think about was going back every time I came stateside. I tried to go back more, but they turned me down. The brass said I had too much valuable experience, so they put me to training pimply-faced draftees down in San Diego. Made a career out of it, though, and I survived. A lot of guys over there didn't."

"How did you wind up here?" Attledge asked, preferring conversation to silence.

"I saw a train coming through Colorado with a great big Department of Defense logo on the side of the engine. The guy in command gave a speech to a group of about two hundred in our little town. At the end of it, he said he needed volunteers for the coming war. Surprisingly enough, no one leapt at the chance to go get shot at. After that he said if we signed up we'd get three square meals and a warm, safe place to sleep at night. Not many of us had anything better going on at the time, so we all volunteered. They sifted through the crowd, and I got in because of my past experience. I doubt I'll see much time with a rifle in my hand, but a guy can hope, right?"

Attledge glanced at the man to see if he was joking, but he hadn't so much as cracked a smile. "You really like it that much? Combat, I mean."

"No one likes getting shot at, sir. It's the adrenaline, not the combat. Nothing like it in the world. You get your body jacked up on it and suddenly you can feel every hair on your head, your arms, all over. Every nerve is jumping with electricity. You can see in damn near pitch black, hear a mouse sneeze a hundred yards away . . . it's a drug. And once you taste it, you chase the dragon. That's just how it is."

Not knowing how to respond to that, Attledge let a somewhat uncomfortable silence settle between them. The older man seemed content to walk without speaking, so Attledge took the time to take in the layout of the camp. There were very few buildings close in around the railroad tracks, and the wide-open gravel lots made for good training grounds. Beyond those was room for several camps, each camp laid out with ten rows of five tents. Daily troop tallies had been sent back to the Facility, so Attledge knew that these tents represented only a small portion of their force in the city, even if they were sleeping two to a tent.

The rest of the men were housed in some of the industrial buildings across the road. As the two of them walked toward the end of the track and away from the open sorting yard, there were more buildings on both sides of the tracks.

Attledge frowned, a bit curious. "Why don't the trains run all the way down to the buildings if that's where we're headed?"

"In case one comes in carrying a bomb. If it blows up back there, then at least the command center and most of the troops and material won't be lost."

"Do you really think that's a possibility?"

"It's not really up to me to think, sir," the older man replied.

They walked in silence again after that. The guide took him from the gravel rail yard to a broad street called Gardner Avenue, which was lined with freight holding lots and a few buildings on both side. Some of the empty shells of boxcars and tractor trailers had been arranged to provide watch posts and defensive positions with machine gun nests and sniper perches.

Farther down the road were construction yards that used to house shipping companies. Teams of uniformed engineers swarmed over box cars and long-haul trailers. They worked with plasma cutters and acetylene torches to cut through the sheet metal sides and open up ports for firing. Some welded hand holds in the interior and ladders up the exterior. When stacked vertically, the ladders would line up, and a person inside the defensive perimeter could easily climb from the ground to the top of the structure.

After walking just over a mile from where the train actually stopped, Attledge and his guide finally stopped in front of a low concrete building with a stucco facade. The building had a green metal roof, and on a sign out front the letters KCTT were scripted in yellow. Rows of tractor trailers with a similar paint scheme and matching logo sat in neat rows beyond the building.

The guide pointed to the sign. "This is the Kansas City Transport Terminal. It's serving as our temporary command operations center as well. Colonel Darius is inside waiting for you." The older man handed Attledge his duffle bag and smiled. "It's been good talking with you, sir. I look forward to working with you in the future. If you'll excuse me, I have orders to go check on the construction teams once we reach this point."

Before Attledge could answer, the older man had turned and, with a purposeful stride, was marching back up the avenue. Attledge watched him go for a moment, then turned back to the former shipping company headquarters. Two of the large bay doors at the far end of the building were open and light from inside spilled out onto the paved parking lot.

As Attledge stepped inside, two men in uniform with black military police armbands around their right upper arms approached him. One man took his duffle bag and the other instructed him to hold his hands out to his side and spread his legs. He complied, and the second officer patted him down for concealed weapons. As the MP ran his hands down Attledge's ribs he paused and carefully drew his pistol from the holster and handed it to the other man who was looking through the duffle bag.

When he was done with the pat down, the MP motioned toward the door into the offices. "Colonel Darius is inside waiting for you, Commander. We'll keep your bag and your sidearm safe for you. Standing order from the colonel—no one goes inside armed, not even him."

Attledge nodded, but he hesitated in the maintenance bay. He had never worn a pistol regularly, even when he'd had his concealed carry permit. But now that he was standing there without the familiar and comforting weight of his sidearm on his belt, he felt nervous and exposed. He was conscious of the MPs watching him as he wiped his palms on his pants to dry them and then knocked on the door to the offices.

"Come in," came a muffled voice from inside.

Attledge opened the door and stepped into what had been the supervisor's office when the shipping company was active. There was a long desk along the far wall with a door behind it that led into the rest of the building. The desk was of simple, industrial construction with a metal frame and a broad veneered top. To the left of the desk was a row of four filing cabinets. To the right on the back wall was an open cabinet with three carbine rifles, several stacks of magazines, and a pair of Colt pistols.

"Commander Attledge, welcome to Kansas City," the colonel said with a smile. He motioned to one of the seats on the other side of the desk from him. "Please, come in and have a seat. We have a lot to talk about."

Attledge stepped inside and let the door close behind him.

Chapter 52

Burden of Command

Colonel Darius stood as Attledge was sitting. He turned and poured two glasses of brown liquor from an unlabeled decanter and handed one of them across the desk. Attledge sniffed the liquor, and it smelled like good bourbon.

The colonel raised his glass. "To the Republic," he said simply.

Attledge nodded. "Cheers," he answered and the two touched glasses. He took a slow sip of what he knew was a smooth, well-aged Kentucky straight bourbon. Bourbon and whiskey had always been his drinks of choice, and this definitely had the taste and feel of a good bourbon, but it wasn't one he was familiar with.

The colonel enjoyed his first sip as well, sitting back in his brown leather chair, a content smile on his face. After a long moment, he broke the silence. "Commander, you have traveled a long way. I'm sure you're tired and there is a lot on your mind, so I will keep this as brief as I can. I felt like we needed a proper introduction, though."

Attledge nodded. "I appreciate that, Colonel. I don't have your experience with these kinds of things. I don't exactly know what the protocol is, to be honest. Am I reporting to you?"

Colonel Darius smiled. "Not exactly. You're not going to be under my chain of command, if that's what you're asking. Not directly, anyway. Temporarily, while you're on this base, there will be some things I am in charge of, yes. But in a larger sense, your mission dictates that you report directly to our friend under the mountain, Commander Price. In those instances, you will be the authority on base, not me."

"What about when we're on the road and away from this facility?" Attledge asked.

"We'll get to that in a minute. I'll be blunt, Commander. I don't know you and I don't know whether to trust you or not. Commander Price places a great deal of trust in you and your judgment, but I'm not so sure. You weren't trained for this, and you don't have a military background to draw from. Not in any real sense. But I've been asked to place some of the men I am responsible for under your command and your authority. Now I've got to decide if that's a move I'm willing to make."

"Would you really disobey a direct order from the commander?" Attledge asked. He was shocked to hear Darius even hint at that kind of insubordination, but he was also more than a little scared of what would happen if the colonel decided against him. More than anything, though, he was angry that Darius would betray Commander Price and the nation like this. The cause they were fighting for was worth more than one man's ego.

"We're a long way from Utah, Commander," Darius said. "And one thing's for sure, the man under the mountain isn't going to stick his neck this far out. Not for you, not for me, and certainly not for my men. So, it's up to me. I won't go so far as to say Price is a coward, but I wouldn't deny it either."

Attledge felt his face redden as Darius attacked Commander Price in the latter's absence. "I doubt you'd say those things if Commander Price were here, Colonel. Or if you were in the middle of one of your daily reports over the sat-net. You're always the picture of polite military bearing in those. Are you rebellious and insubordinate only when your superiors aren't present to defend themselves? Hardly the kind of courage and honor I'd expect from a battle-hardened officer like yourself."

The Colonel's face was unreadable for a moment, and then he broke into a broad grin. "Well, you're certainly loyal. At ease, Commander. I apologize. I had to test your loyalties and your backbone at least a little. Of course I don't really have any intention of balking Commander Price's orders. Have you ever had men under your command?"

Marcus shifted in his seat, thrown off balance by the colonel's sudden shift in attitude and subject. "Only at the facility," he answered, trying to determine if this were another ploy. "I was basically second in command and ran the teams based off the objectives Commander Price set. It was that way before the Blackout, just not in a military kind of way. Or maybe it was and I just didn't recognize it at the time. We all called him Commander from day one, so I guess it might have been."

Colonel Darius nodded. "But never in the field," he said as a statement rather than a question. "You've never been in combat."

"Not directly, no."

"Indirectly?" Colonel Darius prodded.

Attledge hesitated, unsure of how to answer the question, or if he could answer it. "Commander Price once told me that it's never a question that's indiscreet, only the answer to it."

"So, you're not going to tell me if you've ever indirectly led men in the field?" Darius asked.

"I've never been in combat. As for the rest, I'm not sure if I can answer you. So, I can't."

Darius took a sip of his bourbon and leaned forward in his chair.
"You do understand the concept of sensitive information. I'm starting to see why Commander Price put so much faith in you, Commander Attledge. I think we're going to be able to work fine together, and I'd be glad to help in any way I can while you're here."

Darius reached into a drawer by his left knee, and Attledge tensed at the movement, planning how he'd respond if the colonel drew a pistol on him. The only thing he had in his hand was his drink, which he'd throw in the colonel's eyes to blind him. If he got lucky he might be able to dodge the first shot. After that, he didn't know what he'd do, but he knew if the colonel did draw on him and managed to get a second shot, it'd be all over.

The colonel paused, his hand still hidden. "It's okay, Commander. I'm not reaching for a weapon. I'm right handed, so this is the wrong side for that, not that you know me well enough to know if that's true. Still, I'm not going for a gun."

Attledge believed the colonel, but he couldn't completely relax. Like Darius had said, they didn't really know each other that well yet, and Attledge had been burned before by people he thought he could trust. Darius took something out of the drawer and sat back slowly, keeping his eye on Marcus's glass the whole time.

The colonel raised his left hand to show Attledge two books. "Look, that's good bourbon and getting even harder to come by these days. Don't waste it throwing it at me, please."

Attledge relaxed a bit more and offered Darius a nervous smile as Darius slid the two books across the desk. Both had plain white covers with text printed on them in similar style and format. One was called *Asymmetrical Warfare in an Urban Environment* and the other was titled *S.E.R.E.--Search Evasion Resistance and Escape*. Marcus picked up the books and leafed through them. Chapters were laid out like outlines with numbered paragraphs and sections. Diagrams were labeled as figures and high-resolution pictures as images with a numbered coding system for both.

"Those are field manuals we use to help train officers," Darius said. "Listen, plans have changed. It happened while you were en route and out of communication. The three weeks of training we had timed out for you here isn't going to happen."

"Wait, what?" Attledge asked. "What do you mean plans have changed?"

"I'm trying to tell you," Darius said in a calm, measured tone. "You're not going to spend three weeks here training. You don't have the time—not anymore. You and four hundred of our best men are going to load up on a train tomorrow morning and head south. You're taking the Tennessee route to the east into North Carolina because it is the fastest and the most direct. And you're going alone."

It took a moment for the colonel's words to sink in. Attledge had barely become used to the idea of tagging along with him when he made his big push to the east, but then he would have been along for the ride. Now, they expected him to make his own way, alone, with four hundred men under his command?

Attledge felt ill. "Sir, there has to be someone better suited. Or at the very least someone better trained for this kind of thing."

"There probably is," Darius agreed. "But there's one thing they don't have. You're not just on some random mission, Commander. You're going into North Carolina to find Captain Joe Tillman. You've met him before, and he'll recognize you. Hell, if Price is right, he may even trust you. But one thing's for sure, if he sees someone like me coming at him, a stranger with four hundred heavily armed men at his back, he's probably going to get the wrong idea. And the last thing we need right now is a friendly fire incident that could be avoided before it ever happens."

Attledge thought about that for a moment. It made sense, in a strange kind of way, but that was far from comforting. He still had no experience in field command. The entire trip from the compound in Utah had been a simple series of refueling stops along the tracks, and he'd had no part in those. The train's crew had handled them start to finish. Now he was being put in charge of the first wave of the assault into enemy territory. It was madness.

"Commander Price has the utmost faith in your abilities," Colonel Darius said. "And I have the utmost faith in Commander Price. If he says you're the right man for the job, you're the right man for the job. He told me I was the right man for this job, and look at what I've done so far. In another few weeks, this will be a somewhat functional city again, and that's all thanks to Price and his plans. He believes in you and so do I."

"I still think this is a mistake," Attledge insisted, but he couldn't find a better argument than that.

"Don't worry," Darius said. "We'll be in touch as much as possible over the sat-phones and we'll walk you through the training manuals. The men under your command are mostly seasoned veterans and former members of the military. They will help you learn the ropes. Take advantage of their experience, but remember the decision is yours in the end. You're the commander. Weigh the options and go with the one you judge is best."

Attledge took a long, slow sip of his bourbon. "I guess when it comes down to it, I don't really have a whole lot of options, do I?" Darius shook his head. "All right, then. If I'm hitting the tracks again in the morning, I might as well learn everything I can from you tonight. What's your best single piece of advice on command?"

Darius was quiet for a long moment as he stared into his bourbon, a far-off look in his dark gray-blue eyes. "The burden of command," the colonel said, finally breaking the silence that had fallen between them. "They spent a lot of time talking about it my last two years at the Point. Still, we weren't ready for it. At least I wasn't, not really. I don't think anyone can be until it happens."

Colonel Darius glanced up and must have recognized the blank look on Attledge's face. He smiled and gave a small shrug of his shoulders. "I keep forgetting that you didn't come up in this world. The burden of command is the weight of responsibility that comes with having to give a person under your command an order that you know will likely result in his death. When you're in hostile territory carrying out maneuvers against the enemy, there will come a time, eventually, when this happens, and you have to be ready for it. If you hesitate or don't give the order, then you could sacrifice the rest of your men or the mission itself. Sometimes the price has to be paid, and that's all there is to it."

Attledge didn't know how to respond. He had long since accepted the idea that people would die as a result of what they were doing. A war cannot be fought any other way. People inevitably die. That is war. He had never considered, though, that some of their losses would be the result of his own orders as much as enemy fire. It was an uncomfortable awareness that now spun and gnawed at the back of his mind.

"Make no mistake, Commander Attledge," Darius said after draining his glass of bourbon. "You're going into hostile territory against a determined, mobile enemy. People—some of them yours—are going to die. You have to remember your objective and remember the bigger picture. There's a lot riding on this mission."

Attledge drank his last bit of bourbon, and Darius refilled both empty glasses. As he handed Attledge his glass, he stood and pulled a rolled map off the top of a filing cabinet behind him. He cleared out a space on top of the desk and rolled out a detailed satellite map, complete with cities, towns, roads, railroads, and topography. A red line was traced down part of the page running from Kansas City south.

Darius pointed to the end of the red line that was marked with yesterday's date. "This is where the scout team has reached so far. They've cleared about two hundred miles of track, and everything has gone smoothly. When they reach the juncture between I-49 and I-40, they'll turn east and start scouting the rough back into Tennessee. You should overtake the scout team somewhere around Russellville, Arkansas, unless you throttle back when you make the turn and let them gain some ground."

"Commander Price seems pressed for time," Attledge reminded him. "It might be better to push on and just stay a few miles behind the scout team. That way if they run into any trouble, we'll be there for reinforcements. Otherwise, if they get stopped or pinned down, we might lose the momentum we need to keep going."

"Initiative," Darius said. "It's called losing the initiative, and you're right. That might be a better option. But don't get so close to the lead team that you can't stop and reverse course if things get really nasty. You'll have to establish communication with them on your own at that point, and that's another risk."

"What will we do for supplies en route?"

Darius smiled. "Already thinking like a commander. The scout team has some available fuel reserves that they will leave along the track. But their ability to carry extras was limited by their need to provide for their own refueling for the first several hundred miles. You'll have to augment that with what you can find along the way. That means you'll have to organize foraging parties. Keep it basic. Remember, all you're looking for is food, fuel, water. If you can collect a few recruits, fine, but don't stick your neck out for them. We'll have plenty of time to fatten the ranks later."

Attledge nodded. "What do you know about the towns ahead of us?"

As Darius began relaying the bits and pieces he'd been able to find out from some of the local draftees and volunteers, Attledge took a sip of his bourbon. It was going to be a very long night, and he was starting to get a headache already.

Chapter 53

Something To Say

Oct. 26 th 0700 EST

Sunrise was still more than a half hour away, and the woods were dark as Danny moved through the trees. He found a good spot on the ridge of a hill that dropped down into a valley with a small creek running through it. There were tall pine trees on top of the hill and oaks lined the sides all the way down to the edge of the running water. He'd hunted here dozens of times before and always found squirrels' nests all along the ridge line. They would eat in the fields behind Danny when corn and soybeans were in season and then turn to the acorns dropped by the oaks when the fields were bare.

Danny stopped and waited as Uncle Jerry caught up to him. The two stood for a while in silence. Danny took a spot at the foot of a tall pine tree and rested his back against the rough bark. He had a good view of a half-dozen trees in front of him as well as another two dozen down the slope. The sky overhead was light enough to see shapes clearly, and the eastern horizon across the valley glowed red and orange.

Uncle Jerry took a tree a few feet in front of Danny and to his left, facing the other direction. They both squatted for a few minutes listening to the birds chirp as they flew through the scrub brush. Squirrels began chattering in the branches overhead, but

Danny didn't hear any of the scratching noises that would indicate they were out of their nests yet. He watched as the sky grew lighter and the dry leaves rustled off to his right as a few birds hopped around searching for food.

A flicker of movement on one of the pine trees in front of him caught Danny's eye. A squirrel was slowly inching its way down the tree, swishing its tail nervously. Danny waited until it paused on a low-hanging limb to clean its bushy tail. He nocked an arrow and drew his bow. The large diameter pulleys at either end of the compound bow swung down and took most of the weight off his arm. Danny aimed through the tiny peep hole at one of the neon posts that stood out in the dim pre-dawn light.

"So why are we out here, Danny?" Uncle Jerry asked, suddenly breaking the silence. The squirrel in Danny's sight turned and scurried up the tree and out of view.

Danny took a deep breath and let it out slowly, trying not to lose his temper. "I thought we were out here squirrel hunting. At least that's what I'm trying to do. Is there some reason you don't want to eat squirrel today, Uncle Jerry?"

Uncle Jerry snorted. "Boy, you've been hunting squirrels since you were ten years old. The last thing you need is my old ass crawling through the woods and makin as much noise as five other men. So, what am I really doing here?"

"We need to talk, Uncle Jerry," Danny said after a long moment of silence.

"Hell, we coulda done that back at the house," Uncle Jerry grumbled. "At least there we'd be warm."

"I thought this would be better discussed in private. Some of the things I have to say you might not want to hear."

"Like what?" Uncle Jerry asked.

"I wanted you to understand that I am taking charge now," Danny said. "I've had to go to crazy lengths to convince you to agree that what I've said was the right thing to do from the beginning. I've done that for the last time, Uncle Jerry. From now on you take your direction from me. You clear things with me first. That's how it has been for a while now, if you think about it, and that's how it's going to be officially now. This can stay between you and me, or we can make a big thing about it back with the others. That part is up to you and how you take this discussion."

"Funny," Uncle Jerry said, though he didn't sound amused. "That's my land you've been hunting on, my land we're hunting on now. It's my stock you've been trading out of and my pork you've been eating and trading both. And it was my horses you *stole* to make that first deal to begin with. So how do you figure it's *you* that's in charge now?"

"Because like I said," Danny replied, his tone taking an edge, "we're here only because of what I've done and what I've gotten the others to help do. We have the stuff we get from outside only because I set it up. And without that trading with the other group— the group I found—we wouldn't even have the lion's share of that. We'd been going hungry a long time ago."

Danny took a deep breath and tried to calm himself down. "I can use your advice and I can use you as a teacher. With the experience and knowledge you have, you're an invaluable resource. But when it comes to making decisions like a direction we're going to head or a cause we're going to support, that's my call from now on. Because either way, I'm going to be the one actually settin it up and doing it while you sit here at home and hunt squirrel."

"If that's how you feel, I'll do it myself," Uncle Jerry growled, shaking his head so that his white ponytail wagged back and forth. "I'll go out and find stuff and bring it back too. Can't be that hard."

"No. You won't. For one thing, I won't tell you the details of when or where we meet with the other group, so that's gone. You got another ready source of good, fresh, high-quality red meat? Cause I don't. We lose that protein source, whatever else happens, we die. Understand that."

Uncle Jerry stood and strode over to Danny, and as he walked, a squirrel inched its way around one of the pine trees to Danny's left, trying to keep the tree between itself and Uncle Jerry. Danny turned, drew his already nocked arrow, sighted, and released all in one smooth motion. The arrow sprang away from the bow and took the squirrel between the shoulder blades. It was blunt tipped and designed to kill the animal, at least stun it and knock it to the forest floor. A pointed arrow would have impaled the prey and probably pinned it to the tree.

The squirrel squawked once and then tumbled out of the tree, dead. Uncle Jerry scooped it up as he retrieved the arrow. Danny stood as he approached, and Uncle Jerry handed him the squirrel and the arrow together, then took a step back and held Danny's eyes with his own.

After a long moment, Uncle Jerry broke the uncomfortable silence between them. "You know, back in my Daddy's day, when people had a problem, they handled it a different way. Hell, even when I was coming up, we handled things differently. If you had a problem with someone that was serious enough, you might plan a trip like this. And plan 'an accident' if things didn't go the way you wanted them to. Is that what this was? You planning an accident for me?"

Danny shook his head. "Uncle Jerry I should knock you for even thinking that. We're family, for Pete's sake. Get your head on right. I'm not angry at you and I sure ain't trying to hurt you over this. I'm just telling you how it's been, how it is, and how it's gonna keep on being. That's all. Oh, and trying to get enough squirrels that we can grill them instead of stewing them."

"You don't like my squirrel stew?"

"It's not that," Danny replied. "I just like it better on the grill with a little lemon pepper and butter. But that works only if we can do half a squirrel a person that wants one, and if we have butter. Otherwise we gotta stew it to get the most out of the meat. We just had squirrel stew last week. I want something different this week."

Uncle Jerry was quiet again as he surveyed the trees around them, and he had a troubled look when he turned back to Danny. "I'll follow your lead from here on out. You have my word. But I won't kill. Not again. I made a deal with God that if I got out of the war in Europe, I would never take another man's life, not ever. I've had a long life and imagine it ain't too long before I'll have a face to face with the Father, so I would really like to live up to my end of the bargain as much as possible. I'll teach people how to farm, how to hunt, how to track, how not to get tracked. But there are some things I just won't do. If you have a problem with that, then we have a problem."

Danny shook his head. "We don't have a problem, Uncle Jerry. You can teach people how to farm, teach them how to hunt, how to track, how to keep from being tracked, things like that. Teach them what you know about living off the land. That's going to be the bulk of what we have to do anyway, so that's what they need to learn. The fighting stuff will come later."

Uncle Jerry sighed heavily and sat at the foot of the pine tree next to Danny. "I never thought I would see this kind of thing here, on our own soil. Never thought I'd see the day when we had to put a gun in a young man's hand so he could go fight a war not on the other side of the globe, but on the other side of the county. Just don't seem right." He fell silent for a moment and then asked, "So where will you hit them first?"

"Captain Tillman wants to stir up trouble on the northeast side of town. We'll start tracking their foraging teams in that area and ambush a few of them. That seemed to get their attention when he did it the first time, and maybe it will again. He's wanting them looking up here for trouble so he can plan a big hit on their main supply lines."

Uncle Jerry nodded and let the matter drop. "Well, I reckon if we quit all of this yapping we might actually see a few more squirrels. I ain't exactly in the mood for stew either, you know."

Danny smiled and went back to scanning the trees. He had expected more pushback from Uncle Jerry, and he wasn't entirely certain the matter was settled, yet. The real test of whether Uncle Jerry had taken their conversation to heart would be the first time that his way of doing things didn't line up with Danny's. But until then, he was going to take the older man at his word and hope that everything else would work itself out in time.

Chapter 54

Out of the Woods

Oct. 26 th 1100 EST

Arthur felt the young man's forehead, but there was no sign of fever. The group had a decent stock of antibiotics and pain medicine that he'd put to good use. After nearly a full day, the stump wasn't bleeding through the bandages, and there were no new signs of the effects of the venom. It seemed Micah had dodged a deadly bullet, but Arthur knew he wasn't out of the woods yet, not by a long shot.

It would take the wound on the stump of his leg a long time to heal, and as long as it was open, there was the chance of infection taking hold. He could also open the stitches by thrashing around if he woke up in pain, so they had worked hard to keep him sedated and medicated.

"I spoke with his parents," Sue Ellen said from the doors of the church. Micah was laid out in one of the aisles of the church, blankets propping up his head and chest. Sue Ellen stepped fully into the sanctuary and looked down at the sleeping patient. "They know that he's alive right now because you happened to be here at the right time to keep him that way. They're grateful, but I don't think they're ready to say so yet. They're still getting used to the idea that you had to chop off their son's foot."

Arthur nodded and followed Sue Ellen back out of the church. "The young man's doing well," he said once they were outside in the warm fall sunshine. "But you have to be cautious. If infection sets in it'll be damn near impossible to get rid of it. And with the number of major vessels and arteries compromised, it'll turn septic in a heartbeat. I recommend you keep dosing him with antibiotics until the wound starts to close up."

"You're talking like you're not gonna be here to see it through yourself," Sue Ellen said, casting a sidelong glance at Arthur. "We could use people like you around here, Arthur. People get sick and sometimes they need a doctor to get well. Not to mention the people you got with you who are real fighters. We don't run into trouble often, but if we had your group as part of ours, we'd run into it a lot less."

Arthur was quiet for a moment but not because he was really thinking about Sue Ellen's offer. Without coming out and saying it, he was trying to find a polite way to tell her to forget about them hanging around. "I appreciate the offer, and I'll talk it over with the others, but I'm on my way to see if we can find my daughter. I can't stay. Not after we've come so far. I might be able to come back after I've seen her, after I know she's okay. But I can't stay here and just give up on finding her. I couldn't live with that."

Sue Ellen pursed her lips. "I wish you'd rethink that. Like I said, we could use people like you around here. Will you at least stay until Micah is out of the woods?"

Arthur took a long slow breath to buy some time to consider his answer. Finally, he gave a small shrug. "Honestly, it's not really up to me, but I promise I will stay as long as I can to make sure he has the best chance possible. Beyond that, I can't give my word because I just don't know."

Sue Ellen nodded her head but didn't look like she had the answer she wanted, so she decided to accept Arthur's answer—for now. "Well, when you know a time frame for when you'll be moving on, let me know. The people here will want to send you all off with a fitting thank you. I'm pretty sure that young man would be dead if not for your quick thinking."

"Well, I wasn't looking for special favors," Arthur said, an earnest frown creasing his forehead. "I just had to help the young man."

"I know," Sue Ellen said with a smile as she started down the front steps of the church. "That's what makes it special. Don't worry, Dr. Arthur," she called over her shoulder, "we'll talk again soon."

Chapter 55

Groundwork

Oct. 26 th 1800 EST

Vice-President Daniel Arnold pressed the button to disconnect the sat-phone and set the small receiver in the lockbox he used for security. The lid clicked as it locked, and he turned to walk back inside the Chancellorsville Visitor Center. The group had taken over the modest building to serve as their command post and their personal quarters for the night. After inspecting the grounds, Arnold had claimed the defunct theater room as his, and Lieutenant Colonel Hagerston, the force commander, had taken the central welcome hall as his sleeping area. Anyone coming into or leaving the building would have to pass by him at some point.

Arnold stepped inside and found Hagerston seated comfortably behind a desk that had recently been occupied by one of the former administrative clerks. The colonel looked up from a stack of papers and folders on the desk and nodded toward the chair across from him. He didn't have anything else pressing at the moment, so Arnold decided to take one of the chairs, but he deliberately chose the one that the commander had not pointed to.

"Daniel, why don't you have a seat," Hagerston said, making it sound more like an order than an offer. "How are things back in D.C.?"

"The President sends his regards," Arnold answered. "I'm sure he'll want to speak to you in due time. He said to pass along the order to continue along his original path south. For now, that is all you need to know."

"I hardly think that's all I need to know. I need to know a little more about you, Daniel. If we are going to serve together in the field, I need to know the man I have with me. I know the men under my command very well. I was personally involved in most of their training. But not you. I'd never met you before a couple of days ago and to be frank, I don't trust you."

Arnold smiled. It irked him that the other man was using his given name, but he chose not to let it show. Instead, he decided to return the favor. "Well, Lucas, I guess you could read my file, if you had that level of security clearance. Which you don't. So, don't fool yourself into thinking we are serving 'together.' We are not. I serve at the pleasure of the President of the United States. I am under his command, not yours. And you would do well to remember that."

"In that regard," Hagerston said, "we are exactly alike. So, I guess that means we have nothing to gain from making an enemy of each other. Would you agree?"

Arnold considered that statement. It made sense for the colonel to try and feel him out. He would do the same in the other man's position, but as much as the military commander might not trust him, Arnold didn't trust the commander. They were going to be working together and living in close proximity in hostile territory for a long time. Surely that had to count for some kind of trust.

"Perhaps we are missing the forest for the trees, Colonel, " Arnold said. "We both stand within arm's reach of the most powerful man in our respective universe, and that man is President Hall. If we agree to watch each other's backs, then he is the only person we have to worry about. Between the two of us, I'm sure we can keep any other internal or external threats to our positions in check. All we have to do is follow orders and keep a close eye on those around us. What do you say?"

A slow smile spread across Hagerston's face. "Mr. Vice President," he said without a trace of irony, "I couldn't agree more."

Arnold smiled as well. "Glad to hear it. Now, about this road south. We left Alexandria with fifteen thousand men. I would like to arrive at Fort Bragg with at least twice that many. That means we take on new soldiers however we have to. Offer voluntary service to everyone and give more responsibility to those who volunteer and prove their loyalty. See how far we can push them. After that, we draft people into service whether or not they agree. That means conscription."

The colonel reached into his desk and pulled out a pair of cigars. He handed one to Arnold and clipped the end of the one he kept. He offered the cutters to Arnold as he lit his own with a torch lighter. Arnold pulled a small onyx butane torch from his pocket and lit his.

"We won't be popular with the locals if we conscript," Hagerston said. "It's been done before, and people always react badly."

"We will be moving quickly," Daniel said. "That should help keep the impact light. The local population won't have time to work up the courage to attack us before we move on. The president spoke with me about this before I left. His personal order. He wants to overwhelm whatever forces remain when we reach Fort Bragg. And that means we need numbers."

"I understand the order," Hagerston said. "But, if we get bogged down anywhere or if we hit an unexpected road block, then we are screwed. And make no mistake, word of what we're doing will absolutely get out ahead of us. It will get more difficult as we go, and people will likely start resisting."

Arnold took a long, slow drag on his cigar. "Let them," he said as he blew a smoke ring. "They won't resist long."

Chapter 56

Operation Suitcase

Oct. 26th 2300 EST

President Hall sat in a basement room deep beneath the Capitol building. The rooms here were dark and musty, but they were also thick with history. Old paintings and furnishings, the leftovers of two centuries of dead memories, cluttered many of the storerooms and closets, but not all of them. Some of them had always been reserved for the kinds of meetings that didn't make it into official registers and records. These were the meetings where the real operation of power was executed, but few rarely rose to the level of seeing it firsthand.

The man kneeling naked on the cold stone floor in front of him was barely recognizable. His body was a mottled mass of bruises, blisters, and lacerations. His face was swollen and disjointed, looking somewhat like a grotesque caricature of a Picasso. One eye was swollen shut, and the other had blown capillaries and looked as if he should be weeping blood.

The smell turned Hall's stomach.

"Senator," he said calmly, "you have to understand that this is not what I want. I don't want you to suffer. I don't want anyone to suffer, in fact. I simply want the truth. I want to know what you and the late Senator MacArthur discussed. I want to know what he told you and what you told him."

404

The man before him groaned and whimpered softly. He looked up at the president. The one eye that could see was tearing up and pleading. "I ha-have dold the-thuth," he mumbled around a wad of cloth stuffed in his mouth.

Hall leaned forward and took the gag from Senator Coleman's mouth so he could speak.

"I have told you the truth," Senator Coleman whispered around his swollen lips and jaws. "I swear, I've told you the truth. I told him to just say the damned words. Just say the words, whatever he thought. He could do anything after that, just say the words. And I warned him. I warned him about what would happen. I told him you'd kill him and you'd kill me too."

Tears streamed from both eyes now, mingling with the blood on his face and dripping pink and red from his chin.

"I swear, that's the truth," he said over and over. "I tried to tell him, I tried. I swear, please don't ask again, please."

President Hall regarded the man with a thoughtful frown as he crumbled into a weeping and sobbing heap, mumbling over and over in a voice almost too feeble to hear, "I tried . . . I tried to tell him. I warned him . . . He wouldn't listen . . ." Finally, President Hall looked over at the two guards by the door and nodded. They left and he turned back to his guest.

"You were half right," the president said calmly, and suddenly Senator Coleman's blubbering ceased. "I did kill Senator MacArthur but only because he betrayed my trust. I know you didn't betray my trust, did you Senator Coleman? You were loyal and trustworthy, and you've proven that here today. A lesser man might have been tempted to bargain with Senator MacArthur, or possibly even to join the man's cause, but not you. You are far too smart and far too loyal for that, aren't you, Senator Coleman?"

Coleman's head was nodding before President Hall even stopped speaking, and the self-loathing in his one-eyed stare was frightening. But words spilled out of his mouth of their own accord.

"I-I-I w-was loyal, M-M-Mr. President," he stuttered. "I-I s-swear, I was l-l-loyal. I will always b-b-be loyal. Y-y-you have m-m-my word. I w-will take w-whatever oath . . . you w-w-want me to take; I'll s-swear it on a Bible, o-o-on anything. P-p-please, don't k-kill me."

Just then the doors to the tiny room opened, and a man wearing a white hospital coat stepped inside. He had been a doctor, a surgeon, at the Walter Reed National Military Medical Center, but he now served in the FSS.

"I'm not going to kill you, Senator Coleman," Hall reassured the senator. "Especially now that I know the extent of your loyalty. In times like these, a man in my position can never be too sure of the loyalties of those around him except with extreme vetting. I'm sorry for any discomfort you may have suffered, Senator, I truly am. But I can rest easy now knowing that I have your full faith, trust, and confidence. And you can rest easy knowing that you have mine."

The doctor took a brief look at Senator Coleman's injuries and retrieved some supplies from the bag he carried with him. He whimpered as the doctor began gently cleaning his battered face.

"Let the doctor take care of you, Senator," Hall said as he stood to go. "When you've healed, you will resume your normal duties in the Senate. We'll talk again soon."

Hall left the room as the doctor continued to examine Senator Coleman's injuries. The two guards that had been in the room during the interrogation now stood outside the door. Both men snapped to attention as the president stepped out into the dim hallway and made his way to the stairs. The halls of the Capitol were empty except for him and his security detail.

When Hall reached his quarters, he left the security detail at the entrance and closed the door before the commander could raise a protest. He strode over to his private desk and unlocked the bottom left drawer. In the back, buried beneath a stack of unimportant papers and documents, was a small satellite phone. He took a small card from his wallet and dialed the number printed across the back.

The phone barely had time to ring before a voice answered. "This is call sign Domino. Go for authentication. Over."

"This is Eagle One," Hall responded. "Authentication code: Zulu-Alpha-Four-Seven-One-X-ray-Five-Romeo."

There was a brief pause before the man on the other end responded. "Authentication received and confirmed, go for orders."

"Operation Suitcase is a go. Your target is the Kansas City insurrection. Main target is the garrison and command center at the rail-yard. Remember, soldier, these are the people who started this whole catastrophe. They launched the missiles that brought down the grid, they dropped a nuke on New York, and now they're planning to push east and take over the rest of the nation. And you're the only one who can stop them."

The pause was longer this time. "Understood, Mr. President. I won't let you down."

"God's speed," Hall said.

The line clicked and went dead.

Hall pulled a small piece of paper out of one of the seemingly unimportant folders that had buried the sat-phone. Most of the other documents were old tax records, receipts, and bogus shipping orders that he had created simply for camouflage, but this one document was incredibly important. There were twenty-five alphanumeric codes on the page, each with eight characters. The first five codes at the top of the page had already been marked through. He ran a finger down the list until he found the serial number he was looking for and marked through it as well, leaving nineteen numbers untouched.

Hall leaned back in his chair with a satisfied smile on his face. With one strike, he would eliminate a good portion of the enemy's leadership, their fighting force, and their material. Not to mention it would destroy the trains and tracks the enemy had put to use in mobilizing its forces.

As President Hall considered the impact of the order he'd just given, he began humming, "This little light of mine. I'm going to make it shine."

Chapter 57

The Needs of the Many

Oct. 27th 0300 CST

Sticks hated standing watch. He especially hated standing watch on the last shift before sunrise, but he was one of four guards on the northern perimeter of the camp that had drawn the short straw. And that meant his last five hours before sunrise that should have been spent peacefully on his cot were now spent standing in the starlight, waiting. The night was quiet and cool enough that his breath fogged in front of his face, but it wasn't uncomfortably cold.

It was, however, uncomfortably boring. The brief trip to talk with Colonel Darius about the radiation badge had been a respite from the usual drudgery of guard duty, but here he was back on the beat again.

"Chester, want to stretch your legs?" Sticks asked one of the other men standing watch with him.

"Sure," Chester replied.

"Okay, guys, we're going to walk the fence," Sticks said to the other pair of sentries.

The other two nodded, but didn't say anything. Sticks followed Chester through the gate and the turned west along Front Street. Since they had eliminated the FSS garrison in the city, no one really expected to see action on guard duty. Most of the citizens in the immediate area around the camp had already been absorbed and were now uniformed members of what they were calling the National Defense Force. As the camp spread into the surrounding city, they pushed out the dangerous and criminal elements as they went. That made for a relatively peaceful area around the camp and some very boring hours spent on guard duty.

It's not that Sticks wanted an attack to happen, far from it. He just hated standing around waiting with nothing to do. This was why he was walking the fence line for the fourth time in an hour. Thankfully he was on guard duty with Chester, who was nearly as restless as Sticks when it came to standing watch. Sticks had been in the same training group with Chester when they first volunteered, and he'd gotten to know him relatively well. Chester was something of a local legend, having served as an enlisted man in the first Gulf War and then resigning when the twin towers fell on 9/11. After completing Officer Candidate School for the army, he had pulled three tours in Afghanistan and two in Iraq before retiring once more. He was one of the few members of the NDF that had not only been in the military before the Blackout but had seen actual combat.

"When do you think we'll get the orders to move out?" Sticks asked, trying to find a way to break the silence.

Chester shrugged. "When the Colonel decides we've got enough muscle to make it."

"I'm surprised you didn't go with Commander Attledge when he went south," Sticks said. "They're going to be in some of the heaviest fighting soon, from what I hear, and I bet they could have used someone like you."

"I tried," Chester admitted, "but Colonel Darius wanted to keep a few combat vets here to help with training and security. He's got a good head for this kind of stuff, better than some I've served under. As much as I'd love to be at the tip of the sword, there are a bunch of people here who have no experience with combat or military life in general, and they need training. I'm surprised you didn't try to go as well."

Sticks shrugged. "I've seen enough combat for one lifetime," he replied. "I'm not in any real hurry to see it again."

Silence fell between the two men once again as they walked. Memories and emotions from his own time in Iraq rushed to the surface, and Sticks did his best to push them back down again. He'd lost several close friends in Fallujah, and it was still difficult to remember those days without feeling the pain of that loss.

Chester suddenly stopped in his tracks and held up his right hand closed in a fist. Sticks recognized the signal, and his awareness snapped back to reality as he shouldered his rifle and scanned the area around them for a threat. All he saw, though, were shadows cast by the empty industrial buildings and the empty road.

"What do you see, Chester?" Sticks whispered.

Chester pointed down the street. "There was movement. I thought I saw someone cross the road about a hundred yards down. Headed toward the fence."

Sticks squinted hard but couldn't see anything. His eyes weren't as good as they once had been, and the light from the banks of halogen construction lights a few hundred yards away inside the rail yard perimeter were the only real source of light around. The stars overhead cast a little light, but with no moon, the shadows cast by the construction lights were dark and deep.

411

Then, just on the edge of his hearing, Sticks caught the sound of the chain link fence rattling to their left and then, a sharp, metallic snap.

"Shit," Sticks whispered, pointing down the road and toward the fence. "Someone's trying to cut through. We gotta go. Now."

Chester nodded, and the two ran in a low, crouch toward the sound. They had gone seventy yards when Chester stopped them again with a raised fist. He turned and looked at Sticks, pointing to his eyes, then back down the road. He signaled with his fingers that there was one person at the fence line twenty yards ahead of them. Sticks crept up next to Chester and saw the shadowy figured kneeling by the fence. It looked like the stranger was working with a pair of wire cutters to clip through the thick chain link fence. Each pop sent a ripple down the fence.

"Should we just shoot him?" Sticks asked.

Chester thought a moment, then shook his head. "Might be someone desperate and hungry, or something. We can't tell if he's hostile just because he's trying to get into the camp. Could just be looking for food."

Sticks wasn't so sure, but Chester was the one with more experience, so he nodded. Chester stood and Sticks stood with him, keeping his rifle at the ready, just in case.

"Stop!" Chester called in a loud voice as he started forward. "This is Lieutenant Chester Douglass of the . . ."

As Chester spoke, the figure at the fence suddenly stood and turned. There was a flash and a loud pop, and Chester was cut off midsentence as a round tore through his throat. Sticks stood stunned for an instant and Chester half turned toward him, his hands clutching at his neck as blood pumped through his fingers.

Chester fell slowly to his knees, a confused look on his face as his mouth moved, trying to speak.

Another round snapped through the air close enough to Sticks' head for him to feel the wind as it passed. The near miss jolted him out of his shock, and he dropped to one knee and fired his rifle. At least one of his rounds found its mark, and the shadowy figure stumbled backwards and fell, ending the brief, but intense, gun battle. Sticks walked forward and found a man dressed in tactical gear with what looked like a heavy military style backpack on the ground next to him. One of the rounds from Sticks' rifle had taken him through the chest and another through the left eye. Although the assailant was clearly dead, Sticks still kicked a short barreled tactical carbine away from his outstretched hand.

Just then the other pair of sentries that he and Chester had left at the gate came to a skidding halt in the Humvee. One of the men was manning the mounted .50 caliber machine gun and the other leapt out of the cab, scanning the area for any additional threats. When Sticks told the pair that they were clear, the man who had leapt from the cab came over to him while the machine gunner kept a watch on the buildings around them.

"What the hell happened, Sticks?" the man, a sergeant that Sticks didn't know personally, asked. "I thought you two were just going for a walk, and then we heard gunfire."

Sticks pointed at the dead man lying next to the fence. "Chester spotted this guy headed for the fence line, and we came to check it out. I wanted to drop the guy, but Chester was worried about shooting a starving civilian, so he called out. As soon as Chester identified himself, the guy started shooting. He hit Chester in the throat and then I returned fire and dropped him."

"Jesus, is Chester . . . " the sergeant said, looking back at Chester.

Sticks nodded. "He's gone. There was nothing I could do for him."

The sergeant clenched his teeth and shook his head. "Well, let's see what this asshole was carrying."

Sticks waited as the sergeant stepped over to the body and pulled the canvas duffle away from it. He had no desire to see the man's ruined face staring up at the sky again—once had been enough. The sergeant unbuckled the top of the bag and opened it, shining his flashlight inside to get a better look. Suddenly he stood straight as a board and all of the blood drained from his face. The flashlight, still on, slipped from his fingers as he began whispering over and over, "Oh God, oh God, oh God . . ."

"What is it, Sarge?" Sticks asked, taking a step toward the fence.

The other man turned and ran.

"Where the hell is he goin?" the machine gunner asked, pointing down Front Street after the sergeant. "The only thing down that way is the dang river."

Sticks didn't listen. He carefully bent and opened the canvas duffle bag, using the sergeant's forgotten flashlight to look inside. The entire backpack was filled with a large, gray metal cylinder. On the end facing Sticks was a bright yellow circle with a small red circle in the center and three red triangles surrounding it, the universal sign of radiation. There was also a small digital clock display counting down, and as Sticks watched the timer ticked past twelve minutes.

"Oh, God," he whispered.

414

"Not you too," the machine gunner said, snapping Sticks out of his trance.

"Get out of the hummer," Sticks shouted up to the man, who stared back with a confused look. "Get out of the hummer, *now*!!" he called again.

This time the man nodded and climbed down out of the gunner's nest. As he worked his way out of the vehicle, Sticks grabbed the backpack and shouldered it, surprised at how heavy it was. He did his best not to think about why something so relatively small would be so disproportionately heavy, and he hurried up the embankment to the road.

By the time he reached the cab of the Humvee, the machine gunner was standing on the pavement at the back of the vehicle. Sticks carefully set the backpack in the passenger seat of the cab, pulled the handheld short-range radio out, and tossed it to the machine gunner.

"What are you doing?" the man asked.

"No time to explain," Sticks answered. "You're from around here, right? What's the quickest way north out of town? I need to get as far away from people as possible as quickly as possible."

"Uh—take the I-435 loop up to I-35 and just keep headin north," the man said.

Sticks climbed into the driver's seat and pulled a tight U-turn in the middle of Front Street. He jammed the accelerator to the floor and the tires squealed as the heavy Humvee accelerated. The I-435 loop was clearly visible at the end of the road, and he took the onramp going so fast that the back end of the Humvee fish-tailed as he straightened out on the highway. As he drove, Sticks did his best not to look at the backpack in the seat next to him, and he tried not to think about what was inside it. All he could think about were the hundreds of men and women behind him at the rail yard.

The speedometer on the dashboard showed that the vehicle was traveling just under eighty miles per hour, and Sticks had the gas pedal down as far as he could. The highway was mostly empty, but there were a few broken down cars and trucks in the lanes. Thankfully, he was able to dodge his way around them without slowing down too much. After six miles, he saw the interchange for I-35 north, and he took the ramp at full speed. The tires squealed and smoked, but the Humvee kept barreling down the road.

As he left the city behind, Sticks glanced over at the timer and saw he had a little more than six and a half minutes left. Sticks reached over and closed the top of the backpack, resolving not to open it again. The end would come when it came, and he didn't want to watch the timer count down to zero in the meantime.

Tears began to run down his cheeks.

"God," he said softly, "I'm not sure if you're listening or not. It's been a long time since I had anything to say worth hearing, so maybe you changed the channel a long time ago, I don't know. But I've got a feeling I'm going to have a chance for a meetin here in a little bit, so there's some things I need to get out in the open."

Sticks took a deep, shaky breath as waves of emotion rolled over him. "I know I haven't been the best person. There's things I've done, lots of them, that I'm not proud of. I cheated on a girlfriend and broke her heart. I stole three hundred dollars from my second job and never got caught. I lied to my best friend about his fiancé, and they split up because of it. Kelly was so torn up about it she killed herself two years later, and I know part of that was my fault."

Memories he had not allowed himself to think about in years came rushing to the surface, and Sticks' vision went blurry as the tears flowed steadily. "I've killed people," he whispered. "It was war, and it was what we were there to do, to defend our country, but I killed people. I watched them die, the fear and pain in their eyes, and I didn't feel a thing but satisfaction."

Sticks fell silent for a moment, overcome with emotion as heavy sobs shook his entire body.

"I've tried to live a good life, Lord," he croaked when he could speak again. "I've tried, but I know I've failed. Please, Lord, forgive me. Forgive my sins."

The bag beside him began to beep.

Sticks closed his eyes and let go of the wheel, and a smile spread slowly across his face. "I'm coming home, Lord. I . . ."

Chapter 58

A Distant Fire

Oct 27 th 0332 CST

Colonel Darius stepped out of the Humvee in full uniform with polished boots and a holstered nickel-plated .45 caliber pistol at his hip. He had driven out here expecting to die in a cloud of nuclear fire and death, and he was determined to look his best while he did it. Now the driver was saying there was chatter on the radio about the bomb not being there anymore.

"Okay, men, what's going on?" he asked as he approached. "Who's been stacking bodies up next to my fence?"

The commanding officer on the scene, a captain from Iowa whose name Darius could not remember at the moment, nodded to the two bodies. "Chester went on a walk along the fence line with Sticks. That is, I mean . . ." the captain sputtered.

Darius raised one hand. "I know Sticks, Captain. Just tell me what happened please."

The captain nodded and swallowed hard. He was sweating far more than the cool night should have caused. "Well, sir, Sticks and Chester were walking the fence line and they saw someone trying to breach the perimeter. Chester called out and was shot. Sticks returned fire and killed the would-be intruder. They found a package the enemy had been carrying. A bomb, and it had radiation markings all over the casing. And the dead man had this on him."

The captain handed Darius a radiation badge of the same style that the man and his son had brought from Kansas City. Darius turned the badge over in his hands and squinted trying to read the numbers.

"Where is Sticks?" Darius asked, but he was certain he already knew the answer.

"Sir, he . . . he took the bomb," the captain said, and his voice broke. "He took it and took the guard-duty Humvee and started driving. Sir, he just started driving."

Suddenly a flash of brilliant blue-white light lit the sky, and the shadows all around them shifted away from it. Darius flung a hand up in front of his face, but he could still see the light of the flash behind closed eyes and his hand. After a few seconds the light faded slightly, and the colonel let his hand drop. To the north, a glowing cloud rose high into the night sky and Darius could clearly see the bands of fire that twisted into vortexes within vortexes as they rose into the sky and finally dissipated. The cloud itself was lit with a menacing reddish orange glow from beneath in a similar way that low hanging rain clouds used to light up with a reflected glow from the street lights of a city.

But this wasn't that kind of light. It was sharper, harsher, and it meant a large area of fire burned intensely beneath the cloud. The top of the mushroom cloud was lost in the night sky, simply a vague impression of a dark blot that was slowly expanding, but the base of the cloud still glowed on the horizon. Several heartbeats went by and then the unmistakable sharp sound of the blast, dimmed slightly by the distance, rolled over the rail yard.

Darius felt tears well up in him, but he crushed those thoughts for the moment. He couldn't afford that, not right now.

He spun back to face the captain. "Son, I need you to listen," he said, grabbing the captain's shoulder gently to get his attention. The man jumped as soon as Darius' hand landed on his shoulder. "Son, I need you to listen to me. I need you to go back to the barracks and start waking everyone up. I want runners sent to the other garrisons and supply dumps throughout the city. Everyone is to be back here with all of the gear they can carry, load, and drag behind them. Tell the transport crews to prep the trains too. We're leaving in the morning, all of us. They need to get their asses in gear. You understand? Now, go."

The captain turned and ran down the fence line in the direction of the gate as Darius turned and found a lieutenant. "You, go through the camp and tell them the same thing. Everyone needs to get moving on this. We've got a lot of work to do and not a lot of time to do it."

The lieutenant also sped off, and Darius addressed the rest of the men around him. "Search the body for any intel and then bring Chester back inside. We'll bury him in the morning before we leave. He deserves a hero's burial."

The men nodded, and Darius turned to look at the northern horizon where a new light was shining. The dim glow from several minutes before was now a long red swath across the horizon.

"As do you, Sticks," he whispered.

Chapter 59

For a Bit

Mike stood on the road in the early morning sunshine, soaking in the warmth. To his left and behind him a large, open field held the group's tents spread out in a rough semicircle. Their cook fires were going strong and the smell of bacon and powdered eggs teased his nose when the breeze shifted and blew against his back. At the moment, though, the breeze was blowing down the road from his right and he could smell Alyssa's hair. She had found a few travel-size bottles of Pert Plus and had shampooed every morning since.

"I know it wasn't you," Alyssa said, breaking the heavy silence that had separated them all morning. "You didn't choose to put her in that situation. But you almost got my sister killed, and I have had to come to grips with that."

"I didn't know that psychopath Griff would really pull the trigger," Mike said. "Maybe I should have, but I didn't. I thought he was bluffing, and I thought I could bluff harder. But I'm not the one who kidnapped people and put a gun to their heads. As much as I hate to say this, thank God, he chose the guy who had been with us two days instead of your sister when he picked who to shoot first. And once it was clear the kind of monster that prick was, I didn't waste any time with him, did I?"

421

Alyssa shook her head. "No, you did what had to be done," she admitted. "I know that, and I can explain your actions rationally, but I still have a lot of anger about the whole situation, and it has to go somewhere. I know it's not logical or fair to feel this way toward you, but that's still the truth. You did everything you could to keep us safe before that, and since. And I love you for that."

Alyssa stopped, her eyes wide and her mouth hanging open. It was the first time either of them had said the words, though Mike had felt them for a long time. Alyssa blinked and her teeth clicked as she clamped her mouth shut. Red flushed her cheeks.

Mike opened his mouth to tell her he loved her too, but she held up a finger and shook her head. Tears suddenly filled her eyes, and she turned and walked away, back toward the camp. As she went, Arthur passed her on his way to Mike, and Alyssa turned her head away from the older man and kept walking.

Arthur smiled as he walked up to Mike. "It's good to see you two talking again," he said as he shook Mike's hand. "For a while there I was worried that you wouldn't be able to mend the fences. Did you work things out?"

Mike snorted a quick laugh. "I wish I knew," he said. "Half of the time it feels like I get more confused when we talk than when we don't, and this was a perfect example. She just told me she loved me for the first time and then stormed off on the verge of tears before I could even say it back. I don't think I understand women."

Arthur put a reassuring hand on Mike's shoulder. "Son, I've lived with one for more than forty years, and I still don't understand them."

Mike nodded and turned back to the road. He knew it wasn't really necessary to stand guard here, but he didn't want the group to get out of the practice of keeping watch. The best way to make sure the group took security seriously was for him to get involved and take a shift where people could see him right out there along with them. The truth was the little Uwharrie community, as they were calling themselves, had enough people to keep the woods and hills in the area patrolled and clear of most troublemakers. They had apparently shadowed Mike and his group since they crossed the bridge, and no one had even known.

Even now, Mike felt like they were seeing only what this other, larger group wanted them to see. He didn't like the nagging feeling that he was being kept in the dark.

"I guess you probably know why I asked to see you this morning," Arthur began. "Listen, I understand why you want to push on ahead. We've had to go through so much to get where we are, and we're so close now. I get that, but what happened here, I stepped into the middle of it, and things were done on my word, so I have to carry that now. I'm not going to just turn my back on that responsibility."

Mike started to respond, but Arthur held up a hand. "Please, just let me get through what I have to say, then we can talk about it if we need to." Arthur waited and continued only after Mike had nodded in agreement. "If you need to take the group and go, then I understand that call and why you have to make it. To be honest, there are some of our own people I don't trust around here. But I can't go. Not yet. I have to wait until Micah is stable and I know that there's no chance for infection and no lingering effects of the venom. I've got to see this through to the end of it or I won't be able to live with myself."

Arthur paused and looked like he was going to continue but remained silent for a moment. Finally, he gave a small shrug. "I guess that's all I needed to say. Whatever you decide, I'm staying until I know the boy is going to be okay. I took his foot, so I owe him that much."

Mike waited politely for a moment to make sure that Arthur was finished before he replied. "Arthur, I wouldn't ask you to leave if your conscience wasn't clear on it. I respect you too much for that. Besides, I think there are things we could probably teach these people, and I know there are things we can learn from them. I'm not ready to move on quite yet."

"You know, there will be more than a few of our group that aren't happy about the delay. They'll want to get moving again, immediately, and they may split off on their own over it."

Mike nodded. "Yeah, and there are some who won't be happy that we aren't looting this place clean. Not sure how we'll end up dealing with them. I can take it if people want to strike out on their own to go a different direction or because we're holding them back. That's their call. But we can't let people split off because they want to cross that line from trading to taking. If we do, whatever that other group does is on us too."

"That will be a problem, eventually," Arthur said.

Mike smiled. "Without a doubt, but not today. Today we have far simpler things to worry about, like waiting to see if a boy's leg will kill him or not. How long do you think it will take before you can make the call —before you're sure that he won't have anything to worry about?"

Arthur gave another small shrug. "It's difficult to say. I'm not a doctor, after all, at least not the right kind of doctor. I've never had to deal with this kind of injury on a person before. Weeks at least, though how many is too difficult to tell at the moment. Once the wound begins to close, that will be a good sign."

"Do you think they'll let us stay for that long?" Mike asked. "We'll eat every scrap of supplies they've got!"

"I don't think that will be a problem," Arthur said. "From what Sue Ellen said and her reaction when I mentioned that we may be moving on soon, I think they were planning on us sticking around for a while. In fact, I got the impression that if this conversation had gone differently, she might even have grown insistent that we stay. The supplies question is a good point, though. If they can really afford to absorb the extra cost of more than thirty strangers for an indefinite amount of time without endangering their own supplies, that is significant. They must have a lot more than what we've seen so far. Orders of magnitude more."

"And that means they either have a lot more people than we realize," Mike replied, "or they have a gross abundance of materials. Either way, that's valuable information to have down the road. If things work out in Bennett, we could be traveling here to trade with these people."

Arthur smiled and put a hand on Mike's shoulder. "That's one of the ways I know I made the right call throwing mine and Cheryl's lot in with you Mike. You see a life on the other side of this, and that gives me hope."

"I have to hope, right?" Mike said, a faraway look in his eyes. "Otherwise, what's the point?"

Chapter 60

Finding the Mark

Cage drew the arrow back slowly, conscious of the flex in the wooden bow in his hands. When the knuckle on his right thumb was at the corner of his mouth, Cage stopped pulling. The weight of the tension on the bowstring was uncomfortably heavy, but he didn't hear any sounds of wood cracking, which was a good sign. Mr. Levy was standing just behind him and to his left where Cage could just barely see him, and he was nodding.

Cage sighted down the arrow as best he could and tried to visualize the path the arrow would take once it left the bow, arching slightly up, then meeting the target twenty-five yards in front of him. When he felt like he had the arrow just right, he exhaled some of the half breath he'd been holding. His hands steadied and, with a smooth flicking movement, he opened the three fingers holding the bowstring.

The bowstring thrummed and the arrow leapt away from the bow. It arched high, though, and completely missed the stack of hay bales that had been set up as a support for the bright foam target. There was a clatter of limbs and leaves as the arrow disappeared into the forest at the edge of the field.

"Remember when you asked why we painted the ends of the arrows orange?" Levy asked the younger man with a smile. "This is why."

Levy patted Cage on the shoulder reassuringly as they walked toward the line where the woods met the field. "You're picking it up quickly, though, Cage. With your strength and patience, you could become a heck of an archer. Better than I was in my prime, maybe."

"Mr. Levy, I lost all twelve arrows and didn't hit the target," Cage said, shaking his head. "I think I may be too old to learn bows and arrows. You know what they say about old dogs and new tricks."

"Nonsense," Levy said with a wave of his hand. "Best dog I ever had was an old, half-toothless pit-bull stray that showed up one day. He had a brindled coat that, to be honest, was ugly as sin and a scarred and scratched up face. We fed him anyway, and he took to the place and was happy as they come. That dog learned how to sit, lay down, fetch, stay, and all kinds of other things, and I didn't even have to teach him most of it. He just learned it. You ain't ever too old to learn, Cage."

Cage nodded and stepped into the woods with Levy close behind him. They looked for a while and came back with eight of the twelve arrows. Four of them were simply gone. Cage carefully placed the arrows they had recovered back in his quiver, and on the entire walk back to the edge of the woods, his eyes were on the forest floor searching for the other four.

When they were nearly back to the field, Levy reached over and stopped Cage. He pointed up the trunk of a nearby towering pine tree, and about nine feet up, buried in the bark of the tree was one of the missing arrows.

"Don't focus on the dirt so much you forget to pick your eyes up to heaven now and then," Cage said with a smile. "That's a lesson you'd think I'd learned by now."

"It's something we all need to be reminded of every once in a while." Levy replied.

The two walked back out into the field in silence. They stopped at the small pile of whitewashed stones that marked twenty-five yards from the target. Cage set his feet again, but before he could draw, Levy stopped him.

"Hold on a second, Cage," Levy said. "You seem to be aiming high every shot. So, this time, I want you to get set just like you did before and draw the same way. But this time, when you aim and you reach that spot when you feel it's just right to let the arrow fly, I want you to pull down your aim a good two feet. It's going to feel strange at first, but trust me. I think it will help. Let's see if we can get you on the paper."

Cage paused with the arrow nocked, but not drawn. "Mr. Levy, why are you spending so much time teaching me this? I'm not a soldier. I swore I'd never kill again, so you know I ain't gonna use this in Captain Tillman's war."

Levy gave a small shrug. "Maybe not, but you might use it to put a deer on the table," he said. "Or, if you get good enough, maybe some squirrel or duck, too. You have to wait until the ducks land on the water, though. I knew one man back when I was a boy who could shoot them out of the air, but he was half Cherokee, and I'd say that's cheating."

"That ain't a real answer, Mr. Levy," Cage insisted.

"All right, fine," Levy said finally, throwing his hands up, "but if I tell you, then will you get back to work and try what I'm telling you to?" When Cage nodded, Levy continued. "Well, I'm old, Cage. Older than a man has a right to be with the world the way it is. And I imagine I ain't got too much longer on this earth. I want to teach everything I can to everyone I can while I still can, if you understand what I'm saying."

"You could teach this to one of Captain Tillman's soldiers," Cage said, "and then they could hunt *and* use this skill to keep the farm safe, or even win the war. Why me?"

"Look around you, Cage," Levy said, swinging one arm in a wide semicircle, "really look at the world today. Seems to me just about all the world has left is soldiers of one kind or another, on one side or another. Hellfire, there's probably soldiers on sides we ain't even heard about yet. But, when the dust settles and all of these wars are over, what the world's really gonna need is men who know how *not* to be soldiers."

"They're the ones who get to rebuild," Levy said, half to himself. "Now, draw the arrow and try again."

Cage drew the arrow and aimed the same way he did before and then lowered his aim to the point where he was sure he'd hit the ground in front of the target. He let out part of his breath, stabilized his aim, and loosed the arrow. This time the arrow arched through the air and landed with a thunk in the top left portion of the target. It was still a good two feet from the bull's eye and outside even the largest black ring on the target, but he'd hit it.

"There you go!" Levy said. "You're on the paper, and that's an improvement. Let's call it quits there for today, and we'll practice some more tomorrow."

Cage nodded and went to retrieve his arrow from the target. As the two men walked the road that led from the lower fields back up the hill to the farm house, Cage breathed in deeply, enjoying the crisp fall morning. After a while, he broke the silence that had settled over them.

"Mr. Levy, do you really think this war will end? Do you really think there will be anything left to rebuild?"

Levy stopped dead in his tracks and fixed Cage with a serious stare. "Don't you? Cause if you don't, then what's the point of it all anyway? Why keep putting one foot in front of another?"

"Well, I reckon I just figured if Jesus was gonna pick a time to come back, now would be as good as any," Cage replied with a shrug. "The way I see it, at this point, we're all just treading water till he comes."

Levy gave a short chuckle and nodded. "I think that was just as true last year as it is right now," he said. "Now I don't claim to know the good Lord's mind any more than the next man, but if he was gonna come now, why wait until so many good, innocent people died? Why put people through what they're going through—what we're going through—if we're really that close to the end?"

Levy started walking back up the hill. "No, Cage," he said after a moment, "I don't think this is the end. Just another bump in the road."

"This is one mighty big bump," Cage said.

Levy gave a small shrug. "Well, when the good Lord decides mankind needs a kick in the pants, he don't go half-way with it. Just ask Noah."

Cage didn't know how to answer that, so silence fell between them once more. As they walked, Cage couldn't help but think back to the story of Noah and his ark. The analogy to their own current situation fit in more ways than one, despite the lack of a massive boat with two of every animal crammed inside. He couldn't help but wonder where they were in the story. Were they floating on the calm sea, waiting for the waters to recede and land to rise again?

Or were they like Noah in the beginning, sitting in the closed-up ark, waiting for the rain to fall?

Chapter 61

Change in Orders

Oct. 27th 1830 CST

Colonel Darius's face was larger than life on the wall monitor in the Operations and Command Center, and the veins standing out on his forehead and at his temples were clear. The Colonel was clearly under stress, and the strain of dealing with that stress was starting to show. Dark circles had formed under his eyes in a matter of hours.

"Colonel Darius, can you give me a status report?" Commander Price asked for the second time.

Darius blinked. "Yes, sir," he said finally. "Since leaving this morning we have gone nearly a hundred and thirty-five miles. We have picked up thirty-four new recruits since we spoke last. Our options are limited on recruiting, though, since we're having to avoid major cities and thoroughfares, so the numbers are down. We also lost another eighteen deserters along the way at various stops. None of those stole anything like the first wave did, though, so that's good at least. They just disappeared."

"And you're sure these are desertions?" Price asked. "There isn't any chance they've been taken or that you're being shadowed by the FSS? They may have had a force waiting in the area around the rail yard in case you somehow managed to survive the detonation."

Darius shook his head and gave a tired sigh. "I might look like crap, Commander, but I still know how to keep op-sec. in my own command, thank you very much. Sentries have been pulling mobile sweeps for tails and trackers, and they've come up empty every time. We're not being followed. I know how to do my job, Commander."

"I didn't mean to imply otherwise, Colonel," Price said quickly, though in truth he had meant just that. But he was glad to see the colonel had enough fight in him to respond to the suggestion. "Why do you think some of the men have chosen to break ranks?"

Darius snorted. "You mean other than the fact that we had someone try to blow us all up with a damned nuke less than eighteen hours ago? Jesus, Commander, I'm surprised there's anybody left, to tell you the truth! And fact is we've lost less than ten percent since the incident, and most of that's been made up with new draftees and recruits anyway. I doubt we'll lose many more if we keep moving. The farther we get from home for most of these men, the less likely they are to leave the group and strike out on their own. Don't worry, Commander, I'll keep this army together for you, at least until we hit DC I can't promise much after that, though."

Price paused as he carefully considered his next words. He knew he had to tread lightly and reveal only what he could without letting Darius know he was holding something back. It was a fine line to walk with a man who was already so far on edge that his head whipped from side to side like a frightened animal, inspecting every shift in the breeze and rustle of leaves around him. Even now, even after the colonel had done so much and sacrificed so much for the cause, Terry, as Commander Price, couldn't afford to trust him all the way. And that meant he had to hide things as much as he could and deflect or flat out lie about them when he couldn't.

If he could avoid doing the latter by achieving the former, so be it. He could live with that a lot easier than he could live with lying to the man he had sent out to fight a war for him.

"Colonel, there's been a change in your orders. You're not going to Washington. I want you to continue generally east until you hit the mountains in Virginia. There you're going to make a turn southeast and head for Fort Bragg, North Carolina. With any luck, you'll be able to come at the FSS from the north while Lieutenant Commander Attledge hits them hard from the south."

Darius frowned, his eyebrows drawing down and casting his eyes in deep, hollow shadows. "What do you mean we're not going to Washington? I thought the whole point of this little exercise was to take out the traitor calling himself the president. If we're not going to bring justice to that monster, who is?"

"I can't tell you that, Colonel. You'll just have to trust me. It's going to be taken care of. I give you my word. But your forces are going to be needed elsewhere. Understood?"

"I'm not going to lie, I don't like it," Darius said. "I took it as a personal honor to be part of the force that's going to bring that bastard down, and I know a lot of the men did as well. I don't like it at all, not after what he tried to do to us . . . to me."

"I'm not asking you to like it," Price snapped, slamming his fist down on the table in front of him. "I'm asking you to do your duty for the cause. This is bigger than one man's ego or one man's sense of revenge."

"You don't have to lecture me on *duty*," Darius hissed. "I'll follow my orders, *sir*."

Price took a deep breath to calm himself before replying. "I know you will, Colonel Darius. I have every confidence in you and your men. I know you'll do your duty and more, just like you already have. You've more than proven yourself a dozen times over. But the fact is, you were right when you said that morning after the attack that they'd try and hit you again if you stayed stationary. They may try again even with your forces no longer occupying the rail yard, and that's why I can't afford to wait until you reach Washington to act. It might be too late."

"We got almost all of the equipment out of the rail yard, Commander," Darius said defiantly. "Even if they hit that place we wouldn't lose that much, other than the few hundred people still living in that area of the city."

Price shook his head. "If we want to have any chance of rebuilding anything in this country when it's all said and done, we're going to need that rail yard. And eventually we're going to need to clear out St. Louis and retake that junction as well. The rail lines that converge on those two cities can connect the rest of the nation from east to west, north to south. We're going to need that ability to move people, supplies, food. If they hit that rail yard with a surface-level nuke, then even the track that isn't instantly melted or vaporized will be irradiated and toxic for years. If they use a dirty nuke, one salted with Cobalt, then it will be useless for decades."

Price leaned in to the camera. "We simply can't afford that, Colonel. We can't afford to give them that opportunity. I'm going to have to take more drastic measures and deal with that threat immediately. We can't risk the traitor in D.C. deploying more nuclear weapons. Now, I've said what I can say, and I hope it's enough."

Darius nodded but didn't speak. His face looked even paler and gaunter now than it had at the beginning of the conversation.

"Good," Price continued, "then that's settled. I wish I could tell you more, Colonel, but you're not the only one who has to worry about operational security."

Darius's back stiffened at that. "Understood, sir," he growled. "What is our new route into enemy territory? Or is that need to know as well?"

"Continue on the line you're following," Price said. "At Linn you're going to switch onto the Farmington-Harrisburg line. That will keep you well to the south of St. Louis. When you reach Harrisburg, you'll have to make another track change, but we'll go over that when you get there. Obviously, if you have to make some major change to these plans, then you're authorized to break radio silence and contact me. Otherwise, I want to keep signals to a minimum, just in case the enemy is able to pick them up and track them."

"What about supplies?" Darius asked. "We were able to load up most of our meals and a good amount of water, but we'll be running low before we ever get close to Virginia."

Price sighed heavily. "I don't like it, but you'll have to forage as best you can en route. You're going to need to increase the conscription rates as well. We need men, Colonel, one way or another. The enemy may not have our will, experience, or tactical initiative, but they do have us by the numbers. I want you to do your best to fix that before you engage them. Marcus, Lieutenant Commander Attledge, will hit them from the south like a hammer, so I need you to be the anvil that crushes them from the north."

Price was silent for a moment as he let the weight of his words settle on the other side of the connection. Darius nodded once, his face grim. "I understand, sir. We'll be there, and we'll be ready. You have my word. Is there anything else?"

"No, Colonel, that's all for now. Keep your solar panels out when you stop during the day and keep the turbine generators engaged on the trains whenever you're moving. We need to generate power as much as possible. That will give us an edge."

Darius reached up to the side of his transmitter. "I know how to run this show, Commander. Unlike you, I've spent my *career* in the field. We'll get the job done. You handle your end. You've taken the burden of this command, so now it's yours to carry to the end. You understand that, right?"

Commander Price met the colonel's gaze evenly and asked calmly. "Are you questioning my ability or my commitment?"

"Neither. Simply making sure we're clear on expectations. If I do what you're ordering me to and we pull a full-scale assault like that, a lot of people will die on both sides. If we really do surprise them, then maybe we make it out of that, but either way we're going to lose a lot of men, and so are they. If I'm going to have that kind of blood on my hands, I need to know that I've paid the butcher's bill for a worthy cause."

Price smiled a small, sympathetic smile. "My dear Colonel, by the time this is all over, we're all going to have blood on our hands. Too much to ever wash clean."

He reached up and clicked the power button on the remote, killing the video feed and phone call together.

Chapter 62

Zero Hour

Oct. 27 th 2345 MTN

Commander Price reached up and pressed the power button on the small digital video camera standing on his desk. The camera was mounted to a tripod with legs like thick pencils when they were fully extended. He transferred the digitally encrypted video file into a secure message and set it to be automatically sent through the satellite network link to Lieutenant Commander Attledge's computer terminal when a one hour timer expired.

Alone in his office, Price checked his watch and noted the date and time in a log book. He reached up and pressed record on the video camera again. Under his desk was a safe that he entered the combination to and opened without any reference. Inside was a file case with two large combination locks. Each dial was encrypted with independent nine digit combinations.

With a quick twist of his wrists, Commander Price snapped open a plastic security case and pulled out a red card that had the two combinations printed on it. If the system recorded more than three errors in any combination of the two dials, then it would immediately shatter thirteen glass gas packs and seal the locks closed. The reinforced Kevlar and carbon fiber case was nearly impenetrable. And, to make matters worse, it was lined with a hard tungsten carbide shell beneath the woven jacket. The entire system had been carefully engineered to ensure that if too many errors were input, it would become completely and irreversibly inaccessible.

The commander wiped his hands on his pants and began entering the combination on the right dial. He didn't make a single mistake and heard the lock pop open beneath that dial. Then he moved to the left wheel and began entering the combination for that lock, but on the fourth number he missed. He cleared the combination dial and began entering the combination again.

This time he got the second combination correct, and that lock popped open as well. With shaking fingers, Price lifted the lid on the case and reached inside. He pulled out the two security cases under the label XLGM-39-1a. One of the clear cases held a red card, the other held a blue card. With a sharp twist of the top and bottom halves, he opened them both the same way he'd opened the case containing the combinations. The cases snapped open and he took out the cards and set them on his desk.

Price looked into the video camera and said in a calm, even voice, "What I do now, I do of my own free will. I am under no compulsion other than a compulsion of duty to do my utmost to protect this nation from all enemies, foreign and domestic. I alone am responsible for this action."

With his declaration of responsibility done, Price pulled up a window on his work terminal. The screen displayed a launch interface. With the red and blue cards, he entered in the two access key codes to activate the launch system. Technically, the red code was the only one he was authorized to enter, and the blue code was reserved for his second in command. However, at the moment, Attledge was several hundred miles east-southeast of him, and, therefore, unavailable.

After a few key strokes to bring up the latitude and longitude interface, Price selected the target coordinates. He closed his eyes and said a quick prayer, then pressed the enter key and held it. The system beeped twice and then he felt his entire body go numb. He stared at the screen as the message at the top flashed:

Command Accepted, Missile Launch Confirmed, Launch Sequence Initiated

Price checked his watch again and saw the time read zero hundred.

It was a new day.

Chapter 63

The Destroyer of Worlds

Oct. 28 th 0000 MST

In the valley between Mt. Ellen Peak and South Summit Ridge, a silo split down the middle with a shudder of dust and dirt, and the two heavy, reinforced steel and concrete doors that formed the lid slid aside on pneumatic tracks. An alarm sounded, and flashing strobes alerted anyone in the area that they were in imminent danger.

Fifteen seconds after the lid opened and the buzzers sounded, a rumble began deep in the earth, and a gout of flame burst out the top of the silo. The entire valley shook with the sound and the powerful vibration of the intermediate-range missile, based off the decommissioned French S-3, as it launched into the night sky. An intense white light filled the valley and cast the shrubs and rocks in stark shadows for a brief moment as the missile began its initial climb.

The fuel burned quickly, and the missile gained altitude and speed at a frightening pace. It tore through the sound barrier in a matter of seconds and kept climbing and accelerating. At its peak, it was nearly two hundred miles up when it began its turn back to earth.

The warhead detached and began its final descent at more than six thousand miles per hour, creating a massive bright streak as it fell through the sky. Anyone on the ground unfortunate enough to see that streak would have thought, for a moment, that a meteorite had reached the ground.

Then, at exactly 0218:02, the warhead detonated with the force of four hundred and fifty kilotons of TNT at one thousand, three hundred and ninety meters altitude, directly above the Capitol building.

A burst of light thousands of times brighter than the noon-day sun lit up the dark early-morning sky and cast the National Mall in stark shadows for a brief second. The few guards on duty outside the Capitol never had time to register that bright light, as they were vaporized by the intense radiation that traveled along with it. The instantaneous release of energy created a massive fireball more than six hundred meters wide and thousands of degrees hotter than man could endure. Anything directly beneath the fireball was incinerated, and steel began to boil and burn.

The thermal radiation lost energy as it cut through the air at the speed of light, but it still caused third degree flash burns on anyone exposed to the explosion within a nine-kilometer radius. Even at that distance the thermal blast was so intense that it burned patterns of fabric into the skin and caused paper and wood products to smolder and burn. Blindness and retinal burns extended out further for anyone looking in the direction of the blast.

Then the shockwave hit. The air blast traveled downward faster than the speed of sound, but slower than the initial radiation, and impacted the ground with enough force to flex the earth's crust slightly downward. When the surface rebounded, the buildings directly under the blast, including the Capitol, dissolved into smoldering dust and rubble that was sucked into the air by the uprising shockwave reflection. As the reflected shockwave raced across the ground, it overtook the original shockwave that had slowed slightly due to air resistance.

The combined force of the mach-stem, that region where the two shockwaves overlapped, was terrifying. It hit with twenty pounds per square inch over an area two point one six kilometers in radius, covering more than fourteen and a half square kilometers. Even reinforced granite and concrete construction wasn't sturdy enough to withstand those forces, and downtown D.C. effectively disappeared. As far away as the Pentagon, the shockwave shattered windows and caused enough internal damages to kill more than fifty percent of people exposed directly to the full force. Flying debris created missiles that impaled and maimed and killed.

As the reflected shockwave rose, it sucked everything within several hundred meters of ground zero high into the air. The force of the rising shockwave also lifted the raging fireball and created the classic mushroom cloud that was illuminated by the light of fires below. Winds along the surface reached more than a hundred miles an hour as the column of smoke and burning debris rose faster and higher, thousands of feet into the air.

The rushing winds fed the fires lit by the bomb like a bellows in a forge, and soon a firestorm raged across what had been America's capital city. The light of the firestorm caused the rising column of smoke to glow with an intensity that could be seen dozens of miles away.

On the massive eight lanes of Hwy 7, Senator Coleman stared back in the direction of DC, and watched the reddish glow on the horizon grow brighter and brighter. He was just north of a little town called Potomac Falls and had managed to convince his chauffeur to pull their rusted old station wagon over to the side of the road for a brief stop.

"Senator, we need to go," his rescuer and captor said.

The man was a sergeant and a former member of the Army Rangers, the Green Berets, and several other obscure teams that Coleman had never heard of, despite years of classified defense briefings. It was only because of this former special operator's word that he was even still alive.

Reluctantly, Coleman turned away and leaned one hand on the car. He staggered a few steps to the shoulder of the abandoned road and vomited.

"Senator, we really need to go," Sergeant Corbyn said again. "We're making good time, but we're exposed on this highway. We need to get into the mountains and then navigate some back roads away from here, and that means we need to move."

Coleman wiped his mouth with the back of a shaking hand. "For the love of God, man," he growled, "I knew people back there. Good people who are just gone now. Just gone."

The sergeant was silent for a moment before answering in a calm, even tone. "So, did I, Senator, and they died so that you could get out and live. And I had to let them. We're going to get back in this car and drive, and you are going to live. But if you don't do what I'm telling you to do, I'll beat you half to death, put you in this car, and we'll still get back on the road."

The sergeant took a step forward and fixed Coleman with a hard glare. "Now get off your knees, straighten your back, and get moving. There's a war to win, understood?"

Coleman nodded and stood. He stumbled back to the car, shaking off the sergeant's offer to help him. He crawled into the back seat and slammed the door, and without a word, Corbyn climbed into the driver's seat and pulled the car back onto the highway.

They rode in silence and watched in the rear-view mirror the red glow of destruction fade mile by mile.

Pt. III

Chapter 64

Dress Rehearsal

Nov. 8th 0230 EST

Eric crouched next to the unnamed dirt road. This winding path was far from the main paved highways and led from field to field with dense stands of hardwoods in between. Trees on both sides of the road opened into the corner of a broad field, and the road continued around the edge of the field and on through the woods down to a river. But here, it was perfectly angled to form a bottleneck.

Eric motioned and three of the men following him took position on the left side of the mouth of the road, while four men took position on the right, each finding cover behind trees, bushes, and rocks. The two ambush elements had interlocking lines of fire directed out across the open field, the direction their target would approach from any minute now.

Once everyone was in place, Eric took position a hundred yards down the road, more than a third of the way around the field from the corner where his forces were deployed. He checked the height of the moon and waited in the dark shadows beneath the trees that lined the field. Four deer passed within ten feet of him, but Eric stayed motionless, and they eventually moved on across the field and into the tree line on the far side.

Then, on the very edge of his hearing, Eric caught the sounds of people walking through the woods and up the road. He turned and moved silently through the trees back to the corner of the field and his men.

"They're coming," he whispered. "Sounds like one column, maybe ten guys. Wait until the first four get down the bottleneck, then strike."

Eric joined the fire team on the left side of the road and positioned himself at the end of the line farthest into the trees. Soon the sounds of the approaching group became clear. They weren't taking any pains to remain hidden, and the two men on point were actually laughing and joking with each other, taking only an occasional glance into the woods on either side of the road as they entered the bottleneck. Neither made the effort to check for hidden dangers, which was one of the main responsibilities of the men on point.

When the fourth man crossed the threshold into the woods, Eric let out a loud whistle as the signal to attack. The men he had positioned on either side of the road stood and began flashing small pen lights at their enemy. A few of the men in the patrol managed to get their broomstick rifles raised, but it was too late.

If this had been an actual ambush instead of a training exercise, they'd all be dead.

"All right, guys, regroup and head back to camp," Eric said once the commotion had settled down. "Whoever was the commanding officer on patrol, you're with me. Everyone else, follow McClure back to the training camp."

The men who had just been ambushed grumbled and nodded and fell in behind Jacob McClure, a promising young man from the western edge of the county. McClure was a natural leader and at home in the woods as if he'd been born there. The young man who had been in charge of the patrol group was one of the two men on point who had been laughing and joking as they passed Eric's position. As ordered, the young man lingered behind with Eric as the rest headed back to camp.

"What's your name?" Eric asked once they were alone.

"Darin Bolgers," the young man answered, his eyes on the dirt.

"All right, Darin," Eric continued, "tell me what you did wrong. How did you and your men get ambushed?"

The young man gave a half shrug and kicked at a root in the road. "Well, for one thing, we weren't expecting to enter enemy territory for another half mile," Darin answered finally.

Eric shook his head. "That can't be an excuse, Darin," he countered. "You never know in the field where the enemy is going to be. Just because you're handed an intel report that says they're at a certain crossroads or in a certain block of woods, doesn't mean they'll still be there by the time you get there. Once you step outside the fence line and leave your base behind, everything is enemy territory. Remember that."

"Yes sir," Darin said sheepishly.

"Was there anything else?" Eric asked, his tone making it clear that he thought there was.

"I guess we weren't really being too quiet," Darin said with a sigh. "And we weren't checking too good along the trail for enemies, but that's because we thought we were still in the safe zone, like I said."

"In the real world, there is no safe zone, Darin," Eric responded. "You have to assume you're always under threat because in reality, you probably are. You just don't realize it. If you always operate as if there's a threat bearing down on you, you'll be more prepared when one actually happens."

Darin nodded. "Yes, sir. I guess I was so tired from the past few days my head wasn't thinking clearly."

"That's when you're most vulnerable," Eric told him as they began walking after the rest of the group. "When you're tired, when you're distracted, that's when the enemy is going to hit you, Darin. And you have to be ready for it when they do. That's what being a good commander is all about."

"Maybe someone else would be better for this job than me," Darin mumbled.

"Your patrol group is made of people from around your area," Eric said. "I've seen how they react to you. They respect you and take your leadership seriously. That's not an easy thing to train, and it's even tougher to build with a stranger. You need some practice, and you need to work on these strategies, but that's expected. Don't get too down on yourself just because you aren't catching on immediately. The biggest thing is to learn from these mistakes and apply what you've learned to the next round of training exercises so you get better."

Darin nodded, but he didn't look convinced. "I just don't want to screw up and get someone killed," he said softly.

"I'll tell you the same thing my father told me," Eric answered. "You're leading men into combat, Darin. Some of them are bound to fall, and you can't stop that. It's not your job to stop it. It's your job to get the mission done and bring as many of them home alive as you can. We can't ask anything more than that."

"Sometimes I just think the responsibility is too much for me," Darin said, his voice shaking.

Eric put a hand on the younger man's shoulder. "That's a good indication that you're the right man for the job. One other thing, Darin. You're the patrol commander, and that means you never walk point. If you do hit an ambush, the point man's going to be one of the first to go down. If that's you, then who's going to give the orders that will keep the rest of your men alive? If a commander goes down, the rest of the men are thrown into confusion, and that's the worst thing that can happen in a combat situation. Confused men make easy targets. Part of your job as their commander is to keep that from happening."

Eric squeezed Darin's shoulder and then let his hand drop. "You can't do that if you're walking point and you die first," he finished. "Come on, let's get these guys back to camp. We could all use some sleep."

Darin nodded but didn't speak. They walked the rest of the way back to the camp in silence. The group was spread out in a loose column with ten to fifteen feet between them. They alternated which side of the road they kept an eye on, with every other man covering the same side. Now that the training exercise was over, they all had rifles, shotguns, and pistols back in their hands again. Eric watched as the men moved quietly over dry leaves and twigs, keeping watch as they walked, and he was impressed.

He could pick out the men who had come from his group and those that had been part of the element under Darin's command. His men had been at the camp longer, almost from the beginning, and it showed. The more experienced men spent more time with their eyes on the woods and less time watching their feet, but still they stumbled and tripped less than the fresh recruits. They also passed hand signals back and forth, pointing out suspicious

451

shadows or shapes among the tree trunks. The younger, less experienced soldiers tended to whisper back and forth to communicate, creating extra noise and drawing attention to themselves.

In the wrong situation, that could be fatal for an entire group, not just the ones who broke silence. Eric hated to admit it, but the younger group just wasn't ready. Darin would take it the hardest and would probably see it as a critique of his command. The truth was they just hadn't had enough time to develop the combat skills and habits that the older troops were beginning to wear like second nature. With more training and exercises, they would get there, but when the day came to hit the supply lines, Eric would report to his father that this group would need to sit out this run.

There was a sharp snap as a branch behind them broke under the weight of a heavy step. Eric whistled softly, once, and held up his fist. The column froze and dropped to one knee, whirling to face the same way as Eric, down their back trail. Behind him, Eric heard a rustle of leaves as the column fanned out to either side, creating a wedge-shaped formation with Eric serving as the point. He peered into the shadows cast by the dense oak and maple trees overhead.

Another few footsteps came from the woods behind them, and Eric caught the flicker of movement among the shadows cast by the moonlight through the canopy overhead. "That's far enough," Eric called in a loud voice. "If you don't identify yourself now, we're going to open fire. I promise, at this range there's enough firepower trained on you to take you down. Come out slow, with your hands away from your body. If you pull something, you get put down, period."

A long moment of silence passed; then a weak voice called from the woods. "Okay, I'm coming out." A man stepped from behind a tree, his arms held out to either side of his body, the fingers on both hands splayed wide to show they were empty. "I just want some water, if you have any. I'm so thirsty." The man in tattered clothes stumbled forward.

"Stop!" Eric called, and the man stopped so suddenly he stumbled to his knees. "Not one step closer."

The man nodded but didn't speak, so Eric stood and pulled his pistol from its holster and handed Darin his rifle. He unhooked his canteen from his belt pouch and approached the stranger. As he got closer, he saw large, puffy red scars across the man's face in a strange pattern that alternated with thin bands of pale, unmarked skin. At first, he couldn't figure out what he was seeing. Then the man held up a thin hand to block the light from Darin's flashlight, and the pale areas on his face lined up perfectly with the shadows cast by his fingers.

Eric knew of only one thing that could cause burns like that, and the thought of it made the hair on the back of his neck stand on end. "What happened to you?" he whispered as he handed over his canteen.

The man gulped greedily, water spilling over the corners of his mouth, and he began to cough violently. Eric took a step back, just in case he had something contagious.

"I was there," the man whispered, tears running down his cheeks. "I saw it. Saw it happen." He tried to take another drink but ended up coughing again. "I was there. I was in DC"

"Wait, you're from DC?" Eric asked, and he could feel the tension in the men behind him ratchet up a notch. They all knew that the enemy had taken the capital city for their headquarters, and that made anyone and anything coming out of that city suspect.

But the man shook his head weakly, his eyes wide. "Not anymore," he whispered hoarsely. He started to rock gently back and forth, squeezing his eyes shut, as the tears continued to flow. "Not anymore," he repeated. "It's gone. All gone."

"What's gone?" Eric asked, but the man just kept rocking and whispering to himself. Eric bent down and gripped the man's shoulder gently, but the man winced sharply, and fell back, clutching his arm. "What's gone?" Eric repeated.

"The monuments, the Capitol," the man whispered, his eyes wide and staring out at nothing. "The city . . . it's all gone. Washington, DC is gone."

Chapter 65

Weighing Options

Nov. 8 th 0400 CST

Lieutenant Commander Attledge powered up the communications center and waited patiently while the computers ran through a long series of security and systems checks. At the end of that process, the home screen popped up on the small LED screen mounted on the wall of the railcar serving as his office. He selected the secure video transmission option and then entered a seventeen-digit number on the key pad. A small webcam mounted to the top of the screen came to life and showed a red dot as the connection was not yet confirmed.

After a few seconds, the light next to the webcam lens switched to green, and on the LED screen, a video window opened to display a near copy of Attledge's railroad office, except the desk was different and the man sitting behind it was Colonel Darius. It could have been a trick of the lighting or the display of the transmission, but the Colonel seemed to have aged ten years since the last time Attledge had seen him in Kansas City.

"Good morning, Colonel Darius."

The colonel snorted a healthy snort. "It's funny the things we do as a matter of habit that have no connection to reality. Our nation's capital is a smoldering radioactive ruin and the man that did it is our commanding officer. It's four o'clock in the morning, and we are both so terrified of being detected and blown up with a nuke in our own country that we won't tell the other one exactly where we are, even on a known secure channel. Does that really qualify as a 'good' morning?"

"Well, I'm still breathing," Attledge replied with a small shrug, "and so are you. There's that, I guess."

"Optimists make my face itch," Darius growled, his mouth twisted into a sour expression. "Anyway, why did you want to have a little face to face this morning?"

"We are stationary today, waiting for the infantry element to catch up, and I have had a while to roll this whole situation over in my head a little. I just wanted to make sure we've explored all of our options."

"What are you talking about, 'options'? Our orders are pretty clear as far as I'm concerned. And they haven't changed."

"The orders may not have," Attledge said, "but the situation has changed a great deal. When I agreed to take this command and follow these orders, I wasn't serving under the man who had just dropped a strategic level nuke on our own nation's capital. Now I am, and I'm not sure I can reconcile that."

Darius was quiet for a long time, rubbing his eyes as he thought. Finally, he dropped his hand into his lap and leaned his head back to stare up at the ceiling. "You said options, so what are they? What options do you see?"

"Well, we can continue as before. We can keep following orders from Commander Price and effectively pretend that this never happened. I think it's clear that neither of us can live with that option, so it's out from the beginning. At the same time, we can't stop following orders and go our separate ways. We've both been handed pretty big responsibilities and fighting forces to match them. Not to mention the fact that whatever happened in DC, there's still an army on the march south toward Fort Bragg."

Darius nodded slowly. "And there are a lot of innocent people between that army and their target. Thankfully, though, the enemy seems to have stalled. At least for the moment, according to Commander Price's intel."

"Do we trust his word on reconnaissance and intelligence briefings?" Attledge asked.

"I think we have to. He hasn't given us anything that we know is false. At least not yet, so I don't think we have anything to worry about there. It's just a question of whether or not he's told us the whole story about the orders we've been given."

This time it was Attledge who was silent as his thoughts tumbled around large, weighty words like duty, honor, treason, and genocide. "Do you believe him?" he asked. "Do you believe his reasons?"

"You don't?" Darius responded. "Look, maybe I'm in a biased position seeing as how that bastard who used to call himself the president tried to assassinate me and my men with a nuclear weapon. May be a given that I'm not the most objective person to speak up on this—I don't know. I'm not saying what he did was right, but I can understand it. You still haven't spoken to him yet, have you?"

Attledge shook his head. "Not since before he sent the message out about what he was going to do."

"You should," Darius said. "Seriously. You need to hear it from him. Like I said, I may not agree with him, but at least I can understand why he felt he had to do it. And believe it or not, that helps."

The colonel cleared his throat, not quite sure if he wanted an answer to his next question. "You were talking about options, but you laid out only the two most extreme options we have. According to you the only choices we can make are either all-out rebellion and desertion or absolute obedience. I don't think it's quite as black and white as that."

"What else is there?" Attledge asked.

"There's a third option. We focus on what we have to do so that we win this war and settle that first. And then we arrest Commander Price and try him for what he's done. He'll either prove his case before a court martial or he won't and then face the consequences, however it goes."

"That feels like we're betraying him," Attledge said after a moment. "I don't know that I can keep looking him in the eye knowing that we are planning to turn around and slap handcuffs on him as soon as the war is over. That just doesn't seem right."

"Like you said, there's still an army marching south, and that army has to be dealt with. There isn't anyone else to handle this but us, Marcus. We're it right now, and that means we can't afford to just turn our backs on the opportunity to take this country back. Abandoning our mission now won't make that missile magically un-explode over DC. That's already been done, and nothing we can do can change it. But that doesn't mean we should turn our backs on duty and just let that army go unchallenged. We can handle Commander Price and what he's done once the immediate threat has been taken care of."

"What if neither of us lives through the war?" Attledge asked.

Darius chuckled a short laugh. "Well then it won't be our problem anymore. Someone else will have to deal with it."

Attledge smiled weakly. "And you called me the optimist."

"Commander, you should really talk to him," Darius said finally. "You have known Commander Price a long time, a lot longer than I have. You know what kind of man he is, and you know he wouldn't have done something like this if he didn't think it was absolutely necessary."

"So, you think it was necessary, but you still think Price should be arrested and tried for it? How does that make sense?"

"Just because something was necessary doesn't make it right," Darius answered. "In the end, you'll have to make your own decision about it. All I can really tell you is that I'm going to need your help when I take on the FSS troops moving south. If you're there and we can coordinate our forces together, we stand a chance. If it's just me, we'll be outnumbered and outflanked before the battle even begins."

"What made you think of fighting the war first and going after Commander Price afterwards?" Attledge asked, suddenly curious. "I've been wrestling with this thing for more than a week now and I never thought of that as an option. How did you come around to it?"

Darius smiled. "I didn't think of it. Commander Price did."

Chapter 66

On Your Own Two Feet

Nov. 8 th 0840 EST

Arthur was out of breath when he finally made it to the clearing, though he'd never admit it. Micah was already there, of course, waiting on him without even a drop of sweat on his forehead. The young man was strong, and he had taken to the crutches like a natural. He could move confidently and quickly already even across broken ground. In another few weeks when the stump healed completely, he'd probably be able to move more quickly with one foot and two crutches than most men could with two healthy feet.

Right now, Micah was looking out over the valleys and ridges of the Uwharrie as the fall sun bathed them in warm morning sunlight, a deep frown on his face. Arthur stood next to the young man but didn't speak. Spending nearly every moment with his patient over the past week and a half, he'd come to understand the young man's expressions and mannerisms. Right now, he needed time to come to grips with how to say something uncomfortable.

After a while, Micah turned his back on the fall colors that painted the landscape below them. He didn't take a step, though. He simply stared off into the woods to his right.

"It happened over there a little ways," Micah said finally, gesturing with the crutch in his right hand. "There's a big deadfall

460

on the other side o'the ridge. Dumb me didn't check on the other side, just stepped right on over."

Micah paused, his face troubled. He lifted his left leg and rubbed at his calf as if he wanted to scratch it. After a moment, he winced and gave a shudder that ran from his head all the way down his body.

"I felt it when it grabbed my foot," Micah said, and he shuddered again. "It was sharp, and cold at first. Then heat exploded into my foot and pains shot up and down my legs. Felt like I was burning from the inside out. I looked down and saw the rattler's fangs stuck in my shoe. He was trying to pull his head back, but couldn't at first, so he just kept squeezing more of that hot, burning venom in. I could feel it every time it pulsed, and right then, I knew I was going to die."

Arthur looked over at Micah and saw tears streaming down the young man's face as he relived that horrible experience. The pain and fear rolled across his face in waves.

"Then everything pretty much goes black," he said as he wiped the tears away. "Well, more a kind of gray fog that you can't really see through. I remember hearing peoples' voices, like Miss Sue Ellen and Mr. Shaw. And then the axe, I remember the axe and staring at where my foot used to be."

"Micah, I'm sorry," Arthur began, but Micah cut him off with a wave of his hand.

"I didn't bring you up here to guilt trip you. I may not ever win a foot race, at least not a fair one. And I'll never play baseball again, but I'm almost as fast as I ever was on two feet, and baseball was over a long time ago. What you did gave me a chance to grow up, to meet my wife one day and maybe have kids of my own. I owe you the entire rest of my life, however long that is."

Arthur shrugged uncomfortably and turned back to look out over the Uwharrie again. "You're healing pretty well, Micah, and I don't think you're in any real danger of infection at this point. You're obviously regaining your strength quite nicely, and you eat like three grown men. I think you're going to live a long life, Micah, as long as you can stay away from fallen trees and hidden snakes."

Micah turned and looked straight into Arthur's eyes. "And what about the next kid that gets bit? Or the next person to fall and break a leg, the next person to have a heart attack, or catch pneumonia, or a thousand other things that can suddenly kill folks? Who is going to help them get better?"

"Sounds like you've been talking to Sue Ellen," Arthur said. "Those are her words coming out of your mouth."

"Well, she's not wrong," Micah insisted. "We could use a doctor around here, and you know we could. People these days, they get sick and then they don't get better. You could change that."

"Micah, if I stayed here I'd always be the man who chopped off your leg," Arthur said bluntly. "I may not have swung the axe, but that's what people would see every time they looked at me. Say what you want, that's what you'd see every time too. And I couldn't take that. We're only staying long enough to make sure you're going to keep getting better, and then my group has to move on again."

Micah was quiet for a moment, and when he spoke again his voice was soft. "I had a cousin, and he didn't think we should stay here when the Blackout happened. He wanted to leave, try and find a city or a refugee camp, something. One day he did. He left."

Micah looked down and poked at a clump of moss with one of his crutches. "About a month later, Mr. Shaw went out with a group looking for supplies. They found my cousin three days northeast of here. His throat had been cut and he'd been stripped of everything."

Arthur put a hand on the young man's shoulder. "Micah, I'm sorry about your cousin, but your cousin was foolish and went out on his own. I'm part of a group, a large group, and we're large enough that people don't try to give us trouble like that. What happened to your cousin, it won't happen to me."

"You can't know that," Micah said, shaking his head. "I know these woods, Dr. Arthur. I grew up in them my whole life, and all it took was one wrong step to almost end it for me. You never know what's going to be around the next corner or over the next dead tree."

"You're right," Arthur said, "it's dangerous out in the world. There's absolutely no denying that fact. But it's dangerous everywhere, Micah. And there's a chance, if I leave and keep following this road I'm on, there's a chance I might see my daughter again. I have to follow that chance and see how it plays out or I won't be able to live with myself."

Micah was quiet for a long time again, his face somber as he watched the woods around them. "Will you come back to visit? I know it's silly, but I don't have many friends left anymore, not since the Blackout. A lot of them died, some of the families left looking for better place. It's been nice having someone to talk to lately other than my parents."

Arthur smiled. "I promise, Micah, that when we get to Bennett and things get settled, I'll come back to visit. I don't know how long that will be, but I promise I will come."

Micah smiled finally and nodded. "Well, I guess it's okay that you're leaving, then. Besides, if you're getting serious about leaving, then it means my foot—I mean my leg—really is getting better."

Before Arthur could reply, Micah turned and bounded back down the hill, moving fast enough on his crutches to make Arthur nervous. He decided he'd better set off after him.

Chapter 67

Seen Too Much

Nov. 8 th 1022 EST

Joe approached the man carefully. He made sure to stay where the stranger could see him, and he kept his hands still and at his sides. When he was ten feet from the captive, Joe knelt and looked him over.

The man was well built and looked like he was in his mid-forties. A faded Navy tattoo on his right forearm looked like a submarine. His hair was dirty and hung in clumps of dark brown, peppered through with gray at the temples. His face was burned everywhere except for the perfect outline of one hand shielding his right eye.

"Where were you when you saw it?" Joe asked.

The man's eyes dropped to the ground, and he was quiet. "I was on the southeast side of Arlington walking a patrol in a quiet neighborhood of FSS desk jockeys. It was the strangest thing I've ever seen in my life. Suddenly, there was light everywhere, the brightest light I've ever seen. I couldn't help but turn to look at it, but thankfully my hand stayed up out of instinct."

The man showed Joe his right palm, and it had the same puffy red scars as his face. "I think that saved my eyes. A guy walking the beat a few streets over was blinded cause he was facing right at it when it went off. There was no sound at first, just the light and the heat. But I knew what was coming."

The man looked up at the sky, his eyes closed now, lost in memories he could no longer control. "My parents had talked about it before I ever joined the Navy. And then we trained on what to do in the event of a nuke. I dove around behind the houses just before the pressure wave hit. That's when the sound hit too. It wasn't like anything I've ever heard. Loud enough to hurt and make my ears ring, my eyes water, but it was sharp and crisp, almost like the loudest, closest thunder you've ever heard, times a billion."

The stranger shifted his weight, not seeming to notice the zip ties that bound his ankles and wrists. "It blew out windows, ripped doors off hinges, and knocked over vehicles in the neighborhood. A few people were killed by debris that came through windows. They were in bed and their bedroom windows suddenly became shrapnel that sliced through them. We could hear the screams on the street, but everyone was too shocked to do anything."

The man slowly trailed to silence and stared down at the dirt. His eyes were wide and tears streamed down his face. The muscles along his jaw stood out as he clenched his teeth so tight it was a wonder they didn't shatter. When he finally looked back up at Joe, his eyes were swollen and red.

"People came out of their houses, and a lot of them were bloodied and begging for help. The rest of the security detail gathered at my checkpoint and we watched the fires in downtown DC. They spread—kept burning like they were going to burn up the whole world." The man ran his fingers into his hair and twisted them into knots as the zip ties around his wrists pulled tight enough to draw blood. "Some of the people couldn't take it. They snapped. Two of the guards put their pistols in their mouths right there and just pulled the trigger. Another one pulled his and just started shooting people. He killed four people before I could put a bullet in his brain for him."

Joe wanted to say something, wanted to stop the man, but he didn't know how. He couldn't find his voice. He had lived for nearly six years in Washington, DC, after leaving the active duty SEALs. It was a city he knew well and one he felt a close personal affection for that went beyond the deep history or the fact that it had been the nation's capital.

After a moment, the man continued in a whisper. "I tried to tell the people around us we had to go, had to run. Only a few understood. The rest were just too shocked. Most of them just sat there on the ground, staring back at DC. The ones who could think straight came with me. We grabbed what we could and ran. There was an FSS Humvee at the end of our block, so we took it and just started driving."

The silence that settled over the two men when the stranger stopped talking was thick and heavy. Joe's thoughts were racing as he tried to filter through the emotions and images flashing through his head. He couldn't help but think of his time at the Pentagon and the Naval Annex, the people he had known who still lived in and around Arlington. Even if some of them had survived the Blackout and the months since, they couldn't have survived this.

"Where did the nuke hit?" Joe asked after a long moment of silence.

"It looked like it was over the Capitol building," the man said, "or somewhere close. It was pretty dark up until the flash, so it was hard to tell, but that seemed to be the general direction. By the time we got far enough out of the city to look back, it was all burning. The flames were bright and they were everywhere."

Joe was silent for a moment, processing. He fought hard against the emotions that were rising. He stuffed all those thoughts and feelings into a mental closet, shut the door, and locked it. He would come back to them one day, but for now he simply didn't have time. One of the skills that was ruthlessly hammered into every graduate of the BUDS training that marked his initiation into the SEALs was the need for compartmentalization. When the mission was at hand, the only thing that mattered was the objective. Doubts, fears, and everything else had to be put in a separate compartment.

For right now, the mission was getting as much intelligence from this deserter as possible before he had to be dealt with.

"What happened to your group?" Joe asked after a moment. "You said you left with a few others in a Humvee, so why are you walking alone now?"

The man shrugged sharply against his restraints, suddenly in a violent twitch. "We ran out of fuel just this side of the border. Don't know where the rest of them went. I just remember waking up alone one morning. Everything is kind of a fuzzy around then. I guess cause I was still in a lot of pain from my face. And, you know, the rest of it."

The rest of it. A nuclear detonation over the Capitol that likely killed thousands and destroyed the heart of the nation's capital city. That was the rest of it. The thoughts Joe had locked in his mind's closet hammered at the door, but he refused to allow them to take over his consciousness.

"I guess everyone just kind of wandered off," the prisoner continued. "That's what I did. When I woke up alone, I didn't even think about waiting for anyone to get back. I just started walking."

"Are you heading anywhere particular?" Joe asked. "Is there a rally point?"

"Rally point?" the man asked, confused. "You don't get it. It's over. DC is gone, man. I don't know where I'm going. I just know I'm not going back there."

"The FSS," Joe began, his pulse quickening, "are they still operational? You said you were working security, so I assume you were a part of the organization. Are they still functional?"

The man shook his head violently side to side. "I don't know, and I don't care, okay? The army had already left, so who knows what they're doing now. I know I'm done with it all. I just want to stay alive, so I'm going to find the deepest darkest place I can, and I'm going to stay there as long as I can."

"Look, just cut me loose," the stranger panted. "I won't stick around. I'll just keep walking. You don't have to worry about me."

Joe watched as the stranger made his face the very picture of sincere innocence. It would have been a convincing act if not for the wild look in his eyes and the pulsing vein in his temple and along both sides of his neck.

This man was broken. His friendly attitude and straightforward face were a thin veneer over something dangerous. Joe had seen this kind of feral, primal fear in the eyes of enemy combatants in some of the worst areas of the world. When they were captured and realized there was no way out of the trap, they got that look that said if they had the chance they would gnaw off their own arm, or someone else's, to get out of it.

Their prisoner had that look.

Joe leaned forward and locked eyes with the man. "Let's talk about why you have dried blood on your left boot and your right pants leg," he said in a calm, quiet voice.

The man's teeth clicked shut and a sound that could be described only as a low growl emanated from deep in his throat.

Joe nodded and looked at the man for another moment before standing. "You've killed people, and not just in defense. It's in your eyes. Once a man kills and kills again, it sinks in deep and he can't get it out. I've seen it before, and I see it now in you."

Joe turned and started to walk away.

"Wait!" the man called, shifting in his bonds. "We can talk some more, just give me a chance. Untie my hands. Or my feet. Just give me a chance."

Joe didn't turn back. The man had seen too much and had crossed a line. He was dangerous now and would rip out another man's throat with his teeth if he could get to him. Any man was a vicious creature if he thought himself in imminent danger of being killed. They couldn't risk letting this one go.

Joe stopped at the perimeter the trainees had established and motioned for Eric and Oscar to come and join him. The young former college student had proven a natural at military training and exercises and was learning tactical movements quite nicely. He showed real promise. Eric had been at this kind of thing since he was a boy and they ran stalks on each other in the woods.

"Listen, Oscar you stay here with Eric, and you two keep the rest of these young men away from him," Joe said. "We're going to have to decide what to do with him, but we can't just let him go. He's dangerous, and now that he knows we're here, he's a threat. He also said something about an army headed south toward Fort Bragg, so we need to see if we can get any more specific information out of him."

"Dad, what happened to his face?" Eric asked hesitantly.

Because Eric grew up during the tail end of the cold war, Joe had taught his son about the different kinds of threats the nation faced. Eric had chosen to do an AP History research project on the arms race between the USSR and the United States throughout the twentieth century, so he knew a good deal about nuclear weapons. He would have recognized the signature burns from a thermal flash.

"There was an incident," Joe said carefully. "I'm not going to say more than that for now, but you will find out. You just have to be patient. Whatever you do, do not go near and do not talk to the prisoner under any circumstances. I am going to go get Chris back at the training camp, and we will extract this prisoner ourselves. Once we've had a chance to debrief him and get as much as we can out of him, then we'll sort it all out."

Joe looked around at the young men in the patrol. He knew he had talked around Eric's question without really answering it, and he needed to distract him from the subject. "How confident are you that they will hold together?" he asked, implying his own doubt.

"They're good," Eric replied without hesitation. "No question at all. We got this."

Joe started up the road toward the camp. "We'll see. Keep it locked down until I get back, son," he called over his shoulder and then broke into a steady, distance-eating jog.

As Joe ran down the narrow dirt road through the woods and along fields leading back to the church, his mind was racing. If what the man had said was true, then someone had dropped a nuclear weapon right on top of the capital and vaporized a good portion of it. Joe had a twisting feeling deep in his gut that he knew who that someone was.

His right hand went to the small zipper pocket on the left sleeve of his trail jacket and felt the cold, hard weight of Terry

Price's Naval Academy class ring. He had carried it since a stranger showed up out of the blue in a helicopter, handed it personally to him, only to turn around and leave without much more than a good bye.

Now he was beginning to wonder just what that gesture meant.

Chapter 68

First Things First

Nov. 8 th 1800 MST

Commander Terry Price sat alone at a table in the Operations and Command Center. Most of the monitors had been switched off, but a few were still running their tracking programs. His own laptop still tracked a certain transponder far to the east, but it had been a long time since he had risked unlocking the encryption program to check the progress. He would have to soon. He knew that Lieutenant Commander Attledge, once he got rolling, would take very little time to cross the distance.

He had been trying every other hour for days now to re-establish contact with Attledge. He knew his signal was being received; the system could track that. He was simply being ignored, and from more than four hundred miles away, there was little he could do to force his subordinate to pick up the phone.

Still, one could hope.

And so, with the rest of the staff in the chow hall, Price sat alone in the OCC and dialed the patch-in key, signaling over the secure satellite network to Attledge. He flipped a small hourglass in an oak frame, and white sand began to trickle from the top through an impressively narrow neck into the empty bottom, where it formed a small cone-shaped pile. He would continue to signal until the bottom filled with sand, roughly three minutes. Then he would stop.

He heard a click and looked up to see the screen power on as an incoming signal began the security verification process. Price sat up straight and smoothed his uniform. He hadn't actually expected to get an answer and wasn't totally prepared for one.

Once the signal was checked through the various layers of programming security, the image on the screen flickered and Price found himself looking at Lieutenant Commander Attledge. For a moment, no one spoke and the two men simply stared at one another.

Even across the distance and through the electronic filter of both camera and screen, Price could tell that things had changed between them. Their relationship had shifted. He could feel it. At one time, he had been a sort of hero for Attledge, and Price knew that. The young man had made it a point to emulate him as much as possible in both his personality and his work ethic, and it had worked to a degree. Through that process, Price and Attledge had grown to be good friends, and they relied on each other for support, but Attledge had remained the student, the under study.

That wasn't the case anymore. Attledge was becoming more confident about his own abilities, and that was without question a good thing. It seemed, however, from the look in his eyes at the moment, he was also becoming somewhat less infatuated with and impressed by his superior officer.

Price, though, was simply happy to see his friend alive, and he smiled sincerely. "It is good to see you alive and well, Lieutenant Commander," Price said formally. He wanted to make it clear that while hero worship wasn't a requirement of the service, obedience to the chain of command was another matter. "You're making good progress on your mission, I take it?"

Attledge blinked in surprise and a frown furrowed his forehead. "My mission?" he demanded, his voice already heated and angry. "My *mission* is on hold for the moment while I make some decisions. So no, I'm not making progress."

"Decisions about what?" Price asked, certain he would not like the answer.

"Right now, I'm wrestling with the fact that my superior officer, the man who gave me *my mission* launched a nuclear weapon on the nation's capital. We're supposed to be the good guys, right? Aren't we the ones saving the country, not tearing it apart?"

"That's right, Commander," Price snapped. "And what does that mean, to save the country? Do you save the brick, stone, and mortar of DC? Is that what this country is, its monuments and its cities? Because I think it's more than just a bunch of buildings, even very old and historic ones. I think saving this country is about saving the people more than it is about saving the places."

Attledge could feel the heat of his anger. "And how many people did you kill when you turned that key and launched the missile?"

Price dropped his eyes to the floor. "A lot. Too many. But how many more would have died? How many more would have been forced to live in tyranny under that maniac? The traitor tried to use a backpack nuke to destroy Colonel Darius and his group, not to mention his attempt to cut the supply line that has allowed both of you to keep moving east. If that had happened, it would have been the end of the Constitution, the end of the nation, the end of everything. I wasn't going to let that happen. I can't let that happen," Price slammed his fist on the desk in front of him. "I won't let that happen."

"So, your answer to our enemy trying to use nukes against us was to use them instead? How are you any better than the maniac you condemn?"

Price was quiet for a long time. It was uncomfortable to hear his own doubts thrown back at him by his junior officer, but he didn't have a ready response, and that only made it worse. "Maybe you're right. Maybe I'm no better than the traitor who had taken DC prisoner. I don't know. All I know is that I couldn't risk letting that lunatic keep possession of and control over nuclear weapons, not when he had shown how quickly and easily he would use them. I had to act."

Commander Price took a deep, shaky breath and let it out slowly as confidence, self-loathing, doubt, and certainty waged a war inside him. He was watching the satellite feed when the flash lit up the horizon over DC, and it had made him physically ill. For three days, he hadn't eaten a bite and had, at times, contemplated the suspect peace of suicide. But the unfortunate reality was that he couldn't afford that easy escape, not yet. Now that he had done this thing so terrible, yet so necessary, he had to see it through to the end.

"You spoke with Colonel Darius earlier, you said?" Attledge nodded. "I'll tell you the same thing I told him when he raised some of the same questions and doubts that you have raised. I don't have any easy answers for you, Commander. We've all started down a road that I don't think any of us can turn back from, and I'm sorry for that too, for the part I played in putting your feet on this path. You have to understand that we three men are directing the fate of this nation and all of the citizens still breathing within her borders.

And because we carry that responsibility, we don't have the luxury of such sentimental notions as justice and honor."

Price stood and leaned in toward the camera, his face growing large in the display that showed the image Attledge would see. "If you will fight this war for me and see it through to the end, then you can come back here and arrest me. You can try me for treason, or crimes against humanity, or whatever you think fits. I won't resist."

"But first thing's first," Price continued as he leaned back and crossed his arms. "First, we win the war. Then I'll submit to whatever justice you demand of me."

He watched as Attledge thought over his proposal and tried to find holes or loopholes in the promise. Finally, he nodded, though from the expression on his face, he didn't like having to accept even this much compromise. "Very well, but I'm not taking orders from you. I'll stay in contact with Colonel Darius, but I don't trust you as my commander anymore."

Price was already shaking his head. "It doesn't work like that, Commander, and you know it." His voice was hard and cold. "I'm in command, which was part of the deal when you signed up. Now, you'll follow my orders or I will send people after you, and you will be charged with and tried for mutiny, desertion, and treason. There's only one penalty for those crimes in a time of war."

With the press of a button on the remote Price kept in his palm during video calls like this one, he activated a map on the screen behind him. "You were right in this area the last time I pinged your signal." He highlighted the area around Buffalo City, Arkansas. "It's time for you to get moving, Commander. I expect you to be in western North Carolina within forty-eight hours. The freight line you're on stays near rivers and lakes, and there are enough refueling stations along the way that you should have no problem making that deadline."

Attledge was silent for a long moment as he wrestled with himself. Finally, though, some of the tension drained out of his face, and he ran a hand through his hair as he glared at the map over Price's shoulder.

"What about the infantry units? If we're pushing hard to make six hundred miles in two days, they'll get exhausted and we'll leave them in the dust."

"The infantry will just have to make do as best it can. Most of them are in vehicles now, anyway. As long as they can find and scavenge enough vehicles and fuel, they should stay relatively close. You might lose a few, but the main body of the force will be only a few hours behind you at any given point. And even if they fall behind by a few days, so be it."

"Why the sudden urgency?" Attledge asked. "With DC gone, I would think we could take our time getting to North Carolina now."

Price shook his head. "The enemy force is still holding in southern Virginia. If you can get to Joe before they get to Fort Bragg, you might be able to slow them down enough for Colonel Darius to come at them from behind while they're out in the open and exposed. If they get entrenched and start a siege of the base, then it will be next to impossible to dig them out again."

"All right," Attledge said as he stood, "I'll follow your orders, for now. But remember what you said here today, Commander. Once the immediate threat has been dealt with . . ."

Price finished the thought for him. "You know where to find me, Marcus. I'm not going anywhere."

Without another word Commander Price reached up and pressed the button that killed the connection.

Once the line was dead, he sank back into his chair. He was exhausted. He felt like he had run a ten kilometer race up a mountain, but he was relieved as well. Attledge had been angry; that much he'd expected, but he had agreed to continue fighting.

And for now, that was all that mattered.

Chapter 69

Oak Ridge

Colonel Darius stood in the early morning sunlight on a small platform on the roof of the car that served as his office and the convoy's Sensitive Compartmented Information Facility (SCIF). There was a surprisingly large crowd assembled before him, and more than a few wore military uniforms that, while far from new, had been well maintained. There were probably two hundred or more people facing the train in the open gravel and grass lot near the junction with the Eastern Smoky Mountain line that would soon take the convoy north and east into the North Carolina mountains.

As he began his speech, the colonel was acutely aware of where he stood and the relationship this town had to the history of atomic weapons. "Good morning fellow Americans," he said, but as the words caught in his throat, he felt the weight of their meaning. "That simple phrase means a lot more now than it did a year ago, doesn't it?" he asked, and many of the people in the crowd nodded. "I mean, after all, there are a lot fewer of us left today. We've got to hold on tighter because of that and work harder to scrape by. Even with the little we have left, we have to support ourselves and each other. It's tough, I know, but it's what Americans have always done."

Darius paused as people nodded and whispered to each other of shared burdens and sorrows. He waited just a few moments until the whispers began to grow loud enough to be heard clearly. "I know why it's tough. There's a group of people out there. I won't call them bad guys. I think what they're doing is bad—worse than bad—but I don't know about the people. That's between them and their maker. But this group of people, the Federal Security Service, they're the ones that launched the missiles that started this whole thing. They caused the Blackout that crashed society and set us all on this razor thin edge between barely scraping by and dying."

This time when he paused, only angry silence met the colonel's glare. The people were ready to be coaxed now. "The FSS is still at work. They are marching south through Virginia as we speak and headed deep into the heart of the South East, and there's no one to stop them. No one but this army and one other division, both tasked with finding and confronting the worst enemy the United States has faced on its own soil since Robert E. Lee and his Army of Northern Virginia."

Darius leaned forward slightly on the waist-high hand railing that had been screwed into brackets on the roof of the train car. The angle was just right so the pistol in his shoulder holster hung in obvious sight.

"This army is on the move," he continued, scanning the crowd in an attempt to make contact with every pair of eyes he could. "We won't be staying in your back yard for long. We're just pausing to rest before the next big push. We brought our own supplies, so you don't have to worry about us eating you out of house and home while we are around." A couple of faces relaxed visibly at that, and one man with a long white beard fanning across his chest turned and walked away, seemingly satisfied that his personal property would be safe for the time being.

"We are on our way to war," Darius said. "I won't sugarcoat that fact. But I also won't sugarcoat the fact that we are going to need soldiers for the fight. I would encourage anyone who is able to volunteer for this fight. My brother's kids learned about your town in school, about how this place was essential to the Manhattan Project. Without Oak Ridge there would have been no atomic bombs to end World War II on the part of the Allies. In a hundred or two hundred years, when the cities have been rebuilt and this nation is a whole and healed nation again, our great-great grandkids will read about what we do in these days."

Darius stood up straight and tall. "Give them something good to read, my fellow Americans," he said, and a loud cheer erupted from the crowd.

Once the cheering and clapping died down, Darius continued. "Our convoy will be pulling out in twenty-four hours. Until then, there is a general curfew in place. No one on the street past sunset, for any reason. To keep the element of surprise on our side, we need to keep the chatter about our movements to a minimum. To that end, anyone caught trying to sneak into or out of our camp will be considered an enemy combatant and a spy, and they will be treated harshly. Our sentries will do their best to make sure there are no incidents, but I felt like I needed to make that clear."

"Anyone wishing to volunteer and serve their country will receive three meals a day, shelter, and all of the gear and equipment we have for the fight," Darius said, breaking up some angry grumbles about the curfew. "Payment will not be possible until the government is reinstated, but when we win our nation back, I promise the new government will make your service worth your while."

"Jesus, man, a hot meal is coin enough these days," someone from the back yelled, and half the crowd broke into uneasy

482

chuckles. Unfortunately, there was more truth than humor in his words.

Darius smiled and nodded. "Maybe, but we'll keep the tab running just the same. Please, spread the word. We will take anyone who will volunteer. If we don't have room, we'll make room. We need numbers to win this war. Also, I will have quartermasters from the general staff circulate with lists of supplies we could trade and what we're looking for in return, if any of you are interested."

Behind the crowd, a group of former US Army special operations troops had been hastily erecting a flag pole that had a thick, heavy iron base. Having finished their task, they raised a large American flag, and when the crisp morning breeze blew across the lot, it caught the edges and unfurled her for all the crowd to see.

Darius pointed to the flag. "If you'll join me in the pledge, I think that will wrap up this little gathering."

The crowd turned, surprised to find the new flagpole in the empty lot behind them and a group of armed troops in camouflage battle gear saluting Old Glory. Colonel Darius saluted as the crowd did the same, either with a hand over their hearts or with a crisp military salute.

The crowd spoke as one. "I pledge allegiance to the flag of the United States of America, and to the Republic for which it stands, one nation, under God, indivisible, with liberty and justice for all."

With the pledge finished, the soldiers dispersed to pre-assigned security positions around the train and the railroad crossing. The vehicle convoy advance group had already formed a loose perimeter, sealing off the roads and side streets surrounding the interchange. Another group from the vehicle convoy had secured the town itself and would enforce the curfew as sunset approached.

For the moment, though, they were busy handing out recruitment flyers to anyone who would take them.

Darius hadn't lied when he'd said numbers would win the war, and he was painfully aware of the fact that right now, the numbers weren't on his side.

As the colonel climbed down from the platform, a few people in the back of the crowd turned and followed the bearded gentleman who'd been the first to depart. Most of the people, however, waited for the quartermasters to come around with clipboards and lists to talk in small groups of ten to fifteen about the supplies that could be traded.

Darius stepped into his office through a thick sound and bullet proof door, sat down heavily behind his desk, and leaned back in his comfortably over stuffed leather executive chair. He was exhausted mentally, physically, and emotionally. For more than a week he had been pushing the convoy to the absolute limits of endurance, but they had made amazing progress to show for it. They had covered as much ground as light and fuel would let them, averaging a hundred miles every twenty-four hours.

More than once the group had been forced to backtrack and change direction due to blocked paths or dead-ends. Still they had managed to find a way around each detour and put more than seven hundred miles behind them. They made it to Tennessee two full days ahead of schedule as a result.

With Lieutenant Commander Attledge delaying his departure until he crossed into North Carolina, time had been a pressing concern for Darius. He had to make sure his troops were in place before the enemy started moving, and that meant they had to push hard.

This last leg, though, would take them over the Appalachians and down the eastern slope into North Carolina. Once they made it just on the eastern edge of the mountains, they'd be able to hold their place for a while and rest. From that vantage point they would swing down and a third of the way across North Carolina in a matter of hours. When the time was right, they would surprise the FSS army by attacking their unguarded rear.

He hoped Attledge was on the road. He'd tried to make contact with him twice the previous evening and twice before leaving in the early pre-dawn hours this morning, but to no avail. The colonel was curious about how the conversation between Attledge and Commander Price had gone, and he had expected Attledge at least to want to discuss it. The younger man was visibly shaken by the attack on DC, and Darius was hoping that a conversation with his commanding officer and long-time friend and mentor would help to clear his head.

With any luck, Attledge had begun moving this morning just as Darius had, which should account for why he wasn't able to receive or transmit on the satellite network. One of the aspects of war that he hated was the fog of ignorance and the lack of real-time information. He was running in the dark, and that was how mistakes were made.

As the weary Darius ran a hand through his hair, he heard a sharp rap on his door. He took a deep breath and called voice, "Come in!"

The door opened and one of his quartermasters, a man who had been a factory foreman before the Blackout, stepped inside. "Colonel, I have a man here who has information on the FSS."

Darius had hoped to get at least a little time to himself, but it didn't appear that luxury was in the cards. Every time the convoy stopped in a town, there were crowds there to trade for goods, collect information from, and at times sell information to. Usually the exchange of information didn't amount to much, but from time to time the people had something worth paying for. He closed his eyes and willed himself to say, "Very well, send him in."

However weary and desperately tired he might be, he couldn't afford to brush these opportunities off. There was always the chance that information gathered through his casual conversations with civilians could be the difference between a successful mission or a failure.

The quartermaster moved aside and a man in a faded and torn uniform stepped into the office, marched to the center of the room, and presented himself at attention with his eyes perfectly caged.

Darius nodded to the quartermaster and waved him out, then addressed the soldier standing before him. "At ease, Captain," he said after checking the man's lapel. The stranger's rank insignia was still attached, but his nameplate had been torn off the chest of his uniform shirt. "Who are you?"

"Sir, Captain James Withers, 4th Tennessee Mountain Search and Rescue, Army National Guard" the man replied, "reporting for duty."

Chapter 70

An Open Door

Mike stood in the road facing east; his eyes were closed as he soaked up the warmth of the morning sun. The now familiar church was in front of him, and to his left the group was breaking camp for the first time in more than a week. Less than a third of the group was going with Mike. About a third had decided to accept Sue Ellen's invitation to stay and were figuring out the logistics of their new community. About half were following Carter Parker south, and the rest were continuing on with Mike, Arthur, and Cheryl.

It was difficult for Mike to watch the majority of the people who had been under his care since Charlotte leave him and move on to their own paths. He had grown closer to some than he had to others, but he thought of each and every one of them as part of his now extended family. They had become integral parts of each other's lives, and Mike had shouldered the lion's share of the burdens of command and leadership. Now many of those people he had pledged to see safely to Bennett were leaving when they were barely more than halfway there.

Mike heard footsteps, soft and light, to his left, and when the breeze shifted he caught the scent of lavender and honeysuckle. He smiled in spite of himself. "Coming to say goodbye, Alyssa?" he asked, his eyes still closed.

"I guess so," came the hesitant reply. "Maria and I have everything packed and we're ready to go. Sue Ellen said we would get a small house that used to belong to an elderly farming couple. It has some land, a couple of springs, and covers half of two mountains and the valley in between. Would you want to come and see it?"

Mike turned and looked at Alyssa, his stomach twisting and his heart aching, but he shook his head. "I'd better not right now or I'll want to stay. Arthur and I need to make some distance today, so we've got to get moving soon. Besides, that sounds like the kind of place that once you see it you don't want to leave."

Alyssa smiled and dropped her eyes to her feet. "I wish it wasn't like this," she said softly.

"It doesn't have to be," Mike said, and he took a half step towards her. "You can still change your mind, come with us. I . . . I love you, Alyssa. You have to know that."

Alyssa nodded, and when she raised her eyes again tears spilled onto her cheeks. "I do know that. And I love you too. But Mike, you almost got Maria killed," Alyssa whispered. "If her reflexes had been a little slower, or *his* had been a little faster, she'd be dead right now instead of just scarred. I know you didn't do it on purpose and I know you're not the one who pulled the trigger. But I can't risk something like that happening again. Maria is all the family I have left, and I need her. We need each other. And the best way I can think of to keep us both safe is to get off the road and hide. Just find a little corner of nowhere and disappear."

Mike ground his teeth in frustration and shook his head slowly. "I can't do that, not yet. I've made promises—given Arthur and Cheryl, Chip, and the rest of them my word that I would get them to Bennett and that we would have the chance to fight the people that did this. They trusted me and believed me, and now I've got to make good on those promises. And, more than that, I want the chance to fight."

"I know," Alyssa whispered, and she stepped closer, taking Mike's hand in both of hers. She pulled it up to her lips, kissed the back, and held it against her cheek. "Just promise me you will come back to me when it's all done." Mike started to protest, but Alyssa held a finger up to his lips, stopping him. "Promise me that when this is all over and done with, you will come back here and find me and we'll make a life and a family together, Mike. Promise me that, please?"

Mike tried to speak past the lump that had formed in his throat, but he couldn't. All he could do was manage a weak nod, but that was enough for Alyssa. Before he could find his voice again, she pulled his face to hers and kissed him with such sudden, ferocious passion that he almost lost his balance. By the time he regained his balance and thought to return her kiss, Alyssa was already pulling away from him.

"Come home to me," she whispered in his ear, and then she turned and walked away.

Mike stood there in the middle of the road and stared after her for a long time. He wanted nothing more than to run take her in his arms and never let her go again, but he knew he couldn't. He was terrified this would be the last time they ever saw each other or that if he did manage to make it back, he would find that she had moved on without him. Over the past few days resting with the group, things had almost gotten back to normal between them, and he had hoped that Alyssa had forgotten the nastiness with her sister and the raiders who had tried to take her. Now he was watching her walk away and he knew there was nothing he could do to stop her.

A light cough behind him jarred Mike out of his thoughts, and he spun around, his hand going for the Beretta holstered at his hip. Instead of some intruder, he found himself face to face with Sue Ellen. The elderly woman stood on the shoulder of the road in faded gray work pants and an olive button-down cotton shirt, an old white cotton shawl wrapped around her shoulders.

"That looked like a hard goodbye."

"It was," Mike agreed, "and one of your making, I might add. She was happy on the road with me until we found this place, and now she's staying at your invitation. Some men might take offense at that."

"Happy?" Sue Ellen said, one white eyebrow arching over her sharp blue eyes. "Was she really?"

Mike started to shoot back a reply, but something in Sue Ellen's eyes stopped him. Whatever they had talked about, whatever had been said between her and Alyssa, the old woman knew the truth.

"Maybe not, but she would have forgiven me, and she would have been happy again, eventually."

"She's already forgiven you, you clod," Sue Ellen said, shaking her head. "I swear, the older I get the more I think one of these days a man will understand a woman, but it just ain't never gonna be so. She has forgiven you, Mike, and she loves you. That's why she came and said goodbye. If she hadn't, or if she didn't, she would have just been gone."

Mike blinked, taken aback by Sue Ellen's words. He hadn't considered things that way. "Well if she's forgiven me for something I didn't do," he answered, "then why is she still leaving me?"

"She's not," Sue Ellen said, leveling a gnarled finger at his chest, "*you* are the one leaving. She's just stayin put."

Mike ground his teeth, frustrated at himself for being stubborn and angry at Sue Ellen for being right. "Did you come out here to say something in particular, or did you just want to come rub salt in fresh wounds?"

Sue Ellen's weathered face suddenly broke into a grin. "I like you, Mike," she said as she slipped an arm into the crook of his elbow. "You go straight to the point and say exactly what you're thinking. Well, most of the time, anyway. No man says what he's thinking when there's a pretty woman involved, but I stopped being pretty a long time ago. Now I'm just old. Come and take a walk with an old woman."

Sue Ellen started up the road away from the church and away from Mike's group, and since she had him by the arm, Mike had no choice but to follow. They walked for a while, neither saying a word. At first, Mike was uncomfortable and kept trying to find something to say to break the unsettling quiet that stood between them, but nothing seemed worth discussing.

"There used to be a road that came down that ridge over there," Sue Ellen said, pointing off to the right. "There were houses, a mill, and two general stores on the other side of the ridge. Not much, I'll grant you, but at the time it was what passed for a town in this part of the country. Then the Depression hit and things dried up, including that town. The houses all fell years ago, and so did the mill. Last I heard, one of the young'uns said one of the stores was still standing, but it was just a shell. They chase lizards and snakes there in the summer time."

"Why are you telling me this?" Mike asked, a bit confused by Sue Ellen's ramblings.

Sue Ellen stopped and turned to face him, her eyes hard and serious. "I could tell you a dozen stories like that," she answered. "Dozens of stories of farms, shops, even towns just withering away and dying in this area. I've heard the same stories from my parents and grandparents, and I've seen them with my own eyes. But the people here have remained. There's always a remnant that holds on in spite of everything else."

"It's impressive what you've managed to do," Mike acknowledged. "But I don't see what it has to do with me or with my people."

"We're holding on," Sue Ellen answered, "but just barely. Part of the problem is that most of our people are older. They're good people, and strong, but there's just not enough young people here to build a strong future. The people that are staying, they'll help, but most of them are city folk who don't know how to live in the country. And they're not strong, not like you, Mike. We need people like you, like Arthur. People that can make this more than just another withering and dying community."

"I'll tell you what I told Alyssa," Mike said wearily. "I can't stay. For one thing, I've given my word that I would get these people to Bennett—that I would get them to safety. I can't stop now, not when we're so close."

"If it's safety you're looking for," Sue Ellen said, gesturing to the woods and hills around them, "then you've come to the right place. We are in the middle of nowhere. There are freshwater springs and wells all around, and there's more than enough farmland to go around. You could find much worse places to put down roots, Mike."

Mike started to protest, but Sue Ellen raised a hand and stopped him. "I wouldn't ask you to go back on your word, Mike," she said as she patted him on the arm with her other hand. "I know what that means to men, especially a man like you. But I am asking you to come back here. Once you've fulfilled your promises and fought your war, come back here and help us build something for the future, whatever that may be. You don't have to give me an answer now. I know it's the kind of thing you'll have to think about. Just remember that this is a door that's always open to you."

Sue Ellen patted his hand again and started walking toward the woods. Just before she stepped onto an old and almost completely overgrown path that Mike hadn't even seen, she called over her shoulder, "And don't worry, we'll take good care of Alyssa until you get back."

Before Mike could form an answer, she was gone.

Chapter 71

The New Order

The newly ascended President Daniel Arnold sat across from Colonel Hagerston, an untouched glass of bourbon on the desk in front of him. Neither man had spoken in quite some time, but Arnold was content to let the silence stretch. He had made his offer, and now he had only to wait. He had been with the colonel long enough to know how the man would answer. It was just a matter of time.

"And what makes you think you can make this stick?" Hagerston asked. "DC is gone, Daniel. The old government is gone. Why are you clinging to the title and the office like there's still a White House to go home to?"

"The people need symbols, Hagerston," Arnold said as he picked up his bourbon and took a slow sip. "They want something to believe in, something bigger than themselves. That's why our ranks have grown as they have, even since DC was hit. We represent something larger, something they can put their faith in, something they can follow. And if you think a bureaucratic organization like the FSS can inspire people, wait until you see what the President of the United States of America can do."

"The United States are dead," Hagerston said, his mouth twisting with disgust.

494

"That may be true," Arnold replied with an easy smile, "but the people don't realize that, yet. And the longer we can take advantage of that the better it will be for us. President Hall was a fool, but he was a dangerous fool, and people followed him out of fear. We have to convince people to follow us because they think they are doing the right thing."

Arnold slid Hagerston's bourbon closer to him. "If we can convince them of that, then they'll do anything we tell them to. That's the part that Hall never understood. Fear will only motivate a man for so long before he turns and lashes out at the source of that fear. But if you convince a man he's doing the righteous thing, he'll follow your orders forever, no matter what those orders are."

"This won't change our arrangement, though?" Hagerston asked as he took his first sip of bourbon.

Arnold's smile broadened as he realized he had Hagerston hooked now. It was only a matter of reeling him in and landing him. "Actually, it will," he replied, and Hagerston's eyebrows rose. "After all, if the new FSS army is marching with the president at its head, I can't very well be accompanied by a colonel, now can I? That just wouldn't do for appearances' sake."

Arnold swirled his bourbon and watched Hagerston's face carefully as the man turned his words over and tried to decipher their meaning. Just when Hagerston was about to respond, Arnold set his bourbon down and leaned across the desk. "How would you like to be General Hagerston, Supreme Commander of all FSS and Federal States of America's armed forces?"

Hagerston sat back, both eyebrows climbing higher as a slow smile spread across his face. "General Hagerston," he whispered, and the smile deepened. "I like the sound of that." He raised his glass to Arnold and nodded. "To a strong and lasting partnership."

Arnold picked up his own bourbon and raised it in return. "To the new order." Both men drained their glasses.

Chapter 72

Bittersweet

Eager to be on their own way, the group heading south had already left. Arthur had seen them off and had tried up until the very last moment to talk them into staying, though he'd known the whole time his effort was wasted. He knew as well as Mike did that they would miss having that strength in numbers, and that worried him. Now, they were only thirteen, including him and Cheryl. No more bluffing strength that they didn't really have and weren't really ready to employ.

Part of Arthur wished he had been convinced by Sue Ellen's persistent appeals to remain in Flint Hill. The woman was relentless and nearly implacable. Once Arthur had explained that there was a chance Christina was alive, she finally acquiesced and dropped the matter. Though, as with Mike, she had made it clear that the invitation to stay or to return was open.

A good portion of the area's population was elderly, after all, and they would undoubtedly need someone with medical experience on a regular basis for that reason, if nothing else. Arthur could very easily see himself returning to settle down in these hills of the Uwharrie if nothing else worked out. This kind of life, surrounded by this kind of scenery, had always appealed to

497

him, even when he was working fourteen hour days six days a week building his first veterinarian practice.

He knew he couldn't rest until, one way or the other, he'd seen his quest to find Christina through to the end.

Arthur helped Cheryl tighten down the shoulder straps on her pack so that the weight rested on the waist belt wrapped around her hips and buckled in front. Clipped onto the inside left edge of the waist belt was a pocket holster with a .38 special revolver. After years of practice at the range, she had become fast and accurate with the small handgun.

As Arthur was tightening the last strap on Cheryl's pack, she cleared her throat and glanced over his right shoulder with a meaningful look. Arthur turned and found the woodcutter Angus behind him. The towering red-bearded man had an axe slung over his shoulder and an uncomfortable look on his face.

"Doctor," he began, shifting his weight from one foot to the other, "I know y'all are about to leave. And . . . well . . . I wanted you to . . . uh . . . have this." The man held out the axe, handle first, and Arthur hesitated. "It's a Helko Hinterland, the double bit axe I used to . . . well . . . you know. When Micah was bit."

Angus's face went slightly pale as he looked out into the distance over Arthur's shoulder. Arthur took the axe, jarring the woodcutter back to the present. "Well, anyway, I wanted you to have it. I can't look at the thing without seeing that boy and hearing his scream after . . . well . . . you know. Don't think I'd ever be able to use it again, and it's too good an axe to let it sit around here and rust."

Arthur stared down at the axe, wishing he hadn't been in such a hurry to take it now. He swallowed hard and stuck the haft of the axe through the straps of his backpack. "Do you have an extra file I can take to keep it sharp?"

Angus winced as if Arthur had kicked him in the gut. "Doctor, I told you, that's a Helko Hinterland. A carbon file might be good enough for a pressed pot steel axe from the hardware store but never for a Helko. There's a spare sharpening stone in the leather scabbard protecting the bit. You'll want to use a little grease to lube up the stone, then just slide it across like you're shaving layers off the rock. It'll be sharp enough to shave your face with."

"Mr. Shaw, this is really too much. You've obviously got a deep connection to this tool, and I think you should keep it. I don't think I've ever swung an axe except for splitting firewood with a hatchet when we used to stay in the mountains."

But Angus reached out to gently but firmly stop Arthur's hand before he could pull the axe free. He shook his head, a sad look in his eyes. "I do have a special connection with it," he said softly, "but I still can't keep it. I can't take hearing the sound of it shearing through that boy's leg, and then his awful scream afterwards every time I pick the thing up. Just looking at it hanging on the wall of my stall is enough to make my stomach lurch. I need to be rid of it."

Arthur nodded and shook Angus's hand. "I'll keep it safe for you, Mr. Shaw," Arthur said. "Maybe one day you'll change your mind and want it back."

Angus managed a weak smile. "Maybe," he said, and then he turned and walked away.

Mike was waiting by the road with the rest of the group when Arthur joined them. "We ready to go?" Mike asked, and Arthur nodded.

Sue Ellen came up the gravel driveway, her white knit shawl wrapped around her shoulders again despite the warm morning sun. "Arthur, Mike," she said with a sharp sniff, "I wish I didn't have to watch you two leave. We need men like you here, and I hope you'll think about my offer to come back and set down roots."

Arthur couldn't help but smile at the old woman's persistence. "Don't worry, Sue Ellen, we won't forget about you. And with Alyssa and Maria staying here, I don't think you'll have to send any search parties out looking for Mike. When the war's over, I bet even an act of God won't be enough to keep him away."

Sue Ellen sniffed again and tossed her head, lifting her nose into the air so that she seemed to be looking down at the two men, despite the fact they were both at least a head taller. "Well, just make sure you don't go and do something foolish and bullheaded and get yourselves killed."

Mike nodded and started down the road. "We'll do our best, ma'am."

Arthur and the rest were left with little choice but to follow him. A quarter of a mile down the road, just before they rounded a curve, Arthur looked back up the hill at the little church. Sue Ellen's thin frame was still standing in the road, watching them, her white shawl around her shoulders. Arthur raised one hand and waved, and the old woman waved back.

He rounded the bend, and she was gone.

Chapter 73

Through the Night

Lieutenant Commander Attledge watched from the platform atop the railcar that housed his office and the SCIF for the convoy. Two teams worked in tandem to fill the three black tanker cars that were attached to the pair of diesel locomotives at the front of the train. The crews were efficient and skilled, having spent their time at the Kansas City rail yard training for just this task. The rest of the more than four hundred soldiers had split into two groups, with about a third of them going out in teams to forage for more supplies and diesel to leave by the fuel storage tanks, and two thirds providing perimeter security.

The train was parked just south and east of Cleveland, Tennessee, at a large fuel storage facility that had a tight cluster of massive round tanks rising forty feet from the ground. In the pale moonlight, the tanks looked like some form of gigantic mushroom sprouting from the darkness. Only the immediate area around the tanker cars was lit by the portable construction lights the troops had set up, and the darkness outside that small pool of light seemed even deeper because of the contrast.

Attledge checked his watch and rubbed a hand over his eyes. He was exhausted, and he knew the men must be as well. They had pushed hard since leaving Buffalo City, stopping twice only long

501

enough to refill the tanks. With the extra fuel they carried, the infantry convoy had managed to stay relatively close as well. The last time he had spoken to the officer in charge, they were only three hours behind the train and making steady progress. Another party, smaller than the convoy following them, was about three hours ahead scouting their path, and it was these scouts who had alerted him via radio that the fuel storage area was here and usable.

Sending out scouts and keeping a rear guard were both practices that he'd taken from the field manuals Colonel Darius had given him. Though the books were dry in their presentation, they were filled with valuable information. Attledge had spent every free moment studying them and taking notes on their principles. The men under his command had taken note and were beginning to respect his skills more with each passing day.

Attledge was jarred out of his reverie by two sharp, quick whistles from the darkness, followed by two more short bursts and one long one. It was the signal he had developed for the returning foraging parties to let the sentries know they were friendly. But upon hearing the signal, Attledge frowned and checked his watch again. The foraging parties had been gone only twenty minutes or so—not nearly long enough to make an effective search of the area.

Something was wrong. Attledge climbed down from the platform and started walking in the direction of the whistles. Before he'd gone thirty feet, one of the men in charge of a four-man foraging team came running up, his face pale and his eyes wide. The man's hands were trembling.

"Commander Attledge, we've got a problem," the man said without a salute. Because they were moving into potentially hostile territory, Marcus had cautioned the men against saluting and other visible forms of obeisance that would identify officers and enlisted men.

"Sergeant Hardin, right?" Attledge asked, and when the man nodded, he continued. "What's going on, Hardin?"

"Sir, I think you'd better come see this yourself," the man, a retired staff sergeant replied.

Attledge nodded and checked to make sure the Beretta he carried had a round in the chamber. "Okay, fill me in while we walk."

"Sir, there's a residential neighborhood to the east. My group went over to see if there was anything we could use that hadn't been snatched up already. We got to the first houses and were moving slowly, you know, in case someone was still home. Well, there wasn't anyone home, no one alive anyway."

Attledge waited, but the man didn't speak, so after a moment, he prodded him a little to get him talking again. "What do you mean by no one alive, Sergeant?"

Hardin shook his head, his face pale again. "Well, sir, there were people inside the houses. Or what used to be people. Just mostly bones now, and a little bit of clothes here and there. They've been dead a while."

"We've all seen bodies, Sergeant," Attledge said, surprised at how nonchalant his own words sounded. "It's not anything new, even if I wish it was. Why did you bring me out here for this?"

Hardin shuddered and shook his head again, hard. "You'll see, sir. It wasn't just the people in the houses. It was more than that."

Attledge wanted to ask the man more, but something about his voice and the look on his face made him stop. Hardin was a veteran and had seen combat more than once. He had been a volunteer EMT in his civilian life and had seen far more than his fair share of death.

503

To see him this shaken was not something Attledge was prepared for, and it had him worried.

The two men walked in silence and before long arrived at the entrance to the neighborhood. The rest of Hardin's foraging party was waiting for them to return, and they all were visibly shaken, just as Hardin was.

"All right, Hardin, we're here. Take me to the house where you found the bodies and explain to me why you think these bodies are special."

"You don't understand, sir," Hardin said weakly. "The bodies aren't in some of the houses. There are bodies in *all* of the houses. And that's not even the worst of it. Follow me, sir."

Hardin led Attledge to the closest house and pointed. The door stood partially open, but with his flashlight Attledge could see odd markings spray painted on the doorway. A circle was divided into four quadrants and inside each quadrant was a number. He pushed the front door open with the flashlight in his left hand and kept his right hand on the grip of his Beretta.

Inside, the house had been thoroughly ransacked. The bookshelves had been overturned, as had the couch and the upholstered chairs in the living room. Only the coffee table remained upright and undamaged. Two skeletons on the floor had been disturbed by scavengers. Both skulls lay side by side, though, turned slightly. There was one small hole in the back of each round, white bone, and the faces had been shattered by the exit of a bullet. Nearby lay two pairs of wrist, hand, and arm bones with the electrical cord that had bound them still wrapped loosely around the wrists and tied with massive knots.

FSS had been spray painted in large, dark letters across one wall.

Attledge stood still. His stomach was rolling, and he swallowed hard to stay focused on the details of the scene around him. He looked at the pictures on the walls around him and those shattered on the floor. He picked up one photo that had been trampled on, dusted off the boot prints, and carefully laid the picture on top of the coffee table. He forced himself to look at the faces, the smiles, the lives around him displayed in frozen fragments of time. They were someone else's memories, stories no one would ever hear again, but he could remember the images, the faces, the smiles.

These people deserved justice.

Attledge eventually stepped outside to join his men. He took a few deep breaths to steady himself and begin to process what he had just seen.

"Every house is like this?"

Hardin nodded. "Every house that we checked. All of the houses in this neighborhood have the same kind of coded message on the door, but the numbers are different. We haven't figured those out yet, but they all have bodies inside. And there's more."

Hardin led Attledge through the streets to a small playground with a broad, flat grassy area next to the swing sets and jungle gym. At the far end of the field, a large section of grass had been torn up recently. It was obvious that the ground had been dug up and replaced in a haphazard, hurried fashion. Attledge followed Harden, and, just as they reached the edge of the disturbed ground, the breeze shifted and the sick, putrid smell of rotten flesh caught in Attledge's mouth and nose. He staggered against what his body and mind told him they had found, and his stomach heaved again.

"One of my men stumbled on this when the wind changed like that," Hardin explained. "We followed the smell here."

Sticking up from the dirt at the edge of the pit was a small hand, the flesh badly rotted and hanging in bloated tatters from the tiny fingers and wrist. It looked as if a scavenger had recently gnawed it.

Attledge felt his blood run cold.

"I don't know how many are buried here," Staff Sergeant Hardin said, his voice weak with dread, "but . . . I think they're . . . all . . . children."

In an instant, Attledge's blood went from ice cold to boiling hot. Rage threatened to overwhelm him, and his hands began to tremble. He couldn't utter a sound as he began to process what Harden had just said. Few things offended his sense of right and wrong more than the mistreatment of children. He knew the immense scale of loss the nation had faced. He'd seen it in town after town. The people had run out of room and time to bury their dead and, instead, had taken to cremating them rather than risk the spread of disease.

Those left had been broken in heart, mind, spirit and body. They were shells, empty husks, and many couldn't even acknowledge the world around them. Still, they were people. At their core, they were still human beings.

Whoever had done this—whoever had gone from house to house, bound the adults with wire and then executed them—they were heartless. But whoever had saved the children for last—whoever had piled their lifeless bodies in that pit—they weren't human anymore.

They were something else.

"Sergeant, you document every house you have time to," Attledge said in a voice that sounded eerily calm in his own ears. "I want to know addresses, names, occupations, everything we can find out about these people. These families."

Hardin, standing several feet behind Attledge and to his left, made it a point not to turn and face the mass grave when he nodded.

"And Sergeant, find out if they had children."

Chapter 74

Heart to Heart

Nov. 10 th 0430 EST

Eric sat in a small blind on the edge of the woods facing the small, dark ribbon that was the paved road Cutler's Run. He could see the black-top in the light of the moon, a deep, dark scar across the fields a quarter of a mile away. Camouflage wrapping encased the top of a tri-pod deer stand set just back from the edge of an open field with a row or two of short scrubby trees between the stand and the dried soybeans. The elevated position provided an expanded field of view, and it was still difficult to spot from the Run, even in daylight.

This had become the de facto guard post for standing watch over the compound. There would be another guard at the gate and a third walking circuits of the property and rounds up and down the Run. Security was a serious matter these days, and Eric's father was calling the shots for most of this part of the county, or so it seemed. The people who had trained with them at the church accepted his leadership without question, and they came from all over the area. Danny and his uncle were carrying out raids in the northern part of the county on the orders of Eric's father as well.

Eric briefly wondered just how far his father's influence and power would grow. But all of this served only to distract him from the things that were really weighing heavily on his heart and mind.

With everything else going on that he should have been focused on, Eric was hesitant to admit, even to himself, that his thoughts lately seemed to be focused more and more on his upcoming wedding with Christina and their unborn child.

He leaned his head back and stared up at the three-quarter moon in the western part of the sky, along with the scattering of stars bright enough to shine through the glare. It amazed him how many more stars he could see now that all of the cities had gone dark. For a long moment, he emptied his thoughts and simply watched as the heavens spun above him. A noise from the bushes behind him snapped Eric out of his reverie. He sat up and turned halfway around, his rifle going immediately to his shoulder. Eric stopped and did his best to remain totally silent, listening intently, trying to find what he'd just heard. After a moment, a hesitant whistle came from the bushes that sounded like the call of a whippoorwill. Eric smiled and whistled back like a bobwhite and then relaxed.

He recognized the hesitant, slightly garbled whistle that was a decent, though obvious imitation of the whippoorwill. Christina had spent weeks practicing and was getting better, but she still had a long way to go before she could fool the love-struck songbirds. Eric rolled back over and stared once more at the sky as he waited. The stand shook a little as Christina started her climb.

The floor was about four feet on each side with a bench bolted on the back side closest to the woods. Christina reached the top and joined Eric as he watched the stars. She spread a blanket over the two of them and snuggled against Eric's side.

"I figured you'd be asleep," Eric whispered. "Are you sure you should be up this late?"

"It's not late anymore, Eric," Christina said playfully. "If you've already been to sleep once and woken up, then this is early. And trust me, if I hadn't had to pee so bad I thought my bladder would explode, I wouldn't be up right now, early or late, or whatever. I'm still tired, but once I was up, that was it."

"I know the feeling," Eric replied. "I volunteered for the whole night tonight. Didn't make sense to wake someone up when I knew I wasn't going to be able to sleep anyway."

"What's got you up?" Christina asked, propping herself up on one elbow.

Eric rolled on his side and looked at her blue eyes in the moonlight for a long time before answering. "Lately it's been the wedding coming up, our baby. And the raid we're getting ready to carry out. It's getting bigger and bigger. It's all got me worried and on edge and stressed out all at the same time. I've been afraid for so long, it's like I don't even feel it anymore. It's just a part of who I am now, or something. I can't really explain it."

Christina gave him a funny look. "So, getting married and having a child with me makes you scared and worried and on edge?"

Eric frowned, confused for a moment, and then what he'd just said clicked. "That's not what I meant. I mean, it does, kind of, to be honest. This definitely isn't what I had planned when I put that ring on your finger. Not that this is bad. Oh, hell, you know what I'm trying to say. It scares me some, but it excites me too and makes me happy. I guess it's the best scared I've ever been."

Christina smiled and nudged him hard in the ribs with her elbow. "Nice recovery, Slick," she said as she settled back down next to him. "I know what you mean, though. I always wanted to be a mom, but this wasn't what I had in mind when I used to think about it. I thought we'd be married for a few years, maybe buy a house together. After we travel, of course. And then, when we're ready, that's when we'd start having kids."

Eric snorted a short chuckle. "I love that you used to think about things like that. I usually couldn't see much past the end of the week or the first of the month when the bills were due. I mean I wanted all of that other stuff, don't get me wrong. We were just having such a hard time getting by that it didn't seem the right time to start plans."

Christina sighed and rolled her eyes slightly. "We didn't have it *that* bad," she reminded him. "I mean, especially when you consider now. We had it pretty good, actually."

Eric couldn't argue with her about that. Life then had certainly been easier. And, though he had taken it for granted at the time, it had been cleaner too. One of the things that bothered him most these days was the feeling that no matter how hard he scrubbed with sand and soap, he couldn't quite get clean. The house was dirtier too, dirtier than he'd ever seen his Nanny Blossom let it get.

It wasn't that she had slacked off in her housekeeping regimen, quite the opposite. She now commanded a small army of children cleaners who spent much of their time doing chores around the house. They would sweep the floors, beat out the area rugs when the sun was shining, knock down and sweep up cobwebs, dust baseboards, and all manner of other custodial duties. There were just so many people living in and out of the house that it pretty much stayed somewhere between clean and grimy.

"We still do have it pretty good," Eric said after a moment, and Christina, her head resting on his chest, nodded. "We still have power, fresh food, and clean well water to drink. We have a lot of people around us that we can trust and electricity enough from the solar panels to at least remember the world before, especially when we watch a movie or two on the DVD player. I mean, that's got to be more than most people who survived have right now."

"Do you ever feel bad?" Christina whispered after a moment. "About surviving, I mean."

Eric gave a small shrug. "I don't know, maybe," he said, "but that's just how God's worked it out, and it's not up to me to judge that. I just go with it, one day at a time. And the way I see it, the fact that we're all still here is a sign that we should do the absolute best, the most good that we can while we can. Cause someone has to balance out all of the bad that's happened lately."

Christina nodded and wrapped her arms tightly around Eric, her head still on his chest. The two lay like that for a while, watching the night sky turn above them. A couple of shooting stars streaked through the darkness as they watched. Eric would have gladly let the silence stretch between them until the sun came up or sleep shut out the rest of the world. But Christina still had more on her mind.

"Are you scared, Eric?" she whispered, breaking the silence.

"I told you I was, Christina," he replied shortly. "I mean, it's not that I doubt Dad's judgment about the men being ready to do this. It's just that there are so many different things that have to happen in order and with very tight timing. If some critical action happens just a hair too early or just a hair too late, it will throw the whole mission into chaos. And men will die. How could I not be a little bit scared?"

Christina blew out a heavy, exasperated sigh. "Not that," she said, waving one hand dismissively, "you're going to do fine with that. I meant . . . well . . . the other stuff."

Eric frowned, confused. "We both just talked about being a little scared about marriage and having a kid in the middle of everything else. Are you feeling okay?"

Christina shook her head again. "No, not that either. The other other stuff. What the stranger with the burned face told your father."

"Oh," Eric replied, falling silent for a long moment. "You know he ordered us not to talk about it," he said finally, "and there are some parts I won't . . . I can't . . . talk about. But that doesn't stop you from guessing."

Christina arched an eyebrow. "Are you going to make me jump through hoops just to get some gossip from you?"

"This isn't gossip, Christina," Eric said softly. "It's a lot bigger than that. You have to understand. If the wrong person heard . . . or even if some of the right ones did . . . you can't say anything. This is war, and some secrets are so precious that any answer when you're asked is too much answer. Understand?"

Christina nodded. "Was it an attack?"

Eric nodded.

"Was it chemical, whatever burned his face like that?"

Eric paused for a moment and shook his head. No, not chemical.

"Was it heat, then? Like from a fire or an explosion?"

Eric nodded slowly, holding Christina's eyes with his own the entire time.

"What made the fire?" Christina asked in a hoarse whisper.

Eric stopped. This was the question he'd waited for, but he didn't make even the slightest movement. Christina froze, her eyes going wide as she made a guess and then immediately declared mentally that it was too terrible to even voice. She subconsciously gave first her head and then her entire body a shake, almost like a convulsion.

"Did someone burn him? Hold him close to a fire or put acid on him?" Christina whispered, her voice hollow.

She knew the truth. She'd already guessed it in that first moment after Eric had told her it was fire. She'd known then, and she knew now, but she didn't want to admit it to herself. At least, not yet. Eventually, she would be forced to accept what she'd guessed, and she would come to terms with it, but for the moment she was stubbornly mounting a subconscious Hail Mary, reaching for anything she could possibly think of other than the horrible fact that someone had used a nuclear weapon against the United States.

"I can't answer your questions anymore," Eric said. "Like I said, some things you can't offer an answer either way or you're giving something up that can't be leaked."

Christina nodded and let the matter drop. "Was this man part of a larger force? Is a larger force nearby?"

Eric took a deep breath and thought about how to answer that. It wasn't part of what his father had ordered top secret, but it was still pretty sensitive. And the last thing he wanted to do was set Christina's nerves on edge right now.

"Yes and no," he answered carefully. "He was part of the FSS, yes, but he deserted."

"Okay," Christina said, her eyes narrowing. "But that doesn't answer the second question. Is a larger force nearby?"

514

Eric's teeth clicked as he shut his mouth again. After a moment, he shook his head. "That's another thing I can't talk about. If someone was listening and word got out, to either side, it could have very bad effects on morale, on operations. I can't risk it."

This time it was Christina's turn to be silent for a long, increasingly uncomfortable moment. Usually, Eric could read his fiancé at least somewhat well and could understand her thoughts and her emotions by what he saw in her eyes and on her face. But as he looked down at her now, she was unreadable. Eric knew she was wrestling with something, but that was the extent of it. And that troubled him deeply.

Finally, her features softened, and she gave a small shrug. "I guess I never really wanted to be a military wife," she said. "I wouldn't have chosen to be, I guess I should say. It's difficult to watch you go out and put yourself in harm's way. I know a lot can happen, and I don't have control over any of it. That scares the hell out of me."

She paused to wipe a tear from her eye, but her voice was iron strong. "I understand it, and I know you're doing everything you can to keep us safe. I know it's necessary, but it still scares me. I didn't want to tell you because I don't want to put any added pressure on you, especially not now. But I just couldn't keep it to myself anymore."

"It's okay," Eric said with a small smile. "To be honest, I didn't want this kind of life either. That's the whole reason I was in Charlotte, to get away from military life and people I knew who were headed that direction. I never really wanted to go into the family business, but it seems I have a knack for it."

Eric paused and took Christina's hands in his own. He sat up so they were looking at each other rather than talking to the sky. "I told you, it scares me too," he said. "But I'm more scared of what could happen if I wasn't out there. I saw what those FSS monsters were doing on the edge of town. I couldn't take it if something like that happened here, or anywhere else, for that matter—not when I could do something to stop it. Throwing people away like that, just throwing their entire lives away like trash . . . that's just wrong."

"I'm still scared, though," Eric continued softly. "I'm scared that we're not ready, not for something this big. And if we mess it up, we could all die out there. I mean there are maybe a dozen people in the entire group that have seen combat, and three of them live here with us. Maybe six more have had military training higher that ROTC, and that's being generous. And we're going to mount a surprise attack on a mobile enemy with superior numbers and likely superior experience."

Christina shook her head. "You sell yourself too short," she said seriously. "Your father too. Look at what he's done around here. Look at what he's put together at that church. And look at yourself. You've been standing watches and going out on patrols and salvage runs for months now. More than once your back's been against the wall, but you always figured your way out of it. You've done what was necessary every single time you've been put to the test, and you're going to do the same thing now. Between you and your father, and the others, I'm not worried. Not even a little bit."

By the time she was finished, Christina's eyes were burning with intensity. She was utterly convinced that Eric's dad and his army were going to win, no matter what. It warmed Eric's heart to see that kind of absolute faith and trust in their abilities. She wasn't trying to soothe him. If anything, Christina seemed to be chastising him for not having more confidence in himself and those around him.

Oddly enough, it seemed that chastising was just what Eric had needed to break out of the fatalistic thoughts that had been rolling around in his head for the past few days. He smiled and pulled Christina close, and she settled with her back against his chest and his arms around her waist. She pulled the blanket up over her growing belly.

"I'm sure you're right," Eric whispered in her ear. "Everything will come together in the end, and we'll be fine."

Even as Eric whispered the words, he wished he had more confidence in their truth.

Chapter 75

Rallying Cry

The sun was barely up, yet the entire FSS force was assembled in the rolling hills and meadows that a hundred and fifty years earlier had served as a battlefield in the first Civil War. Now, in the midst of what President Daniel Arnold had finally come to realize was the second Civil War America would face, this field would serve not as a battlefield but as a launch platform. Here, the history books would one day record, is where the rebirth of the nation truly began.

President Arnold stood atop the platform that had been raised over the course of the past week and surveyed the troops assembled before him. These were his troops, regardless of what that fool Colonel Hagerston thought. He would maintain the facade of a joint command for now, but, eventually, he would have to deal with the colonel. It wouldn't be easy, he knew, because such a man commanded loyalty in those who served under his command. He had seen the way the men reacted to him, and it was genuine respect they showed him.

If the man proved useful, Arnold could always offer to solidify his position and keep him as a valuable asset. If, on the other hand, he chafed under the president's command and authority, there were steps that could and would be taken. For now, though, he needed the man's experience in battle and wasn't foolish enough to throw that away. Part of his predecessor's problem had been the belief that he was above the possibility of error or oversight. Clearly, given his demise, that was not the case.

Arnold pushed thoughts about his former employer out of his mind. This was a new morning and not the time to think of the dark past he was leaving behind. Today marked a new beginning. Generations ago, his family name had become tainted when a forefather had betrayed the patriots in their war for independence. That ancestor, one Benedict Arnold, had brought generations of shame and disgrace to his family, so much so that some branches of their family had changed their name to attempt to escape it.

Daniel's branch, however, had always worn the Arnold name with a sense of shameful obligation, thanks to the treachery of their ancestor. Now, Daniel would reclaim the honor and glory that his family name deserved. The Arnold name would be etched in the pages of history as the name of the president who resurrected the lost greatness of the old United States in a new guise and under a new name, the Federated State of North America.

Arnold turned to Colonel Hagerston and nodded.

The colonel stepped forward and addressed the assembled troops. "By now, you have all heard what happened in DC. Some of you may have found out when you joined our army. Some of you were actually close enough to see the flash or hear the detonation. Let me say that if you had any doubt, it is true. Washington DC has been obliterated by a massive nuclear weapon."

Colonel Hagerston paused as a few whispers and murmurs were quickly stifled. For most of the troops this was old news, but for some the knowledge was still new enough to be a little unnerving. When silence had once again been restored, he continued.

"Today we are assembled as a unified force to bring justice to those who perpetrated that most recent attack and also launched the attack months ago that brought our mighty nation to its knees. At the head of this fighting force is a man who has served this nation his entire life. He was President Hall's vice president before the cowardly attack that destroyed our nation's capital. He was sent south with this army to help us retake the southeast and then the rest of the nation. I can think of no more honorable, deserving, or qualified man to take up the mantle of responsibility and authority of the office of President of the Federated State of North America."

The troops erupted in a short cheer, though Arnold doubted many of them really knew for what they were cheering. The enthusiasm of a few ignited the self-preservation of the rest who didn't want to appear to be the only people not enthralled by their new leader.

Arnold smiled as he stepped forward and waved to the crowd. "I am honored to fill this office and this role as leader of our new nation. We cannot deny that the old nation, the United States, is done, forever destroyed. It was wiped away in the treachery, blood, and fire of war, but its memory and its legacy will live on in us and in our new nation, the Federated State of North America. That nation begins now, today, with us."

This time the cheer was much more enthusiastic. Everyone wanted to be a part of history, or, at the very least, hear that they were a part of history. If they succeeded, then some of them might actually get their wish. New names would rise out of the crucible of this war, and they would be talked about in revered and hushed tones for generations, the same way patriots like Franklin, Washington, and Jefferson were remembered before the Blackout.

President Arnold finally raised both hands high above his head, and silence was restored. "Colonel Hagerston will now administer the new oath of office."

The colonel turned and held out a Bible. Arnold suppressed the urge to sneer as he placed his left hand on the black leather cover and raised his right. He repeated after the colonel as the oath they had written the night before was read into the microphone.

"I, Daniel James Arnold, do solemnly swear that I will uphold the office of the President of the Federated State of North America. I will defend and protect the state from all enemies, foreign and domestic. I will defend the people with my life, my honor, and my authority. I will faithfully execute the powers, duties, and responsibilities of my office to the best of my abilities, so long as life and duty allow. So help me God."

As the last word echoed over the loud speakers that had been mounted on either side of the stage, another cheer broke out among the assembled troops. This time, Arnold let the revelry go on and on, relishing in the waves of thunderous applause and cheers echoing off the hills and woods around them.

When the cheers finally began dying, President Arnold raised his hand and gestured to Colonel Hagerston. "My first act as your president is to immediately promote Colonel Hagerston to the rank of General and Supreme Commander of the Armed Forces. He will take immediate command over all military assets of the State and will stand second in command only to myself. I have never been a military man and will rely on his guidance in the pursuance of this war. Together, with your help, we will bring swift justice to the insurrectionists, and we will begin to heal and rebuild this once great nation of ours. The future begins now, today."

Once again cheers erupted, and Hagerston waited for the crowd to settle before he stepped to the microphone. "Troops, I have your orders. We break camp at noon. The march south begins today! Dismissed!"

President Arnold and General Hagerston stood side-by-side and felt the waves of cheers roll over them, cheers so loud that the entire platform hummed with their vibrations.

So, this, Daniel thought to himself, *is the sweet taste of power.*

A slow, cold smile spread across his face.

Chapter 76

Right and Wrong

Lieutenant Commander Attledge stood on a small, flat stage that had been constructed using walls from the modular shelter system. The walls were made from prefabricated panels that could be joined using brackets at connection points. When placed flush with each other, they made a solid wall, and by using the correct brackets, corners and angles could be accomplished. For the purposes of the speech this morning, a basic frame had been constructed with one panel on each end and two on each side. The rectangle was eight feet tall and relatively stable. The floor of the stage was simple plywood sheeting and he didn't have a sound system.

The crowd that had assembled stood in the early morning sun, their breaths still fogging from the previous night's chill. These people had been through some hard times, and many of them were thin with folds of extra skin hanging loosely on their newly trim frame. Two men had dark circles beneath their eyes and their loud, harsh coughs were enough to make Attledge wince fifty feet away. After a few moments two of the soldiers providing perimeter control escorted the men away from the crowd.

The silence in the park was deafening.

"I have gathered you here today to bear witness," Attledge began without preamble. "The Federal Security Service has done horrible things here, though I'm sure you're more aware of that than I am, even with all that I've seen. You live here. You survived their inhumanity, somehow." Attledge pointed to the residential neighborhood that bordered the park. "Those families that lived up there, they didn't survive it. The FSS came through, tied them up, and murdered them. Only God knows what they did to the children that wound up here, in this pit before they moved on to another town or another neighborhood."

Attledge drew the crowd's attention to a row of sheet metal panels that had been nailed to wooden signposts mounted in the ground. The paint on the flat sheet metal panels was still wet, but none of it was running. The soldiers who had worked all night in shifts to create these grave markers had taken their time with their work, and they'd been careful to get every name neat and correct.

"Make no mistake, that is a grave marker," Attledge continued. "Each name on that marker lies dead in one of those houses over there or is buried here in this mass grave. We've done our best to account for each person and have found that in some cases, entire families have been wiped out. These were your neighbors, maybe some of them were your family and friends. I know this can't be the only place in the entire city of Cleveland, Tennessee, that this cruelty, this inhumane treatment of innocent people, has happened."

Attledge paused and gave the people a moment to murmur to each other about their own personal losses. Everyone had lost someone at this point, and they all understood the pain and shared in its burden for each other.

"Well, those FSS people moved on," Attledge continued once the whispers had died down, " to do this to other towns, other neighborhoods, other families because right now, there's no one out there to stop them. That means their killing is only going to get worse and more widespread the longer it goes on. Until someone stands up and forces people back to doing right, the ones doing these wrongs are going to keep finding ways to do wrong."

"Imagine if the people who slaughtered this neighborhood get to go on living and killing anybody they feel like killing," Attledge said. More than a few angry murmurs erupted among the crowd. "Imagine if they never face punishment, never face a reckoning for what they have done here, and wherever else they've done. There's no law in this land, not right now. There's no one to hold others accountable for their actions. No one to see that justice is done."

Attledge fixed the crowd with a cold, hard glare. "Our mission is to hold these murderers accountable for their crimes here in your town and to bring the people who were responsible for our nation's fall to justice. We are part of an army that is determined to keep the last remnant of the United States breathing free. We are fighting this FSS with everything we have, and I mean everything, but we need your help. We need our fellow Americans to stand shoulder to shoulder with us because this is your country, too. This is your town, these are your neighbors here in this mass grave, and the people who put them there are still out there, right now, killing more innocent people."

"My men put this marker up overnight," Attledge said, his voice cracking with the anger and the grief born out of all he had seen in the past twenty-four hours. "They worked all through the night, skipped meals, skipped sleep, all because they couldn't let these people die without some recognition that they had lived. The world needs to know they are here, and they deserve justice. That's what it says in the Pledge of Allegiance, right? And liberty and justice for all, remember?"

Attledge paused again, and many of the people glaring back at him had tears on their cheeks or in their eyes. They didn't look tired or worn anymore. His words were awakening in them the righteous outrage that such atrocities should have provoked long ago, but they had been too numb, too shocked, to feel it. Now that he was breaking through that barrier, they were seething.

"Your neighbors deserve justice," Attledge continued. "These children buried behind me deserve justice. Will you see that they have it?"

The crowd roared in response. Their faces were red with rage, their necks straining as fists pumped the air. Now the people felt it, the burning righteous fury within them at the tragic destruction of innocent lives. The air was thick with the lingering smell of death. No longer could they ignore what they had known but had refused to confront.

"This United States Army marches at noon," Attledge shouted as soon as the noise had quieted enough for him to be heard. "Will you march with us?"

The second roar hurt his ears, and Attledge felt his breaths come in hard pants, driven by his fervor for this thing he had been called to do. He raised his fist high in the air, and the people before him pumped theirs in response. He waited until the noise settled before he dropped his hand. Slowly, the crowd fell silent again, but still Attledge waited.

Finally, when the silence had stretched long enough to become uncomfortably still, he broke it. "Bring your guns and ammunition when you come. Bring everything you have because we're going to need it. This war isn't like any other we've faced, not in our lifetimes, because this war is here, right in our own back yards. We can't run from it, can't hide from it. And sooner or later, it's going to come for all of us."

Attledge paused and heaved a heavy sigh. "The only thing we can do is decide how we're going to meet it. What we're going to do when it comes calling on us. Well, for you all, that moment is now. I'm not going to force you into service, though with the men and firepower at my disposal, I could. But I will tell you that if we don't have your help, we won't win this war. We won't regain control of our nation."

Again, Attledge pointed behind him to the mass grave. "And they deserve better than that."

Chapter 77

Chance Encounters

Nov. 10th 1300 EST

Mike knelt next to the road and opened the tightly folded road map that Sue Ellen had given him as the group left the churchyard the day before. She had carefully traced out a route that took the group to Bennett via mostly back roads that avoided major thoroughfares. She had even penciled in distance markers along the way so he'd be able to pace the trip.

He traced a finger down the line from Flint Hill, east along Abner Road to the intersection of Hwy 134 where Abner became Bandy, then down to the Bandy and Ether Road intersection where they'd camped the night before. This morning Mike had led them south down Ether Road, and now, four hours and four miles later, they had just passed Ether United Methodist Church and were going through a small country village.

The houses that had been spaced every half mile or more since leaving the Uwharrie were now much closer and could rightly be called neighbors. When they reached the intersection of Ether Road and Highway 220, they turned south for a quarter of a mile to Hogan Farm Road and then turned east. Just shy of half a mile down the road was the US 73 North overpass. Mike called a halt just before they reached the overpass, and the group ate a cold lunch of salted pork shoulder that had been fried the day before, dried apricots and apple slices, and hard biscuits with honey.

These were the last of the supplies they'd taken with them from Flint Hill. Mike knew they still had thirty miles or more to make it to Bennett, and their supplies were tight. A week of good meals and solid rest had done a lot to cure them of the road weariness they'd all felt when they had entered the Uwharrie Forest. But now they were back on the road and would have to once again become accustomed to eating light and on the move.

"How much farther do you think we have?" Arthur asked. Though he had been a little hesitant to leave, now that they were on the road again, the former veterinarian was anxious to cover ground.

"Well, we've come just a little over thirteen miles so far, and it was around forty to Bennett. I'd guess around twenty-seven of thirty, depending on just how we get there. Sue Ellen traced out a route on the map, but she told me there were other options for most of the roads she had us taking. If we run into a road block here or there, we might have to detour or backtrack to an alternate route."

Arthur nodded. "I know, Mike. I just want to be there and find out one way or another if Eric made it home with our daughter."

"I didn't know him long," Mike said patting the older man reassuringly on the shoulder, "but Eric struck me as the type of man who doesn't break his word. He gave me his word he'd be there and he'd have a place for us if we needed it, and I trust him. I'm sure they made it just fine."

Arthur nodded, and his hand strayed to the handle of the axe by his side. "I know you're probably right. There's just so much that can go wrong out on the road. I just need to see her again, need to know she's okay."

Mike gave Arthur's shoulder one more pat and then finished his light lunch. He washed it down with clean spring water that Sue Ellen had collected for them before they left. She had done everything in her power to get them to stay, short of flat out refusing to let them go, but in the end, she had relented. Mike prayed he would survive the war that was coming so that he would have a chance to return to Flint Hill and thank the old woman for everything she'd done—not just for him but for the whole group.

For now, though, he forced those kinds of thoughts from his mind and focused instead on the task at hand. With lunch finished, Mike stood and led the way east. The pace he set for this leg of the trip wasn't a hard one, but it ate distance steadily at a rate of about a mile and a half every hour. The land was flatter here, and they were able to make up some of the time they'd lost earlier coming out of the hills along the eastern edge of the Uwharrie Forest. As the group walked, the sun fell lower and lower in the western sky behind them and cast longer and longer shadows down the road ahead of them.

Chip worked his way up to walk next to Mike for a bit. "You okay, boss?" he asked without breaking stride.

Mike smiled. "Yea, Chip, I'm okay. Is it showing that much?"

Chip shrugged. "Jess and I have been with you longer than most of the rest. I guess I can see it more when something's bothering you."

"I hate that the group split," Mike said finally. "And I'm not just talking about the ones that stayed behind. At least that I can understand. They found a place that was somewhat close to normal, closer maybe than anything they thought they would see again, so they took it. I can get that. It's the other ones that bother me more. The ones who went south."

"You think they'll cause problems?" Chip asked.

"Maybe, but I don't really think so. There were a couple of saber rattlers who might have tried it if they were in charge of a larger group, like we were before we split, but they're not brave enough to go for something like that if there's a real chance that they might catch a bullet. If they run into trouble, there won't be enough of them to bluff their way out of it like we used to do, and that worries me more than the other."

Chip was quiet for a while. "Well, you can't save everybody, boss."

Mike couldn't argue with that logic, so they walked in silence. "How is Jess doing?" he asked after a small stretch.

"She's okay," Chip answered with a small smile. "She's complaining about her feet hurting, but no worse than usual. I think she just has to get back to walking around on them all day."

"Yeah, we all do," Mike agreed.

Chip patted Mike on the shoulder and fell back to walk with his girlfriend. Mike had had serious misgivings about that pair when he'd picked them up in Charlotte, but they both had proven tougher than he would have imagined, and they both had been stalwartly supportive of Mike and his leadership as the group grew in size. Without their help, things would have become unmanageable for Mike a long time ago. He was glad they had decided to follow him for a little bit longer.

After two and a half miles on Ether Road, the group turned onto Dover Church Road and continued heading mostly east. Three and a half miles later, they came to Dan Road, their next turn off. Mike checked the map, and Sue Ellen had traced one route taking Dan and an alternate. The route that followed Dan was shorter and probably faster, but it took them by fewer houses and places where they were likely to find supplies. On the other hand, fewer houses meant fewer chances to be spotted, and that was the deciding factor for Mike. This group had been through enough troubles on the road, and if he could make it across this part of the country without being seen, all the better.

They turned onto the narrow Dan Road at the Westmoore Fire Department. It was clear early on that this road wasn't traveled much, and as such, it wasn't often repaired. There were potholes and scars in the pavement and long stretches that had thick black squiggly lines where patching machines had sealed the network of larger cracks that threatened to fracture the roadbed beyond repair. Such patches were meant to serve as a temporary fix until the road could be resurfaced, but these were faded with age and beginning to crack and wear down themselves.

The group had been on Dan just over a mile when Mike caught the smell of wood smoke on the breeze as it shifted. He stopped and held one hand up in a fist, halting the group behind him. Instantly, they all knelt and held their weapons at the ready. Arthur and Chip worked their way up next to Mike.

"What is it, Mike?" Arthur asked in a whisper.

"I'm not sure," Mike admitted. "I caught the smell of smoke. First sign we've had of anyone since we crossed Hwy 73."

"Did you see anyone?" Chip asked softly.

Mike shook his head. "Not yet, but if we're smelling their smoke, they can't be too far off." Chip and Arthur both nodded at that, so Mike continued. "Tell the rest of the group to move carefully and get to the bushes on that side," he jerked his thumb toward the left side of the road. "We need to go ahead a little way and take a look."

The two men moved down the line of people, spreading the word, and were back in under a minute. The other nine members of the group did as they'd been ordered and took positions in the thick hedge row next to the road. They were concealed and would have a good view down the road ahead of and behind them, as well as across the twenty yards of open field to the trees on the other side.

Mike, Arthur, and Chip crossed over to the trees on the right side of the road and headed toward the smell of smoke. They'd gone about three hundred yards when the woods opened up to a road-side field. Mike led the three around the back edge of the field, keeping close to the trees. As they went, the smoke grew stronger, and they smelled some kind of food cooking along with the sweet, acrid smell of burning wood.

As they reached the halfway point along the back side of the field, Mike stopped again. They could hear voices through the trees, so he turned and made his way through the dry leaves and dead underbrush, picking his way as carefully as he could. They weren't silent, but they were as close as possible, considering they were moving through woods in the fall.

Just before the edge of the trees, Mike stopped and listened. He could see what looked like old cargo shipping containers stacked in a barren field ahead of him. In front of a few rows of the containers was an open gravel lot where perhaps two dozen men were gathered. They weren't wearing any kind of uniform but looked to be dressed in random pieces of hunting gear. Each man carried a rifle or shotgun on his shoulder and a plate of steaming food in his hands.

Mike's stomach began to growl.

Then, behind them, Mike heard a loud footstep as someone cleared his throat. He spun around and came face to face with a tall, bearded young man who had aimed an expensive hunting rifle right at his chest.

"You three don't make any stupid moves and you might not get hurt," the young man said. "We've got people watching the rest of your group back down the road, and nothing has to happen to them neither. But for right now, I'm gonna need you to set your weapons on the ground and take three steps back. Until I know who you are and who you're with, I can't have you packing."

At that point four more men stepped out of the woods and formed a loose semicircle in front of the group. Those four, plus the two dozen or so men in the clearing at their backs, clearly had Mike, Arthur, and Chip outnumbered, so Mike had no choice but to do as he was instructed. He nodded and took his 5.56mm carbine and laid it on the forest floor with his Beretta. He motioned for Arthur and Chip to do the same. Then they took three steps back.

"Okay," the young man said as he lowered the muzzle of his rifle, "thank you for cooperating. Now, for the time being, you are my prisoners. I wish it would have been under better circumstances, but I'm Brant Thompson. It's nice to meet you."

"And what do we do now that we're your prisoners, Brant?" Mike asked through gritted teeth.

"You'll have to answer some questions," Brant replied, calmly meeting Mike's irate question head on, "and as long as you're mostly truthful, that should be the end of it. But you won't be able to keep heading east from here."

"We'll have to turn around then?" Mike asked.

Brant smiled, and to Mike it looked genuine. "Well, that's part of what we have to figure out, ain't it? Mister you don't realize it, but you've kind of wandered into a live combat zone. It might not be safe to have you just walking around." Brant glanced meaningfully down at the considerable collection of firepower that the three men had been carrying and added, "In more ways than one."

"You're just going to keep us prisoner?" Mike asked, his blood pressure beginning to rise.

Brant shook his head and spread his hands wide. "Now you're putting words in my mouth, Mister. I told you, we've got to figure out what to do with you, and that ain't my call. The captain is going to want to talk to you, I expect, and he'll be the one to let you know what's happening next."

"What captain is this?" Mike asked, not liking the sound of what he was hearing. The young man's soldiers hadn't tied their hands or feet, and Mike thought if he moved quickly enough he might be able to grab his Beretta before any of them shot him. He probably wouldn't be quick enough to actually get a shot off, but it might buy Chip and Arthur the time they need to get their own weapons up and on the men.

That did nothing to help the others back on the highway, though, and Mike knew he couldn't risk it.

"The captain is the man in charge of our army," Brant replied. "He was a Navy SEAL before all of this, and he's a great man. Captain Joe Tillman."

Arthur's head suddenly snapped up, his eyes going wide. "Tillman? Captain Joe Tillman?"

535

"Yeah, that's him," Brant said slowly, watching Arthur with growing suspicion.

Arthur started to take a step forward, and Brant's rifle came back up in a flash, making Mike doubt his earlier thought about reaching for his gun. This country boy wasn't as slow as his accent made him sound.

"Whoa, Arthur," Mike said, holding a hand out to stop the older man. "This guy doesn't know us, remember?"

"But it's Tillman," Arthur stammered. "That's his father, Eric's father's name. It's Joe, and he was a SEAL. It *has* to be the same man!"

Brant frowned, his eyes narrowing. "Wait a second. You know Captain Tillman and Eric?"

Arthur nodded. "Please, young man, tell me, was there a young woman with Eric? A blonde young woman his same age, a fiancé?"

Brant nodded. "You mean Christina, right? Yeah, she's with him. She's alive."

Arthur let out a moan that was close to a wail as he fell to his knees, tears streaming down his face. He kept repeating over and over, "Thank you! Thank you, Jesus, thank you!"

"Is he okay?" Brant asked Mike as he cast a sidelong glance at the older man.

Mike nodded but found it difficult to speak past the sudden lump in his throat. "He'll be okay. He's Christina's father, and since the Blackout he hasn't known if his daughter was alive or dead. Now he knows."

Brant nodded and turned his back on Arthur to give the older man some privacy. He regarded Mike for a long time with an expression that was wiser and more experienced than he would have thought possible in someone so young.

"Look, I can't bring you with me," Brant said after a moment, "but I will go myself and get the captain. If he really knows your friend, then I reckon he will want to see him as soon as possible. And he'll have to clear the rest of you to come in."

Brant's tone changed, and his face grew serious. "One thing I can tell you, though, if you're let in you won't be let out again. This thing is too big to risk people floating around knowing about it. If you're in, you're in until it's done. That's been the policy the whole time."

Mike's eyes narrowed. He didn't like the way that sounded. "What if we don't want to be part of whatever it is you're doing? What if we just want to be allowed to go on our way or back where we come from, either way?"

Brant gave a small, apologetic shake of his head. "I'm sorry, Mister," the young man said, "but you really don't have a choice anymore."

Chapter 78

Stamp of Approval

Colonel Darius sat in a folding camp chair on the platform that was the roof of his personal railcar. The sky overhead was clear of all clouds and the stars were shining. The mountain air was cold enough that his breath fogged in front of his face, and he wore a thick wool jacket. The convoy had made good time through the Smokey Mountains and were now just northwest of Boone, North Carolina, on the edge of the mountains, waiting.

The rail line that Darius was following had been quietly maintained by the Department of Defense since the outbreak of the First World War. It had been deemed necessary to have a way to rapidly move men and material across the country as a matter of national security. Our generals and admirals had seen the tragic effects of not having a means of rapid mobility in war, and they did not intend to become the victims of a mistake that had already been made.

During the Cold War, when the looming threat of an all-out Russian invasion was real enough to be expressed in movies and on television, the government was willing to throw seemingly endless mountains of money at the problem, and as a result the nation was crisscrossed with a vast and intricate network of modern highways and railway lines. Many people were familiar with the interstates that ran like wide concrete rivers cutting through the countryside, but the railways were far less known.

And that anonymity was not accidental. This line ran through a small town called Cades Cove, and it was just above the town that Darius had stopped his convoy. There were fires burning down in the town, but not the kind that meant danger. This was the calm, sweet smell of dried and cured hardwoods burning in fireplaces. The town was living and, if looks were to be believed, thriving.

That made Darius wary.

The colonel looked over at his head of security, a former Gunnery Sergeant in the US Marine Corps named Bartholomew Macon. "Gunny, what do you think? Should we trust him?" Darius asked for the tenth time.

Sgt. Macon gave a small shrug and answered as he had every single time. "Sir, he doesn't seem to be lying. Beyond that, who can really know but him and God? What does your gut say, sir? You're the one who has to make the call."

Darius frowned and chewed on it a moment longer. "All right, bring him up."

The gunny nodded and climbed down the ladder. Darius heard the door to his office open, but he could barely make out the muffled sounds from inside. After a brief moment, his door opened again and the man he'd asked for climbed up to join him.

"Captain Withers," Darius said as he stood, "thank you for waiting, not that you really had any choice in the matter. You surprised me when you showed up in our camp yesterday. And I don't surprise easily . . . or well."

"I'm sorry about that, sir," Withers said in his deep southern drawl. "I listened to your speech, and I've been looking for a way to volunteer for a while now. Just seemed like the right time and the right place."

Darius was quiet for a moment as he mentally ran through what he knew about this man, or rather what he had been told so far. The man's story sounded too farfetched to be believed, but in the colonel's experience those were typically the stories with the most truth to them.

"Captain Withers, please, tell me one more time how you came to be in Cleveland, Tennessee."

The captain was quiet for a long moment but eventually began with a shrug. "Well, like I said before, I was in the army a while back. When I got out, I joined the Army Reserves and then the Air National Guard. I was a crew chief on a Blackhawk back in the army, so the ANG put me on the maintenance crew for a search and rescue detail in the mountains of Tennessee. When the Blackout hit, that's where I went to see if I could do some good. After a while, things fell to pieces around the depot, and the small town went crazy for a little bit with neighbors going after neighbors for things like a case of bottled water or a dozen cans of soup."

Withers paused, his eyes shadowed as he fought his way through memories that he didn't enjoy reliving. After a moment, he gave himself a shake and continued. "Once things settled down around there, I thought it was going to get almost back to normal. Then the FSS showed up. They steamrolled that town in a matter of a couple of days, and when they left there wasn't anything breathing. Half the men got loaded onto flatbeds in orange jumpsuits with about a third of the women and children. The rest . . ."

Darius tasted bile in the back of his throat. "No need to detail that again."

Withers nodded; he really didn't want to go there again. "Well, the other half of the men were *conscripted*, as they called it—pressed into service for an enemy occupying force. And I was one of the ones they called lucky. The FSS got better food and better clothes than the work camps, they told us. That's where the other people were headed. When the FSS pulled out of our town, it was nothing but a shell. We were headed east, deeper into the mountains. Soon as I could, I slipped away into the hills with a few of the other mountain men they'd taken. It wasn't hard to get past their sentries, and we just kept running."

"Why didn't you go back to your post?" Darius asked, though he already knew the answer.

Withers shrugged again, uncomfortable with the answer he would have to give. "Like I said, there wasn't anything left there. Some of the things we saw there . . . well, a man can't unsee what he's seen, but he doesn't have to go back to the place it happened. We just kept walking. Eventually, we made it out the west side of the mountains, and we split up. Some of the guys headed north, some south. I just kept walking west. And then I saw your train stop and I stopped to listen. Couldn't walk away after that, not knowing what I know and knowing what you're on your way to do. I want a chance to make them pay."

Darius pulled out a cigarette and started to light it.

"I wouldn't do that, sir," Withers said, taking a half step forward.

"Why not, Captain?" the colonel asked, the match still unlit in his left hand.

"Well, sir, sometimes in the hills like this the people get bored. I was sitting guard duty with a guy one night when I was still with the FSS. He pulled out a cigarette just like you just did, but he lit it and started smoking. After a few minutes talking, he took a puff, and there was this weird whooshing sound right by my head. The guy, he starts coughing and spitting up blood, and that's when I heard the rifle shot. Got him clean through the throat and he died right there, that cigarette still burning in his fingers. We never did catch who did it, but there was a hunter's camp on the next ridge over. Best we could figure, a local hunter got bored and decided to do some target practice, cause why not? It's not like someone can call the cops on you these days."

Darius set the cigarette carefully on the arm of his chair, unlit. "What do you think now, Gunny?"

"Well, might as well trust him," Macon said from the right corner of the platform.

Withers jumped when the older man spoke. At some point the gunny had climbed back up to the roof and taken up his former position. Darius wasn't sure exactly when it had happened because in spite of facing that direction, he still hadn't seen the former Marine make his return.

"All right, Captain," Darius said, drawing the man's attention once more, "we are going into the town down there tomorrow. I want you by my side keeping an eye on the crowd. Let me know what you see and let me know if you see anyone that stands out. I'm hoping to get a few dozen recruits but could always use an extra set of sharp eyes, and you fit that bill."

Withers nodded and allowed himself a modest smile. "Glad to finally be back in the fight, sir."

"With any luck, there won't be fighting tomorrow, but I certainly appreciate your enthusiasm. And don't worry. Before this war is done, we'll all see enough fighting for a lifetime."

Chapter 79

Strangers and Friends

Arthur woke early with the sounds of their captors' camp already humming around him. Most of the rest of his group were still sleeping in their tents and their bedrolls, but Mike was already up and sitting out by a small cooking fire. Arthur stretched and pulled on a light jacket in the cool morning air as he joined Mike.

"Anything new?" Arthur asked, but Mike shook his head.

"A few groups came and went last night, but I didn't hear anything. There was never a gap in their sentries, not even by a few seconds. These guys might look like a rag-tag bunch of farmers and tradesmen, but they've been taught how to do this stuff and do it right."

Arthur gave a small shrug. "As soon as Joe gets here, it'll all get worked out anyway," he said. "Joe knows me and Cheryl, and we'll vouch for the rest of you all."

Mike's eyebrows climbed up his forehead as he poked at the small fire. "Do you really think it will be as easy as that?" Mike asked after a moment. "I mean, look around you, Arthur. These guys are on edge, bad. You really think they're just going to let two friends and a dozen strangers come strolling in?"

544

Arthur was quiet for a moment. "He's a good man, Mike. You met his son. You know what kind of man he is. Well, his father's the same kind of person. He'll accept us."

"I wish you sounded more confident about that," Mike grumbled.

Arthur was saved from having to think up a response as Chip came strolling up in blue jeans and a stained short sleeve t-shirt. "Good morning, gents," he said as he stretched and yawned. "Sleep good?"

"Not really," Arthur replied at the same time Mike said, "Not at all."

"Well, I slept enough for all three of us, I guess," Chip said.

Arthur was surprised by the young man's nonchalance. "You weren't worried about what was going to happen?"

"After everything I've lived through, not a chance," Chip answered with a half-grin. "I mean if they had wanted to kill us, it's not like we could have done much to stop them. My philosophy is to worry about what I can change and everything else . . . well, just let it go. Makes life a hell of a lot easier."

"Well, I'm not wired like that," Mike said, shaking his head.

"I know," Chip said as he gave another half grin. "That's why you're in charge and I'm just along for the ride."

Just then a young man from the group holding them captive approached the three. "Your group has your own provisions, right?" he asked without introduction.

Mike nodded. "We have enough food for everyone for a couple of days at most. but we're already running low on clean water. You should know, you all took our packs yesterday, and I'm sure you've had more than a peek inside by this point."

The young man whistled over his shoulder and four older men approached with the groups' packs. They dropped them on the ground and turned around without another word. The younger man stayed, though, and fixed each of them with a stare that demanded their attention. "We removed anything you might be able to use as a weapon," he said. "I'm sure you can understand. All of your food, water, and other supplies are still there. We'll give you some of our water, but there's not a lot for us to spare."

"Anything you have would be appreciated," Arthur said, "and thank you."

The young man nodded and then turned on his heel and strode away.

"You're thanking them for giving us our own stuff back?" Mike growled under his breath.

"In case you haven't noticed, Mike, we're not the ones in charge at the moment. Anything we can do to make our relationship with our captors better is smart in my book, even if it's showing a little undeserved gratitude."

"Guys, I really don't think we have anything to worry about," Chip insisted.

Mike was getting a little impatient with Chip's rose-colored glasses. "What makes you so certain?"

"Well, if they meant to execute us, then it wouldn't really be smart to share part of their water supply, now would it? I mean, why give up water to someone you're planning on killing later anyway?"

Arthur frowned. "I hadn't thought of it like that, Chip, but you might have a point."

Mike was unconvinced. "Maybe, but I'm not dropping my guard just yet. Chip, you and Arthur go around and start waking everyone up. Keep it quiet, but tell them to look for anything we can use as a weapon if it comes to that. I mean anything . . . rocks, sticks, tent stakes . . . anything. If we have to fight, it'll get pretty ugly pretty quick, but there's a chance some of us could make it. That will happen, though, only if we're ready when it hits. If they catch us by surprise, we'll all be dead, no doubt about it."

Chip went around to the left side of the camp, and Arthur took the tents and bedrolls on the right. Each person they woke up was given the message to keep an eye out for improvised arms if the need should arise. By the time Arthur returned to the main cook fire, Mike had the packs spread out to one side. On the other side of the ring of rounded river rocks was a stack of five one-gallon containers of purified water, each one still factory sealed.

"They just showed up and handed that over, no questions asked?" Arthur said as he walked up to the fire.

When Mike nodded, Arthur bent and picked one of the gallon jugs and turned it so the lid was pointing down at the ground. He gently squeezed the sides of the plastic container just enough to make the lid bulge, then released the pressure. He repeated the process for each container before speaking.

"It doesn't look like they have any punctures. I'd say they're clear. Honestly, I'm not getting the kind of vibe you would expect from someone planning to poison us. I think if they're going to do away with us, it will be much more straight forward than this."

Mike couldn't argue against that, and neither could Chip, who had returned when Arthur was halfway through checking the water containers. Arthur left Mike and Chip to begin doling out the water to the group, and he ducked back into his pup tent. Cheryl was just rolling out of her sleeping bag and stretching, a forced smile on her face.

"How is it this morning?" he asked.

"Bad, but manageable. My toes are feeling the worst of it right now, like there's a taxicab parked on top of each one. It'll fade with the day. It'll just take time."

"Is there anything I can do?" Arthur asked, but Cheryl was already shaking her head.

"You know there's not, darlin," she answered with a smile. "Maybe tonight you can rub my feet. That's when it will help."

Arthur nodded. This was a dance they played, and they each knew the moves by heart. Still, there was a comfort in the process of it. Neither of them ever said the actual words Rheumatoid Arthritis. At this point they didn't have to. After more than forty years of marriage, they didn't have to name the thing that sat in the corner of every thought, every conversation. They both knew what it was.

Arthur helped his wife dress herself as much as he could. He buttoned her pants and tied the laces at the back of her blouse as well as on her hiking shoes. Arthur knew that Cheryl was in pain by the tightness around her eyes and the way her mouth drew down into a thin line anytime she had to use her fingers or her grip. She hid it well and put on a strong front, but today was going to be a difficult one for her.

When Cheryl was ready, they stepped out of the tent together. Arthur blinked against the sudden light as he helped Cheryl. She patted his hand and smiled. "I'll be all right," she insisted, and Arthur reluctantly let go of her arm.

When Arthur stood he found himself face to face with Eric's father, Joe Tillman. He'd only met the man a handful of times, but that was more than enough to form an impression. He looked different now, though. He was leaner and had a full black beard that was shot through with silver and gray at the corners of his mouth. His hair was longer, too, and he was very tan.

"Arthur, Cheryl," Joe said with a warm smile that never quite touched his eyes, "it's really good to see you both alive. Your daughter is going to be thrilled."

"So, she really is alive?" Cheryl asked, tears in her eyes.

Joe nodded. "Yes, Cheryl, she's alive and doing well. You'll see her before the day is done. You have my word on it."

"And the others?" Arthur asked. "What of them?"

Joe took a deep breath and shook his head slowly. "Like I was telling Mike here, Eric vouches for him, so he can come. And I know you both well enough to let you in, but the rest of your group has to stay here. You all are friends—they're strangers. And right now, we're a little wary of strangers."

"They're good people, Joe," Arthur said. "I've been with them for weeks, some of them longer. Each of them has saved my life more than once, and I've returned the favor. They're good people."

"That may be, but it doesn't change anything," Joe said firmly. "We're in the middle of something here, and they can't be a part of it yet. If you get let in and then decide to leave, I can trust you all not to compromise our operational security. I can't say the same for those people. I don't know them. Until they prove themselves, my people will keep a constant eye on them. If your people don't like that, they're more than welcome to go back the way they came."

Arthur was silent for a long moment. He hadn't expected this kind of cold, cynical response from Joe. The man had changed, it seemed, but then again, they all had. Arthur wondered how he would react if their situations were reversed, and he found he couldn't fault Joe's caution. He hoped the rest of the group would see it that way as well.

"Will our people really be given a chance to prove themselves?" Arthur asked. "Or will they always be at arm's reach?"

Joe gave a small shrug. "If they want the chance, I'll give it to them, but it happens on my terms. They join our army and begin basic training. Whatever their level of past experience, training is an absolute must. They are under my command from that point on until this war is done."

"What if they don't want to fight?" Arthur asked.

"Or aren't able to," Cheryl asked right behind him.

"People are welcome to find an abandoned house or farm in the area and claim it," Joe answered. "There are plenty of those to go around, these days, but we can't take any more in right now. I've already got nearly thirty people looking directly to me to provide for them, and it's got me strained for space and for supplies. Anyone who wants to settle in this area is welcome to, but this whole part of the county is about to turn into one big conflict zone. I'm sure there are quieter and safer places to put down roots."

Arthur looked back at the rest of the group gathered just beyond the cooking fire. They were well within earshot, but not a one of them showed any expression. Mike, on the other hand, looked like a thunderstorm ready to break.

Joe glanced up at the sky and squinted. "The morning's getting on, Arthur. We've got a good ways to go if you want me to make good on that promise about Christina. You ready to go see your daughter?"

"Mike, I . . ." Arthur said as he turned to face him, but Mike cut him off.

"Arthur, you and Cheryl go," Mike said, patting the older man on the shoulder. "You two came here for your daughter. We came here to fight. I'll talk to the group and explain it to them. We'll be fine and we'll see you soon."

Arthur nodded, and his throat was suddenly tight. "Mike, there aren't any words for the gratitude. You got me and my wife here, just like you said you would. I owe you, Mike, and I always will."

Mike just smiled and gripped Arthur's shoulder tighter. He started to speak, but couldn't and, instead, just gripped Arthur's shoulder awkwardly for a moment longer. Cheryl came up to him, a warm smile on her face in spite of the tears streaming down her cheeks. She pulled Mike's face down and kissed him on each cheek and then bent and whispered into his ear for a long moment.

When Cheryl finally let Mike straighten and take a step back, his face was pale, and he looked as if he had a lot to think about. Arthur wondered what had passed between them, but knew better than to ask. If Cheryl wanted him to know, she would tell him in good time. He just had to be patient.

Arthur and Cheryl gathered their packs and shared goodbyes with the rest of the group. It was difficult to leave them behind after sharing the road for so long. As they walked down the gravel drive from the field to the road, Arthur couldn't help but look back and wave every few hundred yards. Finally, they turned a corner in the road and lost sight of the encampment and their captive friends.

Joe walked a little ahead of Arthur and Cheryl with a handful of young men in hunting garb with rifles and side arms ranging around them in a loose security detail. For a while the three of them walked in silence, until the young man Brant joined them. He handed Arthur's shotgun and pistol to Joe, along with Cheryl's pistol. Joe passed them their firearms and then held out the sheathed double bit Helko Hinterland axe to Arthur.

"That's a hell of an axe, Arthur," Joe said with genuine appreciation. "One of these days you'll have to tell me the story behind it."

Arthur chuckled. "You won't believe it when you hear it," he replied, but then his voice turned serious. "Joe, what have you been up to out here?"

Joe was quiet for a long moment before answering. "Trying to get as much as we can and then hang onto it as long as we can," he said wearily. "And praying we survive until Christmas."

Chapter 80

Forward Operating Base

Lieutenant Commander Attledge stepped off the train and stretched his legs. As soon as his boots hit the ground, the security detail of twelve men disembarked behind him, fanning out in front of him and around the front end of the train's locomotive. They were armed but kept their rifles and other firearms at a low ready. The men watched the houses to the left and the lone house to the right as they searched for threats in the morning sunlight.

Nothing moved. There wasn't even a dog barking. For daylight hours, the busy little intersection of the railway and the road was eerily quiet.

Attledge walked down the tracks the hundred and fifty yards to where the steel tracks actually crossed the cracked and faded blacktop of Old Route 80, and eight members of the security detail formed a tight group that moved with him at their center. As they grew closer to the crossing, there was a switch that did something with the track, but Attledge wasn't sure what. He was interested only in the state road designation number stamped on the side of the switch. When he checked it against the number that Commander Price had delivered him the day before, they matched.

Finally, he had reached Faith, North Carolina, or as near to the small town as the railway would come. Attledge looked up and down the paved road and saw no sign of anybody or anything moving. It had been this way since they arrived a few hours earlier. He had ordered the train to halt but had instructed the entire compliment to remain in their cars until ordered otherwise.

Now, in the light of day, the feeling that something was off with this area had only intensified. From the train Attledge had scanned the doors of the houses facing the tracks and had not seen any of the spray paint markings they had come to dread. Whatever was wrong here, it didn't seem that the FSS was to blame, at least not as far as they could tell from the outside looking in.

"Sir, this feels off," First Sergeant Patterson said. "I'm not seeing or hearing anything. It's just a gut feeling, but something ain't right."

A few of the other men who had formed a tight circle around Attledge nodded their heads in agreement. Sergeant Patterson was a former Army Green Beret and a Tennessee native. He had joined the group when they were a week south of Kansas City and their paths had crossed. He was trying to work his way home to Tennessee and figured the convoy would be a safer way to travel than on his own. Over time, though, he'd become a true believer in the cause and was ready to give his life to see the FSS defeated.

Patterson's resume was impressive. He had seen active combat as part of the Special Forces in Central and South America in the eighties and nineties. His group was sent to the Middle East ahead of normal combat operations to soften some of the key targets in both Iraq and Kuwait. He had even been active early in the Afghan war before finally retiring to a civilian teaching post before this war against the FSS had begun. He taught forest and mountain environment close quarters combat and guerilla operations.

With more than thirty years' experience in the field, Attledge was inclined to listen to Patterson's gut feelings. "All right, let's head back to the train," he said, and the group turned back toward the diesel locomotive.

The security detail collapsed around him and formed a tight ring of vigilant eyes watching the streets and areas on both sides of the road. As they approached the crossing, Patterson kept his position at what had been point and watched behind them as they retreated to the train. When they reached the waiting four members of the security detail, the group relaxed slightly.

It was just then that Patterson cleared his throat softly. "Sir, we have a tango," he whispered over his shoulder without turning his head.

Attledge froze as the rest of the security detail took position in a wedge formation with Patterson at the peak. They took a knee and raised their weapons to bear on a figure in camouflaged hunting garb standing in the middle of the tracks. Attledge was framed by four men who didn't drop to a knee but formed a tight knot around their commander and watched for additional threats.

Attledge's hand itched to draw his own side arm, but the security detail had cautioned him against it. As long as they weren't taking active fire he needed to be ready to move more than he needed to be ready to fight. The main objective of this security detail was not to protect the train but to protect Attledge himself. He didn't like the focus that put on him or the fact that it might mean one of these men would give up his life for his, but it was the nature of his position, and he accepted that.

Attledge focused on the figure standing in the tracks and pushed thoughts of potential martyrdom out of his mind. The stranger was dressed head to foot in camouflaged hunting gear that was so realistic in its depiction of an early fall woodland scene that the figure sometimes seemed to disappear against the background of underbrush and trees. If not for the small white squares of cloth held high overhead, it might have vanished altogether.

The figure didn't move. It just stood there, waiting.

"What do you make of it, Sergeant?" Attledge asked.

"Not sure, Commander," Patterson replied, "but with that kind of gear, if he didn't want us to see him we wouldn't have. It could be a bluff or a ruse, but if it is, why did he let us get all the way back to our fallback position before showing face? It would have been better for him if he had come at us at the crossing, not here."

"Hold position and don't open fire until you see something hostile," Attledge said.

Patterson nodded and the rest of the security detail held steady. As long as the stranger didn't make any sudden moves, he would be okay. But Attledge had seen Patterson hit much smaller targets at longer distances with only open iron sights. The scope now mounted to the top rail of his carbine was sturdy and accurate out to five hundred yards, and he could take out coyotes at that distance with a single shot.

Attledge checked his watch and ground his teeth. He was supposed to be on a call with Commander Price in four minutes. He couldn't afford to sit here in what amounted to a long-distance staring contest.

"Patterson, you're on me. The rest of you, keep an eye out around us. If you see even a flicker of movement that looks like someone trying to flank our position, you open up on them. Buy us time and cover to pull back and regroup."

Attledge didn't wait for a response but started walking down the tracks toward the waiting stranger. He heard Patterson catch up and take a position behind and slightly to the right of his right shoulder. From that position Patterson had a clear shot to the stranger.

"If he twitches, sir," Patterson said softly, "I'll drop him. I won't kill him if I can help it. Also, just for the record, not a fan of this course of action. Sir."

"Noted," Attledge replied through clenched teeth. "We couldn't afford to wait. Things are moving now, and we're on a deadline. I'll happily sit through another one of your instructive lectures about the necessity of consideration or some such. But for right now, let me do the talking."

Attledge walked slowly but with purpose, trying to buy time to think about exactly what he was going to do next. When he was a hundred yards from the stranger, he slowed even more. The figure was dressed head to foot in detailed camouflage, complete with what looked like a cloth face shield and some dark sunglasses. The disguise was so complete and so thorough that he couldn't tell whether the figure was a man or a woman.

When he was fifty yards away, the stranger lowered his hands until they were clearly visible and far away from his body. The white streamers were still held tightly in each fist. When he was twenty yards away, Attledge stopped.

"I am Lieutenant Commander Marcus Attledge, United States Navy."

"You're a long way from the ocean, sailor," the figure said in a muffled feminine voice. "You take a wrong turn or something?"

Attledge attempted a smiled and shook his head. "No, we're right where we planned to be. Are you from around here?"

The stranger didn't answer.

"Okay, is this where you call home now?" Attledge asked, trying again to start a conversation.

"Middle of some train tracks?" the stranger asked. "Not hardly. Where's home for you, sailor?"

Attledge managed a smile. "Okay, so we've proven that we don't trust each other. Now, here's the deal. I'm going to be passing through, eventually, but for the next few days at least, the bulk of my men will be in the area. You won't have any trouble from us. You have my word on that. And if you choose to leave us alone, then that's fine."

Attledge paused, and the stranger nodded.

"But let me warn you," Attledge continued, "I have more than four thousand people marching under my command now. They're still arriving at the tail end of this train. The vehicle convoy is over ten miles long when we're moving. My point in saying this is to let you know that you can't dislodge us if you're unhappy we're here. You'd better let that soak in a little bit—four thousand people under arms and well-supplied. I don't know how many people you have in these bushes, but you can't handle four thousand people. If you could our scouts wouldn't have been active in your area two weeks ago without you even realizing it."

One of the small lead weights attached to a white flag hit the ground, and Attledge felt Patterson tense. He raised his rifle in one smooth motion, his finger on the trigger.

"Was that a signal?" Patterson asked, and the stranger shook her head. Patterson was unconvinced. "If it was, you'll be the first one down, understand that. Boss, I don't like this."

Attledge nodded. "Duly noted, Sergeant. To be honest, I'm not a fan myself. But it needed to be said." He returned his attention to the stranger. "If you want to join us, we can talk. If you want to trade, we can talk. But if you're even thinking about causing problems, understand that I don't have the time or the patience. You'll be dealt with. But if you stay out of our way, we'll leave you alone while we're here."

"And what about when you move on?" the stranger asked.

Attledge shook his head. "No promises. Best I can offer."

The stranger thought about it for a moment and then dropped the other lead weight. Slowly, with fingers spread wide and palms facing out, she reached up and removed the wide-brimmed field hat, the dark plastic sunglasses, and a close-fitting camouflage face shield. Beneath was a woman in her late twenties with deep auburn hair and bright green eyes.

"Fair enough," the young woman said, "then that's the best I can offer you. No promises. I'll take it to the people who make decisions, but that's the best I can do. Will you agree to wait here while they decide?"

Attledge glanced at Patterson who gave a half shrug, but never lowered his rifle.

"Will you at least tell me your name?"

The young woman smiled. "Amanda," she said. "My name is Amanda."

"We'll wait here as long as we can. A group our size, though, if we stay in one place for long we end up needing to forage. We prefer to trade and to buy what we need for as fair a price as possible. But one way or another, if we're in one spot more than a few days at the time, we need to resupply, so keep that in mind."

Amanda nodded. "Are there really four thousand of you?" she asked.

Attledge nodded. "Four thousand two hundred and sixty-seven as of the last count," he replied. "That's almost ten times the number I set out with. It's been tough, but we've managed to find good supplies on the road. It's staying in one spot that's hard. I'm leaving to scout our way ahead soon, but I'll be back."

He leaned slightly forward, but Attledge didn't break his stare. "Keep the number four thousand in your mind while I'm gone. If your decision makers decide to do something foolish, that's the number of people you'll be squaring off against. Do you have enough farm boys and squirrel hunters to make a dent in four thousand soldiers?" He paused but didn't really wait for an answer. "You want me to move on as quickly as possible. Don't give me a reason to stay."

Amanda nodded, and Attledge motioned for Patterson to lower his rifle. He did so, but reluctantly.

"How many are there in your group?" Attledge asked.

Amanda smiled and winked. "Not four thousand. I'll let you know what they decide," she called over her shoulder as she turned and walked into the woods.

Attledge was grudgingly impressed with how easily she disappeared into the scrub brush and small trees off to the right of the train tracks. One moment he could see her silhouette moving through the trees, and the next she was gone.

"You sure it was a good idea to let her go?" Patterson asked.

"What do you think? But what else could we have done? I wasn't going to hold her without cause. If she is part of a larger group, taking her prisoner could really be a bad move. If she's not, it's still wrong to violate someone's civil liberties without justification. Plus, she might not be trouble if we just leave her alone. This way we at least have a chance at good relations with whatever group she is part of. Maybe we can land some more recruits. Price keeps saying that numbers matter, so we've got to get as many as we can."

Patterson didn't say anything. Attledge wasn't sure that was because he didn't have anything to say or because by the time he finished talking they were back within earshot of the men they'd left at the train engine. Either way, he was happy not to debate the choice. Attledge had made his decision, and that was that.

Attledge climbed the steps to his railcar and entered his comfortably air-conditioned cabin. He took a moment to activate all of the surveillance cameras along the length of the train, both interior and exterior, and set the program to cycle the video feeds on a loop that was displayed on one of the wall monitors and could be called to the main screen when needed. The recording program was also set to trigger to any camera that detected movement as priority in the loop. At the moment, the images cycled mostly through the interior crew cabins and the exterior mid and rear sections of the train as the security perimeter was established.

The armory was on a dedicated feed that never switched, and a constant cycle of troops moved through the view of the camera as they received rifles and ammunition in groups of three. Each group would split into pairs of mobile sentries with a central over-watch on the roof of the train. The two mobile sentries walked a circuit a few hundred yards out from the train under the direction of the over-watch officer.

Attledge watched the process for a moment to make sure there were no hiccups and then turned to the main monitor that took up the back wall of the office. He powered on the monitor and entered the necessary access commands to activate the video communication system. There was an active request for a connection, so he accepted it, and in a few minutes, was looking at the slowly resolving image of Commander Price in his Operations and Command Center.

When the image was finally fully resolved, the screen flickered a few times as the display and the signal synced. After a few seconds, though, Commander Price was coming in loud and clear.

The look on his face and the impatient edge of his voice made it clear the commander was not pleased with this late start. "Lieutenant Commander Attledge, so glad you could join me this morning."

"I'm sorry, Sir," Attledge said. "I was . . . well . . . delayed by an unexpected introduction."

"Did it go well?"

"We'll see," Attledge replied. "The young woman is taking my offer to the people in charge of this area. Hopefully her return visit will go smoothly."

"Agreed," Price said, and he glanced down at a tablet in his hand. "Well, I see you've reached Faith and Granite Quarry, right on schedule. This is good, Commander. The enemy just started marching, but they are moving slowly. Apparently, they see no need to rush to Fort Bragg now that there are no bosses to report to in DC, so they are taking their time. That's rather unfortunate for the local population that is being overrun and burned out of homesteads in their path."

Price entered a few commands on the tablet, and the display screen on Attledge's end split into two windows. One showed Price, and the other showed a satellite image of the path of destruction and smoke in the wake of the FSS army's march as captured from low earth orbit. It was impressive in its sheer size if nothing else. The cloud of smoke and ash was three miles wide and nearly ten miles long.

When the camera zoomed in, it became clear that small clusters of fires at the ground level were so close their smoke merged and quickly rose into a towering column of black that stained the horizon.

"It looks like they're using the scorched earth policy to a large extent," Price continued, "probably trying to discourage anyone from raising an army to pursue them. That's one reason I think our strategy has a strong chance of succeeding. We won't need to pursue them for long, and we won't have to lay siege to their camp. We hit them while they're stretched out on the road, vulnerable because of their focus on attacking rather than defending. We'll break them before they even make it to Fort Bragg."

"We're still going to need help," Attledge said. "I've gathered as many troops as I can on the way, but I've still got fewer than five thousand men. Unless Colonel Darius has had a heck of a lot more luck than I've had, he's probably not even at four thousand. Your last report indicated that the enemy is already fifteen thousand strong. We're not going to be able to take on those kinds of numbers, not out in the open, and not without help."

"Who said anything about out in the open?" Price asked cryptically. "In any case, I have your coordinates, Commander. Given where you are now and Captain Tillman's trajectory, your best bet to catch him stationary will be at his home for the next twenty-four to forty-eight hours."

"Are you sure that's a good idea? If I show up at this guy's door with three armored troop transports and a bunch of men and guns, he's likely to open up on me with that .50-caliber machine gun that's mounted on the front porch. He didn't seem the type to welcome strangers, sir."

Price smiled. "Well, I'm glad you two have met before, then. I've sent a file with orders and a mapped route to your secure inbox. I want you on the road at sunset this evening. That will put you on Captain Tillman's doorstep by noon tomorrow, even if you move cautiously."

"Three Strykers, each with a four-man crew," Attledge said. "That's going to be my security detail. We'll move fast and, if necessary, hit hard. I hope you're right about this guy, Commander."

"Don't worry, Marcus," Price said, dropping the military formality in an uncharacteristic breach of protocol. "I know Captain Tillman better than I've ever known anyone but my wife. He's a man of honor, through and through, always has been. And one thing about honor, son, it doesn't change. That's what makes it honor. He'll listen to you, and, eventually, he'll agree. You just have to give him a reason to and give him time to see it."

"When do you want me to make contact again?" Attledge asked, feeling marginally more confident.

"After you make contact with Captain Tillman. I imagine he'll want to ask me some questions. But if he takes a drastic turn we're not expecting, then I'll contact you. Otherwise, maintain radio silence as much as possible. And remember, even though they are several hundred miles away, the enemy is on the move."

Before Attledge could reply, Price disconnected the communications link from his end. It sometimes bothered Attledge that Commander Price could exercise that level of control over his systems from across most of the country. It was a clear reminder of who was really in control. After the video feed went dark, Attledge heard a beep from his hardened tablet that was charging on his desk.

He opened the secure data package and ran the decryption programs necessary to access the information. Once the data was unlocked, he opened a file that had a detailed route planned through a satellite mapping and surveying program. The time stamp on the image showed that it was only a few days old. Another map traced the last seventy-two hours of Captain Tillman's movements, courtesy of Price's Naval Academy class ring that had been disguised as a tracking device.

All of the squiggly lines converged on Attledge's destination, the Tillman family farm.

Chapter 81

At First Sight

Nov. 11 th 1700 EST

They had turned down so many small back roads that Arthur was thoroughly lost. It amazed him how confidently Joe would make a change in their heading at an intersection without a map and without hesitation. This was his home turf, and he knew it well. There was a certain comfort in that, and Arthur never even considered the possibility that the small group might have lost their way.

Finally, though, some of the roads began to look vaguely familiar. Several years earlier Arthur and Cheryl had visited the Tillman farm for a family function, and now he began to recognize some of the landmarks. When they finally turned onto the unpaved Cuttler's Run Road, Arthur knew they were close. The road climbed a hill to the top of a wide, flat plateau that rose above the river flood plains that were common in this part of the state. At the top of the plateau, it turned to run the length of the upwelling of granite that formed the roots of this small highland.

At that turn, a small sandy road wound down between two wide, flat fields of dried soybeans. The road cut through a thick line of towering old pine and sweet gum trees a quarter of a mile away on the other side of the fields. A gate that hadn't been there before spanned the white dirt road. Two men stood at each of the pines that formed the natural gateposts, all four of them heavily armed.

But it was the right side of the road that drew Arthur's eyes. There were nearly two dozen graves in the sandy soil, each marked with a simple wooden cross driven into the dirt.

"Was there a sickness?" Arthur asked.

Joe paused, his face unreadable as he looked at each of the graves. "Something like that. People got desperate around here. They needed food, needed water. They knew we had stuff, and they came for it. Some of them didn't take no for an answer."

Joe turned to face Arthur. "We did what we had to do to survive," he said bluntly, "just like everyone else who has made it this far. The handle on that expensive ass axe on your back is stained with blood, and a lot of it. Don't act like you haven't done things, Arthur. Everyone who is alive now has. These people buried here tried to take what we needed to live. They threatened my family. We buried them here so that others who might try the same thing could see the result. Maybe that would scare them off."

"Did it work?" Arthur asked after a moment.

Joe looked pointedly at the graves. "Not every time," he replied.

At a wave from Joe, the men standing watch unchained the gate and swung it open into the homestead. Arthur took a few steps and stopped, stunned at the changes. The field to the left was larger than it had been the last time he had seen it. Trees on both sides of the field had been cleared, their stumps still smoldering in the ground in a few places. Logs were stacked in the inside edge of the field and some had been sawed into sections for splitting.

In front of them, on what had been the broad green yard that had wrapped around two sides of the farm house, rows of tents stood in a neat layout. The tents were different colors and shapes, but each was basically a square with wings that came off either side. They looked like they could sleep anywhere from six to ten people comfortably, more if personal space wasn't a consideration.

The front porch was a raised square patio of concrete, and the front left corner had been built up even more with canvas sandbags that formed sloping walls all the way down to the ground, past the edge of the porch itself. From the top of the small mountain of sand, with a commanding view of the front yard, the gate, and the road immediately beyond, was a .50 cal. heavy machine gun.

On the edge of the field a group of solar panels was mounted on short, stout concrete pilings. A shed at the edge of the solar array had wires converging on it and was obviously a control station of sorts. A few panels secured to fresh wooden scaffolding were mounted to the face of the roof and faced the solar array as well.

Dozens of people milled about inside the gate. Some carried chopped wood toward cook fires in the back of the farmhouse, and some worked with harvested crops. A group of women tossed dried beans and peas on old burlap tobacco sheets, and the dried, crumbling pods were blown away in the soft breeze. The seeds that were left would be kept for planting next season. The same was true for the dried golden kernels of corn a group of young men were scooping into plastic storage containers.

Arthur followed Joe into the compound, his head spinning at the activity. Then, everything seemed suddenly to stop around him as his eyes fell on a young blonde woman pulling laundry from a clothesline. She was turned three quarters of the way away from him and obviously beginning to show the telltale belly bump of pregnancy. Something about the way she held herself, the set of her shoulders perhaps, or the way she reached up and tucked a strand of lightly curled blond hair behind her left ear—something was familiar.

Then she turned and faced him, and their eyes connected. It was his daughter Christina. Her eyes went slowly wide as she saw past the sun-tanned skin, the whiter than gray hair and full beard, and recognized her father. The laundry basked in her hands fell to the ground, and she took a hesitant step forward. Arthur was still frozen in shock, but Cheryl was already moving. She ran across the yard, her arms stretched out in front of her, and met Christina with a hug that nearly lifted her off her feet.

Arthur finally found the will to move and half stumbled and half ran across the yard to join his wife and sweep Christina into a great bear hug that did take her off her feet. Tears were streaming down Arthur's face, and his shoulders shook with violent sobs as he tried to regain control over the rushing torrent of relief sweeping through him. He had never allowed himself to believe his daughter was dead, but he'd never quite allowed himself to believe that he would ever see her alive again. He had been worried the disappointment would be enough to literally kill him if he had held on to a false hope and then never succeeded in finding Christina.

Now, to be standing and holding her in his arms, the relief and joy were almost too much to bear. At first all he could do was whisper, "Thank you!" over and over again. Finally, though, he caught his breath and regained control. He let go of Christina and allowed himself to look at her again from head to toe. She was beaming, fresh tears running down her beautifully tanned cheeks. Her belly was round and swollen, but just in the beginning stages of her transformation from young woman into a young mother.

Arthur placed a rough hand over that bump and looked into his daughter's eyes with a small smile. "You're pregnant," he said.

Fresh tears erupted, and Christina nodded her head. Words began to rush out of her, tumbling over each other in a barrage about marriage and waiting and something about a party with barbecue. Arthur couldn't follow it all, and he didn't care. He put a hand gently on her cheek and shook his head. "Plenty of time for that later, dear."

Cheryl went back to showering Christina with hugs and asking questions that Arthur barely even heard. He turned his head to wipe his eyes and saw Eric standing off to the side, tears in his own eyes. The young man Arthur had known had changed. He was leaner and his face had a hard look to it. A few new scars crossed his face and arms as well, but for the moment he looked unsure of himself, almost nervous.

Arthur broke away from Cheryl and Christina, walked up to Eric, and took the young man in a firm hug. When he finally took a step back, Arthur shook his hand. "Thank you," he said. "You got my daughter here safely. I don't think I can ever repay that debt."

"She wanted to go look for you," Eric said, looking down at his feet. "She wanted to, but I said we had to get out first. I planned to go back, I did. But things got bad here, and we couldn't risk it. They needed me. But she wanted to go back. I'm sorry I didn't listen."

Arthur shook his head. "You were right to go, Eric, and you were right to stay," he said firmly. "Ask your friend Mike, when you see him. Things got bad in Charlotte, probably worse than they did here. We almost didn't make it out alive. You did the right thing getting Christina to safety first. That's your job as her husband, right? Well, you did it. And I'm glad you did. You don't owe us anything, Eric, certainly not an apology."

Eric frowned. "Wait, what did you say? My friend Mike? Mike is here? He's with you?"

"He was, but he stayed back with the rest of our group. Your dad said he could come, but he didn't want the rest of our people to get nervous. I don't know how well you got to know each other before you parted company in Charlotte, but he's changed Eric. He's changed since I've known him, and I'm sure he's changed since you got to know him."

A hardness entered Eric's voice as he gave a half shrug. "I've changed too, Arthur. I'm just glad Mike's still alive. We're going to need all of the help we can get."

"Well, you won't have to work too hard to convince him to fight," Arthur said. "It's practically all he talks about lately. He's become obsessed with lashing out, fighting back against the enemy. I don't think it's healthy, to tell you the truth."

The sun was low in the western sky, casting long shadows across the yard as Arthur put an arm around Eric's shoulder and drew him back to Cheryl and Christina. "Well, there will be plenty of time to worry about that. Right now, I just want to take it in that we're all here, alive and well, and safe after everything. Nothing else is more important than that at the moment, not to me."

Cheryl nodded and gave Eric a tight hug and kiss as well, fresh tears spilling down her cheeks. She tried several times to say something elaborate and heartfelt but got too choked up to speak each time and finally settled on a half-strangled, "Thank you."

Christina gasped and pulled Eric over to her. She whispered softly in his ear for a moment, and then he straightened and nodded. "If it will make you happy, babe, then it will make me happy too," he said cryptically. "But we'll still have to do the big party on Thanksgiving or my mom will go crazy. She's been making all kinds of plans for this shindig, and I think she might be more excited about it than we are."

Christina nodded, a grin splitting her face. "Can I tell them?" she asked, and when Eric nodded, she turned to Arthur and Cheryl and took one their hands in her own. "Eric and I are getting married. You both knew that. We were going to have the ceremony on Thanksgiving here at the farm, but that was before today, before now. He and I agree that there's no reason to wait. Now that you two are here, we can get married now, and we both want to. With everything else that's happened, I don't want to wait one more second to officially start our life together."

Arthur's eyes filled with tears, and he nodded. Neither he nor Cheryl could find the words to speak, so they just drew Christina and Eric both in for a hug. Arthur felt an odd mix of pride and pain as he kissed his daughter on the forehead, realizing that in a very short time he would have to let her go. But knowing now the kind of man that Eric had become and how strong and capable he'd proven himself to be, Arthur knew she'd be in good hands. And then a new thought hit him, and he nearly fell to his knees.

Arthur was going to be a grandfather.

Chapter 82

The Hard Way

Nov. 11 th 1945 EST

President Daniel Arnold stood at the head of the column of armored troop transports and tanks in a full battle-dress uniform, complete with Kevlar flak jacket and a helmet with the Presidential Crest emblazoned on it. The town councilmen of Orange, Virginia, were assembled before him, each with three personal guards. The four council members and twelve guards were still outnumbered more than two to one by the president's entourage.

It was a simple, yet effective show of force. Arnold had set the terms of the agreed meeting via messenger and then had broken those terms in a flamboyant fashion. The council was set in their place for a moment, it seemed. But as the introductions wore off and the conversation about terms of occupation began, the town council balked. They weren't resigned to the notion of the military taking over their city and drafting their population, and they began to resist.

Arnold shook his head. "You don't seem to understand, ladies and gentlemen," he crooned in his most soothing voice. "General Hagerston is absent from this meeting, not out of a lack of respect for your position but because he is already laying plans to put your little town to siege. If it comes to that, we'll simply cut off your supplies and starve you out while we eat everything for a three-mile radius. Then we'll salt the earth and ruin your fields."

Arnold's tone was not just matter of fact; the crowd felt the brutality of this tyrant's words and knew his threat was only a breath away from becoming reality. "However, if you open your gates and don't harass our soldiers, I promise we will move on as quickly as possible and do as little permanent damage as we can. But the needs of the State are great at the moment, and those needs must be met by the citizens. It's time to pull our weight on behalf of the Federation."

The council members sat motionless and silent.

"I have twenty-four thousand men behind me," Arnold reminded them. "At your peak before the Blackout you would have been outnumbered six to one. What about now? How many of you are left? A third? A fourth? You can't hope to stand up to our numbers, and you know it. Don't risk getting all of your people killed over some foolish sense of pride and patriotism."

Finally, Arnold leaned forward and motioned for the council members to lean forward as well. The guards around each council member tensed visibly, but no one made a move to stop the four representatives.

"If it will make you feel better," Arnold said, "I'll exclude you and your families from the official pool for the draft. Then you have nothing to lose and everything to gain. You'll be heroes for averting an attack on your sleepy little town and furthering the cause of the Federation."

The council members all exchanged meaningful looks as they leaned back.

"Perhaps we should clear the room?" Arnold suggested, and the council members nodded. The security personnel all left the portable shelter that Arnold had provided as a meeting place. The interior of the tent was cooled by a solar air conditioner and lit by solar-powered LEDs.

When the door finally closed, President Arnold presented each member with an official pardon and exemption. The members read through the document, looking for any possible loopholes. The language, though, was iron-clad and had no possibility for misinterpretation.

Satisfied, each member of the council signed the paperwork transferring legal control and authority to President Arnold and his chosen military leadership structure. They would be subject to the president's direct command until otherwise ordered by act of the Federal Senate. Not a single one of the four signatories even bothered to ask what the Federal Senate was. They merely accepted that the document declared how long they would be controlled by an outside authority.

The whole process turned Arnold's stomach, in a way. It confirmed all of the worst aspects of humanity he'd come to suspect infected society. As soon as they were presented with an avenue for personal gain or enrichment, people grabbed it, no matter how many tens of thousands had to suffer as a result.

Then again, when he considered his own life, such ruminations always made him more than a little uncomfortable. He pushed those thoughts out of his head as the last of the four members of the council finished signing.

Arnold took the document and smiled. "Thank you for being reasonable in accepting these terms. Now, by my order, every person within your town between the ages of fifteen and fifty will be hereby conscripted and forced into service for the State. You are hereby placed under command of General Hagerston who serves at the pleasure of the president as the Supreme Commander of the Federal Army of North America. He will be your commanding officer, second only to my own authority as President and Commander in Chief."

"What about our deal?" one of the council members demanded. "You just said you'd exempt us!"

Arnold's smile, more a derisive smirk, caught the council members more off guard. "I lied," he said with a small shrug. "Good luck appealing those papers to anyone. I've instructed my soldiers to ignore them."

The council members' faces paled, but one dared to speak. "We'll go to the Federal Senate."

"You're welcome to," Arnold said, contempt evident in his smile and his eyes. "They were meeting at Capitol Hill until it was vaporized in a nuclear attack a few weeks ago. But you're welcome to go and present your case. If you can make it through before the radiation sickness kills you, that is. For now, you are stuck with me. There is no Senate."

One by one the council members realized they had been deceived. Outside, their guards had been disarmed and bound hand and foot. The ones who could be reconditioned and retrained to follow the new order would be integrated into the forces. The ones who couldn't would be neutralized.

Arnold shrugged his shoulders uncomfortably as he thought about it. He preferred not to focus too long on the inevitable collateral damage that resulted from his tactics. It was a necessary evil in pursuit of the greater good. So far none of the small towns had required more than twenty percent of their populations be liquidated to reach the conscription goals, and most resistance collapsed well before that point. Once it became clear that the Feds believed no price was too great to encourage obedience, things stopped being difficult.

Still, that meant thousands of lives had been snuff out and thousands more ruined, yet Arnold's army marched on, chewing its way south. It was an awesome thing to ride at the head of the leviathan. The army he was building was going to be unstoppable as they faced small towns and the occasional city. Once he secured Fort Bragg, he would have the hardware he needed to push a ground war across the country.

Already Norfolk had been hardened into a secure naval port for the fleet of loyal ships, although that loyalty had already begun to dwindle away when President Hall was still alive. Now that he and most of DC were gone, Arnold knew he couldn't count on help from the sea, not yet. He was on his own, and that meant he had to grow his ground force as large and as powerful as he could.

One step at a time, Arnold reminded himself as the tanks and armored personnel carriers throttled up their engines. He climbed into the observation seat in the lead tank and gave the order to advance. They hit the town so quickly the residents never stood a chance. They were subdued and gathered in the central square in a matter of a few hours. It was dark by then, and lights had been set up to shine on the impromptu stage the troops had built.

President Arnold climbed that platform and addressed the residents with the signed surrender of the town council in hand. "I have here the surrender, unconditionally offered and signed by each member of your council. They are, at this moment, serving the Federation Army to their full capacity, and shortly you will join them. Any citizens between fifteen and fifty will report to the registration officers for assignments. Today is a glorious day! The day you get to repay your nation and serve tomorrow's generations by defending the State."

Arnold leaned forward, gripping the microphone so hard his knuckles were white. "Congratulations," he growled.

Soldiers began moving through the crowd, checking the identification of those trying to leave. Unless they were clearly outside the age range, they were held for questioning. A few fought at first, but they were made examples of, and people quickly fell into line. These were conscripts, so some would inevitably escape. The majority of those would be caught and used as deterrents to future desertion.

A few would make it out for good, though. That was the reality of dealing with conscripts. Still, the majority would be too frightened to even attempt escape, and that meant the ranks would swell, which was Arnold's goal for the moment. He would gather as many soldiers as possible, one way or the other.

After a few moments of observing, Arnold left the draft divisions to do their work. Back in his tent, safely surrounded by a ring of security personnel, he joined General Hagerston in planning their next move south. Eventually they would pass Greensboro, North Carolina, and pick up Highway 421 South. That route would take them within twenty miles of Fort Bragg, and it would keep them off the major thoroughfares in the process.

With any luck, in a few weeks they would have Bragg surrounded and would strike without warning. If things went well, they would take the whole base before Christmas.

Chapter 83

Intuition

Nov. 11 th 2330 EST

The highway out of town and back to the train was steep and dark. The moon and stars didn't really make much of an impression under the trees on the steep slopes overlooking Valle Crucis, NC. The security detail with Colonel Darius were clearing the path ahead and had quickly moved out of sight when they first left town more than an hour ago. For a long time now it had been only Colonel Darius and Captain Withers on the hike up the dark highway.

They had spent the last six miles in total silence, each listening for any sign of either the scouts ahead of them or pursuit behind them. The valleys were eerily silent, though, and even the sporadic hoots of owls in the tree tops back in the valley seemed to echo forever.

"So, what did you think?" Colonel Darius asked when he was finally satisfied that they weren't being followed.

"The people were honest, but not open," Withers said without hesitation. "They're definitely holding stuff back, but what they did offer up was true, which is a good sign."

"How do you figure that?" Darius asked.

579

"Well if they were planning to try something that could piss you off," Withers replied with a small shrug, "like maybe trying to kill you, well they wouldn't want you knowing the truth if they missed. Then you could use that to hurt them. They'd just lie to you first so that if you lived you knew only their lies. And from what I could tell, they're probably telling you the truth."

"Probably?" Colonel Darius asked as he paused to catch his breath. "What do you mean probably? I took you down there with me to eliminate the word probably from the equation."

"Colonel, like I said before, mountain people are tough to read," Withers replied with a straight face and not a hint of irony. "Sometimes you just can't tell if what they're saying is what they're really saying, and sometimes you can."

"Well that doesn't exactly clear up the muddy water," Darius replied, shaking his head.

"Sir, all I can say is I know people like that. I grew up with them my whole life. It's part of why I was stationed where I was. And they're the kind that if they don't like what you're saying or they feel backed into a corner and threatened, then they'll smile in your face all day long while the sun is shining. But once it gets dark, you better watch yo' ass. They're gonna come for you one way or another."

Darius chewed on that for a moment. He didn't like the sound of it, and the fact that they were hiking through essentially pitch-black mountain back roads didn't help ease his apprehension one bit. For a moment, he felt like he could feel eyes hidden in the trees and the rocks around them burning across his skin, as if he were being watched from a thousand different angles at once.

He pushed those thoughts aside and asked his next question. "How many FSS do you think were there?"

Darius had an answer in mind, and it was already too high for his liking. He had avoided asking the question because he felt sure that Withers was going to, at the very least, confirm his suspicions and may well have seen some agents that the he had missed.

Withers thought about the question carefully before answering. "Three at the least. There may have been as many as five or six, but there were at least three. I saw each of their ID badges briefly as they were looking at goods during the trading session. The others were just suspicious, but those three were definitely FSS. Probably field scouts for a larger force."

"What makes you say that? They could have been former FSS conscripts like yourself."

"I guess they could have been, but the first thing I did when I finally got clear of that group was ditch my ID tag. I'm sure they have some kind of positioning device on them or in them somehow. I wedged mine into a log and sent it down a river as soon as I could."

"You've got a point there," Darius said.

The colonel opened his mouth to ask another question when he heard a sudden whiz and a pop overhead. A loud snap on the bare rock face to the right of the highway marked the point where the rifle round hit. It ricocheted away with a whir and then the report from the rifle reached them. Already the sound was echoing off the rocks, trees, and distant peaks on the other side of the valley a couple of miles away, making it impossible to tell from what direction the shot had come.

Both Darius and Withers dropped instantly to their stomachs, each man scanning around him, looking for an attack. Their carbines wouldn't be much good at long distance in the dark, but close in they would be deadly. Darius tensed, waiting for the first wave of an assault that never came.

"Do you think they'll take another shot?" he asked after another moment, his heart still pounding in his ears.

"I doubt it," Withers replied. "I think it was just a message to get us moving again. If they had really wanted to do more than that, they already lost the initiative. But, just to be on the safe side, I say we save the rest of this conversation until we reach the train."

Darius nodded. "Sounds like a solid plan to me," he said, already moving more quickly up the shadowy road. The two hadn't gone more than fifty yards when the security detail came running back down hill, weapons drawn and at the ready.

"We heard the rifle," the sergeant in charge said. "Point us in the right direction and we'll go find 'em."

Darius shook his head. "No, stand down Sergeant. If we send out a search and eliminate squad tonight, that might be just the excuse the people down there are waiting for to launch an all-out attack on us. And, to be honest, I'd really rather avoid killing them if we can. They seem like nice people, after all, so let's not give them an excuse to do something stupid."

The sergeant reluctantly stood down, but he decided to keep his men deployed closer to the two officers for the rest of the hike to the train and waiting convoy. The rest of the walk passed without incident, and it seemed the captain had been correct. The well-timed and perfectly placed shot had been simply a reminder that they were not alone.

Once they were back in his office and it was just the two of them, Darius finally began to relax. His hands started to shake slightly, so he laced his fingers behind his head and leaned back in his office chair to stare up at the banks of LED lights overhead. He had taken live fire before, enough during the course of his career that he'd lost count of the individual instances. But no one could take close fire at night and not get at least a little rattled when the adrenaline rush finally filtered out.

"What do you think our chances of getting a few recruits are?" Darius asked, breaking the silence that had settled between them.

Withers barked a short laugh and shook his head in disbelief. "We just got shot at on the side of a mountain, and you're asking how many people will join us? I love your optimism, Colonel, but a better question might be how many will try and kill us?"

"You don't think any will volunteer to join the fight?" Darius asked again, a little deflated this time.

"If you had a good week to devote to convincing people, maybe, but one day that had a handful of recruiting speeches scattered through it, along with not-so-vague overtures of force? No, I don't think we'll win any one over that quickly, not here. It's a shame too, cause these people have been fishing, hunting, tracking, and what not since they were old enough to run. They'd make a hell of an asset, if we had the time."

"Your advice, then, is not to move on at first light like I said we would in the speeches?" Colonel Darius asked.

"You can't do that now, sir," Withers said. "You already made a promise to be moving by a certain time. If you go back on your word, they won't trust anything you say after that. I think you don't have much choice here. You'll have to take what you can get tomorrow morning if anyone volunteers and then hope you can count on the people for a favor if you ever need it. But the fact that we just had a warning shot fired over our heads is a pretty clear message that our welcome has some pretty severe limits on it already."

Colonel Darius snorted. "Well, I guess it's a little comforting to know that if we all get killed in this battle we're rushing toward, then at least there will be some stubborn holdouts here in the mountains that the FSS can break its teeth on for a while."

"I think the FSS knows that," Withers said, his tone serious. "That's why they've been especially ruthless in the mountain towns. They're softening those communities so they'll be weaker in the beginning of the war."

"They've been doing that same kind of thing all across the country," Darius said, shaking his head. "It's not specific to the mountains. They're displacing the population en masse so they can relocate them. It's a good way to subjugate people that might otherwise be a threat. Relocate them to unfamiliar territory and they're a lot less likely to cause issues. The Soviets did the same thing in the early years of the USSR, and it helped quell local disturbances and prevent large scale rebellions."

"Then it sounds like the FSS is taking a page right out of the Soviet playbook," Withers said, and he turned his head to spit but thought better of it since they'd moved inside.

"The only thing missing so far are the camps," Darius said. "In the USSR they had work camps and reeducation camps both to deal with the cases in between total converts and hopeless rebels. I know there have to be camps somewhere. I just don't know where."

"Georgia," Withers said with unsettling certainty. "The camps are down in Georgia. And I helped load some of the trains that were headed there."

Chapter 84

Unannounced Guests

Nov. 12 th 0415 EST

Joe's eyes popped open, and he lay motionless for a few moments, straining his ears. The doorknob to the bedroom door rattled again, softly, as someone started to turn it. In an instant, Joe was out of bed with his Glock 19 in his hand, muzzle half-raised toward the door. As the door opened, Joe hit the thumb switch that clicked on a high intensity LED light attached to the bottom rail of his pistol.

Eric was framed in the circle of bluish white light as he pushed the door slowly open. He stopped for a moment, his hands outstretched and his eyes wide, and then Joe released the thumb switch and killed the tactical light.

"Jesus, son, that's a good way to get shot," Joe whispered. "What's up?"

"I think you need to come to the gate," Eric said, his face serious. "We have some visitors, and one of them claims to know you."

"Is it someone local?" Joe asked as he swung his feet over the edge of the bed. Beth rolled over and mumbled something, but she was back to sleep before Joe could even ask what she'd said.

Eric shook his head. "If what this guy says is true, they've come halfway across the country. You should come and see for yourself.

Whoever this guy is, he's traveling with some serious hardware, and I get the impression this is just the tip of the iceberg."

Joe nodded. "I'll be out in a second. Meet you at the front door."

Eric backed out of the room and pulled the door closed. Joe slipped on the rest of his clothes in silence and in the darkness. He belted on the holster for his Glock and positioned the pistol on his right hip. He grabbed his M4 on the way out and paused just long enough to give Beth a kiss.

Outside, Joe followed Eric down the front steps and across the yard. He glanced up as he walked past the edge of the machine gun nest, manned by Oscar on this watch. The young man gave him a thumbs up signal, and Joe kept walking. Before he got halfway across the yard, Joe picked up the sound of large diesel engines idling. He quickly checked his rifle to make sure a round was chambered and that the safety was in the off position.

"I didn't want to say anything in there where Christina or mom could hear," Eric whispered to his father as they walked, "but this guy is the same one that showed up on a helicopter a couple of days after the Blackout. He's got friends and armored personnel carriers with big guns. I don't think he's bluffing."

Joe placed a hand on Eric's shoulder and gave it a squeeze. "You did good coming to get me, son. How are you doing?"

Eric blinked. "Uh . . . all right, I guess." The question had caught him off guard, just as Joe had intended. "A lot going on the past few days, you know. Maybe a little nervous."

"Well, that's understandable," Joe said as he stopped at the edge of the yard, still barely out of earshot of the front gate. "Listen, everything's going to be okay. I know you thought there would be another couple of weeks before the wedding and now everything's kind of happening at once. That unexpected change could freak anyone out."

Eric shook his head. "That's not it, Dad. I'm glad I'm marrying Christina tomorrow. The sooner the better, as far as I'm concerned. It's the baby. That's what's got me freaked out. We don't have a doctor or a hospital for delivery, nothing."

Joe smiled and gave Eric's shoulder another reassuring squeeze. "Son, it'll be fine. Humanity was having babies for thousands of years before the first hospitals. Things will work out."

Eric nodded, but he didn't look convinced. Unfortunately, Joe couldn't take the time to talk and reassure him more at the moment. He had bigger fish to fry.

Joe nodded to the men at the gate as the two of them approached, and the men unchained and opened it ahead of them. Joe and Eric walked up the road two hundred yards to a row of three armored personnel carriers. A semicircle of well-equipped men with rifles and shotguns were arrayed in a semicircle sweeping down to the right and left toward Joe and Eric.

No one had a weapon raised, but Joe had the distinct impression that it wouldn't take much for that to change or for the men in the machine gun turrets atop each APC to suddenly take aim. The men facing him were tense but not afraid. They held themselves like soldiers, professional and confident, and that worried Joe a great deal.

Standing in front of the lead APC was a man who resembled the one that had stepped out of a Blackhawk in the field a few months earlier. This man was harder, though, and more dangerous. He wore a solid month's beard growth, it looked like. There were a few single gray hairs here and there, but they were still rare enough to be more proof of youth than anything else. This man had grown into the responsibilities that rode heavily on his shoulders and showed in the clenching of his jaw. He was wary, cautious even, yet confident at the same time.

"Captain Tillman, it's good to see you again," the young man said, holding out his right hand. "I am sorry for the early hour, though. I hope you'll understand that I'm trying to move at night and attract as little attention as possible at the moment."

Joe looked down at the young officer's hand, but he didn't take it. "What are you doing here, Commander?" Joe asked bluntly. "Last I saw you, you were headed back to Utah on a helicopter. I liked that view a good bit better than the one I'm looking at now."

"Commander Price sent me," Attledge said carefully. "And he didn't send me alone this time, Captain."

Joe nodded to the twelve or so men facing him. "I can see that. My question, though, is why did he send you at all?"

The lieutenant commander smiled apologetically. "You don't understand, Captain. This is just my security detail. I have more than four thousand men under my command at the moment, with recruitment efforts still under way."

This time it was Joe's turn to blink in shock and surprise. "Wait, what did you say? Four thousand men? Jesus, that's an army! Why are you bringing your army here?"

Attledge shook his head. "Not my army, Captain. Your army. Commander Price ordered me to find you and report with this fighting force to your command, sir."

Joe shook his head trying to process the onslaught of shocks Attledge was delivering in rapid fire. Four thousand men was a sizeable force, if properly equipped and trained. With some light armor like the APC's or a few tanks to augment their forces, that many men could be nearly unstoppable in open country.

"Wait," Joe said, part of Attledge's statement finally registering. "What do you mean my command? You're joking, right? I came to the middle of nowhere to escape trouble, not to lead some damned army. I was in the Navy, anyway. There's got to be someone else better suited for this type of operation."

Attledge's jaw clenched, and his face began to redden. "With all due respect, sir, I brought these men halfway across the country, some of them well over a thousand miles, on the promise that you would lead them in battle and give them a prayer of winning. You owe us more than 'a someone else,' sir. At least listen to what Commander Price has to say."

"Listen to him?" Joe grated, his temper rising. He took a step toward the young officer, and the security detail instantly came to the ready. Joe was honored they still thought of him as such a threat, but he resolved to move carefully as he took a step back, his hands raised and open. "You want me to listen to your boss?" Joe asked as the security detail lowered their rifles once more. "Tell me this, was he the one who hit DC with a nuke?"

"Yes," Attledge responded without even a breath of hesitation.

Joe staggered back a step as if struck. He had suspected it was Terry, but he hadn't really wanted to believe it. How could a man sworn to protect the country, to defend the Constitution with his life, do such a thing? Joe's mind spun. He'd known Terry longer than anyone still in his life with the exception of his wife. And the man he'd known could never have pushed the button to wipe out any city, much less the symbol of everything he'd devoted his life to protecting and serving.

"You need to listen to him," Attledge insisted. "I have the equipment to allow you to talk to him, face to face, over satellite connection. Give him ten minutes, sir, please. People have died to get us here. Please don't let that be for nothing, Captain, not without at least listening to why."

Joe pondered that a moment. "Fine. You have the equipment with you now?"

Attledge nodded. "Yes, sir. I have a portable communications unit. The connection usually isn't great, but it's enough to get the job done in a pinch. I have a much stronger receiver back at my base, though, if you'd be willing to come back with me."

Joe was already shaking his head. "No deal," he said firmly. "You come with me, alone, right now, or we don't have a deal. You're the one that showed up on my doorstep with your hat out, Commander. Don't forget that. Now, what's it going to be?"

Attledge thought for a moment and then gave a half shrug. "What about my men?"

"They can stay right where they are. Trust me, by morning this will have spread far enough that they won't want to be caught outside my protection. I expect your position will be surrounded by daybreak. Word travels fast in a small town, Commander."

Attledge retrieved two hardened cargo cases from one of the APCs. He allowed Joe to open both and inspect the contents. He expressed some concern about the rough handling of a few of the more delicate pieces of equipment but other than that gave no objection to the search. When Joe was satisfied, he took the commander's two side arms, a belt knife, and a boot knife for safe keeping.

Attledge gave orders for the men to rotate watches and resting parties to recharge as much as possible. A crew was to be awake at all times, though, and ready to pull out at a moment's notice. Once the orders were in place, he followed Joe back down the white sand driveway toward the farm house. As they walked, Eric led the way with Commander Attledge behind him as Joe brought up the rear.

"So, Commander Attledge," Joe said as they walked, "how did you know exactly where to come to find me? I've been moving around a lot in the last few weeks, and I can't believe it was pure, random luck that you just happened to come to my home and find me on my first extended trip back in weeks. So, how did you do it?"

Attledge was quiet for a long moment before answering. "Sir, I . . . I would prefer you asked Commander Price about that," he stammered. "I wouldn't be comfortable . . . that is, I'm not sure if he's . . . well, I don't know how he'd want me to answer that, sir."

Joe grunted. "So, it was the ring, wasn't it? Does it have a tracking device in it?"

Even in the dim predawn light cast by the moon and stars, it was clear that Commander Attledge's neck and ears flushed deeply. Still, to his credit, he didn't offer any further comment on the subject.

"It doesn't matter," Joe said brusquely. "He knew I would keep the ring for him, and I did. It's not your fault, in any case. I was just curious. I shouldn't be surprised that Terry would tag me, I guess, given everything else. But I admit, I am a little."

"To tell you the truth, sir," Attledge said, weariness thick in his voice, "not much Commander Price does surprises me anymore."

"Even dropping a nuke on our nation's capital?" Joe growled. "That didn't surprise you?"

Attledge didn't respond, and they walked in silence for a while. Joe worked to get his temper back in check. He needed a level head to handle this situation, and he didn't have one at the moment.

"Where do you want to make the call?" Attledge asked. "I can set up anywhere that I get an unobstructed view of the southern sky. At least that's the theory."

Joe shook his head. "We're not doing this yet. I need some time to finish sleeping and to get prepared. And besides, there's someone that I think both you and Commander Price need to meet face to face."

"Who is that?" Commander Attledge asked.

"A prisoner—a former FSS soldier who was stationed in DC until a couple of weeks ago. I'd like to hear Commander Price explain his rationale to him. As for you, Eric will get you water and some food while you wait, if you need it. Otherwise I'll see you again in a couple of hours."

"But Captain," Attledge insisted, "the enemy is already on the move. Please, won't you consider making contact now?"

Joe snorted. "Is this enemy less than four or five hours from our doorstep?" Attledge shook his head. "Good, then I have time to catch up on my sleep. Relax and make yourself comfortable, Lieutenant Commander. I'll let you know when I'm ready."

Before Attledge could respond, Joe nodded to Eric and then turned and strode away, leaving the other two men behind him to work out the details. Joe climbed the steps and entered the farmhouse by the front door, his mind racing. There was a lot he wanted to get done in the next few hours before his video call to Price, but he certainly wouldn't be sleeping as he'd told the lieutenant commander.

He had to wake everyone up for this. They needed to hear it when he heard it so they could make a decision together because Joe had a feeling that what was about to happen would affect more than just the few dozen people taking refuge with him at the homestead. A decision that big deserved to be made by more than just one man.

Joe walked carefully and quietly back into the front bedroom that he shared with Beth. He opened and closed the bedroom door noiselessly and managed to cross all the way to the bed on the old creaky floor without a single misstep. However, as he settled his weight onto the edge of the bed, Joe gently reached over and gripped his wife's upper arm. He gave her a light but purposeful nudge, and her eyes popped open almost immediately.

"It's just me," Joe whispered. Beth's eyes focused on his face and she started to speak, but Joe placed a single finger over his lips. "It's still very early, but something's happened and I need your advice and your help."

"Is everyone okay?" Beth asked, barely stifling a yawn that likely would have woken half the house.

Joe nodded. "Yes, everyone is fine. I just need your help. Remember the helicopter that landed?" He reached into his shirt pocket and pulled out Terry Price's Naval Academy ring. He explained to Beth the conversation he'd just had with Attledge, the man who had been on that helicopter. He was back, but by land this time and apparently with four thousand men under his command.

By the end of Joe's explanation, Beth was sitting up, hugging her knees to her chest, her chin resting on her knees. She shook her head firmly, her jaw clenched. "I know you, Joe Tillman," she hissed in a low whisper. "Whatever else you set your fool ass mind to, you will marry your son and Christina before anything else is done. You hear me?"

Joe spread his hands. "Whoa," he said leaning back away from the onslaught. "Look, I didn't bring this guy here. I didn't invite him. He just showed up. I told him I didn't want any part of a war, but if this is as serious as I think it is, I don't know how I can say no."

Beth fixed Joe with a firm glare and leveled a finger at him. "That's exactly what I'm talking about, duty, and honor, and country and all of that. I want you to promise me that this once you will put something else first. Perform the wedding ceremony and let our only son go to war with a wife and child waiting on him back home."

Beth paused, tears streaming down her cheeks. "At least that way," she continued after a moment, "he'll have something to fight to come home to."

"I haven't even agreed to anything yet," Joe said.

Beth wiped her eyes and smiled as she patted him on the back of one hand. "I think we both know you will, though, because it's the right thing to do. And you always do what's right, even when the cost is too damned high."

"The problem right now," Joe whispered to her in the darkness, "is I can't tell yet what's right, if anything *is* right anymore. I'm lost."

Beth shook her head and pulled Joe's hand close to her heart. "You're not lost. You're right here, and you're not alone."

Joe didn't know what words to say for the gratitude and relief he felt, so instead he simply nodded and kissed Beth's forehead. No more words were necessary. They sat together in the darkness, waiting for the sun to rise.

Chapter 85

Better Than Expected

Nov. 12 th 0600 EST

Colonel Darius stood outside the train, his breath fogging heavily in the morning grayness. The early cold snap had been accompanied by low, heavy clouds that were a nearly uniform steel gray. The air had the sharp, crisp smell of snow that reminded the colonel of the smell of an old deep freezer thick with frost.

He had slept surprisingly well the night before despite having a sniper shoot at him from the pitch-black darkness. If he had dreamt, he couldn't remember his dreams. That was a welcomed blessing and a change from several weeks of night terrors that brought back uncomfortable memories of his active duty as a Special Forces operator. Memories he thought he had long buried were once again haunting his nights.

The colonel blew into his coffee mug, and a cloud of steam rose into the cold air. He took a sip of the dark, black brew and smiled at the bitterness and the heat. There were hints of vanilla and hazelnut on the back end of the sip, and the colonel's smile broadened. Darius had always been a man of modest tastes, but he indulged himself in some simple pleasures like gourmet coffee, fine bourbon, and high-grade pipe tobacco. This morning he was sipping a medium French Vanilla and Colombian bean coffee that had been sourced from a local chain shop on the western border of Tennessee the week before.

As he watched the eastern sky inch closer to dawn, one of the perimeter sentries approached from the railroad tracks. "Sir," the man said with a quick salute that he held until Darius returned it, "there are some men from town who say they want to join. You said last night for us to come and find you if that happened."

Darius nodded, surprised by the unexpected news. "Search them for weapons even if they've already handed some over. Then send them through with an escort. I'll be waiting in my office, Specialist."

The man saluted again before turning and jogging back down the rail road tracks the way he'd come. Darius took another sip of his coffee as he climbed the steps and entered his office. He'd hoped to have a quiet morning for once and to be able to enjoy the sunrise, but that wasn't in the cards, it seemed. He sent word for Captain Withers to join him as soon as possible, and then he sat down behind his desk and finished his coffee, savoring the last few sips.

It was more than a half hour later when Withers finally came in, still tugging his uniform into place. He gave a crisp salute, though, and stood at attention in front of the colonel's desk, waiting for instruction. The man was professional and resolute, that much was certain, but Darius was still uncertain whether to trust him or not. Something in the back of his mind was warning him that the junior officer's simple sincerity could be a carefully crafted mask.

After all, the captain had admitted to serving in the enemy's ranks and had made no secret of what he'd done and what he'd learned while there. At times Darius found himself wondering whether or not his attack of moral conscience was sincere or an expertly devised cover, but, given that so far, Withers had proven good to his word, Darius had no choice but to trust him for the moment.

"Captain Withers, I need your help this morning. It appears that you were wrong to be so pessimistic in your estimation of our recruiting efforts. We have a group who have offered their services being escorted to the train as we speak."

"I see," Withers replied cautiously, "and what exactly is it you need me here for?"

"I want you to help me screen the recruits—see if you have an impression that any of them are worth keeping under temporary surveillance."

"I'll do my best, sir," Withers replied. As instructed, he took a spot to the colonel's left and back against the wall, where an attendant would have taken station.

"All right," Colonel Darius said once Withers was in place, "I'll let the sentries know to send in the first recruit."

Darius pushed a button on the communication control console and gave the necessary orders to the sentries standing guard outside. The two officers watched on the closed-circuit security feeds as the first recruit was pulled away from the group and ushered up to the door by one of the security officers. The rest of the group sat in a row on the ground, ankles crossed, and hands resting on their knees in plain view. There were twelve men left outside, though two of them sat with more distance between them and the rest of the group.

The man that entered the office was a little less than six feet tall with broad shoulders and a strong frame. His face and hands were tanned from the sun, but he was still young enough not to have wrinkles or gray hairs in his beard or on his head. His eyes were an intense hazel as he met the colonel stare for stare.

"I understand you'd like to join our group," Darius said, and the man nodded. "What's your name?"

"Hunter Cullock, sir. And yes, sir, I would like to join up. Hunter's voice was surprisingly soft, given his rough appearance, and was thick with a southern drawl. "I'd like to do my part, sir."

"Do you have any skills that will be particularly valuable?" Darius asked.

Hunter gave a half shrug and scratched at the right side of his beard. "I dunno. I grew up my whole life here in the valley. I can hunt and fish with the best of 'em, I can skin and butcher a dear in less than thirty minutes, and I can track a week old cold trail better than a red bone hound."

"Can you grow your own food too?" Darius asked, and Hunter nodded enthusiastically.

"Oh yeah, I can grow any kinda food you want. I grew up on our family's farm until I was grown, and I've always kept at least a small garden at the house."

"Do you know the rest of the people with you?" Darius asked. "Do they have similar skills as you do?"

Hunter thought for a moment. "I know most of 'em," he answered hesitantly, "but there's two that showed up about a month ago looking for a place to stay. The ones from around here are good folk, solid and down to earth. Them other two I can't really vouch for outside of what I've seen of 'em in the past few weeks, but they seem okay, I guess. They just kinda keep to themselves and whisper a lot. "

Darius looked over at Withers who gave a small half shrug and a nod. The colonel turned back to Hunter. "See the sergeant outside and he'll get you set up and registered. You'll go through a training period and then a proving period. Then we'll toss you in the mix. Do you have any questions?"

Hunter hesitated a moment after the dismissal. "Thank you, sir. There would have been more of us that came, but we needed to keep enough to hold the town and the roads. Those FSS assholes you talked about in town, they cause trouble sometimes down along the bigger highways. So far, we've been able to discourage them from coming out here into the hills, but it's only really a matter of time."

"I understand, Hunter," Darius replied. "A man needs to know his home is being defended. We'll see what we can do to help out in that regard."

"Well, sir, if that's what you're thinking, I know who you should talk to," Hunter said as he pointed to the security camera footage of the waiting group of men. "This guy with the not quite curly hair and the stubble, his father is one of the big important people on our town council. When he picks a way, most of the rest of them fall in line behind him."

"Thank you for the information," Darius replied. "What's his name?"

"Well, he'll tell you that if he wants to. That ain't my place to say, but if there's any of our people that have weight in town, it's him. Can I go now, like you said?"

Darius nodded, and Hunter left the office by the same door he'd entered. Outside he spoke briefly to the guard at the foot of the steps, then was ushered over to a waiting sergeant who had already taken inventory of the recruit's personal effects.

"Should we take the big shot's son next or save him for last?" Darius asked Withers.

Withers thought about it a moment, then shook his head. "Wait until last. Take one of the two shady characters instead. If they're going to be a problem, then better we find out about it sooner rather than later."

Darius nodded and gave the order over the communication system to bring in one of the two men sitting off to themselves. The sentry walked over and tapped the man closest to the railcar on the shoulder. The man stood and followed the sentry back to the door and came in as instructed.

It was immediately apparent that this man was different from Hunter. His face was clean shaven with just a solid morning shadow that looked as if it would normally be getting shaved off right about now. His clothes weren't nearly as stained as Hunter's, and the few stains that showed were faded with time and many washings. His hair was trimmed, though not short.

"I understand you'd like to volunteer for the army," Darius said. "What is your name?"

"Montgomery Alexander Clayton, but I go by Alex," the man replied, "and yes, I would like to volunteer."

"Fair enough, Alex," Darius said. "Do you have any skills that will be especially helpful to the war effort?"

"Probably not," Alex answered truthfully. "I cut hair. I used to do it mostly with clippers, though I actually went to stylist school. Now it's all scissors, and I think I enjoy it more than I did. But fighting a war, I don't know much about that."

"Why do you want to join?" Colonel Darius asked.

"It just feels like the right thing to do," Alex replied immediately. "And besides, this is way too big to sit on the sidelines. Our grandkids will read stories about us and these times. I want to give them something to read about, I guess. I just want to do my part, whatever small part that is."

Darius looked back at Withers. "Do you have any questions, Captain?"

Withers shook his head as he tapped commands on a small tablet connected to the train's computer and data storage systems. The inventory from each of the recruits had been entered as items were inspected.

"I can confirm that Mr. Clayton had one pair of hair shears in his pocket and five more pairs in his pack, along with a total of thirty-seven combs."

"See the sergeant outside," Darius said. "He'll get your information and get you registered as a recruit. I'm sure we'll make good use of you keeping the soldiers neat and trimmed. One thing history proves time and again is that a dirty army is a sick army, and a sick army is a weak army. And in times like this, a weak army is a dead army."

Alex thanked the colonel and left.

"Well, there's something definitely different about him," Withers said after Alex was gone. "I don't think he's a threat, just someone that is awkward and off-putting in some vague way."

"Well, he can be useful around here cleaning the men up a little," Darius said.

He gave the orders for the second of the loners to be ushered into the office. The sentry waited as the second man was brought forward. As soon as the man's face was framed in the monitor, Withers stepped forward, close to the screen, and examined it in detail. When he turned back to Darius, there was a certainty in his expression that was unmistakable.

Withers pointed to the face on the monitor without turning to look at it. "I know that man. We were in the FSS together after I was drafted. He was a volunteer, a fanatic. He's dangerous, sir."

"How can I know that what you're saying is the truth?" Darius asked, "I haven't known you that long, Captain. I trust you in some things because you've proven yourself, but you're telling me this man is an active and committed enemy agent. That could have some very serious repercussions for him if you're right, and for you if you're wrong."

Withers thought for a moment, then snapped his fingers. "He has a scar that runs from the outside corner of his left eyebrow, across his forehead, and ends just a little in front of and above his right ear. When he's not wearing a hat, he keeps long hair parted on the left and combed over the portion of the scar that's in his hairline What goes across his face was stitched together with skill so it's hard to see, but he'll show it to you, if you ask. It's from a bar fight when he was twenty-two. He got hit across the face with an empty beer bottle by a drunk biker. The biker thought he was someone else and attacked him, so this guy fought back and put the biker in the hospital for two weeks. He loves to tell that story. When he comes in, ask him about the scar and see what he says."

Darius examined the man's face, but after a moment he shook his head. "I don't see a scar."

"The hospital flew in a plastic surgeon to stitch him together," Withers replied without hesitation. "The guy did a good job, so it's tough to see. Look at the corner of his left eyebrow and you can see where it's split in two. The scar runs right through it."

Darius could just make out on the poor resolution of the security camera what looked like a faint line in the man's eyebrow. He was far more uncertain of it than Withers, but he gave the order to have the man ushered into the office. Once the prisoner was frisked again by the sentry and Darius pressed the electronic release for the lock on the front door, the prisoner stepped inside.

For a long moment, nobody spoke. Darius watched the stranger closely to see if there was any spark of recognition in his eyes for Captain Withers. For a long time the man simply stared at a point on the floor just in front of Darius's desk. When he finally brought his eyes up, his expression was carefully controlled.

"So, I understand you want to join the army as well," Darius said, breaking the tense silence. "Do you have any special skills that would make you valuable?"

The man smiled a cold, calculated smile that never quite touched his eyes. "Yeah, I'd say so."

"I don't want to be rude," Darius said carefully, "but it looks like you have seen some combat, maybe?"

The man blinked. "I don't follow you."

"Your scar," Darius replied bluntly, "is it from combat?"

The man reached up to run the fingers of his left hand across the faint line across his forehead. "Oh, that," he said with a chuckle. "No, that was from a rowdy episode when I was younger. A case of mistaken identity between me and a biker. I got hit with a beer bottle and it sliced me open pretty deep. It took more than a hundred and sixty stitches to close my head up, but I was home by the next morning. I put the guy who did it in a hospital for two weeks."

"You can handle yourself, then?" Darius asked, and the man gave another cold smile and nodded his head. "That could come in handy if we ever find ourselves in close quarters combat, which we most certainly will. The sergeant outside will give you your kit. Welcome to the army."

The man nodded and stepped outside to stand next to the waiting sentry. Withers took a breath and started to say something, but Darius held up his hand, stopping him in his tracks. The colonel entered a string of commands that isolated the sentry's communication channel.

"Specialist, I want you and the rest of the security division to keep an eye on this guy. Don't give him access to any weapons under any circumstances and secure all sensitive and above intelligence. I don't want this guy getting close to anything that we don't choose to let him get close to, got it?"

Outside the sentry gave a single firm nod to the camera he knew was watching, and he personally led the prisoner away.

Once he was gone Darius turned back to Withers. "Before you ask, Captain," Colonel Darius said calmly, "yes, I believe you about who this man is. And if we take what you said as truth, then he has either been sent here to kill someone or he's a spy. Either way, the fact that we know who he is gives us an advantage. We can now use him without his knowing it."

"This is dangerous, sir. I know that guy. I've seen what he's capable of, and he's dangerous. Even with people watching him he can be slippery. And I believe if you let him in this camp, even under surveillance, it's going to end in trouble."

Darius shook his head. "Let this be a lesson to you, Captain, from Sun Tzu himself. The only good enemy spy is the one you have identified that is unaware his cover is blown. Disinformation delivered through a trusted source can be devastating to the enemy's tactics. It's a risk, but it's worth the reward, even if someone has to pay with his life."

"Even if that someone is you?" Withers asked seriously. "Even if it's someone else?"

"We should be so lucky that he goes after me, if he's an assassin," Darius answered. "I never have fewer than four guards within earshot of me, so odds are, even if he is successful, he won't get out of it alive if he goes after me. He's much more likely to pick a target that would actually impede the operations of the army. Someone that is more accessible and, therefore, more vulnerable than I am."

The colonel's voice was heavy as he continued. "Even if he does and even if he's successful in carrying out his mission, it will be worth it if the right disinformation can find its way from his hands to his handlers in the enemy ranks. We could set the entire enemy army up for ambush and failure before a shot is even fired. It could save thousands of lives."

Darius was quiet for a moment. Then he raised his eyes from his desk and turned to meet the captain's penetrating gaze eye to eye. "Ask yourself, Captain, if it's worth it. Ask yourself what you would do in my shoes."

Withers didn't know what to say to that, so he stood in silence, and after a time Darius rose and walked through the door into his living quarters at the back side of the car.

Chapter 86

The Longest Day

Nov. 12 th 0722 EST

Eric stood next to his father as the sun slowly crept over the horizon. Light filtered through the mostly bare hardwoods and scattered long leaf and loblolly pines when the sun was still very low. In the summer time, it wasn't visible until much later in the morning, thanks to the thick canopy, but now as soon as it broke the distant horizon the red sphere was clear.

The morning air was damp and chilly enough for their breaths to fog slightly. By the middle of the day it would probably be warm enough for shorts again, but right now the cool, almost clammy air called for pants. Mornings like this hinted at the coming change to winter; although, in the South it was often difficult to predict when one season would fade into the next. Sometimes there were warm snaps into the low eighties even into December, so a few cold mornings this early might not mean anything at all.

Even Eric's granddaddy had said he thought the winter would be rough, and when Levy spoke about these kinds of things, it was a good idea to listen. Eric didn't quite understand on what his grandfather based those seemingly certain statements about the coming weather months in advance, but more often than not he was right when he made them. Granddaddy had predicted the bad storm season that had seen four hurricanes impact the coast, one of them riding the Cape Fear far enough inland to still be a category three hurricane when it hit Bennett.

Eric's father looked over at him without quite turning his head. "Twenty-four hours, son—twenty-four hours from now, this moment, you'll be getting married. How do you feel?"

Eric thought about it before he answered. "Excited and I guess a little anxious to get it done. I mean, if I could snap my fingers and make it now, I would. I'm just ready to do it."

Joe smiled at him and nodded. "Believe it or not, I remember the day before I married your mom. That was thirty-one years ago this year, but I still remember it. And I felt the same way. I was just ready to get there already. Then the morning before the wedding, my dad, Grandpa Tillman, had a talk like this with me, and he gave me something valuable. Something I'm going to do my best to pass on to you, now, and that's perspective."

"Perspective?" Eric asked, doing his best to keep his tone level. "Okay, Dad, let's talk about perspective. There's a convoy of military vehicles that has crossed most of the country at great risk to themselves and others just to find you, and they're waiting out on the main road right now because you told them to wait. How's that for perspective?"

For a moment Eric's father didn't have any reply, and he looked a bit shocked at Eric's outburst. Finally, he gave his head a small shake, and his tone was serious. "That wasn't what I was talking about, Eric, and I think you know it. We will get to the bottom of that, but not right now. Right now, this is more important. I need to say some things and I need to know that you're going to hear me. I mean really hear me, Eric. Forget about the rest of the world for a minute and just hear me. The rest of the world will still be there tomorrow afternoon, I promise."

Eric blinked, suddenly overwhelmed with emotion, and he nodded without speaking. The words he wanted to say just wouldn't form for him.

"Good. First off, I love you, son, and I'm proud of you. I maybe don't say that enough, but I want you to know it, and I know you're in a hurry to get married. I understand that. But you're going to have the rest of your life to be married, Eric, and I don't doubt for a second that your marriage with Christina will last that long. You two are made for each other. There's just no question about it."

Eric's father patted him on the shoulder with one hand as they looked out at the sunrise. "This is the last day of your single life, Eric. Enjoy it and savor it. Remember all of the experiences along the way that brought you to where you are right now, in this moment, and be thankful for each one of them—the good and the bad. Remember that without each one of those experiences, and how they shaped who you are, you might not be here. Your past is a part of you, and so it's part of your future. Remember that while you're creating your past."

For a moment, his father fell silent and Eric wiped a few tears away that he hadn't realized he was going to shed. After a while, his father squeezed his shoulder and broke the silence that had fallen between them.

"You haven't been a kid for a good number of years, but you'll always be my kid. And you know that I'm always here for you, no matter what. Take some time and think about what you want to do today and then do it. And this time tomorrow I'll be telling you to kiss you lovely wife. I'll be around if you need me, but remember that once the rest of the house is awake, you won't get to see Christina again until she walks down the aisle."

After a brief pause, his father turned toward the door. "Whatever happens, son, you'll be fine. Remember to pray to God, remember to love your wife and family, and remember to fight the enemy with everything you have. That's all any man can do, really."

Before Eric could reply, his father patted him on the shoulder and walked across the front porch and into the farm house. Already Eric could hear sounds from inside, and they were getting louder, especially in the kitchen. That was his mother and grandmother making sure everyone knew it was time to get up. The reward for crawling out of bed with the sunrise was a very tasty and hearty breakfast.

But it seemed there was always work to be done afterwards, and this morning proved no different. Eric's mother handed out biscuits cut in half with thick slabs of country ham and sausage sandwiched between the layers. Some of the biscuits had purple blackberry jelly spilling out of the sides instead of protein, and Eric made sure to grab two of those.

He drank sweet iced tea that had enough sugar to make his teeth tingle and was as cold as the solar-fed refrigerator could get it without freezing the jug solid. There was fresh bean coffee, the real stuff, not the flash frozen field rations he was used to cooking up while on patrol. The food and drink were some of the best he'd had in months, and it set the tone for the rest of the day. Still, Eric couldn't help but wonder where Christina was and what she was going through at the same time.

After a while Brant and Eric stepped outside with Justin and Oscar close behind them. When all four of them were in the open, Brant put a hand on Eric's shoulder. "You've been my best friend for longer than I can remember, and since the Blackout, your family has taken me in and made me one of your own. You are like a brother to me, Eric. Congratulations, man, I love you."

Brant reached into his pack and pulled out a tall, wooden box that had a deep, dark finish and an aged gloss, and he handed it to his friend. Intrigued, Eric undid the clasp on the top right edge of the box and found a bottle of The MacAllan 25yr. o. single malt scotch. Folded up and nestled in the side of the green felt lining was a note.

Eric unfolded the note and knew immediately that his father had written it. He read through the words a couple of times, tearing up each time, and then he folded the note and put it in his pocket. He didn't mention it again after that. He didn't even want to think what such a bottle would have cost before the Blackout. It must have been top-shelf expensive then, and now, an even more exorbitant price. It almost didn't feel right to drink it without his father with him.

"Before you say anything," Brant said, "I have to tell you something. Your father is terrifying."

"What are you talking about?" Eric asked, confused at Brant's description of his father.

"He came to me," Brant said, gesturing to the two brothers, "and probably to them to, and kind of hinted around to the fact that it would be bad for the ones who let him down on his son's wedding day. He never came out and said exactly how or why it would be bad, just that it would be very bad. Then he handed me that bottle of scotch and the note."

Eric looked again at the bottle of scotch in his hand and wondered where and how his father had managed to find it.

"Anyway," Brant continued after a moment, "your father made it clear that your bachelor party was for the bachelors, and he wished us all well. He said we could do whatever we want as long as it doesn't involve hanging around here all day. The only catch is

610

we have to be back here by tomorrow morning at sunrise, ready for you to get hitched. Any ideas?"

Eric thought about it a moment. A slow smile spread across his face and he nodded. "I know just the place. Pack an overnight, some good clothes, and your bow."

"Where are we going?" Brant asked, curious but more excited about spending the day with his best friend.

"Back to school," Eric said with a cryptic smile.

Confused by Eric's response, Brant frowned for a moment and then walked back over to the porch with Eric. Four packs were already waiting along with four bows, complete with full quivers as well. There was a note sitting on top of Eric's pack with his name on the outside, written in his mother's hand. He picked it up and carefully unfolded the paper.

The note was short and simple, *For the road. Stay safe. I love you. Mom.*

Even with the simple message, Eric suddenly felt his emotions welling up again. He swallowed the lump in his throat and focused on getting his pack situated on his shoulders so the waist strap took most of the weight off his back and spread the load over his entire frame. Eric's bow was a Bear and it was built to be strong, lightweight, and accurate. With a thick leather wrist strap and a good counter-balance, he barely felt the weight of it, even with eight arrows in the side quiver.

Eric led the way to the gate and through it onto the dirt driveway that would take them to Cutler's Run and eventually to his bachelor party. He couldn't help but smile as he thought about the bottle of scotch in his backpack, wrapped in a towel and a sweatshirt to keep it as safe and as cool as possible. Tonight was definitely going to be a night to remember.

Chapter 87

Answers

Joe stood at the back of one of the armored personnel carriers that formed Lieutenant Commander Attledge's convoy with his prisoner kneeling in the sand next to the road. A small, collapsible satellite dish had been raised on the roof of the heavily armored vehicle, and thick cables ran down to a series of power supplies, filters, amplifiers, and eventually into a pair of laptop control units. One laptop showed the image that was being broadcast in the upstream feed and one showed the image being received in the downstream feed.

Joe's own reflection stared back at him from the left, the sound muted to prevent a feedback loop. The right side of the screen was still static at the moment, but Commander Attledge had assured him that soon it would resolve into a live feed from the mountains of Utah where Terry Price had built his hyper-secret information storage facility.

Joe looked at the young officer standing across from him and studied Attledge's features. He'd aged in the few months since Joe had first seen him, and there was a new wariness about him. The man never stood perfectly still for long; he was constantly shifting and glancing over his shoulders. His eyes also never rested in the same place for more than a few breaths before they were back

613

scanning the perimeter or the horizon. This was a man who was used to watching his back at all times. There was a new scar, faint and shallow, that ran completely around the commander's throat. It looked almost as if someone had tried unsuccessfully to garrote him.

Most of the men with Attledge were older than he was, and they bore the scars of battle, some faded with age and some bright and fresh. None of them looked at the prisoner, including Attledge himself. Their eyes seem to slide past the scarred man kneeling in the dirt without really seeing him or acknowledging his presence. To these men he was just another enemy who hadn't realized yet that he was already dead.

Attledge had tried to explain the things they'd seen on the journey across the Midwest and the Appalachian Mountains, but he hadn't been able to make it through more than a handful of sentences before he was overcome by the raw reality of the death and destruction he had seen. He stared at the prisoner and then turned his back and didn't let his eyes touch the man again. The rest of the soldiers had given him that same kind of withering glare at some point in their own silent introspection, and then they had mentally erased the man from the equation of their mission.

Finally, after what seemed an eternity, the screen on the right beeped three times and then flickered. When the image stabilized again, it showed the interior of a high-tech command center. A man with closely cut gray hair and a clean-shaven face that looked vaguely familiar faced the camera. He wore a battle uniform of digitized woodland camouflage colors and carried a holstered .45 caliber pistol on his right hip. When their eyes met, Joe saw in this stranger the friend he'd known decades ago.

For a moment, memories washed over Joe that threatened to destroy his self-control and his focus. They had been through so much together, from BUD/S class all the way through the ranks of the teams. Joe had stood as Terry's best man in his wedding and was at the hospital the night his twins were born. He was also at the hospital the night Terry's wife and one of his daughters died in a horrifying accident. That night was the last time he'd seen his friend face to face.

Commander Price smiled at first, but then a few silent and seemingly unnoticed tears ran down his hollow cheeks. He looked very tired and his smile wavered. "Captain Tillman, good morning and good to see you, sir," Price said before Joe had a chance to speak. "I trust Commander Attledge relayed my message and my request?

Joe was silent for a long time, his mind racing. He could see his old friend in the old man that stood on the other side of that screen. The years had not been kind to Price, and the weight of his burdens showed in the lines of his face and the dark circles under his eyes. His body was beginning to twist downward at the shoulders and neck, and he had lost weight. He was four years younger than Joe, but at the moment he looked a good ten or fifteen years older.

"I have someone here who would like to talk to you," Joe said finally. "This man was just a little more than five and a half miles, about nine kilometers from the epicenter. He was on guard duty for the FSS in a neighborhood when your missile detonated over the Capitol."

Joe pulled the man to his feet and unbound his hands. He fixed the prisoner with a hard glare. "Don't try anything, or I will put you down."

The man nodded and looked at the ground as Joe stepped back away from the cameras. "You wanted to find the man who blew up

DC, right?" Joe asked the prisoner, and he pointed at the screen. "That's him."

The man slowly raised his eyes and stared at Commander Price, who stood up a little straighter and squared his shoulders, meeting the man glare for glare. Joe watched as his old friend took in the man's puffy, scarred face and forearm. The only part of his face that wasn't scarred from deep burns was the outline of his hand in front of one eye. That patch of skin was eerily clean and healthy but had turned an angry red. His breath was coming in ragged, heaving gasps.

"Why?" he asked, his right hand clenched so hard that it trembled. "What did I ever do to you? I was standing watch over some suburb as part of a civilian guard force, and, suddenly, I'm flash burned and stumbling down a charred alleyway. What did I ever do to deserve that?"

"Collateral damage," Price replied without hesitation, "that's what the textbooks call it. Insufficient explanation, perhaps, but there it is. I didn't mean to burn your skin to a crisp, sir, but I had to destroy a particular enemy with a certain degree of certainty unavailable by any other means. You see, we had just been attacked by your boss, 'President' Hall. He used a nuclear weapon just hours before, and my army narrowly escaped being vaporized in Kansas City as a result."

"You almost got toasted by a nuclear weapon and decided it would be a good idea to return the favor? That sounds like revenge," the man spat back at Price. "Well, look what your revenge did to me. I can still smell the stink of my own skin and flesh as it was seared in the heat flash, the smell of cooking meat mixing with the acrid smoke of melting nylon as it burned my nose. Our uniforms were dark blue, black, and gray, and they soaked up that heat. I have scars of the pattern of the weave all along my arms and back. Sometimes I wake up from nightmares with the stink of that smell in my nose and on the back of my tongue."

The prisoner was panting in short, quick gasps now, and a string of spittle hung from the burned left corner of his mouth. "There was one guy, Marshall, but everyone called him Martian. He had half of his shirt melted into the skin on his left arm. He was about a half mile closer than I was, pulling a supply run back to the neighborhood. Nobody knew what to do, and he wouldn't stop screaming. Finally, he just reached up and ripped the rest of his shirt off and took half his skin with it. Everything got infected and he died two days later, whimpering like a starving pup."

The man's eyes seemed to focus once again on Price, and the unburned streak turned a deeper red. "We were people, for God's sake. I guarded a neighborhood and Martian—Marshall—he was in charge of supplies kinda like a grocer. We were ordinary people living an ordinary life, and you killed him and damn near killed me. Did you ever think about us? Did you ever even stop to consider the people you were going to kill and burn and melt? That 'collateral damage' you were talking about?"

Tears were running down Price's cheeks now, but he met the prisoner's angry glare without flinching. "Yes, I did," he replied in a frighteningly calm, soft voice. "I thought about you, and I prayed about you, and I wept over you. But I also thought about and prayed over and wept over the three hundred and ninety million people that called this nation home before the attacks, before the Blackout. And I thought about all of the ones who had died as a result and how we're probably down to a half of our numbers this time last year, maybe a third. And it's all because of what that soul-less monster Hall did. And then I thought about how that monster was using you and your friend and all the tens of thousands of people who had already bought into his propaganda."

617

Commander Price paused, his hands clenched in fists so hard his entire body was trembling. "That monster was doing everything he could to take over, to put the few people we have left in this country firmly under his boot and under his thumb for the rest of his life. We owe our dead countrymen better than that. We owe them more than that. We owe it to them to make sure that those monsters that did this do not win." Price slammed his fist down on the table before him hard enough to make a crystal ashtray jump. "And I will do anything in my power to make sure that we pay our debt."

"I don't owe anyone shit," the prisoner spat back at the screen. "I paid my debts, I paid my taxes, and I worked my job in that city for seventeen and a half years. I did my time, and I was finally getting my easy, cushy reward. That's what that assignment was supposed to be, easy. A reward for years of quiet, obedient service. It was a post at home, away from the front, away from the fighting. Christ, man, there were families there!"

Joe walked up behind the man and smacked him in the back of the head. "All right, that's enough. Kneel down and shut up."

The prisoner glared pure hatred at Price's face in the screen, but he did as he was instructed. Joe stared at the back of the man's head for a long moment, an array of thoughts and feeling churning through him. This man, this prisoner, was broken. He'd tried six times already to get to the guards and escape. He had knocked over one of the guards Joe had sent with him to the latrine and tried to tear the man's throat out with his teeth. Luckily the guard's buddy had been just a few steps behind them and was able to knock the prisoner unconscious before any permanent damage was done.

He was dangerous, and he was broken inside and out. Joe knew what had to be done.

Price was still talking, his eyes focused on the prisoner as Joe turned his back and pulled out his Beretta 9mm. Joe stared at the handgun, a knot in the pit of his stomach. He knew the man was dangerous. Some of the things he'd admitted to doing while on the road were sick, and there was no telling what kinds of things he'd kept secret. Joe didn't like the idea of having to execute the man, but he knew it had to be done. As Joe wrestled with his conscience he heard the young officer chime in with an opinion that Price didn't like. The two were going back and forth when Joe turned back around, the Beretta in his hand, and the conversation suddenly stopped.

Commander Price's eyes were locked on the Beretta and so were Attledge's. The prisoner had turned halfway around and the first thing he saw was the handgun. At first, the prisoner's eyes bulged with shock, but then they narrowed and a slow smile spread across his face.

"Good," he whispered, "it's about time. Put me out of my misery, please. I can't sleep at night, and when I do sleep I wake up screaming. I'm constantly remembering pain I never really felt and I can't really feel what's going on with my skin anymore at all. I can't even get my plumbing to work so I can soak up some sympathy sex. I got nothing left for this world. It all got taken by him." The prisoner jerked his head back in the direction of Price's image.

"Wait," Price said. "Joe, you can't. This man might have vital information, and even if he doesn't, he's still a prisoner of war. He's still a person, Joe. You can't just shoot him in cold blood like some animal gone rabid."

Joe's eyes slowly rose to meet Commander Price's. "It's Captain Tillman," he growled.

He leveled the pistol and fired three shots in rapid succession. Two rounds took the man just to the right center of his chest, and one took him just below the left eye. The prisoner jerked hard once and fell forward, dead before he hit the dirt.

Chapter 88

Promises

Nov 12 th 0815 MST

Shocked by what he had just witnessed, Commander Price stared at the screen as the man who looked like his friend calmly waited for the suppressor to cool enough for him to unscrew it from the barrel of his pistol. The suppressor went in a small pouch that was attached to the inside of his belt, and the pistol went back in the holster strapped to his leg. Captain Tillman stood, one hand idly twisting what looked like a faded bottle cap on a leather lanyard, and looked down at the corpse at his feet.

After a few moments, Tillman raised his eyes again, and they were cold and hard with hatred. "There was going to be only one outcome for that man, ever. He was an enemy of the nation, a traitor. He deserved to die and that's what he did. I just wanted to make sure that at least once you came face to face with the price some people paid for your war, Commander."

Price felt his throat closing again and swallowed hard to try and stop it. He had been nearly overwhelmed with a panic attack the moment he had seen the executed prisoner's scarred face. Only one thing was known to make those kinds of scars and that was a nuclear blast. He'd seen those scars many times in his nightmares, rows upon rows of puffy, scarred faces staring their hatred and

621

their accusations at him. Those dreams would drive him sweating and screaming from sleep and into the darkness around him.

In the end, Tillman was right. Though the man had been burned and maimed beyond belief with scars across his skin as well as his mind, he was still a committed enemy soldier. After all, he had said himself that this was his reward for a life of service.

Before Price could bring up that point, though, Tillman continued speaking in a tightly restrained tone. "You asked whether or not the commander here delivered your offer, and I never answered you. He did. He offered me the command of field forces here in the Southeast, and he explained why I should take the position. An army of more than twenty thousand will be passing within thirty miles of my home, and I guess that kind of makes neutrality a non-starter at this point."

"I will lead your army, Commander Attledge," Tillman said without looking over at the man, "but that makes you under my chain of command now. If you don't like that you can go back to your boss in Utah. That's up to you. I'm stuck fighting this fight, no matter what. But when this is done, if I am still breathing, I'm coming after you, Commander Price. I don't know enough to judge what you did, to be honest. Not yet. But I know you will face a reckoning for what you've done. I will make it my life's mission to make sure it happens, even if I have to deliver it myself."

Price couldn't help but smile. "Well, you know where I'll be, Joe," he said. "It's not like I've got anywhere else to go."

Tillman didn't respond, so after a moment Price asked to speak to Attledge privately. Tillman made no move to leave, though, so Price had no choice but to talk with an audience.

"Lieutenant Commander Attledge, you and I both know what you need to do, but I want you to hear me say the words. Your orders are to accept Captain Tillman's commands in all things. You're under his chain now, and I wish you the best. It's been an honor to serve with you, Commander, even if that feeling isn't mutual. I want you to know I respect you and I am proud of you, if that matters anymore."

Commander Price stood to attention and Attledge did as well. Attledge raised a slow salute, and once Price had returned it, he keyed in the commands to break the satellite connection. Once the link was broken, Price sat for a long moment staring at the dark screen. He felt as if he'd lost a member of his family, and a strange mix of pain and panic gripped him for a moment. He was overcome with nostalgia and the memories of working with Marcus over the years and the close friendship they'd developed.

But, for now, for the nation, this was how it had to be.

"I had hoped that would go better," Price said when he finally turned his back on the screens. "I had expected a rocky reunion, but nothing like that. The man I knew wasn't even there. This man is cold, calculating, and merciless. He executed that prisoner in cold blood and didn't even seem fazed by it."

"You launched a nuclear missile against the nation's capital," the Chief said from his position next to the door, "and you're calling *him* cold blooded and merciless?"

Price started to bite off a retort but stopped short. The chief was right, of course, though he didn't like hearing it. "Do you really think he'll come after me?" Price asked after a moment.

The chief thought about his answer a long time before replying. "I don't know Captain Tillman personally, but I've known people like him. If he says he's coming after you, then he's going to come after you. You know him, Commander, what do you think he'll do?"

"I thought I did," Price whispered to himself. "I thought I knew him, but now I'm not so sure. He's changed, but I think you're right. I think he will come, too."

The chief nodded. "When he does, will you fight it?"

Price didn't hesitate when he answered. "No, I won't fight it. When I launched the attack against DC, I made the decision to accept whatever consequences come out of it. It was my call, my move, and it's my responsibility. I knew that I would probably have to face a court-martial at the very least and possibly a war crimes tribunal. Whatever happens, though, this is my burden to bear. And who knows, maybe by the time Captain Tillman is finished with the conflict in the East he will have had time to come to an understanding of what I did and why."

"And what if he decides to give you the same verdict that he gave his prisoner?" the chief asked.

Commander Price was silent for a long moment. "When I was nineteen I made the decision to devote my career and my life to the United States Navy. When I did that I also decided that I was ready and willing to give my life for my country and for my countrymen if the need should ever arise. It's been nearly forty years since that cool October morning in North Boston, but nothing's changed about my commitment to my country. If that's the price I have to pay, then I'll pay it with as much courage and dignity as I can."

The commander turned back to the wall monitor and keyed in a series of commands that brought up a satellite image of the eastern United States. The image focused in on the Southeast, then on North Carolina, and finally zoomed in to show the central area of the state. Superimposed on the satellite image were major highways and state roads, city and county names, bodies of water, and three blinking lights. One of the lights was just barely visible in the

624

northwest corner of the display and marked the position of Colonel Darius's column in the edge of the mountains. The other two lights were very close together, one representing Lieutenant Commander Attledge and the other Captain Tillman.

Price zoomed in on the area around Attledge and Tillman. "Those men are going to need to know best places to hit the enemy so they can choose where to attack. That's on us, Chief. We've got to help them figure out where to make our stand."

Chapter 89

Memory Lane

Eric crouched at the edge of the woods and scanned the open kickball field in front of him. There was a red clay diamond to the left, complete with bright white bases and a broad fringe of grass between him and a cinderblock wall. That wall would come up to just over his bellybutton now, but when he'd been a student at Boone Trail Elementary, it had been head high or taller. That wall marked the lower edge of the playground and the upper boundary of the kickball field. Moss was thick on the face of the cinderblocks, but the wall wasn't sagging or bulging anywhere.

Up the hill three swing sets were positioned in a row. The see-saws were gone now, but the monkey bars and the rolled steel jungle gyms still stood. The concrete basketball court and another two swing sets lined the right edge of the playground, and that was it. At the very top of the hill was a thick layer of asphalt that had served as a parking lot for delivery trucks, teachers' cars, and other official vehicles.

The sun was bright overhead and the entire field between Eric and the top of the hill was empty. The windows of the old brick elementary school looked out over the abandoned and partially overgrown playground like a sad vigil. Weeds had sprouted through all of the paved areas and the poured concrete of the basketball court. Morning glory vines crawled up and over the monkey bars and the metal jungle gyms so that the bottom halves of both structures were tangled masses of flowers and leaves.

Eric led the way up the hill from the kickball courts. He smiled as he walked through a haze of memories and a flood of long-forgotten emotions. He could remember the smell of the snow cones they'd had in third grade the afternoon he'd gotten his first kiss. He'd chosen grape and had dropped more than half of it on the hot blacktop when a yellow jacket landed on his hand. Later, on the bus ride home, a girl with pigtails and in a pink polka dotted dress gave him a kiss on his cheek and whispered for him not to tell anyone.

He could still feel the rough gravel and dirt the day Brant had pushed him down after a disagreement over a game of dunkball. The two wouldn't speak for more than a month, and that was the closest their friendship had ever come to ending. Eric still couldn't remember what had started the fight or what Brant had said that had hurt his feelings so much that he'd taken a swing at his best friend. He could only remember the hurt and the fear he'd felt at the idea that they might not be friends anymore.

Eric shared some of his memories with the others, and some he kept for himself. By the time they reached the top of the hill they were all laughing, and both Eric and Brant were wiping tears from their eyes at the same time. They had grown up together from before kindergarten and knew all of the same people and all the same stories from their time in and around these brick walls. After this school, they'd been in the same classes in middle and high school as well. But this is where everything started to grow into what would become a lifelong friendship for both of them.

The afternoon was bright but cool, and the constant breeze out of the northwest brought with it a high layer of thin, steely-gray clouds that cooled the air even more. Eric led the group to what had once been a loading dock on the back side of the school between the auditorium and the cafeteria. Using the raised concrete dock as a bar, Eric pulled the bottle of scotch from his back and poured four glasses of the deep amber liquor.

He handed the three glasses out to his companions and took the fourth for himself and raised it high over his head. "Here's to the last twenty-eight years of our lives bringing us inexorably together to this moment, here and now. I can't think of any better friends to share this day and this scotch with. And I can't think of any three men I would rather trust my life to than you three right here. We've been through a lot together, Brant you and me especially. But I want all of you to know I think of each and every one of you as brothers."

Eric started to get choked up, and Brant reached over to grip his shoulder. "All right, Mr. Weepy Eyes, can we drink this scotch now? I've been wanting to taste this stuff since your dad handed it to me."

Eric smiled and nodded. "Cheers," he managed to get out past the lump in his throat.

They all clinked their glasses, and then Eric took his first sip of twenty-five-year-old scotch. The flavors were cleaner, crisper, and smoother than anything he'd ever sipped. There was no trace of bite or burn as he swallowed, just a firm and glowing warmth that spread out from his middle and made him smile. This was what scotch was meant to be. When Eric looked around, he saw each of his friends staring into his glass with the same kind of wide-eyed awe and appreciation that he felt showing on his own face.

"Gentlemen, it's a hell of a time to be alive. You realize that if we make it through, these are the days that our grandkids will tell stories about, right?"

"You really think we'll have grandkids around to tell those stories?" Oscar asked.

Eric smiled and nodded without hesitation as he took another sip. "Absolutely. Some of us will, anyway. And for those that don't make it long enough to meet their grandkids, we'll tell your stories too."

"Enough of that depressing bull crap," Brant said with a wave of his hand. "This is a bachelor party and it needs to be a lot more fun than that. Eric, do you remember when we had the dunkball tournament our fifth-grade year?"

"Dunkball?" Oscar asked.

"Yeah, it's kind of like basketball," Eric replied, "but not really. You see the two metal monkey bars down there? Those were the goals. Shooting the ball didn't count. We had to dunk it through the bars, hence the name of the game. Fouls were few and far between and we basically had to draw blood before we were penalized. Two people to a team, two teams to a game. We usually played first team to twenty-one wins."

Brant nodded. "It was the most fun on the playground, and it was where all of the action was. Well, our fifth-grade year we got the grand idea to have a tournament. We worked out a rotation of teams between the two fifth-grade classes and the two fourth-grade classes. It lasted a week, and at the end of it there had been four fist fights and three friendships broken completely, and we still didn't know which team was the best at dunkball."

Eric and Brant both laughed at the shared memory while Jordan and Oscar just looked confused. "I don't get it," Jordan said finally. "Why would you choose to come to an old school for your bachelor party? I mean, I know there aren't exactly that many options available anymore, but a school? That seems pretty lame, even today, man."

Eric gave a small shrug. "I guess this place has a lot of history for me and my family. Granddaddy and Nanny both came here from first grade on. Granddaddy dropped out his eighth-grade year to work on the farm, but my mom and Nanny went from first grade through twelfth grade. I came here up until the sixth grade." Eric took another long, slow sip of his scotch. "My life and who I am was shaped by what happened in these halls a long time before I even set foot in them. Besides, this place was abandoned twelve years ago and everything that could possibly be scavenged or stolen is already gone, so I figured it would be secluded."

"Yeah, I don't really feel like dealing with outsiders today," Brant said with an uneasy shift of his shoulders.

When all four of them had finished their first drinks, Eric nodded toward the door behind them. "Come on, let's find a way inside," he said, a mischievous smile tugging at the corners of his mouth.

They tried, with no luck, to push in through six doors, all with thick latches and heavy padlocks. The doors and the frames were old and the paint faded where it hung on at all, but the wood was still strong. Finally, Eric found a four-foot piece of heavy steel rebar that was three inches thick standing in an outside corner. It was the largest and thickest piece in what looked like a stack of forgotten scrap metal.

It took a couple of hard swings, but the weight of the rebar was enough to finally break through the latch on the door to the back of the loading dock. The heavy hardwood door swung inward on hinges not accustomed to such sudden and violent movements. The top hinge seized, but the door's momentum was too much to stop, and the metal bands snapped. The door smacked the wall of the hallway it opened into and rebounded back at Eric, but he caught it with his foot.

Eric stood holding the door with his foot, listening for any movement or sign of life from the inside. After a long moment, he nodded to the others. "I don't hear anything. Come on."

Eric leaned the rebar against the corner of the wall just inside the door and then turned to grab his bottle, his glass, and his backpack. He led the others into the dark interior of the school, his flashlight in one hand and his pistol in the other. Eric and the others all had their bows hanging from the shoulder straps. In a close fight, they needed something with a little more actual firepower, so each of them carried handguns at all times.

The loading dock door opened into a short hallway that had only one exit into the back of the kitchen. This part of the school was dark with very few windows. From the front of the school, the cafeteria and lunchroom were below ground level. From the back of the school, this was the ground level, designed that way to make for easy loading and offloading of supplies. Once they had made their way into the kitchen, the light was brighter from the windows along the front side of the lunchroom. Eric lowered his flashlight a little bit and paused as memories flooded over him again.

The tables and chairs were gone, and the floor had been pried up in several places. Ceiling tiles had collapsed in the back corner, and it smelled of old wetness. But Eric remembered it as it had been when he stood in line for lunch every weekday school was in

631

session. This was where he'd started the International Cheese Lovers Club of Boone Trail Elementary School in the third grade. The whole thing fell apart when everyone realized the only international cheeses they'd eaten were mozzarella and parmesan, and both were served on pizza twice a week.

Eric led them up the stairway that opened into the first-floor hallway. It was reassuring for him to see the same odd mix of sadness and nostalgia reflected in Brant's features. So much of their early life had been spent here, and those memories that had long since been given up for gone were floating back to the surface. It was too much to put into words, so Eric led them silently through the shadowy hallway past darkened classroom doors. The ceilings overhead were tall and arched, and the floors were thin planks of hardwoods polished with decades of flooring oil until they were such a deep, dark brown they looked black.

They rounded a corner and passed several more classrooms on the left. A large set of double doors on the right opened into the auditorium. Two aisles ran down a slow grade to a stage that was perhaps fifteen feet lower than the doors that opened into the hallway. A balcony overhead extended over the first five rows of seats. As a boy, Eric had wondered what it would be like to sit on the balcony with the auditorium full of people, but it had been off limits since before he was born. The chains across the twin stairwells had become permanent fixtures of the school to the point that they had rusted in place.

Eric led the group down the aisle to the stage. "This is it. We've got a roof over our heads, open space, and easy access to the outside. It's perfect."

"Perfect for what?" Jordan asked.

Eric gave a shrug. "I don't know. This is my first bachelor party, to be honest. I guess we finish the scotch and trade stories or something."

Brant smiled. "I've got a better idea." He reached into his backpack and rummaged around for a moment and then produced two new decks of cards and a small metal case holding poker chips. "Let's play some cards."

The four young men took a moment to spread their bedrolls around and get their things positioned in a rough circle in the center of the stage. They had brought a handful of small, battery-operated fluorescent lanterns that provided more than enough light to see their cards. Once they had everything in place, Brant passed out the red, white, blue, and green chips in even stacks.

"The game, fellas," he said as he shuffled one of the decks of cards, "is Texas Hold'em. No limits on bets. You can go all-in at any time. Small blind is one white chip, big blind is two white chips. Make the best five-card hand you can, and good luck. Let's play some cards."

Eric poured everyone another round of scotch as Brant dealt the first hand of poker.

Chapter 90

Borrowed

Christina stood in front of the tri-fold mirror in the corner of Nanny's bedroom, every angle of her reflected in the panes of glass around her and in miniature on the flat brass framing that connected them. Her mother Cheryl, her future mother-in-law Beth, and Nanny stood behind her, all beaming with pride and love. No one spoke. Tears were streaming down all four of their faces as they shared this moment. It was the first time she'd had her dress on since the final adjustments and alterations had been made a few days earlier, and it was so beautiful it took her breath away.

Beth Anne was standing in the doorway, smiling with a quiet, professional pride. She had been instrumental in making some of the more complicated alterations to Beth's and Nanny's old dresses. Elements of both had been combined to form a sort of hybrid contemporary, classic look.

The top third of the dress was stitched from the lace that had made up most of the outer layer of Nanny's dress. Beth Anne had fashioned that lace into a form fitting overlay that closed with hooks and clasps up the back. It covered Christina's shoulders, arms, and torso down to her waist. Beneath the overlay was a satin bodice that formed the inner support of the dress. The bodice was reinforced along the back seam where ribbon laces would allow it to open and close to an extent in an attempt to help support the weight of her growing belly. The skirt flared slightly when it came out of the bodice and was made from thick silk and satin layers over the frame of Beth's bell-shaped prom dress that had hung in her mother's closet for more than forty years. Christina loved the way that it swished when she turned and swayed.

As Christina was standing transfixed by her image, Nanny took a thin lace veil from the small oak box that Beth was holding. The flower and vine pattern perfectly matched the pattern on the lace overlay. She stepped up behind Christina and placed the veil on her head and pulled it over to cover her face.

"There," she said, patting Christina's shoulder with a weathered hand, "now you look like a bride."

"I don't know what to say," Christina said through sniffles and tears. "I never thought I could look so beautiful."

Christina wiped tears away and took a moment to regain her composure. Her hormones were taking advantage of the fact that she was already excited and on edge and they were playing havoc with her emotions. The dress looked like it had come from an expensive boutique or high-end bridal shop. Beth Anne had been more than modest when she described her skills with a sewing machine as simply okay.

Cheryl dabbed at her eyes with a tissue and turned to face the other women. "I just want to say thank you for taking care of my baby girl. Those words don't seem like enough, don't feel like enough. Not for what you've done for her. You took her in, gave her a home, this dress. Thank you just isn't enough for what I feel."

Beth smiled and put an arm around Cheryl's shoulders. "We're all just glad you're here now, in time for the big days that are coming."

"Well, the fabric may be something old, but the dress is new," Beth said to Christina with a smile.

"The veil can be your something borrowed," Nanny said.

Cheryl reached up and unclasped the only necklace she ever wore and nodded for Christina to lift her hair and turn around. Cheryl carefully clasped the thin necklace at the back of Christina's neck and let the pendant, a small pear-shaped blue sapphire framed in a cushion setting of white gold and tiny diamonds, sit on the outside of her shawl. The blue sapphire caught the blue in her eyes.

"Your father gave this to me on our wedding day," Cheryl whispered as she put her chin on Christina's shoulder and looked at her daughter's image in the mirror. "It can be your something blue. You are so beautiful, Christina. And I am so proud of you, honey, so very proud of you."

Christina couldn't find the words to reply, so she simply returned her mother's hug and felt herself sobbing again. After a moment, her mother stepped back and Christina straightened herself and wiped the fresh tears from her cheeks. The rest of the women were busy for a moment drying their eyes as well.

"Okay, sweetheart," Beth said, stepping forward, "now that we know everything fits and that you're going to be just about the most breathtaking bride ever in the history of brides, let's get all of this off of you before something tears or snags. We still need to eat supper and then we've got to start getting nails and hair started for in the morning."

Beth helped Christina lift the veil over her head and carefully replace it in the padded wooden case. "We'll pull your hair up in the back like you asked and maybe have one or two of your blonde curls down along the side of your face and down your neck. That sound about right?"

Beth pulled Christina's hair back and twisted it up with a couple of strands hanging down here and there in the front. Christina liked the way having her hair pulled up called attention to the sapphire from her mother. With that settled, they began the process of helping Christina out of the dress. Getting into and out of the contraption was difficult enough that she needed help. It was going to make using the restroom more than a little interesting tomorrow.

When Christina was finally back in her cutoff blue jean shorts and sleeveless yellow t-shirt, she looked over her shoulder at the door to the front part of the house with longing. "Are you sure I can't see Eric?" she asked again. "I mean, I get the whole don't let the husband see the bride on the wedding day thing, but we're not getting married until tomorrow. Why can't I see him today? Besides, it's not exactly like we're strangers," she said, placing one hand on her small, round baby bump.

"For one thing," Beth said firmly, "you're getting married at sunrise for some damn reason. So, you won't have a whole day to avoid seeing him, and that means that happens today. Consider it a test of will power. Besides, Eric's not even here right now. Men go through their own rituals before a wedding, just like us women. And what they do is their business, and what we do is our business. As long as everyone ends up at the right place at the right time, I think it's probably better that it stays that way."

Nanny stepped up next to Christina and patted her hand reassuringly. "Besides, honey, you'll have the rest of your life to spend with your husband," she said with a warm smile. "This is your last chance to spend time with just us ladies here, and there's another thing. You miss Eric right now, a great deal, and he misses you too. When you see each other tomorrow, it will be very special moment. You'll see a different look in his eyes when he sees you for the first time in your dress, with your hair and makeup and everything else exactly right. It will be a look unlike anything you've ever seen before, and you won't ever see that look again. It's one of the most special moments in a couple's life, honey. It's been more than fifty-five years now and I still remember the way Levy looked at me on that warm day in September and can't help but smile when I do."

Cheryl nodded in agreement. "And there will come a time when you will need that memory. You'll be in the middle of some big argument, fight, or whatever and you'll be so hurt and angry and disappointed that you're going to be at the end of your rope. And that's when you need the memory of that look in his eyes and the way tomorrow feels for you. You'll need to be reminded of that from time to time because you'll face some hard patches."

Cheryl squeezed her daughter's shoulders. "Things were tough for me and your father starting out as newlyweds. We were broke, didn't know what we were going to do for money, and both of us were still in graduate school. Our first Christmas together as husband and wife I traced pictures from a children's coloring book onto felt and decorated them, then sewed them together with cotton stuffing in the middle, poked a string through the top, and called it an ornament. We still hang some of them on the tree every year. But at the time, things weren't so good."

Christina knew the ornaments she was talking about, and she knew the story too. It was one her mother and father liked to tell sometimes while decorating the tree, or after presents had been opened Christmas morning. Hearing the story at some point during the holidays had become something of a family tradition. But this was the first time the story hadn't ended with the part about still hanging the ornaments.

"Your father and I had some problems early on, more than we ever let you know about before. Things got bad for a while, and then you came along and things got better. But for a while there it was touch and go, and one of the things that kept me holding on was the memory of those first days and that first Christmas together. We had nothing but each other and were content with what we had. I think for a long time we were chasing that feeling of contentment with happiness, and the two aren't the same thing. Learn to be happy with just each other, honey, and nothing else will matter."

Nanny pulled Christina over to the bed and they both sat down on the edge of the mattress. Nanny took both of Christina's hands and held them for a long time before she spoke. "There are going to be some lean, hard times ahead for you, dear," Nanny said after a moment, her high-pitched voice thick with emotion. "You and Eric are gonna have to learn to lean on each other a lot. I think it's going to be for you two like it was for my momma and daddy when I was growing up through the Depression. Momma and Daddy leaned on each other, and sometimes on the whole community, but they got by. And they helped others get by."

Nanny took a tissue from up her sleeve and dabbed a tear off Christina's cheek. "I know you're nervous about tomorrow," she continued without breaking stride. "And I know you're scared for the baby. But honey people been having babies a lot longer than they've had hospitals. We'll find a way to make it work. You'll see. We'll take care of y'all, don't you worry. You're already family, honey, even if you ain't quite said the words yet."

Christina put her arms around Nanny's tiny frame and gave her a warm hug. "When I thought about this day and dreamed about it," Christina said after a moment, "I imagined myself surrounded by friends from high school and college. Maybe a few of my close sisters from the sorority too. There would be a fancy sunset wedding and a massive party afterwards. But even if I could have had that dream wedding, I don't think I could have possibly felt one ounce more loved than I do right now."

Nanny patted Christina's hands. "Oh honey," she said with a smile, "we're just getting started. Now, let's talk about nail polish."

Christina couldn't help but laugh, and for just a little while the concerns and stress of the circumstances evaporated. For the time being she didn't have to worry about where their next meal would come from or if it would be safe from thieves and brigands when it came. She didn't have to wonder about sanitation and keeping everyone clean and healthy. She didn't even feel the worry and stress of wondering what the future would be like for her unborn child.

Right now, for this small moment, she was safe, she was loved, and she was cared for, and that was all that mattered.

Chapter 91

Echoes

Mike looked at his watch and chewed on his left thumbnail. It had been sixteen minutes since he heard the shots in the distance and the guards around the camp had gone tense. No one was expecting gunfire that close to this position. The surprise and worry were clear on every single face. The guards and sentries were professionals, though, and they quickly returned to their duties. The group might look like a rag-tag group of country boys, but they had good bearing.

As he watched the woods around him, Mike couldn't help but feel disgusted with himself. He had made a choice years before to become a rescue swimmer in the Coast Guard and had dedicated his life to saving the lives of others, often at great peril to his own health and safety. It was more than a career choice—it was his passion and his way of life. He had pulled people, gasping for breath, out of the water seconds before the end, and he'd lost some that he couldn't reach in time. But no matter what, he had done everything he could to save every single one he could.

And now here he was sizing up these young men, some of them little more than boys, and trying to gauge how many of them he could kill before they took him down. Odds are he could only get

641

two, maybe three, and that wouldn't be enough to buy the rest of his group time to escape. There was no way they could challenge the group outright because they were outnumbered more than two to one. He missed the numbers he'd commanded before their run-in with the town of Flint Hill.

Mike checked his watch again—eighteen minutes since the gunshots.

A twig snapped from the tree trunks off to Mike's left, and a familiar voice called, "Thunder."

The leader of the group guarding them, a young man named Shane, called out the response. "Flash."

Captain Tillman walked out of the woods, seeming to materialize out of thin air. A little behind him and moving only marginally less quietly, was a younger man that Mike hadn't seen before. The newcomer wore an official Navy combat uniform, though, and there were other men with them moving through the trees. Mike caught only glimpses, but he counted at least three other armed men in combat gear, bypassing most of the sentries without their even realizing it. They ranged out from the main group and in a matter of seconds were gone.

These were the real pros. Captain Tillman, Eric's father, strode through the camp with the calm confidence of a man who knew he was in charge. He wasn't flashy about it. He simply walked with a singular purpose and force that refused to be interrupted. Brant saluted the captain as he approached, and Tillman returned the gesture.

"How have our guests been behaving, Shane?" he asked bluntly.

"No incidents to report, sir. They've been quiet for the most part, although I get the feeling that a couple would like to talk if they got the chance. If nothing else, just to hear a stranger's voice for a while."

"Good job, Shane," Tillman said, patting the young man on the shoulder. "I'll take it from here for a while. You and your men go down to the creek and follow it to the river. Wait there for me and I'll come get you to come back to your post when it's time. If any of you brought snares or fishing lines, put them to use until I come get you. The more you catch the more you'll have to eat."

The younger men all moved off through the trees, making less noise than Mike would have thought possible for a group so large. They moved separated from each other, walking among the trees at odd intervals with each man picking his own path. By spreading out their ranks they made less impact on the landscape. If they had moved through in a single column the way they marched along the roads, then all of the damage to the leaf litter would have been concentrated in a tight ribbon along the forest floor. That would be easy sign for even a novice tracker to follow.

When they were gone, Joe turned to the four men that were still in sight. "Sweep the area once, make sure the sentries are in place, and report back," he said, and the men disappeared into the trees in two pairs. Once they were gone, Tillman turned back to Mike and motioned for him to follow as the captain walked away from the rest of the group's camp.

"There's a lot happening at once," Tillman said when they were a few dozen yards into the woods, "and I apologize if it feels like you and your people have been neglected. That's not what I intended, but when people look to you for decisions you have to be there to make them. Mike, Eric has vouched for you and so has Arthur, so you are guaranteed a place here."

Tillman paused, his expression unreadable for a moment. "The truth is, Mike, I don't really know you, but people I trust do. Even they don't know the people you're with, not really. I mean Arthur says they're all good people, but most of them you picked up on the road here. People who were desperate, and I get that, believe me. But desperate people will do whatever they need to do in order to survive, Mike, and that might mean masking who they really are."

Tillman gave a small shake of his head. "As a leader, I can't let my people be put at risk like that, but as a person I'm not going to just slam the door in their faces. They're going to have to go through the training camp like all of our local volunteers. It's a way to make sure everyone has common training as well as a way to weed out threats that might try to infiltrate our ranks."

Mike felt as if a great pressure bearing down on his back and shoulders had suddenly lifted. They were done with the road, done running, for at least a time. He had refused to let himself feel it until this moment, but he was bone weary from the road. His feet and legs ached constantly, and there was a gnawing hunger deep in his bones that he couldn't shake. Many days in a row of burning more calories than he was getting had taken their toll on him both physically and mentally. Only grim and stubborn determination had kept him from collapsing a long time ago.

"Thank you," Mike managed to say as he fought to control his relief and his gratitude. "We'll prove ourselves. You won't be sorry."

Tillman nodded. "In the morning, my men will escort your group back to the church where our training camp is located. They will get a good hot meal, and they'll be entered into the camp's log. All of their weapons will be inventoried, along with ammunition, but none of it will be taken. You should know, and you should let your people know, that we are at war. There's a no tolerance policy for criminal infractions. Anyone who robs others, assaults them, rapes them, or kills them is subject to immediate and summary execution on completion of a tribunal."

"Wait, what?" Mike asked, his shock more than a bit evident. "You're just shooting people? Jesus, this isn't the wild west."

"No, it's North Carolina. And yes, if someone is a threat to that extent, we will take them out, period. We can't afford not to, Mike. But listen, we haven't had to use this policy yet. It's in place so we hopefully won't have to."

"Listen, Mr." Mike paused and corrected himself, "Captain Tillman, that's just wrong."

The captain's jaw clenched as he met Mike's indignant glare. "And what do you suggest, Mike? Should we imprison rapists and give them food out of my kids' mouths to keep them alive? We can't afford that. Should we let them go and banish them with knowledge of our camp, our numbers, and our security? We can't afford that either. So, what option do we have, Mike? You tell me."

Mike stood in silence, unable to answer the ruthless onslaught of cold, calculated logic.

"I didn't think so," Tillman growled. "Have you seen the inside of the prisons since this started?" Tillman asked and then shook his head when Mike said he hadn't. "I didn't think so. People just closed the doors, locked them up tight, and left the inmates in most of them. Who knows how many people starved to death behind locked cell doors after the guards just stopped coming. All because when it finally hit the fan, society just couldn't afford to keep them alive anymore. Was that more humane?"

Tillman took a deep breath and visibly took control of himself. When he opened his eyes, and looked at Mike again, he was a mask of unreadable, controlled patience. "That's the last time you will question my orders, understood? I'm not here to debate command decisions with anyone, especially a fresh volunteer without a rank. If you don't like it, you and your group can go back the way you came, no harm no foul. But this is the way I run things, and if you want to be under my command, you have to get behind that. You have to get behind me. Understood?"

Mike nodded. "Yes sir."

"So, what's it going to be, Mike? Are you staying or are you going? Because I don't have time for the bull crap."

"I came all this way to join in the fight," Mike replied. "The real fight, not just randomly taking out FSS grunts here or there. I wanted to make a real impact, let them know what it felt like. I'm not about to tuck tale and run now."

"Good. I'm glad that's your decision. I wouldn't want to have to explain to Eric why you aren't at his wedding tomorrow."

"Eric's getting married tomorrow?" Mike asked, taken aback.

Tillman nodded. "And he wants you there with them. He said you helped them a lot early on and they wouldn't be here if not for what you and your partner did."

Mike snorted a short laugh. "It's more like I wouldn't be here if not for your son, Captain Tillman," he admitted. "I had no clue what was going on, but Eric remembered you and your talks with him years ago about what could happen. He's the one who told us we had to get out of town and fast, and he was right. I didn't listen to him, but he was right."

Tillman place a hand reassuringly on Mike's shoulder. "You'll get your chance to make them pay," he promised. "But right now, you need to go talk to your people and let them know that first thing in the morning they will be heading to a new camp to begin training. Make it quick, too. We don't have a lot of time, and I want to get you back to the farm before supper."

Mike nodded and walked back to the camp alone. The rest of his group was gathered in front of his tent, waiting. "All right, listen up," Mike began, and he explained what Captain Tillman had told him about the training camp and their policies. When he went over the part about the no tolerance for criminal activity, a lot of the people in the group started murmuring amongst themselves. "I know it's not what we're used to," Mike said. "But we're all good people here. As long as we keep to ourselves and do what we're told, there shouldn't be any problems. Just don't let things get out of hand, and if someone steps out of line don't try to handle it yourself. Report it first."

"What about you and Arthur?" Chip asked. "Where are you going to be?"

"I have to be at a wedding in the morning, believe it or not," Mike replied. "It's Arthur's daughter, Christina, and the guy who saved my butt when this whole thing started. After that, I'll come and join up with you at the camp. If you're going through training, then so am I."

Chip smiled. "A wedding? Does that mean we need to go find you a tux?"

The rest of the group laughed at the joke, and Mike joined them. They felt the relief too. He could see it. Already they were standing straighter, and they were drawing a new kind of strength from each other. He couldn't remember the last time they had shared a laugh and let the stress slip away.

For as long it lasted, it felt good to be off the road.

Chapter 92

The Last Hand

Nov. 12th 1845 EST

Eric looked at the two cards in front of him one more time and then checked the three cards in the middle. With the flop cards, he already had a straight from two to six. He pretended to consider the hand for another few seconds and then casually tossed in twice the minimum bet. One by one the other three players folded, and Eric raked in the chips to add to his lead. If the cards kept coming in his favor, he would be able to take out at least one and possibly two of his competitors before long, and then it would be him and Brant heads up again.

Two of the three games they'd played so far had come down to him and Brant, but this time Eric was ahead in chips, which gave him the advantage. The last two times that had happened Brant had been in the lead, but they were still tied with Oscar at one game apiece. Eric had managed to come back from behind once, and he was hoping that now that he was in the lead he would be able to break their tie.

The bottle of scotch was more than two thirds gone, and they each had a healthy buzz going, but they weren't drunk. At first, they had exchanged stories and laughed at the memories, but they'd been silent for a while now. With the good memories inevitably came the memories of people, friends and loved ones they all had lost.

As Oscar took his turn shuffling the cards and dealing them, Brant spoke for the first time in a dozen hands. "Are you nervous about tomorrow, Eric? Or scared?"

Eric shook his head. "I thought I would be. I thought I would be terrified of it, but I'm not. I guess more than anything I'm excited and anxious to get it done. We've been waiting so long and talking about it and planning it. I mean it's not going to be anything like what we thought when we started seriously thinking about it a year ago. But it's still going to be me and Christina saying the vows, and when it comes down to it, I guess that's all that really matters to me."

Brant reached over and patted Eric on the shoulder. "I'm happy for you, man, and jealous, but mostly happy."

Eric smiled. "Thanks, and don't worry, we'll find a wife for the rest of you, eventually. After all, it's going to be up to us to repopulate, right?" Eric said jokingly.

Brant nodded, his face serious. "You're right, man. If we're going to have any hope, we'll have to build our numbers back up."

"I was just kidding around," Eric said, "but you're right. My dad's focused on the war and on survival, which is good, but if we don't have a next generation, then what are we fighting for anyway? You three better get serious about finding a wife, soon."

"And where do you suggest we look?" Oscar asked.

Eric snorted a short laugh. "That's up to you guys," he replied with a grin. "I've already found mine."

The conversation died down again as the cards were dealt. Several hands passed with the guys folding to the big blind, refusing to risk more chips than absolutely necessary. Finally, Eric found himself in the small blind with one white chip, and his pocket cards were an ace and a jack of clubs. Both of the brothers had tossed in two white chips, and Eric decided to slow play his hand by simply calling the blinds. Brant, who had paid the big blind that hand, checked and Oscar dealt a card that was burned and placed it face down to the left. Three cards face up made the flop a ten and an eight of clubs with a two of diamonds.

Eric checked, and the bet went untaken all the way around the table. Oscar burned another card and put the fourth card, called the turn, face up in the middle. It was a five of clubs, completing Eric's flush. He knew he had the best possible hand, but still he checked to Brant. This time, Brant raised, and then Oscar immediately went all in. Oscar had more chips left than Justin, so Justin went all in to call him. Eric called Oscar's bet, and Brant folded. The action happened so fast that, in a blink, two of the players were all-in and at Eric's mercy.

Oscar burned a card and turned the last card over, the king of diamonds. The river couldn't help anybody, and since they were all in already and Eric had called the bet, it was on him to flip over his cards. He turned over his ace and jack of clubs for the flush, and both of the other players groaned. Oscar flipped over two pair, Jacks and twos, and Justin flipped over three eights, but neither had enough to beat Eric's flush.

The deal went to Eric this time, and he paused before shuffling the cards. "Listen, guys, this has been fun," he said, "but I think I'm ready to go back. I know we're supposed to be out all night and everything, but that's just where my head's at. I think I'm ready to go home and get ready to get married. So, Brant, I say we let the next hand be the last hand."

"Your call, Eric. We're here for you, man. If you're ready to go back, we'll go back. We don't have to play another hand."

"Yeah, I think we do," Eric insisted. He shuffled the cards and dealt them each two. "You are too much like me, Brant, and if we leave this undecided in a tie, it'll eat at the both of us. One way or another, someone's got to win it."

Brant nodded, and they each checked their cards. Brant pushed his cards all in and Eric immediately called. They flipped them over at the same time. Brant had the ace of hearts and two of spades, and Eric had a pair of threes, the three of hearts and the three of clubs. For the moment, Eric was ahead, but Brant's ace had him seriously worried. All it would take would be for one of the other three aces to fall and Eric would be all but assured defeat.

Eric took a deep breath, burned a card, and placed the three-card flop on the stage in front of him. The flop was the ace of diamonds, two of clubs, and three of diamonds. Eric had locked in three of a kind to beat Brant's two pair, but Brant could still make a full house and beat him. Since they both were all in, there was nothing for Eric to do but burn a card and place the turn card on the stage. It was a jack of diamonds and no help to either of them.

"This is it," Brant said, "last chance for a river boat."

Eric smiled as he burned a card and turned the last card, often called the river, face up on the stage. It was a king of spades. Eric's three of a kind had held out against Brant's two pair.

"Good job, Eric," Brant said, "that was a good hand to end it on, I think. Now, are you ready to go get married?"

Eric smiled. "Yeah, I think I am," he answered.

"All right, then, buddy," Brant said, pulling Eric up to his feet, "let's get you home."

Chapter 93

Welcome Senator

Nov. 12th 1850 MST

Commander Price stood inside the OCC, staring at the maps on different wall displays. Colonel Darius was holding his new position outside of Goldsboro, waiting for the FSS army to get closer to the North Carolina, Virginia border before moving again. Marcus and his group were still holding about an hour west of the Tillman farm and Bennett, North Carolina. And, most importantly, the enemy advance seemed to have stalled in the middle of rural Virginia.

He had positioned the pieces as best he could, and now it was time to wait and see how they played out in the coming confrontation. He could do little to change it now that he had handed command over to Captain Tillman. There were six people in the room with him working various tracking and signal stations. They represented nearly a quarter of the entire shift that kept the basic systems at the facility running.

There were seventy-two technicians rotating through three shifts. This was about the least number of personnel Price felt he needed to safely run the facility, and he didn't plan to downsize the staff any further. If anything, he was contemplating pulling some more of the security teams back from their field positions. It was becoming clear that the enemy had invested little in establishing a foothold in the Central Plains states and had focused most of their

653

effort on the East Coast. The West Coast was still essentially dark to him, and if Price could deploy some units across the Rockies to begin gathering data there, the information would be helpful.

Just the day before, one of the satellite communications techs had reported making brief contact with a weather satellite over the Anchorage area. Apparently, a good portion of the Pacific Fleet was at anchor there riding out a nasty early-winter storm. Before long they would have to make a decision about whether they were going to head south for the winter or head back out and try to make the trip all the way to Hawaii.

Price was nudged out of his thoughts by the chief. "Sir, they're at the gates."

Price nodded. "Get the security detail assembled and have them meet us at the main gates."

The chief nodded and stepped back out of the room, already speaking into the small communications unit attached to his chest rig. By the time Price had closed out of the secure tracking programs, shut down all of his sensitive command protocol programs, and stepped out into the hallway, his security detail was waiting to escort him.

As Price moved through the corridors of the facility, the security detail formed up around him. Two men were in front and two behind, with another on each side of him. Of course, the ever-present chief was at his left elbow, but not quite within arm's reach.

When the group entered a new section of the corridor, motion sensors in the light banks overhead activated the lights. The same system shut the lights down after they'd passed, leaving the group in a travelling pocket of lit corridor amidst a river of darkness ahead and behind. It was a disconcerting effect overall and an unfortunate byproduct of the power saving systems in the sub-levels of the facility. The effect was less pronounced above ground as windows along the exterior walls allowed some natural light inside.

On a broad shoulder of the south ridge of the Henry Mountains, part of the high plateau had been artificially leveled and extended into the side of the mountain a few hundred feet. In the exposed bedrock face of the mountain, a set of massive exterior blast doors had been set, anchored into the solid granite. Three sets of redundant interior blast doors had to open before the massive gears on the exterior gates could begin the slow, arduous process of swinging the massive gates outward.

Price stood in the interior loading bay and keyed the necessary commands into an interface at the door. The alternating airlocks and blast doors lowered in sequence, opening a broad corridor that ended in the final exterior blast doors. Those massive gates began to swing slowly outward as he led the security detail forward.

By the time the gates were fully opened, Price and his guards were striding out into the early November evening. The air was cold, and his breath fogged in the crisp north wind. Waiting on the landing pad were two makeshift armored cars, commonly called technicals, and one Humvee. One was a modified pickup with a mounted .50-caliber machine gun on a swivel in the bed. Another was a Wrangler with a .30-caliber mounted on the light bar.

There were a dozen men arrayed around the vehicles, all of them armed except one. The middle-aged man in the center of the formation looked like he would rather have had a sidearm than a security detail. Several weeks of rough, unshaven stubble covered his cheeks and neck.

"Welcome, Senator," Price said without preamble, "to the Henry Mountains in Utah. This is the nerve center for the United

States National Defense Force. We are currently prosecuting a hostile war against the Federated State of America and against the Federal Security Services that operates as the military wing of the FSA, formerly under the command of a self-proclaimed President Hall. I think you're familiar with him."

Senator Coleman's eyes narrowed slightly and he hesitated. "You know I am," he growled. "The madman shot one of my colleagues right in front of me, almost *through* me. What is the point of this? I was told I was coming here as a guest. What the hell is this?"

"Senator Coleman, you swore an oath to a man who was clearly violating the Constitution," Commander Price replied, "and you violated the oath of office you took yourself. From where I am sitting, you stand accused of treason and dereliction of duty, unless you can present a convincing case otherwise."

"That's going to be tough," Coleman said coldly, "considering I saw in the rearview mirror a mushroom cloud rising over what used to be the nation's capital. And now you accuse me? I did what I had to in order to survive, sir. Did I say some words and sign a paper? Yeah, I did. And that kept me from getting shot through the heart on the floor of the Senate. You have no idea what Hall was like near the end. He was rabid. You could see it in his eyes. Every shred of humanity he once had was gone."

"From your perspective, you were in fear for your life and did what was necessary?" Price asked calmly, and Senator Coleman nodded. "I see. And how much more would you be willing to do if you thought the entire nation was in jeopardy? How far would you go if you thought that America itself was about to be erased from the face of the map, truly and permanently? Is there any limit to what you would do to save the nation if you could?"

The senator thought for a long time before answering. "Hypothetical situations are a waste of time and energy," he said finally.

Price shook his head. "This is no hypothetical situation, Senator. You said it yourself, there was a mushroom cloud over DC. And I put it there. I don't deny that. But so far everyone seems to think it was some act of monumental betrayal to launch such an attack against the nation's capital city. My defense is that it was a military necessity. We had just survived one attack with a man-portable nuclear weapon. Our backs were against a wall, and if we didn't act and act swiftly and decisively, there was a good chance the entire fighting force still loyal to the United States of America would be lost in the next attempt. I had no choice but to do what I did."

Coleman frowned. "Why are you trying so hard to convince me of why you did what you did? It's already done and over with, and you've clearly still got enough power to do just about whatever you want to at the moment. What do you care what I think?"

This time it was Price's turn to hesitate. He was suddenly unsure how much to reveal and how much to hold back. "I know that at some point I will have to answer for the strike on DC. I knew that when I made the decision to launch the missile, and I won't try to hide from that. I did what I had to do to protect the nation and the Constitution as my oath requires."

Price paused and took a deep breath before continuing. Much of his future depended on Senator Coleman's answer to his next question. If he'd misjudged the man, then this might all have been for nothing and could even be the final nail in his coffin when his inevitable tribunal occurred.

"I want you to represent me when that day of reckoning comes," Price said. "You were there. You saw the man yourself. You know how dangerous he was, how infected he was by his own lust for power. That man was already responsible for tens of millions of deaths when he tried to vaporize the US defense forces. One man willing to sacrifice himself so the rest of his brothers and sisters in arms could live is the only reason that attack failed. I couldn't wager that the same kind of providence would prevail the next time. Not when I had the means to decide the issue myself."

"You want me to help you prove that it was okay to nuke Washington, DC?" Coleman asked. "My name will go down with yours and Benedict Arnold's for all time if I do."

Price smiled. "Perhaps, but only if you lose. If you win you'll be remembered with the likes of John Adams. He got the British officers acquitted of the Boston Massacre, and they still made him president."

Coleman shook his head. "I don't want to be president. Don't even talk like that."

Price chuckled to himself. "Does that mean you'll take the job? Be my counsel?"

Coleman hesitated. "We've come a long way, Commander, as you are aware. If I say no are you going to abandon me out here in the middle of nowhere with nothing to survive on?"

Price shook his head. "You're welcome to stay here at the facility regardless of whether you represent me or not, Senator. The way I see it, you're the last remnant of the legitimate civilian government of Washington, DC, from before the Blackout. That earns you a seat at the table, if nothing else does, and with everything you've been through, that counts twice."

"Then I'd like some time to think about it before I make any commitment," Coleman replied, visibly relieved. "This is all a little overwhelming, to be honest, and I just need some time to process it."

"That's understandable. But you should understand that until you give me a reply, one way or the other, your access to certain parts of the facility and to the general staff will be severely limited. You have no security clearance to even know this place exists, despite your position as a senator, and that hasn't changed since the Blackout."

"Don't worry," Coleman replied with a cold, humorless smile, "I know what it's like to be locked in my quarters."

Price chose to ignore the barb and, instead, turned and motioned for them to enter the facility. The security team that had accompanied the senator across more than half the country remained outside. They would take the vehicles over to the hangar for maintenance and reload. Once the vehicles were secured, the men would be debriefed and given hot meals and warm beds.

Price's security detail expanded to include Senator Coleman, and they ushered him through the blast doors as Price turned and headed for the interior of the facility. When they all were back inside the corridor, Price entered the access keys and commands, and the blast doors began swinging closed. Coleman stood and, without comment, watched them.

When the doors were finally sealed, the senator heaved a heavy sigh of relief. "I never thought I'd be so happy to be inside someplace."

"Follow me and I'll show you to your quarters, Senator," Price said. "Later you can join me for dinner, and we can discuss your trip here."

Price didn't wait for Coleman to respond before he started down the long corridor. He had already exposed himself more than he was accustomed to by asking for the senator's help in the company of so many people. Unfortunately, though, there wouldn't be any getting around that. Until the senator accepted the role, he would be under guard, which meant whenever Price met with him, others would have to be present. At least this way there was no chance that some random person in the halls heard Coleman's decision first.

The last thing he needed right now was rumors among the staff about a pending trial or tribunal. Managing the staff's stress and anxiety levels was difficult enough without the constant fear of legal action. That weight was his alone to bear for the time being, and he meant to keep it that way.

Chapter 94

Father-Son Talk

Joe stood in the white sand road and waited. He could hear them coming down the quarter-mile-long driveway, laughing and joking. None of their words sounded too slurred, but they were still a ways off, so it was difficult to tell. The moon was high overhead, and slowly, four shapes resolved out of its dim light, and as they grew closer Joe could see Brant, Eric, Justin and Oscar, their packs with them, bows in hand.

Joe walked out to meet them. "Brant, you take Oscar and Justin on to the house. I need a minute with Eric. Take his pack with you if you don't mind."

The three young men gave Eric a pat on the back as they left, and Brant took Eric's pack for him. Joe led Eric back up to the paved Cutler's Run, and they turned down the highway. They walked in silence for a while, Eric following a little behind Joe but keeping pace. When they reached the point that Cutler's Run intersected Highway 902, Joe turned left and led Eric up the hill and around a curve to the first house, the McDougalds'.

Joe stopped in the driveway, hesitating for a few seconds before he spoke. "You know this house, Eric. The McDougalds were out of town visiting their son in Philadelphia when the Blackout happened. No one has heard anything from or about them, and at this point, I doubt they're coming home. With you and Christina starting out, you need a place of your own. You need that space and that privacy."

Joe reached into a pocket and pulled out a set of new keys that he handed over to Eric. "It's yours, son," he said. "I put the new locks on myself. There are six panels in the back, hooked into the house. It's not much, but it's enough to run a freezer or two, a window air conditioner, the plumbing, and a few LED lights."

Eric took the keys and stared at them in his hand for a moment. "I don't understand," he said after a moment. "You're giving me a house?"

Joe nodded. "Come on, I'll show you around," he said, putting an arm around Eric's shoulders and walking him to the front door. "The locks on the front and back doors match, and they're new, like I said. The original plan was to put three more clusters of solar panels in the back to give you a good surplus of power if you need it down the road. We thought we'd have another few weeks before the wedding, so we didn't have time to get them hooked up."

Eric unlocked the front door, and the two of them stepped inside. A pair of lamps in the living room to the right filled the room with a soft light from the LED bulbs. The couch and two loveseats were upholstered in simple brown leather. To the left of the foyer was an office with a large desk and a fireplace. A short hallway led to a large family room with another fireplace. The good-sized kitchen was connected to the family room and opened into a dining room that had a door into the hallway as well. There was a bathroom on the main floor and another upstairs with the three bedrooms.

The furniture was sturdy and tastefully upholstered. The walls seemed bare with all of the pictures taken down and the empty frames stacked against the walls. A few paintings and prints and one large wooden pendulum clock were placed around the rooms. The air smelled a little musty but not as bad as Eric had imagined it would, and it was comfortably cool in the house. The central air was working, for the moment, but they wouldn't be able to run it all the time. There were two window units, one in the family room and one in the master bedroom upstairs. Between the three systems and the two fireplaces, they should be set for climate control.

"I don't know what to say, Dad," Eric admitted when they had made their way back downstairs after the tour. "When did you even have time to put this together?"

"I had some of the guys and gals working on it here and there," Joe said with a sly half-smile. "While you were out on patrol or guarding the herd, we'd sneak a work crew out here to get some things done. Like I said, we thought we'd have a little more time, but it's definitely livable. And now you and Christina can put your own touches on it together, as a family, the way it should be with a first home."

Joe stopped in the kitchen and leaned against the refrigerator, facing his son. "Listen, Eric, it's never easy when you start out in a marriage. Your mom and I, we had some rocky patches early on, but most couples do. The thing is, things are going to be extra tough for you and Christina a few different ways. Not the least of which being you've got a kid already on the way. Things are going to be tough. There's just no getting around that."

Joe took a deep breath and tried to control the emotions that were thick in his voice. "Remember that your mom and I are always here for you two and so are Arthur and Cheryl. We're here for you, all of us, to help carry those burdens and help get you through the hard times. But most importantly, you've got to learn to lean on each other. You're going to need that support and that strength that only your wife can give you. Believe me, I know. There's no way I could do what I need to without your mom standing right there with me."

Joe stepped forward and put one hand on Eric's shoulder. "Son, the real reason I wanted to bring you out here tonight was just to let you know how proud I am of you, of the man you're becoming. All of the best parts of me I see in you, only better. If that makes any sense. I'm sorry, son, I'm not big on speeches, never have been."

"I don't know, Dad," Eric replied. "You seem to be doing pretty well to me. And you should know that everything I ever learned about being a man, a husband, and a father I learned from you. If you're proud of the man I am becoming, then it's because I had a good example to start with."

Joe pulled Eric in for a tight hug as he fought with the conflicting joy and pain of letting go of his son as a boy and accepting the fact that he was now a man in every sense of the word. It was a proud, yet painful, moment for Joe as a father.

"I love you, Eric," Joe said as he stepped back from the hug and dried his eyes. "Now, get a shower and get some sleep. I'll be back out here early, around first light, to bring you back to the farm. Tomorrow is going to be a long and joyful day, so try to get at least a little shut-eye."

Joe turned and stepped outside before Eric could answer, closing the door behind him. As he walked down the steps, he checked his carbine just to make sure he still had a round chambered. The rifle was on safety, as it always was when he was on the move and not under direct fire, but he liked to know that it was ready just in case.

It also gave his hands something to do while he tried not to focus on the fact that his little buddy, his son, was, in truth, on his own now. He had his own family, his own wife, his own child on the way. Somehow the little bundle of fingers and toes that came into his life in a hospital room one late January night in nineteen eighty-two was now a man.

Joe felt an odd mixture of pride and anguish, love and loss as he walked away from Eric's new home. They were beginning to expand the boundaries of the farm, which was important. Joe planned to control the entire county by the end of the new year, if possible. But that would take time. This first house was a test to see if his plan would work. If the systems integrated well, they would be able to set up homesteads all over the countryside. And more than military power, that's what the people were going to need come spring—farms.

Chapter 95

By The Power

Eric waited under the broad green canopy of a single massive oak tree that stood roughly in the center of the long, broad field to the left of the Tillman homestead. Eric wasn't sure how old the tree was, but it had been a towering giant for as long as he could remember. There were multiple photos of Eric's granddaddy standing in front of the tree, both as a young man and as an adolescent, and it was already a full-grown giant then. It was old, probably well over a hundred years old, and it had been a big part of his growing up.

Eric had played under that tree while his parents and grandparents worked the farm, first in the tobacco fields and then setting up the solar panels one pair at a time. After the farm had officially stopped raising crops for sale, there had been at least as much work to do, possibly more. It had started with the solar panels and then wells were dug and cisterns and sealed tanks were dug into the ground around the farmhouse. They had been in the process of fixing the old hog house at the bottom of the hill when the Blackout hit.

All the while, the oak tree had stood tall and strong in the field. And now, Eric was standing beneath it with his father in front of him and Brant to his right. Standing on the flat top of the field

666

drainage dike was the entire homestead group. They were split into two columns, and all were dressed in relatively clean, respectable clothes. Eric had seen each of them beaming as he walked in. Toward the back of the group was the thin, weathered man that looked like Mike, but he was twenty-five pounds leaner than Mike should have been. Bill waived at him with his left arm, showing off his growing range of motion, now that his gunshot wound had healed completely. And then came his family with his mother and his grandparents in the front row behind him and to his right. Cheryl was behind him on his left, across the aisle and on the front row.

His father, standing in his full dress white uniform, complete with gloves and cover, and his ivory-handled sword at his hip, smiled at him. The Bible he held was the one that Eric had given him years before—the same one he read every day on his job at JFCOM. For a moment, he looked more nervous than Eric had ever seen him, but then his eyes grew wide, and he smiled. Tears filled his eyes, and he turned to Eric and nodded.

Eric turned just as the first deep golden rays of sunlight broke over the tree line in the east. Everyone had turned to watch the bride, but Eric wouldn't have seen them even if they'd been facing him. For the moment, the only thing that existed in the world was Christina.

She stood framed in the soft golden sunrise, a bright smile dancing on her face. Her dress was stunning. As Arthur walked her down the aisle, Eric's eyes blurred with tears for a moment. He had always thought of her as pretty, even striking, but in that moment, he was completely and utterly floored as if it were the first time he'd ever seen her. She must have seen it in his face because she smiled and blushed prettily as she and her father neared the oak tree. When they reached Joe and Eric, Arthur stopped, and after another half step, so did Christina.

Joe cleared his throat. "Who gives this woman to be married to this man?"

"Her mother and I," Arthur replied. He turned to Christina and cupped her face in both of his hands for just a moment, and then he leaned over and kissed her cheek through her veil. He wrapped his arms around her and whispered in her ear.

When he finally stepped back, Arthur turned and placed Christina's hand in Eric's. He walked over to stand by Cheryl and pulled a handkerchief from his back pocket to dry his eyes. Christina paused just long enough to wipe two large tears from the corners of her eyes. Then she let Eric take her other hand as well.

Eric knew his father was talking, but he wasn't sure exactly what he was saying. All he could think about was how beautiful Christina was and how much he loved her. When the time came, Joe had to nudge him to remind him it was his turn to say the words.

Eric smiled. "I do," he said, and Christina laughed, another tear trickling down her cheek.

She said, "I do," when it was her turn, but Eric was positive she hadn't really heard the question.

"Then, by the power vested in me by your mutual love and trust, and before God and all of these witnesses, I now pronounce you husband and wife."

Those words Eric heard loud and clear. For him, at that moment, time seemed to grind to a halt. Everything crystallized into one instant of pure clarity, and his brain scrambled to catalogue every minute detail. He would always remember the way the sun danced in the sapphire and diamond pendant around Christina's neck and mirrored the sparkling blue of her eyes. He would remember the way her golden curls were pulled back and up into a tight nest at the back of her neck, only a few stray strands hanging down on either side of her face, framing it perfectly. The way her face glowed with love would forever be etched in his mind and on his heart.

He breathed in and let that breath out slowly, his first as a married man.

"Eric, son, you may now kiss your bride," Joe said finally.

Eric wrapped his arms around Christina, pulled her close to him, and kissed her slowly and tenderly. Then he pulled back and, with a huge grin and teary eyes, said, "Wife."

"Husband," Christina replied, her hands on either side of his face.

They kissed again, and their family and friends cheered and clapped and whistled. After a moment, Eric and Christina turned to wave at the crowd. They ran down the aisle as people tossed handfuls of glitter scavenged from the new elementary school down the street from old Boone Trail.

When they reached the end of the aisle, they stopped and kissed again. This time the kiss was longer and more passionate, and at the end Eric held Christina close to him and felt her cry tears of joy and relief against his chest. Neither of them said a word because neither of them had to. For the moment, all was right with the world, and they were more than just content.

No matter what tomorrow might bring to them, or heap on them, right now they were together, they were happy, and that was all that mattered.

Epilogue

Battle of Bear Creek

Nov. 16th 0745 EST

Eric shifted his weight slightly to his left and felt blood rush back to his right foot, making it tingle and itch. He resisted the urge to stomp his foot against the metal bottom of his tree stand, though it was tempting. He wasn't deer hunting, so he didn't have to remain perfectly motionless and quiet, but it would be best if he didn't draw attention to his position. Thirty-five feet up an old hickory tree long the side of Howard's Mill Road, he was too exposed to risk being seen and blowing the whole operation.

Four hundred and fifty feet down the road was the concrete and steel bridge across Bear Creek, their chosen ambush point. He couldn't see it from this distance, but Eric knew there was a spike strip stretched across both lanes of the highway. They'd scavenged it from a local police department, and placed about two thirds of the way across the bridge.

If everything went according to plan, at least one, possibly two, of the trucks would roll over the spike strip, disable their tires, and form a natural road block at the end of the bridge. The other two or three trucks in the rear would be trapped. That's when Eric would strike, taking out the driver of the back truck, creating a boxed in kill zone. At that point, the flanking elements on both sides of the bridge would take over and eliminate any remaining targets on the bridge.

Eric's only real orders were to take out the rear driver, but he had also been given the green light to take out targets of opportunity as he saw fit, so he planned to stay on his rifle until the last threat was neutralized. From his elevated position, he would be in a perfect position to provide cover fire for the flanking attackers.

The plan was the result of a group effort on the part of Eric's father, Commander Attledge, and Bill, the former Texas Ranger. Chris had wanted to be a part of it, but he was in charge of the rear guard back at the cow pasture. If things went sideways at the ambush and Joe's group came under threat, then Chris and his rear guard would be called in via short-wave radio, and since he wasn't going to be in the action, he'd excused himself from the discussion.

Eric cupped his hands to his face and blew into his fingerless gloves to warm his fingertips. It was starting to get quite cool in the mornings, and he didn't want stiff fingers when it came time to pull the trigger.

Just then, on the edge of his hearing, Eric caught the unmistakable sound of diesel engines. He shifted his weight again, moving to make sure that the tree trunk would be between him and the enemy convoy as the trucks approached. Once they passed him, he'd have a clear shot at their backs, but for now he had to make sure that the tree was hiding his frame or they might lose the element of surprise.

Eric huddled as small as he could in the lightweight two-piece deer stand. He couldn't see his outline in the shadow cast by the tree he was sitting in, which was a good sign. Behind him, the sound of the engines grew louder as the trucks grew closer, until Eric heard the swooshing sound of a passing vehicle as the pickups sped by one by one. There were five trucks in all, and the first two had men in the beds, but they appeared to both be sleeping.

As the last truck passed him, Eric reached into his pocket and pulled out a small two- way radio. He clicked the transmit button on the side twice to send a signal to the rest of the team that the targets were moving into the kill zone. He positioned Tom's sniper rifle on the gun rest and flipped up the caps on the scope. With his right thumb, Eric clicked off the safety and began slowly and deeply breathing, getting his heart rate and breathing in sync.

The lead truck was rolling over the bridge when, suddenly, it hit its brakes. The driver must have seen the spike strip, but he was going too fast to stop. There was a loud pop as all four of the truck's heavy tires blew out, and it screeched sideways to slam into the concrete wall on the left side of the bridge.

The second truck slammed on brakes as well, but it was following too close to the lead vehicle and it too ran directly over the spike strip with all four tires. The last three trucks managed to stop before they hit the trap, though just barely for the third truck in the line. For a moment, none of the people in the trucks moved as they sat in stunned silence. Then the passenger riding in the bed of the lead truck slowly climbed to his feet, one hand holding his head. Eric was watching through the scope on his rifle as the man's hand came away from the back of his head stained with blood. The man climbed out of the bed of the truck, stumbled, and collapsed onto the pavement.

The second truck had stopped just before crashing into the back of the first one, and the two men in the cab climbed out to check their tires. The man in the bed of the second truck hopped out as soon as the truck stopped moving. He ran over to the man bleeding on the pavement, a medical bag in his hand.

Eric focused on his breathing.

The last truck slowed and finally stopped twenty feet back from the end of the bridge. The other four trucks were actually on the concrete span, and the men were getting out and looking around in confusion. The driver for the rear truck rolled down his window and stuck his head out to yell something.

Eric breathed out half of his breath and held the rest.

The man leaning out the window of the truck paused, and for a moment he was still as he listened to the men up at the wrecked first truck shout back.

Eric squeezed the trigger.

The rifle report was muffled from the two-foot-long suppressor on the end of the barrel. Eric's aim was true, and driver of the rear truck jerked as the round entered the back of his neck at the base of his skull. It was an instant kill shot, and the man never had a chance to feel the bullet. For a moment, all of the men on the bridge stopped dead in their tracks, their faces turned towards the vehicle at the rear of the convoy.

Suddenly, everything happened at once. The man in the back of the second truck leveled his rifle in Eric's direction, scanning for a target, so Eric's next round took him just to the right of the center of his chest. The man slumped forward, his rifle slipping from his hands. The passenger in the rear truck opened his door and spun out with a carbine in his hands. Eric heard rounds snapping through the trees around him as the men on the bridge opened fire.

Then, just as Eric felt the cold, sinking fear of death grip him, four soldiers burst from the trees on either side of the road at the end of the bridge. They opened fire in coordinated bursts at the same time that six more men attacked from the other end of the bridge. In a matter of seconds, the brief burst of fighting was over, and there was an eerie silence that settled over the road.

The man who had climbed out of the bed of the lead truck struggled to reach his rifle, a half-applied bandage hanging from his bloodied head.   Eric watched as one of the soldiers from the commander's group walked up, calmly leveled his sidearm at the injured enemy, and pulled the trigger three times.

Eric closed the caps on the ends of the long-distance scope and clicked the safety to the safe position. The battle of Bear Creek was over. Eric's fingers were shaking as he tied the thin para-cord rope around the sniper rifle and lowered it to the forest floor. Once the weapon was secure, he began the process of descending the tree.

First, Eric faced the tree trunk and sat on the curved gun rest so he could slip his feet into the harnesses attached to the lower section of the tree stand. He picked his feet up, and the bottom section lifted away from the tree. Eric extended his legs as far as he could and then pressed his feet down, causing the angled teeth on the front edge of the stand to grip into the tree trunk. Eric test his weight on the bottom section, then stood on it and lowered his safety rope. Next, he picked up the top section of the stand and lowered it so he could once again sit comfortably.

Eric repeated the process, climbing down the tree four to five feet at the time. It was a laborious process, but it went rather quickly. Still, by the time he was standing on the leaf litter of the forest floor, he was sweating and out of breath. He wiped his forehead clean and climbed out of the tree stand, untied the safety line that secured his rifle to the metal frame, and then untied the rope that tied the two halves of the tree stand together. Once those ropes were removed, Eric unlatched the cables that held each half of the stand to the trunk and stacked the top half in the bottom half.

The two safety ropes tied the stand together, and there were straps through the bottom of the stand that let Eric wear it as a backpack. He stood, shifted the weight of the stand until it was comfortable on his shoulders, and then picked up his rifle. With great difficulty, he made his way through the fifteen yards of woods between his tree and the edge of the road. The stand was meant to be used on trails or in deep woods, but in the dense underbrush that grew along the verge of the highway, it was difficult to navigate without getting caught on small scrub trees or tangled in painful briars.

By the time Eric broke through the trees and onto the blacktop, his face and arms were scratched, and the transport team had already arrived and loaded all of the supplies on the ATVs. Captain Tillman was coming up the highway toward him, a grim smile on his face.

"We did well," Tillman said. "You did well, son. We took out the whole enemy force without a single casualty. We captured rifles, handguns, ammunition, and enough water, food, and medical supplies to keep our tactical teams going for a month or more in the field."

Eric nodded, wishing he felt better about what they'd just done. "What's next?"

"Next, we take Commander Attledge and his men, and we liberate Bennett," Tillman said. "Then we get ready for what's coming. We get ready for all-out war."

There wasn't much that Eric could think to say in response, so he simply held the rifle out to his father, but Tillman shook his head. "You hang onto it, Eric. You're the best shot of anyone I've seen since Tom himself. And given what's coming, you're going to need it again."

Eric sighed heavily, but kept the rifle. He followed his father across the bridge as the last of their soldiers began dousing the bodies and trucks alike in diesel fuel. Everything that could be scavenged from the scene of the ambush had been, and now it was time to destroy the evidence. As the rest of them cleared the bridge, one last soldier poured a trail of diesel fuel down the road fifty feet. Then he screwed the top on the gas can tightly, handed it to one of his partners, and lit a road flare he pulled from his back pocket. The soldier tossed the road flare onto the fuel trail, and the flames raced back toward the bridge.

With a whoosh, the pile of bodies and trucks burst into flames so intense that, from a hundred feet away, Eric could feel them drying the sweat on his back. Just up the road from the bridge, a group of ATVs and Strykers waited to carry the assault team home. As he loaded the tree stand and sniper rifle into one of the Strykers, Eric cast a last glance at the raging inferno on the bridge and the towering column of thick, black smoke climbing into the early morning light.

<u>Character List</u>

Alphabetical by last name

Arnold, Daniel: Hall's second in command. Daniel served as Hall's personal assistant and secretary years ago when the two first met. He was then promoted several times through Hall's personal organization and helped Hall run three failed election campaigns. Eventually it was Arnold who convinced Hall to pursue civil service rather than election, and Arnold who steered him towards a career in Homeland Security. Arnold is one of the few people left alive that Hall feels he can even partially trust.

Attledge, Marcus: Commander Price's second in command. Attledge was never in the military. He began working for Price as part of the team constructing and managing the data systems at the Facility. Since the Blackout he was drafted into the National Defense force and given the rank of   Lt. Commander. He serves as Price's second in command and has been integral to coordinating resistance efforts.

Boltzman, Chris: Former Air Force Special Ops worked as a battlefield medic. Was with Joe in the watch room when the Blackout occurred. Brought his wife and young child with them out of Norfolk south to the Tillman homestead.

Boltzman, Meg: Chris's wife. Meg helped the group get out of Norfolk with a Humvee for transportation. She has also helped with the children and upkeep of the homestead.
Chris and Meg's kids: 1) Mary Boltzman (2)

677

Brecken, Tom: Co-worker of Joe's, former special operations military. Was with Joe in the watch room when the Blackout happened. Left Norfolk with Joe and took refuge with his wife and children at the Tillman homestead. Has helped with security since.

Brecken, Jen: Tom's wife and mother to their four children. She fled Norfolk with her family shortly   after the Blackout event and has been a vital part of the homestead since. Since four of the children are hers, most of her time is spent watching over the children at the homestead. She organizes classes, teaches basic education, and helps with other chores.

Tom and Jen's kids: 1) Trey Brecken (11)
2) Matthew Brecken (8)
3) Sarah Brecken (6)
4) Elisha Brecken (3)

Buchannan, Mike: One of two park rangers present at the park where Eric and Christina witnessed the Blackout EMP attack. Mike helped the group get out of the park and evade capture. Mike chose to remain in Charlotte when Eric left so he could find Claire's daughters and let them know how their mother had died. He has taken shelter with a small group of refugees at the White Water Center in Charlotte.

Campbell, Arthur: Christina's father. Arthur is a former veterinarian from Charlotte. He met up with Mike's group at the White Water Center and has been with them ever since. He helped nurse Mike back to health after an infected gash on his arm nearly killed him.

Campbell, Cheryl: Christina's mother.

Campbell, Christina: Fiancé of Eric Tillman. Christina was with Eric when the Blackout occurred. She left Charlotte with him, leaving behind her parents and the city where she was raised. She helps with the gardening and food preservation at the homestead. She is also teaching the younger children basic reading, writing, and arithmetic.

Coleman, Shawn: Senator from Kentucky. Another surviving member of the old Congress, Coleman is more of a go along to get along kind of person who has been intentionally keeping a low profile. His principles don't align with the FSS or their agenda, but he also doesn't want to risk his own life for those principles. Not yet, anyway, though he accepts it may come to that. He is forced to participate in a sham trial of Senator MacArthur against his will, though he does his best to fulfill his duties.

Daley, Bill: Former Texas Ranger, was at the park where Eric and Christina were camping when the Blackout happened. Bill provided transportation out of the park for the group, and he was shot at a convenience store. Eric saved his life with a quirk of historical battlefield triage, packing sugar into the wound to stop the bleeding. Probably saved Bill's life. He has been with the group ever since.

Daley, Imogene: Bill's wife. Former EMT with over 40 years of experience. However, she was overcome with shock at Bill's injury when he was shot. Helped later with some of the various medical issues.

Darius, Charles: Colonel US Army (active). Col. Darius was the commandant of an Army Special Operations survival skills training facility in Idaho until the Blackout. He received word from Cdr. Price that resistance efforts were underway in response to the attacks and he answered the call to serve as one of the battle field commanders of the NDF. Col. Darius is a seasoned warrior and tactician with decades of front-line experience.

Davis, Carlton "Chip" : Young man who survived in Charlotte by sheltering in a pharmacy. Former student at CPCC in the college transfer program. Isolated for most of the time since the Blackout. Offered shelter to a young woman, Jess, who worked at the gas station next door.

Demetrius, Gauge "Cage": Former inmate in a state prison, Cage's cell doors opened after a lightning strike sparked the electric security system just enough to trip the breakers. Cage met Eric and Joe on the road and has been with them ever since. He is Levy's close companion and friend now, learning much about fishing, hunting,

trapping, and farming from the elder veteran. Since committing a
crime of passion as a young man, Cage has sworn a vow of
nonviolence before God and he takes it very seriously. He also
knows most, if not all, of the Bible by heart.

Fitzpatrick, Nicholas "Chief": Master Chief Petty Officer US Navy SEALs.
He was assigned to be Lt. Commander's personal bodyguard after
an assassination attempt nearly took the young officer's life. He
has served as Commander Price's personal body guard since
Commander Attledge was sent into the field.

Gandry, Gilbert: Beth-Anne's elderly father. Former farmer who sold his
land due to tax debts and pressure from encroaching
industrialized farms and mass-production subdivision housing.
Gilbert is a veteran of both World War II and Korea. He also has
decades of experience farming and homesteading. He is a skilled
hunter and fisherman, though his eyesight is failing.

Gandry, Maimey: Beth-Anne's elderly mother. Experienced farming and
raising chickens and rabbits for food. She is a skilled hunter and
can still hit a squirrel in the head at fifty yards with a .22lr.
Maimey also worked as a midwife's assistant and briefly as a
midwife in her younger days.

Grayson, Danny: A resident of the area around Bennett and near the
Tillman homestead. Danny was caught stealing beef from Brant's
herd shortly after the Blackout. Joe and Danny worked out a deal
and the two have been trading since. Danny agreed to help Joe in
his fight against the FSS detachment in Bennett.

Hagerston, Conrad: Colonel who is promoted to General and Field
Commander of the FSS. In command of the army that begins
marching south towards Fort Bragg. This is the first organized
military movement in the field from the FSS since the first days
after the Blackout event. Hagerston is eager to prove himself in
combat.

Hall, Phillip: Self-declared President of the newly christened Federated
State of North America. Hall is the apparent mastermind behind
the attack that resulted in the Blackout. A former Under Secretary

of the Department of Homeland Security, he coordinated the attack and subsequent coup that overthrew the old US government. He was promised aid from Russia if he attempted his coup, but that aid never materialized. Hall consolidated power quickly and ruthlessly. He has been ruling through an iron-fisted FSS bureaucracy and military apparatus.

Henderson, Alexis "Alex": A young Marine who was working as an MP on base in Norfolk when the Blackout occurred. When Joe, Tom, and Chris decided they were going to take their families and flee the city, Henderson briefly tried to detain them. In the end, he joined Joe's group and has been with him ever since.

Jacobs, Betsy: Called "Aunt Betsy" by practically everyone on Cutler's run except for those in her immediate family. She is elderly, but far from frail. A strong farmer's widow who runs her own farm despite being in her late seventies. She is the matriarch of the Jacobs family, the other extended family that shares the Run with the Tillman-O'Quinn family.

Jacobs, Paul: Aunt Betsy's son and Steven Jacobs' father.

Jacobs, Steven: One of the young men who lives on Cutler's Run with his family. Stephen volunteered early on to help out with security at the homestead. He has helped serve guard duty and patrols and is now a member of the National Defense Force.

Masterson, Greg: The leader of the FSS group in control of Bennett. He is reclusive and rarely comes   out into open view of the public, but his orders are followed unquestioningly by his men and the same is expected of the rest of the subjects in Bennett.

MacArthur, Timothy: Senator from Tennessee. One of the few surviving members of the former Federal Government of the United States. He decides to take a principled stand in support of the Constitution when pressed into service in the newly assembled Federal Senate, the sole legislative body in the new government.

MacPhail, Benny: Pharmacist and owner of MacPhail's Pharmacy in Bennett prior to the Blackout. Joe confronted a desperate mob in front of the store shortly after the Blackout and though Joe later looted Benny's inventory, he also saved the pharmacist from the angry mob. The two parted on less than friendly terms, however.

Marsha: Former store manager at Lowe's Hardware in Bennett. She is now the leader of a small group of survivors that has taken refuge in Lowes. They have used generators to power parts of the store, but keep the interior of their domain a closely guarded secret.

McCarthy, Alyssa: Daughter of Claire, Mike's partner. Alyssa lived on the north side of Charlotte in the Lake Norman area. Mike went in search of her after her mother died shortly following the Blackout EMP attack. She has been with Mike ever since.

McCarthy, Claire: US Park Ranger. She took charge at Crowder's Mountain State Park and helped organize the evacuation of the campers. She also saved Eric's life when a man drew a gun on him the morning after the Blackout. Claire was killed when an air strike destroyed the Buster Boyd Bridge over Lake Wylie. She is survived by her two daughters.

McCarthy, Maria: Younger daughter of Claire, Mike's partner. Mike and Alyssa rescued her from an FSS refugee camp in the Steele Creek area of Charlotte shortly following the Blackout EMP attack. She helped Alyssa, Arthur, and Cheryl nurse Mike back to health after a gash on his arm became severely infected.

McCormick, Terrence: Young man who helped Maria in the refugee camp. He joined with Mike and the sisters after the FSS camp, but left with most of the group when Mike fell gravely ill from an infected arm. He hasn't been seen or heard from since.

O'Quinn, Blanche: Mother of Beth Tillman. A survivor of the Great Depression, Blanche is a source of strength and wisdom for the homestead. Her knowledge of food preservation and other home craft help the group survive through the winter. She also has a deep knowledge of folk medicine and herbal remedies available from the forest.

O'Quinn, Levy: Father of Beth Tillman. Levy is a World War II veteran
    and a lifelong farmer. His   knowledge of farming, food
    preservation, fishing, hunting, trapping, and stone knapping will
    be invaluable. Levy defers to Joe's judgment in most things
    concerning the war, but he still exercises his authority when it
    comes to the farm and general principles. He attempts to pass on
    as much knowledge as he can to his family and to the refugees at
    the homestead.

Paglio, Micah: A boy from Flint Hill. He is injured and Arthur has to break
    off his negotiations with Sue Ellen to attend to the boy. The
    incident is a major turning point for both groups.

Price, Terry: Commander US Navy (retired). Former member of the
    SEAL team member and Naval Academy graduate. Price attended
    the academy with Joe and they went through BUD/s together.
    Price served under Joe in the SEALs. He then became the
    commanding officer at the Utah Facility. Commander Price has
    been directing resistance efforts and commanding loyalist US
    forces against the FSS since the Blackout.

Prichard, Sue Ellen: Elderly woman who is the de facto leader and public
    face of the Flint Hill community. She meets Arthur on the road
    and the two begin negotiations of a sort. Despite her small size
    and advancing years, Sue Ellen is still strong and active, with an
    acute mind.

Ramirez, Justin: One of two brothers who were close friends of Brant
    Thompson before the Blackout. They attended college together.
    Justin is the younger brother by 18 months. He follows his older
    brother's lead in most things, but the two often butt heads on
    smaller issues. Justin helps out around the homestead with farm
    chores and hunting/gathering food.

Ramirez, Oscar: One of two brothers who were close friends of Brant
    Thompson before the Blackout. They attended college together.
    Oscar is the older brother by 18 months and is the leader of the
    two. Oscar helps with work around the farm as well as helping
    with security of the homestead and the herd.

Richards, Beth-Anne: Single mother who lived on a farm in Southern Virginia. One of her sons fell and broke his arm the day of the Blackout. Joe was flagged down and Chris set the young man's arm so it would heal. After initially being left at their home, Joe later returned and persuaded the   family to evacuate for their own safety. She has helped at the homestead with farming, food preservation, child-care, and general work.

Beth-Anne's kids: 1) Shawn
2) Steven: Boy who broke his arm the day of the Blackout

Sgt. Macon: An assistant to Colonel Darius and part of his command cadre. Sgt. Macon is a trusted advisor and was one of the men at the Colonel's wilderness survival training school prior to the Blackout. He is an active duty Army Special Forces Operator with combat experience in Afghanistan, Iraq, and Central America.

Sgt. Patterson: Former Green Beret, Sergeant Patterson volunteered to serve in the National Defense Force just south of Kansas City. He quickly rose through the ranks as a result of his previous service, and he serves as a valued key member of Cmdr. Attledge's command cadre.

Shaw, Angus T.: Wood cutter from Flint Hill. Also head carpenter for the community. He is a skilled craftsman and master carpenter by trade from Kentucky.

Taylor, Jess: Worked at a gas station next to the pharmacy where Chip took refuge. The two sheltered together and became romantically involved. Jess doesn't take the isolation well and it takes her some time to reintegrate and adjust to life with a group.

Thompson, Brant: Eric Tillman's lifelong best friend. The two briefly attended college together where they had a falling out that lasted for several years. After reuniting in the aftermath of the Blackout, Brant took refuge with Eric's family. Brant also became equal partners with Eric's father, sharing the responsibility of protecting Brant's family cattle herd as well as sharing the beef and the profits from trade that the cattle bring. Brant serves as an important element in the militia and defense of the homestead.

Tillman, Beth: Wife of Joe Tillman, Beth serves as the matriarch of the Tillman homestead. She lives on the farm where she grew up with her parents and a growing number of refugee survivors of the Blackout. Years ago, Beth's parents deeded the farm to her in a move to protect her from taxes   should the pair die unexpectedly. As such, the homestead is known as the Tillman Homestead.

Tillman, Eric: Son of Joe and Beth Tillman. Eric is a former college student who, following his college   career, lived and worked in Charlotte, North Carolina until the Blackout. immediately following the EMP attack, Eric led a group of tourists out of a state park and away from wildfires sparked by downs aircraft in the wake of the EMP. Eric has grown into his increasing role as a soldier, but his conscience still wrestles with the harsh realities of the new world.

Tillman, Joe: Captain in the US Navy SEALs (retired). Cpt. Tillman is a Naval Academy graduate who spent more than twenty years in the field. He then served more than fifteen years as the senior officer of the watch at US Central Command. When the Blackout occurred, Cpt. Tillman led a group of fellow contractors out of Norfolk and to his family farm in North Carolina. Since then Captain Tillman has worked to secure the family's position and expand their network of survival support. Cpt. Tillman is also considered one of the senior leaders of the last remaining forces loyal to the old American Republic.

Tippy: A very special young man who helps his father navigate from St. Louis to Kansas City with an important message for Colonel Darius. Tippy and Sticks become friends and Tippy talks to Sticks, a rare event for the young man. His father is moved to near tears watching the two interact.

Tyson, Hunter "Sticks": An enlisted volunteer for the National Defense Force. He serves under Colonel Darius in Kansas City. Sticks is known for his sense of humor and his sense of duty.

Williams, Jerry D. : Danny's uncle and the owner of the butcher shop where Danny has been getting much of the supplies traded with the Tillman homestead. Danny is the de facto leader, but Jerry still exercises his authority when he can. Danny is careful to make Jerry feel like he is running the show, even when it is clear to most of the people with them who is really in charge.

Withers, James: Captain US Army (retired) and Captain US Army National Guard (active). Marcus met Captain Withers when he first ventured across the country to deliver Commander Price's class ring to Joe. He was in charge of an Army Air National Guard base in eastern Tennessee that provided mountain rescue capabilities to local law enforcement and emergency service providers. He gave valuable jet fuel to Commander Attledge free of charge and was instrumental in the success of his mission.

www.ingramcontent.com/pod-product-compliance
Lightning Source LLC
Chambersburg PA
CBHW051053030726
47504CB00006B/1611